THE Underground Railroad BRIDES COLLECTION

9 Couples Navigate the Road to Freedom before the Civil War

Barbara Tifft Blakey, Ramona K. Cecil,
Lynn A. Coleman, Cecelia Dowdy, Patty Smith Hall,
Terri J. Haynes, Debby Lee, Darlene Panzera, Penny Zeller

BARBOUR BOOKS
An Imprint of Barbour Publishing, Inc.

Print ISBN 978-1-68322-632-1

eBook Editions:
Adobe Digital Edition (.epub) 978-1-68322-634-5
Kindle and MobiPocket Edition (.prc) 978-1-68322-633-8

Published by Barbour Books, an imprint of Barbour Publishing, Inc., 1810 Barbour Drive, Uhrichsville, Ohio 44683, www.barbourbooks.com

Our mission is to inspire the world with the life-changing message of the Bible.

ecpa Member of the Evangelical Christian Publishers Association

Printed in Canada.

Contents

Emma Underground

by Barbara Tifft Blakey

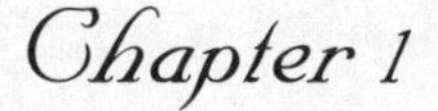

Chapter 1

Schenectady, New York
1851

Emma Trebor stood with her husband, Paul, on the church steps as their youngest daughter, Catherine, sat beside her groom in the flower-bedecked carriage. A chill breeze scuttled dry leaves across the cobblestones as the sun shone thinly in a cloud-streaked sky.

Emotions battling within, Emma smiled and waved. Of course she was happy for her daughter—more than happy—she was thrilled. But, oh, she would miss her.

As if Catherine sensed her turmoil, she turned backward in her seat. Their gazes met and she mouthed, "I love you, Mother." Then the carriage rounded the corner, out of sight.

Emma turned toward Paul, but he had already left her side. She shook off the disappointment and smiled at well-wishers offering their congratulations. Normally she felt invisible to the community, but duty insisted they acknowledge her today, and she soaked it in. While the children had all been home, being an outsider was more an inconvenience than hurtful. As long as she had her daughters to pour her love into, she didn't *need* other relationships. But one by one, her girls had married and moved away. Catherine was the last. Her new home in Boston was miles and miles away.

Planning the wedding had consumed Emma for months. What was she to do now? "Shame on you," she chided herself. "Feeling sorry for yourself on Catherine's joyous day." But there was no denying the ache in her heart.

Paul sent word that he'd be detained and for her to go home without him. Emma sighed. She wasn't surprised, but she'd hoped they'd ride home together. And talk.

As the carriage bumped along, she wondered if this was her future. To be alone. That mistake she'd made—that horrible mistake happened over twenty years ago. How long had she struggled with agonizing guilt? Yet God's love had overcome her self-reproach. Even as she rode along now, she felt His compassion and mercy, knowing she didn't deserve them, but resting in the knowledge that in His eyes, she was forgiven.

At home, her lady's maid, Beulah, helped her undress. "We'll miss her, won't we, ma'am?"

"Yes, so much." Emma smiled at her aging servant. Beulah's once ebony hair had turned gray; wrinkles creased her black face. "Will you mind so much with just me to take care of?"

"Oh, I think it will be just about right. Give my aching bones a bit of rest." Beulah gathered the day's garments and headed out of the room.

"Wait, Beulah. Would you like to sit awhile with me—perhaps have a cup of tea?"

"Oh, thank you, ma'am, but"—Beulah bowed her head—"it's best we keep things as they've been, don't you think? It's been a long day, and I'm eager to get to bed, if you don't mind."

"I don't mind at all. You are right, of course. I hope you sleep well." Emma forced a smile. Did the heat she felt in her cheeks show? She shouldn't have put Beulah in such a spot as to decline a request. She respected her maid's wisdom and faith, but their relationship had always been as employer and employee. Why was that? Had Emma kept her at arm's length, or was it Beulah who remained aloof? Was their lack of closeness a result of her terrible deed?

Alone in her room, with the festivities behind her and the night stretching before her, Emma fluffed her pillow, turned on her side, then her back, then her side again. Errant thoughts attacked as they hadn't for years. "Why tonight, Father? I know You forgave me many years ago, so why does this haunt me tonight?"

She slipped from her bed, lit the lamp, and read from her Bible, but not even that soothed her heart. Praying helped, but as soon as she uttered, "Amen," the restlessness returned. Perhaps a cup of hot chocolate would assuage her. She slipped into her robe, left her room, and crept down the hallway, hoping not to disturb her husband.

A second thought paused her. Perhaps if Paul were also awake, they could talk. How did he feel about all four daughters married and established in their own homes? Lingering outside his room, she raised her knuckles to rap on the door. He might invite her in. No. She hadn't been in his private quarters in twenty years. She lacked the courage to intrude now.

The flickering candle cast eerie shadows as Emma tiptoed down the stairs. She was too old to be afraid of the dark, but the creaks and groans of the manor unnerved her. The grandfather clock chimed two as she hurried down the hallway. What was that noise? It came from the back of the house. The kitchen door closing? Was Mandy up? Perhaps the cook also had trouble sleeping after such a big day.

It would be nice to share a cup of hot chocolate together. Reminisce about Catherine. And Julia. And Lydia. And Charlotte. They hadn't been all together since Christmas two years ago.

Emma appreciated Mandy's culinary skills and all she did for the family, but the only discussions they had involved menus and grocery lists. Not that Emma hadn't tried to be friendly, but like Beulah, the cook remained aloof. Perhaps tonight could be a new beginning.

She pushed through the swinging doors into the kitchen, surprised to find it empty. She set the candle on the worktable then peered out the window to see if anything moved outside.

A light flickered from the stables. She couldn't discern a shape in the shadows, but had no trouble distinguishing the sound of a cantering horse.

Paul rode away on Perseus, aware of the light winking in the kitchen window. It was probably Mandy, nursing a cup of tea, or Beulah, rummaging for a biscuit. They both knew about his involvement with the Underground Railroad and would not question his late-night disappearance. If it were Emma in the kitchen? That was unlikely, but if it were, he'd figure out something to tell her.

Riding in the dark heightened Paul's senses. His ears strained to detect unnatural sounds. His eyes darted from one shadow to another, every muscle tensed to react if necessary. As he reached the maple grove, Perseus slowed. Paul loosened his rein, allowing his horse to pick its way along the narrow path.

He should have come earlier to check on the *freight*, but the wedding prevented it. Ah, the wedding. How beautiful Catherine had looked. He'd been startled when he saw her in

Emma's wedding dress, her features a replica of her mother's twenty-six years ago. It had taken him back, momentarily, to that glorious, happy time when Emma was the world to him. He prayed Catherine's resemblance to her mother was only outward. Surely none of his daughters possessed her capacity for duplicity.

And yet. Through all the years raising their four daughters, he'd never seen her lose patience, nor heard a complaint about having four babies in six years. By anyone's standards, she was a devoted and selfless mother. If he didn't know better—if he hadn't seen her treachery with his own eyes—he'd believe her incapable of the slightest hint of cruelty. But he had seen. He did know. He couldn't let himself forget.

Not with freedom seekers' lives at stake. Others might refer to the poor souls as runaway slaves, but to him they were much more than that. Industrious. Resourceful. Courageous. *Freedom seekers.*

Paul ducked to avoid a low branch and urged his mount on. Although his cotton mill was a popular *depot*, he hadn't expected any *freight* for another three days. The information had been scanty this time; he didn't know how many to expect, their ages or gender. He'd provide food and water now, assess their needs, then bring more provisions after the workday ended. Nothing gave him more pleasure than helping the fugitives.

His situation was perfect. He purchased cotton for his mill in Virginia and smuggled out one or two slaves each trip. In all the years he'd been involved, his wagonloads of cotton had not been searched or even stopped. Other conductors used his mill as a safe house as well. Since the Fugitive Slave Act had passed a year ago, a few conductors had experienced a bit of trouble from bounty hunters, but none close to Schenectady.

Paul laughed to himself. He'd like to see a pattyroller try anything in Schenectady. The community was an antislavery stronghold. In fact, Amos and his wife, Hannah, escaped from a plantation in Georgia fifteen years ago. They felt so safe, they chose to stay right there and not continue to Canada—operated a blacksmith shop on the north end of town. Every man in the county would fight to protect those two. A meddlesome bounty hunter might find himself floating facedown in the Hudson River if he caused trouble.

Pausing at the edge of the woods, Paul scanned the area for anything out of the ordinary. He doubted the precaution was necessary, but lives were at stake. It comforted the runaways to know procedures were adhered to, even in safe havens such as Schenectady.

He entered the redbrick mill. After lighting the lantern, he waited for his eyes to adjust then climbed the wooden steps to his office on the third floor. He knocked on the door hidden in the closet to alert those inside that he was coming in. He took a deep breath and steeled himself for what he'd find behind the door. It was this moment, this very moment that added meaning to his life. It was never pretty, but it was always powerful.

He opened the door and a woman and two children stared at him. Fear and pain filled their eyes. Where was the hope?

"I'm sorry I couldn't get here sooner." Paul removed the two canteens crisscrossing his back and handed them to the woman.

She passed them to the children. "Thank you, sir. Thank you." Her hair was covered with a blue bandanna, her clothing tattered and soiled.

"I'm Paul." He handed her a basket filled with apples, cheese, and bread.

"I am Tabitha. These are my children, Isaiah and Leah."

Paul nodded to each one. "You are welcome here. You are safe."

He sat on the floor. Now for his second favorite part. "Tell me your story."

Tears coated Tabitha's words, but none slipped from her eyes. "We started out together from Virginia, me, Samson, and my chilluns. But they sent the hounds after us. Samson said we should split up. I ain't seen him again. I wanted to wait longer, but the conductor said we gotta go."

"Samson is your husband?"

Tabitha shook her head. "No. Not yet. We's gonna be married in Canada."

Chapter 2

Emma listened as the hoofbeats faded away. Through the darkness, she made out neither horse nor rider, but suspected it was Paul. Who else could it be? Clancy, the stable hand? Unlikely.

But where was he going at this hour? She had half a mind to follow him, but discarded the idea as foolishness. He was probably as restless as she and needed air. If not for the moonless night, a ride sounded good to her as well. When he returned, perhaps they could talk.

Loneliness engulfed her like fog creeping along the river. She slumped into a chair and raised her eyes heavenward. "What do I do now, Father?" With a series of deep breaths, she quieted her anxious thoughts and waited for calmness to prevail. When it did, the words flowed from her. "You've been so good to me, Father. I have four beautiful daughters, a wonderful home. I've no right to ask for more, but You've promised the desires of our heart. Please, show me how to reconcile with Paul. I'll do whatever it takes, if You will show me the way."

She kindled the fire in the cookstove and heated a pan of milk then added cocoa, vanilla, and sugar. The hot chocolate warmed her, but she yearned to share it with someone. An hour passed. No rider returned. No household help appeared. She went back upstairs and wandered into Catherine's room then the vacant rooms of each of her daughters. Their years together had passed so quickly, although it didn't seem like it at the time. Then she was content with her life—she hardly missed Paul. She should have, but the girls kept her distracted. She hadn't considered how everything would change when her daughters were grown and married.

Emma returned to her room and grasped her Bible. It fell open to Psalm 130. "*Out of the depths have I cried unto thee, O Lord. Lord, hear my voice; let thine ears be attentive to the voice of my supplications. . . .*"

The clock chimed four, rousing Emma from a light slumber. Her first thought was of Paul. Had he returned? She put on her robe then stood in front of his door. She could peek in to make sure he was there. Her fingers grasped the doorknob, but it was not so easy to break a twenty-year-old habit. Her hand dropped. She'd wait for breakfast. He never missed the morning meal.

Unsettled, Emma returned to her room. Riding in the dark was not safe. What if his horse had tripped and he had fallen? What if he needed help and no one knew? She chided herself for being ridiculous. He was probably in bed, sound asleep.

But what if he wasn't? She could go to the stables and see if Perseus was there. That might ease her mind.

Emma changed quickly into her riding clothes. Her boots thudded on the wooden stairs, louder than she wished for such an early hour. She passed through the house and out the back door. Darkness swallowed the light of her single candle and she stumbled a few times. A dog barked in the distance. Nearing the stables, she heard a horse snort and stamp.

She reached out for the latch, but the door swung open. A man filled the frame. "Oh!" Emma gasped. Was it Paul or the stable hand? The shadows concealed his face. She stepped back.

"Emma!"

Paul. Thank goodness, he was safe. As her anxiety fled, she longed to hug him, but the moment passed. Emma wrapped her arms around herself.

Paul rubbed his jaw. "You startled me." What was she doing out here? What did she know about his absence? Why was she wearing her riding clothes? It was too early for an outing. He forced a smile. "Were you headed somewhere?"

"No. . .I. . .well. . .saw you leave last night and wondered if you were back. And I thought if you weren't, maybe you'd had an accident or something." Emma looked down. "Maybe you needed help." She glanced back up.

Confusion clouded her eyes. For a moment he wished to comfort her, but held himself back, fearful she'd return the affection, and he wasn't prepared to handle that.

She'd seen him leave. What could he say, if she asked where he'd been? So far he'd never lied to her to keep his secret—she'd been too preoccupied with raising their daughters to notice his absences. He didn't want to start lying now. "I'm sorry to have worried you. I'm fine, as you can see; however, I am eager to catch some sleep."

"Yes, of course." Emma turned from the stable toward the house. "Look, there's a light on in the kitchen. Mandy is probably up. Are you hungry? Would you like something before you return to bed?" Her voice sounded artificially light, as if she were forcing cheerfulness. Was she covering up something?

"No, I think sleep is what I need most. Go on ahead. I just remembered some instructions I want to give Clancy. I'll be right along."

He watched her return to the house. She looked small and fragile alone in the dark. He ached to take her hand and see her safely inside. Instead he waited until she reached the back door, just in case she tripped, then he reentered the stable and found the groom.

"Clancy, I want you to let me know if Mrs. Trebor goes on any late-night rides."

"Do you want me to detain her?"

"No. But tell me if she leaves and how long she is gone."

"Should I follow her?"

"No. Not yet. Let's see what happens. I may be overreacting."

Paul delayed a few more minutes before heading into the house, hoping Emma wasn't waiting for him in the kitchen. He didn't want to face any questions—but why hadn't she asked where he'd been? Her not asking was as troublesome as if she had.

The smell of coffee met him before he opened the back door. Mandy looked up as he entered. She reached for the pot.

"None for now, but keep it hot for me, will you? I'm beat."

"Yes, sir." She edged closer and lowered her voice. "What we gonna do about her nosing around? She gonna find out; I just know she gonna find out."

Paul frowned. "She will if you keep talking right here in the kitchen."

Mandy wrung her hands. "But what we gonna do?"

"I don't know. I'm too tired to think. We'll pray for God's continued protection."

With four long strides, Paul was out of the kitchen, but he paused at the foot of the stairs, puzzling over something Emma had said—that he should "return to bed."

If she'd looked in his room, she'd know he'd not been to bed, so she wouldn't suggest he return to it. Instead of checking his room, she went to the trouble of dressing and going out to the stable to see if he was home. In all these years, then, had she never entered his room?

Had she never come in to watch him sleep, as he did her? Of course not. It was a silly thing to do, yet he had continued the practice year after year. Many a night he'd sat in the chair near her bed, gazing on her face, her beautiful, angelic face. Some nights he'd been unable to stop himself from kissing her hand or the top of her head, love for her welling inside. Most nights he contented himself with just watching her sleep. Doing so helped him keep his distance during the day. It helped him keep the facade in place.

But this new knowledge tugged on his heart. Was it respect or indifference that kept her out of his room? And now was she truly worried about him riding in the dark, or did she suspect something? She was dressed to go riding. If he hadn't been home, where would she have ridden to look for him?

Emma heard her husband pause outside her door. She sat still, her heart pounding in her ears. Would he come in? She stared at the doorknob, willing it to turn, willing Paul to walk through the door, to envelop her in his arms, to kiss her again. He'd loved her once. Couldn't he love her anew?

His footsteps continued past her door, and she sank back into the chair. Where had he been? He'd been gone for hours. One didn't ride for hours in the dark without a purpose. But one could be gone for hours, riding only a short distance.

Did he have a mistress? Pain pierced her chest as if she'd been stabbed with a knife. It had been years since they'd been intimate with each other. Could he have found solace elsewhere? She bit her lip to keep from crying out. It wasn't fair. She'd never locked her door; she'd have welcomed him anytime. He was the one who rejected her, not the other way around. Sometimes she dreamt he came, that he looked at her adoringly and kissed her hand. Such pleasant dreams.

But now—what was happening? Was he seeing someone else? Emma rose from her chair and paced the room, wringing her hands. With whom was her husband meeting?

Perhaps no one. She was overreacting. He might have fallen asleep or lost track of time as he pondered their married daughters. He was a good man. His integrity would prevent him from indiscretions.

Emma knelt on her prayer pillow and stilled her mind. She envisioned coming before the Great I Am and poured out her heart. She rose from her prayer with renewed strength and conviction. Not only would she reconcile with her husband; she'd make peace in the community and friends among her servants. Beulah might believe it was best to leave things as they were, but Emma couldn't. She had all this love to give. All the attention and care she'd poured into her daughters needed a new outlet, but more than that, she felt God's leading in this endeavor. He wanted her to reconcile, and so she would.

Eager to begin the day, she chose a blue outfit and laid it out. How frustrating that fashion dictated corsets and tiny buttons down the back, making it impossible to dress oneself.

A half hour later, Beulah bustled into the room, huffing a little.

Emma smiled. "Did you sleep well, Beulah?"

"Yes, ma'am, thank you." She tightened Emma's corset. "Do you have a special day planned?"

"Yes, Beulah, I do. A very special day that involves Mr. Trebor, our household, and our community." Emma was giddy with anticipation. Today was the beginning of a new life. She hugged Beulah, felt her lady's maid stiffen, but squeezed gently before letting go. "I know you believe things are better left as they were, but it's time I showed you how much you mean to me. Prepare yourself. There will be more hugs coming."

At the top of the stairs, Emma drew in a deep breath. Beulah hadn't hugged her back, nor smiled at the declaration of more affection to come, but Emma hadn't expected the change to be easy. Even so, by the time she was ready to enter the breakfast room and face Paul, her mouth felt as dry as burnt toast.

Her husband looked up as she entered. "Good morning, dear," he said. "I expected you might sleep late, considering our eventful day yesterday."

"Good morning." She drew in a deep breath. "Paul, I must speak with you." She moved her plate setting from her usual spot at the opposite end of the table to his right side.

His brow furrowed as he watched her. "Of course, dear, but I haven't time this morning. I'm needed at the mill, you know." He started to rise.

She put her hand over his, pausing his exit. "Please eat breakfast with me."

He didn't look at her, kept his gaze toward the window. "I'd love to, dear, but really I can't. I'm sure you understand." He slid his hand from under hers and hurried from the room.

Emma sat alone, her determination unaltered. If he had no time for her at home, then she'd join him at the cotton mill.

Chapter 3

Emma lingered, drinking her tea, mulling over her brief encounter with Paul. He had left before finishing his breakfast and had made no eye contact. Because he didn't want to be alone with her? Guilt over his nocturnal activities?

She'd never doubted Paul's fidelity before. He seemed above that sort of thing, but she was easy to deceive. She'd been duped before with disastrous results. Had he played her false all these years? Appearing upright and honest—a devout man of God—all the while carrying on an affair?

Perhaps she should give up the idea of reconciliation and plan a trip to New York City. Charlotte, her eldest, often asked her to come. The city was festive in the winter, and with Charlotte's connections, there'd be plenty of social opportunities. And her eldest had been married three years; mightn't there be a baby on the horizon? What a happy distraction that would be!

But no. She wouldn't leave. Not yet, anyway. She loved Paul, and if he still cared for her, they could begin again. Unless. . .he'd taken a mistress. . . .

Her heart reached heavenward. She closed her eyes and whispered, "Dear God, don't let it be too late."

Of course it wasn't too late. God would not be urging her if it were. She was jumping to conclusions. Paul had been out one night that she knew of. These doubts attacking her heart were not heaven sent.

"Are you finished, Mrs. Trebor?" Mandy carried a tray to clear the breakfast dishes.

"Oh! Yes. Thank you, Mandy." Emma rose. "Will you tell Clancy, please, that I would like to take the buggy to town?"

"Yes, ma'am." The cook collected the leftover eggs and sausages onto her tray and left the room.

Emma walked to the window overlooking the garden. Most of the blooms were spent; only a few asters and chrysanthemums remained. They'd be gone too after the first hard frost. The garden's bleakness subdued her mood further.

She turned from the window and pulled a cord hanging near the door.

A bit out of breath, Beulah appeared.

"Please sit down a moment."

"Thank you, ma'am, but I'm fine to stand. Is there something you need?"

"Do you remember that blue-flowered chintz we bought too much of for Catherine's trousseau? We made a dress from it, but there were yards and yards left."

"I remember it."

"Could you gather it for me, please, along with my sewing kit? Put them in a hamper for traveling."

"Yes, ma'am."

"And I was wondering, Beulah, if you'd like to come with me. I'm going to sew garments for the poor with the women's auxiliary."

Beulah's gaze met Emma's. "I'll get ready."

"But do you want to come?"

"I want to please my employer."

"Beulah, I'm asking for your honesty. If you truly want to please me, then you'll give me sincere answers, not what you think I want to hear."

Beulah rubbed her forehead. "For this particular question or all the time?"

"All the time."

Beulah planted her hands on her hips. "Why do you want to use that fancy chintz for poor people's clothes? It's gonna be soiled and tattered in no time."

"Maybe so, but don't you think poor people like pretty things too?"

Beulah's smile grew slowly then flooded her face. "They sure do. Yes, ma'am, they sure do."

Paul's gaze drifted to the third-floor windows as he neared his cotton mill. Noise from the machines drowned out his arrival and covered any sounds the hideaways might make.

Before heading up to his office, he checked the shed holding his supply of cotton. Each bale weighed five hundred pounds, and there were two left; he'd need more soon. Perhaps he'd go himself this time. The round trip could take a fortnight and would be a way to avoid Emma. Maybe in his absence, she'd find a hobby to replace mothering their daughters. She needed something to do, but he couldn't have her looking his way.

Although—what if they could recapture the life they'd shared the first years of their marriage? He'd come home after a hard day, and she'd greet him with a smile, admiration shining from her eyes. They'd share the frustrations and successes of the day with each other, listening to and caring for one another. Sometimes they'd ride around the estate together. Other times they'd dance, just the two of them. He could feel the softness of her hands in his, inhale her fragrance as she leaned into his embrace.

Paul shook himself from his daydream. He had no business entertaining such thoughts. Nothing good would come of it. He'd not put the freedom seekers at risk over his own pleasure.

He sought his foreman, Joe, among the carding machines. Carding was the most dangerous job in the mill, and Joe oversaw the men running the machines carefully. The huge, rotating cylinders, covered with thousands of sharp wire teeth, could maim or kill a careless worker. Fortunately, no such accidents had occurred at Paul's mill, a fact he attributed to his overseer's constant attention. "Where's Joe?" he shouted over the noise of the machinery to one of the carders.

The man pointed upward.

Paul ascended the steps to the second floor, where women spun the carded, clean cotton into threads that were wound onto large wooden bobbins. He smiled at the children playing marbles in a corner near a window. Their job was to remove the full bobbins and replace them with empty ones, but the task left free time for play. He was glad for that. A part of him was sorry that children as young as ten had to work, but he was thankful to provide jobs that didn't entirely rob them of their youth. He spoke with one of the boys, raising his voice to be heard over the machinery. "Have you seen Mr. Joe?"

The boy nodded. "Trouble with a warper." The youngster had several full bobbins he was carrying to the third floor.

"I'll take these for you." Paul continued up the stairs, where the warpers and weavers worked. The room was quieter than the lower floors, with a rhythmic pulse as weavers worked the cotton warp and weft threads into fabric, yet even here there was a constant din. He handed the spools to a woman working a warper. "Have you seen Joe?"

"I believe he went to your office, Mr. Trebor."

It wasn't as if his office was off limits to his foreman, but it wasn't common for him to come up to the third floor, even to visit his wife and daughter, who worked on the looms. "Joe," Paul called as he entered the room.

"Yes, boss." His overseer stood in front of the closet leading to the secret room, where the family was hidden.

The men's eyes locked. Neither smiled. Paul spoke first, his face nonexpressive. "Have you checked the freight?"

"Yes, sir."

"Is it ready to go?"

"Unfortunately, it can't leave until the next stockholders' meeting." Joe walked to the door. "I'd better get back downstairs."

Paul nodded as he processed the code. The freight—the freedom seekers hiding in the secret room—couldn't leave until the stockholders—those financing the escape—could get funds to purchase berth on a ship heading through the canal to Canada.

Paul contributed to the stockholders' fund, but he wasn't in charge of managing it. The current freedom seekers were safe in the cotton mill, but he was expecting another delivery in two days—one large and one small *bale*. Hiding five people in one location was risky. Too risky.

Suddenly, above the din, a voice shouted, "Fire!"

Chapter 4

Emma parked the buggy in front of the First Presbyterian Church and glanced at Beulah. "I'm not sure where the women's auxiliary meets. Reverend Bachus will know."

"They meet at the Potters' home." Beulah met Emma's gaze. "At ten."

Emma looked at the dainty clock circled in diamonds and rubies that she wore as a pendant. It read ten fifteen. "We're late." She turned the buggy around and urged Apollo to a trot. It took only a few minutes to travel down the street and around a corner to get to the Potters' modest abode. Mr. Potter was a barber, with a shop on the canal. His means were simple, but the home was well cared for.

Emma paused at the front door. She dreaded being late. Perhaps it would be wise to wait until next week, when she could plan her arrival to coincide with others and not draw attention by her tardiness.

"Are you having second thoughts?" Beulah huffed under the weight of the fabric-filled hamper.

"Yes." Emma nodded. "But we're here now. We'll go inside." She knocked, a bit louder than she intended.

Mrs. Potter answered. Her eyes widened momentarily; then a smile replaced the surprise. "Mrs. Trebor, how lovely to see you. Oh, and Beulah too. Please come in."

Their hostess led the way to the parlor. As they entered the room, the hum of conversation stopped, and all eyes watched Emma. Warmth spread from her neck to her cheeks, but she drew in a deep breath and straightened her back. "Good morning, ladies. I apologize for my tardiness."

"Nonsense. We are just getting started." Mrs. Potter gestured to an empty settee. "There's room right there. Please have a seat."

Beulah placed the hamper between them as she and Emma sat. Emma forced cheerfulness into her voice. "I've brought fabric from Catherine's trousseau, but of course I'm happy to work on whatever needs doing." Why were they still staring at her? Emma shot a smile around the room. "I wasn't sure what was needed more, children's clothing or women's."

She glanced at Mrs. Potter, hoping for a friendlier countenance. She was not disappointed. "It's all in demand, my dear, even men's clothing for that matter."

Emma opened the hamper and pulled out a length of the chintz material.

"We're sewing for the poor, my dear." Mrs. Linde, on her left, scowled. "Why would you bring *that*?"

Beulah lifted her chin. "Because poor people like pretty things too."

Emma looked about the room. Ten women filled the chairs, not counting her and Beulah, and at the moment not a one was speaking. Remarkable.

Disapproving silence settled over the room.

Mrs. Potter picked up a half-finished child's dress made of a drab olive-green cotton. "Catherine's wedding was beautiful, was it not, Mrs. Linde?"

"Yes. It was beautiful." The sour woman focused on her sewing as if it required every ounce of her concentration.

Mrs. Potter glanced at Emma. "Did you make her gown?"

"My mother and I did. It was my wedding dress, and now I suppose it belongs to my four daughters."

Silence again. Small talk was not Emma's forte. Mrs. Potter was trying to bring normalcy into the room, but now even she stitched away without speech.

None of the women were strangers. Every Sunday morning they smiled and nodded at her coming and going from church, but she knew so little about them. Too little to know what to say to take the attention off herself and onto one of them.

Did the warmth Emma felt on her cheeks show? This was a mistake. Why did she think she could show up and make friends? The women had gone from staring at her to not even looking at her. That she was not welcome was as obvious as a blackberry stain on a white apron. She rose. "I'm sorry. I just realized I left my favorite thimble at home. Perhaps Beulah and I will return next week." She faced her servant. "I'm sorry, Beulah."

Mrs. Linde's gaze never left her work. "Let her stay. We'll see she gets home all right."

When the door closed behind her, Emma paused on the porch. Why had she ever thought she could waltz back into the sewing circle after all these years, as if she'd never left? Was she still being ostracized for her long-past sin, or had she done something else to offend them? Well, she didn't need them. She could sew for the poor at home.

Except, how would she bear one lonely day after another? Keeping her hands busy was only part of the solution. Her heart needed an outlet as well.

Mrs. Linde's voice came through the closed door. "I don't care, Lillian Potter. You shouldn't have let her in. It's too risky. That's all I'm saying. It's too risky."

Emma left the porch pondering why it was *risky* for her to rejoin the sewing circle. Nothing about her person could possibly put anyone in peril. She understood they might feel justified punishing her for her past, but how did that fit with risky? Something secretive was going on that everyone in that room knew about.

Including Beulah.

"Fire! Fire!" The words echoed through the mill. Paul flung open the secret door. Wide-eyed stares met him.

"You are safe—at least for the moment. I must go downstairs to assess the situation."

Tabitha nodded. "What do we do?"

"Right now, nothing. If you smell smoke before I get back, then climb out the window near my desk. There is a ladder attached to the outside wall and you can crawl down to safety."

Tabitha's eyes revealed her fear, but she nodded. "I understand, sir. We stay here, as long as we can, but if we must, we crawl out the window."

Paul shut the door behind him and raced from his office to the second floor. Smoke had filtered in, but not alarmingly so. He continued to the first floor, where smoke billowed about, but the water brigade had already quenched the blaze. He found Joe shouting at a stranger. Male workers gathered around. The females huddled together near the stream, keeping their children with them. Some still had buckets in their hands.

"Move aside." Paul pushed his way through a dozen men. "What's going on?"

Joe poked the chest of a burly man. "This yahoo tried to burn down the mill!"

"Touch me one more time and you'll be floating down that there creek." The man stepped forward, chest jutted out.

Paul wedged himself between Joe and the stranger. "You start that fire?"

"What if I did?"

"Then you've got some explaining to do." Paul spoke conversationally, but he smoldered inside. "To the sheriff." He looked over his shoulder at Joe. "Fire out?"

"Yes, boss."

"Damage?"

"Just to the bale shed."

"So not a problem with the carder?"

"No, boss, it's like I said. This lunkhead started the fire. Walked in the bale shed smoking a cigar."

The crowd of men murmured. They glared at the stranger, hands fisted.

Smoke swirled from the small structure. The wind gathered it and tossed it skyward, along with gray ashes. Remnants clung to the ground.

The fire damage to the shed might be minimal, but no one would buy smoke-infused cotton.

A faint sound stilled Paul's heart—the scrape of a window opening. Perhaps no one else heard it over the sound of voices. He forced himself not to look toward his office window—but Joe looked up. The stranger's gaze followed Joe's.

Paul cleared his throat. "What's your business here?"

Without taking his eyes off the window, the stranger put a cigar in his mouth and took out a match, as if to light it.

Paul slapped the match from the man's hand. "Get off my property and don't come back. I see any sign of you, and you'll be talking to the sheriff." He'd like to march the stranger to the sheriff's door right now, but that would mean a fight. He wasn't afraid and his workers would help, but he just wanted the man gone, for the sake of the freedom seekers.

The stocky stranger curled his lip. "I ain't afraid of no sheriff, but I'm done here anyway." He mouthed his unlit cigar, sauntered to a nearby apple tree, and mounted a dapple gray mare.

"Everybody, back to work," Paul called out. "Show's over."

A muscle in Joe's jaw twitched. "That's it? You gonna let that fire-starter walk away?"

"I just want him out of here." Paul lowered his voice. "Protect the packages." He glanced up at the window. What had the stranger seen?

Chapter 5

As Emma drove the buggy toward the cotton mill, she chastised herself for leaving the sewing circle so quickly. She was made of stronger stuff than that. And Mrs. Linde's attitude might change once Emma asked for forgiveness.

She had never publicly confessed her wrongdoing. In the beginning, her shame held her back. She didn't deserve the community's clemency, so she didn't seek it. They didn't know the months she spent in anguish, until God's persistent love won and she accepted His mercy. By then the pattern of her avoiding social contact was set, and she made no attempt to correct it. She hadn't even prayed about it—which puzzled her now. Why hadn't she tried to reconnect with the community? Her daughters provided an outlet for her affections, but was that the only reason? Had her pride played a role?

She'd go back next week, arrive on time, and be better prepared—perhaps bring a small gift for Mrs. Potter. Maybe a beaded reticule. She'd begin making it that evening. Peace settled in her soul. God would strengthen her for the tasks ahead, if she relinquished her vanity and let Him guide her.

As she neared the mill, a stranger on a dapple gray loped toward her. He reined his horse to the edge of the narrow road, stopped, and removed the cigar from his lips. "Good day, ma'am."

Nodding politely, she smiled and urged her horse on. At least strangers treated her civilly!

Near the mill, the air smelled of charred cotton. Its pungency stung her eyes. Had there been a fire? Was everyone all right? She urged Apollo into a trot. The buggy bounced along the rutted road.

Joe was outside as she stopped near the apple tree. "Good day, Mrs. Trebor." He helped her down from the buggy.

A mountain of charred cotton lay in the yard, along with countless bits of blackened fluff.

"What happened, Joe? Is anyone hurt?"

"No one was injured, but there's a financial loss." He gestured to the bales.

"That's unfortunate, but it's a blessing everyone is safe."

"Yes, ma'am."

Emma retrieved a covered basket from the floor of the buggy. "I've brought a picnic for Mr. Trebor. Do you know where I might find him?"

"He was here a minute ago. I'll send one of the men to get him."

"Thank you, but that's not necessary. I'll find him." Emma headed for the door.

"Really, ma'am, it's no trouble. Still a bit smoky inside. The air is better out here."

"The workers are back inside?"

"Yes, ma'am, but—"

"Thank you, Joe. I'll be fine." Emma smiled at the foreman then opened the narrow door. He was right—the odor was much stronger inside. Breezes wafted through the open windows along the length of the first floor, helping to rid the large rectangular room of the acrid smoke. Emma's eyes watered.

As she ascended to the second floor, the smoke was less annoying, and on the third floor, it was barely noticeable. Paul's office door stood ajar. She tapped on the frame then listened for him to bid her enter. After a moment, she knocked again, louder, then stepped inside the office. "Paul?"

Was that a woman's voice? She followed the sound. In a closet?

Paul's voice sounded from the other side of the wall. "Don't worry. Our secret is safe."

Who was Paul speaking with? And where? And what secret?

The woman's voice sounded again with words too quiet to decipher.

There must be a room on the other side of the wall, but how did one enter it? She saw no door. She left the closet and Paul's office and examined the wall from the outer angle, but found no entrance into another room.

Puzzled, she reentered the office just as Paul exited the closet.

There must be a door she hadn't seen before. "To whom were you speaking?"

"Emma! What are you doing here?" Paul composed himself as quickly as he could. He planted on a smile. "I mean, you surprised me."

"I heard a woman's voice. Who were you with?" Emma's gaze pierced him. She stepped toward him as if to look into the closet.

What could he say? He knew the day might come when he'd be forced to lie to protect the fugitives, but now that it was here, words failed him. "I see you brought a basket. Lunch?"

"Yes, I thought we might have a picnic under the apple tree." Emma's face was flushed. Her hands trembled. "You were speaking with someone."

He faked a cough to avoid answering. "Excuse me, dear. The effects of the smoke, I imagine. Shall we go outside?" He coughed again as he took the basket from her and tucked her arm under his. A glance at her face smote his heart. Pain cloaked her tear-filled eyes, her drawn cheeks. He swallowed against the lump in his throat as he escorted her from his office along the loom-filled room. What would he do if she asked him about the voices again? He trusted she wouldn't as long as there were workers around to overhear.

But she did.

"Paul, I heard your voice. And a woman answered."

"You must be mistaken, dear. Perhaps you heard workers through my open window." He closed his eyes a moment. *Forgive me, Father.* "Anyway, as you can see, the morning hasn't gone well with the fire and all, and I've a lot to do. It was kind of you to come, but in the future, perhaps you can send word of your intentions, and I'll let you know if it's a convenient time."

Cringing at his own words, he walked her outside then toward the buggy. He withdrew his arm from hers and set the basket on the floorboard. He hated being so cold. Despised the fact that he was causing her pain. He didn't trust her, couldn't let her discover his secret, but he didn't want to hurt her. Not like this.

This wasn't a problem when the children were home. They should have had more.

It took everything he had, but he steeled himself, cementing the barrier between himself and his wife. "And, dear, don't wait supper for me. I'll be delayed tonight."

Quivering sobs threatened to burst from Emma's bosom. She had heard a woman's voice, and Paul had dismissed her. Fear and anger clashed over the renewed suspicion of a mistress. And then sorrow and shame and guilt attacked. It was too much. All too much. Her anguish threatened to scream its pain, but she clamped her lips together and climbed into the buggy. She swallowed hard, trying to find the strength to utter a calm goodbye, but the task was too difficult. She couldn't breathe. Couldn't look at him. Every muscle tensed. Go! Run! Flee!

She slapped the reins against Apollo's back. The buggy jerked and they were off. Tears blinded her. She doubled over, covered her face with her hands, bit her lip to keep from crying aloud. The buggy bumped and jolted without direction, but Emma didn't care. Nothing existed but this all-consuming pain. She sat upright, her fists clenched in anger, then doubled over again as sorrow battled her wrath and left her limp.

When her emotions subsided, she found herself near a creek on the outskirts of town. Apollo had pulled the buggy off the road and nibbled grass poking through the fallen magenta leaves of a maple tree. How long had they been there? She got out of the buggy and washed her face in the creek. Emotionally exhausted, she leaned against a hollow cottonwood stump and watched red and amber leaves float lazily by. One would think she had cried herself out, but the tears loitered near the surface, ready to overflow again had she the energy to let them.

As the afternoon turned chilly, Emma rose and returned to her buggy, but getting it back on the road proved difficult. Apollo couldn't get the buggy over the muddy ridge onto the road. Even getting out to lighten the load didn't help. Emma stood near her horse's head, urging him to try harder, but it was no use. The wheels spun in the slippery grass, and he could not gain traction.

As Emma started to unharness Apollo from the buggy, hoofbeats sounded.

The cigar-smoking stranger riding the dapple gray she'd met earlier pulled up. "Are you in a bit of trouble?"

"Yes." Emma sighed. "It seems getting off the road is much easier than getting back on."

"May I help?"

"Would you? I'd be most grateful."

The man dismounted and scrounged under the nearby trees. In less than ten minutes he brought up small branches and twigs and scattered them on the slippery grass under the wheels. "Try now."

Emma stood at Apollo's head and gently tapped his hooves with her riding stick. "Walk."

The horse strained. The buggy's wheels gripped the ground. In minutes it stood solidly on the road.

"Thank you ever so much, Mr.—"

"Steeple. Uriah Steeple at your service." He made a slight bow. "And you are?"

Emma hesitated. This was not the way introductions were done, but considering the help he had provided, how could she be so rude as not to answer? "I'm Mrs. Paul Trebor. And again, thank you."

"It's a pleasure to make your acquaintance."

Emma climbed back in the buggy and took the reins. "You've made an unpleasant day more bearable. Again, thank you."

"Good day, Mrs. Trebor. Perhaps we'll meet again."

Chapter 6

Clancy greeted Emma as she neared the stables. He helped her get out of the buggy and unhitched Apollo, all without saying a word.

"Thank you, Clancy."

"Yes, ma'am."

Emma drew in a deep breath and strode toward the house. As she entered through the back kitchen door, conversation between Mandy and Beulah stopped. They were sitting at the worktable drinking tea, but rose suddenly as if caught doing something wrong.

"Please, don't get up." Emma pulled out a chair and joined them. If she wanted to establish friendships, she'd have to face her past head-on. There'd be no moving forward until she did. She sent a prayer heavenward for wisdom to say the right words then looked at her servants. "I wish to speak with you."

Their eyes showed their distrust.

Emma started to force a smile then realized this situation demanded honesty, not just with words, but with her emotions as well. She pushed back her hair with sweaty hands. "You have both been with me a very long time. Beulah, you've taken care of me since Paul and I were married. Mandy, you came after Catherine's birth. You have both been faithful members of this household."

Emma paused, looking from face to face. Neither servant smiled. Beulah's hand trembled slightly as she sipped her tea. When she set down her cup, it clinked against the saucer.

"I have not deluded myself thinking that your loyalty is to me. And the fault is mine." Emma drew in a deep breath. "About twenty years ago, I did a terrible thing. You weren't here, Mandy, but did you hear about it?"

Mandy nodded slightly.

"And what did you hear?"

Beulah blurted out, "What you want to bring up all that for? It's done and over."

"Yes, it is done, but it is not over." Emma sighed. "It certainly isn't forgotten. I've not acknowledged my wrongs publicly. I want to start with my household. To ask your forgiveness."

Mandy folded her arms across her chest. "Have you spoken with Mr. Trebor?"

"I'm speaking with you now." She turned to Beulah. "What do you remember about that day?"

"I wasn't there. I didn't see anything."

"But you heard the stories."

Beulah nodded.

"What did you hear?"

"You really want me to say? Because once the words are out, they can't be taken back."

Emma's gaze locked with her maid's. Without breaking the connection, she said, "Earlier today I told you I always want your honest opinion. Now I'm telling you I want honesty and openness in every conversation."

"You caused that poor little girl's death." Beulah spat out the words.

The accusation pierced Emma, taking her breath away. She sat a moment, unable to speak. Then strength entered through the words planted in her heart. *"The truth will set you free."*

The truth was Jesus. He was the One to break the chains. He had already forgiven her. He would help her face this. First with her household, then with the community.

"Yes, I did." Emma's tears flowed unchecked. "I let ignorance and pride overrule me, and the consequence was disastrous. Can you forgive me?"

Beulah's eyes narrowed. "How could you have done it?"

"I won't make excuses. There are none. My actions were deplorable in every way."

Mandy's chair scraped against the floor as she stood. "Then how can you ask our forgiveness?"

"Because I must." Emma's shoulders drooped, and her head dropped. "Whether or not you give it is not under my control."

Mandy remained standing. "It ain't my forgiveness you need. It's too late for that little girl, probably too late for her mama and daddy. You need to beg God for mercy."

"I have." Although her vision was blurred with tears, Emma looked into Mandy's eyes. "It took almost a year before I could accept it, but our gracious Father granted me forgiveness. His love is stronger than our vilest sin. I do not deserve His mercy, but He has given it to me."

Mandy sank back into her chair. She dabbed at her eyes with her apron.

Beulah's tremulous voice broke the moment. "I want to hear you tell the story. I want to hear it from your lips."

Emma swallowed hard, then began. "The sewing circle had been making clothes for the poor, or at least that's what we said aloud. Most of us knew that while some garments went to the less fortunate, most went to the runaway slaves who flowed through town. I was proud that Schenectady welcomed those poor souls. I was also prideful of my sewing and liked to make pretty dresses to show off what I could do. Sometimes I made dresses for the poor and runaways to match the ones I made for my daughters. That way everyone would know which garments I made. It was foolish and prideful." Her sin attacked her as she spoke. She felt the ugliness of her transgressions. The words clogged her throat.

After a few moments, she continued. "We had been warned in church that a slave owner was on his way to claim back his property, but I didn't think he had a chance against the antislavery community, so while I heard the warning, I did not take it to heart. I especially did not consider a woman would have anything to do with it.

"At the church picnic that day, a stranger, claiming to be passing through from Albany, commented to me on the number of well-dressed children she'd seen. I explained that the women's sewing circle made serviceable garments as well as nice dresses for the poor, so there was little or no difference in their Sunday best compared to others.

"She oohed and aahed over a number of garments, none of which were ones I'd sewn. I grew determined to show off my skills. I'd given a dress I was particularly proud of to a little girl that morning, and I knew where the family was hiding. I persuaded the stranger to come with me."

"You did what?" Mandy's eyes widened. Her back straightened.

"I have no excuse." Emma's ragged breath choked off the words.

Beulah shook her head. "There's no excuse, but times was different then. No pattyrollers to dodge. Slave owners didn't chase freedom seekers this far north. But the runaways was still careful, cuz lives was at stake. They hid most days, but sometimes, on a particularly nice day, they'd come out and enjoy the sun a little." She looked at Emma. "I ain't making no excuse for you, just telling it like it was."

Mandy's posture relaxed. "Still don't see how you could do it."

"In hindsight, neither do I. But I never suspected this woman was a slave owner. I did not see anyone following us. It is no excuse for what happened, but it is the truth. Pride had an ugly grip on me." The last words gushed from Emma, and she broke into sobs. She had God's forgiveness, so why did this undo her?

Beulah reached across the table and took Emma's hands. "You led that woman and her husband right to the freedom seekers."

Emma nodded. She spoke between sobs. "Beautiful day, outside in the sun. By the time I realized—two adults—clapped in chains! A little girl crying for her mama. Her mama screaming for her to run—the boom of the gun. The child fell, so much blood."

Emma was there again, saw it all again. She couldn't breathe, couldn't think, but she heard again the child's screams, saw again the mother's terror-filled eyes. Emma's pain was uncontainable. She rocked back and forth in her chair, wailing, wailing. She had done this. It was as if she had pulled the trigger herself. God had forgiven her—why did she feel this torment again?

Mandy's arms encircled her. "It's all right. You're all right."

Beulah knelt in front of her, crooning, "Hush, child, hush."

Emma's cries subsided to hiccups. A few deep breaths helped her gain more control.

"I'd like to know about the money." Beulah's voice was as soft as dandelion fluff. "Did you accept the bounty?"

"No! Yes." Emma closed her eyes. "The woman thrust a wad of bills in my hand. She laughed and thanked me for my help. Said I deserved the reward. I don't know why I didn't throw the money back at her, why I didn't run for help. I've thought over and over of what I should have said and done, but I just stood there, as if paralyzed. Everyone came at the sound of the gunshot, but it was too late. Then Mr. Trebor escorted me home."

Mandy rubbed Emma's shoulders. "You've never told anyone this story, have you? Not even Mr. Trebor."

Emma shook her head. "At first I was so appalled at what had happened, I couldn't face anyone. I couldn't forgive myself, so how could I ask mercy from others? I thought Mr. Trebor might ask me about it, but he never did. By the time I accepted God's love and compassion, a pattern had been set, and I didn't know how to break it. Now I see that my pride was again the culprit. It was easier to distract myself with the children than to face the community."

Mandy and Beulah retook their chairs. The three women sat quietly for a few moments before Beulah broke the silence. "The community believes you purposely led the slave owners to the freedom seekers' hiding place for the bounty money."

Emma's gaze drifted from Beulah to Mandy and back again. "Is that what you believe too?"

Chapter 7

Paul rubbed his temples against the mounting tension headache. The freedom seekers hiding in the cotton mill were not safe. Emma had heard them and she might act on her curiosity, but worse, the dubious stranger who started the fire may have seen something in the office window.

Paul had to send the family on. The stockholders reported a lack of funds, but he couldn't wait.

He could use money from his safe at home to purchase their passage on to Canada. He'd have to fabricate an excuse to tell Emma why he took the cash—perhaps he could replace it before she discovered it missing.

But there was also the matter of incoming freight. He'd have to warn the conductor not to stop. Display the *danger* signal. Many homes used quilts on a porch railing or a lamp in a window. Paul had a white sign with words painted in black: NO COTTON DELIVERIES TODAY.

He'd never had to display it, and couldn't remember where it was put—after all, it'd been unused for over fifteen years. Finally he found it in the rafters of the bale shed. Smoke damage had changed the white to dark gray. The words no longer stood out boldly. In fact, they were difficult to see, but it would have to do. He hung it on the nail on the front side of the shed and headed to town. He wanted to talk to the sheriff about the fire-starting stranger. He found the lawman in his office.

"Well, Paul Trebor." Sheriff Martin rose from his chair. "Don't see you often in town this time of day."

"How are you, Sheriff?"

The two men shook hands, then the lawman sat and gestured for Paul to take a chair. "I'm pretty sure you aren't here to inquire about my health."

Paul shook his head. "Had trouble with a stranger today."

"What kind of trouble?"

"He walked into my bale shed with a lit cigar. Started the thing on fire."

"Why didn't you bring him in? You got enough men to do it."

"I wish I had, but he wouldn't have gone quietly; there'd have been a fight, and I just wanted him gone."

The sheriff frowned. "Much damage?"

"Two bales of cotton ruined, what with smoke and water. No one was hurt. I don't know if there's much you can do now, but I wanted to report it in case there's more trouble."

Sheriff Martin picked up a pencil. "Got a name or description I can take down?"

Paul described him in as much detail as he remembered, including the dapple gray horse.

"Did he say why he was there?"

"No, and that's got me concerned. I don't know who he is, why he showed up at my mill, or why he wanted to ruin my cotton. Unless"—Paul's gaze met the sheriff's as he finished his thought—"unless he's a bounty hunter."

The lawman set down his pencil then caught it before it rolled off his desk. "That what you figure? Makes sense. A bounty hunter setting fire to cotton could smoke out the freight. But you know I can't do anything to obstruct a hunter. Fact is, if he wants my help, I'm obliged to give it to him." He locked eyes with Paul. "And you need to be real careful about what you tell me."

"I know. You have to obey the Fugitive Slave Law."

"Have you considered that if I arrest him and he contends your accusations, he'll have the right to examine the premises?" The sheriff stood. "If freight is found there, it won't matter that he started a fire."

"Why, Sheriff Martin, you know I'm a law-abiding citizen, doing my best to run a little cotton mill. Don't know what kind of freight you're talking about. 'Course I don't want anyone nosing around, but that's just protecting my business interests."

"Glad we cleared that up."

Paul wasn't quite ready to leave. "There's something else. With the bales ruined, I have to either go myself or send someone south, leaving the mill shorthanded for ten days or longer."

"That works to the advantage of the bounty hunter—um, I mean fire-starting stranger." The sheriff rubbed his stubbly chin. "Can't you delay the trip until this sorts itself out?"

"I could, but without cotton, the mill shuts down. I've got workers to think about. How will they pay their rent or buy food if they don't work? For that matter, how do I supply the factories with fabric if I haven't any cotton? They'll look elsewhere, and I'll be out of business."

The sheriff walked around the edge of his desk. "I'll help any way I can, but my hands are tied when it comes to bounty hunters."

"But not arsonists."

"Nope; I can deal with fire starters, if that's what you want."

"I'm not sure. Maybe hold off on tracking him down. Could be he's moved on."

Outside the sheriff's office, Paul looked up and down the street. Schenectady had grown. He didn't know everyone in town anymore, didn't know whom he could trust. Whoever went after the cotton needed to return with more freedom seekers, but with bounty hunting growing more and more prosperous, helping freedom seekers was getting riskier. Was it right to send someone else into that sort of danger?

But first things first. The freight at the cotton mill had to move on. He'd get the cash from the safe and make the arrangements as soon as possible. He'd prefer to return home after Emma retired, but he needed to act now.

The two servants didn't answer Emma's question. Neither met her gaze. She repeated her question. "Will you forgive me?"

Mandy sat with arms folded across her chest.

Beulah scowled, her brow furrowed. "Why now? After all these years, why do you bring this up now?"

"The Lord is prodding me to let go of my pride and confess to the community. He's been urging me all these years, but I refused to acknowledge it. His forgiveness has been my sole comfort, but He is asking me to follow James's command, 'Confess your faults one to another.'"

The servants sat stiffly. Tension mounted in the room.

"I know this has been a long time coming. Much too long. I have no excuses, but I hoped you'd believe me. . .and forgive me."

Beulah shook her head. "I know you to be a devout mother and kind employer. I'm thankful for that. You've asked for my honest response, and this is my thought: You've had twenty years to come up with that story."

Mandy nodded. "And it's a good one. A dandy. But I've heard good stories before."

Apparently consoling a sobbing woman was not the same as believing her. Emma rose from her chair and stumbled from the room, her sight blurred by tears. She'd not break down in front of them again.

On her knees in her room, she cried out, "I did my best, Father, but it fell short. Please don't ask me to try again. I can't. I can accept being alone the rest of my life, as long as I have You. I don't deserve the community's forgiveness. I don't deserve happiness with Paul. As long as I know You love me, I don't need anyone else."

The peace she'd experienced before eluded her. She was deceiving herself. She could no easier live without someone to love than she could fly to the moon. She sat at her writing desk and penned a note to her eldest daughter:

Dearest Charlotte, I pray this finds you well and happy. I'm wondering if you are amicable to an extended visit. I'd love to come soon and perhaps stay until Christmas. . . .

Chapter 8

Clancy took Perseus's reins as Paul dismounted near the stables. "Don't put him away," Paul said. "I'm heading out again. But you might let him drink."

He entered the manor through the french doors leading from the garden to his study. A lamp cast shadows into the room. He swiftly moved to open the safe.

"Good evening, Paul."

He turned quickly. "Oh, Emma. You surprised me."

"I didn't intend to startle you, but I've been waiting. I'd like to talk."

She deserved an explanation for the voice she heard at the mill, but he couldn't give one. She couldn't know about the freedom seekers, and he didn't want to lie. "I'm sorry, but it will have to wait. I really haven't time at the present." He cringed inwardly at the look on her face.

"Surely you aren't going out again? What business could you possibly have at this hour?"

He detected frustration in her voice. "My dear, business is done at every hour of the day. Now, if you'll excuse me, I'm in a bit of a hurry."

Instead of leaving the room as he thought she would, she stepped nearer. "Please, Paul. It is ever so important." Her voice was a soft whisper, filled with longing.

She drew even closer. A whiff of her perfume teased him. She leaned into him; her gaze connected with his then dropped to his mouth. Her lips parted. He yearned to take her into his arms and kiss her, to ease the hunger in her eyes.

He moved away. "I'm sorry, dear. Perhaps we can speak in the morning." He grasped her elbow and escorted her from the room. He felt her body tremble, and his heart responded with its own quivering.

He shut the door quickly, before his emotions sabotaged his determination. He returned to the safe, retrieved the cash, and left the same way he'd entered. Even as the door shut, his inner being urged him to stay and listen to her. She was, after all, the mother of his children.

The only woman he had ever loved.

Or ever would love.

No, he argued with himself. The lives of freedom seekers were more important than his own happiness. And Emma could not be trusted in those matters.

As she heard the study door close, Emma pushed into the room.

He was gone. She knew he would be, but the empty room caved in on her.

She sank to the floor. Again tears flowed straight from her broken heart. She'd begged him to stay and he had brushed her off.

Did she mean so little to him?

Or was it that someone else meant more?

She rose from the floor then noticed the safe was not closed tightly. She strode to it. The usual papers were all there, but cash was missing.

Why had he taken it? For business? Or something else?

Such as a rendezvous with another woman. If he were seeing someone, what chance did she have? Perhaps this was part of the price she had to pay for her sins. God's forgiveness did not include erasing consequences. But why was her heavenly Father urging her to reconcile if it was too late?

Taking deep breaths, she sat in his chair. A battle rose within her.

Let him go, one voice said. *He'll hurt you more.*

Fight for him, said another.

Just leave—go to your daughters. They love you, the voice argued.

Paul knocked on Joe's door, aware that he was about to violate an Underground Railroad code. To protect everyone, stationmasters did not identify themselves to conductors. He had the money to buy passage, but he didn't know which ship to use. Who was the contact? What was the safest route? It would be better if his foreman did it.

Joe answered his knock and stepped outside. He looked up and down the street. "What are you doing here, boss?"

"You're my foreman—can't I talk to an employee after work hours?" Paul handed him his messenger's bag. "There's enough cash in here to book passage on a ship for the freight at the cotton mill."

"Yes, boss. I'll take care of it. But. . .tonight's ship has already left. It will be tomorrow evening at the earliest, possibly the night after, before the cargo can be loaded."

"But more freight is coming. We don't have that long." Paul rubbed his temples. "I know you'll do the best you can."

Joe scuffed the ground with his shoes. "Sure don't like that stranger nosing around."

"I reported him to the sheriff. Gave his description. I'm hoping he's moved on, looking for greener pastures."

"Not likely." Joe looked up at the moon then met Paul's gaze. "Not if he's a bounty hunter and saw something in your window."

"But if he had seen something, wouldn't he have challenged us right then? He'd have been within the law."

"The workers were itching for a fight. If the stranger saw something in that window, he was smart to wait for another day."

"You set a night guard, right?"

Joe nodded. "Sure did. And boss, what are we going to do about the cotton? We'll have to shut down the mill if we don't get more soon."

Paul rubbed his chin. "I know. I'm thinking I ought to go this time. Assess the increased danger. Sure hate to leave right now, though."

"Yeah, boss. We need you here."

Emma went down to breakfast after she was sure Paul was gone. She'd determined to avoid him until she heard back from Charlotte about her proposed visit. Her presence was obviously uncomfortable for Paul, and it was unrealistic to suppose he'd tell her the truth if he were having an affair. God might be disappointed in her for giving up, but she didn't know how to continue.

In the meantime, she'd make garments for the poor and send them with Beulah to the women's sewing circle. But she wouldn't make plain, drab things. She'd make beautiful clothes as if sewing for her own children—but not because of pride this time. She'd do it for the sake of the poor. To give them the joy of having something pretty. She'd pour her love into the dresses, and then when she was with her daughters, she would relieve her emptiness by caring for them.

There was one more thing she'd do before she left. She had no peace about it, but she couldn't leave without knowing whom Paul was seeing. She was not deluded into thinking it would make any difference between them, but she wanted to know.

Likely she'd find answers at the mill, upstairs in his office.

Chapter 9

Paul stuffed papers from his library desk into a leather case. "Yes, I'm leaving. It can't be helped." The words came easily to Paul because they were true. It was a bad time to be absent from the mill, but he couldn't in good conscience send anyone else. The increased pressure from bounty hunters meant he needed to assess the new dangers, perhaps establish a new route or reevaluate the whole process. Even so, Emma's stoic expression surprised him.

"I understand. The fire destroyed the cotton bales and we need more." Emma's chin lifted. "How long will you be gone?"

"Ten days at least, perhaps as long as a fortnight." Why wasn't she asking for them to talk now, before he left? The previous night, when they were together in the library, the same room they occupied now, she'd begged him to talk. He didn't want to then, and certainly didn't want to now, but what had changed? What had been so important then that no longer mattered? He assumed she wanted to ask about the woman's voice she'd heard in his office, and he was happy to avoid the topic, but why had *she* dropped it?

"I hope you have a pleasant trip. The weather has turned quite chilly; you might want to pack extra warm clothes."

"Yes, thank you, dear, for the reminder." Paul's eyes sought her face, but she was looking down as if to avoid him.

"I suppose you have a lot to do to get ready. I shan't keep you." Emma hurried from the room.

Since Catherine's wedding day, Emma had been seeking him out. It had made him uncomfortable, but now that she was pulling away from him, he was more uneasy. Something wasn't right. Perhaps he should speak with her before he left after all.

Emma released the breath she'd been holding and sank onto the parlor chair. She'd succeeded in keeping her composure in Paul's presence. The entire time she wanted to ask him who his mistress was, and if the Jezebel was going with him. But she'd held her tongue and responded with civility. She'd not beg him to talk again.

He was leaving in the morning. She could avoid him that long.

The less contact she had with him, the easier it would be for her to go to New York City. Charlotte's answer regarding the visit would likely come before he returned. She could be gone within a fortnight. But first she'd discover who his mistress was.

She'd go to the mill after he left, find the hidden room, and look for clues.

For now, she'd sew. The needle flew in and out of the flowered print chintz. She focused on making tiny, even stitches, and the garment took life.

Several hours later, she ran out of thread. She could send Beulah to town to get more, but she'd rather go herself than speak with her maid unnecessarily.

She saddled Apollo herself. The ride to town was pleasant in the afternoon sun. Autumn colors decorated the hillsides, and the smells of ripening apples and pumpkins wafted on the air. She arrived in town feeling content if not joyful.

As she entered the general store, she looked around to see who else was there. Mrs. Linde fingered a drab-brown cotton fabric. She glanced Emma's way and nodded politely, but made no effort at conversation.

Emma blushed then chastised herself for her emotional reaction. This woman had chided Mrs. Potter for allowing her to join the sewing circle then said something about it being risky. Did everyone in the room know about her husband's affair and feared exposing the guilty party? Was that the risk?

She caught her breath. It could be someone in the sewing circle! She glanced around the mercantile. It could be someone in the store. She fought the urge to rush out and return home as quickly as possible. Instead she examined a beautiful blue silk fabric. "Mr. Dodd, nine yards of this, please."

As she carried her purchases to her horse, Uriah Steeple bowed from his saddle and tipped his hat. "Ah, Mrs. Trebor. How are you? Has Apollo been staying on the road?"

"Yes, Mr. Steeple. Thank you again for your help the other day. I am indebted to you."

A silent alarm sounded to beware of this man. He had done her a great service, it was true, but why was he waiting for her outside of the mercantile? She tied her packages onto the back of her saddle and mounted. "Have a good day."

"Oh, Mrs. Trebor, might I have a word?"

"Certainly." She cringed as he rode his horse next to hers. She'd had no ill feelings about him when he rescued her, but his nearness now unnerved her. Apollo flexed his ears back, shook his head, and stamped.

Mr. Steeple blew out cigar smoke. "I'm in Schenectady on business, seeking a missing person for my client. I wonder, may I count on you to report to me if you see this child?" He showed her a sketch of a little Negro girl, about ten years old.

"A missing Negro?"

"Her family is devastated. They fear the worst. There are unscrupulous men about who will kidnap a child like this and sell her as a slave. It's even happening to adults."

Emma sighed. "I know the Fugitive Slave Law has opened the door to this kind of thing."

Mr. Steeple shook his head. "It's terrible, I tell you, but I've a talent for locating missing persons, and I take pleasure in reuniting families. So may I count on your help?"

"Certainly." As Emma rode off, she considered Mr. Steeple's words. Her heart felt for the child's parents. How terrible to fear your child had been kidnapped. And how silly she felt for the distrust she had for Uriah Steeple. Then she wondered, if he was good at locating missing persons, might he be good at exposing mistresses?

Before Paul left with the wagon, he gave Mandy a note to pass on to Joe. He'd hoped to speak with Emma before he left, but she had retired to her room with a headache the previous night, and he thought it uncaring to wake her so early this morning.

As he drove the wagon southward, he let himself dream of a life with her as his partner.

How fulfilling it would be to share the freedom seekers' stories and to work together to help them. He'd need to protect her, of course. He'd not want her trapped by a bounty hunter. She was naive—too easily duped, as his own actions proved. How many husbands would be able to deceive their wives for as long as he had?

It occurred to him that he'd never heard her story of what happened all those years ago. Had her naïveté played a part then? He knew what he'd seen, but what if there was more to it? He tried to remember why he'd never asked her and came up blank.

His heart stuttered as he considered how he refused to listen to her not just the past few days, but ever since the tragedy. What if she wasn't as guilty as she appeared? The thought stabbed deeply.

Emma remained in her room, reading her Bible and praying until she was sure Paul had left. Her prayers left her feeling tender toward her husband. She doubted her assumption of infidelity. Would the community esteem him so if he were having an affair? Might there be another explanation for his late-night absences and the woman's voice? She couldn't think of what and wished she could ask him about it.

Their lives might have been much different if he had ever asked her about her actions twenty years ago.

On her request, Beulah brought up a breakfast tray. It frustrated her that her maid didn't believe her story, but the only real difference between then and now was Emma knew what Beulah thought, where before she'd been in the dark. She couldn't fire her for openness when that's what she had demanded from her.

Emma gave her credit. She'd been a faithful maid, especially considering what she'd believed all these years, and still did her job with gentleness.

After breakfasting on toast and tea, Emma gathered the tray and headed down the stairs. As she neared the kitchen, she heard the two servants talking. It was tempting to eavesdrop, but she pushed through the door without pausing. The women stopped talking immediately and faced her.

"Good morning, ma'am." Mandy took the tray from her. As she did so, Emma saw something fall from her hand and land under a chair, but she ignored it. What did it matter if the two women passed notes? "I'll be in the sunroom sewing," she announced and left.

No sooner did she reach her destination than she decided she wanted another cup of tea. She returned to the kitchen. The room was empty but the note was still under the chair. Faceup. Revealing Paul's handwriting.

Her breath caught as she picked it up. The words brought her to her knees.

The note read:

We risk detection at the mill. Have to find a new safe place. Let me know where. Hide the note with the new location in the cottonwood stump. You know which one.

So, there it was. Right in front of her. His plans to meet with someone secretly when he returned. The missive fell from her trembling hand. It fluttered to the floor, carrying her dreams with it.

Chapter 10

I don't need the buggy today, just Apollo, please." Emma walked to the stables herself rather than sending Mandy with the message. She could barely look at the cook, let alone speak to her. It wasn't just that the woman didn't believe her story, but Paul had trusted this servant to deliver his note, meaning Mandy knew about the affair. How many times had she and Beulah laughed at her behind her back over this?

She returned to the house to change into her riding clothes, but walked around to the front door, rather than face Mandy in the kitchen. The extra steps were worth it.

When she was ready, she returned downstairs and called for her lady's maid. "If you're going to the sewing circle today, I've several garments I'd like you to deliver."

"Yes, ma'am, but I thought you were going back."

"I've changed my mind. May I count on you to deliver the dresses?"

"Of course." Beulah turned to go then paused. "Ma'am, do I still have permission to speak frankly?"

Emma stared at the black woman before her. *Why not speak frankly about my husband's mistress? Why not speak frankly about his secrets and indiscretions?* The words swam in her mind, but she held her tongue. "No, Beulah. You were right before. We should keep things as they were." Although that was not possible. She couldn't un-know that her household staff thought her a liar and a murderer, all the while protecting her husband's secrets.

She rode quietly to the mill, letting the crisp autumn day lift her spirits. Everywhere she looked she saw the beauty of God's creation, and she let it minister to her. Her soul responded to the blueness of the sky, the colors of the leaves, the chirping of birds. Even if her world was falling apart, God's faithfulness upheld her. She rejoiced in the knowledge that He loved her despite her failings and shortcomings. Experiencing God's love and mercy helped smooth the edges off the judgment she received from others. Even if her husband couldn't love her, God did, and that mattered more than all the husbands in the world.

Except. . .Even now as she rode through the forest, even as her spirit relaxed in the arms of her God, there was an unrest, and she understood its message. "Why, God?" she called aloud to the limb-crossed sky. "Why do You want me to reconcile, when he's already chosen someone else? You saw how I tried with Beulah and Mandy—how can You ask me to keep trying?"

As the mill came into view, her questions went unanswered. Joe greeted her as she tied Apollo under the apple tree. "Hello, Mrs. Trebor. I didn't expect you."

That Joe was uncomfortable was obvious. Did he know about Paul's affair as well? She had trouble meeting his eyes. "Good morning, Joe. I won't keep you from your work. Carry on."

"You know that Mr. Trebor isn't here, and the mill isn't a safe place. The machinery can be dangerous."

"Yes, I am aware of Mr. Trebor's absence, and thank you for the warning, but I don't plan on running any machinery." She'd been at the mill a number of times, so why was Joe warning her now? To dissuade her from entering?

She strode up one set of stairs and then another. On the third floor she paused outside Paul's office, her hand shaking on the doorknob. What would she find inside? Did she really want to do this? If she found a clue to the identity of Paul's mistress, she wouldn't be able to go back to when she didn't know, just like she couldn't take back her confession to Beulah and Mandy. There were some doors, which once you walked through, you could never return the same person.

Uriah Steeple ducked around the corner as the sheriff crossed the street. He'd been in town over two weeks, and people were beginning to notice him. Not a good thing. They weren't all as gullible as that Mrs. Trebor. He needed to speed things up. Chances were those shadows he saw in the mill window had already been transported away, but there'd be others, he was sure of it.

He'd been out to the mill a few times after work hours, but the guard was alert, and he couldn't gain access upstairs. It was a nuisance the fire hadn't flushed anyone out. He'd used that trick successfully a number of times. Didn't have to worry about arson charges when the runaways appeared.

He'd kept watch on the ships in harbor as well. A couple of times a week, one or more headed up the Hudson into Canada. Those were the ones to watch, but he hadn't seen anything suspicious. Yet.

Mrs. Trebor was his likeliest resource. Sweet and gullible, just the way he liked them. He had to be careful not to overplay his hand, but what luck that he had come across her at the side of the road when he did. Quite the damsel in distress.

He smiled and sucked on his cigar as he hid in the trees.

He'd just have to figure out a way to rescue Mrs. Trebor again. Build her confidence in him. Get her to trust him.

Paul drove slowly along the rutted road. The mules strained uphill, pulling the wagon overflowing with cotton. When they reached the top, he took a side lane and stopped near a decrepit barn. He waited in the inky black night, listening, listening. Tree branches scraped together in the breeze. Twigs snapped. Leaves crunched. Deer? Porcupines? Bounty hunters? Stumps looked like crouched men. Was someone hiding behind that rock?

After several moments, he jumped down from the wagon and led the mules to a trough. As he pumped water for them, his eyes peered into the darkness. The signs were wrong. A barred barn door meant water the mules and keep going. An open door meant pick up the freight.

The door was closed. Not barred, but not open. Blown shut by the wind? Unbarred by a hunter on to their scheme? Waiting inside? Outside?

He couldn't just ride on. Not if there were freedom seekers inside without food or water. As the mules drank, he approached the barn door. It creaked loudly as he opened it. He lit his lantern and entered, lifting the scant light to illuminate the dark corners.

A whisper reached his ears. Someone was there. But who? A freedom seeker or a bounty hunter? He pretended to look for oats in stacked grain bags as he tied a blue handkerchief around his neck—the signal to let any runaway know he was the next conductor.

He caught movement out of the corner of his eye. "Is it safe?" Whispered words carried hope.

Paul put a finger to his lips. Something felt wrong. He held up his palm as if to say *stop* and went back outside. The mules had stopped drinking. Their upright ears twitched, and they looked to the south of the barn.

Could be a deer.

Or not.

He led the mules away from the trough and backed the wagon into the barn. A figure moved as silently as a shadow toward him. Paul handed him a canteen and a bag filled with biscuits. Then the runaway crawled into the false bottom of the wagon. The process took less than two minutes.

A boot scuffed the ground outside. Paul whirled around. "Who's there?"

Chapter 11

Emma opened the office door and stepped inside. The desk was as tidy as the one in Paul's study at home. She searched the closet first—where the woman's voice had come from. She saw no door, but there had to be.

Emma felt along the sides of the wall, along the floor. She stood on a stool to feel higher up on the wall and then the ceiling. And that's where it was. *Click*. The secret door opened.

It was not what she expected. Certainly not a lovers' nest. There was a mattress on the floor, a table with four chairs, two candles, and a washstand. Nothing more. No windows. No carpet. Nothing remotely romantic.

But it was a secret room. And there had been a woman in it.

She took her time searching the room and Paul's office, but found nothing suspicious.

As she rode from the mill, Emma gave Apollo his head. She couldn't imagine a mistress being satisfied with such a meager room. Whoever it was would know Paul could provide much better accommodations. She prayed, "What does it mean, Father?"

These words came to her mind. *"Be not overcome with evil, but overcome evil with good."*

It was not the comfort she'd anticipated. "What do you mean, God? I'm being overcome with evil? What more good should I do? I confessed to Beulah and Mandy. You saw where that got me. And I'm not trying to punish Paul; I just want to know who has taken my place."

Apollo began to veer off the road, but Emma checked him. Then she saw it was the same place he had pulled off with the buggy, and the little creek beckoned to her. She dismounted and led her horse along the worn path to the edge of the stream. As he drank, she leaned against the familiar hollow stump and continued praying.

When she quieted her mind and stopped arguing with God, she understood His words to her. Mandy and Beulah were wrong not to believe her, but God would have her forgive them and do good to them, instead of avoiding them and acting as if she were guilty. God had forgiven her at great cost; she need not ever claim that guilt again. In that gracious freedom, she could overcome all things by loving those who didn't love her.

Even Paul? She dropped Apollo's reins and covered her face. "It is asking too much!"

A gunshot blasted nearby. Spooked, Apollo reared. He galloped away, crashing through the brush along the creek.

"Apollo!" Emma's heart pounded in staccato rhythm to the horse's thudding hooves. He could hurt himself with the uneven footing or trip on the dangling reins. "Apollo!"

A man shuffled into the lantern light—unshaven, rumpled, and carrying a rifle. "Whoo-hoo! Caught ya, red-handed!"

Paul lifted his lantern to better see the stranger facing him. "I don't know what you're talking about. Caught me red-handed at what? Getting my cotton out of the night air?"

The stranger scowled. "You expect me to believe that? What kind of fool do you take me to be?"

"Look, mister, I don't know what you think I'm doing, but I don't want any trouble. I've used this barn for years on my way home—it's a good place to water the mules, keep the cotton dry overnight, and get some shut-eye myself." Paul climbed up on the wagon and took the mules' reins in his sweaty hands. "But if you have a problem with me being here, I'll leave. Like I said, I don't want any trouble."

The stranger blocked the doorway. "If'n you don't want trouble, then you won't mind me searching your wagon."

"If you don't want trouble, you'll get out of my way." Paul slapped the reins against the mules' back. They stepped forward.

The stranger stood his ground. "I got the law behind me. Fugitive Slave Act says I can detain anyone I suspect is transporting slaves."

"This wagon is full of cotton. If you think I've got runaways aboard, you're crazy. There isn't room for another pound of cotton, let alone a grown man—or a child, for that matter."

The bounty hunter walked alongside the wagon, jabbing the barrel of his rifle here and there into the cotton bales.

The mules kept walking out of the barn.

"Why you in such an all-fire hurry to get shut of this place?" The stranger cradled his rifle in his arms and walked to the front of the wagon.

" 'Cause all I want is a little sleep, and I'm not going to get it here."

"Tell you what, you get down from the wagon, and we'll have ourselves a little campfire. You can get some shut-eye. I'll keep watch over the wagon for you." The stranger snickered. "I'll watch it real good."

The false bottom was about a foot and a half deep. It was a terrible way to travel, but worse to wait. He couldn't stop all night with a freedom seeker trapped in that small space. Nor did he want to give the bounty hunter any extra time to examine the wagon. The false bottom was well hidden, but not invisible.

Should he get off the wagon as the stranger said, or make a run for it?

A run for it with mules?

Yeah, right.

Emma fisted her hands. "Apollo, come back!" But the horse was nowhere in sight. Then suddenly galloping hooves splashed through the creek. A rider sped by in a blur, but she recognized the dapple gray. Mr. Steeple to her rescue again?

He returned with Apollo in tow. "I believe this belongs to you." He handed her the reins.

"Thank you, again." Emma felt her cheeks flush.

"You are welcome." Mr. Steeple dismounted. "My own mount bolted. It was perhaps fortuitous you were not riding when the pistol fired. Whoever shot that gun should be horsewhipped."

Emma drew a deep breath. She took this man's appearance as a sign from God that she should seek his help. After all, he'd shown up twice now when she needed someone. This was a prime opportunity to request Mr. Steeple's assistance to find Paul's mistress, but it was hard to ask. She opened her mouth several times, but the words wouldn't come. Her pride had caused her problems before. She needed to humble herself.

"Is there something on your mind, Mrs. Trebor?"

Apparently he had noticed.

"Yes, actually there is, but I'm hesitant to ask. It's personal." Emma stared at the ground. She swallowed against the lump in her throat. A voice cautioned her to be careful. She heard it and ascribed the warning as against her stubborn pride. She would humble herself. She would defeat pride.

"Mr. Steeple, I have reason to believe my husband is. . .seeing another woman. I fear it has been going on for some time, and I've determined to travel to my eldest daughter for a while to sort things out." Her gaze remained fixed on the ground as she spoke. "But before I go, I want to know who the woman is. I'm not seeking revenge or any type of retribution; I just want to know who she is. Will you help me?"

The words were out. She could not take them back. But she did not feel relieved.

"Mrs. Trebor, I hate to ask this, but are you sure? What evidence do you have against your husband?"

Did she have to say? Yes. If he were going to help her, he needed something to go on. She told him about the late nights, his secretive ways, the hidden room, and the note she'd found. "I'll pay you, of course."

She bowed her head as she remembered the missing cash from the safe. "I cannot pay you in cash, but I have this." She removed the clock pendant from around her neck—a present from Paul—and handed it to him. "The diamonds and rubies are real. I believe it has value."

Uriah pocketed the jewelry without examining it. "I know this is hard, but I think I can help."

Emma's eyes lifted to his face then strayed toward the creek. Her gaze landed on the stump. "Oh! This could be the stump mentioned in the note."

A worn trail led from the road to the creek, right past the hollow stump. Maybe all she had to do was wait. Wait and see who responded to Paul's message.

Uriah Steeple grinned. Luck was certainly his friend. He had planned to spook the horse when he shot off the gun. Then he'd show up—a knight in shining armor to rescue her. He hadn't anticipated the gullible woman would give him everything he needed to capture her husband—and pay for the privilege as well.

Paul got down from the wagon. "Looks like we got off on the wrong foot." He extended his hand. "My name's Paul Trebor. I came to Virginia to buy cotton and take it to my mill in Schenectady. I've been doing it for over fifteen years without any trouble. Now I know you folks here in Virginia have trouble with slaves running away and Northerners helping them. But President Fillmore hails from New York, you know, and without him, I doubt the Fugitive Slave Act would have passed."

It galled Paul to put on such a show when he knew the danger this fellow presented to his freight, but what was that saying? Keep your friends close and your enemies closer?

He kept up the friendly banter until the bounty hunter shook his hand. "I'm LeRoy. Sorry to make trouble, but there's a regular highway of runaways escaping north, and I'm doing my patriotic duty to stop it."

Paul rubbed the stubble on his chin. "If it's as bad as you say, I might need to buy my cotton someplace else. I can't afford to be challenged every step of the way. Maybe I should try Kentucky."

"You don't want to do that. You can't grow decent cotton in Kentucky. Virginia needs good folks to buy our cotton. Tell you what. I got something for you." LeRoy pulled a wooden token about the size of a half dollar from his pocket. Carved in the center of the circle were the letters *VPU*.

"What does this mean?" Paul turned the disk over in his hand.

"Virginia Patriotic Union. If you get stopped, just pull this out and show them. You won't have no more trouble. In Virginia, anyway."

"Thanks. Thanks a lot." Paul shook LeRoy's hand again. Now wasn't it just like God to take a dangerous situation and turn it around for good? If the token was worth anything, it could make his future trips south as easy as falling off a horse.

Paul waited for LeRoy to leave then hustled the mules down the road. Hours later, he stopped near a stream and let out his passenger.

"It'll be best if you don't sit within the light of the fire." Paul handed him beef jerky and an apple. "I'm Paul Trebor."

"I'm Samson, and thank you, sir. Sure do appreciate your help."

"It's an honor." Paul settled against a tree trunk. The freedom seeker leaned against a wagon wheel. "You're alone," Paul said. "Are you leaving someone behind or meeting up in Canada?"

"Meeting up in Canada, except my woman probably thinks I'm dead."

"You left together and got separated?" Paul breathed in deeply. This was a familiar story.

Samson nodded. "Yes, sir. I drew away the ones after us to give my Tabitha and the chilluns a chance to escape."

"Did you say Tabitha? She have two children with her, Isaiah and Leah?"

"Yes, sir. How do you know their names?"

"I've seen her and the children. She told me you two were to be married in Canada."

"Praise God, praise God." Tears flowed like rain down Samson's cheeks.

Chapter 12

Emma sewed. She made dresses and men's shirts. She told herself as soon as she finished the one she was working on, she'd purchase serviceable material and make sturdy work clothes, but the nicer, prettier fabric always won out—even for the men's shirts.

The letter from Charlotte arrived, welcoming her to come and stay as long as she wanted. Emma's trunk was packed. As soon as she heard from Mr. Steeple, she'd be off on the next train. Hopefully before Paul returned home.

On Sunday, Emma went to church. Without Paul by her side, she felt vulnerable. Not even the women from the sewing circle returned her smiles. The Reverend Bachus was courteous as always, asking about Paul and news from her daughters.

As Emma headed downstairs to the basement with a bundle of new clothing, Reverend Bachus stopped her. "Mrs. Trebor, may I take that for you?"

"Thank you, Reverend, but it's not necessary." She shrugged. "I'm just adding to the collection for the poor."

He edged past her and reached for the bundle. "I'm headed down anyway. I can take this from here."

As she released the bundle, she had the impression the reverend didn't want her in the basement. Why would he be heading that way, when his flock milled around outside waiting to shake his hand?

Suddenly Mrs. Linde was at her side. The same Mrs. Linde who had looked the other way when Emma smiled at her before services. "Mrs. Trebor," she said. "I wanted to thank you for your many donations for the poor. You do have a flair with a needle." She took Emma's arm and escorted her back up the stairs.

God said to love her, Emma reminded herself. "I enjoy sewing, so it's a blessing to me to be able to contribute."

They reached the top of the stairs, but Mrs. Linde kept hold of Emma's arm. "When will Mr. Trebor be back?"

"I think anytime." Emma wondered at the attempt at small talk. What was going on? She allowed Mrs. Linde to walk her to her buggy.

"Good day, Mrs. Trebor. I hope you have a pleasant afternoon."

Uriah had spent hours hiding behind a spruce tree on the opposite side of the creek from the hollow stump. Cold had seeped into his very bones, but his patience paid off. Just before sunset on his second day of surveillance, Joe appeared on the path. He watched the foreman slink toward the creek. He held his breath when the man's gaze swept toward the tree. But

Joe put the folded paper into the stump and hurried away.

Uriah counted to one hundred before he slipped into view, crossed the creek, and retrieved the note. "Eight bundles of wood. Presbyterian church. Pattyroller watching."

Uriah's grin grew. The message was easy to decipher. He now knew there were eight runaways hiding in the Presbyterian church, and just as important, they'd identified him as a bounty hunter. He'd overstayed his welcome, but he'd not leave without his prize.

It was afternoon when Paul arrived back in Schenectady with his load of cotton. Normally he'd drive straight to the mill and hide the freedom seeker in his secret room, but the station had been compromised, and after bringing Samson so close, he couldn't risk it. He stopped at the path leading to the creek and retrieved the message from the hole in the top of the stump. It would let him know his next steps.

He unfolded the paper and read it. So a total of eight were hiding at the church. That was risky. The ships must be well watched not to have shipped out any packages. Maybe Tabitha and the children were among those still waiting. Wouldn't that be a grand thing!

But what excuse would he have for stopping at the church with a load of cotton?

He'd have to bring Samson home with him. Hide him in the stables until dark, then get him to the church.

From the sunroom, Emma watched Paul pull in with the empty wagon. Her heart stuttered at the sight of him, but she quieted it. God was asking her to be loving, and she would. She'd ask her husband no questions. She'd be kind and gracious.

The wagon disappeared around the corner of the stable, and Emma returned to her sewing. She strained to hear Paul's footsteps in the hallway. She knew he'd not come to the sunroom, but still she listened. Even so, she was surprised when he entered.

"Beulah said I'd find you in here." He met her gaze and smiled.

Emma rose. "I hope your trip was successful."

"Yes, very." He stepped toward her. "I need to clean up and make a trip to town. When I return, I'd like to speak with you."

Emma's heart stopped. What did he mean? To tell her about his mistress? No, his face was too tender, his voice too compassionate for that. Had something happened on the trip to soften his heart toward her?

Now that was wishful thinking. First of all, he was cleaning up and going to town first.

Maybe she could go with him.

Dusk settled before Paul came down the stairs. Emma approached him in the hallway. "I have a completed garment to donate to the poor. May I ride into town with you? I could drop it off at the church."

Paul's eyes widened slightly, and he appeared disturbed. "I'm sorry, my dear. It won't do just now. But I shan't be long and we'll talk."

Emma stepped back. She pasted on a smile she did not feel. "Of course." She watched him leave, her heart shrinking with each step he took away from her.

"Beulah," she called. When her servant appeared, she said, "I'll be leaving tomorrow on the first train. Will you make sure my trunk is ready to go?"

"Yes, ma'am."

"And when Mr. Trebor returns, please tell him I've a headache and gone to bed."

"Yes, ma'am."

Uriah walked along the docks. Ships were preparing to sail, but as yet he'd discovered no sign of the runaways. He had considered charging into the church and arresting them on Sunday just to cause a scene and upset the do-gooders. But he couldn't pass up the opportunity to see the look on the Trebors' faces when each realized what the other had done. He chuckled to himself.

Even though Paul would be arrested and have to cough up a large sum of money, possibly losing his mill, it would be Mrs. Trebor who would suffer the most. The foolish woman would blame herself the rest of her life for thinking ill of her husband and causing his demise. He rubbed his hands together in glee at the pain he'd cause.

And it would all happen today.

Sounds of horse hooves brought Emma to the window again. Had Paul returned so soon? He hadn't had time to get to town, let alone come back home. Perhaps he'd changed his mind! Maybe he'd come back for her.

It was the dapple gray horse. Mr. Steeple. Probably coming with news.

News she no longer wanted to hear. Trusting God would protect her heart, not knowledge. She could no longer remember why the identity of Paul's mistress mattered. It was better if she didn't know, then she wouldn't be able to picture them together. Nameless and faceless was better after all. Putting it all in God's capable hands would give her the peace she sought. That's what He was telling her. *"Do not be overcome by evil, but overcome evil with good."* Sneaking around trying to uncover secrets was not overcoming evil with good.

She opened the front door herself when he knocked. "Good evening, Mr. Steeple." She did not invite him inside.

"Good evening, Mrs. Trebor. I've already asked your stableman to saddle your horse. I believe you'll want to come to town with me."

"I'm sorry, Mr. Steeple, but I've changed my mind. I no longer want to know the woman's identity. But I appreciate all you've done for me."

"I see. Well, I still think you should come with me. There's doings you'll want to witness."

"I'm sorry, Mr. Steeple. I've a headache, and I'll be leaving in the morning. I've a lot to do."

She started to close the door, but Steeple reached through and grabbed her arm. "I insist you come."

She pulled back, but his grip held. He dragged her onto the porch. Emma yelled for help. Screamed and kicked.

"Let go of her!" Clancy had brought Apollo around. He dropped the horse's reins and punched Steeple in the jaw.

Steeple stumbled off the steps and fell to the ground. He was on his feet in a moment. "You'll be sorry," he shouted, then mounted his horse and raced away.

Emma trembled. What had just happened? Why had that man turned on her? She'd thought him an ally.

"Are you all right, ma'am?"

"Yes, Clancy, thank you. I think I'll sit here on the steps a moment."

As Emma sat, she put the puzzle pieces together in a different way.

Paul's late-night expeditions, a hidden room, a woman's voice, a secret message didn't necessarily mean an affair.

What if he were involved with the Underground Railroad? She ran through the house to the kitchen. "Mandy! Beulah!"

"Yes, ma'am?"

"Paul's late-night excursions, they were to the cotton mill, where he hid freedom seekers. Am I right?"

The servants stared at her, fear in their eyes. It was enough of an answer.

"Oh no! I've done it again."

But this time she'd not let fear paralyze her. She'd act.

If it wasn't too late.

Chapter 13

As Paul drove the buggy toward town, he felt both cautious and excited. He'd hidden Samson behind the buggy seat, covered with a blanket. It was not an ideal situation, but they had a short distance to go.

Possibly, Tabitha and Samson would be reunited in a short while. He wanted to see that moment. It gave him great joy to know he had a part in making it happen. But he couldn't let his enthusiasm cloud his judgment. It would be devastating to come so close and be discovered.

Dusk lingered. He parked at the church and waited for Joe to join him and for darkness to deepen. He quieted his nerves by humming "Amazing Grace."

A familiar-looking, cigar-smoking man strolled his way. When the sheriff appeared with several deputies, Paul smelled the trap. He whispered, "Samson, stay low. We got trouble."

Paul yelled, "Hie!" and snapped the whip, but it wasn't enough. The stranger grabbed the horse's halter, and the buggy stopped.

"Arrest him, Sheriff."

"You got to produce the runaways first." Sheriff Martin shook his head as he met Paul's gaze. "This your arsonist, Paul?"

"Yep."

"Sure do wish you'd have pressed charges. Meet Uriah Steeple, bounty hunter."

Uriah reached into the buggy and pulled the blanket off Samson. The black man jumped out and ran. Uriah pulled out a revolver and fired.

Samson fell.

Paul tackled Uriah, but the sheriff pulled him off. "He's within his rights, Paul. It galls me to say it, but you know it's true."

Uriah grinned. "Don't figure that one's going anywhere fast, but come with me, Sheriff. There's more inside."

Clancy exchanged horses for the tired mules. Emma grasped the reins, shouting, "Hie! Hie!" as Beulah and Mandy tried to stay seated in the wagon. Arriving in town, her heart stuttered. She was too late. Townspeople had gathered, most holding torches. She stopped the wagon far back from the scene.

Paul and Joe were handcuffed near the buggy. Eight people sat tied together in the church courtyard, four adults and four children. A man lay on the ground nearby, blood oozing from his leg. Heart-wrenching wails filled the air.

No one appeared to have noticed Emma's arrival. She turned to Beulah and Mandy and whispered, "Take the wagon behind the jailhouse." Silently, she got down.

Her mind whirling, Emma stood behind a tree, watching the scene. She had no plan. Sending the wagon behind the jailhouse was a hunch. She had no idea how it would help, other than keeping her servants safe.

"You all should know," Uriah shouted so everyone could hear, "that I have Mrs. Trebor to thank for the success of this little roundup. She told me about the secret room at the mill and the hollow stump where I found the message. Even paid me." He held up Emma's pendant.

The crowd murmured, but it was the look on Paul's face that smote Emma's heart. She fought the urge to run to him and explain, but what could she say? Uriah was telling the truth.

"Okay, people, the show's over. Go back to your homes." The sheriff gestured for Paul and Joe to walk in front of him. Two deputies supported Samson. Uriah held the ropes tying the runaways together.

An idea came to Emma. It wasn't much of one—it could backfire horribly—but she had to do something. She waited until the crowd moved away from the church then unhitched Perseus from the buggy.

Uriah's words about Emma pierced Paul's heart. It couldn't be true. He looked at Joe.

"She found the secret room, boss. Mandy delivered the message to me, that's all I know."

So she had discovered the secret room. Had he really thought she wouldn't look?

The procession flowed toward the jailhouse as the community followed, yelling jeers and taunts at Uriah. He grinned back then jerked on the rope he held, causing several captives to fall.

A deputy grabbed the rope from him. "Get out of here." He brandished his gun. "If I were you, I'd find someplace to lay low. This crowd might turn any minute."

Uriah slunk off.

Anger welled up inside Paul. He didn't care about himself. He'd be fined a large sum, perhaps lose his home and the mill, but that was nothing compared to what these freedom seekers would endure. All would be severely punished by their masters. Some would die. Some would wish they could die.

He slowed his pace to match that of the deputies walking with Samson. "Did you see her, Samson? Tabitha is still here with the children."

Samson stopped moving. "Not safe in Canada?" Tears coated his words.

As soon as Emma was out of town, she urged Perseus to a full gallop. A diversion was needed. Something big. Something that would force everyone to help.

Like a fire.

She couldn't set fire to a building in town. That could be catastrophic. The whole town could suffer.

But the mill was a short distance from town.

With trembling hands, Emma touched the match flame to a ball of cotton fluff in the bale shed. She blew on the sparks then fanned the tiny tendril. When strong flames appeared, Emma mounted Perseus and raced back to town, shouting, "Fire at the mill! The cotton mill's on fire!" She rounded the corner behind the jailhouse as the streets filled with men running for the mill.

Mandy and Beulah were still in the wagon.

"In five minutes, drive to the front."

Emma dismounted and ran around to the front of the jailhouse. She barged in, startling the deputy on duty. "The mill is on fire! What are you doing here?"

"Somebody's got to guard the prisoners."

"I'll guard them. If the mill burns, a lot of people will lose their livelihood. Go! Help!" Would the deputy trust her as a guard? He would if he believed the things Uriah said.

He hesitated.

"If you care at all for Paul, you'll do all you can to save his mill."

The deputy ran out—with the keys.

Emma searched the desk, the drawers, the walls for another set. Finally she found them on a hook on the inner side of the desk. She ran to the cells and unlocked the doors. "There's a wagon waiting. Hurry. Go!" She glimpsed Paul run past, but there was no time to talk.

"Get in," Paul yelled, and jumped on the wagon seat. Joe sat next to him. The runaways helped Samson into the back of the wagon and jumped in themselves.

"Hang on," Paul shouted then asked Joe, "Can we get them on a ship?"

"No ships in port sailing north for two days." Joe rubbed his forehead.

"Then our options are limited." Paul flicked the reins again and turned the wagon toward his home. It wasn't safe, but it might buy time until they could think of something else. Nine people bounced in the back of the wagon as Paul raced home.

When Paul stopped in front of the manor, Joe's brow furrowed. "Inside the house? Not the stable?"

"I want them in my home. And I'll shoot anyone who tries to come after them."

Emma rode Perseus down the road to the mill. On the way she passed the path to the creek and noted Uriah's dapple gray under a tree. She'd like to stop and give Mr. Steeple a piece of her mind, but more important was saving the mill—from the fire she started.

A water brigade was already set up, and she joined the ranks, risking recognition by the deputy. But she had to help. It was her husband's mill.

The bale shed was destroyed. Windows were broken in the main building, but it was made of brick and less susceptible to fire damage.

Had anyone recognized her as she rode through town shouting, "Fire"? She counted on the darkness, the surprise, and her horse's speed to disguise her. If she were suspected of alerting the town, there would be a lot of questions to answer.

With the fire out, men milled about. Emma shrank back into the shadows. Most of them had heard Uriah's accusations, and some probably believed him. Helping put out the fire would not vindicate her. She listened to the chatter.

"Wonder how it started."

"Hey, I saw that Steeple's horse on the path to the creek."

"Think he did it?"

"He tried once before."

"Why'd he want to burn the mill?"

"Punish Paul for helping the freedom seekers."

"Who else could it be? Nobody in town has anything against Paul."

"You say you saw him by the creek? Let's go."

Emma rode back to town and waited in the sheriff's chair for the deputy's return.

"Hey! What happened here?" The sheriff walked in smelling of smoke. "Mrs. Trebor, can you tell me why you are here and the prisoners are not?" He shoved a handcuffed Uriah Steeple into a cell and locked it.

"Yes, sir, I can. The mill was on fire, and I wanted every able-bodied person to help fight it, so I badgered your deputy to let me guard them."

Uriah shouted from his cell, "You got to arrest her, Sheriff! She let my runaways go!"

The sheriff planted his hands on his hips and faced Uriah. "Now why would she do that? According to you, she went to a lot of trouble to help you round them up. Don't make sense that she'd let them go."

"I confess, Sheriff, that I didn't stay to guard them. I thought about the fire and my husband's mill, and I had to help, so I left my post and went to the mill. Can you arrest me for deserting my post?" Emma rose from the chair.

"No, Mrs. Trebor. You are not a deputy. You didn't have a post to desert."

Uriah rattled the cell bars. "Somebody let my runaways go. I want them back."

"It could have been most anyone in town. Without a clue, I'm not going to waste my time investigating." The sheriff sat in his chair. "Why don't you go on home, Mrs. Trebor? It's been a long night."

"Thank you, Sheriff. But one more thing. What has Mr. Steeple done that you've arrested him?"

"Arson. Started the fire at the mill. I'll keep him in custody till Paul can come in and press charges."

Emma's conscience bothered her as she drove the buggy home. Uriah was in jail for the fire she'd started. She'd have to go back and confess, of course—after the freedom seekers were safely on their way to Canada.

Chapter 14

Emma wasn't surprised when she arrived home to a houseful of strangers. She laughed aloud to see children in her daughters' rooms.

But there was Paul to face. He had wanted to talk before the night's debacle. Did he even want to see her now? She went to her room and prayed. "I misjudged my husband. You tried to tell me. My distrust led to disaster. Thank You for rescuing me."

At the knock on her door, she rose. Paul entered her room.

Emma's throat constricted. Sweat coated her palms. She waited for him to speak but kept her gaze on the floor. She couldn't bear his censure tonight.

"Can we talk?"

She nodded.

They sat on the window seat.

"How much of what Uriah said was true?" His voice was neither accusing nor tender.

"All of it. I didn't know you were hiding freedom seekers. I thought you were having an affair. I uncovered secrets and told Steeple because I thought it would expose your mistress." Emma's head remained bowed. "I'm so sorry."

"When did you discover I had no mistress?"

"After you left this evening, Steeple came and urged me to accompany him, but I refused. He turned ugly, and if it hadn't been for Clancy, I may have been in danger. Then I put the clues together in a different way. We—myself, Beulah, and Mandy—came as quickly as we could to warn you, but I was too late."

"That's what Mandy said."

The room fell silent. Emma could not look up. She couldn't meet his eyes, couldn't endure his disapproval. She should have known better than to entertain thoughts of his infidelity. He was a good, good man. Better than she deserved.

Paul broke the silence. "Mandy also told me another story. One that happened twenty years ago."

Emma glanced up. "But she doesn't believe it."

"She does now. And I do too." He took her hands in his. "I was wrong not to ask your side of the story. I was wrong to think so ill of you. Will you forgive me?"

"Yes! Can you forgive me?"

Paul took her in his arms. Their tears mingled as their hearts re-joined.

He whispered in her ear, "Can we start over, Emma?"

She leaned into his embrace.

"Do you love me, Emma?"

"Yes, yes, yes." She smothered his face with kisses until she found his mouth, and a long-overdue passion built.

Early the next morning, Paul rode into town, waved at Uriah through the jailhouse window, then stopped at the Presbyterian church. After speaking with Reverend Bachus a few minutes, he left, smiling, and returned to the manor.

He found Mandy in the kitchen, whispered instructions to her, then bounded upstairs, taking two steps at a time.

Samson swung open his door before Paul had a chance to knock. "Something wrong?" Worry lines creased his face.

"No, nothing's wrong." Paul entered the room Samson shared with another male freedom seeker and shut the door. "Been through a lot lately, haven't we?"

The men nodded, their eyes cautious.

"But today is for celebrating."

Samson shook his head. "We ain't in Canada yet."

"That's true. But the bounty hunter is in jail and Sheriff Martin won't be letting him out anytime soon. No one knows you are here. I say we celebrate, Samson, with a wedding."

"You mean today?"

"What's Canada got that we can't provide right here, this afternoon?"

"Yes, sir!" Samson almost danced a jig, but for his wounded leg. "Have you spoken to Tabitha?"

Paul grinned. "Didn't think that my place."

Samson raced down the hall as if his gunshot wound didn't exist.

Emma's brow furrowed as Beulah entered her room, wedding dress in her arms.

"Do you think we could use this again?"

"I suppose, but I'm confused." Emma fingered the smooth satin fabric. "Who?"

Beulah explained about Samson and Tabitha. "They want to get married today, right here. I think this will fit her."

Joy flowed through Emma. "Of course! Bring her in, have her try it on."

Delectable smells of fresh-baked bread and roasted chicken wafted through the manor as Mandy put the freedom seekers to work helping her prepare a wedding feast.

Paul found Emma gathering the few remaining mums from the garden for Tabitha's bridal bouquet. She blushed as his gaze met hers, and he took her in his arms again.

"Joe has secured passage for our guests. They'll leave around midnight on a ship going to Canada."

"So we just have to keep them safe until then."

Paul nodded then whispered in her ear. "Emma, will you marry me—again?"

A few unexpected guests showed up with Reverend Bachus. Mrs. Linde and Mrs. Potter embraced Emma, tears glistening. "Forgive us?" they asked.

She kissed their cheeks. Everything she'd ever wanted was coming true.

After Reverend Bachus united Tabitha and Samson, Paul and Emma stood before him.

She held Paul's hands as the reverend blessed them. Gazing into Paul's eyes, she felt his intensity. Never again would she doubt his devotion. This wonderful man loved her, and now trusted her as well.

If the guests were confused by the double wedding, they kept it to themselves, for one thing was obvious to everyone: underground weddings were the best of all.

Barbara Tifft Blakey lives in the Pacific Northwest on five wooded acres with Terry, her husband of forty-plus years. She is best known for her award-winning, literature-inspired language arts program, *Total Language Plus*, which she created over twenty years ago and is used by thousands of homeschoolers. Barbara teaches Sunday school and enjoys speaking on various topics to Christian women's groups. She and her husband have four grown children and five grandchildren. She enjoys camping at the ocean and is an avid soccer fan. During the daylight-challenged winter months, she reads, crochets, bakes, and plots her next novel.

Follow the Christmas Star

by Ramona K. Cecil

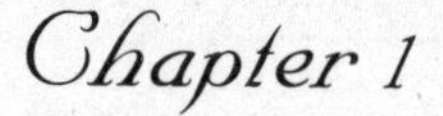

Chapter 1

Madison, Indiana
1850

Ah, don't cry, Dahlia." Edith reached out and brushed away the tear meandering down the little girl's dusky cheek, her heart crumpling. "I'll be back every Tuesday to teach you and the other children." She gave Dahlia a brave smile. "And maybe you can come visit me in Lancaster."

Dahlia sniffed and ran her hand under her nose. She looked up from wrapping Mother's prized alabaster vase in an outdated edition of the *Madison Courier*, fresh tears glistening in her sad brown eyes. "I know, but it won't be the same. I won't be able to come and see you whenever I want to like I do now."

Despite Edith's desire to comfort Dahlia, she knew the girl was right. Life *wasn't* going to be the same. Nothing had been the same since Mother's death from cholera five months ago. And now that Father had resigned his position as president of Applegate Pork Packing Company to accept a teaching position at the Eleutherian Institute eleven miles north in Lancaster, her life would again change.

Edith gazed around the familiar parlor of the home she'd known all her life, and her heart constricted. Father's new position at the institute came with a house.

An involuntary shudder slithered through her at the memory of her first look at the run-down structure she would soon call home. The thought of living in any strange house, let alone the decrepit building that she and Father had toured last week, felt at once saddening and frightening.

"I can do all things through Christ which strengtheneth me." The scripture from Philippians that had encouraged her since she'd first learned of the impending move buoyed her spirit. She must stay focused on the institute's mission that she and Father had joined: the education of all regardless of race or gender, especially those freed from slavery.

Still, however noble the mission before them, it didn't negate Edith's sadness in leaving Madison. At least she'd managed to convince her brother, Edwin, not to sell their beloved home outright but instead to rent it to an employee of the family's company he now headed.

Fighting back her own tears, Edith forced her lips into a stiff smile and pulled Dahlia into a warm hug. While she cared for all her students—the dozen or so free black children she'd taught in her home over the past year—nine-year-old Dahlia Taylor was her favorite. With her quick wit and engaging personality, the girl had entangled herself in Edith's heartstrings. In truth, Dahlia had become an invaluable asset in the classroom, and Edith wasn't sure she could have managed packing away everything for this move without Dahlia's help. "We'll be seeing each other often. Edwin and Sophie have agreed to let us use the music room at their home once a week for a classroom."

She gently pushed Dahlia away and schooled her voice to her best stern teacher tone. "Right now, we need to finish packing up this room." She managed a smile. "And tomorrow

I could really use your help packing the books in the library if your mother can spare you."

Dahlia nodded, her dark eyes brightening with enthusiasm. "I'll ask Mama, but I'm sure she'll let me come."

The faint sound of a door creaking open followed by footsteps echoing in the library down the hall surprised Edith, bringing her to her feet. "Father must have returned earlier than he'd expected." When he'd invited her to accompany him to Lancaster for a faculty meeting with the other members of the Eleutherian Institute, he'd told her it would be an all-day affair. Longing to spend as much time as possible in her childhood home, Edith had declined, opting instead to stay and, with Dahlia's help, box up some personal items to take to Lancaster.

She took the wrapped vase from Dahlia's hands and nestled it into the wooden crate with other wrapped glass bric-a-brac. "Would you please go to the library and ask Father to carry this crate to the wagon? It's a little heavy, and I wouldn't want to drop it."

Nodding, Dahlia popped up from her crouch beside the crate and sprinted out the door. She returned a few seconds later, her dark eyes the size of dollar pieces. "Miss Edith, it ain't Mr. Applegate! Or Mr. Edwin, either."

"It's *not* Mr. Applegate, Dahlia. *Ain't* isn't a word." Edith started for the door, curiosity laced with growing concern eclipsing her teacher's impulse to correct her student's grammar. She struggled to affect an unconcerned smile and lowered her voice to a near whisper. "You stay here, Dahlia, but if you hear any commotion or trouble, head out through the kitchen and fetch Mr. Edwin."

The heavy footfalls still echoing in the library suggested sturdy male boots. Edith's heart thumped harder. Could a brazen thief have heard that she and Father were moving out and decided to take advantage of a supposed uninhabited house in full daylight? Perhaps she should have grabbed the iron poker from the parlor fireplace before heading out to confront the intruder.

Whatever she'd expected to find in the library in no way matched the reality of what she saw. The sight brought her up short in the doorway, her pulse slowing as bewilderment replaced her mounting fear. Unless thieves had taken to dressing in gray broadcloth coats with matching beaver hats, starched white shirts, and black string ties, she doubted that the man standing in the middle of the library's parquet floor and looking up at her grandfather's portrait above the fireplace posed a threat to her or her property. Still, the audacity of the man to enter her home uninvited sparked her ire.

"May I be of assistance?" Edith didn't try to blunt the sharpness in her voice.

The man jerked around to face her, his comely features reddening. He hurried to remove his beaver hat, revealing a thick shock of sand-colored hair. "I beg your pardon, miss. I was of the understanding that the house was unoccupied."

"Yes, I expect you were." Edith drenched her words in sarcasm. She met his blue-eyed gaze with an unblinking glare. "You have exactly thirty seconds to either explain your presence or leave the premises before I go fetch Sheriff Wharton." She kept one foot on the hall side of the threshold in the event that she needed to make a hasty retreat.

To his credit the intruder stood his ground, his complexion returning to a normal hue. He gave a deep bow, sweeping his hat in front of him. "Wade Beaumont at your service, ma'am. I was invited by my employer, Edwin Applegate, to peruse the place in advance of taking up residence here." His thick Southern accent, while pleasant to Edith's ears, at the same time alarmed her. The new Fugitive Slave Act had put every abolitionist as well as the free blacks north of the Ohio River on keen alert. Edith sent up a silent prayer that Dahlia had already left the house through the kitchen. Though her brother tended to be a bit gullible, she couldn't imagine that Edwin would hire someone who might jeopardize the freedom of those they'd worked so hard to help bring out of bondage.

Mr. Beaumont's well-shaped lips, beneath a neatly clipped mustache, quirked up. "So if you are the cook here, as well as the cleaning lady"—his gaze settled on her dust-covered apron—"I like my coffee black and my johnnycakes with plenty of butter and maple syrup. And assuming there is still a bedstead somewhere in this domicile"—his gaze panned the room void of furniture—"I'll want a bed-warmer run over my sheets as the October nights here are turning uncomfortably chilly."

"Oh no, I am not..."

A mischievous twinkle glinted in his eyes.

Indignation roiled in Edith's chest. The insufferable man was teasing her! How could Edwin have hired such an oaf?

Stiffening her spine, she stood at her full five feet three inches. "I, sir, am Edith Applegate, Edwin Applegate's sister. This is. . .was my home." To her horror, a distinct tone of sadness crept into her voice, evoking a look of sympathy from Mr. Beaumont.

"Please accept my humble apologies, Miss Applegate." He closed the distance between them in three long strides. "I fear your attire led me to a false assumption."

Before Edith had a chance to decide the sincerity of his expressed regret, Edwin walked into the room with Dahlia in tow.

"Ah, Wade. I see you've met my twin sister, Edith." Edwin's wide smile and bright voice rankled like fingernails down a chalkboard. Later Edith would scold him for not informing her of Mr. Beaumont's planned visit. Edwin's face swung to Edith, his naturally ruddy complexion deepening. "Sorry, Sis. I understood you'd be accompanying Father to Lancaster for the day. Mr. Beaumont is Applegate Pork Packing's new accountant. Wade and I met four years ago when I traveled south on that business trip for Father." He gave Wade a smiling nod. "We spent some time together in Natchez, and he impressed me greatly as a man of fine character and with a keen mind for business and mathematics. So when I ran into him outside the Madison Hotel two weeks ago and learned he was looking for an accounting job, I knew he was heaven-sent to us. He'll be moving into the house later this week as a resident caretaker of the place."

Wade Beaumont cleared his throat. The sparkle in his eyes infuriated Edith while at the same time, sent her heart into a somersault. "I'm afraid that Miss Applegate and I have gotten off on bad footing, which was my fault entirely." One sandy brown brow quirked up. "I'm assuming it *is* Miss, though my earlier assumptions have proved quite flawed."

"Miss Edith ain't, *isn't* married," Dahlia piped up, correcting her grammar.

Wade smiled at Dahlia. "I'm assuming you are unmarried as well."

Dahlia giggled and nodded, but then her smile faded and her expression turned serious. "I'm not gonna get married. I'm gonna be a teacher like Miss Edith."

Wade's grin vanished, causing new alarm to flare in Edith's chest. If he were an incognito slave hunter, the notion of blacks, especially a black girl learning to read let alone teach, would likely repulse him.

His brow furrowed, and he leaned down toward Dahlia as if examining her.

Edith's heart vaulted to her throat. Did Dahlia resemble a slave girl he'd been sent to find? Before Edith could step between Wade and Dahlia, he reached out and felt behind the little girl's ear.

"What is that behind your ear?" His look turned astonished as he held up a quarter-dollar piece. "Do you always carry money behind your ear?"

Dahlia's eyes grew large. "I didn't know it was there."

Wade handed Dahlia the coin, his face serious. "If I were you, I'd check my ears more often." His grin returned. "You never know what you might find there."

While Wade's parlor trick eased the tightness in Edith's chest, it didn't diminish her concern for Dahlia's safety. "Dahlia, you'd best hurry on home and take that money to your mama."

Dahlia's dark brow crinkled. "But it ain't—*isn't*—mine."

"Of course it's yours." The corner of Wade's mouth twitched as if restraining a grin. "I found it behind your ear, didn't I?"

Delighted, Dahlia clutched the coin and scampered out the library door.

"That was very nice of you," Edwin said, putting voice to Edith's own sentiments.

Grinning, Wade shrugged. "Just a sleight of hand trick I learned during my time on the riverboats." He turned a bright smile to Edith. "I like to keep in practice."

While Edwin seemed to know and trust this man, Edith didn't. She folded her arms over her chest and glared at Wade.

"So, Mr. Beaumont, I've seen your skill at sleight of hand. What experience have you in accounting?"

Edwin cleared his throat with a disapproving sound. Edith chose not to look at her twin's expression.

Wade grinned. "Before my time on the riverboats, I spent several years keeping the books for my father's business near Natchez, Mississippi."

"And is your father in the pork packing business as well?" If Edwin wouldn't subject the man to a critical interview, Edith would.

Wade's grin evaporated. "No. He owns a cotton plantation."

Chapter 2

Wade eased himself onto the feather bed and lay back, emitting a sigh of contentment. After three years of sleeping on riverboat bunks, he'd forgotten the pure luxury of a proper feather bed.

Rays from the setting sun streamed through the bedroom's west window, casting a red-gold hue on the room's east wall. The light, dappled by the shadow of an ancient oak tree's branches outside the window, danced over the wall as if to a merry tune beyond Wade's hearing. The faint rumble of some sort of conveyance rolling over the gravel-paved street filtered in.

Wade pulled the quilt up to his chin as he'd done as a child when the winter evenings grew chilly. Here, on the north side of the Ohio River, the cool weather came earlier than it did down in Mississippi. In the fading light, he noticed the fine needlework of the quilt done in a large star pattern made up of red, yellow, and orange fabrics on a snowy white background. The Star of Bethlehem pattern, Ma had called it. How had he remembered that? Memories of Ma reached back ten years, before her death. Odd how an object like this quilt could call such memories forward from the recesses of his mind. What would Ma think of him, up north, working for Yankees?

As he retreated from such speculation, thoughts of another woman blew in like a warm summer breeze. Edith Applegate. Now there was a woman he'd like to know better.

He ran his thumb over the quilt's tiny stitches. Was it her hands that had fashioned this bed covering? He liked to think so. The image of the girl he'd surprised in the library the other day flashed before his mind's eye. While Edith Applegate's coloring matched her twin brother's to a T, hers was packaged in a far more appealing form. His pulse quickened in response to the memory of her trim, petite figure marching into the library as if going to war. What spunk it must have taken for her to confront what she undoubtedly supposed was an intruder in her home.

Renewed admiration sparked in his chest. Edwin had mentioned his twin sister to Wade on more than one occasion, so he'd had little doubt of the woman's identity the moment she'd stormed into the library. But somehow her dust-covered and somewhat disheveled state had made it impossible for him to resist teasing her.

Warmth that had nothing to do with the smoldering embers in the fireplace filled him at the remembered vision of her, a riot of coppery curls framing her alabaster angel-like face, golden freckles sprinkled over a pert nose, and agate-brown eyes flashing in anger then darkening with fear. Fear of him.

Wade closed his eyes to expunge the sight, but it remained. Since his employment at Applegate Pork Packing, he'd learned of the Applegate family's involvement in the abolitionist movement. Little wonder that the fair Edith had regarded him with suspicion and even fear. The memory of the horror in her eyes when he'd disclosed that his father owned a cotton plantation in Mississippi once again pricked his heart. Convincing her that he posed no threat to her, her family, or the adorable little Dahlia and others like her would not be easy.

Wade's deep sigh filled the darkening room, blotting out the soft popping of the banked fireplace embers. He'd never backed down from a challenge, and winning Edith Applegate's friendship, if not affection, would doubtless prove a considerable one.

A sense of resolve solidified in his chest. He would not allow his pedigree and Southern accent, which Edith Applegate obviously found abhorrent, to prevent him from becoming better acquainted with his employer's enchanting sister.

Edith halted in sweeping four years' worth of accumulated dirt from the front room floor. Though aware that the house had sat unoccupied for several years, she'd found its sad state of disrepair both surprising and daunting. As she gazed at the pile of soil—the contents of which, she'd rather not speculate—mounting in the middle of the floor, she fought despair. She'd worked for nearly an hour and the room still looked as grimy and dingy as it had when she'd begun. She leaned against the broom handle and blew out a deep sigh as tears filled her eyes. How on earth would she make this place habitable for her and Father, let alone decent enough for entertaining company?

"And we know that all things work together for good to them that love God, to them who are the called according to his purpose."

For once the familiar words from the book of Romans, which she'd leaned on for solace since Father first announced their move, rang empty.

Lord, why?

As despondency enveloped her, the question that had screamed through her heart since her and Father's first night in this forsaken abode slunk out again to torture her. How this change in their lives could better serve God's will escaped her. So far Father's classes consisted of five students, and two of them were children of other faculty members. Furthermore, she feared that the family business would suffer without Father at the helm. According to her sister-in-law, Sophie, Edwin felt overwhelmed in his new position as president of Applegate Pork Packing. All in all, Father's abrupt change in career that had precipitated this move seemed a folly of monumental proportions.

Mother had often said that Father required a rudder to keep him on course. That thought brought with it a deluge of guilt and regret. Edith had failed to provide that rudder and, in so doing, had failed Father, Edwin, herself. . .everyone. She should have been more forceful in her attempts to convince Father to decline this teaching job and stay on as president of Applegate Pork Packing. If she had, everything would be as it was and they'd still be living in the home they loved instead of this squalor. They were doing God's work right there in Madison—in their own home. Now Edith's students from Madison's free black district were restricted to one day a week of classroom time instead of five. The memory of Dahlia's tearful goodbye at the close of class last Tuesday tore at Edith's heart.

As she opened the front door, the *caw, caw* of crows in a nearby cornfield punctuated the bright air. A stiff gust of wind sent a shower of russet maple leaves fluttering across the porch boards. She lifted her face to a sky so blue it almost hurt her eyes. Despite the undeniable beauty of the countryside, she missed the town of Madison. She missed home.

A fresh spate of tears she couldn't hold back flooded down her cheeks. While she and Father struggled to further the abolitionist movement in Jefferson County, a riverboat gambler and former slave owner resided in the home she adored, likely plotting ways to undermine the abolitionist cause and perhaps even put Father in jail.

A surge of anger dried her tears and shot renewed strength into her arms as she swept a broom full of dirt out the front door, sending a dark cloud of unmentionable filth into the crisp October air. Despite Edwin's assurances that Wade Beaumont posed no threat to anyone except perhaps careless bookkeepers within the company, Edith wasn't convinced. Even more maddening was Father's cavalier attitude toward her concerns. While he well knew of Edwin's tendency to be too trusting, having chided his son about the fault since Edith and Edwin were children, he'd shrugged off her worries saying, "These decisions are Edwin's to make now. I'll be kept abreast of the business, but I've handed your brother the reins and he must find his own way."

Frustration bubbled up inside Edith. She released it with a mighty swipe of the broom, sending another cloud of dirt into the air.

"Whoa!"

Edith looked up into Wade Beaumont's smiling face and myriad emotions exploded in her chest, each vying for prominence. In the end, anger won out.

"What are you doing here?" Gripping the broom handle as if it were a weapon, she stepped out onto the narrow porch.

"I'd hoped to receive a more cordial greeting than on our initial meeting, but I suppose one shouldn't hope for too much." His nonchalant grin poured fuel on the anger sizzling in Edith's chest. "At least you missed me with the dirt."

"As you said, one shouldn't hope for too much." Edith clipped her words, her tone as dry as the dirt she'd swept out the front door. Wade Beaumont was far too smooth. His Southern charm may have beguiled the sort of females with whom he'd likely associated on the riverboats, but it wouldn't work on her.

His grin widened, threatening to turn her flaring anger to a conflagration.

Father's frequent admonition to never show emotion to an adversary popped into Edith's mind. To calm herself, she inhaled a cooling breath of autumn air and propped the broom handle against the front door. "What can I do for you, Mr. Beaumont?"

"I've come to bring your father the company's weekly reports." He held up a small leather satchel.

"I'm afraid he hasn't yet returned from the institute, but you can leave them with me and I'll see that he gets them." Edith held out her hand to take the satchel, questioning the wisdom of divulging the fact that she was alone.

Wade lowered the satchel and held it against his thigh. "I was really hoping to speak with your father. There are some matters. . .company business, that I'd like to discuss with him." He gave her a sweet smile. "I'll wait."

"As you wish." Edith turned to head back into the house.

"Your little friend came by the house yesterday."

Edith whirled back to face him, fear leaping in her chest. "Dahlia?" Dahlia's parents, especially her father, Mose, were active in the Underground Railroad, the network that helped fugitive slaves cross the Ohio River to freedom. Edith would need to speak to Dahlia and warn her about talking to Beaumont.

"She helped me locate some needed items in the kitchen and, in turn, I found another two-bit piece behind her ear." He grinned.

Edith's back stiffened, and she glared at him. "Dahlia is a sweet, intelligent child with a big heart. I trust you will not take advantage of or attempt to buy her charity in the future."

His smile evaporated, and his sandy brows pinched together in a frown. He met her glare with an unflinching look, and for the first time, she saw anger flicker in his blue eyes. His voice remained low, his tone measured. "Miss Applegate, I do not take advantage of children. I like Dahlia very much, for all the qualities you mentioned." A soft smile replaced his momentary frown. "In truth, she brightened my day." He opened the satchel and slipped out a paper that looked like the lined paper Edith had purchased for her students' class work. "When I told her I was coming to see you today, she asked me to deliver this."

Edith stepped down from the porch and took the paper he held out to her. As she perused its contents, her heart contracted and the words on the paper blurred through her tears. Dahlia had written in careful cursive, *We miss you, Miss Edith*, and signed her name. The rest of the students had, in turn, printed their names and sentiments on the paper, which they'd embellished with pictures of flowers and hearts.

Edith brushed the tears from her cheeks. "She must have worked so hard on this. She'd only begun practicing her cursive letters last week." She glanced up at Wade, looking for any sign of disapproval on his face, but found only smiling compassion.

His voice brightened. "Besides delivering the paper from your students, I did hope to see you. I wanted to thank you for all the amenities you left for me in the house. I hope your generosity has not inconvenienced you or your father. If so, I would be happy to purchase my own household necessities."

Edith shook her head. "That is kind of you, but Father and I have everything we need." She glanced behind her at the stone building a third the size of their house in Madison. "As you can see, all of our belongings would not have fit into this house." Before she'd learned who would be moving into their old home, she'd felt good imagining another family using and enjoying the household goods they had to leave behind. She struggled to resurrect that feeling of benevolence. "You are more than welcome to use everything we left in the house, Mr. Beaumont." In spite of herself, Edith felt her attitude toward Wade Beaumont begin to thaw.

"I must say, I'm especially fond of the quilt you provided for my bedroom—the one with the yellow, orange, and red star pattern." Wistfulness crept into his voice. "My mother had one that was done in the same pattern. She called it the Star of Bethlehem." He gave her a shy, almost boyish grin. "When I was little, I actually thought it *was* the star of Bethlehem." He gave a soft, embarrassed-sounding chuckle. "I hadn't thought of that in years." He shook his head as if trying to shake the cobwebs from his mind. "Anyway, your Star of Bethlehem quilt has made me feel very much at home."

Edith's heart melted, thinking of the little boy who'd believed that somehow his mother had managed to capture on a quilt the star that led the wise men to the Christ child. "I'm sure that memory still makes your mother smile."

"I like to think so, though she died ten years ago." His voice softened, and his eyes glistened with moisture.

"Oh, I am sorry," Edith said, and meant it. "I lost my own mother this past May."

"Yes, Edwin told me. I am sorry for your loss as well." He reached out and covered her hand with his.

While surprised by the gesture, Edith felt no impulse to draw her hand away from his warm touch.

Kindness filled both his voice and eyes. "I'd like to tell you that the loss gets easier to bear as the years pass, but I'm afraid that hasn't been my experience."

For a long moment they shared an empathetic gaze. Wade broke the silence.

"Miss Applegate. . .Edith—"

"Ah, Mr. Beaumont!" Father came striding up, a wide smile stretching his bearded face. "I see you found our humble abode. I hope all is well at the house in Madison."

Wade took his hand from Edith's and turned to greet Father, leaving Edith feeling bereft and causing her to wish that her parent had waited a moment later to appear.

Chapter 3

Wade put the ink pen in its well, sat back, and rubbed his eyes. The odors of the pork packing operation filtered into his dusty, closet-sized office. After two weeks of employment, he'd become, if not oblivious, at least accustomed to the smell of the place.

An unexpected sense of contentment washed over him. A month ago he never would have imagined he'd be keeping books again and certainly not for a pork packing company, but it felt good. He'd forgotten how much he enjoyed the mathematics of accounting. With less than five dollars in his pocket when he'd disembarked the sternwheeler *River Star* three weeks ago, he thanked his lucky stars for having made the chance acquaintance of Edwin Applegate outside the Madison Hotel. Or, as Ma would have said, reciting the first line of the Doxology, *"Praise God from whom all blessings flow."*

As exciting as he'd often found life on the riverboats, the vagabond existence had grown stale. The monotonous moving from card game to card game, hoping and praying that Lady Luck would bring enough money to keep body and soul together while not garnering so much that it angered a drunken card player to the point of shooting him, had become tedious. The day he watched a man shot to death in front of him, he knew he had to leave that life. Ma's voice reciting Proverbs 4:14, *"Enter not into the path of the wicked, and go not in the way of the evil men,"* had sounded as clearly in his ear as if she'd been standing beside him. The next day he got off the boat at Madison, trusting God to provide him a living. God provided him with Applegate Pork Packing.

Wade leaned back in his chair that creaked in protest with his movement. Yes, he could well abide the malodorous smells coming from the processing side of Applegate Pork Packing knowing that he had a home and featherbed waiting for him every evening and that on Saturday Edwin Applegate would deliver his wages in the form of a bank draft. And of course, there was Edith.

A soft sigh puffed from his lips before they stretched in a smile he couldn't suppress. The sight of her last Friday had set his heart galloping. He couldn't help smiling again at the memory of her armed with her broom as if ready to do battle. His pulse quickened. While her coppery hair and flashing brown eyes had fit the October day perfectly, her spunk reminded him more of a summer storm. In truth, he couldn't blame her for viewing him as some sort of adversary. Of course she must see him as a usurper, especially since Edwin had given her no prior warning of the arrangement he'd made with Wade. She might even wonder if Wade intended to somehow finagle the property away from her and the senior Mr. Applegate.

That first night in the Applegate home, Wade had vowed to win Edith's friendship. So when Edwin mentioned that his father desired to stay informed of the company's business,

Wade had offered to deliver a weekly accounts report to the elder Mr. Applegate in Lancaster in hopes of seeing Edith. He hadn't imagined he'd have an opportunity to speak with her alone, so Friday's visit to Lancaster had far exceeded his hopes and felt like a small but definite step toward his goal. The memory of their shared gaze as they commiserated over the loss of their mothers wiped the smile from Wade's face but sent pleasant warmth radiating through him. In that moment he'd felt a connection with her. He must build on that connection and find a way to disabuse her of the notion that he harbored any nefarious schemes to legally wrest her home from her and her father. Something he'd noticed last evening on the bedroom chifforobe dresser might be just the thing to help win her trust.

Excitement for his plan bloomed in his chest then withered. Friday seemed a long time away from midday on Tuesday.

He blew out an impatient breath. As Ma always said, *"Anything worth having is worth waiting for."* And Edith Applegate was certainly worth waiting for.

The clock in Mr. Applegate's office down the hall began chiming the noon hour. Wade closed the open ledger book on his desk and stood. Perhaps he would avail himself of the restaurant in the Madison Hotel for his midday meal.

"Wade." Edwin Applegate poked his ruddy, bespectacled face into Wade's office. "Sophie mentioned this morning that she and Edith would be making pork and vegetable stew today and asked me to invite you to our noon repast."

Wade's heart did a little hop, not because of the stew that did sound delicious, but at the opportunity to see Edith three days earlier than he'd thought.

"Why, yes. Thank you, Mr. Applegate. I'd like that very much." Forcing a nonchalant tone to his voice, he tried to rein his heart to a slow canter. "Restaurant fare does get tiresome." A smile he couldn't control stretched his cheeks taut.

As they walked the three blocks from the company building to Edwin Applegate's home, Wade allowed Edwin to monopolize the conversation, which ranged from the week's business to the latest antics of his eighteen-month-old son, Archie.

"Neither Sophie nor I can imagine how the little scamp got out of his crib, let alone opened the pantry door. But there he was on the kitchen floor, all covered in molasses and cornmeal." Edwin leaned his head back and let out a hearty guffaw.

Wade managed to produce the expected chuckle as he turned up the collar of his wool coat, fending off a chilly breeze blowing from the Ohio River. "My mother loved to tell about all the mischief my brother, Jube, and I would get up to." As much as he would like to inquire if Edith would be joining them for the meal, three years of playing card games for a living had taught him not to reveal his hand.

Edwin turned a curious face to Wade. "Is Jube your only sibling, or do you have other brothers and sisters?" He angled a shamefaced grin at Wade. "Sophie's always scolding me for not inquiring more into the lives of my employees."

"No, it's just Jube and I." Wade managed a tight smile and focused on the street in front of them, hoping Edwin would move on to another subject. He'd rather not divulge more about his family or the real reason he left their plantation outside Natchez.

"Ah, here we are." Edwin stopped in front of a two-story brick home, situated about halfway down the block. "And there is Father's horse and buggy." He nodded toward a handsome roan mare attached to a neat black phaeton—the same one Wade had noticed parked behind the Applegates' little stone house in Lancaster. "I'm not sure if I mentioned that Edith holds classes here on Tuesdays now."

Wade's heart thumped harder. Before he could get a word past his drying lips, Edwin spoke, his smile widening. "I can almost smell that stew now." He unfastened an impressive wrought-iron gate gaining them access to a neat leaf-strewn yard bisected by a brick walkway that led up to a white-pillared front porch. He turned and fastened the gate behind them. "Can't be too careful," he said with a grin. "Or we're liable to be chasing Archie all the way down to the river."

Wade followed Edwin inside where delicious aromas welcomed them into a narrow foyer, making Wade's mouth water.

Edwin took off his hat and coat and hung them on a coat tree in the corner and invited Wade to do the same. "There's a water closet down the hall if you'd like to wash some of that ink off your hands while I let Sophie know we've arrived."

Wade glanced at his ink-stained hands and grinned. "A hazard of the accounting trade, I suppose. Yes, thank you, I think I will."

A few minutes later he exited the washroom and nearly bumped into Dahlia carrying a chubby toddler.

Dahlia shifted the little boy whom Wade assumed was Archie Applegate on her left hip and smiled up at Wade. "Hello, Mr. Beaumont. Are you havin' lunch with us?"

Wade smiled back. "Yes. I understand we'll be dining on pork stew."

Dahlia nodded as Archie squirmed in her arms. "I helped Miss Edith cut up the carrots and taters before we had class." She set Archie, who'd begun fussing, on his feet and glanced down the hall behind her. "I'll show you the music room where we have class after I take Archie to his ma, but you can go on in there if you want."

"I'd like that, Dahlia. I'll see you in the music room." He gave her a parting smile and headed down the hall, a tendril of sadness curling around the wonder sprouting in his chest. *If only Ma could have seen this.* Wade had found the world that he and Ma dreamed of back in Mississippi, a world where black and white children learned together and grew up as equals. On the southern side of the Ohio River, such a world had seemed fantastic, but here the Applegates and others like them were making it happen. While the scourge of slavery still existed here on the north side of the Ohio River, the winds of change were blowing in as surely as the autumn gusts off the river. And Edith Applegate numbered among the driving forces. *Mahli chito.* The Choctaw word for tornado that he'd learned from the old Indian who'd taught him and Jude to fish along the banks of the Mississippi River came to mind. Yes, Edith Applegate was a whirlwind—a force of nature.

Wade stepped into the room at the end of the hall and stopped short, his heart bucking against his chest like an unbroken colt. Edith stood over a writing table gathering lined papers—much like the one Dahlia had asked him to deliver to Edith last week—into a neat pile.

She looked up and greeted him with a smile. "Mr. Beaumont. I see you've accepted Edwin's invitation to dine with us." She put the papers away in a desk drawer. "I trust you've worked up a good appetite. Sophie, Dahlia, and I made enough stew to feed a small army." A beguiling dimple dented her left cheek, making Wade wonder why he hadn't noticed it before, and then he realized he hadn't seen her smile until this moment.

Dahlia skipped into the room. "May I show Mr. Beaumont where I sit for our classes, Miss Edith?"

"Of course, Dahlia." Edith stepped from behind the desk.

Dahlia grasped Wade's hand and towed him across the room's oak floor to a spot about a yard in front of Edith. I sit here in front so I can help Miss Edith. 'Course I sit in one of them chairs." She pointed to several folding carpet chairs propped against a wall.

"*Those* chairs," Edith corrected in a gentle tone, her fetching dimple becoming more pronounced with her suppressed smile. "You should know, Mr. Beaumont, Dahlia is my true right arm." She smiled at Dahlia, who beamed beneath her praise. "I'm not sure I could get through a class without her."

Edwin walked into the room with Archie in his arms. "Sophie tells me that the lunch table is set, so I suggest we all head that way." His smile stretched his thin mustache into a straight line above his lip. "My good wife may be small in stature, but I'd advise you not to get on her bad side."

Everyone except for Archie, who had a thumb stuck in his mouth, shared a laugh and followed Edwin and his son across the house to the dining room.

"Wade, let me introduce my wife, Sophie." Edwin strode to the end of a long cherry-wood dining table to stand beside a pretty young woman who would have looked much shorter if not for her blond curls piled high on her head. He glanced down at his wife, whose height barely reached his bicep. "Sophie, this is Mr. Wade Beaumont, our new accountant."

Sophie Applegate rounded the table and held out her hand to Wade. "I am pleased to meet you, Mr. Beaumont. Edwin was quite pleased to find someone of your caliber to fill the accounting position and care for the Applegate home."

"Thank you, ma'am. So kind of you to say so. And thank you for inviting me to your lovely home to share this meal." Wade thought he detected the hint of a frown on Edith's face the instant before he bent to plant a cursory kiss on Sophie's hand.

Dahlia sat beside Archie in his high chair while Edwin held a chair out for his wife. Wade hurried to do the same for Edith, earning a tepid smile and murmured expression of thanks from her.

When all were seated and Edwin had offered a prayer of thanks for the meal, the conversation turned to family matters.

Feeling awkward, Wade focused his attention on his bowl of stew.

"Is the stew to your liking, Mr. Beaumont?" Sophie's kind smile suggested she sensed his unease.

Thankful to be brought into the conversation, Wade dabbed his mouth with his linen napkin and returned her smile. "Very much, Mrs. Applegate. In fact, I must say this stew rivals the stew our Hattie used to make back home."

Edith, seated across the table from him, set her spoon down with a clink and fixed him with an unsmiling glare. When she spoke, her voice held a sardonic dryness. "I assume Hattie is your slave?"

Chapter 4

Regret curled in Edith's middle as she stepped out onto the porch, Mother's cut glass vase in hand, and looked westward down the dirt road. Once again she cringed at the memory of Wade's reddening features, Sophie's soft gasp, and Edwin's disapproving grunt at her tactless remark last Tuesday concerning the Beaumont family's cook. While her assumption was undoubtedly correct, embarrassing Edwin and Sophie's luncheon guest did nothing to help rid the country of the scourge of slavery.

Her nagging sense of remorse must stem from disappointing Edwin and Sophie, for surely Wade Beaumont, as any slaveholder, deserved her reproach. Besides, she *had* murmured an apology to appease her brother and sister-in-law if not Wade.

"And when ye stand praying, forgive, if ye have ought against any: that your Father also which is in heaven may forgive you your trespasses."

The verse from the Gospel of Mark flitted into her mind like a pesky insect. She shook her head to shoo it away.

She headed across the road where goldenrod and purple asters decorated the meadow and filled the air with fragrance. Since Father insisted on hosting Mr. Beaumont every Friday when he came to report on the business as well as the house in town, she was determined to present their new domicile in as refined a light as possible. While she could do little to bring any true elegance to their dingy abode, freshly cut flowers would add a splash of brightness. Last Friday when Father had apologized for the condition of the house, Wade's look had turned near piteous.

Pride lifted Edith's chin as she strode toward the meadow of wildflowers. Though Father had laughed and chided her, saying, "Do not try to make a silk purse from a sow's ear, daughter," since Tuesday she'd worked until every muscle ached and her hands reddened to make the little stone cottage more presentable. She wouldn't be pitied, least of all by the Southern slave owner who now occupied her beloved home.

She reached into her apron pocket for scissors to clip the flowers but found only two small balls of lint. An exasperated sigh puffed from her lips, and she turned to head back to the house.

At the sound of a horse approaching, she looked up to see Wade riding toward her on a fine black stallion.

For a fraction of a second, the thought to hide among the tall flowers skittered through her mind. Too late.

Wade waved and let out a hearty "Hallo!"

Edith managed a halfhearted wave as he dismounted and walked toward her, leading his steed by the reins.

"Good day, Miss Applegate." He doffed his gray John Bull hat and hung it on the saddle pommel. Something about his cheery mood and the broad smile marching across his handsome face grated against Edith's nerves.

"Good day, Mr. Beaumont." She managed to push the chilly salutation through unsmiling lips.

"And what a beautiful day it is." His gaze turned to the woods beyond the meadow, resplendent in the showy reds, oranges, and yellows of October. "I can't get enough of the vivid colors of the leaves here in autumn. Our trees back home in Natchez show some color this time of year but not nearly to this extent."

"Is the color of our trees the reason you're here instead of back in Mississippi, Mr. Beaumont?" Edith didn't try to keep the sarcasm from her voice.

Wade showed no sign that he noticed. "It would almost be enough of a reason." He perused the colorful hillside. "Wanderlust enticed me to the riverboat life, but after three years I grew weary of life on the river." He turned his smiling gaze back to her. "I needed an occupation and place to lay my head at night, and your brother offered me those, so here I am." He held out his arms with his hands palms up. When he lowered them he looked her in the eyes and his smile gentled. "We have known each other for the better part of a month, Miss Applegate. It would please me greatly if you'd call me Wade, and if I might be so bold, I humbly beg your permission to call you Edith."

"As you wish," she mumbled, when in truth, she wished that his request didn't cause her heart to do odd flips.

His gaze moved to the flowers surrounding her then to the vase in her hand. A muscle twitched at the corner of his mouth. "While I appreciate the gesture, you needn't trouble yourself to pick a vase full of flowers on my account, Edith."

Anger sizzled inside Edith's chest. The man was insufferable! He doubtless intended to goad an angry retort from her, but she would not give him that satisfaction. Calming herself, she willed her voice to a tone as cool as the gusting October breeze. "I assure you, Mr. Beaumont," she said, intentionally disregarding his request to call him Wade, "the flowers are not on your account. I simply enjoy fresh flowers in the house." She glared at him and raised her chin even higher. "At our home in Madison I would cut roses from the bushes beside the front door until the frost killed the last blossoms, but since I no longer have access to my roses, I must make do with the flowers I have." Hating the renegade tears that sprang up in her eyes, she batted them back.

His maddening grin widened. "I am happy to report that the roses you speak of are still blooming to a fare-thee-well." He cocked his head, and his features took on a thoughtful look. "Perhaps I will clip a few and bring them in to decorate my. . .uh, the library," he said, correcting himself.

The smoldering anger inside Edith blazed. What impudence to refer to their library, or any part of their home, as his own! The urge to stomp away from him gripped her, but pride kept her rooted to her spot.

He turned and looked toward the house. "Well, I will leave you to it. I assume your father is at home?"

"Yes, he is." The notion of admitting her mistake of forgetting the scissors to Wade felt repugnant, but she saw no way around it. "I might as well join you and Father at the house. I'm afraid there will be no flowers. I seem to have forgotten my scissors."

"Please, allow me to be of assistance." He reached into his inside coat pocket and pulled out a small folded knife, flicked open the blade, and began cutting lengths of asters and goldenrod. His tone turned wistful as he worked. "Asters were one of my mother's favorite flowers."

The anger that Edith had labored to restrain withered, replaced by curious surprise. "Why, they were one of *my* mother's favorite flowers as well." Could Edwin have mentioned such a trivial fact to Wade? She discarded the cynical thought the moment it popped into her mind. That Edwin was cognizant enough of Mother's floral preferences to voice them in a conversation, let alone a conversation with another man, seemed beyond absurd.

Wade handed her a stem full of the purple blossoms. His gaze that met hers turned so tender that her heart did a somersault. "It seems that we may have more in common than you might have imagined."

Before Edith could gather enough air in her lungs to answer, his sandy brows shot up.

"That reminds me. I found something personal in the house that you must have overlooked when packing for your move here." He walked to where he'd tethered his horse to a low-hanging cottonwood bough and reached into a saddlebag. When he handed her the small shiny object, she gasped.

A new well of tears that she didn't try to hide sprang up and flooded down her cheeks. "Mother's daguerreotype." Unashamed, she lifted her drenched face to him. "I'd assumed it must still be among the unopened boxes as I hadn't yet found it." Unexpected gratitude bloomed in her chest. "Thank you, Wade." And she meant it.

The tenderness in his eyes threatened to unleash a fresh spate of tears. "I do hope it helps to make your home here feel more like. . .well. . .home."

"Thank you, Wade," she repeated, fighting an astonishing urge to hug him. "This was so very kind of you."

"I know that I treasure the picture I carry of my own mother." He pulled a gold watch from his green brocade vest and opened it to reveal the image of a middle-aged lady tucked inside the watch's lid.

"She is lovely." Edith's smile came far easier than she would have imagined.

"So is yours." Wade reached out his hand and cupped hers holding Mother's picture. "Something else we have in common, I'd say."

That night Edith lay awake long after she'd gone to bed, her roiling emotions robbing her of sleep.

She turned her head on her wet pillow to gaze at Mother's picture illuminated by pale rays of the full moon flooding through her bedroom window. Thoughts of Wade Beaumont unleashed a war of conflicting emotions within her chest. How could she feel tenderness for a man whose family practiced a way of life that she abhorred?

In an attempt to sling Wade's image from her mind, she rolled onto her back and worked to cement a more rigid defense around her heart. She'd lambasted Edwin for his naïveté in hiring Wade in the first place. She too must guard against falling prey to the slick Southerner's wiles and not forget that, for three years, he'd practiced the art of deception on the riverboats. What had seemed like a gesture of kindness in bringing her mother's picture could well be a calculated effort to win her affections in hopes of garnering information about those locally involved in the Underground Railroad.

The uncharitable suspicion crumbled as it collided with the memory of the genuine kindness in Wade's eyes when he handed her Mother's picture. Other memories set her pulse racing: his handsome smile, his gaze that seemed to peer into the depths of her soul, and the touch of his hand on hers that had sent pleasant tingles up her arm.

She gazed up at the ceiling and felt her defenses crack like the aged plaster above her head. But somewhere between wakefulness and slumber, the realization that Wade had never said why he hadn't returned to Mississippi registered in her consciousness.

Chapter 5

"Are you tearin' out Miss Edith's roses?"

Edwin stopped his work with the shovel to turn and face Dahlia's large, horror-filled eyes. He strained to suppress the grin tugging at his mouth and schooled his lips to a serious expression. "No, ma'am, I would never do that." He went back to working the shovel beneath the bush's roots. "I noticed that this little bush is being swallowed up by the bigger ones on each side of it. It'll likely die if it's not moved." He angled a glance at Dahlia and allowed his grin free rein. "I thought I'd take this bush to Miss Edith when I go to Lancaster later today. Last time I was there she mentioned that she missed her roses."

Dahlia nodded, her dark braids bouncing on her shoulders. "She does miss this house somethin' fierce."

Sadness that matched Dahlia's tone settled in Wade's chest along with an unreasonable sense of guilt. Since moving into this place, he'd worked hard to maintain the home as he'd promised Edwin he would do. He'd fixed anything he'd found in disrepair and had even hired a woman to come three times a week to keep the place spotless. Still, he couldn't shake the nagging sense of guilt he felt about occupying the home Edith missed so much.

Dahlia's voice brightened and her face lit up in a wide smile. "Miss Edith will like havin' roses again." She cocked her head as she eyed the dark, upturned soil around the rose's roots with a critical gaze. Her expression turned serious, and she gave an approving nod. "Pa says that November is a good time to move bushes."

Wade smiled. "That is a good thing to know." For the first time, he noticed the paper in Dahlia's hand. "Do you have something for me to take to Miss Edith?"

Dahlia nodded again then shivered as a cold gust of wind whipped at her gray wool cape and sent brown leaves whirling across the yard.

Edwin wiped his hands together to knock off bits of drying soil. While he enjoyed Dahlia's company, he needed to get the child out of the cold. He glanced up at the slate-gray sky. "Let's go inside. I have a good fire going in the library, and Mrs. Sage is in the kitchen making bread." He gave her a wink. "I bet if you ask her politely, she'll give you a glass of milk and a warm slice of buttered bread."

Dahlia's smile widened. "Ms. Jenny knows me. She's a friend of Ma's."

Inside, the delicious smell of baking bread met them, setting Wade's mouth to watering and making him glad he'd hired such a good baker for a housekeeper.

In the library he tossed another piece of wood into the fireplace, sending orange sparks up the chimney, then turned to Dahlia. "What do you have for Miss Edith?"

Dahlia handed him the lined page of paper filled with large penciled script. "It's all about how I want to one day go to school at the Eleu—Eleutherian Institute. I had to copy that word from a paper Mr. Applegate gave my pa."

Wade perused the childish cursive. "This is very good, Dahlia." He gave her a big smile. "I'm sure Miss Edith will be very pleased, and I have no doubt that you'll be attending Mr. Applegate's class someday." He carefully folded the paper and tucked it into his vest pocket. "I'll give this to Miss Edith first thing when I arrive."

A rapping sound at the door intruded. Answering it, Wade stood stunned.

"Jube!" he said when he finally found his voice again. "How on earth did you find me?"

Wade's older brother grinned at Wade's gaping mouth. "A fellow down at the Madison Hotel told me you were here. Asked me if I was any kin of the Beaumont fellow living in the old Applegate place." He shook his head. "I figured you were still ridin' the riverboats unless another gambler had shot ya and fed ya to the fish." His short burst of laughter faded as he peered over Wade's shoulder into the library. "Ya gonna invite your brother in?"

"Of course." Wade stepped aside to allow Jube to enter. Remembering Dahlia's presence, concern flared in his chest. While he hadn't yet inquired as to Jube's business in Madison, he had a strong suspicion as to what had brought his brother so far north. Since the age of sixteen, Jube had relished and excelled in hunting runaway slaves.

Wade quirked a smile he couldn't sustain toward Dahlia. "You'd best go to the kitchen and ask Mrs. Sage for that bread." To his relief, she scampered off.

A look of admiration filled Jube's face as he stepped into the library and his gaze scanned the room. He doffed his black, short-crowned top hat, sending a strong scent of pomade wafting to Wade's nose. "It looks like you've done very well for yourself, little brother." His smile faded when his gaze fastened on the doorway Dahlia had exited through. "But you really should've been more forceful with the girl." He turned a critical frown toward Wade. "You always were too easy on the slaves."

Wade shrugged. Better to let Jube think that Dahlia belonged to him. Like most slave catchers, Jube had no compunction about snatching free blacks in the North to take back south.

Jube's expression brightened as he continued to look around the room. He pursed his lips and let out a low whistle. "You must have got a lot better at the card table than I remember to afford a place like this."

"It actually belongs to my employer. I'm presently employed as an accountant with Applegate Pork Packing."

"Done with the river, are you?" A smirk pulled up the corner of Jube's mouth and he emitted a soft snort. "Never knew anyone fonder of numbers than you." He frowned. "At least when you were at home Cypress Hill's books always balanced." He cocked his head and his left brow shot up. "If you want to do bookkeepin' you could always come back home, ya know. I reckon Pa's hired and fired half a dozen bookkeepers since you left."

"How is Pa?" Wade needed to move the conversation away from any talk of him returning home to Mississippi. Also, while he had little interest in Jube's answer, his brother would expect him to inquire after their parent's health.

A momentary scowl crossed Jube's face, and then his expression brightened again. "He's well for a man his age." He gave a mirthless chuckle. "Ornery as ever."

"I'm glad to hear it." Wade forced his lips into what he hoped resembled a smile. "So what has brought you to this fair river town, Brother?" Another compulsory but unnecessary question. Jube was doubtless on the trail of runaway slaves.

"After escaped slaves, as you might have guessed. A male and female from Cypress Hill and three males and two females from Belle Terre." He cocked his head and fixed Wade with an intense gaze. "We trailed them to Carrollton, Kentucky, then lost the trail. Rumor has it this town is on the Underground Railroad." His gaze narrowed. "A fellow down at the Madison Hotel says it's a hotbed of abolitionists and claims that your employer is one of 'em."

Wade trusted that his years of perfecting an unreadable poker face would mask the unease churning in his midsection. Shrugging, he willed a nonchalant tone to his voice. "Never inquired about the gentleman's politics." He forced a light chuckle. "Just happy for the job and the decent roof over my head."

Jube snorted, and his gaze returned to roving the room. "Doubt you'd tell me if you knew." A smile replaced his dark expression, though it did nothing to soften the hard look in his green eyes. His voice rose in a confident lilt. "No matter. If there are runaways here, me and the boys will find 'em. We'll turn in the abolitionists hidin' 'em too."

Wade prayed that his brother would enjoy no such success. While Edith and her father's interest in the education of the free black population suggested antislavery leanings, Wade had no knowledge as to the family's involvement in the abolitionist movement, or to what extent. He also prayed that Dahlia would leave via the kitchen after enjoying her treat.

Smiling, Wade clapped Jube on the shoulder. Like a dog, his brother had always had the ability to smell fear, and Wade mustn't allow him to get so much as a whiff of his concerns. "Have a seat." He motioned toward a wing chair beside the fireplace. "I'll have my cook make some coffee to go with the fresh bread she made, and we can catch up over our repast."

Jube shook his head, sending a wave of relief washing through Wade. "Sorry, Brother, but I'm afraid we'll have to save our reminiscences for another time. I have an appointment with a Mr. Rea down at the hotel." He slipped his gold watch—the one Pa had given him for his eighteenth birthday—from his maroon brocade vest. "And it seems I'm already five minutes late."

Wade walked his brother to the door. "I trust you'll be in town for a while?"

Jube shrugged as he slipped the watch back into his vest. "Until we've turned over every rock lookin' for those runaway slaves."

"Then I look forward to a longer visit at your earliest convenience." His conscience chafed against the lie.

"As do I." Jube settled his hat over his slicked-down auburn hair. He opened the door then paused, his gaze dropping for a moment to the threshold. When he looked up again at Wade, his expression held uncharacteristic concern. "Take care, little brother, that your misguided sense of justice doesn't lead you to the wrong side of the law. When the boys and I cast out our net, be advised that we'll pull in whatever we catch. We won't discriminate between Northern carp and Mississippi catfish."

Two hours later, Jube's warning, or perhaps veiled threat, still rode heavy on Wade's mind as he guided his horse down the dirt road toward the Applegates' little Lancaster cottage. Thankfully Dahlia had remained in the kitchen until after Jube left. Wade had considered warning the girl about his brother and the other slave catchers, but no sense in causing the child night terrors. Besides, Dahlia's pa had likely already learned of Jube's and his men's presence. More than once Dahlia's unguarded comments about her parents and activities at their Georgetown church had caused Wade to suspect that the free black family was somehow involved in the Underground Railroad. Each time she'd seemed about to accidently divulge any such information, Wade had hurried to change the subject. The less he knew about those kinds of activities, the better. While his sympathies lay with those fleeing oppressors like his own family in Mississippi, to outright defy the Fugitive Slave Law felt like a bridge too far.

Not mentioning Jube's presence to Dahlia had made sense. Whether or not to inform Edith, however, was an entirely different matter. Wade's shoulders sagged beneath the burden his brother had laid upon him. He gazed at his saddle's pommel as if he might find the answer in the leather's dark grain. Teaching free blacks and even supporting the abolitionist cause—legal activities north of the Ohio River—did not make the Applegates lawbreakers. Any mention of Jube's appearance to Edith would undoubtedly be interpreted as Wade accusing her and her father of unlawful activity.

With each step of his horse the burlap bag containing the rosebush bumped against his leg. Wade expelled a deep sigh. In the weeks since he brought her mother's picture, he'd felt Edith's attitude toward him warming. Instead of her earlier cool to almost hostile demeanor, she now regularly greeted him with a warm smile and wave. Last Friday, while waiting for Mr. Applegate to return from the institute, they'd sat together on the porch and discussed the company's business. To his surprise and delight, Edith had shown a business acumen that, to Wade's mind, far outdistanced that of her twin brother.

A grin tugged at the corner of Wade's mouth. He'd commented that she, instead of her brother, should be running the company. When she agreed, they'd shared a laugh, and he'd felt their bond tighten.

Wade's smile evaporated as the plodding horse brought him within sight of the cottage. Since this morning when he'd acted on his impulsive notion to dig up the rosebush and take it with him to Lancaster, he'd fretted about how Edith might react. His heart had quaked more than once imagining her viewing his good intentions with horror, accusing him of stepping outside his authority and, worse, of ruining her mother's rosebushes. He didn't need the added worry of wondering how she might receive a mention of Jube and his slave hunters.

No. Wade would not jeopardize his budding relationship with Edith to mention an unexpected visit from his brother with whom he'd been estranged for three years and who'd likely be gone in a few days.

At the sight of Edith sweeping dead leaves from the porch, Wade's heart bucked. The gusting November wind played with loose strands of hair framing her face while it painted her alabaster cheeks a deep rose-pink. For a moment he sat still on his horse and drank in her beauty.

She looked up from her work and greeted him with a wave and smile that sent his heart galloping. "Wade. I didn't hear you coming." While he'd like to attribute the breathlessness in her voice to his appearance, exertion with the broom had likely left her winded.

As he dismounted he struggled to think of a clever reply. "The wind probably covered the sound of my approach." Feeling as awkward as a schoolboy with his first sweetheart, he glanced up at the dark gray clouds chasing across the sky. "It looks like it might rain," he said and groaned inwardly.

She seemed not to notice the stupidity of his comment. Her smile widened as, broom in hand, she descended the two stone steps. "Or snow." She looked up at the sky. "I *am* so looking forward to the first snow of the winter."

Wade's heart throbbed imagining the two of them snuggled together in a sleigh, a pair of dappled grays whisking them over snow-covered fields.

"Father should be home in a few minutes," she said, yanking him from his pleasant muse.

The memory of Dahlia's paper in his vest saved him from standing and gaping like an imbecile. "Dahlia asked me to deliver this." He eased the folded page from his vest pocket.

When she took it from his hand, their fingers touched for an instant, sending delightful shivers up his arm. Her brown eyes sparkled as she perused the girl's work. "Oh, this is so well written." She lifted glistening eyes to him as she refolded the page. "I must show this to Father. He will be so pleased."

"I brought you something else as well." Wade's heart hammered in fear of how she might respond as he lifted the burlap bag bearing the rosebush from his horse's back. "You'd mentioned that you missed the roses from your old home, so I brought you one of them."

Her eyes grew wide and her mouth gaped in a look of stunned incredulity that confirmed his worst fears.

Chapter 6

Is your rosebush bloomin' yet?" Dahlia paused in gathering the other students' slate boards from their otherwise empty chair seats.

Edith looked up from grading the day's arithmetic assignment and pressed her lips together to suppress her grin, reining it to a small smile. "No, I'm afraid it won't bloom again until next spring, Dahlia. But I do appreciate your father fertilizing it for me."

Dahlia nodded as she resumed collecting the slates. "Pa says there's nothin' better for roses than horse manure."

Once again, Edith was forced to restrain a giggle, not because of Dahlia's comment about the manure but from the memory of Wade's face at her reaction that he'd brought her the rosebush. At his horrified expression she'd realized that he'd misinterpreted her surprise. To her shame she'd found the temptation to prolong his misery a few seconds longer too strong to resist. When she'd finally assured him that she wasn't angry that he'd dug up the rosebush, the relief on his face had forced her to press her fingers to her lips to keep from laughing.

The memory of her mirth faded, replaced by a sweet emotion she wasn't yet prepared to name. It seemed impossible that a few short weeks ago she'd dreaded Wade's weekly visits. Now, she found herself so looking forward to them that the sound of an approaching horse on Friday afternoons caused her heart to skip. To her great joy, Father encouraged her to join him and Wade in their discussions of the company's business. Each week, she reveled in surprising Wade with her knowledge of the workings of Applegate Pork Packing. His blue eyes had lit when he learned of their shared love of numbers, and on more than one occasion, they'd engaged in animated discussions over how best to improve the company's profits, mental sparring matches he seemed to relish as much as she did.

Her smile evaporated. Despite Wade's considerable charms, she must never forget that he hailed from a world far different from hers, a world that bought and sold human beings with the same indifference that Applegate Pork Packing dealt in swine.

Her stomach churned at the thought. A jarring reminder of that ugly reality had come last evening when Father brought home news from the institute that a group of slave catchers had appeared in Madison, aided by no less than the county's former sheriff and hot pro-slavery advocate, Robert Rea. This morning in the mercantile as she waited to purchase pencils, her friend and minister's wife, Rosaleen Hale, had verified Father's unsettling news.

Fear slithered through Edith. Yes, she needed to keep a close watch on her heart concerning Wade Beaumont and remind Dahlia to do the same.

"Edith." Sophie, with Archie perched on her trim hip, poked her head into the room. "Mr. Beaumont came by to inform me that an unexpected situation has arisen at the plant, so Edwin won't be coming home at noon to take you back to Lancaster." Sophie's eyes and voice expressed her regret as she bounced her son on her hip. "You'll either have to wait until Edwin comes home later this afternoon to take you back to Lancaster or stay the night here."

Edith shook her head. "Father has invited the director and his wife to a luncheon at our home tomorrow, so staying here is out of the question." Disappointment squiggled through her. If she hadn't given in to Father's insistence that he drive her into Madison each Tuesday to hold class and have Edwin drive her home, she wouldn't be stranded without her own buggy. "I'm afraid I have no choice but to wait for Edwin." As much as she dreaded the thought of a two-hour ride home in the cold darkness, causing Sophie to feel guilty about it would not change the situation. She stifled a sigh and forced a smile. "Don't fret, Sophie. If Edwin is willing to drive me home after a hard day's work, I can certainly put up with some chilly night air."

Relief smoothed out the worry lines creasing Sophie's forehead, and her expression brightened. "While we're waiting for Edwin, you can help me plan the Christmas party for the company employees."

Edith gathered up her students' work papers and grinned at her sister-in-law, who loved nothing better than planning a party. "Christmas is over a month away, Sophie. Isn't it a bit early to be planning a party?"

Sophie shifted a fussing Archie to her other hip and gave an exasperated huff. "Edith, there is ever so much to consider in planning a party, and we'll be holding it the week before Christmas, a scant three weeks from now. So no, this is not a moment too soon." Her eyes sparkled, and her voice took on an excited lilt. Sophie was in her element. "Of course we must both have new dresses. I'm thinking red for me, and with your coloring, you always look absolutely divine in green, but which shade of green I haven't yet decided. Oh, and I was looking in *Godey's* the other day and saw the most angelic baby gown worn by Queen Victoria's little boy." She giggled and gave Archie a squeeze. "I absolutely *must* have one made for Archie."

Edith stifled a groan. The prospect of spending all afternoon enduring every mind-numbing detail of Sophie's party plans far exceeded her dread of facing a cold buggy ride through the November evening. Blocking out Sophie's prattle, her mind raced in search of an alternative way home as well as an excuse not to wait for Edwin. "I do wish I could get word to Father that I'll be arriving home so late. I hate the thought of him coming home to a dark house with no prepared supper, and, of course, he will be worried sick about me." The truth of her words somewhat assuaged her conscience at being less than forthright in why she'd rather not stay. "I suppose I could rent a horse and buggy from the livery."

"I'd ask Pa to take you home, but he's down at our church with..." Dahlia piped up then clamped her mouth shut as if she'd said more than she should have.

"I would be more than happy to take you home." Wade walked into the room, sending Edith's heart vaulting to her throat. His gaze bounced between Sophie, Edith, and Dahlia. He fingered the gray brim of his John Bull hat. "Forgive my intrusion, Mrs. Applegate. Miss Applegate." He nodded in turn at Sophie and Edith. "I wanted to stop by and pay you and Miss Dahlia my respects before I headed home, and I couldn't help overhearing your conversation." His gaze settled on Edith, and his grin widened. "I've recently purchased a phaeton and a fine gelding to pull it. I'd be honored if you were the first to share a ride with me in my new carriage."

Sophie's face pinked, and before Edith had a chance to respond, she shook her head. "Of course we thank you for your kind offer, Mr. Beaumont, but you must realize that it would not be prudent for Edith to accept such an offer without a chaperone."

Heat rushed into Edith's face, and she wished the floor would somehow swallow her up. "I'm sure Mr. Beaumont didn't mean—"

"I was thinking that perhaps Dahlia could accompany Miss Applegate and me to Lancaster." Beyond a slight redness to his complexion, Wade seemed unfazed by Sophie's insinuation. "With her mother's permission, of course." He gave Dahlia a fond smile.

Dahlia began hopping up and down. "Yes, yes! I've never rode—ridden—in a phaeton." She turned pleading eyes to Edith. "You did promise that I could come and visit you sometime at your house in Lancaster, and Ma said if you asked me, I could. I'll run home and ask Ma right now!" Before Edith could stop her, Dahlia raced out of the room.

A half hour later Edith, Wade, and Dahlia all scrunched together on the phaeton's plush green velvet seat with Dahlia wrapped in a quilt and perched on Edith's lap.

"I do hope you ladies are comfortable." Wade glanced at Edith as he guided the handsome dappled gray gelding down the road leading out of Madison.

Edith shifted Dahlia on her lap. "Yes, thank you." She angled a smile at him. "I'm surprised at how roomy the seat is for a phaeton."

"One of the reasons I bought it," he said with a grin as he flicked the reins on the horse's spotted rump. "The salesman assured me that this seat would easily accommodate a lady's widest skirts."

At his light comment, Edith experienced an odd twang in her chest. "Then I assume you plan to regularly squire ladies in this carriage?" Edith's voice sounded tighter than she would have liked.

His laughter rang in the early afternoon air, and a snoozing Dahlia stirred on Edith's lap. "One must prepare for any circumstance." A grin lifted the corner of his blond mustache. "And, as it turns out, the first passengers in my carriage are of the female persuasion." His expression turned serious. "I was wondering if I might have the honor of escorting you to the company Christmas party next month? That is, if you're planning to attend."

Edith's pulse quickened. Hopefully the chill in the air would account for any extra color in her cheeks. To cover her disconcertion she affected a horrified tone. "Miss Sophie's Christmas party? I'd best be on my deathbed."

"Then I have hope of squiring you to the event?" He kept his gaze focused on the road ahead.

"No."

His shoulders sagged, and even in profile, a stark look of disappointment dragged down his features.

Edith had to stifle a giggle while bubbles of unexplained joy bounced around in her chest. "I mean, I'll be staying with Edwin and Sophie that week to help with the party, so I won't require an escort to the event."

He turned to face her and a spark of hope flickered in his blue eyes. "Then may I be so bold as to ask if I might squire you *during* the party?" An uncharacteristic look of confusion came over his face. "Unless, of course, your father"—his voice tightened—"or someone else has already secured that privilege."

Edith struggled to keep her smile in check. "Father will doubtless spend the evening in conversations about politics and business, leaving me on my own."

"Then if no one else has laid claim to your company for the evening, it would be my great pleasure to squire you at the Christmas soirée."

The distant sound of warning bells rang in Edith's brain. She ignored it along with her vow to gird her heart against Wade's charms. After all, as his companion for the evening, she could keep a close watch on his activities. Despite the hollow ring of that justification, her response leapt from her mouth as if of its own volition. "Yes, I would like that very much."

Hours later as Edith and Dahlia worked together tidying up the kitchen after supper, her niggling regret concerning her agreement to accompany Wade at the Christmas party scratched harder at her conscience. While it would be awkward and perhaps even unwise to rescind her acceptance of his offer, she at least should warn Dahlia about the rumored slave catchers lurking around Madison.

She handed Dahlia a freshly washed plate and tried to think how best to broach the subject without frightening the child too much. "Have you heard of slave catchers, Dahlia?"

Dahlia nodded as she took the plate and began drying it with a towel. "They are bad men from down south who chase after runaway slaves."

"That's right." Edith lifted another clean plate from the soapy water. "Have your parents told you to beware of them?"

Dahlia nodded again as she took the wet plate from Edith. "Pa told me to stay clear of anybody I don't know who talks with a Southern accent."

"Then I'm surprised your ma allowed you to ride here in Mr. Beaumont's carriage."

She grinned up at Edith. "Oh, I know Ma and Pa don't mean Mr. Beaumont, 'cause he's nice and I know him. Bedsides, if he wanted to snatch me and take me down south, I reckon he'd have done it already." She shrugged as she ran the towel over the plate. "All I asked Ma was if I could come and stay the night here with you."

Dahlia's mother doubtless thought Edwin would be driving them. Fear at the little girl's innocent naïveté leaped in Edith's chest and honed a sharper edge to her tone. "You must not be so trusting, Dahlia. There are rumors of slave catchers around Madison. Mrs. Hale told me that the leader is a tall man with brown hair that comes over his ears, a crescent-shaped scar on his cheek, and answers to a given name something like Jeb or Jude."

Dahlia's eyes grew large. "That sounds like the man that came to visit Mr. Beaumont when I was at your Madison house last week. Mr. Beaumont called him Jube, and I think the man said he was Mr. Beaumont's brother."

For a long moment Edith stood mute as fear gripped her. Her insides writhed, threatening to reject her supper onto the kitchen floor right in front of Dahlia.

"What's the matter, Miss Edith? You look like you're gettin' sick." Dahlia's little forehead puckered with worry lines.

Through sheer will, Edith managed to breathe again and keep her supper down. She folded her arms across her chest to stop herself from shaking. Anger flooded through her, washing out her shock and fear; anger at Edwin for bringing Wade into their lives, anger at Wade for his duplicity, but mostly anger at herself for allowing Wade to beguile her with his Southern charms and wriggle his way into her affections. At the memory of her impulsive agreement to let him squire her at the Christmas party, her stomach churned again.

She fixed Dahlia with her sternest look. "You must stay away from Mr. Beaumont. Do you understand me?"

A pained look crumpled Dahlia's face as tears filled her eyes. "But Mr. Beaumont is my friend."

"No, he is not!" The words came out harsher than Edith intended, and her heart twisted with remorse when Dahlia began to cry.

Edith sighed as she knelt and pulled Dahlia into her embrace. "I'm sorry I spoke so harshly, but you must understand how dangerous it is for you to be anywhere near slave catchers." She wiped the wetness from Dahlia's cheeks. "Until we can determine whether or not Mr. Beaumont is in any way connected to slave catchers, you must not go near him or our old house in Madison." She cradled the girl's face in her hands. "Promise me you will stay away from that house and Mr. Beaumont."

Dahlia nodded. "I promise," she murmured.

"Good girl." Edith forced a smile and stood again on shaky legs.

Dahlia gave Edith a quizzical look. "But if Mr. Beaumont is so bad, why did you say you'd go to the Christmas party with him?"

Edith stood speechless, having thought Dahlia was asleep during her conversation with Wade in the carriage. As she grappled for an answer, a soft rapping sounded at the front door.

Edith stepped into the front sitting room to see Father open the door to reveal Dahlia's father, Mose.

"Pa." Dahlia stepped from behind Edith, and disappointment dragged down her voice. "Ma said I could stay the night here and you'd come for me in the morning."

Mose put a hand on his daughter's head, but no hint of a smile touched his lips. "I'm not here for you, child. I'll be back after you in the mornin', just like Ma said." He looked at Father. "The first passengers have arrived."

Father nodded. "I'll show you to the place."

Edith's mind raced, trying to comprehend what was happening. She looked from Mose to Father. "What do you mean, 'passengers'?"

Father turned a grave face to Edith. "It is for this reason we have moved here, Daughter."

Chapter 7

Edith's hands shook as she reached behind her neck and tried to tie the black velvet ribbon attached to Mother's best cameo pendant. The prospect of attempting to appear serene and unaffected by Wade's presence tonight felt daunting. Since the evening three weeks ago when she'd learned that their Lancaster home was a stop on the Underground Railroad, she hadn't drawn an easy breath. In the past twenty-one days she and Father had provided sanctuary for two more groups of runaways, concealing them by day in a hidden compartment behind a false wall in the apple cellar. Father explained that with the passage of the Fugitive Slave Act, the governing board of the Eleutherian Institute had decided that someone needed to occupy their little cottage in order to utilize it as a stop on the Underground Railroad. While it hurt that Father hadn't told her the real reason he'd taken the teaching job at the institute when they moved to Lancaster last fall, she understood the need for secrecy. Also, by keeping her ignorant of their greater mission, he'd allowed her to remain unburdened by the knowledge in the event that she was questioned.

When Edith shared what Dahlia had told her about Wade's brother, Father decided that they could no longer risk Wade's weekly visits. Instead Father now traveled to Madison to review the company books. Unsure how she could face Wade again, let alone allow him to touch her, Edith's first impulse had been to renege on her promise to let him squire her for the Christmas party this evening. Father had disagreed, saying that after curtailing Wade's visits, any further changes might pique Wade's and his brother's suspicions, putting Edith, Father, and any runaways hiding on their premises in danger. Father also suggested that Edith use the occasion of the party to engage Wade in conversation and learn of his involvement, if any, in slave hunting.

Edith gazed into the dresser mirror and heaved a tremulous sigh. Her heart stung with a painful twinge of disappointment, and she pressed her hand against the bodice of her bottle-green watered silk frock. As she now faced her image in the looking glass, she must face the truth. She had wanted to believe that Wade had no interest in dragging people back into bondage and so she'd allowed herself to care for him.

Hot tears sprang into her eyes and slipped down her face. She brushed them from her too-rosy cheeks with trembling fingers. The evening's excitement could explain her flushed face but not her unsteady voice or hands.

Happy chatter of arriving guests wafted up from the music room below, sending new waves of dread washing through her.

Dear Lord, You must help me do this. Please help me do this!

Two quick raps on her bedroom door sent a jolt of panic through her.

"Edith, are you ready? Guests are arriving and Edwin can't deal with them all. We'll need to divide and conquer." Impatience lent an edge to Sophie's voice. "Edwin says I take forever to get ready, but even I have been prepared to greet guests for the past half hour."

Somehow Edith stood and crossed the room on wobbly legs to open the door to her sister-in-law. "I just need to tie this ribbon better. I would hate to lose Mother's cameo." Her conscience chafed against the lie. While she felt relatively confident in the knot she'd tied, the delay would gain her a few extra minutes to bolster her courage before heading downstairs.

Smiling, Sophie gave a happy gasp and clasped her hands together as she looked Edith up and down. "Oh, I knew you'd look wonderful in that color of green." The compliment held a hint of self-congratulation.

Edith gave her sister-in-law a fond smile. "Your judgment in choosing frock colors remains impeccable, Sophie. And you look absolutely gorgeous in that red silk dress." She let a teasing tone creep into her voice. "My brother had better stay close to his wife tonight. I expect all the gentlemen's eyes will be on you this evening, and I wouldn't want Edwin to feel forced to defend your honor."

"Oh don't be silly. I'm an old married lady and a mother at that." Sophie batted the air with her hand in a dismissive gesture, but the sparkle in her blue eyes told Edith that she lapped up the compliment like a cat with a bowl of cream. She cocked her head at Edith, and her tone turned teasing. "Speaking of admiring gentlemen, a certain Southern gentleman is among the early arrivals, and he inquired after you specifically."

Edith's pulse quickened to the pace of a crazed metronome. "I—I can't go down yet."

Sophie huffed. "But you look perfect."

"My neck ribbon still needs retying." She must buy one more moment to calm her nerves before facing Wade.

Sophie huffed again. "Oh, fiddle-dee-dee! Turn around."

Edith did as Sophie asked and heard her sister-in-law grunt as she sensed the shorter woman go up on her tiptoes to reach Edith's neck.

In a quick moment, Sophie untied and retied the ribbon, then gave her work a final pat. "There, your mother's cameo is secure. We must hurry down. Our guests await."

Edith had no choice but to follow her sister-in-law down the curved staircase that ended in a wide hallway opposite the music room, which already hummed with the cheerful sounds of the milling guests.

As she descended she focused on each step so as not to trip on her hem and send both herself and Sophie tumbling down the stairs. So her heart shot to her throat when, safely on the landing, she looked up into Wade's smiling face.

The intense look in his eyes took Edith's breath away. His gaze never budged from her face as he took her hand and pressed it to his lips, sending delicious tingles up her arm. "Forgive my rudeness for staring, Miss Applegate, but you are the most ravishing creature I have ever had the pleasure of clapping eyes on." A sad, almost pained smile touched his lips. "I have missed you, Edith."

Her heart reciprocated the sentiment, but the compliment stuck in her throat. In truth, she'd never seen Wade look handsomer than he did this evening in his black frock coat; white, high-collared shirt; and blue silk necktie that exactly matched his eyes. Desperate for a diversion, she looked in search of Sophie, but her sister-in-law had joined the other guests in the music room. Praying for guidance and poise, she tucked her arm around his proffered one and willed her lips into a smile. "How very kind of you, Mr. Beaumont. Shall we join the others?"

As they stepped into the music room, Rosaleen Hale, seated at the piano, began playing the "Jenny Lind Polka."

Wade stepped back and gave Edith a deep bow. "Will you honor me with this dance, Miss Applegate?"

"Of course," Edith murmured and found herself swept among the other dancers. For once she silently thanked the Lord for giving her a sister-in-law who loved parties. Her feet flawlessly executed the dance steps she knew by heart, and the polka's quick tempo precluded her from having to make conversation.

When the dance ended and everyone applauded Rosaleen's playing, Wade gave a low whistle. "Whew, that was exhilarating." He offered Edith his arm. "May I get you some refreshment? Eggnog or perhaps some sweet cider?"

"Thank you." She repeated the sentiment in a silent prayer of thanks to the Lord, welcoming any respite from Wade's nearness that kept her heart in contortions. "Perhaps some cider." She searched the room for Edwin, Sophie, Father, or anyone she knew who seemed unengaged in conversation.

Wade turned as if to go for the refreshment then turned back to her again. "Edith, are you angry with me?" The pained look she'd seen in his eyes earlier returned. "If I did or said something to offend you when I took you home in my carriage some weeks ago, I am grievously sorry for it."

Only that you would drag other children of God into unspeakable bondage. Praying that the uncharitable thought didn't show on her face, she quirked a smile that her lips refused to sustain. "I assure you that you did nothing that day to offend me, Mr. Beaumont."

An odd look crossed his face before his smile returned. "Then I am most relieved." Giving her a stiff bow, he headed off toward the refreshment table.

Edith crossed the room to the piano where Rosaleen Hale sat flipping through pages of music. It struck her that the frugal minister's wife wore the same rose-colored silk dress she'd worn five years ago at another of Sophie's parties when her husband had proposed marriage.

Rosaleen settled the music sheets on the piano and smiled at Edith. "Good evening, Edith. It looks like Sophie has managed another successful party."

"It does seem to be her gift," Edith said with a little laugh.

Rosaleen grinned. "You look to be having a good time, but I must say I'm wondering if it was the polka or your handsome companion that has you blushing."

Edith pressed her hands to her warm cheeks, and her smile dissolved. Glancing around, she lowered her voice to a conspiratorial tone. "I would not have agreed to let Mr. Beaumont squire me for the evening if I'd known earlier that—" She glanced over at the refreshment table to assure herself that Wade was still engaged in conversation with Edwin. "I believe the slave hunter you warned me about is his brother."

Rosaleen nodded. "And I believe you are right." She took Edith's hand and an understanding look gentled her expression. "Edith, just because Wade's brother's heart is turned a certain way doesn't mean that Wade's heart is turned the same. Jacob has spoken to Wade on more than one occasion, and he believes that Wade is cut from different cloth." She smiled. "Ezekiel 18:20 says, 'The righteousness of the righteous shall be upon him, and the wickedness of the wicked shall be upon him.' Don't judge Wade for his brother's actions."

The anguish grinding inside Edith crept into her voice. "I'm not judging him for his brother's actions, Rosaleen. I just wish I could be sure he's not involved in the same wickedness."

"Then ask him," Rosaleen whispered as she glanced past Edith's shoulder. "He's coming this way now."

Edith's heart sprang to her throat, and she turned to see Wade walking toward them with two steaming cups of mulled cider.

Wade handed Edith a cup and acknowledged Rosaleen with a shallow bow. "Mrs. Hale, may I commend you on your wonderful piano playing? I've never heard a polka done better on the pianoforte."

Edith gave her friend a fond smile. "Rosaleen could have played for audiences in New York City, but she decided to marry a minister here instead."

Wade laughed and Edith wished she didn't like the sound so much. He pressed his hand against his heart. "Ah, fame and fortune forsaken for love. Then it must be true love indeed, ma'am."

"True indeed." Rosaleen glanced across the room where her husband, Jacob, stood talking with another gentleman. She shifted her gaze back to Wade. "Should I play a waltz, do you think?"

Wade looked at Edith. "Yes, please. But don't begin until Miss Applegate has finished her cup of cider."

Rosaleen shuffled through her sheet music. "I have a rather new Christmas tune, 'O Holy Night.'"

Edith managed to get a few sips of the cider past her tightening throat as Wade and Rosaleen discussed other waltz options.

At length Wade set his cup and saucer on one of Sophie's little marble-topped parlor tables and, with Edith's murmured permission, put hers with it and took her hand. "May I have this waltz, Miss Applegate?"

Wishing she could think of a reason to say no, Edith looked at Rosaleen for help. Finding none, she nodded and found herself in Wade's arms in the middle of the room as Rosaleen began playing the waltz.

After two bars of the dance Edith relaxed in his arms as they twirled among the other dancers.

Wade smiled. "You dance divinely. I must confess I'm surprised."

"Why?"

"Your reluctance to partner me in the dance made me wonder about your proficiency. Or is it that you don't care to dance with me?"

"Are you a slave hunter, Wade?" That she'd blurted the question chasing around in her mind surprised Edith.

A stunned look replaced his smile, and for the first time, he missed a step in the dance. He recovered the momentary stumble. "Ah yes, you would have heard about my brother, Jube. And no, I'm not a slave hunter." A flash of anger crossed his blue eyes, but whether at having to defend himself from the charge or being found out, Edith couldn't say.

"And why should I believe you when your brother and his band of slave hunters appeared in Madison only after you arrived here?" Edith executed a twirl then glared up at him. "I'm not as gullible as Edwin, which I would need to be to believe that you have not kept in correspondence with your. . .family."

The dance ended and Wade and Edith joined in the applause for Rosaleen's playing.

Wade took Edith's hand. "Come, we need to talk." He led her to an unoccupied settee. When they'd been seated, he rested his arms on his upper thighs and clasped his hands together. "In truth, I've had no contact with my brother or father for over three years now." He shifted his gaze from his hands to her face. His throat moved with a swallow, and a look of pain filled his eyes. "From childhood, I found the institution of slavery sickening. Pa began taking Jube and me on hunts for runaways when we were just boys."

The distant look in his eyes seemed to gaze beyond the festive atmosphere of the party swirling around them. "Parents and their kids all screaming as Pa and the other catchers tore them away from each other and sold them down the river, never to see one another again. And then there were the beatings. . ."

He shook his head as if to dislodge the picture in his mind. "I believe our country's founding fathers ascertain in the Declaration of Independence that all men are equal, and that should apply to all people, regardless of skin color." His eyes turned watery. "My mother felt the same way, but Pa wouldn't hear a word of it." His brow furrowed in a scowl. "I believe it's what put Ma in an early grave."

"I'm sorry." Edith put her hand on his as her own eyes filled with tears.

Wade shrugged. "After Ma died I grew tired of the daily arguments with Father about the subject of slavery, so I left our plantation, boarded the next riverboat, and never looked back." He narrowed an intense gaze at her eyes. "No one was more surprised at Jube's appearance here than me. You have to believe that."

"I do." Edith squeezed his hand. While her heart broke for him, joy flooded her chest and happy tears mingled with the sad ones slipping down her face. "I'm sorry I accused you of engaging in such wickedness. Please forgive me."

Wade shook his head, took her hands in his, and gave her such a sweet smile her heart ached. "Nothing to forgive. What else *would* you have thought?" For a long moment, his gaze dropped to their clasped hands. When he looked back up at her, his expression turned serious. "Edith, I know that you and your family are sympathetic to the abolitionist movement. To what extent I know not, nor do I care to. But please be careful. Jube is ruthless, and he won't make exceptions because of your family's connection to me."

For the rest of the evening Edith's heart danced along with her feet as she partnered Wade in every dance. As they waltzed to the tune of "God Rest Ye Merry Gentlemen," she knew she'd lost her heart to him.

"Thank you for a wonderful evening," Wade murmured later as he lifted her hands to his lips and pressed a warm kiss on both of them, setting every nerve in her body firing like fireworks on the Fourth of July. Hope shone in his unwavering gaze. "May I call on you soon?"

Edith nodded. Though Father had declared Wade's visits too risky, he didn't know Wade's story. When he learned of Wade's feelings about slavery, he would doubtless have no problem with welcoming him to their home again. "Yes," she finally managed, wondering if he could hear her hammering heart.

After Wade and the other guest had left, Edith's heart still waltzed as she worked to put the music room back to rights. She passed a window that looked onto the back portico and thought she glimpsed Wade's profile. Sure that she must be mistaken, she slipped behind the table holding the little decorated Christmas tree and peered through the window.

Outside on the porch Wade stood talking with another man. The other man, almost a head taller than Wade, struck a match to light a cigar. The momentary orange glow illuminated one side of his face and Edith could make out a crescent-shaped scar.

Chapter 8

Wade exited the jewelry store with a new spring in his step. Though less than two weeks had passed, it seemed an eternity since he'd held Edith in his arms and their hearts had beat as one as they waltzed over her brother's music room floor. He'd hoped to visit her the next week and ask her father's permission to court her, but when he suggested to Edwin that he take the company records to Lancaster as he used to, Edwin had shaken his head, saying his father was sick in bed with a bad cold. "Half the town seems to have come down with the coryza. I'm just glad we got the Christmas party over. I'm keeping Sophie and Archie inside near the hearth."

Every day hence Wade inquired into the elder Applegate's health as well as that of Edith, who, thankfully, seemed to have escaped the sickness. Finally this morning Edwin, at Wade's inquiry, announced that his father once again enjoyed robust health, forcing Wade to suppress a whoop of joy.

Smiling, he patted his chest above where he'd tucked the little box from the jewelry store. Now if Edith accepted both his gift and his request to court her, his cup, as the scriptures said, would overflow with blessings.

As he strolled down the snow-dusted boardwalk, a sight outside the tobacco store across the street wiped the smile from his face. Two fellows who stood there talking looked a lot like Jube's cohorts.

Wade hadn't seen his brother since the night of the Christmas party when Jube came by Edwin's home to ask Wade to return with him to Mississippi, so Wade had assumed that Jube and the others had long left Madison. While Jube's uncharacteristic show of brotherly affection had touched Wade, he'd declined the offer without hesitation or regret. The differences between his view of slavery and that of Jube and their father—the differences that had driven Wade from Mississippi three years ago—remained.

Curious, Wade crossed the street. Careful to stay out of sight of the men, he made his way to the alley beside the tobacco store. Staying close to the building, he craned his neck to listen to their conversation.

"Now that Jube's back on his feet again, we'll be headin' over to Lancaster tonight to search that Quaker school and the little stone house across from it." The man paused to take a bite off a plug of tobacco. "Word is," he said around a jaw full of chaw, "the place is a station on the Underground Railroad."

The other man nodded and spat out a brown stream. "Feller by the name of Applegate lives there with his girl. Pa of the feller Jube's brother works for." He gave a derisive snort. "A bunch of abolitionists accordin' to Bob Rea and others here who feel as we do." Anger hardened his lowered voice. "Rea says if we can catch that Applegate bunch hidin' runaways, he'll push to get the old man put behind bars."

Fear for Edith and her father shot through Wade like a lightning bolt. The man had said they'd be raiding the house tonight. Darkness came by six o'clock and it was already past noon. Moving with both speed and stealth, he made his way to the back of the tobacco store then ran the rest of the way home, his heart hammering as much from urgency as exertion.

Not stopping for a midday meal or to don a heavier outer coat, Wade saddled his horse with less than steady hands. He could no longer afford the luxury of remaining neutral about the subject of slavery, nor could he concern himself with how Edith and her father might receive his warning. His contention to Edith that he didn't care to know the extent of her family's involvement in the abolitionist movement had blown away on the December wind. With the prospect of prison facing the woman he loved and her family, the time for beating about the bush had passed.

Pushing his horse as hard as the weather conditions allowed, Wade traversed the snowy roads between Madison and Lancaster in record time. At least the snow flurries had stopped and the sky had cleared.

Jumping from his horse, he scaled the stone steps to the front door in two strides. His pounding heart matched the blows of his fist on the door. *Dear Lord, let them believe me, and help us conceal anyone hidden here.*

Edith opened the door and stood stunned. "Mr. Beaumont," she finally managed when the breath had come back to her lungs. "Edwin never mentioned you would be coming today. Is there a problem at the plant?"

"No, but I *have* come with urgent information." Wade took off his hat and circled the brim in his hands. "Please, may I come in?"

The temptation to deny his request, call him out for a liar, and shut the door in his face tugged hard. In the end, a lifetime of practiced etiquette and Christian charity compelled her to invite him in.

"Mr. Beaumont. To what do we owe this visit?" Father's voice behind Edith held as frosty a tone as she'd ever heard from her parent.

"Mr. Applegate. Edith." Wade's gaze swung between them as he kept turning his hat in his hands, his look so genuine, so intense, that Edith had to remind herself that he couldn't be trusted. "My brother, Jube, and his slave catchers are convinced that this house is a station on the Underground Railroad."

Edith felt the blood in her veins freeze. When it began flowing again, her heart hammered. Had Wade come to inform them that he planned to report them to the sheriff for being in violation of the Fugitive Slave Act?

"And where did your brother get such a notion?" Nothing in Father's voice betrayed the tumult Edith knew he must feel.

"I do not know, sir, nor is it important." Impatient urgency gave a sharp edge to Wade's voice. "I do not know if you are hiding people on these premises, but if you are, you must know that Jube and his men are more than thorough in their search for runaway slaves." His throat moved with a hard swallow. "They will not leave a stone unturned."

Remembering Father's maxim that a winning army remains on the offensive, Edith raised her chin in defiance. "If you brother and his men are waiting somewhere outside, you have our permission to invite them in and they can look for themselves." While Mose had alerted them to expect a "package" this evening, no guests resided at present.

Wade shook his head. "They are not outside, but they *are* coming this evening." His gaze locked on Edith's. "Please, you must believe me. Like I told you at the Christmas party, I'm on your side. I wish to protect the runaways too."

"Is that what you told your brother on Edwin's back portico after the party?" Edith hated the tears filling her eyes. "I saw you out there talking with him. Were you telling him how you'd duped me into believing you are not a slave catcher?"

Wade groaned and closed his eyes. When he opened them again, his gaze narrowed to a near glare. He frowned and emotion thickened his voice. "I am not a liar, Edith. I meant every word I said to you. Jube came to ask me to return with him to Mississippi, but I told him that while I will always care for him and Pa and will continue to pray for them as Ma did, I cannot go back to that life." His look turned pleading and his voice softened. "Please, you must believe me." Moisture welled in his blue eyes. "If you like, I will put my hand on the Holy Scriptures and vow that what I've told you is the truth."

Warmth filled Edith's chest, melting the icy block of distrust she'd allowed to encase her heart concerning Wade since the Christmas party. To her shame, Father spoke first.

"There is no one else here now, but I have word that Mose Taylor, Dahlia's father, will be bringing passengers tonight from Georgetown." Father stepped toward the pegs on the wall that held his hat and coat. "We must warn Mose not to come."

Edith shook her head. "No, Father. You must not go out into the cold. You could get a setback and catch your death."

Wade nodded. "Edith is right, Mr. Applegate. You stay here. Edith will show me to Mr. Taylor's home."

Father sighed but nodded agreement. "Of course you are right." He gave Edith and Wade an encouraging smile. "I'll stay here and pray that you reach Mose before he leaves with the group, but I will prepare the hiding place for the passengers in case they arrive." He touched Wade's shoulder. "You can leave your horse here and take my horse and buggy."

Wade shook his head. "A horse and buggy would be too slow. Besides, my brother knows my horse. If he should arrive in my absence, it would alert him that something is not right here." He grinned at Edith. "If it won't offend your sensibilities, we'll need to ride tandem on my horse."

In truth, Edith couldn't have described the sensation curling in her chest at his suggestion offensive. Hoping he didn't notice any deepening color in her warming cheeks, she lifted her chin. "Decorum must take second place when lives are at stake, Mr. Beaumont."

Indeed, thoughts of decorum never entered Edith's mind as she and Wade covered the roads between Lancaster and Madison at a near canter, her arms wrapped around his waist. The icy December wind, the lengthening afternoon shadows, and even the uncomfortable riding position felt trivial in comparison to warning Mose and his group of runaways.

When they finally reached Jefferson Street in Madison's Georgetown district, Edith guided Wade to the Taylors' home. She peered around his shoulder at the line of neat two-story stone houses crowded close together. "It's the green one between the white and ochre-colored houses."

Wade nodded, dismounted, and helped her down.

Edith slipped into his arms and for a moment the world and the worry that had consumed her mind over the past hour and a half vanished. As their gazes met, an understanding passed between them that needed no words. The next moment his lips found hers and they floated in a beautiful sphere devoid of all thought.

His horse shifted and emitted a soft neigh, slamming Edith back to reality.

Wade released her and cleared his throat, an almost embarrassed sound as if he regretted the kiss. His voice—the first words she'd heard from him since they'd left Lancaster—sounded dispassionate. "Go knock on the door. I'll tie up the horse."

Her face burning and her heart hammering, Edith somehow managed to scale the two stone steps to the door on wobbly legs.

In answer to Edith's three soft raps, Polly Taylor opened the door. Her eyes grew wide with a look of alarm and she clutched her throat. "Miss Edith," she said, her voice a near squeak, "is Dahlia all right?"

"I haven't seen Dahlia." Confusion and mounting fear mingled in Edith's chest.

"Come inside." Polly's sharp glance bounced between Edith and Wade, who'd joined Edith on the steps. She moved aside to allow them entrance. Without another word, she bade them follow her to a small room next to the kitchen. There Mose lay on a little bed swathed in a green and yellow comforter.

"Mr. Taylor." Audible relief filled Wade's voice. "We've come to advise you not to make that planned trip to Lancaster, but I see you're in no shape to go out tonight."

"No." A spate of coughing interrupted Mose's answer.

Polly eyed Wade with suspicion.

Edith put a reassuring hand on Polly's arm. "It's all right, Polly." Her pulse quickening, she gave Wade a fond smile. "Wade is an abolitionist too. He wants to help us."

Wade stepped behind Edith and cupped her shoulders with his hands, sending delicious warmth through her. "My brother and his band of slave hunters are planning to search Mr. Applegate's house in Lancaster tonight for runaways. We came to warn you not to take passengers there tonight, but I see our concerns were for naught."

Polly crossed her arms over her chest and began to shake, a look of terror twisting her comely features. Gasping, she pressed her hand to her mouth. "Oh dear Lord, no. My baby, my baby!" Tears streaming down her face, she looked at her husband, whose look of anguish mirrored her own. "Oh dear Lord, help us. What have we done, Mose?"

Fighting the fear rising like floodwaters in her chest, Edith grasped the distraught woman's arms. "Polly, what are you talking about? Where is Dahlia?"

Mose began to sob. "We heard that slave hunters were comin' to search all the houses here in Georgetown." His dark eyes brimmed with anguished tears. He shook his head. "We thought that Lancaster was safe." He looked at Edith, and his tortured expression that pled for understanding ripped at her heart. "Dahlia begged us to let her guide them to your place. Said she knew she could find it, even in the dark. The people promised to take care of her." His voice snagged on the ragged edge of a sob. He gave Edith and Wade a vacant, helpless look. "If them slave hunters find Dahlia with the others, they'll take our baby away with the rest of 'em and sell her down south."

Chapter 9

Wade knelt beside Polly and took her hands in his as fear and anger swirled in his chest. He strove to keep his voice both calm and confident. "Mrs. Taylor, I will find Dahlia and bring her back to you safely. I promise." As he gazed into the frantic face of Dahlia's mother, he prayed he could keep his promise.

Edith stepped to Mose's bedside. "How many are with her?"

"Four; a husband and wife and two young men." Mose sniffed and dabbed his wet eyes with his shirt cuff.

Wade rose from Polly's side to join Edith. Noticing the fringe on her blue wool scarf quivering, he marveled at the steadiness of her voice. Seized by the desire to reassure her, he slipped his arm around her waist. He reached his free hand out to Mose Taylor, who gripped it as if clutching a lifeline. "I will bring Dahlia back to you, Mr. Taylor, you have to believe me. But every moment is precious. What route have they taken?"

Eager to head out in search of Dahlia and the runaways, Wade struggled to take in Mose's directions. The thought that he and Edith might have passed the group somewhere between Lancaster and Madison felt maddening. Edith's confident nods lent calming assurance. She knew this country far better than he.

Wade joined Edith in reiterating parting words of comfort and reassurance to the Taylors before heading out in search of Dahlia and the runaways.

Edith's confident voice in Wade's ear directing them through the winter gloaming along roads, country lanes, and rutted cow paths bolstered his own courage. Yes, this was the woman he wanted—needed—at his side each day for the rest of his life.

By the time they neared Lancaster, the pale light of a full moon bathed the countryside beneath a canopy of sparkling stars strewn across the inky sky.

"Stop." Edith put her hand on Wade's shoulder as he guided the horse through a little copse of pine trees bordering a wood. The warm breath of her whisper felt delicious against his ear. "I think I saw something move in those trees ahead."

Wade reined the horse to a halt, and before he could stop her, Edith slipped off the animal's rump. He dismounted and followed her through the trees.

"Dahlia, is that you? It's Miss Edith." The urgency in her whispered voice held a measure of restrained panic.

A soft rustling of dead leaves to their left drew his attention.

"Miss Edith?" At Dahlia's faint but distinctive voice, relief swooshed through Wade.

The next moment Dahlia's face appeared out of the darkness from behind a Scotch pine tree, her eyes wide with surprise. "What are you and Mr. Beaumont doing here?"

Edith fell to her knees and embraced Dahlia. "Oh, praise the Lord! Thank You, Jesus!" Emotion thickened her whispered voice, muffled against Dahlia's head. She started to stand

and stumbled as if her legs wouldn't support her, and Wade reached out to help her up. "Mr. Beaumont and I have come to take you back home, Dahlia. It's not safe for you out here."

Dahlia gave her head a defiant shake. "I can't go back until I get the people to the tunnel behind your house." She turned and headed back into the trees, and Edith and Wade followed.

In a clearing between the pines and a blackberry thicket huddled a man and a woman—the woman wrapped in a dark wool cape. Two other young men crouched near them. At the sight of Wade and Edith, every dark face registered alarm.

Wade looked at the man with his arm around the woman. "You must go back to Georgetown. There are slave hunters about."

The man narrowed a suspicious glare at Wade. "And why should we believe a white man with South Mississippi on his tongue thicker'n molasses on bread?"

Edith stepped forward. "Because he's with me and my father, and I run the station where you're headed."

Dahlia gave a definitive nod. "You can trust Mr. Beaumont. He's my friend."

Wade's heart melted at the little girl's affirmation, and he gave her an appreciative smile before turning back to the man. "You're right, I *was* born and raised in Mississippi, but like Dahlia and Miss Applegate, I'm an abolitionist too." It felt good to finally embrace the term he knew defined him.

The wary looks on the faces of the four began to fade, and the man who'd questioned Wade reached a hand out to him. Wade accepted the gesture of friendship. "I'm Sam, and this is my wife, Ida." He cocked his head toward the two young men who looked to still be in their teens. "That there is Joe and Simon."

Joe and Simon shook Wade's hand in turn while Ida nodded her greeting from where she huddled beneath the pine tree.

Wade turned back to Sam, who seemed in charge of the group. "You can't go on to Lancaster. I heard the slave hunters say they planned to search Mr. Applegate's home this evening."

Sam crossed his arms over his chest and glanced down at his wife. "Ida's six months on with child. She won't make it all the way back to Madison, and she'll freeze out here in the woods tonight." He shook his head. "We gotta go on."

Frustration bubbled up inside Wade. "Did you not hear me, man?" He flung his arm out in the direction of Lancaster. "If you go on to the next station, they'll find you and send you all back to slavery!"

"No, they won't." Edith's small, calm voice broke in. "Father says the house has been searched several times in years past and no one was ever able to discover the hiding place. If they can get to the house ahead of the slave hunters, they will be safe."

The *clop, clop* of horses' hooves along the nearby road brought everyone to silent attention. As the riders neared, their muffled conversation became audible.

"I'm about froze. How much longer is it to that place anyhow?"

"Quit yer bellyachin', Jake. Only about another mile, I reckon." Jube's voice jarred Wade.

When the riders had passed beyond earshot, a sense of urgency gripped Wade. He turned to Edith. "Do you think you can find your way to the house?"

Edith nodded. "I think so."

"I can find it," Dahlia said in a loud whisper. "I know I can."

"Good girl." He patted Dahlia's cheek then turned back to Edith, a brew of emotions roiling inside him. "I think if I make enough racket I can lure them a mile or so away and give you enough time to get everyone into the hiding place." He rubbed his hands down her arms as he gazed into her eyes. Too many things to say and no time to say them. "It's in God's hands now. All we can do is pray and trust Him to take care of us."

Edith squeezed his hands, her smile as brave as it was encouraging. "The Lord has gotten us this far. He'll get us the rest of the way home."

The temptation to kiss her lips became too strong and he allowed himself one moment of bliss before turning to Sam.

"Sam, I need you to holler, 'Come on, we gotta go this way.' I'll make a ruckus and head in the opposite direction. When you hear the slave hunters pass, hightail it to the house as fast as you can."

Sam narrowed his eyes at Wade. "Why can't you do the hollerin'?"

Wade swallowed and prayed he wouldn't lose the man's trust. "Because at least one of them will know my voice."

To Wade's relief Sam nodded and proceeded to follow his instructions. The next moment Wade heard Jube holler, "Come on, boys, they're over there!"

His heart pounding, Wade jumped on his horse and headed southeast, thrashing through the thickets and underbrush with as much noise as possible. A moment later the sound of pounding hooves behind him grew louder. For the better part of a mile he managed to stay a few yards ahead of his pursuers. From time to time Jube would call out instructions to his men, assuring Wade that none of the slave hunters had broken away and headed back toward the house.

"We got 'em, boys!" The shouts grew louder—closer.

A gunshot echoed in the darkness, and something whizzed past Wade's head. There was no way they could get a bead on him in the dark woods, but his thrashing could draw a lucky shot. His insides clenched at the notion that his brother and childhood companion might take his life.

The instant that thought formed in his mind, something struck the back of his shoulder with the force of an oak plank. Searing pain like a white-hot poker shot through his upper back.

"In here. Hurry!" Having sent Dahlia on to the house some fifty yards away, Edith directed Sam, Ida, Joe, and Simon into the tunnel that led to the cellar. "You'll have to make your way through the dark, but the tunnel opens up to a little room with cots, food and water, a lamp, and a box of phosphorus matches." At Sam's nod she closed the wooden door and covered it with the cut elderberry bush Father used to conceal the tunnel.

Since they left Wade, the safety of Dahlia and the runaways had dominated her thoughts. Now as she neared the house, concern for the man who owned her heart gripped her. Two faint pops that might have been gunshots had sounded in the distance. Had Wade evaded Jube and the other slave hunters? Was he lying somewhere in the darkness hurt or. . . Tears filled her eyes as panic rose. She pushed it down. No, she mustn't think such things. Wade had said they must trust God, so until she knew otherwise she would believe that God had led him safely back to Madison.

The night darkened as clouds obscured the light from the moon and stars. The intermittent flurries of earlier that day began again, increasing to a steady snowfall. She squinted through the milky veil at the welcoming light shining through the kitchen window. At least the new snow should obliterate any tracks that she and the others had made.

As she rounded the back of the house on her way to the kitchen door, something grabbed her arm. Her heart vaulted to her throat and she emitted a yelp that Wade stifled with his kisses.

The questions swirling in her mind, the whereabouts of the slave hunters and why Wade was here instead of on his way to Madison, drifted away with the falling snow as she luxuriated in the arms of the man she loved.

When he finally released her lips, she rolled her head against his shoulder and he groaned in pain.

Alarmed, Edith stepped back, out of his arms. "What is the matter, Wade? Are you hurt?"

Wade nodded and groaned again. "We need to get inside. I was able to give them the slip, but they could show up here any minute."

Inside the kitchen that smelled of sausage, potato soup, and apple cider, Father greeted her with a warm hug and prayers of thanksgiving. Dahlia, seated at the table, smiled up from her bowl of soup.

Father took Edith's wool cape. "You have them safe, then?"

"Yes, but Wade is hurt." Edith fought the panic rising in her voice.

Frowning, Father turned his attention to Wade.

Wade winced as Father helped him off with his coat, and Edith stifled a gasp at the red stain spreading across the shoulder of his white shirt. "They got off a lucky shot." He looked at Edith and grinned through a wince. "Or not so lucky for me."

Dahlia dropped her spoon into her bowl with a clank. Her dark eyes, growing to the size of half-dollar pieces, filled with tears. "Are you going to die?"

Wade smiled. "Someday, little one, but not tonight."

Edith's mind raced. If Wade's brother and the other slave hunters found Wade shot, they'd know he had helped the runaways. Schooling her face to a calm expression, she turned to Dahlia. "Dahlia, you know where we keep the sheets?"

Dahlia nodded.

"Bring me a sheet and one of Mr. Applegate's frock coats, please."

Dahlia hurried off on the errand and returned with the items within seconds.

With Father's and Dahlia's help, Edith tore the sheet into strips, which she wrapped around Wade's injured shoulder, staunching the bleeding to a faint pink smudge. She tied a final knot in the bandage. "Tomorrow we'll send someone from the institute to fetch Dr. Morgan from Madison, but tonight you must appear unscathed."

Father helped Wade on with the coat. "Do you think you can hold up, son?"

Wade, whose complexion had paled, grinned and nodded. "I have no choice."

Three sharp raps sounded at the front door.

Edith, Wade, and Father exchanged knowing looks. Edith headed to the front room with Father and Wade behind her. She opened the door to a tall man in a heavy black overcoat and a felt low-topper hat.

The man doffed his hat, sending the scent of lanoline to Edith's nose as she stifled a gasp at the crescent scar on his cheek. "I believe my brother is within. Jube Beaumont at your service, miss." He glanced behind him where two men stood near the road with three mounts then gave Edith a toothy grin. "I do believe that is Wade's horse tethered outside."

"Brother." Wade sauntered to the door. "What brings you out to the countryside on this snowy winter's night?" The lilt in his voice held a convincing tone of surprise.

Something between a grin and a sneer twisted Jube Beaumont's upper lip. "Tom, Jake, and I are on the trail of a bunch of runaways." His gaze turned to a glare. "But you know that, don't you?"

"So you told me back in November." Wade shrugged, and Edith marveled at how he covered a wince with a grin. "Thought you'd headed back to Mississippi after we spoke outside Mr. Edwin Applegate's home some weeks ago."

Jube's brow lowered. "Got sick. Laid up at the Madison Hotel for better'n a week." His jaw jutted. "While I was there I heard it rumored that this place is a station on the Underground Railroad. Thought I'd come and take a look around." He turned a dazzling smile to Edith. "With your permission, of course, miss."

Father stepped to the door. "All manner of wild rumors swirl around the Madison Hotel, Mr. Beaumont. But you and your friends are more than welcome to come in and look around if it would ease your mind." Smiling, he motioned toward the front room. "Please, come in and warm yourselves. We have hot apple cider if you'd care to partake."

"Thank you for your hospitality, Mr. Applegate. I believe we will." Jube beckoned the men outside to join him. The three trooped into the front room, and Jube made perfunctory introductions.

Edith glanced at Wade and marveled at his constitution. If she didn't know of his injury, she'd never guess he carried a bullet in his shoulder. He showed no sign of discomfort except for tiny beads of sweat breaking out along his hairline. She needed to get him off his feet.

She motioned around the room at the sofa, settee, and wing chairs. "Please be seated, gentlemen. Dahlia and I will bring you some hot cider."

Jube shifted a narrowed gaze between Dahlia and Wade. "Isn't she the girl I saw at your house last month? What's she doin' here?"

Wade emitted a soft groan as he lowered himself to a wing chair, but his brother and the other men did not seem to notice. "Dahlia will be staying awhile with Mr. and Miss Applegate."

Alarm flashed in Edith's chest, and she hurried Dahlia to the kitchen while keeping a keen ear turned toward the men's conversation.

"Hmm." Jube's murmured voice sounded skeptical. "By the way, Wade, what are *you* doing here?"

"As you may know," Father said, "your brother is employed by my family's business. Part of his duties is to keep me apprised of financial reports."

Jube gave a derisive snort as Edith and Dahlia returned to the front room, each carrying two cups of steaming cider. "Never knew a feller who loved numbers more'n my bookish brother here. Now me"—his voice turned sugary, and he gave Edith a rakish grin as she handed him a cup of cider—"I'm a man of action."

"Speakin' of action," piped up the man called Jake. "Ain't we gonna search this place for runaways?" He quaffed his cider in two loud slurps and pushed away a strand of dirty blond hair straggling into his face.

Jube took a sip of cider and set the cup down on its saucer with a clink. "Forgive my uncouth companion, Mr. Applegate, but the time *is* late. I wouldn't want to overstay our welcome." He gave Father a cold smile that never reached his eyes. "We will avail ourselves of your offered tour now." He looked at the man called Tom, and his voice turned hard. "Find the cellar and check every cubbyhole."

Tom nodded as he ran curled fingers across his dark, stubbly beard, put down his cup, and headed to the kitchen.

For the first time alarm flashed in Father's eyes. He rose. "I must inform you that this house belongs to the Eleutherian Institute, and you will be held responsible for any damages."

Jube put a hand on Father's shoulder. He glanced at Wade, who remained seated and looked even paler than before. "I promise you we will leave the place as we found it." His grin twisted to a sneer. "Minus a few runaway slaves, perhaps."

As Jube, Tom, and Jake scoured the inside and outside of the house, Edith prayed they wouldn't discover the whereabouts of Sam, Ida, Joe, and Simon. The minutes dragged as she, Dahlia, Wade, and Father waited in silence in the front room.

"Nothin' down there, boss." Tom's voice sounded from the cellar's top step.

Jube emerged from Father's bedroom. "They've gotta be here somewhere. Bob Rea said so."

Alarm leapt in Edith's chest when Wade began to close and open his eyes as if struggling to stay awake. Catching her look of concern, he rallied and gave her a brave smile and wink that touched a deep, sweet place in her heart. He shook his head and sat up straighter, and she stifled a sob imagining the pain that action must have cost him. She could trust this man with her life. She prayed he could trust her with his.

The front door opened, letting in a burst of snow, a whoosh of cold air, and the straggly-haired man called Jake. "Couldn't find nothin' outside."

The three men gathered in the front room. Jube smiled at Father though his green eyes shone with contempt. "It seems there is nothing for us to find here, Mr. Applegate. Or your hidin' place is more cleverly concealed than we have time to ferret out. Either way, we will take our leave." He stepped to Wade, who now stood. How he found the strength to stand, Edith couldn't imagine.

For once, Jube's expression turned somber, almost sad. He put his hand on Wade's bad shoulder and Edith held her breath, but Wade never flinched. "Goodbye, Brother. The invitation to come back home to Cypress Hill still stands." Edith thought she saw moisture glisten in Jube's eyes. "It's too cold up here in the winter for our Southern blood."

Wade's throat moved with a hard swallow as he shook his brother's hand. "I think I like it up here." He glanced at Edith. "And I've found something to keep me warm."

Jube laughed. "Take care, Brother." With that he left the house, his posse in tow.

When the hoofbeats of the men's horses faded, Wade collapsed to the floor.

Chapter 10

Wade!" His name came out in a strangled cry, constricted by the fear clutching at Edith's throat. She sank to the floor beside him, tears flooding down her cheeks. She touched his face and pulled her hand back, horrified at the heat that met her fingers. "He's burning up."

Father patted Edith on the shoulder. "We must get him into bed. You stay with him; I'll get help. Dahlia, you go prepare the bed in the guest room, please."

Left alone with her beloved, Edith felt her heart rend, releasing a bevy of prayers for God to spare his life. Grasping his hands, she crawled to heaven's mercy seat. *Please save him, Lord. Please, please. . .*

The next moment Father appeared with Sam, Joe, and Simon. The three younger men carried Wade to the bed Dahlia had prepared. Edith and Dahlia sat at Wade's bedside as he lay in a fitful sleep. Ida, who insisted she could bring down Wade's fever, tied cloths filled with cut onions to his wrists and ankles.

"Never seen it to fail," she said, giving Edith an encouraging smile. "Me an' Sam, we owe our lives to all our angels along the way. 'Cause of folks like you and Mr. Wade here, our child will be born into freedom, not slavery." She patted the mound beneath her apron. "Got to do all we can for our angels." She grinned at Dahlia and cupped the girl's face in her hand. "'Specially our littlest angel. Your ma and pa should be proud of you. I jist hope my child has half your spunk and courage."

When Ida had left the room, Edith looked at Dahlia. While proud of Dahlia's courage, she needed her to understand the gravity of the risk she'd taken. "You did a good thing, Dahlia, but you do know that what you did was very dangerous, don't you? It could be you lying here injured instead of Mr. Beaumont." She glanced at Wade and her throat constricted. "Your mother and father are beside themselves with worry, not knowing if you're alive, dead, or on your way south into slavery." She gave Dahlia the sternest look she could muster. "Promise me you won't take off on your own again until you're old enough to take care of yourself."

Dahlia emitted a frustrated huff. "But I wasn't alone. Sam, Ida, Joe, and Simon were with me." She shrugged and toyed with the poultice tied to Wade's wrist. "Besides, after what happened to Mr. Beaumont, I reckon Ma and Pa won't let me lead people to a station again until I'm grown."

The question that had earlier nibbled at Edith's curiosity but was later lost in the evening's events bubbled again to the surface. "You've traveled here only a handful of times. However did you find your way to within a mile of the house in the dark?"

Dahlia shrugged again. "I just followed the Christmas Star."

Edith couldn't help grinning. "You mean you followed the North Star."

Dahlia frowned and shook her head. "No, it wasn't the North Star. It was brighter." She gave an emphatic nod and pointed to the ceiling. "It was in the sky, right over this house. It's Christmastime, so I know God put the Christmas Star in the sky to guide me here."

Edith smiled. "I'm sure you are right, Dahlia. Now you must go on to bed. Ida and I will tend to Mr. Beaumont, and early in the morning Mr. Applegate will take you back to Madison when he goes to fetch Dr. Morgan."

Throughout the night and next morning, Edith and Ida fought the fever ravaging Wade and prayed for God's mercy and healing. When Dr. Morgan finally arrived and removed the bullet from Wade's shoulder, a measure of the anxiety gripping Edith drained away.

Dr. Morgan smiled over at Edith as he washed the blood from his hands in the pan of warm water she'd brought a moment earlier. "The bullet came out cleanly and the fever is down. He should make a full recovery."

"See, I told ya." Ida crossed her arms over her chest. "I told ya the onions would work."

Dr. Morgan dried his hands on a towel and rolled down his shirtsleeves. A grin teased at the corner of his mouth. "Yes, I think you can take those poultices off now."

"Thanks, Doc," Wade muttered in a raspy voice. "Dreamed I was lost in an onion field."

Tears of relief sprang into Edith's eyes as she hurried to the bedside. "You're awake."

Dr. Morgan shrugged his coat onto his six-foot frame. "I'd say it's not onion fields, but slave hunters you need to avoid, Mr. Beaumont." He eased his low-crowned beaver hat over his black hair. "It may relieve your mind to know that I have it on good authority that the three slave hunters who've been poking around Madison for the last month or so were seen early this morning embarking a sternwheeler headed south."

"Thank you, Dr. Morgan," Edith managed past the wad of relieved tears gathering in her throat. While other slave hunters might come to Madison in the future, she doubted that Jube Beaumont would ever return. How two men so different could be brothers strained her understanding. She smiled down at Wade, and her pulse quickened when he returned her smile and gripped her hand.

When Dr. Morgan had gone and Ida went to the kitchen to begin the noon meal, Edith sat on the chair at Wade's bedside. Guilt at thinking he had colluded with Jube and the other slave hunters pressed hard on her heart. "I'm sorry I mistrusted you." She lifted her gaze from her clasped hands in her lap to his dear face, blurred by her tears. "Can you forgive me?"

Wade reached out, took her hand, and pressed it to his lips. "As I told you at the Christmas party, there is nothing to forgive. Through you I've found the purpose for which, I believe, God has brought me to Jefferson County, Indiana." He licked his lips and turned a distant look toward the window on the south wall. "All her life my mother hated slavery, but she felt powerless to change it." His smile turned sad. "She often said she hoped that someday I could." He looked at Edith. "For three years I wandered without purpose. I forgot the words from Proverbs that Ma always quoted; 'Trust in the Lord with all thine heart; and lean not unto thine own understanding. In all thy ways acknowledge him, and he shall direct thy paths.' Last night I felt God's direction, His hand of purpose on me. For that, I like to think my mother is smiling in heaven."

"Perhaps she and my mother are smiling together." Her heart throbbing, Edith squeezed his hand. "My mother liked that verse too. She always said that we will never get lost if we just look for God's guiding light." She met his smile with her own. "Last night Dahlia told me she saw a bright star in the sky that led her to the house, and she's sure it was the

Christmas Star God had put there to guide her."

He gave a little laugh. "I believe Dahlia, because God used a star to bring me to you, the steamboat *River Star*."

His eyes widened as recollection bloomed on his face. "I'd completely forgotten." He shifted his gaze to the chair in the corner of the room that held his clothes. "Look in the inside pocket of my coat and you'll find something I have for you."

Bemused, Edith did as he asked and found a small black velvet box.

His voice turned as soft as the fabric covering the spring-hinged casket. "Open it up. It's for you."

Edith lifted the box's lid and gave a soft gasp at the lovely oval-shaped porcelain pendant decorated with a sprig of painted purple asters. The sight misted through her gathering tears. "Oh, Wade, it is beautiful. Thank you."

"When I saw it I thought of you and that day last October when we picked the asters together." His voice gentled. "And I thought of our mothers."

Edith walked to his bedside, love and regret curling together in her chest. "I'm sorry I have no Christmas gift for you."

He reached for her free hand. "Perhaps you do. All I want is your love, my darling, if you're willing to give it." His intense gaze felt as if it reached all the way to her soul. "Last night God gave me my purpose. Today I pray He gives me you. I want to devote the rest of my life to helping those in bondage find freedom, and I want to do it with you by my side. Edith Applegate, would you do me the great honor of becoming my wife?"

Tears gushed as Edith's heart overflowed with love and joy. Nodding, she managed to murmur, "Yes," through her tears, then bent to allow her intended to seal their engagement with a kiss.

Behind her, she heard Ida twitter and whisper, "Praise Jesus."

The next day—Christmas Day—Wade insisted on rising from his sickbed to join Edith and Father in seeing Sam, Ida, Joe, and Simon off to the next station.

While the men exchanged handshakes, Ida gave Edith a hug and whispered in her ear, "He's a good man. Now you take good care of him, ya hear?" She leaned back out of the hug and smiled into Edith's face. "I'll be prayin' for you."

Fighting tears, Edith pulled Ida in for another hug. "And I will be praying for you." She wiped a tear from her cheek that she couldn't hold back. "I so wish I could see your baby when it's born."

Ida glanced north across the snow-covered countryside. "And I'd love for you to see her, but this is way too close to the line. We got to keep goin' north." She grinned and put her hand on her extended belly. "For some time now I've been feelin' this baby's a girl. If I'm right, maybe I'll name her Dahlia."

"Dahlia would love that." A new spate of tears washed down Edith's face.

For the next several minutes Edith and Wade stood on the porch with their arms twined around each other as they and Father watched the four travelers climb into the hay wagon of another conductor on the Underground Railroad.

"They will make it to Canada; I know it." Father's declaration rang with confidence. "Can't think of a better Christmas gift than that." He grinned at Edith and Wade. "Except maybe knowing that I'll be gaining a new son in the coming year." He glanced southward then turned back to Edith and Wade. "Speaking of gifts, I'd like to give the two of you the house in Madison for a wedding present."

Overcome with emotion, Edith could find no words as she gave her father a hug that nearly toppled him. The thought that she'd be returning to the home she loved and be sharing it with the man she loved seemed like a blessing too abundant to comprehend.

Wade shook Father's hand. "Thank you, sir, but, like I told Edith, I plan to devote the rest of my life to helping people escape bondage. Won't you need us here to help with this station?"

Father shook his head. "Between the institute and the abolitionists in Georgetown, I'll have plenty of help. And you both will play an important part in the abolition movement from the house in Madison." He smiled at Edith. "As your mother used to say, my dear, we'll always find our way in life if we follow God's guiding light."

Wade squeezed Edith's waist and gazed into her eyes, his blue ones shining with love. "Or as Dahlia said, follow the Christmas Star."

Ramona K. Cecil is a wife, mother, grandmother, freelance poet, and award-winning inspirational romance writer. Now empty nesters, she and her husband make their home in Indiana. A member of American Christian Fiction Writers and American Christian Fiction Writers Indiana Chapter, her work has won awards in a number of inspirational writing contests. Over eighty of her inspirational verses have been published on a wide array of items for the Christian gift market. She enjoys a speaking ministry, sharing her journey to publication while encouraging aspiring writers. When not writing, she enjoys reading, gardening, and visiting places of historical interest.

Under the Sails of Love

by Lynn A. Coleman

Chapter 1

Savannah, Georgia
1860

"Come quick," Charlotte whispered, signaling for the runaway slaves to hide in the old childhood fort. She'd been hiding men and women there for six months. Soon it would be too hot, and her family would be leaving the plantation for their summer residence in downtown Savannah. Slaves were like cattle and oxen to her father. He didn't see them as equal to him or anyone with lighter-colored skin. The slaves stayed behind year after year and worked in the rice fields. It was hard and hot work. Worse, they never earned a penny for their labor. Over the past couple of years, Charlotte had become convicted that slavery was wrong and that slaves were real human beings—not chattel to serve her or others. She had no problem with servants if they were paid for their work and treated respectfully.

Her frustration had grown to the point where it overflowed.

"Quick, get in here." Charlotte held back the covering that hid the small mound where men and women could hide and have a safe place to sleep for the night. She'd taken her childhood fort and converted it to aid the slaves in their quest for freedom. Unfortunately, she never knew if one or more of them made it to the North, but she hoped and prayed they would.

The small family huddled in. "I'll bring some food when it's safe," she whispered, and closed the door-like opening and reset the fallen branches and Spanish moss to keep it from appearing as anything more than an old forgotten heap.

She quickened her pace. Her parents would begin to wonder where she'd been if she didn't make an appearance within the next few minutes.

"Miss Charlotte, you best be gettin' yourself over here. Come on." Maggie was the house slave who had been cooking for the Kimbrels since before Charlotte's birth.

"Coming. I lost track of time."

"Uh-huh, I's knows what you be doin'. Don't you be—" Maggie stopped for a moment. "Come and get it, Miss Charlotte. I cooked some mighty nice vittles for you this evening. The house sure does smell real good."

"Charlotte," her mother's voice called out. "What are you doing out there?"

"Sorry, Mama. I was down by the river and lost track of time."

"Maggie, make sure she's cleaned up. James Tyler is coming to dinner. With any luck he might just find Charlotte desirable and set his cap for her."

Charlotte rolled her eyes but kept her peace. Her parents could not find out what she'd been doing. If they did, they'd marry her off to the first man possible.

Her mother nodded and headed toward the dining room.

"Git in here!" Maggie pushed her through the doorway. "What am I's goin' to do with you?"

"I'm fine."

"And the good Lord Hisself is the only One who can look over fools." Maggie wagged her head. "Git to your room, and I'll be there to tighten that corset. I's set your lime-green dress out for tonight's dinner."

"Thank you, Maggie."

Charlotte headed up to her room. The only real question she had was whether her own slaves knew what she was up to. Had they helped the other slaves in the past six months? It was a risk to ask. It was safest if no one knew for certain.

Charlotte undressed and cleaned up at the basin and pitcher of water always placed fresh each morning in her room. No doubt she lived a pampered life. From sunup to sundown she didn't have a thought or worry that couldn't be handled by one of her father's slaves. Charlotte sighed.

She stepped into the dress laid out on her bed to prevent wrinkles. She closed her eyes. She'd forgotten the corset. No dignified Southern lady would dress without a corset, not for something as formal as a dinner with guests. She removed the dress in time for Maggie to slip in through the servants' corridor. "I's here, Miss Charlotte."

In no time, the corset was laced, the dress on, and a fresh pair of shoes adorned her feet, unlike the mud-caked ones she'd had on earlier. "You's look real fine, Miss Charlotte. Mr. James. . .he be a fool not to notice."

"Thank you, Maggie, but I hope he doesn't notice too much." James Tyler wasn't a bad man, as far as she knew, but he was twenty years her senior and had a belly that extended far more than one should.

"Trust the Lord, miss. He knows what's best."

Charlotte bit her lip. How did God allow such cruelty to slaves? Then she reminded herself of the story in the Bible of the people of Israel and how long they were captive in Egypt.

The doorbell rang. Charlotte shuffled out of her room and down the stairs. Two men stood in the entrance, James Tyler and a rather handsome younger man. Charlotte couldn't help herself and smiled. Tonight should be an enjoyable evening.

"Mr. Tyler, a pleasure, and who might this gentleman be?" Mother asked as Father shook Mr. Tyler's hand.

"May I introduce you to Captain Zachery Browne. He hails from the North, but we won't hold that against him." James Tyler laughed at his own joke. No one else responded in kind. "I hope you don't mind that I brought a guest. Captain Browne is leaving port in the morning, and I thought he might be able to help you with some of your transportation costs. He's offering me quite a fair price for my exports."

"Always happy to meet a potential business contact," Father said as he shook the captain's hand.

Charlotte's four other siblings entered the room. Davis, two years her junior and just like their father; followed by Randall, two years younger than Davis. Pearl, the only other daughter, was suffering the afflictions of being sixteen years old. Last but not least, Stew, who broke the two-year pattern by showing up ten years ago, four years after Pearl. Of all her siblings, Charlotte spent most of her time with Stew.

Father gave the introductions as they all stood there in line and smiled. Respect and manners were of high importance in the Kimbrel household. After a few social pleasantries in the parlor, all were called to the dinner table. Mr. Tyler's place card sat next to Charlotte's. The servants had added another setting for Captain Browne. Before anyone noticed,

Charlotte placed Mr. Tyler's place card at a new setting then scurried back to her own chair and set Captain Browne's next to hers.

Stew was on her right. Captain Browne on her left. Charlotte glanced across the table and caught her mother's eye. She hadn't fooled anyone. Mother was wise to the subterfuge. Conversation was polite until Captain Browne said, "No, sir, I do not have any slaves working for me."

Zachery tried to be polite. The evening had been tolerable. But he found it difficult to hide his emotions on the slave issue, which was why the owners of the shipping company were hinting this might be his last run to any of the Southern states. More and more Northern shipping companies were avoiding the South. Tensions were rising in the country with regard to slavery. Zach saw it. His bosses saw it. He felt the Southerners saw it too. Perhaps it was even worse in the South, judging from Mr. Kimbrel's reddening face.

Miss Charlotte squirmed in her seat.

Davis stood and threw his cloth napkin on his plate. "I ask you to leave, sir!"

Zachery wiped his mouth with his own napkin and nodded. "Forgive me for insulting you. I merely voiced that I do not have slaves working on my ship. I am captain of a Northern vessel, and we have a policy against it. And since it is not my ship, I am obliged to respect my bosses' directives."

"Sit down, Davis," Mr. Kimbrel said. "I understand your plight, Captain Browne. No offense is taken. We are sensitive to the Northern intrusion. We do not have children working in our factories. Each state, North or South, has their own version of slave labor. Don't you agree?"

Zachery didn't want to agree but couldn't argue the point. He didn't believe in children working in factories as much as he didn't agree with a man owning another man. "Fair enough." He held up his wineglass and turned it toward his host. He knew he shouldn't have come to dinner tonight, but he had to keep James Tyler preoccupied for the evening while his men took care of some business. For the past year he'd been running hidden cargo on his ship, and while he knew his time of sailing slaves to freedom was coming to an end, he didn't want to go home empty-handed.

Placated, his host and the oldest son calmed down. The conversation shifted. James engaged their host.

"Is that really your position on slavery?" Charlotte whispered.

"I take it you have different views?"

Charlotte nodded then smiled. "Tell me about your ship, Captain Browne." She glanced in the direction of her mother. Zach caught on. "She's a fine vessel. She was built in Bath, Maine. As you may or may not be aware, Bath has one of the richest histories in building wooden boats. The *Lady Grace* is one of theirs. She's fifty-seven feet long and has a width of twenty feet. Her draw is low at six feet. She can't go too far up the Savannah, but there are some rivers she can sail in."

"How long have you been a captain?" Randall asked.

Mrs. Kimbrel went back to her conversation with Mr. Tyler. "To answer your question, Randall, I started as a cabin boy at the age of twelve. I come from a sailing family, so I have been on sailing vessels since before I could walk. I've been a captain for three years now. It was a lot of work, but the owners saw that I was a man of honor and sober mind, so I was given an opportunity. They were pleased. I not only have the responsibility of the owners of the vessel, but I also have to meet the needs of my customers."

"Where have you sailed to?" Charlotte asked. He could see the wanderlust in her pretty blue eyes. She was a fine-looking young woman.

"Around the world. I've been to the Far East, Europe. . .but most of my work since I became captain has been on the east coast of America."

"I'd like to travel someday," Charlotte admitted. "Mother speaks of England and Paris with such a fondness—"

"They are beautiful cities," Mrs. Kimbrel interjected.

"I prefer to stay here in Savannah." James Tyler voiced his opinion. "It has all the culture I need."

"Me too." Davis sat up. "There isn't another city like Savannah."

"Have you traveled much, Mr. Kimbrel?" Zachery asked Davis.

"Nah, don't need to. We got it all right here. We live on the plantation most of the year and in the city during the hotter months. There, a man can have a different female escort every night if he were so inclined." Davis grinned.

Charlotte squirmed. She definitely had a difference of opinion with her brother. Zachery turned toward Charlotte. "Where else would you like to travel to, Miss Charlotte?"

"Oh, I don't know. I've read about so many different places. Some are so deep in the interior of a country it would take a year to visit."

"Such as?" Zachery enjoyed the fire starting to ignite in Charlotte.

"The Iguazu Falls in Argentina. I suppose that isn't too far inland, but what about the Amazon River? I've heard it is dangerous and man-eating fish live there."

"Piranhas, yes, which in part explains my desire to stay on the oceans." Zachery chuckled.

"Don't sharks attack people?" Pearl asked.

"Goodness! Such conversations coming from my daughters."

"Sorry, Mother," Charlotte and Pearl said in unison.

"I understand that to meet a man who has sailed around the world is rather interesting, but I'm certain there are topics he can speak to that are far more edifying."

The servants, or rather house slaves, came and cleared their dinner dishes as they made the table ready for dessert. Zach could feel Charlotte's curiosity rise. Truthfully, she had captured his attention as well. After a delicious peach cobbler, Mr. Kimbrel led the men to his study and closed out the women and his youngest son. Zach prayed he wasn't in for another discussion on the values of slavery. He'd heard his share over the years, and he definitely did not share the views of most Southern plantation owners.

Mr. Kimbrel lit a cigar and leaned against a large mahogany desk. "So, Captain Browne, do you fancy my daughter?"

Charlotte wanted to eavesdrop, but she had some food she needed to get out to the runaways. She went to her room, changed, and slipped into the kitchen without her mother noticing. Maggie was still cleaning up. "Don't you be sneaking out there tonight, Miss Charlotte. I knows what's going on. I's take care of it."

"But—"

"Don't you never mind. I's knows."

"I can't let you get caught. You'll be whipped for sure."

"I's knows what I's doing. Trust me."

"I'll let you feed them, but I'm taking them to freedom tomorrow. I can walk slaves down the street and no one will be the wiser. You can't."

Maggie nodded. "How many?"

"Three—a man, his wife, and a toddler."

Maggie shooed her away. Charlotte stepped onto the servants' stairs. "Who were you speaking with, Maggie?" Mrs. Kimbrel asked.

"Just some slave talk. I's planning a real fine breakfast for ya in the mornin'."

"Nothing too fancy. I ate too much this evening. You did a fine job, Maggie. I appreciate it."

"Ain't nothin'. Just doin' my job."

Charlotte needed to be more careful. She slipped back up the stairs to her room. She was putting not only the slaves she was helping escape in harm's way, but also her own slaves. They would be blamed if the runaways were caught. No one would believe she was the one helping them escape. They'd rather think she was trying to cover for the slaves to help them avoid punishment.

"Charlotte!" her mother called. "Can you come down here, please?"

Fear washed over her. Charlotte stepped out of her room and approached the stairway.

"What are you wearing?"

"Sorry, Mother. I was changing into my nightclothes."

Her mother waved her back up the stairs then turned her attention back to their guests. "I'm sorry, Charlotte is indisposed at the moment," she could hear her mother say.

The next morning Charlotte attended to her chores then slipped out without further notice. She scurried to her hiding place. The plan was to have the male runaway push them down the Savannah in a pole boat and help them buy passage on a ship.

Maggie's husband, Jed, came over to the dock. "Can I help you, miss?"

"No, we're fine."

"And how will you be bringing the pole boat back?" Jed asked.

"Oh."

"Let me come with you and stay with the boat," Jed pleaded.

"Are you certain?"

"Yes, miss. We's too old to run now."

"Thank you, Jed."

An hour later, they were in Savannah proper, and Charlotte was looking at the various ships, trying to find the right one to purchase passage for the family. The gentleman she usually worked with who helped process and hide the runaways at the church was out of town. She walked the streets, which were cobbled with old ballast stones from various ships that had come to the harbor. Mounds of cotton bales and barrels full of molasses and sugar syrup gave a unique smell to the air when mixed with the brackish water of the river.

The stern of one ship read the *Lady Grace*. She scanned the crew loading cargo. Standing next to the gangway was the familiar stance of—"Captain Browne?"

He turned. His smile brightened. "Miss Charlotte. A pleasure to see you this fine morning. How can I help you?"

"Are you heading north?"

He stiffened at her question then answered, "Yes."

"May I purchase passage for this family?"

He narrowed his gaze then grabbed her by the elbow, moved her away from her runaways, and whispered, "Are you trying to have me arrested?"

"What? No. I simply want to purchase tickets for these slaves to visit up north."

"Don't lie to me. You're smuggling them, aren't you?"

She clamped her mouth shut. If she admitted it, she could be arrested.

"Fine," he said, and she hurried back to her runaways. "Get on board." He cracked a whip.

People turned, noticed he was moving slaves, and went back to their business, ignoring the captain as he placed them on his ship.

He came back. "Do you have papers?"

"Of course not."

"You are something. Does your family know?" He pointed to the ship.

"Of course not."

He wagged his head. "I'll try to get them safely to the North, but there are no guarantees. Do you know your father offered your hand in marriage to me last night?"

"He what?"

"Seems he thought we had a lively conversation."

Heat infused her cheeks. She relaxed her stance.

"Seems he's concerned that his twenty-two-year-old daughter hasn't married. He offered me a thousand-dollar dowry."

Catching her voice, she asked, "What did you say?"

Zachery Browne chuckled. "I said I'd consider it. Truth be told, this is quite possibly my last trip to the South. My employers are losing interest in dealing with businesses down here."

"That's fine. I don't think my father would approve of our courtship."

Zachery laughed. "My dear Charlotte, you have no idea how much your father and brothers are concerned by your Yankee thoughts."

"My Yankee thoughts?"

"Seems that you have expressed the wrongness of slavery on more than one occasion. Which was enough to convince James Tyler that you wouldn't be a suitable wife for him."

"Thank the Lord for that blessing." Her face momentarily brightened.

"You're a rare jewel among women, Miss Charlotte. I can offer you passage to the North as well, but I won't be offering my hand in marriage."

"That's a relief." She paused. "My place is here. I have a purpose working in. . ." she lowered her voice, "the Underground Railroad."

"I am well acquainted with the secrecy. But you are far from discreet. You marched these slaves down the boardwalk without a care in the world. Your father is well known. His slaves are well known. Don't you think someone would recognize you at some point?"

"Perhaps. But I've been freeing slaves for six months now."

Captain Browne shook his head. "You are a marvel, Miss Charlotte. Have a good day."

He turned and left her standing there on the ship-lined wharf. The heat of the sun and the rotting fish upset Charlotte's stomach. She turned and headed back to Jed. Her father was trying to marry her off. Worse yet, he and her brother Davis didn't want her around. What did she have to go back home for?

Charlotte told Jed to return to the plantation and to let her parents know she would be staying in Savannah for a night or two. She then headed straight to the bank and withdrew most of her money. She stopped at a couple of stores and purchased a carpetbag, some clothes, and other items for travel. Life in Savannah had just ended. She glanced back at Bay Street and headed toward the wharf. She might just be the first white woman to ride the Underground Railroad.

Chapter 2

Zachery couldn't believe the predicament he'd gotten himself into. Not only did he have three extra runaways on board, for a total of seven, but now he had a Southern belle taking up his quarters. He rubbed the back of his neck. "How'd that happen?"

"Cap?" his first mate questioned.

"Just mumbling."

Frank laughed. "You've been doing that a lot since we left Savannah."

"Don't remind me." Zach looked over his map and took his readings. "Two more hours until we hit Port Royal."

"Yes, sir. That's what I figure. Tides running with us."

Zach nodded. "I'd better go to my quarters and see if Miss Kimbrel is in need of anything."

Frank snickered. "Better you than me."

"You'll have Charlotte duty tomorrow."

"She ain't bad to look at but. . .can I swab the decks instead?"

"You mean I'm stuck with this duty?"

"You're the captain." Frank whistled and focused on the compass heading. He'd been Zach's first mate for the past year and a half. They worked well together, and Zach could trust him with any task at hand.

Zach headed to his quarters and knocked on the door. "Miss Charlotte?"

"I'll be right there," she answered through the closed door. The ship shifted to starboard. Zach glanced back at Frank. He nodded and continued sailing toward Port Royal. He stood on his tiptoes to see what Frank was avoiding. Spotting nothing, he focused on the door opening in front of him. Her pale blue eyes stared into his for a moment. He cleared his throat. "I've come to let you know we'll be stopping in Port Royal for a couple hours. If you'd like to stretch your legs."

"Thank you, Captain." She stepped back into his room and closed the door. Zach didn't know if that meant she would be getting off the ship or not.

He shook his head. She was beautiful, but she had a mind of her own. He turned and headed back to the helm. "What was that jolt for?"

"Porpoise. You know I love sailing with them." Frank laughed.

Zach took the helm. "Get the cargo ready for delivery," he ordered. Frank left, and Zach focused on the compass and the various landmasses. Port Royal was actually an island in the middle of Port Royal Sound, with Hilton Head Island on the south and Philips Island to the north of the entrance. To reach the port for Beaufort, South Carolina, he'd travel farther up the river. But since Port Royal served his purpose, he didn't need to go farther, and his destination to the north was a higher priority. The large marsh and grassy fields extended into the bay, but a good navigator had no trouble going around them.

As they made it to the island, Zach sailed past the fishery docks and on to the cargo area. One of his runaways had family in town and wanted to get a message to them. Zach found an excuse to pick up some oysters. Word had it that good oysters could be found in Port Royal. Not to mention, he had four additional passengers to feed on this voyage.

Onshore he found some canned oysters and bought several cases to bring north and a bushel of fresh ones for his men and their trip north. He also purchased a thousand pounds of rice. Stores in the North would be running low. Of course, most Northerners preferred the potato. He checked over the inventory to see if there was anything else he wouldn't be bringing north for a while. "Indigo. I'd like ten pounds of that, please." The salesman smiled, obviously happy for additional sales. "You are certain you want forty-five hundred grams?"

"Yes, please. I have a textile company who will be glad to have the brilliant blues made from it."

The salesman nodded and went to work wrapping ten pounds in one-pound packages of brown paper and sealing them with string. The smaller packages would make it easier to sell.

The door to the warehouse opened. Miss Kimbrel entered. "May I help you, miss? This isn't the place for a lady. If you walk down Paris Avenue, you'll find a mercantile more to your liking," the merchant offered.

"Do I have time, Captain?" She glanced at him with her piercing blue eyes.

Zach nodded. "Certainly. I'll have one of my men fetch you if we are ready to depart before you return."

"Thank you." She exited the warehouse, and the merchant looked at him. "She's a passenger?"

"Yup. I'm bunking with my mates."

The man laughed and finished packing up the indigo. "Enjoy your voyage." He wagged his head. "Ain't no place for women on a working man's vessel. Your men don't mind a woman being on board?"

"They haven't quit yet."

He nodded and went back to his inventory.

Once everything was loaded and Miss Kimbrel wasn't back, Zach started to ask Jake, one of his men, to go fetch her. Zach spotted her marching down the street, her skirt fluttering behind and being forced forward as she took elongated steps toward the ship.

Zach rubbed his face with his handkerchief and stuffed it back in his pocket. "Never mind, Jake. She's a-coming."

"I can see that, sir. All I can say is I'm glad she stayed in your cabin. Ain't right to have women on board a working vessel."

"I know, but, well, I can't explain it, but she needed this trip as much as some of our other passengers."

Jake nodded and went back to work. Once Miss Kimbrel was on board, the ship departed. Zach piloted the *Lady Grace* out of Port Royal Bay. After they were past the outer islands, he set their course north and gave Frank the helm. Out to sea, they could let the slaves out of hiding and give them freedom to roam the decks. If, however, a ship approached, the signal was given, and they went back in hiding. Bales of cotton stacked to appear to be more than there were made for an excellent hiding place.

The first day of sail out of Port Royal was uneventful. A storm blew in the next morning.

Charlotte held her stomach. It rolled and flipped with the rocking of the boat. She needed fresh air. But she didn't feel safe roaming the ship. Why, she wasn't certain. She felt safer in the captain's quarters. The room was lined with wooden shelves, a desk, a bed, and a nightstand. There was also a small table and chairs for the captain's meals, she presumed. The room had no feminine touches, and it spoke volumes about Captain Browne's tastes in literature and art.

The ship bucked to the right, or starboard, or whatever side of the ship it was. She turned herself around and faced the door to the room. *Port, the left side of the ship.* Left *has four letters, so does* port. Charlotte decided she could remember it that way—she hoped.

Her stomach rolled with the next wave. She turned around and walked toward the stern of the ship, where a couple of windows faced where they'd been. The angry ocean rolled. Rain spat against the windows. Surf splashed against them as well. Or maybe it wasn't the surf because they were higher up, weren't they? Charlotte didn't know. She'd never traveled by ocean before. Only by train, and that was limited to two trips up to Augusta with her entire family. Father wasn't a traveler. Mother enjoyed traveling, but Father ruled the roost. Her heart cinched knowing her parents would be worried. She'd mailed a letter in Port Royal to her parents, explaining she'd left Savannah to travel the country up to New York and she might possibly take a trip to Europe. She would mail them as soon as she arrived. She hoped and prayed that her parents wouldn't put together that she'd left on Captain Browne's ship. Then again, it would be a logical assumption. *Father God, please do not let any harm come to Captain Browne because he granted me passage on his ship.*

A ray of sunshine split the clouds but was immediately swallowed up by the thick gray clouds. Charlotte smiled, confident that God would honor her prayers.

A loud bang rumbled the door in its frame. Charlotte carefully went to open the door. A sailor dressed in drenched oilskins stood there and nodded. "Miss Kimbrel, the captain said to stay in your cabin. It is not fit for you to be walking on the decks."

Charlotte snickered then nodded.

"Someone will bring you food later."

The thought of eating turned her stomach. She was certain she turned a shade of green. "Just broth would be nice."

He nodded and grabbed hold of the rail. Charlotte closed the door as she heard Captain Browne call out to drop sheets. *Sheets?* She peeked out and saw the sailors lowering the sails farther. So sheets were sails, hmm. Maybe by the completion of the voyage, she'd understand the sailors' language.

A few unseemly words wafted through the storm. Perhaps not all their language, she mused. She closed the door and settled back inside the cabin. Her best bet was to lie down or sit and read. She sat down and opened her Bible. The words seemed to roll with the ship. She closed the Bible and lay down on the bed.

As the ship calmed, Charlotte woke from her nap. She glanced at the wall clock. She'd been asleep for hours. She jumped out of bed, straightened her clothing, and opened the door. The ship was active with sailors scurrying around on the decks. The runaway slaves were on the deck too. She glanced at their hiding place. It was secure. One of the men glanced at her then looked above her to the area where the captain navigated the ship. She stepped out.

"Good afternoon, Miss Charlotte." Captain Browne's voice flowed over her raw nerves like honey.

"Good afternoon, Captain. How bad was the storm?"

He shrugged. "Not that bad. We might be in for some weather again, so I suggest you get some fresh air while you can. If you don't mind, I need to gather some dry clothing from my quarters."

She thought he'd removed his clothing the first day. Perhaps not enough. "Of course not, it is your room. Thank you again for letting me stay in there."

He bent at the waist. "My pleasure, miss." He reached to take her hand but didn't. He stood and tipped the brim of his hat. "Enjoy the calm, miss." He slipped to her side and stepped past her and into his room.

Charlotte grabbed hold of the railing and calmed herself. She wasn't here to fall in love. She was here for freedom. But what did that mean? Where would it take her? What would she do?

Zach gathered another pair of wool pants and a coat from his closet in his quarters. He scanned the room and sniffed. It had a pleasant floral odor. He couldn't place the fragrance but knew it came from one of her perfumes or powders. Women were always fussing to make themselves more beautiful. His mind drifted out of the room and to the railing where he had left Miss Charlotte. His heart quickened. He took a deep breath and calmed himself. She was beautiful, but she was born the daughter of a plantation owner. He had nothing to offer a woman of her station. Yet he was a captain. The rank was honored among certain people of society.

He had humble roots. Granted, his father had land and a few acres set aside for him and his family to farm one day. But how does a captain farm? Mother did most of the work. Miss Charlotte had slaves to work for her. She wouldn't know the first thing about fending for herself or her family.

Zach shook off such ill-conceived thoughts. Yes, she was beautiful. Yes, she cared for the slaves she helped escape, but. . .

He closed his eyes for a moment then gathered his clothing and left his quarters. She stood at the rail in virtually the same position. "Miss Charlotte?"

She turned. Tears trailed down her face. He stepped closer. "Can I help you?" His heart went out to her. He didn't understand her tears, but he never really did understand when women cried. He just felt helpless and wanted to help.

She shook her head and looked down at her feet. Her boots were the same pair she had worn when she arrived at the dock in Savannah.

"Was it the storm?"

"No, Captain. The storm was not good for my stomach, but I am wondering what I shall do when I arrive in the North. I am not trained. I was raised to be a hostess, to run a household, take care of the house slaves, and I had looked forward to having my own family one day. Now I shall not have any of those things. I pray I shall find good and honorable work. Perhaps I was rash leaving my parents' home as I did."

Zach paused for a moment. She was rash. But then again, he didn't like the idea of her being subjected to marriage to a man she did not care for all because she held different opinions than her parents. "I cannot answer those questions, but I will pray for you and for God's guidance."

She smiled. His heart fluttered. What was the hold this woman had over his heart?

"Thank you, Captain. Again, I apologize for any inconvenience I am to you, your ship, and crew."

"Nothing to mention, Miss Charlotte. Pray for guidance. The Lord will direct your path."

She nodded and turned back to the railing and scanned the deck.

"Good day, Miss Charlotte." He left her there, not knowing what to do or say. She certainly was in quite a predicament. *What would the owners of the vessel say about my extra passenger?* Zach squared his shoulders. He'd deal with that when the time came. *"Do not worry about tomorrow"* floated through his mind as he recalled Jesus' teaching from his Bible reading and Sunday school. Obviously God cared more than enough to take care of Miss Charlotte once she arrived up north. But she was correct. Without skills, she would find work difficult and low paying. Zach said another prayer for Charlotte Kimbrel and slipped into the men's quarters to change from his wet clothing into the fresh outfit. He knew most of the men would be working in their wet clothes for another hour. He needed to maintain focus and keep healthy in order to secure safe passage for his men, their cargo, and the runaway slaves, who faced challenges similar to Charlotte's. But the runaways had skills and trades to fall back on. What would a Southern belle be capable of?

Based on what little he'd seen over the years, not much. They were to appear pretty but let their slaves do all the hard work. He thought back on Charlotte's hands, silky smooth, not the hands of a laborer. Zach fired up another prayer for Charlotte. How was she going to survive?

Chapter 3

Charlotte prayed until her knees could no longer take the hard and moving floor beneath them. She didn't have an answer. She seemed to have more questions. The knock on her door pulled her from the spiraling thoughts.

"Yes?"

"Miss Kimbrel, the captain asked me to bring you your dinner. May I come in?"

She opened the door. A small boy, perhaps ten, stood there with a plate covered with a metal lid. "Thank you."

He smiled. His freckled cheeks filled with joy. His red hair was similar to the captain's. She examined him more closely. "Are you the captain's son?"

"No." He shook his head then leaned in closer. "He's my uncle, but I'm not supposed to talk about it. Can't have the crew thinking I'm getting special favors."

"I see."

"Most of them know. We don't hide it. But when new crewmen come on board we wait for them to learn it on their own. That way they know I'm a hard worker and not just here because my uncle is the captain."

"Sounds like a logical decision." She smiled, instantly liking the lad.

"May I?" He lifted the cover of the plate and glanced over to the table.

Charlotte stepped back and swept her hand, ushering him inside. "Yes, thank you again."

"It is my pleasure. You're a lot more pretty to look at than the sailors."

Charlotte giggled. "What's your name?"

"Bradley William Browne the third at your service." He bowed ever so slightly then stood up straight and smiled.

"May I call you Bradley?"

"Brad is fine. Everyone else calls me that except for the men. They call me *boy*."

"I see. And how long have you served with your uncle?"

"Three months. Dad is a farmer like my grandfather is now. I'm like my uncle Zach. I live for the sea. Of course, most of the men in my town work on ships, or they farm. Farming is fine, and I don't mind it, but I love the adventure of the sea. There are so many interesting places to go and see." He glanced over to her dish. "You best eat your dinner now. Ain't no telling when the wind will kick up again."

Charlotte placed a hand over her stomach. She wasn't certain she wanted to eat yet.

Brad nodded his head and smiled. "Takes a bit to get used to. But don't you worry. You'll get your sea legs in a couple of days."

"Thank you."

He headed for the door and turned back toward her. "You might like to take a walk on the deck tonight. The stars are brilliant, and if I'm done with my chores, I'll be happy to show you how we navigate by the stars."

"That would be splendid. Thank you again. I look forward to it."

Brad gave one confident nod and slipped out the door.

She went to the table and lifted the lid off her plate. Two slices of ham, a boiled potato, a roll, and a pile of grayish green beans—her least favorite vegetable—waited for her. So much for broth, she mused. Once she had been served green beans that were still green and enjoyed them. But this Southern way of boiling them for hours in bacon fat just didn't appeal to her. Yet she loved her collard greens cooked that way. Charlotte shrugged and sat down. She placed the cloth napkin over her lap, clasped her hands, and prayed a blessing over her food.

An hour later she made her way out to the deck and stood for a moment as her eyes adjusted to the darkness.

"Good evening, Charlotte." The captain's voice slid down her spine like warm cane syrup.

She spun around with such vigor she lost her footing. He reached out and rescued her from falling.

"Careful, my lady. You must acquire your sea legs before moving so quickly on board a ship." He grinned.

She couldn't make out the brilliant green of his eyes, but they seemed to sparkle in the moonlight.

"Thank you. You have rescued me again, Captain." She stood up but instantly felt a longing to be back in his arms. Instead, she brushed her upper arms.

"Are you cold?" he asked.

"I'm fine, thank you. Your nephew suggested I take an evening stroll on deck and he'd show me some of the stars and how to navigate a ship by them."

Zachery Browne's chest and shoulders heaved with a chuckle. "He is learning, but he has a long way to go. Perhaps I can be of assistance."

"That would be an honor, but I would not wish to harm young Bradley's sensibilities in the matter."

Captain Browne sobered. "Thank you. He would be very happy to show you. I'll fetch him for you." He stepped to her left.

She reached out her hand and touched his forearm. "I wouldn't mind adult companionship, if you have some time later."

The captain nodded. "If I can, Miss Charlotte, it would be my honor."

What was the connection she was feeling with Captain Zachery Browne? She never would have suggested such a thing back home on the plantation. Of course, her father would have locked her in her room until she was sixty if she had made such a forward comment or gesture. *Dear Lord, guard my heart.*

Zach watched as Brad shared his knowledge with Charlotte. The boy had remembered just about everything he'd taught him so far. He did misname two stars, but for three months of training, he was doing really well.

"Cap?"

Zach turned at the sound of Frank's voice.

"Do you want me to take first or second watch this evening?"

"First. I'm going to get some shut-eye while I can. Have them wake me for the third watch."

"Yes, sir. I'll have Daniel take the second," Frank offered.

"Good." Zach took one more glance at Brad and Charlotte and turned toward the men's quarters. Most of the crew would be up on deck. Those who were designated for third watch would be going to sleep soon. It would help if he could fall asleep first. The hardest part of giving up his living quarters was the snores of the other men. When he was younger, he didn't seem to notice. But since he'd been sleeping in his own quarters for a couple of years now, he enjoyed the peace.

He rolled into the hammock, placed his hat over his eyes, and fell fast asleep.

"Captain," a hoarse voice whispered. Then his body was jolted. "Cap, get up."

Zach sat up. "Sorry, thanks."

"You're welcome."

Zach rolled out of the hammock and watched John slip in. It was the way of the ship. He headed toward the galley, poured himself a cup of thick coffee, and headed up the ladder.

The sky was dark, the horizon darker. Soon the horizon would begin to lighten up, but not before the darkest part of the night hit. He took the lantern and glanced at his watch. Ten past four. He sipped the bitter coffee. He couldn't put it off any longer. He needed to find a better cook for his ship. He took a second gulp of the swill and dumped the rest overboard.

"You're relieved."

"Thank you, sir." Daniel stepped back, and Zach stepped up to the helm. "Helmsman is being relieved. . . ." Daniel spouted out the heading and position of the rudder.

"Helm has been relieved. . . ." Zach finished reciting the same coordinates. "Good night, Daniel."

"Night, Cap."

Zach followed protocol for the sake of the crew and rules of the sea, but he enjoyed a closeness with his first and second mates. The *Lady Grace*, being a smaller schooner, had a limited crew, and Daniel had been with him for a year now.

Zach glanced at the compass and followed the line of sight on the horizon. In front of him was complete blackness. He turned to the port and then to starboard, again nothing but blackness. He turned for a moment behind him and saw what appeared to be the red and green lights of a ship at least five miles away, perhaps more. It was a dull enough glow that he pulled the binoculars out and sought a better inspection. It wasn't abnormal to have another ship traveling the seas at night, but when carrying runaway slaves, one took precautions. Zach called out to Daniel, hoping he hadn't fallen asleep yet.

A few minutes later, Daniel came out, shuffling into his jacket. "Captain?"

"Round up the slaves and hide them."

"Yes, sir."

"Low or no light, Daniel."

"Aye, aye, Captain."

Daniel scurried off in the darkness.

Zach kept steady on course. There was no need to fret and possibly no need to hide the slaves. But he didn't want to risk it. He was still in Southern waters with North Carolina or Virginia on his port side.

"Seaman, come grab the helm," Zach called out to the seaman on duty for the third shift. He grabbed the sextant, glanced at his watch, and measured the angle from Polaris, the North Star, and the horizon—which at this hour was a calculated sight.

Below, on the main deck, Zach watched the slaves work their way into the hiding place.

Daniel returned. "All accounted for, Captain."

"Thank you, Daniel. Go get some rest. I suspect we'll know more after the sun rises."

Daniel nodded and retreated to the crew quarters.

Zach finished his calculations and examined the map. They were 33.8° north and 77.7° east, which put them about twenty miles east of Bald Head Island, North Carolina. Two more degrees north and they'd be changing their heading toward New York City. With his calculations done, he relieved the seaman at the helm and continued on his course. The ship behind drew closer. Zach couldn't help but wonder if it was running under steam or was a larger vessel with more masts and sails.

He prayed his precious cargo would be safe.

As the sun came up over the horizon, the ship behind them was no more than an hour back.

Miss Kimbrel came out of his quarters. She scanned the ship and smiled as she focused on him. "Good morning, Captain Browne."

"Good morning, Miss Charlotte."

She climbed up toward the helm, and her face fell as she saw the approaching ship.

"Do not fear, Miss Charlotte. I am aware and have hidden our cargo."

She nodded. "Is there anything I should do?"

"Could you see if the cook has made a fresh pot of coffee?" He handed her his mug.

"I'd be happy to. Where's the kitchen?"

"Galley," he corrected. "On a ship we have galleys, not kitchens."

"Why. . ." She let her words trail off.

Zach chuckled. "It does take some getting used to. The galley is through those doors and down a deck. I'm certain you'll find it. Just follow your nose. By now the cook should have fed most of the men."

Charlotte nodded and headed toward the door. A ship really wasn't the place for a woman. On the other hand, she was a sight more pleasant to look at first thing in the morning than his crew.

Charlotte found the galley and marveled at the small space. The pantry at her parents' home was larger than the ship's galley, and to think it fed nearly twenty men three times a day. . . *How?* she wondered.

"Can I help ya, miss?" A man with broad shoulders and a once white but now very dirty apron stood by a butcher block with a knife in his hand and a hunk of red meat on the block.

"Captain Browne asked me to fetch him some coffee." She held up the mug as proof of her reason for being there.

"Aye." He pointed to the coffeepot sitting on the stove. "Over there, unless you need me to pour for ya."

"No. Thank you."

"The boy will be bringin' ya breakfast up to the room in a bit."

"Thank you."

He nodded and went back to work slicing the red meat into small chunks. She guessed beef stew was for dinner tonight. She poured the thick black coffee into the mug and set the pot back on the stove. As she left the small area, she realized everything had a place. She supposed it needed to be that way in order to function. "Good day, sir."

"Good day, miss."

She was a few feet down the hall when she heard voices. "Ain't right havin' a woman on the ship."

"Maybe, but she ain't bad to look at."

The men snickered. Charlotte hustled out of the area and up the stairs. She didn't mind hearing comments about her beauty as much as she minded the issue of it not being right to have women on ships. Didn't women travel? How else did female folks travel from Europe to America? She thought she had heard similar grumblings before when they were in Port Royal.

She marched up to helm. "Do the men have issues with my presence on board the ship?" She thrust out his coffee.

"Some." Zach Browne took a sip and glanced at the compass.

"Why? That doesn't make a bit of sense. Don't women travel by sea all the time? How does one get from Europe to America, or for that matter from America to Europe, without taking a journey on a ship? This is ridiculous. Why?"

Zach chuckled. "You're pretty when you're upset."

She plopped down on a stoop of some sort. She imagined it was used for sitting. *You couldn't stand the entire time you were at the helm, could you?*

"Yes, women travel on passenger vessels. But working vessels like the *Lady Grace* aren't meant to have the fairer sex on board. And there is a rumor—a tale, if you will—that when a woman is on board, bad things happen. It's a fantasy, but nonetheless real in some sailors' minds."

"That's just silly."

Zach chuckled. "I agree. But it is the way of the sea."

"The ship's coming closer." She pointed off their stern. She could make out the men standing on the deck. "Why are they so close?"

"I suspect we're in for trouble."

"Why?"

Zach shrugged. "Relax. Trust me to handle it." He leaned into her. "Marry me?"

"What?"

"I can't lie. Say that you'll marry me, and I can introduce you as my fiancée."

"Of all the silliest. . ." She glanced back at the ship. The men were carrying weapons. "Sure."

Zach smiled and kissed her cheek. "Thank you. We will break our engagement as soon as possible."

Charlotte stilled. The crash of the waves on the bow of the other ship danced on the water. "Ahoy!" a few of the sailors called out.

"Ahoy," Zach replied and waved. "You're taking the wind out of my sails."

"Captain wanted to say hello," one of the sailors responded.

A man walked up to the side of the vessel that had come alongside theirs. "Ahoy, *Lady Grace*."

"Ahoy. What can I do for you, Captain?"

"Seems there's a man in Savannah looking for his daughter. Thought I ought to let you know. I presume this is her."

Zach smiled. "This is my fiancée, Charlotte Kimbrel. Her father offered me a thousand dollars to marry his daughter. I foolishly didn't take the money, but I"—he reached out his hand to Charlotte, who grasped it and held on for dear life—"or rather, we decided it was love at first sight, and she's coming north."

The other captain laughed. "I would have taken the money."

"I agree. But this way Charlotte knows I'm marrying her for love not money."

The captain nodded. "Rumor spread through Savannah she was probably on your ship. Folks saw her board."

"Where are you headed?" Zach asked.

"England. You?"

"New York City and then on to Boston."

The captain scratched the back of his neck. "Aren't you far east for New York?"

"I change direction a degree north of here and set a heading for New York."

"Odd way to sail. Rough waters for such a small craft."

Zach chuckled. "I know it isn't the normal shipping lane, but it's what I was taught, and I'm comfortable with it."

The captain nodded as his ship began pulling ahead. "Fair wind, my friend."

"Fair wind." Zach waved as the four-masted schooner eclipsed his ship and captured all their wind. Zach fell off and waited for the wind to fill his sails again.

"Are you in trouble? Have I put you in a position where you could be arrested?"

"We'll be fine. You can break our engagement now."

"No thanks. I think we should stay engaged until you are safe."

Zach laughed. "Honey, I did it for your safety not mine."

Charlotte stood. "And I, sir, am choosing to remain engaged for your safety." She squared her shoulders and walked down to her cabin. . .his cabin. . .their cabin. She chuckled. If they continued the engagement to the point of actual marriage. . . A full belly laugh erupted as she entered the captain's quarters. She could have fun with this new state of being.

Chapter 4

Zach couldn't wait to be relieved. Why, oh why, did he ask Charlotte to be his fiancée? At the moment it seemed the prudent thing to do. Now? *Oh Lord, help me.* He had no plans to marry. The single life seemed in order for a sea captain. He loved the sea. He loved working on the sea. A wife? He shook his head, took in a deep breath, and eased it out slowly. He wasn't really engaged to be married. Technically he was, but. . . "I'm an idiot." He laughed and headed down to the galley for his breakfast.

The cook seemed a bit gruff. "Mornin', Oscar."

"Mornin', Captain. I'll fry you up some eggs and bacon. Ain't got no more biscuits, but I can slice you up some bread."

"Bread will be fine, thank you." Zach sat down at one of the tables and composed himself for a few minutes while he waited on his breakfast.

Oscar set the plate in front of him. "Word has it you're marrying our female passenger. She gonna be travelin' with us all the time?"

Word certainly flew around a ship. "I honestly don't know." He wasn't going to deny his engagement being what it was, but he wasn't going to speculate on a future with Charlotte either.

"Well, I'm givin' my notice then. I'm old school, and a workin' vessel ain't no place for women. It's bad enough we're harboring runaway slaves. Now you're fixin' to have a woman on board. No, sir. Sorry, sir, but I just can't have no woman walkin' around my ship."

Zach wanted to laugh. The ship didn't belong to the cook. It didn't even belong to Zach. But he was the boss of the vessel. Instead, he nodded. Oscar was fair in the cooking department. Zach had been considering getting another cook anyway. This took that burden off his shoulders. "I accept your resignation." Zach held out his hand.

Oscar wiped his hand on his dirty apron and grasped the captain's hand. "Men are foolish when it comes to women," he mumbled.

"Perhaps so." Zach stared down at the crispy fried eggs—too crispy. . .nearly charcoaled. His impromptu engagement was serving another purpose. He smiled and ate the less-than-desirable meal in front of him.

Bradley came running in. "Here ya go, Cook." Bradley plopped the empty plate on the counter. "She said to say thank you."

Oscar grumbled. Bradley shrugged and spotted Zach. Zach finished swallowing and said, "How are you doing, Brad?"

"Fine, I finished my math last night. And I read a chapter before bed. Nicholas Nickleby's situation isn't the same as slavery, but forcing others to work for you and pay and feed them nothing. . .in a way it kinda is the same." Bradley sat down.

"In a way, it is similar. Slave owners tend to keep their slaves in good health because they need them to work the farms and plantations. But they treat them as if they are property. Whereas Squeers in the book is merely scamming money from the parents of the children he's taken in."

"Yeah, that's kinda why I said it's similar but not the same."

Zach smiled. "You're a smart boy. Did you do your history assignments?"

"Some, but I spent time with Miss Charlotte teaching her about the stars and navigation."

"I saw that. You're learning well. However, you did confuse two stars."

"Which ones?"

Zach closed his eyes and tried to remember. "I forget at the moment. But I'll remember later, and we'll go over them tonight."

"Yes, sir. I promised Mom I'll keep up with my studies. She said I could stay at sea as long as I continued my education."

Zach ruffled Bradley's red curls, similar to his own. "I made the same agreement with your grandmother. You're doing great."

"Thanks. Well, I better git goin'. It's time for our special cargo to stroll out on the decks."

Zach nodded, and Bradley ran off.

"Can't believe you're wasting that boy's time with book learnin'," Oscar said as he continued to scrub the morning dishes.

Zach chose not to engage the man in further conversation. He had picked up Oscar about three months ago, but he wasn't fitting in with the crew. In four or five days, if the winds held, he'd be saying goodbye to the man.

The chair scraped across the floor as Zach stood up from the table. "Thank you for breakfast, Oscar."

Oscar grunted. "Yes, sir."

Back on deck Zach watched as the seven slaves came out of hiding. He wondered if any of them knew how to cook. He approached the man whom Charlotte had brought on board. "Excuse me," he called over.

The man stood about five foot seven, had dark brown skin, coiled hair, and a wide gap between his front teeth. "Yes, suh, how can I's help ya?"

"What's your name?"

"My peoples call me Caleb. My owner called me Nigger Twenty-Three." He looked to the deck of the boat.

"Caleb." Zach spoke just above a whisper. "When asked again, your name is Caleb. Don't say anything more about your previous owner to strangers. Do you understand?"

"Yes, suh." Caleb looked up at him.

"Look me in the eye, Caleb." Zach paused and waited for Caleb's brown eyes to engage with his own. "That's right, Caleb. Stand proud and confident."

"Yes, suh."

"I'm wondering if you or your wife know how to cook for a crew?"

Caleb's smile blossomed. "My wife's name is Ruth, and she's a mighty fine cook, Captain."

"Great. May I hire her to cook for the rest of our journey?"

"Oh no, suh. I's can't accept payment, not when you's bringing us to freedom."

Zach reached over and put his hand on Caleb's shoulder. "We'll settle that later on. Come introduce me to Ruth, and I'll bring you down to the galley. Cook might not like it. Then again, he might be happy not cooking for the rest of the week."

An hour later Ruth, Caleb, and their little one were in the galley cleaning and taking inventory. Oscar was just as happy to be paid for doing nothing the rest of the trip. He took a bottle of rum with him as he left the kitchen. Zach had suspected the man was drinking on ship but hadn't caught him.

Zach finished working with the navigation, adjusted their heading toward New York City, and settled down for a restful morning.

Charlotte hated to wake up Zach, but rumors were spreading. She'd received half a dozen congratulations from various members of the crew. Brad, the cabin boy, skipped in and out of her room, or rather, Zach's room, several times this morning, cheery with the news of the engagement.

"Captain, may I speak with you?"

Zach blinked. His thick, wavy red hair spiraled down his forehead. He combed it back in place with his hands. "Miss Kimbrel, how can I help you?" he said as he stood up.

"I'm sorry to interrupt your sleep."

He waved and shook his head. "Nothing is too much for my fiancée." He chuckled.

"That's the problem."

"What?" Zach narrowed his eyebrows together. She had to admit he was pleasant on the eyes, with his thick red hair and straight nose. She could get used to looking at his face for years to come. Charlotte shook off the thought.

"This engagement. It isn't right. My parents will. . . Perhaps they wouldn't object, but getting engaged in the real world of society—one does not do such a thing." She huffed. "I'm a proper girl and I can't have—"

He clasped her shoulders and turned her to face him. "If you wish to end our engagement now, I will do so. I merely suggested it as a means to protect you in case we had pirates coming upon us. Not that the worst of the worst pirates would care if you were engaged, married, or single."

Charlotte chilled at the thought. "The entire crew is aware and have congratulated me."

"I know. News travels fast on a small ship. It does, however, protect you against any of my men who might not have high moral character. Staying in my cabin and being under my care is enough to protect you, and saying we are engaged would give a man additional pause."

Charlotte sighed. "It feels wrong. I know and you know it is not real."

"Oh, it is real. If you asked me to marry you as soon as we arrived in port, I would honor my word. I would not have offered if I were not serious."

"But we don't know one another."

"Agreed, and you and I both know I did it to protect your virtue. I merely am stating that I am a man of my word, and if the situation were to arise, I would honor my word. However, I am well aware of our differences and that we do not know one another, so I would not subject you to such a marriage. If you wish for our engagement to end, it shall end at this very moment. If you wish to continue under my protection as my betrothed, then I shall honor that as well. The matter is for you to decide."

Charlotte closed her eyes and looked down at their feet. Zach pulled her into an embrace. She felt his protection and strength. A calm washed over her. What would it be like to be in love with this man? She leaned into his embrace and wrapped her arms around him. "Thank you," she whispered.

"Come with me to my quarters. I have a matter to discuss with you. We shall leave the door open to ensure a proper respect for your virtue. Or we can invite my nephew in the room as a witness, whichever you prefer."

"The door open should suffice." She stepped back and out of his embrace. "Bradley is quite excited about our engagement."

Zach nodded. "I'll explain to the boy about our arrangement when we go over his studies."

Charlotte led the way toward the captain's quarters. Being engaged did give her further protection, but she still wondered if it was right. What would God say about such a strange arrangement?

She stepped up on the open two-step stairway to the level above the main deck, though still not as high as the deck where the captain and others steered the ship, which sat above the captain's quarters.

He reached for the door and opened it for her. He waited for her to enter, a gentleman for certain. Charlotte was intrigued by him. With each moment they spent together, she grew increasingly desirous of learning more about him.

"Miss Kimbrel." He waved his hand for her to enter then latched the door to remain open.

"What is it you wish to discuss with me, Captain?"

"Your runaways."

Charlotte stiffened. She didn't know anything about these people, just that they were traveling the Underground Railroad from Augusta. "Yes?"

"I've hired Caleb and Ruth—"

"Who?"

"Your runaways, Caleb and Ruth."

"Oh, I apologize. I never know any of their names. I simply help them for a night by giving them food and shelter. Generally, I bring them to the First African Baptist Church. From there, I don't know where they go or how they go. Unfortunately, the Reverend Campbell was away and unable to help with this family, which is why I sought to purchase their passage north." She sat down on one of the seats under the windows at the stern of the ship. The fresh air was a welcome relief.

"I see." Zach sat down in the opposite chair. "Well, I've hired them to work the galley until we arrive in New York. I can bring my runaways to Freedom Church on Church Street. However, I bring them in irons so as not to attract the attention of the agents hired by Southern owners. I don't have two additional sets of irons. The baby doesn't require them. I recommend that we take them on to Boston, if you think they won't mind."

Charlotte shook her head. "I have no say in the matter. Whatever you think is best. I'm certain they'll find it to be a wise decision."

"Did you help your own slaves escape?"

"No, I'm sad to admit. Father would have figured it out, or worse, he would have beaten our other slaves in order to gain information as to where they were. Apart from Father's temper, he does feed and treat his slaves fairly well, at least from what I've observed of others. And to the best of my knowledge, he has not impregnated any of our slaves in order to have more. They breed well on their own."

"They are not cattle," Zach defended.

Charlotte closed her eyes. "I know. I do not wish to sound insensitive. My world is. . . was. . .very different from yours."

"Forgive me, Charlotte. I believe in hiring a man and paying him fairly for his wages. I don't believe in ownership of another. I'm not against a bondservant if the owner of the bond keeps the agreement. I have seen abuse in those kinds of arrangements as well. The issue of slavery is heating up in our country, and I foresee life becoming very difficult for the Northern and Southern man.

"I'm hopeful that the next president will help end the divide that is growing in our country. But I fear if Lincoln wins, the South will revolt. And if Breckinridge wins, the North will revolt. I am concerned."

"I have read some about Mr. Lincoln. Obviously, my father and brothers are for Breckinridge. There was not so much as a positive note spoken on behalf of the other party."

"I understand. Now with regard to your slaves—"

"They are not my slaves."

"Forgive me, your runaways. Would you be so kind as to speak with them and mention the option of staying with the *Lady Grace* until we reach port in Boston?"

"I'd be happy to."

"Thank you." Zach stood and took a step toward the doorway, then turned back to her. "With regard to our engagement. . ."

Charlotte chuckled. "I will acquiesce to your wisdom."

Zach chuckled. She enjoyed the lilt of his laughter. "Good day, Miss Kimbrel."

"Good day, Captain Browne."

Zach's mouth watered even before the food hit his lips. The savory smells coming from the galley had his stomach leaping for joy.

"Thanks, Captain," one man after the other said as they exited the galley.

"Good?" Zach asked.

"Yes, sir." Each man grinned.

"Good evening, Captain Browne," Caleb said as he entered. "May I's serve ya, suh?"

"Thank you, Caleb. But on this ship the men go to the galley window and gather their own dinner."

"I knows, suh, but you are the captain," Caleb pleaded.

"Very well, thank you." Zach sat down and waited for the man to serve him. The room looked cleaner, smelled a lot better and—his eyes caught sight of the beautiful stew coming his way. The aroma made his stomach dance. "It smells wonderful."

"My Ruthie is a mighty fine cook, Captain."

Zach plunged his spoon into the bowl and slipped the delightful morsels into his mouth. He moaned with pleasure as his taste buds screamed in joy. "Yes, she is," he confessed. "Thank Ruth for me."

"I's will, suh, I's will." Caleb backed up from the table and headed back toward the galley door.

Zach ate his dinner in record time. He wanted another bowl even though he was full. Beside the bowl was a fluffy roll. *How'd she make this?* He lathered on some butter and bit into the soft bread and groaned.

Frank sat down beside him. "That good, huh?"

"Frank, your taste buds will thank you."

Frank dove in. "Oh my. Can you hire her on for all of our travels?"

Zach chuckled. "I was thinking the same thing."

Frank slurped his soup bowl. He probably ate his as fast as Zach. "Goodness, this is good." Frank cleaned his bowl with his roll. "Do you think there is enough for seconds?"

"Couldn't hurt to ask." Zach motioned for Caleb to come over to their table. "Caleb, does Ruth have enough for a second bowl?"

"I's afraid not, suh. She simply finished cooking what the cook had started."

No way Oscar started this stew. She must have added to it. "Would you ask Ruth to draw up a list of supplies she would need to prepare the meals for the ship?"

"She doesn't write, suh. I's don't either."

"I tell you what, Bradley the cabin boy does. It will be good practice for him to write out the list for your wife."

"Thank you, suh." Caleb bowed.

Zach was about to tell him he didn't need to bow but decided against it. A lifetime of habits would take a while to break. "Has a dinner tray been brought to Miss Kimbrel?"

"Yes, suh. Your boy brought it to her an hour ago."

"He's my nephew, not my son."

Caleb nodded.

"Where's your little one?"

"Asleep in the kitchen, suh."

"Keep a rope on him so he doesn't fall overboard."

"Yes, suh. I's do that, Captain," Caleb said as he bowed and stepped back toward the galley door.

"This is great," Frank said as he licked his fingers. "I'm already salivating for breakfast."

Zach chuckled.

"So when were you going to talk to me about this sudden engagement? I thought you were never going to marry," Frank said as Charlotte entered the galley.

Chapter 5

Charlotte stopped. Had she just heard correctly? Did Captain Browne never intend to marry? He glanced over at her as his smile slid down and redness infused his neck. Frank turned.

"Sorry, Cap." Frank took his bowl and hustled out of the dining area.

Charlotte placed her tray in the galley window. "Ruth, dinner was wonderful."

"Thank ya, miss."

"The kitchen, I mean, galley, looks wonderful too. A far cry from when I saw it this morning."

"Thank ya, miss. I's cleaned real hard, but there is much more to do."

Charlotte nodded. She didn't doubt that the galley was a mess. She glanced at the apron Ruth was wearing. It had a spot here and there but it was basically clean.

She didn't turn around but sensed Captain Browne stood behind her. "May I speak with you, Miss Kimbrel?"

"Certainly, Captain. Are you on first watch?"

"Yes."

"Then I will see you later at the helm."

"Charlotte," he whispered in her ear. He placed his hand upon her shoulder. "I wish to explain."

Charlotte nodded. "Later, if that is all right with you, Captain. I would like to speak with Ruth, please."

"Of course. I shall wait my turn. A very fine meal tonight, Ruth, thank you. My nephew Bradley will be coming tomorrow to write a list of supplies you need for the galley."

"Thank ya, suh." Ruth beamed.

Charlotte focused on Ruth and Caleb and the suggestion Captain Browne had for them, rather than the comment she'd just heard. They weren't really engaged. Why did it bother her so? Why did his touch calm her when she was troubled?

"Ruth, Caleb, if you have a moment, the captain asked me to discuss something with the two of you."

Caleb came over. Ruth took off her apron and came out from behind the galley window. "Is the captain unhappy?"

"No, no, this has to do with your flight to freedom."

Both of them sobered and waited for Charlotte to speak. Charlotte glanced around the room. Seeing no one, she continued. "When we arrive in New York City, he's suggesting that you stay on the ship and continue on to Boston. Apparently many men wait in New York for runaways to bring them back home. The others he will bring off the ship in irons and take to safety."

Caleb nodded. "Iffen the captain says we should stay on board, we will stay." Caleb wrapped an arm across his wife's shoulder. She nodded in agreement.

"I'm certain the crew will appreciate you staying on, especially after dinner tonight."

Ruth and Caleb beamed with delight.

"Tells the Captain we's will stay. We trust his wisdom."

"I do too." The sting at hearing Frank's comment about Zach never marrying didn't hurt her wounded spirit quite so much. He told her he proposed for her safety and recommended they continue in such a state until she departed the ship. But where should she get off? New York? Boston? She didn't know. *Dear Lord, what is my purpose?* "I will tell him, thank you."

Ruth wrapped her arms around Charlotte. "Thank ya, miss. We's probably be back in Georgia if you's hadn't helped us."

"Thank the Lord. He seemed to work all of this out for everyone's benefit." Charlotte smiled. Did she really believe that? *I'm trying, Lord.* She headed back up to the main deck. It was a little before the first watch. She glanced up at the helm to see if Captain Browne was there. He wasn't. She slipped into her quarters, shut the door, and let her emotions flow into her pillow. If she had returned home, her life would be the same, perhaps another dinner or two with another would-be suitor. Although Mother and Father were running out of eligible men.

She sat up and wiped her eyes. She opened her Bible to Proverbs 31 and its passage about the virtuous woman. She'd never measure up, but there had to be something she could do. She was smart. She had passion. Could she continue to work for the Underground Railroad? Not really in Boston. Should she get off in New York? Were there places and people there who would benefit from her help?

She opened to Psalm 37 and read verse 3: "Trust in the Lord, and do good; so shalt thou dwell in the land, and verily thou shalt be fed."

She read the verse again. Scriptures about not worrying about tomorrow flooded over her. *Trust, trust, trust. Isn't that always my problem, Lord?* She placed her Bible back on the stand next to the bed. Captain Browne was trustworthy. He might not want to marry one day, but he was a good man. Of course, how would it be for a wife to live with a sea captain who was gone for months at a time? Did she really want that kind of a life? Not really.

She straightened her dress then went to the mirror and washed her face and touched up her hair. She had a duty to serve the captain well as his fiancée even if it wasn't a real engagement. She could still be a good testimony to his kindness. She stepped outside. The night sky was filling with stars. She remembered her lesson from Brad the other evening, and his knowledge of the sexton. She looked for the North Star. Polaris, he called it. She found the Big Dipper and followed it up to Polaris and smiled. Perhaps the captain could educate her on a few more stars.

She stepped up the stairs to the helm. "Good evening, Captain. It's a gorgeous night, isn't it?"

"Splendid, but it dulls in comparison to you."

Charlotte blushed, grateful she was too far away for him to see her rosy cheeks. "There is no need to flatter me. I am fine with what was said earlier. I am curious as to why you have chosen not to marry."

"It seemed the practical thing to do. My mother worries all the time. I can't imagine what a wife would do with a husband who is constantly at sea, the responsibility to raise the children alone if something were to happen to me. It's too great of a risk."

"Perhaps," she said. "It might also be too great of a loss never to have loved at all." She sat down where she had earlier in the morning at the time of their supposed engagement and prayed for Zach and contentment with his decision, if it was what God wanted for him.

Zach thought about Charlotte's challenge about love all through the night and the following day. The winds were great and they would make New York by morning. The men adjusted the bales of cotton so that no one was the wiser. The runaways were not happy about the idea of being put in irons. Charlotte had softened the blow, and they all agreed to his wisdom. The agents from the Southern plantations were growing in number. He didn't know whom to trust, except for his old contacts.

"Charlotte," he whispered in her ear. "I know you were hoping to go into the city, but I'm concerned about Oscar and what he might say. Take Caleb, Ruth, and the little one up to my cabin. If anyone comes on board and asks, order them to stay in the room. Personally, I think he's too drunk to make sense to anyone, but. . ."

She reached out and touched his forearm. "I understand."

He clasped his hand over hers. "Thank you." He stood up straight and bellowed out, "Captain's debarking the ship. First mate is in charge."

A round of "ayes" circled around as the men continued to unload the freight. He led the slaves off the ship and through the streets until they were at last on Church Street. He entered Freedom Church.

"We don't cotton to men in chains here," a stranger bellowed.

"I am aware. Where is the reverend?" Zach proceeded to unlock the irons.

The men smiled and embraced him one at a time. "Thank ya, Captain."

"My pleasure. Go in peace and with God's grace."

"Thank ya, Captain."

"What's goin' on here?" the same man called out with a bit less anger.

"These men have come to Freedom Church," Zach said. The real name was A.M.E. Zion Church, but no one really called it that.

"He's our deliverer; he brought us here," one of the runaways said.

"Go in peace," Zach said and slipped out of the church with the irons in hand. He hated the things, but they played an important role in gaining freedom for the slaves he'd been able to deliver to the North.

He went to the market and filled the order for Ruth. He couldn't wait to eat whatever she made. The woman was the perfect mess cook. Now, if he could get the owners to agree to his hiring Caleb and Ruth. They were hardworking. The galley never smelled so good. The cleanliness of the place was another blessing. He wired the owners and let them know of his arrival in New York and his anticipated arrival time in Boston. Then he headed back to the ship.

He walked up the gangplank. A couple of men stood at the end of it, their backs to him.

"You will not enter this ship. You have no authority," Charlotte huffed, pointing a rifle at them.

"I told ya we're looking for runaways, miss. We have every right," one of the men said.

What totally surprised Zach was the way Charlotte stood with a rifle aimed at the men's chests. "This is not your ship. You have no authority, and I am weary of your blustering, gentlemen," Charlotte said. She caught his gaze. "Afternoon, Captain. These men claim to have your authority to enter this vessel."

The men paled.

"I do not recognize them. Thank you, my dear. You are a splendid fiancée." He turned toward the men. "Now, by whose authority do you claim to have a right?"

"Sorry, we must have the wrong ship."

Zach held up the irons. "Shall I hold you until the authorities come?"

The men ran down the plank and across the pier. They were halfway up the road when he and Charlotte laughed. "Wonderful job, Miss Charlotte. I might just need to keep you around. Where is Frank?"

"There was a problem with one of the deliveries. He's over at the dockmaster's office straightening it out. Although I suspect those men might have something to do with the confusion. I'm fairly certain they were looking for Caleb and Ruth."

"Then we will set sail as soon as my men come back and our cargo is loaded. Go let Caleb and Ruth know they are safe."

"We's knows, suh." Caleb came out from behind a bundle. "Miss is mighty handy with the gun."

"I'm certain she is." He turned toward Charlotte. "How many men are still on board?"

"Six or eight, I think."

He glanced up and saw the red and white pilot flag. "Do you know where the pilot is?"

"At the helm," Charlotte answered.

He smiled. "You're learning."

"Thank you."

"Take care of Caleb and his family. We'll be pulling away from the dock as soon as possible."

"Understood." Charlotte hustled over to Caleb and hurried toward her temporary quarters.

He joined the pilot at the helm. "You've got quite a woman there." The pilot grinned.

Zach laughed. "You have no idea. Do you mind staying around for a bit longer? I think we'll be heading out as soon as possible."

"If you wish, I can. Say. . .for a fiver."

Five dollars was highway robbery, but the pilot was no fool. He'd witnessed the goings-on and certainly understood that Caleb and his family were runaways. "Fine." Zach held back from grumbling.

Frank arrived a few minutes later. "What's going on here? The entire dock is abuzz."

"Oscar," Zach said.

"Oh." Frank scanned the ship. "I'll gather the men."

Zach nodded and waited. He counted the men. One by one they came back on ship and went to their stations. The fresh supplies he'd purchased from the market had arrived. With his purchases he added some fresh apples and Concord grapes, a childhood favorite of his.

Frank came up the gangplank. "All aboard, Captain."

"All aboard. Cast off." He turned to the pilot. "Take her out, sir."

The pilot went to work ordering the men to maneuver the vessel away from the loading dock and out of the very full harbor. The pilot exited the ship with his flag when they were safely out of the congested area. Zach couldn't imagine taking ship after ship in and out of one location. He loved the open ocean, the night sky. . . Charlotte's blue dress swayed with the ship. She was a distraction.

"Miss Kimbrel," he called with a wave.

She came over. "Yes, Captain."

"I sent the telegram you asked me to send to your father."

"Thank you. How much do I owe you?"

"Nothing. Keeping those men off my ship was payment enough."

She started to open her mouth and closed it. Instead, she nodded. She turned to walk away. He reached out and grabbed her elbow. "Miss Kimbrel, have dinner with me this evening?"

She cocked her head as if to ask him why. He chose not to explain further and let the silence hang between them. "I'd be honored, Captain."

"Thank you. I'll make arrangements with the cook."

She raised her eyebrows. Hadn't he been the one to encourage using Caleb and Ruth's first names when referring to them? "Ruth," he corrected.

"I'd be happy to speak with Ruth. She's been teaching me some about food preparation. She's young but has a lot of knowledge about running a household. Her mother worked for their master in the kitchen, and Ruth grew up working alongside her mother."

"I am not surprised. She is a mighty fine cook. I'm hoping the owners of the vessel will allow me to hire Caleb and Ruth for future voyages."

"You said you were making your last journey to Savannah. Where will you be sailing to next?"

"I don't know. My month's leave is coming up when we return. I'm sure I'll have several meetings with the owners, but for now I'm uncertain."

Frank hollered out orders.

"Excuse me, I must work. I shall see you for dinner in my quarters at five."

Charlotte's smile caused butterflies to flutter in the pit of his stomach. "Five would be nice."

She turned and stepped down to the main deck. Maybe the good Lord had a reason and purpose in creating women. Maybe he should reconsider the issue of remaining single the rest of his life. He shook off his foolish thoughts and joined the first mate at the helm. He knew his goal and purpose.

By evening they were nearing the end of Long Island and heading toward the Cape and Islands. By morning they would be passing Hull and heading into Boston Harbor. He needed to work on some of the facts he'd received from other captains about hauling cargo from New York and Boston down to South America and back. Coffee, sugar, molasses, and chocolate were always in high demand and seemed profitable.

He approached Charlotte's quarters. He chuckled to himself at the very thought that his cabin had become hers.

Charlotte slipped into the dress she'd worn to Savannah the day she booked passage on the *Lady Grace*. The clothing she had purchased in Savannah was more conducive to travel. This was her fanciest dress, even though it was a walking dress. The hoop was much smaller than those of high fashion. A full hoop skirt would not serve well with sea travel. In fact, this dress could be of better service if it didn't have a hoop at all.

The gentle rap of the captain's knock pulled her away from the mirror with one final brush of her hands across her hair. She pulled the door open. The captain was wearing the same outfit he'd been wearing earlier in the day. Perhaps she had been reading too much into the invitation. "Good evening, Captain."

"Good evening, Miss Kimbrel. May I come in?"

She was about to say, "Of course," but decided to let her hand speak for her as she waved him into the cabin. "Bradley should be here with our dinner soon."

"Thank you. If you'll pardon me for a moment, I need to write a few things down in one of my logs." He sat down at his desk.

He looked comfortable behind the desk, as if he and the furniture belonged together. "Is the desk yours or a part of the ship?"

He turned and smiled. "Mine. My father and I built it after I earned my commission as a captain."

"It's beautiful." She traced the edge with her finger. She'd admired it before but looked at it in a new light. "This really is quite nice."

"Thank you." He went back to his notations.

"Evenin', Miss Kimbrel," Bradley said as he stepped through the open door carrying two plates of food. "I'll be back with your drinks in a moment."

Bradley ran out of the room. The enticing aroma coming up from the plates tickled Charlotte's nose. She lifted the lids. "Captain, you won't believe—"

"Oh my," Zach said and abandoned his pen and ledger. "I really need to convince the owners to let me hire Ruth."

Charlotte chuckled. "Bring them a plate of her food."

"What a splendid idea." He sat down and draped his napkin over his left thigh. He paused for a moment. "Would you mind if we pray before we eat?"

"No, not at all."

Zach nodded. "Father, we thank You for Your many blessings. We ask for Your grace and protection for the former slaves who are now in New York and for the three still remaining on this ship. I also ask for Your guidance for Miss Kimbrel and her future. Protect the men and the ship. In Your precious Son's name, amen."

"Amen." He didn't ask for prayer for himself. *Hmm.*

"This smells like heaven on a plate."

Charlotte examined the feast before her. The plate was filled with pulled pork, baked beans, corn bread, and glazed carrots. Ruth had outdone herself tonight. Charlotte had made apple tarts, something Ruth had never seen or had before, but the tarts weren't served yet. How was it possible for Ruth to cook so much in such a small kitchen?

"Charlotte," Zach said, taking her hand and holding it in his own. "I wish to speak with you about your future."

Moisture built up on her palms; her heart raced. She was falling for this kind sea captain. Was he falling for her?

Chapter 6

Zach's throat thickened. Charlotte's eyes sparkled with affection. He glanced down at their hands. He hadn't meant to be so forward.

"Here's your drinks," Bradley said as he stepped into the room.

Zach released her hand. "Thank you, Bradley."

Bradley shrugged off the comment. "Have you tasted it?"

"We were just about to," Charlotte said.

"It has your seal of approval?" Zach asked his nephew.

"Yup, and she made enough for seconds. She has this sauce you can pour on the pork that is yummy. It's not ketchup but sorta like it, different tastin' though."

"The South makes this sauce for cooking pork on a pit or grill," Charlotte said. "They baste the meat over and over with the sauce. It's really good." She then scooped a forkful of pork into her mouth.

Her delicate pink lips... Zach closed his eyes. Where did that thought come from? He forked some meat and concentrated on the food. "Yum. Tell the cook I'll have seconds on the pork with some of that sauce, please."

"Yes, sir." Bradley saluted and ran out of the room again.

Charlotte chuckled. "When you were a boy did you run around the ship as much as Bradley?"

"At least as much, if not more. My captain would tell me to slow down, but I learned later he'd time me."

The rest of the dinner continued with light conversation and chuckles as they shared some of their childhood memories.

Bradley stepped in and brought the apple tarts. "I don't think I can eat another bite," Charlotte said as she wiped her mouth with her cloth napkin.

"Can I have yours? Miss Charlotte made these and they are really good," Bradley praised.

"Charlotte?"

"I know little in the kitchen, but Maggie taught me a few things when Mother wasn't looking."

"Well now, if Miss Charlotte made this I will have to try one." Zach picked up one of the tarts and bit it in half. Bradley's eyes bulged. Charlotte's did as well. The sweetness of the apples and cinnamon danced on his tongue. He chewed and swallowed without being able to savor it because he'd bitten off too much. He washed it down with some lemonade. "This is really good."

"Thank you."

Zach took his time eating the remaining tart, savoring the sweet confection.

"If you like these, you would love my peach cobbler. We have a lot more peaches in Georgia than apples."

"I look forward to the opportunity."

"Captain, I need to finish my studies. May I be dismissed?"

"Yes, sir. I'll check on you before you go down for the night." Zach ruffled Bradley's hair. "You don't have to be formal in front of Miss Charlotte."

Bradley relaxed his stance. "Oh, good. I thought maybe with you two getting married and all. . .but I didn't know. When can I call her Aunt Charlotte?"

"After the wedding," Zach replied without thinking.

Bradley nodded. "Good night, Miss Charlotte." He ran out so fast Zach stared out the open doorway.

"That was the perfect opportunity to be honest with the boy," Charlotte grumbled.

He turned to face her. Her posture was rigid, her cheeks flushed. "I know, you're right, but it wasn't the time."

She bounced to her feet and began to pace. "I don't understand you, Zachery Browne. You propose for my sake, never intending to marry. You won't allow me to break off the fake engagement for my sake, and when I suggested you should at least tell Bradley the truth, you don't. And then you spend time with me, as if you are courting me, only to. . .what? Pretend to keep up this charade? I don't understand you."

Zach took in a deep breath and held it for a moment. "First of all, I did propose for your sake, not mine. Second, I do not need to explain to you my life choices. Third, if I were to marry someday, it could not be to a woman like you."

"Like me?" Her temper was showing now.

"I didn't mean—"

"Like me?" Her voice ratcheted up another notch.

"Charlotte, please, let me explain."

She crossed her arms across her chest. "Please leave, Captain, before I say something I will regret."

"But—"

She pointed to the door.

He nodded and exited before he said something he might regret. All he wanted to do was wrap her in his arms and make the pain go away. What foolishness was that? He marched up to the helm and sent everyone away. He needed to be alone, to cool down and try to figure out what just happened. How could such a pleasant evening turn so quickly?

Charlotte paced back and forth in her room late into the evening then tossed and turned in bed. The boat's rocking motion seemed to stop. Were they in port?

She tossed off her covers and dressed faster than she'd ever done before, even when she was sneaking off to help the runaway slaves. She pulled open the door to see nothing but flat sea. They weren't in port. The sails lay flat on their masts and booms and whatever else held the sails in place. "What's happening?"

"No wind." Zach's voice flowed down her spine like warm tea with honey. He stepped closer. He was behind her, but she sensed him closing the gap between them. "Miss Charlotte, Charlotte, I want to apologize for last night. I was rude, and my behavior was uncalled for."

She grasped the rail tighter. She could not give this man another piece of her heart. She'd given him too much already, and he didn't even know it. She nodded that she forgave him.

He placed his hands on her upper arms. "Speak to me," he whispered.

Charlotte's legs were about to betray her. She mustered up the courage and spoke. "You are forgiven, Captain."

He released her and stepped away.

Charlotte continued to hold on to the rail. She couldn't move. Her legs felt as solid as ice in her sweet tea on a hot summer's day. They wouldn't support her for long. The men were scattered about the ship, doing nothing. It was a scene she'd never seen before since starting this journey. Some men were working with rope. One was whittling a piece of wood. Another was fishing, but most were simply sitting, doing nothing.

Wind was necessary to fill the sails to move the ship—but no wind. She thought back to some of the hot steamy days in Savannah where the air didn't move. The slaves would fan Mother all day long. She and her brothers would play in the river to keep cool.

"Winds will change, miss," Frank, the first mate, said as he passed her, heading up to the helm. "They always do."

She thought back on that twenty-four hours later when they were still motionless. The captain had put the men to work, polishing all the brass, checking all the lines, cleaning the deck, and anything else he could think of just to help the men focus. Charlotte still hadn't spoken with the captain. She supposed she hadn't forgiven him deep in her heart.

She stood by the open windows, staring at the flat ocean. Nothing moved. It seemed peculiar and unnatural.

A knock at her door broke her thoughts. "Come in," she said, without bothering to turn around. The only one who came to her room was Bradley.

"Charlotte, we should talk." Zach's velvet voice spilled over her jangled nerves.

She turned and faced him. Her eyes betrayed her. "I'm sorry, Zach."

He was beside her, and she was in his arms in two steps. "I didn't mean to hurt you. I spoke poorly. I was trying to say a wife of a sea captain spends many days and months alone. She has to do all the work at the house, raise the children, farm, can the food, provide the education, and keep everything running. I know you were raised to be a great hostess, but—"

She placed her finger to his lips. Goose bumps spread up her arm. "I understand. Unfortunately, my heart has gone out to you," she confessed.

He closed his eyes. "I'm sorry. I just know I am not the right man for you. You deserve a husband who will be with you to share your joys and sorrows." He released her and stepped away. "I wish I were, Charlotte. You are a remarkable woman. You fought your family and traditions. You helped several men and women gain freedom. And you won over the hearts of my men, which was no easy task. I-I. . ." He stepped closer to the door.

She reached out to him. "Pray, Zach, and I will as well."

He nodded and slipped out the door. She stood there for a moment. Relief washed over her. She had finally admitted to him her feelings. Now it was in God's and Zach's hands. He had a valid point. She couldn't imagine not seeing her husband every day, or their children not seeing their father. Perhaps her love for him was genuine, just not marital love?

Charlotte slipped back to the window and looked at the still water. "Father God, direct us in Your path, not our own."

She left the room and headed to the galley. It was time for another cooking lesson. And if she were going to be living on her own, she would need to know how to prepare meals.

Zach climbed the rigging to the top of the mast. He had men who could do it, but he wanted to be alone, and the top of the mast afforded an excellent choice when out in the middle of nowhere and going no place. He'd already missed his deadlines with the cargo. Some of the cargo might rot if the wind didn't pick up soon.

"Father, I care for Charlotte, I really do. But my life and life choices are not good for a wife. I have been content in my single life. I have not regretted that decision, but now I am faced with a woman who is making me question whether I made the right choice. Remove these feelings if she is not to be my wife. I want to protect her, love her, but I cannot allow. . ."

A story from the Bible came to life in front of him. He recalled the story when Peter was up on a roof praying and the vision of a sheet descended in front of him with all the food choices, including the restricted ones. And how Peter fought God because of his faithfulness to remain true to Jewish traditions regarding food.

Zach's stomach knotted.

He looked down on the sails and sheets below him, flat and dormant. It was time to change the course of his life. The decision he'd made earlier as a young man was good for that season. But now he was being led to live another way. Zach laughed out loud and worked his way down the mast. A gentle breeze began to blow.

Zach laughed even harder. "I am listening, Lord. Thank You."

By the time he reached the main deck, the sails were filling with air. Frank was at the helm. He waved, and Frank waved in return as he barked out orders. The men scrambled to their places. It was time to go home. He marched over to his quarters and knocked. No answer. He knocked again. Again, there was no response. He opened the door, closing his eyes. "Charlotte?" he called out. Not hearing a response, he opened his right eye, then his left. She wasn't there.

Zach rubbed the stiffness out of his neck. If the winds continued, he would have eight hours to admit his attraction to Charlotte before she left the *Lady Grace* into parts unknown.

She couldn't be far. They were on a ship, he reasoned. Zach exited her quarters and began his search.

Chapter 7

Charlotte packed her bag. She prayed she would find housing and a job soon. Her finances were such that if she was very frugal she could survive for six months, perhaps more if she found a job working at a place where food was served. The past few days working with Ruth she'd learned she enjoyed cooking and baking. She had a long way to go, but hopefully she'd find work that would allow her to learn new skills.

The gentle knock on her door was like a sledgehammer coming down. Her time was up. The freedom and protection she had from Captain Browne ended as soon as she walked down that gangplank. Which could be as soon as the dinner hour.

"Miss Kimbrel," the captain's voice called out. "May I enter?"

Charlotte eased out the breath she'd been holding since she heard the knock. "Yes, sir," she answered, but remained standing next to her bag.

The door creaked open. "Charlotte, forgive me."

She closed her eyes. Tears threatened to fall but she managed to hold them back. "There's nothing to forgive, Captain."

"But there is. Please turn around and face me." His voice was gentle. As always, it calmed her rattled nerves.

And to think a week ago he was a stranger. Now she couldn't imagine life without him. But he was confident in his declaration of being like the apostle Paul and remaining single all of his life. She squared her shoulders, straightened her spine, and turned to face him.

"You are so beautiful, Charlotte."

She averted her eyes. She didn't have the strength to look into his again, knowing what she now knew.

"Forgive me." He knelt down at her feet and grasped her hands in his. "I don't know how to say this except to speak as truthfully and honestly as I can. I spent some time in prayer about you and me and my commitment, and I feel that the Lord has given me permission to no longer remain single. I can move into a different life. . . That's not right. How can I say this? That I'm no longer bound to the commitment I made as a younger man to remain single, that I'm free to take you as my wife."

Charlotte pulled her hands away and stepped back. "What?"

Zach stood up. "I know I'm not making sense, but do you recall the Bible story about Peter seeing a sheet with all the foods he was now allowed to eat?"

Charlotte could feel her eyebrows move closer together. She nodded.

"Well, Peter never ate anything unclean by Jewish tradition, but God was saying that now it was permissible for him to no longer keep that commitment, that he was free to eat pork, ham, lobster, and all sorts of things. My singleness is like the Jewish tradition of eating kosher, and now God is saying it is all right for me to change my sheet lines and change direction. I have feelings for you, Charlotte. I've been fighting them, but I do have them. I would be honored if you would be my wife."

Charlotte stood there amazed, confused, and not certain what to say. "But you said it yourself: I wouldn't be able to handle being a wife of a sea captain who was gone so often and for so long. I don't know how to farm or store and preserve food for the winter. I can sew, and with Ruth's help I've learned to cook a few more things, but—"

"Shh." He pulled her into his arms. "We'll work those details out. All I need to know right now is that you love me enough to be my wife."

What should she say? "Where would I live until a proper time has elapsed for us to be married?"

"Charlotte, what is proper with regard to our relationship? I'll marry you tonight when we arrive in port and we can find a minister to marry us."

She touched his forehead. "You're ill, aren't you?"

Zach chuckled. "Never better." He cradled her face in his hands. "I have to go. I don't want to, but I must. Can we continue this conversation?"

She met his gaze. She could see the love shining in his eyes. He was sincere, and honesty and truth bored into her from the depths of his soul. "Yes," she whispered.

"Thank you, my love, thank you." He brushed his lips on her forehead. The warmth and softness melted the rest of her resolve. How could her life change so quickly?

The ship shifted, tacking. She'd been told what the movement was when the ship changed position to catch the wind. Zach's sea legs kept them upright. "Is it safe to say you and your decision to marry were tacking?"

"Hmm, I hadn't thought about that, but yes, I reckon I have. My goal is still the same, to live an honorable life and be a good witness for the Lord. But now I'll have a wonderful woman by my side."

The clang of the captain's bell rang out. "I'm sorry, I really need to go."

"I'll be here when you return."

"Thank you, Charlotte. I love you."

He disappeared out the door before she could reply. "I love you too," she said to the emptiness of the room.

"Where were you?" Frank bellowed.

"Sorry, I had business with Miss Kimbrel."

"Oh, sorry."

They went through the traditional relieving jargon, and Frank left the helm and headed toward his bunk. He turned and faced Zach before he went down the stairs. "You're going to marry her, aren't ya?"

"If she'll have me, I am."

Frank wagged his head back and forth. "Must be true what they say about women being a bad omen on a ship." He laughed.

"If this is bad, I'll have her on every voyage."

Frank waved and hopped down the stairs.

The idea of Charlotte traveling with him sounded wonderful. Caleb came up to the top of the stairs but didn't step off them. "May I's come closer, suh?"

"Of course, Caleb. What do you need?"

Caleb stepped up and walked over to the helm. "I's don't want to be ungrateful to alls ya is doin' for me and the missus, but we don't want to stay workin' on the ship. Our little one, Lizzy, is too small for a ship."

"Ah." Zach kept his hand on the wheel and an eye on the compass.

"We's be honored that ya wants us, but. . ."

"I understand. A ship is a dangerous place for a baby."

"Thank ya, suh." Caleb bowed and stepped back toward the stairs.

"Do you know anyone in Boston or around the area where you can find some work?" Zach asked.

Caleb turned. "No, suh, but the good Lord, He's been watchin' o'er us."

"True. I'll be praying for you."

"Thank ya, suh. We's appreciate 'em."

Caleb left, and Zach started to pray. He'd grown closer to Ruth and Caleb than any of the other runaway slaves he'd helped bring to freedom.

Zach's shift ended. Charlotte waited for him on the walkway deck to his quarters. "Hi," he said. "I wasn't expecting to see you. I thought you'd be asleep by now."

Charlotte giggled. "After what you proposed a few hours ago? You have a lot to learn about women, or better yet, me."

"I look forward to discovering every nuance that makes up the whole of you."

"Ah, but I haven't said yes yet."

He wrapped his arm around her shoulders and led her to the bow of the ship. Would she turn him down? No, he didn't believe so. "Which part of what I said has you unable to sleep?"

He helped her to sit on the bow, leaning against the cabin, and sat down beside her.

"All of it. I can't imagine marrying a man without a proper courtship. On the other hand, my decision to leave home in the manner that I did. . .does make me question whether or not I need to conform to the social norm."

"If it will make you happier, I shall wait one year."

"But"—she paused—"I do not know where to live. Where to find employment. How would we court if you were out to sea? So many questions, yet your suggestion makes sense. But where would I live when you are at sea? If I remember correctly from our conversations, you do not have a house or home. I would find it odd to live in your parents' home, especially if you went out to sea right after we married."

"I have land to build a house on. My father has given me a piece of his farm. My family lives outside of Salem in Danvers. It's good farmland."

"But I don't know how to farm."

"No, but my parents and brothers do. They will help you."

Charlotte nodded.

"Charlotte, I have a good savings. I could take a leave of absence for six months and we could build the home together."

Charlotte nodded.

"I am not a mind reader," Zach continued. "You must speak with me in order for me to understand your thoughts."

"You might think this is Southern of me, but what if we have Ruth and Caleb work the farm? I'm not saying as our slaves, but as our hired servants. I know you wanted to hire them to work on the ship, but..."

"What a splendid idea." Zach smiled. "Caleb spoke with me earlier and said that he and Ruth thanked me for the offer to work on the ship but they didn't believe it was a safe place for Lizzy."

"That's wonderful for me, not you, I suppose."

"If I ate as well as I have been for the past few days I would gain too much weight. No, I think we would be better served if Ruth helped you around the house. What about children?"

"What about them?"

"How many would you like?"

"Ah, well, in high society it is not expected that you have too many children."

"You do realize we shall not be living in high society. Being a captain, I am awarded some decorum and respect, but..."

Charlotte placed her hand on his chest. "I am not saying I want to be a member of high society. What I was trying to say in an indirect way was that I am willing to wait and see what the Lord grants us with regard to children."

"Ah."

"I can be direct, but I do know how to be delicate in conversation."

"I understand, and I appreciate directness and sensibilities. Now, we must settle one more item before we retire for the evening."

"What's that?"

"Are you going to marry me tomorrow or a year from tomorrow?"

Charlotte giggled. "Tomorrow."

He took her in his arms and kissed her. At first it was a sweet, gentle kiss, but then it deepened. Charlotte's heart fluttered. She was very glad she'd chosen to marry tomorrow.

They arrived in Boston by early morning. The ship was unloaded within two hours. Ruth made a light lunch for the six of them, including Bradley, as the crew left once the boat was anchored in the harbor.

Zach left to speak with the owners of the ship and give them an accounting of his various travels, as well as the financial logs and money he still carried. By two, he returned with a much smaller sailing ship, his own. The six of them—Caleb, Ruth, Lizzy, Brad, Zach, and herself—sailed to Salem Harbor and arrived by dinnertime.

He glided the ship to the dock with ease. A small group of people met them there. "Who are they?" Charlotte asked.

"My family and the pastor of our church, I hope. Otherwise we're not getting married until tomorrow." He winked.

"How?"

"I sent them a telegraph message and told them I was getting married and asked them to bring the pastor."

Charlotte chuckled. "I should have known. I thought it odd you didn't bring me into Boston. I thought we were going to marry there."

"I hope you don't mind. I want my family to be a part of our lives, and I wanted you to meet them before you married me. You might not want to once you meet them." Charlotte smiled. Zach was an incredible man and an excellent planner.

A man with red hair and a chin similar to Zach's stood at the end of the dock. "Hey there, little brother," he called out, "you couldn't have timed it better. We've only been waiting for an hour."

"Charlotte, this is my older brother, Russell." He tossed Russell a rope. "He's the one who will inherit most of the farm. He's a fair farmer too, but I wouldn't say that in front of him. His head might swell."

Russell stood prouder after securing the rope to the pilings. "You're sure you want to marry this man? He's not normal—living on boats. Ain't got no roots, just rudders."

Charlotte laughed. "I like your brother," she said to Zach. Turning to Russell, she added, "Zach is a bit different, but then again, so am I."

"Oh, she'll fit right in. Hi, I'm Edith, Zach's mom." She extended a hand to help Charlotte step onto the dock. "Pleasure to meet the woman who finally got this man to settle down."

"Hey now," Zach defended. "Russ, help me with the baby."

The crowd hushed.

Zach reached into the cabin and pulled out Lizzy. Ruth came next, and Caleb followed. "Family, this is Lizzy, Ruth, and Caleb. They've agreed to help me and my wife-to-be build and farm our land. They'll also help take care of Charlotte when I'm out to sea."

Murmurs of welcome gradually swept through the crowd, while hugging and shaking of hands went around the small circle. Charlotte looked back at Zach. She'd never seen him so happy. Well, maybe this was the second time she'd seen him this happy. No, wait, the third. The first was when he told her his insight from the Lord about changing his life course. The second was when she agreed to marry him the next day. And the third was right now, encircled by his family.

"Is the reverend here?" Zach asked.

Charlotte stiffened. It was really happening. She was going to get married.

"Right here, Captain Browne."

Zach wrapped his arm around her waist. "Can we marry right here, right now?"

"If you wish." The reverend smiled. "But your mother set the church up real nice."

"Mom?"

"I couldn't help myself. You know me and weddings. You're the last of my children to marry. I had to send you off well."

"Do you mind, Charlotte?" Zach asked.

"No. A church wedding sounds perfect." Charlotte snuggled into Zach.

"Head to the church, folks," Russell called out. He leaned toward Zach and Charlotte. "Good choice. There's a feast, and Mom and the girls went out of their way to fancy up the church."

"Grandfather's cottage has been cleaned up for you and Charlotte. I'm afraid we didn't set up quarters for your servants. They are servants, right?"

"Yes, we hired them," Charlotte said.

"Good. Don't fret none. We'll find them a place to stay," Russell added.

Within ten minutes, the boat was secured at the dock. The wagons were loaded with all the family members and the reverend. Zach and Charlotte sat with him on the way to the church. He pumped them with questions about their relationship and passed on some advice about marriage.

Before long they were married and sitting at a table, eating some of the food the ladies of the family had cooked earlier that day. Charlotte sat back and marveled at all the changes in her life. Last week at this time she had discovered the small family fleeing for their freedom. Today they were free.

She reached over and took Zach's hand. "Thank you."

"For what?"

"For being the man you are. You helped me save the runaways, and you rescued me as well."

He leaned over and kissed her. "You rescued me too."

"I never asked, but why is the ship named *Lady Grace*?"

"Ah, well, the owners are from England, a husband and wife. The wife holds the English title of lady, while he is a lord, and her name is Grace. Thankfully, I don't captain their other vessel."

"Why? What's the name of that one?"

"Lord Nibley."

"Nibley?"

Zach nodded and smiled.

"Do they have other ships?" Charlotte asked.

"Not yet, but they're looking to increase their fleet. I reckon they'll start using their children's names."

"Hmm."

"So how does it feel to be Mrs. Zachery Browne?"

"Good. Strange, and like it may not be real."

"Oh, my dear, it is real." Zach took her hand and stood up. She followed his lead. They said their goodbyes and were promised not to be bothered until dinnertime, when they were expected to join his parents at the main farmhouse.

The cool night air hit. Charlotte took a deep breath. "It smells of pine and oak with a slight hint of flowers. I don't smell the saltwater, though."

"It drifts in on occasion when the tides and air are just right. But the harbor is a ways away, as you discovered on our long trip here." Zach paused. "I love you, Charlotte."

"I love you too."

He guided her to a carriage and helped her inside, then ran around to the other side. "Russell is going to take care of the horse and carriage after I get us to my grandfather's cottage."

She snuggled next to Zach. This was right. She had a purpose—to be the best wife and mother to Zach and their future children. She also believed she would be teaching Ruth and Caleb how to read and write, as they would be teaching her how to do the many things she'd never needed to do. She would miss her parents and maybe even her life back in Savannah, but she had made the right decision to help the slaves to the road to freedom. She didn't know it would include a journey on a ship for herself as well.

"Zach?"

"Hmm?"

"Aren't the sails called sheets on a ship?"

"No, the sheets are the lines attached to the corners of the sail that help us direct the wind flow into the sail. Why do you ask?" He continued to hold the reins and direct the horse.

"I was just thinking about the freedom for the runaways and how my voyage gained me love and a husband. And if the sails were sheets, as I thought they were, it was interesting that God would remind you of Peter's vision with the sheet. But I guess that doesn't fit, does it?"

"Not exactly." Zach paused for a moment. "The sheets in Peter's vision were God's love and blessing on all the foods Peter was now allowed to eat. A freedom, if you will."

"Sails of love," she whispered. "We fell in love under the sails of God's love."

"And we'll continue under the sails of His love." Zach reached over and wrapped his arm around her. "I love you."

"I love you too." And she did. She didn't know much more about her future, but she knew she would always be protected by God's love. . .and Zach's.

Lynn A. Coleman is an award-winning and bestselling author of *Key West* and other books. She began her writing and speaking career teaching how to utilize the internet. Since October 1998, when her first fiction novel sold, she has sold thirty-eight books and novellas. Lynn is also the founder of American Christian Fiction Writers Inc. and served as the group's first president for two years and on the advisory board for two years. One of her primary reasons for starting ACFW was to help writers develop their writing skills and to encourage others to go deeper in their relationship with God. "God has given me a gift, but it is my responsibility to develop that gift." Some of her other interests are photography, camping, cooking, and boating. Having grown up on Martha's Vineyard, she finds water to be very exciting and soothing. She can sit and watch the waves for hours. If time permitted she would like to travel. She makes her home in Keystone Heights, Florida, where her husband of forty-three years serves as pastor of Friendship Bible Church. Together they are blessed with three children, two living and one in glory, and eight grandchildren.

The Bakery Bride

by Cecelia Dowdy

This is the bread which cometh down from heaven,
that a man may eat thereof, and not die.
—John 6:5

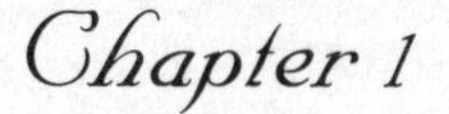

Chapter 1

Philadelphia, Pennsylvania
1859

"Son, when are you going to get married?"

Oh no, she had to go and mention that. His mother acted as if he were the only unmarried, upper-class Negro man in Philadelphia. Joseph Adams ignored her and shoved the paddle into the hot, wood-fired masonry oven. He pulled out the thick, crusty loaves of bread. Thin fingers of sweat trickled down his face. He set the paddle of hot bread onto the counter and flexed his aching arms. The pain reminded him of his late-night excursion with other free black abolitionists. He'd been unloading supplies into the church, getting ready for the next group of runaway slaves they were expecting. The yeasty scent of the bread enveloped him as he sighed and wiped his forehead with a towel. Hopefully, his headache would go away soon.

"Boy, you hear me talking to you?"

"Mother, I hear you." Did she honestly think he could predict when he'd be getting married? His mother's mouth pressed down while she arranged loaves of bread into large square baskets. Her bony shoulders drooped. She'd been so miserable since Father died one month ago.

Joseph focused on the rough pine walls and two empty slab tables in their bakery. Visions of sitting with his father at those tables, talking about life, filled his mind. He eyed his mother. She hadn't been eating as well as she should be, and she'd lost a lot of weight. He was worried about her, but when he tried to get her to see the doctor, she'd get upset. He heard her crying every night. He hoped she'd soon heal from her sadness. He figured her grief was what was making her act so irrational about his future.

He pointed to the office in the back room. He briefly eyed the stacks of parchment papers and inkwell resting on top of the antique desk and focused on the painting of his late father centered on the wall. "Didn't you tell me you had to do some bookkeeping today?" Maybe if he got her focused on something else, she'd stop asking him about holy matrimony.

She shook her head, the red kerchief on her head bouncing with the movement. "You never answered my question about marriage."

No, he hadn't. She'd asked that question at least ten times over the last month. His response hadn't changed, so why bother answering? "Mother, I don't want to talk about marriage." He again gestured toward the office. "If you don't want to do the bookkeeping, then why don't you go and rest for a bit." He figured she could sit in the chair and prop her feet up. Maybe close her eyes for a few minutes.

"No, if anybody should be resting, it should be you. You got up before I did." In spite of her words, she made her way to the office. She dropped into the chair and propped her feet onto a stool and leaned back. "You were up hours before I was." She closed her eyes.

Indeed he was. He missed having his father in the bakery, helping out in the kitchen.

Now he had to work even harder since they had yet to hire someone to take his father's place. Working the extra hours made him sick, literally. Thoughts of running away from the family business and never looking back rushed through his mind. How nice it would be to never bake another loaf of bread. The loud screech of the door opening invaded his thoughts.

Joseph focused on the small, dark-skinned woman who strolled into his shop. A few black curls peeked from beneath her bonnet. As soon as he spotted her full lips and sculpted cheekbones, he paused. He could look at this woman all day. He took a deep breath, for he realized he'd stopped breathing. Her sharp eyes scanned the redbrick walls and rough wooden tables. He wiped his sweaty palms on his apron and approached her. "May I help you?"

"I's come about the job."

They'd just started looking for a replacement for his father. The few people who'd inquired had not passed his mother's approval. This was the first time they'd ever tried to hire a non–family member for their business. He cleared his throat and stared at the woman. Her skin was the color of the dark chocolate they sometimes used in their flaky, crescent-shaped croissants. He asked the first question that popped into his mind. "What's your name?"

"Ruth."

Ruth. The name suited her. He studied her warm, cocoa-brown skin and her cheap gray dress. Scuffed brown shoes covered her dainty feet. When he again focused on her face, she looked away, as if embarrassed.

Realizing his staring made her uncomfortable, Joseph glanced away and cleared his throat. He schooled his face to a stern, businesslike expression before shifting his gaze back to her. "Ruth, have you worked in a bakery before?"

"No, I—"

"Do you need my assistance, Joseph?" At Mother's voice, Joseph's stomach curled with dismay. Ever since his father died, Mother had watched his every move, as if she didn't trust him to run the bakery on his own. She focused on Ruth. "Did I hear you asking about the job?"

Ruth dipped her head. Mother scrutinized the young woman. "Yes'm. I's come to see about work."

Mother peered at her. "How did you know about this job?"

"Cyrus Brown says you lookin' for a baker."

Mother scrunched her eyebrows. "Who is Cyrus Brown?"

Ruth folded her arms over her chest. "He's an abolitionist over at the church."

"An abolitionist told you about this job?" Her voice vibrated through the room.

Joseph groaned inwardly. The last thing he needed was for Mother to get upset about the abolitionist movement. If she found out he was involved with the Underground Railroad, she'd have a conniption for sure. She'd often told him they should give money to the cause, but not get actively involved. He figured she was scared. She'd been so distressed since his father died that he had not found the right time to tell her about his recent involvement.

Mother cocked her head and squinted at Ruth. "How would an abolitionist know about this job?"

"Mother, it doesn't matter. Ruth is here now, so we need to consider her for the position."

Ruth nodded toward Joseph. "Thank you. I's glad you said that."

He gestured toward Mother. "Ruth, this is my mother, Elizabeth, and I'm Joseph Adams."

Ruth nodded at Joseph before focusing on his mother. She dipped her head. "Pleased to meet ya, ma'am."

Mother didn't acknowledge Ruth's greeting. Instead, her dark eyes assessed her like a hawk. "I can't have someone working in our bakery who talks like that."

Joseph cringed. He needed to step in, and Mother needed to tone down her elitist attitude. Their family had been free for two generations and had amassed a considerable amount of wealth. Mother wore their upper-class status like a badge, making sure everybody knew they owned their own business and catered to both white and black elite clientele. "She doesn't have to talk to anyone. I'll wait on the customers." As long as Ruth knew how to bake, he was sure she'd fit into their business.

Mother's chin jutted out. "I'm in charge around here. She just won't do."

Ruth's dark eyes snapped to life, and she stood taller. She folded her thin arms over her chest and looked directly into Mother's face. "I's can bake bread better than anybody around here. Lets me prove it."

Mother stepped back, obviously stunned. Joseph smiled. People rarely stood up to his tall, overbearing, and outspoken mother. Joseph liked Ruth's spunk. Someone like Ruth was just what they needed around here to put Mother in her place. He needed to hurry up and give Ruth a chance before Mother got crazy and forced her to leave the bakery. He gestured toward their oven. "Come over to the oven, Ruth."

With quick steps, she followed him to the workspace behind the counter. She glanced at the dough trough, the wood-fired masonry oven, the large counter space. She then took note of the sacks of flour in the corner. She seemed to be taking everything in, an inventory of her new surroundings. "You gots any nuts, berries, dried fruit. . .cinnamon?"

Joseph opened the cabinet and removed dried cranberries, raisins, and a canister of cinnamon, pushed the items toward Ruth, then glanced at Mother and grinned. Mother remained uncharacteristically quiet. Usually when she met someone, she enjoyed dominating the conversation. Her silence told him she was either impressed or speechless—and it took a lot to make Mother speechless.

Ruth took the paddle, plunged it into the trough, and scooped some dough onto the counter. She then stopped and glanced around. "Do you have any dough that's already been set out to rise?"

"Yes." He rushed to give her the filled wooden bowl he'd placed near the oven earlier. She dumped the dough onto the workspace and sprinkled flour on top. Then, with deft hands, she worked the dough, sprinkling in the cinnamon, nuts, and dried fruit. Her small, delicate hands looked so lovely. . . He could imagine watching her knead dough all day. She stopped working, turning toward him. "Where's the other stuff?"

He frowned. What was she talking about? "Stuff?"

"To bake your bread. Sugar and stuff like that."

He pointed toward the cabinet. "I'll go get what you need."

She shook her head. "I'll get it." She opened the cabinet and studied the shelves. She removed containers, opened the tops, and sniffed each one. Their containers of spices were clearly labeled, so he figured she just wanted to make sure their spices were fresh. She stopped sniffing and looked directly at him. "Don't watch me." The command flew from her mouth as her dark eyes pierced his.

Goodness, he hadn't been expecting that. He focused on Mother. Her narrowed, dark eyes and pressed mouth indicated her building anger. Joseph's hopes for Ruth earning a position in their bakery deflated.

Not wanting to crowd Ruth, Joseph left her side and strolled over to Mother, who gestured at Ruth as she leaned toward him. "Don't let that foolish girl give you orders. No way is she working here." Despite her whispered voice, he wondered if Ruth could hear her.

"Mother. . ." Joseph's grip on his temper slipped at Mother's imperious attitude.

He eyed Ruth again. It appeared she'd dumped some herbs and spices into a bowl. He wondered what she'd put into the dish. She dumped the contents into the dough and her hands again kneaded the mixture. Soon, she'd made four perfectly round small loaves. When she finally stood back and pressed her fists against her waist, he joined her behind the counter.

"I usually lets this rise for a hour. But I knows you don't want to wait."

Joseph figured Ruth knew Mother was uneasy about hiring her, and she wanted them to taste her bread as soon as possible. She took a pinch of flour and turned toward the large, beehive-shaped brick oven. Orange flames licked from the back of the baking hole. She tossed the flour into the oven. The cloud of flour floated down on the brick surface. The white powder slowly darkened from the heat. Her beautiful lips moved. He figured she was counting how long it took for the flour to brown. She then gave a little nod, took the handle of the large paddle, and shoved the loaves into the oven. Her lips continued to move silently. He wondered if she was counting, or praying. . .or what. She cleaned up her mess on the counter and returned the bowl to the cabinet.

A delicious fruity scent soon filled the kitchen. Joseph's mouth watered. He had been so busy he hadn't stopped for dinner that afternoon. The heavenly scent grew stronger, and Joseph's stomach rumbled. About twenty minutes later, Ruth lifted the paddle and quickly removed the hot, crusty loaves of bread. The dried fruit peeked through the cooked dough.

He opened the cabinet and removed the butter crock. They waited for the bread to cool slightly before Joseph sliced open one of the loaves. Steam exploded from the bread, releasing more of the delicious scent. He slathered butter on two thick slices of bread and carried the extra slice to Mother.

She eyed the delicious-smelling bread. Her eyes sparked with curiosity. She accepted the bread and took a hearty bite.

His stomach rumbled again as he bit into the bread. Heaven help him. This bread tasted amazing. The combination of fruit, nuts, and cinnamon exploded in his mouth. He closed his eyes. Melted butter dribbled down his chin. He gobbled another bite. He wiped the stray butter away with his hand. There was something else in this bread too. . . some other spices. . .what were they?

Mother gave him a critical glance. "Joseph, don't forget your manners. You're eating like a street beggar."

He stopped eating. Bristling at Mother's caustic tone, he scowled at his outspoken parent. She'd eaten her entire slice of bread. He'd never seen her consume such a large slice of bread so quickly. It figured she berated him for eating too fast when she'd done the same thing.

Well, he didn't need to ask Mother if she wanted to hire Ruth. He already knew how she felt by the way she eyed Ruth's tasty bread sitting on the counter. Mother wanted another slice but was too proud to say so. He was taking matters into his own hands. He focused on Ruth, coaxing her into the corner. Mother hovered, but he didn't care. He needed to get Ruth to agree to work for them before another bakery snatched her up.

Her dark brown eyes appeared pensive and serious, and her pretty mouth drooped. Concern about being hired shone on her face. Well, she could stop worrying. Before he offered her the job, he had to ask her one question. "What did you put into the bread?"

She blinked, focusing on him. "I can't tell you."

He jerked back. "Why not?"

"That's my secret bread. If you want more of my bread, then you gots to hire me."

Well, he already knew some of the ingredients. . .so that was a start. But what if he wanted to make the bread? What if Ruth were sick or delayed from coming to the bakery? How would he manage to make this bread if she wouldn't tell him what was in it? Well, he'd figure all of that out later. For now, he just needed to make sure they hired Ruth. He offered his hand. "Ruth, would you like to work in our bakery?" He mentioned the wages they'd offer. Her pretty brown eyes widened. He wasn't sure if she was pleased or if she was upset because she wanted more money.

Her face split into a huge grin as she shook his hand. "Yes, I accept."

Mother narrowed her eyes. She approached them and pulled Joseph away from Ruth. "I need to talk to you."

He sighed and followed his mother into their office. He eyed the fountain pen, inkwell, and parchment papers that littered the desk. He wished Mother would focus solely on her bookkeeping duties and leave the hiring up to him. "Joseph, you can't hire that girl without my permission."

"I just did." It was high time he stood up to Mother.

"Well, you're paying her too much money." One reason their family had accumulated so much wealth was because Mother watched every penny they spent. She did the bookkeeping with a keen eye, always looking for ways to save money. "That girl is poor as they come. I can tell by the kind of clothes she's wearing. She's desperate for a job, and you could've offered her a much lower wage. She probably would've accepted it."

He shook his head. He didn't agree, not one bit. "Mother, Ruth is worth every cent I offered." He wasn't going to argue with his mother about this. Sometimes, talking to her just made him so tired. He often wondered if she was so miserable she just wanted to argue for no reason. "I'm not a fool, Mother. You know just as much as I do that our customers will be lining up to purchase Ruth's bread."

"Well, let me tell you something, Joseph. That girl is here to bake and nothing else." She glared at him, folding her thin arms over her chest. "I saw you looking at her. If you even think about courting her, then you are a fool, the biggest fool I've ever seen in my entire life."

Joseph turned on his heel and stormed toward the door, knocking his knee against the desk. Pain shot through his joint as parchment papers scattered onto the floor. He had to get out of there. No way could he stay in Mother's presence for another minute. He limped toward the front of the bakery.

"Joseph, get back in here and pick up these papers."

The scent of Ruth's delicious bread lingered in the hot air. He pushed the door open and breathed deeply, limping outside and into the sun.

"Joseph!" his mother yelled from the door, but he'd already limped halfway down the street. No way would she follow him. She wouldn't risk losing income by leaving the bakery unattended.

He finally dropped onto a bench beneath a huge oak tree. Bright sunlight sliced through the branches as the leaves danced in the wind. A man in a black suit rushed by, checking his pocket watch. Joseph closed his eyes and tilted his face toward the sky. He rubbed his aching knee and tried to calm down. He figured if he'd stayed around his mother another minute, he might have said something he'd later regret.

Chapter 2

Ruth smiled as she scurried down Market Street. The strong scent of animals filled the air as horse-drawn wagons maneuvered down the road. She stopped, leaned against a tree, and closed her eyes. *Jesus, thank You so much! I's blessed to find this job!* She opened her eyes and continued down the street at a slower pace. Folks in business suits rushed by, and a little boy stood at the corner, hawking candles.

Joy bubbled through her like boiling water; she just couldn't resist. She turned at the next corner and ran the last block toward the rooming house where she stayed. Miss Tilley, one of the boarders, unexpectedly came around the corner, and she ran right into her.

Miss Tilley's spectacles jerked to an angle, and she dropped her dinner pail and school satchel.

"Oh, I's so sorry." She rushed to help the schoolteacher gather her belongings.

"My goodness, Ruth, you were running like somebody was chasing you."

"I's sorry, Miss Tilley." She really wanted to be sure the schoolmarm was okay. "Anything I can do to help?" She handed the woman's dinner pail and satchel to her.

"Ruth, I'm fine. I just want to make sure you're okay."

"I's fine, delighted, actually."

"Well, glad to hear that. Why don't you come in and tell me why you're so happy? In the few days you've been here, I've never seen you look so delighted."

"I's be glad to tell you about it."

Miss Tilley opened the door to the rooming house, and Ruth followed her inside. The schoolmarm, the daughter of the elderly rooming house owner, looked at least ten years older than Ruth's eighteen years. She followed the older woman into the sitting room.

The sun beamed through the open drapes, highlighting the large pine table and chairs. A bookshelf nestled in the corner filled with several titles. Ruth ran her fingers over the spines. A longing to be able to read the words printed on the books' pages gushed through her. She pushed the longing aside as Miss Tilley went into the adjoining kitchen. She reappeared with a plate of sugar cookies. She placed them on the table and soon returned with two tin cups of water. "We can have ourselves a little snack. I'd told Ma I'd been craving some sugar cookies, so I'm glad to see that she baked some."

"I's can bake some good cookies. I don't mind doing that for you, but I's going to be busy working at the bakery." They settled into their chairs as she smiled and bit into a cookie. She enjoyed the delicious sweetness and took a sip of water, and then she told her friend about getting the job at Adams Bakery. "Miss Tilley, I's so glad to get this job. That's why I was running down the street. Not only is I glad, but I'm also worried."

Miss Tilley nodded, her wise, kind eyes focused on Ruth. "You mentioned you couldn't read the labels on the spices, so you sniffed them to see what they were?"

"Yes'm. Elizabeth. . .I mean, Mrs. Adams, didn't seem to like the way I talked. If she finds out I can't read, she might fire me."

Miss Tilley reached across the table and took her hand. "Honey, I doubt she'll fire you. From what you just told me, Joseph gobbled that bread as if it was the best bread he's ever tasted. I imagine customers will be flocking to Adams Bakery to buy your bread." She squeezed Ruth's hand. "That woman is as stingy as a miser. She watches her pennies, that's for sure. As soon as those profits start rolling in from your bread, there's no way she'll fire you."

"Really?" She wasn't so sure if money would be enough of an incentive for Elizabeth to keep her on staff.

"I can almost guarantee it. But if you want my advice, if I were you, I wouldn't tell her you're an illiterate former slave. If she ever asks you the question directly, then you can tell her, but otherwise, I'd keep that information to myself."

Ruth frowned. "Why? I's not scared of her." She sat up straighter in her chair. "I's not ashamed of being a former slave." She certainly didn't have control over where she was born and raised, so it was wrong of Mrs. Adams to hold her past against her.

"I've known both Elizabeth and Joseph for years. If she doesn't like someone, she'll make them miserable. For that matter, even people she does like she makes miserable. That woman has been sad and upset for a while, and her negative attitude has gotten worse since her husband passed."

"Her husband died? That's so sad." Ruth mentally sighed, able to relate to Mrs. Adams's pain. The woman was probably sad and needed some cheering up. Ruth needed to try to figure out what to do to make Elizabeth feel better.

"Yes, her husband's recent death is sad." The schoolteacher released Ruth's hand and gestured toward the bookcase. "I've noticed you looking at those books lately. I think it might help you working in the bakery if you learned to read and write. I could even teach you proper English, if you wish."

Ruth felt as if the schoolmarm had read her mind. On her journey home from the bakery, she'd wondered if learning to read, write, and speak properly would help with her transition to this new area.

After she'd been granted her freedom in her master's will, she'd been able to relocate from Maryland to Philadelphia. Arrangements had been made for her to have an abolitionist escort to her new home. In Philadelphia she'd become acquainted with Cyrus Brown, the abolitionist pastor at the local church. She'd only been there for a few days, and during that time, she'd found herself amazed and homesick at the same time. The city of Philadelphia proved far different from the huge Maryland farm where she'd lived her entire life. Seeing the tall brick buildings and crowds of people each day was still jarring. It would take her a while to get used to her new environment.

It was also an amazing shock to her system to see blacks free, a few owning businesses, often walking down the streets unescorted. She certainly wasn't used to encountering a family like the Adamses, a black family with wealth. Just knowing a Negro could have money made her feel good inside, made her feel hopeful. Maybe there would come a time when *all* blacks were free. What a wonder that would be. *Lord, please help those still enslaved.*

Miss Tilley patted her arm. "Ruth? Are you all right? I asked if you'd like to learn to read, but it seemed you were daydreaming."

"I's sorry. Just thinking about my trip from Maryland." She dipped her head. "Yes'm. I'd like to learn to read."

She nodded. "Good decision. Learning to read will open your world up to so many things." She paused and took a sip of water. "I was also thinking you could help with the abolitionist movement. Both myself and my ma have been active for a while. Since you're a former slave, you might be interested in helping slaves to escape to freedom. The church I attend is a stop on the Underground Railroad. There's an abolitionist meeting there in a couple of days. After you return from the bakery, maybe we can have our first lesson and then go to the meeting."

"Me? Helping with the Underground Railroad?" She honestly couldn't imagine how she could help. What skills could she bring to the cause? All she could do was bake bread and cook an appetizing meal.

"Ruth, I can tell you're hesitant. But being a former slave yourself, I'm sure you realize how important it is for people to escape to freedom. Don't be scared. We pray before all of our meetings, and we feel led to do this."

Freedom! The feeling was so new to her that she was just getting used to it. The taste of freedom was so new and fresh, almost like tasting the sweetest nectar for the first time. She still wasn't used to not answering to her master. Her life had proved a whirlwind of change, and she didn't want to risk making wrong decisions. Feelings of inadequacy churned through her like sour butter. She'd been thinking of assisting with the Underground Railroad ever since she'd gained her freedom.

"But Miss Tilley, I's don't know what I can do to help. You's know I can't read. Can't write either."

"Harriet Tubman can't read or write. She's been wanted for years. She's the biggest advocate for the Underground Railroad. You don't need to be educated to help others." She patted her hand, stood, and gathered her dinner pail and satchel. "I've got to go and prepare my lessons for tomorrow. Just think about what I've said."

After they'd finished visiting, Ruth made her way outside to the small garden. Miss Tilley had shown her the herb garden, and she had volunteered to keep it thriving. The May sunshine enveloped the thriving plants with warmth.

She'd also planted some seeds that she'd brought up with her from Maryland. It'd probably be a week before they sprouted. She took a filled watering can and liberally sprinkled her seedlings and the other plants with water. She sniffed the aroma of rosemary, thyme, oregano, and other herbs. She used combinations of these herbs to give her bread a unique, distinctive taste.

Small paper sacks lined the edge of the garden. When she'd journeyed to Philadelphia, she'd brought bunches of her dried herbs with her. She opened a sack that held one of her unique combinations. She sniffed. Since she couldn't read, it wasn't possible to label the packs of herbs. Instead she deduced the contents by sniffing. This sack contained her unique herb combination, which paired nicely with the cinnamon and raisins she'd used in the bread this morning. She'd hid the herbs in her satchel and was glad Joseph had done as she'd commanded and not watched her.

In due time, Joseph and his mother would figure out she snuck her own herbs in the bread. However, if she was discreet about it, she might hide her secret for a long while. She hoped to keep her secret as long as possible. After watering the plants, she went up to her room, looked out the window, and studied the street. A few couples walked together, holding hands, though the supper hour was drawing near. She studied the redbrick buildings surrounding her, still astounded that Philadelphia was now her home.

The scent of vegetables and meat drifted from the kitchen downstairs. Miss Tilley's mother had started supper. As she stared at a horse-drawn buggy clomping down the street, she again recalled her home.

She missed Maryland. No, she didn't miss not getting paid for her job, but she missed the other slaves, her friends, and the bit of camaraderie they'd shared. When she'd left, her departure had been bittersweet. Yes, memories filled her mind, some good and a lot bad. She squeezed her eyes shut, recalling how she'd lost the only man she'd ever truly loved. The death of the man she'd loved on an adjoining plantation still shook her to the core. She squeezed her hands into fists, her eyes still closed.

The pain from slavery ran deep, and she had to do what she could so that others didn't suffer too. Granted, her suffering was probably minor compared to what others had experienced, and were still experiencing, in their days of slavery. She leaned against the wall and wiped away the unwelcome tears from her eyes. She again recalled the abolitionist meeting to which Miss Tilley had invited her. Yes, she'd be going to that meeting. She'd do all she could to help abolish slavery.

Chapter 3

Joseph shoved the last bite of beef into his mouth and washed it down with water.

"Joseph, stop eating so fast."

He needed to get to the abolitionist meeting tonight. No way was he telling Mother about that. He didn't want to be late. He would've skipped supper so he could get to the meeting on time, but he figured it would have aroused Mother's suspicions. They were having supper late that evening for a good reason.

Mother had gone over the accounting ledgers for the last couple of days. Since they'd hired Ruth, their profits had increased by 25 percent. Just seeing the increase of income in two days' time had somewhat pacified Mother about hiring her. She still barked at Ruth with a stark tone, but he figured in time, Mother would learn to treat her with the respect that she deserved. He certainly hoped so.

"I've got something to do tonight."

"What's that?" She narrowed her eyes and gave him a shrewd look. "Joseph, you better not be hiding anything from me."

"Mother, I'm a twenty-five-year-old man. Stop treating me like a child. I don't have to tell you everything I do."

She frowned and pushed her plate away. At least she'd finished half her supper, which was a blessing. Her appetite seemed to have returned since they'd gotten extra money into their coffers. "Are you going to call on Francine tonight?"

"No." The beautiful Francine was an upper-class black woman whom he'd escorted to one formal event. The woman proved whiny and clingy. One evening alone with her was enough for him to determine they did not belong together.

"Then where are you going?"

It was none of her business. He pushed his chair back, stood up, and kissed her cheek. "I'll see you later, Mother." Hopefully she'd be in bed by the time he returned. The last thing he needed was to have her subject him to an inquisition when he came home.

Ruth's hard shoes pounded on the cobbled street as she rushed to the abolitionist meeting.

The last couple of days working in the bakery had been busy. She flexed her aching fingers. She'd never kneaded so much bread each day. When she'd been a slave on the big farm, she'd cooked, cleaned, and baked a few loaves of bread daily.

Working in a bakery was much different than kneading bread for farmers and workers.

It'd been a blessing that she'd been able to keep up with the orders. People lined up down the street to purchase her herbal, cinnamon, dried-fruit bread. Joseph's hazel eyes had been laced with kindness when he'd seen her rushing to keep up with the orders. She'd been so tired, and he'd kindly offered to help bake the bread, but she didn't want him to know her secret recipe.

A young man rushed by so quickly, he bumped right into her. She blinked, and her steps faltered as the scent of male sweat—and corn—filled her nose. *Thomas.* But this man smelled just like her deceased beau. "So sorry, miss." He bowed his head, and her heart skipped; his cinnamon-colored skin, tall, lanky frame, and deep voice reminded her so much of her beloved. He raised his head. His almond-colored eyes sparkled with warmth. She released the breath she'd been holding. Of course, it wasn't Thomas. The man gave her another smile and rushed away.

Salty wetness slid down her cheeks. She swiped the tears away. Thomas had been dead for over a year, yet that was the third time since his passing she'd imagined seeing him. The first two times had occurred while she was still living on the Maryland farm as a slave. How foolish could she be? Thomas had died, he'd been buried, and that was that. Slavery, that's what had killed Thomas. If he had not been a slave, she figured he'd still be alive.

The conditions of Thomas's death still haunted her. He'd lived on an adjoining farm and had taken ill. His master didn't send for the doctor, thinking he could treat Thomas himself. They concluded Thomas had contracted cholera. If the doctor had been summoned immediately, he might have lived. His death had hit her hard. She'd continued working in the kitchen as if in a trance. She couldn't eat, couldn't sleep. She'd been like a walking phantom, unable to fathom life without her beau. They'd discussed getting married, jumping the broom. She was about to approach her master about her intended plans just before Thomas died.

She continued to wipe her tears as she spotted the small, redbrick building of the church, where flocks of people entered. Ruth stopped, took a few steps back. She swallowed and took a deep breath, recalling the last time she'd been in a crowd so large. A slave who'd tried to escape an adjoining farm had been beaten. She'd witnessed the poor man being beaten so hard. He'd died a few days later.

"Ruth, are you all right?"

Her heart skipped when Joseph touched her shoulder and pressed a white handkerchief into her hand. She blinked and suddenly realized she'd been crying. She sniffed. Her nose was running too. She mashed her lips down, squeezed the handkerchief, and closed her eyes. She'd done so poorly. She only cried when she was alone. If she was careful, she could avoid tears in public. Well, the few times she'd spotted someone who resembled Thomas she'd lost control, unable to keep her emotions hidden until she was alone.

Now, Joseph had seen her cry. She certainly hoped he didn't think she'd be a weak, sniveling woman while working in the bakery. She considered herself a strong woman, and she didn't want Joseph to think otherwise. She took a deep breath and stood up taller. She needed to pull herself together. She had to focus on helping with the Underground Railroad and worry about her grief later.

"I's okay." She wiped her wet eyes and blew her nose. She figured she could clean Joseph's handkerchief and return it to him later. She tucked it into her battered reticule and again focused on the crowd of people entering the church.

"Why are you crying?"

"Slavery. Thinking about it makes me sad." She didn't want to tell him about the beating she'd witnessed, or about Thomas.

"So you're here for the abolitionist meeting?"

She nodded. "Miss Tilley was supposed to come with me, but she's sick." Before the meeting, Miss Tilley was supposed to start teaching her the alphabet so she could learn to read. Before she'd left for the meeting, she'd stopped by her room and had seen the metal sick bucket beside her bed. Miss Tilley said she had a stomachache and couldn't attend the meeting. Her ma had been tending to her. Ruth had some dried mint leaves and had brewed them into a tea and given it to Miss Tilley's ma to give her. "Might help with her sick stomach," she'd advised.

She'd been disappointed she'd have to attend the meeting alone. She didn't realize Joseph was a part of the abolitionist cause. Strange that Miss Tilley had not mentioned this when she'd invited her to the meeting a couple of days ago. Her heart skipped as Joseph touched the small of her back and led her inside the church. Lanterns were lit and crowds of folks flocked to the hard wooden pews.

They took the last two spots on the back pew. She spotted some whites amidst the mostly Negro crowd.

Joseph touched her hand and gestured toward the group of whites. "Those are Quakers." He mentioned their names. "They've been working with the abolitionists for a long time, trying to stop slavery."

She nodded. This was the first time she'd ever seen whites and Negroes openly meeting together. She surveyed the church, studied the rough wooden cross in the front of the room. *Jesus, I really needs You right now. Please take my sadness away.* Seeing Joseph had been a somewhat welcome reprieve to her sadness. She discreetly studied him while they waited for the meeting to begin. She'd been relieved when he didn't ask her more questions as to why she'd been crying.

Joseph was probably one of the handsomest men she'd ever seen, besides Thomas. His skin was cinnamon-colored. His complexion reminded her of a loaf of lightly browned bread. He was tall, muscular, and hardworking. His curly hair was light, too, like the color of dust. The color of his eyes was captivating. His eyes weren't dark brown, like hers; they were light, like the skins of the hazelnuts she'd once chopped for a pie.

Over the last few days, she'd caught him staring at her. For some weird reason, she felt he could see deep into her soul. When they'd taken their dinner break, his mother had hovered, as if afraid to leave them alone to eat. She'd sensed he'd wanted to talk to her, ask her questions about herself. When his mother had left to deposit money in the bank, a couple of skinny street beggars had shown up. Joseph knew them by name and had given them a loaf of bread and some milk.

She figured the beggars knew when his mother wasn't around, they could come seeking food. Joseph had been so kind, asking them questions about their lives, and he'd encouraged them to come to church. The beggars had left by the time his mother returned. She'd been touched by his kindness. She'd been thinking about his interaction with the vagrants all day. She might as well ask him about it. "It was mighty kind of you to help the street beggars today."

He raised his thick eyebrows. "Those two have been coming around for a few years. I've been praying for them. I think you know Mother doesn't realize that I feed street beggars."

She nodded. "Would she be upset about a loaf of bread and some milk?" It'd be upsetting to know Joseph's mother would withhold food from someone for a few pennies of profit.

Surprisingly, Joseph chuckled. "Hard to say. She might not say anything initially, but since I do it every week, yes, I could see her objecting." He touched her hand, and her skin warmed. "I hope working with Mother doesn't bother you very much. She's always been controlling, but she's gotten much worse since Father died."

Ruth nodded. "I's sorry to hear that. Miss Tilley told me your pa passed. Anything I can do to make your ma feel better?"

His mouth dropped open, and he appeared speechless. He then focused on her again. "Ruth, that is so nice of you to ask. I honestly don't know what could help Mother feel better except some prayers."

She nodded. That sounded like a good idea. She almost felt ashamed she'd not thought of praying on her own. "All right. I'll be praying for your ma and for you too. I figure it's hard on both of you, since your pa passed."

"Thank you." He tilted his head, studying her for a few seconds. "What about you, Ruth? Are your parents still alive?"

Since she never knew her parents, she didn't know how to answer.

"Everyone, time to start the meeting." Cyrus Brown rescued her from responding to Joseph's question. She figured he'd ask her about it again someday. But she'd rather wait until she'd been working at the bakery for a while before she shared something so personal with him.

Cyrus leaned on his cane as he made his way to the podium. She'd heard he was close to eighty years old. He'd even revealed his health was starting to decline.

Cyrus's kind eyes stared at the audience. "The Lord wants us to do all we can to abolish slavery. We've already helped so many slaves to escape, but we must help more." He bowed his head, and Ruth lowered hers and closed her eyes. She focused on Cyrus's words. "Dear Lord Jesus, please be with us tonight as we try our best to abolish slavery. Please let Your Holy Spirit be with us during this meeting." He paused for so long that Ruth peeked at the front of the room and spotted Cyrus wiping his eyes. She pressed her hands together and closed her eyes again. "Please be with all of the slaves who are on the run right now, Lord. Help them to find freedom. Amen."

"Amen," Ruth whispered.

Cyrus opened his mouth and his deep voice boomed throughout the church. The words of "Amazing Grace" rippled through the church as others joined in with the song. Ruth smiled, camaraderie and familiarity sweeping through her being. She sang along with the crowd, glad to hear her voice blended in well with the others. Joseph's strong voice also filled the room, and she stole another peek at him. They shared a smile when the song ended.

He touched her hand and liquid warmth spread through her. "Amazing Grace" was her favorite Christian song. Her master had allowed the slaves one hour of worship every Sunday. During that time, they sang hymns to the Lord. A few times, a traveling preacher had spoken to them.

Cyrus cleared his throat. "If it's the Lord's will, we're expecting some slaves to come through within the next two weeks."

Murmurs filled the room. Cyrus waited until the people had quieted before he continued to speak. "For those of you who are new to the movement, we have to provide meals, a bath, clothes, and shelter to the runaways." Ruth focused on Pastor Cyrus's words as he spoke about the movement, giving a summary of all the duties that were involved to keep the movement going. "We also need volunteers to provide encouragement, and we need to be sure we have plenty of supplies. . ." Ruth kept eyeing Joseph. He focused on Cyrus, leaning forward. He appeared spellbound by Cyrus's speech, and she realized Joseph seemed happier here, in church, then he'd ever appeared at the bakery.

She sniffed. Joseph smelled nice, like freshly baked bread and spices. The delicious scents of the bakery clung to him, making him that much more appealing.

"I also want to announce that I'll be stepping down as pastor. I'm getting old, and I don't know how much longer I'll be able to pastor this church."

Murmurs again rustled throughout the church. Cyrus closed the meeting with a word of prayer. Joseph then looked directly at her. "Ruth, would you excuse me for a minute?"

When Cyrus dismissed the meeting, Joseph raced toward the podium.

Chapter 4

Joseph approached Cyrus. His brown, bald head shone under the light from the lanterns. Several people came toward Cyrus, but Joseph pulled the pastor aside. What he had to say could not wait. "Reverend Brown, I'd like to be considered as a pastor for this church." As soon as Cyrus had made his announcement, excitement slipped through Joseph like a raging fire. Since he'd started coming to this new church, the sermons had moved him. He'd taken to reading the scriptures more often, and he'd also started memorizing passages.

He'd also been talking about scripture to the street beggars he fed each week. He often worried about the vagrants and had asked for Cyrus's advice when ministering to the homeless men.

"Joseph, I'm not surprised. I was hoping you'd say something."

His conversations with Cyrus about scripture, ministering, and the abolitionist movement were like nourishment to his parched soul. He craved being in this church the way a thirsty man craved water. He suddenly wondered if Cyrus had been secretly guiding him toward pastoring the church. But was he qualified? After all, he'd never even given a sermon.

Cyrus clapped him on the shoulder. "Prepare a sermon for the church service in two weeks. I'll let the deacons know you are interested. We may need you to preach for a few weeks before they decide to allow you to be pastor." He cleared his throat. "I'll still be around to guide you if you're chosen as pastor."

Joseph opened his mouth, about to ask another question, but Cyrus shook his head. "Joseph, I have to get home. It's past my early bedtime and my knees hurt. We can talk about this some more later, but for now, that's what you need to do."

Joseph nodded as Cyrus leaned on his cane and made his way through the crowd. Several tried to stop him to speak, but he waved them away, apparently exhausted. Eager to share his news, he glanced at the pews and found Ruth in the back, patiently waiting. Ruth was easily the kindest, most patient woman he'd ever met. Any woman who could work with Mother and not lose her temper deserved a reward.

He quickly made his way over to her. "Thank you for waiting. Can I escort you home?"

He was rewarded by her bright smile. She quickly nodded. They exited the church and started down the cobblestone street. A horse-drawn carriage passed by as street lanterns spilled light into the semidark night. He eyed Ruth as they strolled down the street. Her bonnet was neatly tied, covering her dark curls. He ached to remove it and see her hair.

She'd kept her head covered with her bonnet while working in the bakery. They'd been so busy he'd not had a moment alone with her. Longing to see her outside of the confines of the bakery, without Mother's hovering, resonated within him. They could always use help with the movement, and he figured she might be willing to help him tomorrow.

"Ruth, tomorrow I have to go to the printers to pick up the pamphlets to distribute with some of the volunteers. Would you like to come with me? We could meet up with the rest of the volunteers and hand out the literature to people on the street, asking for their support for the movement."

Her pretty brow furrowed, as if she were worried. She chewed on her lower lip. "I be glad to do that, Joseph."

"Wonderful. We can go after I close the bakery tomorrow. Mother will be leaving right before closing because she has an errand to run. So she won't bother us."

"Your ma don't know about your involvement in the Underground Railroad?"

He swallowed and shook his head. Ruth was a nice, honest woman, and he sensed he could trust her. "No, she doesn't." He sighed. "If she knew, she'd be extremely upset."

Ruth stopped walking and looked directly into his eyes. Her brown eyes sparkled beneath the lit lanterns. She clutched her reticule as if she were nervous. "Joseph, you should tell your ma about your involvement. Don't be scared of her. Besides, won't she eventually find out if you're passing out literature on the street?"

Not only was Ruth beautiful and honest, she was courageous. He figured she wouldn't keep something like this from Mother if she were in his position. "Philadelphia is a big city. I could probably do this for a long time before she found out."

"Why wait? Tell her now. Won't she be even angrier if she finds out on her own?"

Ruth had a point, but he didn't want to tell Mother about his involvement yet. The time just wasn't right. He didn't want to hear her objections while he worked in the bakery every day. She already complained enough as it was. They continued walking, and he squeezed his hand into a fist. He ached to hold Ruth's hand, but he didn't know if it was a good idea. Sure, he thought about Ruth every night before going to bed, and he loved seeing her in the bakery. But he figured it was too soon to let her know of his attraction to her.

"Joseph, I thinks you making a big mistake, not telling your ma about your abolitionist involvement."

He didn't want to talk about Mother anymore. Just talking about his mother was ruining a perfect spring evening. It was time to change the topic. "So, Ruth, where did you learn to bake bread?"

Her pretty eyes widened for a second, and she hesitated. It almost appeared as if she didn't want to share this information with him. "I worked in the kitchen on a big farm for a long time. The owner died. I's then decided to work in a bakery instead."

He paused, noticing the tightness in her cheeks and her hands shaking slightly. She seemed suddenly nervous. He didn't want to scare her off with too many questions. He figured she'd tell him more about herself as they got to know each other better. They approached the rooming house. They slowly walked up the steps. "When you see Miss Tilley, tell her I hope she feels better."

She nodded. "I'll do that."

Thoughts of kissing her pretty lips rushed through his mind. He took a step back. He couldn't risk kissing her. He didn't know if it was the right thing to do, and he honestly didn't know if she'd welcome his attention. Instead, he touched her cheek. "Good night, Ruth."

"Good night, Joseph."

He stayed on the steps until she unlocked the door and entered the house.

Ruth removed her apron and eyed Joseph as he moved the ashes with a wooden stick, putting out the fire in the beehive-shaped oven. Gray smoke curled up from the baking hole as the flames died. She wiped the sweat from her brow. It'd been a long workday, and they'd sold many loaves of bread, just as they'd done the previous days. Her bread continued to be popular at the bakery, and she'd overheard customers asking Joseph questions about her.

When he'd walked her home the previous evening, her heart had skipped. When he dropped her off at the door, she wondered if he'd kiss her.

She was glad he hadn't. When she'd gone to bed last night, she'd dreamed about Thomas. Although she enjoyed the time she'd spent with Joseph, she doubted she'd ever get married. Thomas's death still haunted her. She still thought about the conversation she'd had with Miss Tilley. She found that her desire to help with the movement had grown in just a few days' time.

She wanted to help as many people as she could to find freedom. She also wanted to tell them about Jesus. She felt that was her calling in life. She honestly didn't think she was strong enough to fall in love again. She sensed just helping others in the movement was what she wanted to focus on. Being courted by a man was not something she wanted to do right now.

She sensed Joseph wanted to ask her questions about her background to find out more about her.

Once, his ma had caught him staring at her, and he'd looked away as if he were embarrassed. During the day Elizabeth hovered, her eyes narrowed like a hawk. Whenever Joseph was about to speak to her, Elizabeth would appear, almost as if she suspected Joseph's interest in Ruth. Well, the woman should learn to calm down and not spy on her son. Even though Joseph seemed as if he were interested in getting to know her better, she knew once he found out she was an illiterate former slave, he'd avoid her like the plague.

His mother had such a strong hold on him that Ruth wondered about them. She treated Joseph as if he were a child instead of a grown man—a handsome grown man with light brown skin and amazing eyes. She'd overheard some of the young, female patrons flirting with him when they came into the bakery. He'd always rebuffed their advances.

Another thing about Joseph that proved troubling. Except for yesterday evening, she never saw him smile. He was always frowning, and he bristled whenever his mother came around, as if he resented her presence. He baked bread almost mechanically, as if he had no choice.

He removed his apron and came toward her. "Are you ready, Ruth?"

She nodded. His ma had left about thirty minutes earlier, and it was time to go to the printers to fetch the literature. She was still eager to learn to read. It was kind of sad she was passing out literature and she didn't even know what it said. Miss Tilley promised they could start their lessons right before bed that evening. She squeezed her hands together, eagerly wanting to learn to read and possibly write. Imagine that, writing her own name!

Joseph held the door open and they stepped outside onto the sidewalk. The hot sun beat down on them as they started walking along the cobblestone street. Joseph reached for her hand.

She shook her head and took a few steps away from him. She wanted him to hold her hand, but didn't think it was a good idea to allow herself to become smitten with Joseph, not until he knew all of her secrets. His attention would never grow into a fruitful relationship, so it was probably best if she didn't encourage his attention.

"You don't want me to hold your hand?" The disappointment in his voice made her pause.

"We don't know each other very well, and. . ."

He shook his head. "We can discuss this later, Ruth. I'm sorry if I offended you." He took quick steps, and as sweat poured down Ruth's brow, she forced herself to quicken her pace to keep up with him. She struggled to walk so fast, and her foot caught on a loose brick and she stumbled. She cried out, and Joseph turned around and caught her. "Ruth, I'm so sorry."

His deep voice washed over her like cool water on a hot day. His strong arms wrapped around her like a glove, and he smelled nice, like freshly baked bread. She looked into his hazel eyes and couldn't think of what to say. Her tongue seemed glued to the roof of her mouth. She took a deep breath—she couldn't let Joseph make her feel so unsettled. She cleared her throat and finally found her voice as she stood upright. "You sure do walk fast. You wasn't walking this fast last night."

"I want to get to the printers before they close, and I'm eager to start handing out the literature. I didn't remember you probably would not be able to keep up with me." He shook his head for a few seconds. "Accept my apologies, please. I should have been more considerate."

She didn't trust herself to speak. Her attraction to Joseph was as real as the sun shining from the blue sky. She figured her attraction would go away. She'd just been irritable from the heat, and she'd been afraid of falling on the street. Flustered, that was the way she'd been feeling, and Joseph's rescue had made her feel a bit better. "I's okay." He really did seem to feel bad about his mishap.

He slowed his pace, and soon she was strolling beside him. She almost stumbled again, but he quickly touched the small of her back, breaking her fall. "They need to replace some of these cobblestones."

Finally, they walked at a leisurely pace. The late afternoon sun shone on them with warmth. Ruth wiped her brow. "Sure is hot out here."

"Yes, it is hotter than normal today." He continued walking slowly, his feet clomping against the street. She had a lot of questions she wanted to ask him, but she wasn't sure if her curiosity would encourage him to ask more questions about her background.

"Ruth?" His deep, sultry voice interrupted their silent walk.

"Yes?" Looked like he had something he wanted to ask her too.

"You said we don't know each other very well. That's true. We haven't really had time to get to know one another since Mother is always watching us."

That was an understatement. She figured since they were working together every day, it'd make sense to know something about one another. She gulped as they turned a corner. A horse-drawn carriage clomped down the street as folks rushed by. Hopefully, he didn't want to get too personal. She wasn't ready to tell him everything about herself. She figured it might be best to focus on him. "You mind talking about your pa?"

He frowned.

She touched his arm. "I sorry. I understand if you don't wants to talk about him."

He patted her shoulder. "I don't mind telling you about him. I was close to Father. He taught me so many things. I enjoyed working with him, more so than Mother. My father was the most honorable man I've ever known. I miss him."

She squeezed his arm. "Thanks for telling me." She wasn't sure why she wanted to know more about Joseph's relationship with his father. Perhaps she wanted to understand his relationship to his kin because she'd never had contact with many of her blood relatives.

The printers was just down the street. She wanted to ask her question before they arrived. "I have another question for you, Joseph."

He focused on her with his amazing eyes. "Really? What's that?"

"Why you so unhappy at the bakery? You seem happier when you're not there."

"If I had to explain, it would take me all day." He took a deep breath and looked directly into her eyes. "I hate working in the bakery."

Her eyes widened at his blunt statement. "Do your ma know?"

He shook his head, the tortured look returning to his handsome face. "I'm sure she suspects. A mother should know her own child, right?"

She shrugged. She'd never known her own mother, so it was hard for her to comment. "Why do you stay? Can you work someplace else?"

He dropped onto a nearby bench, and she sat beside him. She wanted to be Joseph's friend, and she hoped he'd feel comfortable confiding in her eventually. She honestly did not know what else to say. Just to be able to work and get paid was a new experience for her. She couldn't imagine not liking any job if you were paid.

He took a deep breath. "My family has been free for two generations. This bakery has been in my family for a long time. It's just expected that I work there and make my living, but I'm miserable. Mother's attitude makes it worse."

Ruth couldn't understand. After all, she loved baking bread. She felt at home in the kitchen and couldn't imagine doing anything else for a living. "Well, what would you do if you's could choose?"

"I have plans to do something else, Lord willing." He paused and peered directly into her eyes. "Ruth, I didn't get a chance to tell you last night. You know I went to talk to Cyrus after he announced his retirement?"

She nodded.

"I want to be considered for the position."

"You's leaving the bakery?" She couldn't keep the shocked tone out of her voice. If his ma found out, she'd have a huge fit. Ruth imagined his ma would make her life even more miserable if Joseph were not around. If Joseph became pastor of the church, Ruth figured she might have to find another bakery to hire her. She sure didn't want to endure Mrs. Adams's sour treatment if she could find the same wages elsewhere.

But if Joseph was called to be a pastor, who was she to judge? She recalled his kindness toward the beggars. She sensed he enjoyed ministering to others, so she needed to have faith things would work themselves out if he was appointed pastor.

"If I get the position, then yes, I'd be leaving. Mother will be disappointed."

She sure would be. Ruth didn't want to be anywhere near the bakery when Joseph told his ma his news. She didn't want him to get the wrong idea about her reaction. "I's happy for you, Joseph. I hope you gets appointed."

He smiled; his hazel eyes sparkled with warmth. "Thank you, Ruth. That means a lot to me."

He jerked his thumb toward the printers down the street. "We need to pick up the literature before they close."

She scampered to keep up with him as he rushed to the printers.

Ruth offered the literature to a well-dressed man. "Help stop slavery." She said a silent prayer of thanks when he accepted the paper.

"Help stop slavery." Joseph handed the literature to another passerby. The woman balled it up into a wad and threw it on the street. She glared at them before hurrying by.

Ruth had gotten used to the mixed reactions of the crowd as they'd handed out literature. After they'd gotten their leaflets from the printers, they'd met up with the group of abolitionists she'd met at church the previous night. Standing beside Joseph, hearing his deep voice as he offered the leaflets to the passersby. . .she felt his passion. Pride, that's what she felt. She felt proud to stand here beside him and hand out the literature.

"Joseph!" The high-pitched female voice rocked Ruth's core. She eyed the woman who sauntered toward Joseph. The lady sported an expensive frock and polished, buttoned shoes. Her skin was the color of a lightly browned loaf of bread, toasty. She carried a black umbrella to shield her pretty face from the sun. By far, she was the most beautiful Negro woman Ruth had ever seen. Her entire appearance screamed money, wealth. . . Ruth figured this gal was part of one of the elite black families in the area.

The woman fingered Joseph's lapel, her eyes downcast. "Why have you not called on me?"

Ruth's heart skipped a beat, and she was glad she hadn't allowed Joseph to hold her hand earlier.

"Francine. . ." Frustration and. . .something else tinged Joseph's deep voice.

Try as she might, Ruth just couldn't stop staring at this beautiful Negro woman. Joseph's crestfallen expression also had her enthralled.

Chapter 5

Joseph narrowed his eyes. *Lord, please help me not to lose my temper.* "Francine, what on earth are you doing here?" Her perfume clung to his nostrils like an annoying ant. He took a few steps away from her.

She batted her eyelashes. "I came to see you. Joseph, you have not come to call on me since you took me to the cotillion a month ago. I just wanted to see you."

He'd never in his entire lifetime encountered such a bold and beautiful woman. Francine may have been beautiful, but her beauty was outward. He just couldn't warm up to her. A few weeks before he'd escorted her to the cotillion, she'd spotted him feeding the beggars as she rode by in her carriage. He had not realized she'd noticed his actions until she'd boldly confronted him about it on their way to the ball.

"I can't believe you'd feed *those* people, Joseph. Your mother told me you give to the Philadelphia charities. You don't want those people in your bakery."

At that time, he'd hauntingly realized Francine sounded just like Mother. He didn't even want to ruin his day thinking about the abhorrent time he'd had at the cotillion.

"Joseph?" Her voice rose, just a bit, as she fingered his shirt. "Why aren't you speaking to me?"

He eyed Ruth as she continued to pass out pamphlets. She appeared busy, her bonnet covering her dark curls. She glanced his way for a few moments before continuing her chore. Her pretty mouth appeared pinched. Perhaps she was upset about Francine's unexpected arrival. Hopefully Francine would be on her way so they could return to their duties. "Francine, I've been busy." He showed her the pamphlets in his hand. "I'm in the middle of my abolitionist duties." He took a deep breath. "Listen, don't you want to abolish slavery?"

She narrowed her eyes before boldly offering her parasol. "Hold this for me, please." Another trait of hers that proved bothersome—she commanded him as if he were her personal worker. He swallowed and grasped the handle of her parasol. She then opened her fancy black reticule and removed a folded object. She opened her rose-decorated fan and waved it in front of her face in quick movements. She then accepted her umbrella. "It's hot out here today."

"Perhaps you should go back into your carriage." He was determined to get back to his duties, and having Francine around was not helping with his mission.

She narrowed her eyes. "Does your mother know about your involvement with the abolitionists?" It was no surprise she refused to answer his question about slavery.

He certainly could not lie to Francine, yet Mother's knowledge was none of Francine's concern. He'd tell Mother when he was ready. "I don't want to talk about her now. I'm busy."

She pursed her red-painted lips and again fingered his collar. "Well, the charity ball is coming up..."

He resisted the urge to groan. The charity ball. Mother had been hinting about the event for the past week, openly wondering why he'd not yet asked to escort Francine. Well, one evening of Francine's company was enough to last him a lifetime. No way was he going to ask to be her escort. He couldn't be rude to her, so it would probably be best if she left before he said something he'd regret. He gestured toward her carriage. "I don't want to make you late, Francine. It appears you were on your way to an engagement. I will speak with you another time."

He then turned to the next passerby, his back turned toward Francine. He supposed he should help her up into the carriage, but she'd already fingered his shirt twice and openly flirted with him. He recoiled from the notion of giving her yet another opportunity to flirt. As he handed a pamphlet to the dark-suited gentleman, he caught Ruth's open stare.

Over the next few days, the pretty woman Ruth had spotted on the street haunted her mind.

Francine. That's what Joseph had called her. Since the day they'd handed out the pamphlets, Ruth had spotted Francine twice. She'd brazenly come into the bakery, bothering Joseph as he waited on customers. His mother enjoyed Francine's impromptu visits. The two of them had spent a full half hour in his mother's office. She had even asked Ruth to bring back a pot of hot tea and slices of her cinnamon, fruit bread with butter.

She'd overheard Francine's praises for the bread through the closed door. His mother had laughed, stating they'd hired a new girl. She'd also made it seem as if Joseph's business acumen had made their bakery even more successful.

She'd wanted to step into Mrs. Adams's office and tell Francine that *she* had helped make their business more successful, and *she* was most likely the best bread baker in all of Philadelphia. She gritted her teeth as she overhead their chatter behind the closed door. Joseph's ma still thought of her as nothing more than a hired hand—she didn't seem to want to acknowledge the talents she'd contributed to the bakery.

Well, there was nothing she could do about that. *Lord, help me with my anger.* She was here to do a job, and she continued to be grateful for her employment. She didn't need to think about Mrs. Adams's chatter right now. She had some more bread to bake. As she kneaded dough, she thought about the dream she'd had the previous night.

In her dream, Thomas had been stumbling in the darkness, blind, unable to see her standing right in front of him. She'd screamed, tried to get his attention. Joseph had stood in the distance, studying her with his intense hazel eyes. Francine had screamed at Joseph, but he'd ignored Francine's tirade. She'd awakened from the dream, stunned and confused. She'd been so upset she'd had to drink a cup of lavender tea to calm her nerves. She'd finally managed to fall back to sleep.

She ached to ask Joseph the nature of his relationship with Francine. He was cordial toward Francine. But it was hard to tell if he was smitten with the beautiful young woman. Thoughts about Francine and Joseph twirled through her mind like windblown seeds as she approached the rooming house after work. Miss Tilley occupied one of the kitchen chairs. She nibbled on a cookie while sipping a glass of water.

"What's wrong, Ruth? You look like you're about to cry."

She'd been so emotional since she'd come to Philadelphia. She'd been finding it hard to keep her emotions hidden until she was alone. "Nothing."

Miss Tilley patted the empty chair beside her. "Come on and sit down. We have a few minutes to visit before we start your lesson."

She'd been having a lesson every night since the schoolmarm had recovered from her stomach illness. Ruth had started looking at the newspaper. No, she could not read it, but she knew the first letters to some of the words. Oftentimes, she caught herself listening to customers while they talked. When she heard words, she found herself trying to figure out the first letter of the word. She'd been surprised when Miss Tilley told her that *cinnamon* started with a *c* not an *s*, as Ruth had assumed. She still had a lot to learn, and she was grateful the Lord had placed Miss Tilley in her path to teach her how to read.

She pulled out a chair and selected a cookie. Gingersnap, one of her favorites. She consumed the entire spicy cookie and enjoyed a sip of water. She'd not spoken of her weird feelings about Joseph to anyone. But she needed someone to talk to, and Miss Tilley seemed like she wanted to help. She took another sip of water before gathering her thoughts. "I's. . . I—" She paused. Miss Tilley had been teaching her the proper way to speak. She'd been trying hard to say *I* instead of *I's*. Sometimes she forgot, but she figured with enough patience and tutoring from Miss Tilley, she'd soon read and speak properly. Maybe Mrs. Adams would then feel comfortable enough for her to wait on the customers.

"I. . .am confused."

"Confused? About what?"

She told Miss Tilley about her dream the previous night and about how her heart thudded whenever Joseph was around. She spoke of Francine and about how her interaction with Joseph made her feel uncomfortable. "He is so handsome and strong. Plus, he cares about helping to end slavery."

Miss Tilley smiled and took her hand. "Ruth, there's nothing to be confused about. You're obviously sweet on Joseph. There's nothing wrong with that. He's good-looking, charming, and nice as can be." She cleared her throat. "Are you upset because he's not smitten with you?"

"Miss Tilley, my problem is, I just can't get him off my mind. But I needs to. I'm not supposed to be with anybody."

Miss Tilley frowned and pushed her tin cup aside. "What do you mean?"

"God called me to help people escape from slavery. I's. . . *I* feel the Lord led me here to help people escape through the Underground Railroad."

"Dear, I don't understand why that's a problem. You *are* helping with the abolitionist movement. So is Joseph. I'd imagine that would make him a perfect beau for you; that is, if he shares your feelings."

She shook her head. Miss Tilley just didn't understand. Not at all. "I'm not supposed to be with anybody. I'm spending the rest of my life alone, without a husband or children." She squeezed the older woman's hand. "I'm supposed to help men, women, children escape from slavery. I'm going to spend my life helping other people. Alone. That's what the Lord wants me to do."

"Oh, Ruth." Miss Tilley's kind, thoughtful voice filled the kitchen. Her eyes shone with curiosity, and something else that Ruth couldn't quite put her finger on. "Why do you honestly feel the Lord has called you to be alone your entire life?"

"Well, I's. . . *I* was going to jump the broom back in Maryland to Thomas."

"Thomas?"

"My beau in Maryland."

"What happened?"

Her eyes teared and she wiped the wetness away, unable to hide her pain. "He died, Miss Tilley. He lived on a nearby plantation. He got sick. His master didn't call the doctor soon enough. If he had not been a slave, I think his master would have called the doctor and gotten him the help he needed. *Slavery* killed the only man I ever wanted to marry. He been dead for eighteen months now. I still think about him every day."

"Ruth, I want you to do something for me."

"What?"

"Pray about it. You're still not over Thomas, but that doesn't mean you should remain unmarried for your entire life. Our lives are full of seasons, and maybe you *are* called to be single, but maybe the Lord wants you to be single for now. After you're over Thomas, maybe the Lord will see fit to open your heart to a man's love."

"I just don't know, Miss Tilley."

"Honey, listen to me. Listen to your heart. You like spending time with Joseph. Maybe being with him is part of the process of healing, learning to cope with your pain from losing Thomas."

Ruth continued to think about Miss Tilley's advice while she opened her primer to start her next lesson.

Chapter 6

Psalms, Proverbs, Ecclesiastes. . .Matthew, Mark, Luke, John. So many books of the Bible. Joseph flipped through it, staring at the pages. He leaned back against his chair, eyeing the stacks of parchment papers littering Mother's mahogany desk. Since she was out on an errand, he'd taken liberties and was using her office for the afternoon. Ruth had agreed to come fetch him if any customers came into the bakery. He continued to work on his sermon to present himself as a candidate for pastorship. He wasn't sure which verses he wanted to use.

He was still unclear about his message. He'd been praying to the Lord, seeking His guidance, as he prepared the very first sermon of his entire life. He wrote a few notes down on the paper. He needed some ideas, quickly. Time was running out, and he wanted to be sure he gave a sermon that would please Jesus, as well as the congregation. *Oh Lord, please help me.*

He rubbed his tired eyes. He'd been up late the previous night, reading his Bible and praying. Thankfully Mother had slept soundly and did not know he'd been up half the night. He sighed and patted his full stomach. He'd just consumed his dinner of fried chicken, a hard-boiled egg, two crisp apples, and several slices of Ruth's cinnamon and dried-fruit bread. She'd just slid several loaves into the oven before he'd entered Mother's office. The delicious scent filled the air with decadent sweetness. He'd been watching Ruth, still wondering how she made her wonderful bread. She shooed him out of the kitchen whenever she baked her loaves, and he longed for the day when she trusted him enough to tell him her secret recipe.

Secrets.

Ruth was full of them. He longed to take her into his arms and kiss her sweet, rosebud-shaped mouth. Her dark cocoa skin looked lovely beneath the sun shining through the bakery windows. He sensed a wall between them, a barrier. He'd caught her openly staring at him a few times. He was unclear as to if she was merely curious about him or if she had something else on her mind.

He'd wanted to find out more about her, but she'd been strangely quiet when he asked too many questions. Her responses had been vague, and he was unclear as to if his questions made her uncomfortable or if she truly did not enjoy talking to him. He supposed she may feel uncomfortable because of Francine's visits. The woman proved a bothersome thorn in his side, and he hoped Ruth did not mistakenly think Francine was his sweetheart.

He sniffed again. He could use a few more slices of bread. . . Bread! That was it! He plopped back into the chair. Bread—that would be the subject of his sermon. Spiritual bread. He opened his Bible and flipped through the pages. He scribbled, writing and mumbling to himself. He recalled which scriptures mentioned bread. He dipped his pen into the inkwell then scribbled some more. A loud knock broke his concentration. It couldn't be Mother. She'd never knock. It had to be Ruth. He figured she needed his help with some customers. "Come in."

Ruth opened the door. Her dark eyes settled on him. She looked lovely. Apparently, she'd gotten a new bonnet. Her head covering was bright red, and it contrasted nicely with her dark hair and mahogany skin. "You's. . . *You* said to remind you to stop. . .stop working when the bread was done."

He'd noticed Ruth had been doing that a lot lately, correcting her speech. He figured she'd found someone to teach her proper English. She probably was learning how to speak so she could be even more of an asset to their bakery. After all, if she spoke properly, then Mother would let her wait on the customers.

"Yes, that I did." He stood up. Mother said she'd be gone for an hour. He figured he'd have ample time to put his work away before she caught him working on his sermon. He'd made some good progress during her absence. He pulled out his pocket watch and checked the time. He still had fifteen minutes before Mother returned.

Ruth bobbed her head once and turned away, as if to return to her duties up front.

"Don't leave yet."

She slowly turned back around. "Yes, Joseph?" Her voice, sweet as honey, washed upon him like a river. During the workday, she seldom spoke unless he asked her something directly. She seemed more comfortable talking to him when they were away from the bakery. He certainly understood how intimidating it could be, trying to have a conversation with Mother hovering nearby.

"You've been working here for two weeks. It's payday."

Her pretty dark eyes rounded, and she raised her becoming eyebrows. "Payday?"

Before Mother had gone to bed the previous night, she'd finished reviewing the ledgers for the last two weeks. Their profits had increased so much from Ruth's bread that she grudgingly agreed to let Ruth have a few cents extra per day as a bonus. He was amazed he'd been able to convince his miserly mother to do this. But Ruth deserved it. Folks had been lining up in front of their bakery in the early morning for the last fourteen days to purchase Ruth's bread. Mother had been humming about the increased profits, and he'd had to gently remind her last night that Ruth was the sole person responsible for their increased profits.

If Ruth chose to leave, then their profits would decline.

He doubted Mother wanted that to happen.

"Yes, it's payday." He had not discussed when she'd get paid when they originally hired her. He knew she was staying at Tilley's Rooming House, so he figured she owed for her room and board. He opened the drawer and pulled out a small sack. He quickly counted out her wages and approached her. He pressed the money into her small, flour-stained hands.

Her lips quivered as she counted out the cash. "But Joseph—"

"There's extra in there for your bonus."

Her eyes shimmered. She was going to cry? He'd thought she'd be excited about the extra funds. "Thank you." Clutching the money in her fist, she leaned toward him and pulled him into a hug.

She smelled lovely, like cinnamon and spices. His heart pounded as he returned her hug; her delicate body fit into his arms perfectly. He now realized she cried tears of joy.

"I's. . . I'm going to take the bonus money and give it to the abolitionists. I want to do all I can to stop slavery." She gave him a little nod again and swiped her tears away before rushing back into the bakery.

He blew on his papers and made sure the ink was dry before he folded them into a neat square and shoved them into his pocket. He then made his way back into the bakery and stole a look at Ruth, who placed the freshly baked bread into baskets.

She was a strong, beautiful woman. Prayerfully, if he was patient, she just might agree to court him.

Ruth sighed as Joseph dropped into the empty seat beside her. The oil lamps glowed in the crowded room as Cyrus Brown took the podium. He cleared his throat before speaking. "The runaway slaves should be here in less than a week. We've been making all kinds of preparations. We have the supplies on hand, and we figure we will be hiding them underneath the church for a few days before we help them to the next station." He paused for a few seconds. "We also want to be sure we give the runaways ample provisions to take with them when they go to the next station. We've been making sure we have plenty of dried meat, bread, and potatoes for them to take with them on their journey." He continued to state what they needed to provide.

Her heart swelled. She hoped and prayed the runaways made it here. *Oh Lord, please help the runaways to find freedom. Please let them escape from slavery.* As Cyrus Brown continued to speak about their preparations, she recalled the funds she'd made from working at the bakery. Joseph had paid her a few days ago, and she still found it hard to believe she'd actually earned her own money. When she'd first received the money, she stayed up half the night, thinking about her funds. She found a loose floorboard and placed her money in her hiding place. Her heart swelled as gladness filled it. This was the very first time she'd ever been paid.

Joseph shifted in his seat, making the pew creak beneath his weight. He looked tired. He'd mentioned to her during their dinner break that he'd been up late the previous night working on his sermon. Far as she knew, his mother still didn't know about his involvement in the abolitionist movement or about his wanting to be a pastor. Well, he needed to have a backbone and tell his mother. Sure, she'd be upset, but why keep it a secret?

Thankfully, she had not seen Francine in the bakery over the last couple of days. She still wondered about the bothersome woman. She'd caught Joseph watching her all day. She sensed something was on his mind. Well, one thing that had been on her mind was that hug. She could not believe she'd hugged Joseph when he'd paid her wages. His arms had felt big and strong around her. Being held by him made her feel safe, just for a few moments. His large, muscular build, light brown skin, and hazel eyes. . . She pushed those unwelcome thoughts away. *Lord, I'm sure attracted to Joseph, but, there's nothing I can do about it.*

Thomas still hovered in her mind. His death still haunted her dreams, and she recalled how he kissed her when he'd asked for her to jump the broom. Well, she couldn't focus on that right now. She just needed to be sure she was ready when the runaways came. That was all she was concerned with right now.

"I'd like to close with a word of prayer," Cyrus announced from the podium. She bowed her head, and her heart skipped when Joseph took her hand. Her hand felt warm and protected in Joseph's large palm. As Cyrus prayed over the runaways, she took deep breaths and listened to every word that came out of the pastor's mouth. He ended the prayer, and she and

Joseph joined in with their amens.

She stood up and took a deep breath. Joseph stood up beside her. He focused on her, his hazel eyes serious. "Ruth, can I—"

"Ruth. Joseph." Cyrus ambled over with his walking stick. "I wanted to talk to the two of you." He cleared his throat. "Joseph, since you want to be considered for the pastorship, I think it's best if you be there when the runaways arrive. You can help minister to them. I'll come and find you as soon as they get here. Do you know your whereabouts over the next few days?"

Joseph nodded. "Pastor, I'll either be in the bakery or at my home. I doubt I'll be elsewhere."

Cyrus focused on Ruth. "What about you, Ruth?"

"Me, Pastor?"

"Yes. I figure we should find you too. I think you should help minister to the runaways. I've received word that they'll often have to forage for herbs when they're on the run. I've heard you have a passion for drying herbs and cooking with them. Do you have some dried herbs to spare for the runaways?"

"Oh, Pastor." Her heart swelled. "Yes." She mentally thought about all of the herbs she'd dried. Miss Tilley's herb garden was thriving, so she could easily dry more herbs to replace what she'd donate to the runaways.

Joseph frowned. "I didn't realize they'd need herbs."

She turned toward Joseph. She'd need to explain this to him. "Yes. They's. . . They need them to help them to be healthy. They can also provide some nourishment." She went on to explain that echinacea could help them not to get sick and that mint could help an upset stomach. "They can use the herbs for tea too."

She focused on Cyrus. "I's. . . I'll be at the rooming house or at the bakery over the next few days."

Cyrus nodded. "Good. I'll be sure to come fetch you as soon as they arrive so that you can assist them." He gave them another nod before making his way toward another church member.

"I hope the runaways make it. I've been praying about them whenever I think about them," Joseph commented.

Ruth nodded. "Me too. I really want to help them find freedom." She also wanted to tell them about her own journey from Maryland to Philadelphia. Of course, she was not an escaped slave, but she had a lot to share about how she'd made a new life for herself, getting paid to bake bread and helping the abolitionists.

Joseph touched her elbow. "Ruth, before we were interrupted by Cyrus, I was about to ask you something."

"Yes?"

"May I walk you to your rooming house?" He balled his hands into fists, and his light brown skin reddened. He looked nervous, nervous as a schoolboy. What in the world did he want to speak with her about?

Chapter 7

Joseph eyed the food-laden table. He'd successfully transformed the bakery into a nice dining space for himself and Ruth. The crude wooden table had a cloth laid over it. He'd closed the shutters on the windows so the early evening light wouldn't shine on them.

He needed total privacy this evening. The only other person who knew about his private supper with Ruth was Cyrus. He'd wanted Cyrus to know where to find him and Ruth if the runaways arrived this evening. He'd also confided to the elderly pastor about his feelings for Ruth, and Cyrus had encouraged him to make his feelings known to her. If Ruth shared his feelings, then he knew they had a rocky road in front of them. Once Mother found out how he felt about Ruth, she'd have a fit. He could imagine her bony shoulders shaking with rage when he made his intentions known to her.

He lit the candles and eyed the chicken and ham he'd prepared as soon as Mother had left for the day. She had a charity meeting to attend, and he imagined Francine would be there too. He could imagine Francine speaking with Mother, upset that he'd not asked her to the charity ball. He closed his eyes and imagined Ruth in a fancy dress. Her dark hair would be uncovered, and he imagined her loose curls would dangle down her slim back. She was so pretty, he didn't think she needed the face paint that some women used. She looked perfect just the way she was.

After the abolitionist meeting the previous evening, he'd escorted Ruth to her rooming house. He asked her to supper, and she surprisingly agreed. His request had startled her. He could tell by the way her eyes widened. Well, he was tired of hiding his feelings, and now it was time to do something about it.

A loud knock sounded at the door. He'd locked the door earlier, so he figured it was Ruth. He opened the door and smiled. Ruth sported the dress she'd worn to church last Sunday. She also wore a fancy bonnet; it was red, and a pattern of flowers decorated the headpiece. She clutched her battered reticule as if she were nervous. He finally found his voice. "Ruth, so glad to see you. Come in." He took her hand and guided her into the room.

Ruth's hand warmed as Joseph led her into the bakery. Her mouth dropped open when she spotted the fancy meal. Candles flickered in the semidarkness. She blinked, her mind spinning. Well, when Joseph asked her to come to supper, she wasn't sure what to expect. She'd spoken with Miss Tilley after the abolitionist meeting the previous night. The schoolmarm had advised her to speak with Joseph and tell him the truth about her background. "There's no need to keep secrets from him any longer." The older woman had then reminded her that the only reason she'd initially told her to keep her background a secret was because she was concerned about Elizabeth Adams's reaction.

Joseph's mother could be quite intimidating, that was for sure. But Ruth could handle her. But she honestly didn't know if she could handle the growing attraction between herself and Joseph. "This. . .looks so nice, Joseph." She still struggled to use proper speech, but Miss Tilley had been great with her lessons. She'd advised her to think before she spoke, giving her time to recall the rules of English. Thinking first proved tiresome, but she'd been improving, and that was the important thing.

"Thank you, Ruth. Come and sit down." He led her to the table and helped her into a chair. He sat across from her, still holding her hand. He bowed his head. "Lord, thank You so much for Ruth's company tonight. Please allow me to open my mouth and say the right words to her. Please also be with us as we share this meal together. Please, Lord, be with me as I continue to work toward my pastoral endeavors. And Lord, please be with the runaways as they make their journey to Philadelphia. Amen."

Ruth squeezed his hand. "Amen." They feasted on flavorful fried chicken, fried ham, flaky biscuits slathered with butter, and fresh peas. Ruth resisted the urge to lick her lips. Miss Tilley had also been teaching her proper table manners, but sometimes Ruth longed to forget those proper etiquette rules and just be herself. Was it possible to be proper about everything as a second nature?

"What's the matter, Ruth? You were frowning." Joseph gathered their dirty dishes.

She ignored his question. "You. . . Do you need help with the dishes?" She figured he was going to take them back to the kitchen to wash them.

He stopped gathering their dishes. "No, I want to know what you were thinking a few seconds ago."

She inwardly winced. She'd come to tell him the truth about herself, so maybe this was a great time to start.

"Why don't we have dessert before you tell me what's on your mind."

Oh, so he had dessert too? He abandoned their table and went behind the counter. He returned with a yellow cake. A thin glaze was drizzled over the top of the confection, and cherries decorated the top. He sliced two generous pieces and plopped them onto their plates. She wanted to eat the cake with her fingers. Instead, she followed Joseph's lead and sliced into the cake with a fork. The moist, delicate cake melted on her tongue. Sweetness exploded in her mouth.

"Joseph, this is so good. I likes it." She inwardly groaned. In her excitement she'd forgotten about her proper English, but Joseph didn't seem to notice as he ate his cake.

"Thank you."

She was a great bread baker, but cakes were not something she made very often. Her master only allowed them to bake cake for birthdays and holidays. They each ate two pieces of the wonderful cake. Afterward, Joseph served up some hot coffee with milk and sugar.

"So why were you frowning a few minutes ago?"

Could she open herself up and be completely honest with him? She sighed and looked into his hazel eyes. The candles flickered in the darkness, and she figured she needed to be honest with him. Joseph had been kind to her. She realized she actually trusted him. She took a deep breath. "I's. . . *I* was thinking about the table manners Miss Tilley has been teaching me. Your food was so good, I wanted to eat it with my fingers."

He laughed. The loud, wonderful sound filled the small bakery. His eyes twinkled as he looked at her. "I understand. Mother still chastises me about eating fast, and I'm a grown man."

Ruth nodded.

He took her hand. "So why has Miss Tilley been teaching you table manners?"

"I wanted to learn to read, write, and speak proper. She been teaching me table manners too."

He raised his eyebrows. Thankfully, he didn't interrupt her. "Joseph, I was a slave. My master set me free when he died." He squeezed her hand, as if encouraging her to continue. She told him all about her master's death and her journey from Maryland to Philadelphia with the help of the abolitionists. She mentioned how Cyrus helped her to find the job at the bakery, and she also told him about Thomas's untimely death. "Joseph, I was in love with Thomas. I still am. . . I still dream about him. I sometimes think the Lord wants me to be single for the rest of my life and help other people escape slavery."

He frowned, and his hazel eyes no longer sparkled, but he continued holding her hand. "Ruth, you can't—"

A loud banging on the door shattered the silence. Joseph dropped her hand and rushed to the door. He unlocked it and opened it. Cyrus Brown stood at the door, his balding head shining amid the streetlamps. Leaning on his cane, he poked his head into the bakery and spoke to both of them. "The escaped slaves are here. We need your help."

Ruth blew out the candles and joined Cyrus and Joseph at the door. Looked like it was going to be a long night.

Joseph opened the door to the secret room underneath the church. Ruth eyed the five occupants. A tall, lanky white man was laid out on a pallet in the corner, snoring. She assumed he was the conductor. Two boys, both looking to be around ten years old. A man and a woman. The couple held hands and the woman rubbed her stomach. They sat on the pallets on the floor and leaned against the wall.

They guzzled water from tin cups. Ruth narrowed her eyes, unsure of how hard their journey was. "Don't drink too fast," she advised them. She feared if they drank a lot of water too quickly, they might get sick.

They nodded, and she poured more water for them. They sipped it and then nibbled on bread, their dark eyes tired. She and Joseph and Cyrus ministered to the runaways for an hour before more church members arrived. The church members agreed to stay with the runaways so that Joseph and Ruth could leave.

"I'll be back tomorrow," she commented. Ruth wanted to tell the runaways about her experiences in a new place, and she hoped she could provide some guidance for them. She also needed to bring the herbs Cyrus had requested. The runaways were supposed to stay for a few days before continuing their journey toward Canada.

Before she and Joseph left, they joined hands with Cyrus and the other church members. They formed a circle around the slaves and the sleeping conductor. They bowed their heads. Joseph cleared his throat. "Lord, we come before You today to seek help. We want to help these people escape to Canada. Please let Your Holy Spirit guide them. Please protect them and help them to stay strong and healthy during their journey. Amen." His voice boomed throughout the room and the sleeping conductor opened his eyes for a few seconds before falling back to sleep.

Joseph touched each of the runaways before he led Ruth out of the church. Her heart skipped when he held her hand as they made their way toward the street. Fatigue weighed upon her like a ton of bricks, and she sighed. *Lord, please help me to get a good sleep tonight. I don't want Elizabeth to get angry with me when I can't stay awake to bake the bread tomorrow.*

"Joseph!" Elizabeth's stern voice pierced the dark night, causing Ruth's heart to thud.

She rushed toward them, her mouth pressed tightly, and her bony shoulders shook with apparent rage. She glared at their joined hands. "What is the meaning of this?"

They'd barely left the church when Joseph's ma appeared. How had she found them?

"Mother, what do you want?"

"I saw Francine at the charity meeting, and she told me about the church where you've been worshipping. She claims you're involved in the abolitionist movement. Is that true?"

"Mother, we can talk about this later. I—"

Elizabeth screeched, tears coursing down her cheeks as she again eyed their joined hands. She rushed away.

"Joseph, you need to go after your ma."

"But I want to be sure you get home."

She gestured down the street. "I's be okay."

He shook his head. "I've only seen Mother this angry once in my life. You cannot talk to her about anything when she's so upset. I must wait until later to speak with her."

Ruth disagreed—he needed to go after his ma. She chewed her lower lip as he held her hand while escorting her to the rooming house.

He then pressed his lips against her forehead. "After we get some rest, we need to finish the conversation we started earlier."

Unable to sleep, Ruth arrived at the church a few hours before her workday started. She knocked on the door, and a church member answered and led her to the hidden stairs behind the church. They walked down the steps, and Ruth pushed the door open, entering the secret room. Surprisingly, the couple was awake, but the boys and the conductor were sleeping. She nodded toward the couple who were sitting up on their pallets. "Hello, I didn't get a chance to introduce myself earlier. My name is Ruth."

"Hello, Ruth." The man greeted her and introduced himself and his wife.

His wife rubbed her belly. "I's two months pregnant," she announced.

Ruth raised her eyebrows. She'd heard that pregnant women usually could not make the trip because it was too difficult for them. She figured since this woman was only two months pregnant, she wasn't as fragile as a woman who was further along with a pregnancy.

"I hope your baby is born free. I have faith it will happen."

The woman bopped her head. "Thank you."

She removed her herbs, and over the next hour, she showed them the different herbs she was providing to them. She told them to sniff each one so that they could identify them. "Drink the echinacea each day as a tea. If you can't find water, then chew it. It'll help you to stay healthy." Once she was finished telling about the herbs, she focused on telling them about her life. "I just want you to know how the Lord has guided me from Maryland to

Philadelphia as a manumitted slave. I work now and receive wages, and I want you to know that it's possible for you to get a job too. I prayed for this every day, and I wants you to pray for freedom and hope for a better life." She took a deep breath as she began telling them about the events that led up to her journeying to Philadelphia.

Chapter 8

Two days. Joseph didn't know if he could last another day like this. Mother had not spoken to him, not one word since she'd found him holding Ruth's hand. He was also worried about his sermon. Tomorrow he'd be presenting his sermon to the church, and his stomach had been tied up in terrible knots.

He'd been fasting, asking the Lord for guidance regarding his mother's attitude, his feelings for Ruth, and his sermon. He'd noticed Ruth's dark eyes on him, as if she were questioning his silence. He figured she'd say something when she was ready. They'd never finished their conversation they'd started during their special supper. He just found everything so overwhelming. He couldn't focus on his mother's caustic attitude, his feelings for Ruth, and his sermon at the same time. So he decided he needed to concentrate solely on his sermon for now.

He'd been happy to discover the runaways had left late last night for their next stop. He continued to pray for them whenever they crossed his mind. *Lord, please help them to find freedom.*

As he put out the fire at the end of the workday, Ruth approached him. "Joseph? You okay?"

He took her hand. "No." He lowered his voice. "I've never seen Mother so angry for such a long time."

"She is upset. I can tell." Pausing, she stared at him for a few seconds. "Your sermon is tomorrow, right?"

He nodded.

"I've been praying for you. I hope you do well."

He nodded and hugged her. "Thank you, Ruth." He studied her as she left, still recalling they needed to sit down and talk. Well, after his sermon was over, and after Mother cooled down, then he'd speak with Ruth. He pulled out his pocket watch. Mother would probably be leaving to go home soon. Well, he didn't want to delay speaking with her any longer.

He knocked on her office door. "Mother. I need to speak with you."

Even though she didn't respond, he opened the door. Surprisingly, she wasn't going over the numbers. She sat in her chair and stared out the window. Tears coursed down her sunken cheeks. He pressed his handkerchief into her hands. "Mother, when was the last time you've eaten?"

She shrugged, refusing to look at him. Mother could be so impossible when she got into one of her moods. He went up front and found a few pieces of Ruth's bread. He buttered them and poured a large cup of water. He returned with the small meal. "Eat, Mother. Then we can speak about what's troubling you."

She stared at the plate for a long time, almost as if she'd never seen a plate of bread before. She then bit into the bread and sipped the water. Once she'd finished eating, he closed the shutter on the window and sat on a chair in front of her. "Mother, my affections for Ruth should not upset you like this."

"Affections?" She spat the word as if it left a bad taste in her mouth. "I saw you looking at that dreadful girl when she first came into our bakery. I never should have hired her. I'm firing her on Monday."

His heart skipped, and he narrowed his eyes. "No, you aren't. Mother, I know how much you love money. Our coffers have greatly increased since Ruth's employ. Father would be ashamed of you right now."

Her mouth dropped open. "Don't talk to me about your father."

"Mother, we must talk about Father. You've not been yourself since he died. You don't eat half the time. You cry every night. I know you miss Father, and you are sad, but don't let your sour attitude cloud your judgment."

He closed his eyes. *Lord, help me to say the right words.* "Even if you were to fire Ruth, it won't solve anything. I'm going to ask Ruth to court me."

"No." Her voice echoed in the small room.

"Mother, is this what you want? To be alone?"

"What do you mean?"

"I hate working in our bakery. I'd be happier if I never baked another loaf of bread in my life."

She pressed her bony hands together, sobbing. "Joseph. . ."

"I want to be pastor at my new church." He then explained that Cyrus was retiring. "If they like my sermon, I may be voted into the pastorship, Lord willing."

She shook her head, the red kerchief on her head bopping. "Joseph, you are not thinking clearly. That girl put these horrid ideas in your head. She told you to become a pastor. I'll bet she even convinced you to join the abolitionist movement."

"That girl has a name, Mother. It's Ruth, and you'd better learn to say it. As far as the movement, I joined myself. I feel called to help others find freedom. I started doing this shortly before I met Ruth." He paused and licked his lips. "I felt unfulfilled at our old church, so I joined another and became involved in the movement."

"Son, just give them some money for the cause. You can help that way."

"Mother, no."

She grabbed his hand, tears streaming from her eyes. "I hear that kind of work is dangerous. What if a slave catcher comes and pulls a weapon on you while you're helping those runaways? Son, I've already lost your daddy. I don't want to lose you too."

His heart thumped as he pulled his mother into his arms. "Mother, I'm sorry." He'd never stopped to think how this would affect her. Mother always wanted to act tough and in control. Well, she needed to understand she couldn't control everything. "I promise I'll be careful." He released her. Hopefully, she wasn't still angry. He may as well be honest with her about everything. He was tired of hiding things from her, hoping to keep her from one of her moods. "I want to help people. I was talking to Cyrus about this the other day, and he said I was already pastoring and did not know it."

She frowned. "You were talking to Cyrus about what?"

He sighed. "Pastoring. When you make your trips to the bank each week, I let some beggars into the bakery. I feed them, but I also talk to them about the Bible and salvation. Mother, they have questions, and I can't answer them all, but I want them to know that God is watching out for them. I want them to have faith. Can you understand that?"

She gasped. "You've been letting homeless bums into our bakery? Do the customers see them?" She actually looked as if she were in pain and was about to cry again.

"I take them into the back."

"Into this office?" She screeched the words as if she were having a fit.

"No, Mother, into the room where we keep our extra supplies."

Well, he didn't want to upset her further. He feared she might faint if she realized how much bread and milk he gave away each week.

"Son, if I can't change your mind about the movement and pastoring, then please listen to my reasoning about Ruth. She'll never fit into our world. She's not the right woman for you. She's poor, and she talks like an uneducated slave."

"Because she *was* a slave."

She cried again. "Oh my. . .she was a slave?" Her hands shook, and Joseph rushed to get her more water.

"Mother, calm down. Don't make yourself sick with worry."

She dropped the cup of water and it spilled onto the floor. Joseph mopped up the mess with a towel. "Ruth's a manumitted slave. She's free now and is trying to make a fresh start. Your negative attitude toward her is not helpful. Ruth is a sweet, lovely, God-fearing girl, and you'd see that if you'd just give her a chance." It proved galling and embarrassing that his mother would not learn to accept Ruth.

"But Joseph. What about Francine? She's more your type of girl. Just give her a chance. She's beautiful, rich, upper-class. . ."

"Mother, I can't control my feelings. I don't love Francine." There was something about Francine that bothered him. He didn't trust her, and the thought of spending more time with her made him uneasy.

"Oh, you *love* that dreadful girl Ruth?"

He gritted his teeth. No way could he continue to speak with Mother when she was like this. Besides, he needed to go over his sermon a few more times before he spoke to the church tomorrow. He turned and left the office.

Ruth sat in the front pew of the church. She'd gotten up early, wanting to make sure she got a seat in the front so that she could hear Joseph. Miss Tilley had still been eating breakfast when Ruth left for the church. Ruth had been too nervous to eat. She'd been up half the night, praying Joseph's sermon would make an impact on the congregation.

She'd also spent the night thinking about their supper that had been interrupted right after the runaways arrived. Since they'd assisted the runaways, Joseph had been so quiet. He'd seemed like he had a lot on his mind, and she knew he had a lot to handle with his mother's moodiness as well as preparing his sermon. Miss Tilley had encouraged her to speak with Joseph tomorrow. If his sermon was well accepted by the congregation, then he might be in a better mood to talk.

Heaven help her, she was still unsure about Joseph's feelings toward her. Sure, they'd shared a candlelit supper, but she still had Thomas on her mind. However, she finally admitted to herself that her thoughts of Thomas weren't as strong since she'd become involved with the abolitionist movement and had spent more time with Joseph. She found herself admiring Joseph so often, craving his company.

Were these feelings about Joseph God's way of nudging her to see that she may not want to be alone for the rest of her life?

The murmuring from the crowd snapped into her thoughts. She gazed around the sea of folks who were waiting to hear Joseph speak. She scanned the crowd and didn't spot Elizabeth. She hoped Joseph had finally told his mom about his pastoral endeavors. However, if he did tell his mother about his plans, she could imagine Elizabeth not supporting her son. She'd probably be distressed and refuse to hear Joseph preach.

What a rough life, living with Elizabeth Adams.

Ruth smiled when Joseph walked up to the podium. He looked so handsome in his brown suit and polished shoes. He clutched his black Bible in his large hands. He placed it on the podium and then looked directly into the audience. He looked directly at her. His hazel eyes sparkled as he gave her a small, nervous smile. "Good morning," he greeted them.

"Good morning."

"Let's start with a word of prayer." He paused for a few seconds. "Lord, please be with me as I deliver the first sermon of my life. Please open up the ears of this congregation; allow them to understand my words. Help them to find spiritual guidance from my sermon. Please, Lord, continue to be with the runaways as they travel to Canada. Please allow them to arrive safely at their destination. Amen."

"Amen," the congregation murmured.

"Most of you know that I'm a baker. I recently lost my father, and I run the bakery with my mother. Every day we bake bread, and that bread brings sustenance to all those who purchase it. They may eat it for breakfast, dinner, or supper. Well, after you eat that bread, you're going to get hungry again. But God's Word is just like that bread. . .except it's bread from which we'll never grow hungry again." He lifted his Bible and flipped the pages. "Please turn with me to. . ."

Ruth listened, transfixed by Joseph's strong, confident voice. He continued his moving sermon. Once he was finished, the entire congregation clapped. Ruth scanned the crowd, noticing some of the church members cried, their brown cheeks stained with salty tears.

Joseph smiled before bowing his head and closing with another prayer.

Ruth grinned. She ached to go up to the podium and tell Joseph just how proud she was that he'd written such a moving sermon. The congregation had barely started to leave when Francine strolled into the sanctuary. She wore a yellow dress, and her dark curls bounced against the fabric. "Joseph." She cooed his name as if she were a bird calling out to her mate.

His light brown skin reddened as he turned toward Francine. The rest of the congregation stopped and stared—Francine proved a beautiful sight. She looked so glorious that Ruth could imagine the men aching to stare at her all day.

"Joseph." She spoke his name again, and he appeared speechless as he patiently stood at the podium. Francine soon stood beside him. She then looked out at the audience, toying with his lapel. "You can't go without announcing our betrothal to your church." She then kissed him on the mouth.

Ruth's heart sped up, and she rushed from the church. She heard Miss Tilley's voice over the drone of the audience, calling out to her, but she just couldn't stay. Tears of shame rushed down her face.

Chapter 9

Joseph banged on the door. The door squeaked as it was swung open. Miss Tilley's eyes widened behind her spectacles. "Joseph. You were just here an hour ago."

"Ruth still isn't here?"

"No. I already told you if she showed up that I'd let her know you were here."

But if Miss Tilley told Ruth he'd been here, that still wouldn't make things better. He needed to *talk* to her. He didn't want to wait until tomorrow when she showed up to work at the bakery. It'd been two hours since Francine had pulled that terrible shenanigan. "Miss Tilley, you've known me for a long time. You know I am *not* engaged to Francine. That woman is nothing but trouble, and she fabricated that whole encounter this morning." He wouldn't be surprised if Mother had schemed with Francine too. After he'd unsuccessfully tried to find Ruth, he'd gone to his house. Mother had not been there. Her absence proved disturbing since she always rushed home after church for Sunday dinner. He had to wonder if Mother was with Francine right now, trying to come up with another scheme to hurt Ruth.

Miss Tilley touched his arm. "I know you're not engaged to Francine, but now you've got to convince Ruth." She paused and leaned against the doorframe. "You know, since you were here earlier, I've been thinking..."

"Yes?" He'd take any advice he could get. All he wanted to do was fix things with Ruth.

"Ruth once told me she'll sometimes go for a walk in Fairmount Park on Sunday afternoons. You might find her there." She threw her hands up in the air. "I apologize for not thinking about this earlier. But—"

He patted her shoulder. "Thank you. Don't apologize. I'm grateful for your help." He rushed down the steps. He needed to get there as soon as possible. His Sunday shoes clomped against the cobbled street as he rushed toward the park. Sweat beaded on his forehead and rolled down his face. He could imagine Mother's reprimands about his running down the street on a Sunday afternoon. Mother needed to realize protocol was not always relative to the situation at hand. Sometimes, when you needed to get something done, you must do all that was within your power to make it happen, even if you broke a few social rules. Winded, he rounded the corner and approached the park. *Lord, I need Your help. Please help Ruth to understand she doesn't need to live her life alone. Please, Lord, be with her as she listens to what I have to say.*

He rushed into the park. Flowers bloomed and the sun shone on the bright green grass. He slowed to a walk as soon as he spotted Ruth. She sat on a bench, staring up at the sky. The breeze blew, and the leaves of the maple tree danced in the warm spring breeze. He focused on Ruth, and she looked toward him. Their eyes locked like two pieces of a puzzle. "Ruth, please don't run away."

Thankfully, she stayed right on the park bench. Good. Now all he needed to do was rectify everything. He approached the bench and noticed Ruth's red eyes and tearstained cheeks. Well, looked like he had some explaining to do. Now they could continue the conversation they'd started days ago.

Ruth eyed Joseph as he plopped onto the bench beside her. He'd obviously been running. Sweat clung to his face, and she noticed his strong, muscular arms beneath his sweaty shirt. His mouth mashed down as if he were angry. Well, he'd told her not to run away, so she wouldn't. She'd listen to his words.

"Ruth, I'm sorry." He reached over as if he wanted to take her hand, but then he pulled his hand back.

She figured he didn't want to make her angry. Well, she was mighty angry, so angry she didn't know what to say.

"I'm not engaged to Francine."

"She *kissed* you."

"I didn't return her kiss. I didn't even know she was coming to our church today. She worships at Mother's church. I think Francine and Mother came up with a plan to make you upset." He touched her face.

She sensed the aftermath of her tears had dried onto her skin, and she probably looked frightful.

"Looks like they succeeded. . .making you upset. I hate seeing you cry, Ruth."

This whole conversation made no sense. "Why would your ma and Francine want to upset me?"

He reached for her hand, and this time he took it. He cradled it in his large palm and kissed each of her fingers. "I like you, Ruth. When I made supper for you, I did that because I wanted to ask if I could court you. I never got around to asking because the escaped slaves arrived. Then Mother was in one of her moods. I told her I wanted to court you, and she got upset." He paused and took a deep breath.

Joseph looked so tired and tormented. The circles beneath his eyes and the droop to his comely lips made her realize just how many troubles he carried on his broad shoulders.

"Mother mentioned Francine would be a perfect mate for me. I got mad. I think Mother wanted to make me change my mind about Francine. That's why I believe she sent Francine to the church today, just to make you jealous."

Goodness, he really wanted to court her? In spite of his mother's objections and his social standing, he still wanted to court her, a former slave? But could she really let Joseph court her? She liked him too, but she didn't know if she wanted to have anybody court her now, or ever. "Joseph, I like you too."

He grinned. "I'm glad to hear that, Ruth."

"But remember what I told you when we shared supper?"

"You feel called to help people escape slavery. You don't want to be attached to anybody. You were in love with Thomas, and you still think about him."

Well, that was a blessing. He was a man who listened. He'd heard all she'd revealed to him that day. She considered herself to be a strong, courageous woman, a woman who was destined to be alone, doing good for others. But she couldn't deny the feelings she'd developed for Joseph Adams over the last few weeks. "I don't know what to say."

"Would you like some time to think about it?"

She nodded. She figured she'd be spending the next few days praying, hoping the Lord would see fit to show her what to do.

The soft classical music drifted from the closed front door of Joseph's home. If memory served him correctly, it sounded like Mozart. He frowned as he slowly opened the door. He softly closed it and placed the antislavery notices he'd recently picked up from the printers on the hallway table. He then quietly followed the sound of the music. He spotted Mother in the sitting room, her back toward him, playing a flute. She finished playing the classical song.

She sniffed. "I didn't realize you'd be home so soon." She placed the flute onto a nearby table and turned toward him. Her face was wet, but she no longer seemed angry. She just seemed sad, and her shoulders drooped. Looked like she was tired too.

He slowly approached her. His mind stirred with so many questions. Confusion filled his soul as he dropped onto a chair beside her. He offered her his handkerchief. "Mother? You can play the flute?" In his entire life, he'd never known her to play anything. He didn't even realize she enjoyed music.

She slowly nodded, wiping her face. "I used to play a long time ago. After I married your father and became involved with the bakery, and had you. . .time just got away from me, I guess."

Well, that didn't explain much. Why would getting married and having a baby make her want to stop playing the flute? He needed to understand what was going on with her. "Why are you playing now?"

She shrugged. "I guess I'm just so sad about you not taking a liking to Francine. Everything I've been working so hard for is just ruined. Playing used to help me escape from my problems. Decided to try it again now, I guess."

"Why do you say everything is ruined? I don't understand."

"Son, when I married your father. . .well, we wanted to start a family."

He nodded. He still had tons of questions he wanted to ask her but sensed he needed to let her open up to him when she was ready.

"You're not my firstborn. I had two other children before I had you."

His heart stilled. "What?"

"You heard me. I had two children before you. Both of them died when they were infants. Then I had you. You were sick as a baby but you survived. Son, I've always been so proud of you. You're charming, good-looking, compassionate, sometimes too compassionate. Before your father died, I promised him I'd help you find the perfect wife. Both of us felt Francine would be a perfect match."

"Mother, I've explained—"

She touched his hand. "I know. I've just been so focused on doing what I and your father felt was right for you that I haven't been paying attention to how my actions have affected you. Son, I just didn't want to further alienate you. I don't want to lose you."

"Mother, you will never lose me. I will always love you and be your son." He took her hand and squeezed it. "Is there anything else you want to tell me?"

She nodded. "I have to be honest with you. I schemed with Francine. I agreed to her meeting you at the church and kissing you. You're so smart you probably figured that out on your own."

He nodded, still holding her hand. "Yes. Mother, you hurt Ruth. I like her. I honestly don't know if she'll agree to court me, but even if she doesn't, I know that there's no future between me and Francine. I can't be with a woman I can't trust."

"I'm sorry, Son. I really am. I now realize I took things too far, and for that I'm truly sorry."

He nodded. "I forgive you." A miracle had just occurred. He couldn't believe that Mother had actually admitted she'd been wrong. Well, he needed to tell her something that might make her feel better. "I like hearing you play. You should do it more often."

She actually smiled. He then abandoned his seat and made a pot of coffee. He spent the entire evening talking to his mother, asking her questions, hoping that he could help erase the rift that had grown between them.

Ruth lay on her bed and stared at the ceiling of her bedroom. It'd been two days since Joseph's question about courting her. A loud knock on the door interrupted her thoughts. "Come in."

Miss Tilley came into the room. She pushed her glasses up on her nose. "Have you been all right?"

Miss Tilley seemed to be able to know when something was bothering her. She may as well be truthful. "No."

"Your mind has been wandering the last couple of days during our school lessons." The older woman pulled her chair up to the bed and took a seat. She patted Ruth's leg. "You've made excellent progress on your lessons. Your speech has improved."

"Thank you, Miss Tilley." She'd even started reading some of the simple children's nursery rhyme books. She'd been working hard on learning her letters, and she figured in due time, Mrs. Adams might let her wait on the customers in the bakery. The woman barely paid her any attention. She often wondered if Mrs. Adams noticed her speech had improved since she'd been hired to work in the bakery.

Miss Tilley cleared her throat. "I worked with Joseph this evening."

"You did?" This was surprising. She didn't realize Miss Tilley would be helping Joseph.

"Yes. I helped him to hang some antislavery notices. We're trying to get some more people to come to our next abolitionist meeting. We're expecting some more runaways in a couple of weeks."

She'd known Joseph was going to be hanging notices, but she didn't realize he'd be doing that this evening. Normally, she would have assisted him with the task, but she'd seen him all day at the bakery. She needed some time away from him to think about his offer of courtship.

"How are things going at the bakery?"

"I's. . . I've been working hard like usual."

"Are you getting along with Mrs. Adams?"

She resisted the urge to roll her eyes. "She don't. . .doesn't talk to me, Miss Tilley. She doesn't look at me. Only reason I'm still there is because of my bread. The profits are good, so she tolerates me."

"How about Joseph? He was mighty upset about what happened last Sunday with Francine. He told me you two talked at the park."

"Yes, we talked." She then told Miss Tilley about Joseph wanting to court her. "I don't know if I should let him court me. I wonder if I'd be happier by myself."

"Have you prayed about it?"

"Yes, a lot."

"What do you feel in here?" Miss Tilley touched her chest. "In your heart?"

"I like Joseph. It made me mad when Francine kissed him. I hated seeing her around him when we were passing out the pamphlets earlier this month."

"Are you still sad about Thomas?"

"Not as much since I've started working in the bakery. I still dream about him, think about him."

Miss Tilley nodded. "Grief can be like that sometimes. When my pa died, it was awful. Took me a while to get used to his being gone. I still think about him a lot."

Ruth nodded. "Sorry about your pa."

She waved her hand. "It happened a long time ago. Now, tell me how you feel about Joseph."

"I like Joseph. He's kind, honest, and trusting. I like how he helps people."

"Are you referring to his helping with the abolitionist movement?"

"Yes, but I'm also talking about his helping people in the city. He feeds homeless people and tells them about the Bible. He really cares, and seeing him care for folks like that, feeding them, wanting to nourish their souls"—she swallowed and continued to gather her thoughts—"makes me feel happy in here." She pressed her hand to her chest. "My heart gets glad just seeing him minister. Plus, he's handsome. I could sit and look at him all day."

Miss Tilley grinned. "I think you know what you need to do, Ruth."

She frowned. "I do?"

"What would Thomas want you to do? Do you think he'd want you to be alone for the rest of your life?"

She'd never thought of it like that. She knew Thomas would want her to be happy.

"Ruth, from hearing you speak, you want to spend time with Joseph and get to know him better, but you are scared of being hurt again." She took Ruth's hand and squeezed her fingers. "Don't be afraid to love again. The Lord wants you to be happy, and if being with Joseph brings you happiness, then you should let him court you." Miss Tilley hugged her then left the room and closed the door behind her.

Joseph pulled out a chair for Ruth. They'd just closed the bakery, and Mother had already gone home. Mother was still strangely silent during the workday, clearly unsettled about his affections for Ruth. She still didn't speak to Ruth, but at least she no longer glared at her like she used to. Ever since she'd told him about her deceased children and her aspirations for him as her only living child, it was like a barrier had been removed from between them. For the last couple of nights, they'd shared coffee and had a decent conversation. He was finding things out about his mother he'd never known, and he'd encouraged her to consider playing the flute as worship to God.

He eyed Ruth as she sat in her seat. Earlier, she'd requested to speak with him after closing, and he'd gladly agreed. *Lord, please let Ruth agree to my courtship.*

She removed her bonnet and he admired the bunch of curls gathered on her head. He sat beside her as she pulled her dinner pail from the floor. She reached into the pail and removed a small wrapped parcel. "This is for you." Her dainty hands shook as she gave him the package. She looked nervous. Well, he was nervous too.

He studied the package before untying the knotted twine. Two heart-shaped sugar cookies were nestled within the folds of paper. "You baked these for me?"

She nodded. "I's. . . I like you, Joseph. I baked these for you to let you know that my answer is yes. I want you to court me."

He grinned and pulled Ruth into his arms. She smelled like vanilla and cinnamon. He took her soft, dainty hand and squeezed her fingers. He bit into the thin confection, and the taste of sugar and vanilla exploded in his mouth with delicate sweetness. He offered the cookie to Ruth and she took a small bite.

He then leaned toward her and kissed her beautiful lips.

Epilogue

One year later...

Joseph strolled to the podium, holding his Bible. He relished his role as pastor of his church. He'd been the pastor for almost a year, and he was still amazed he'd been chosen to replace Cyrus Brown. He scanned the audience, his eyes resting on Ruth. She sat in the front seat, her hands resting on her large pregnant stomach. Mother sat right beside her. It had been a rocky road getting the two of them to get along.

After he'd asked Ruth for courtship, they'd spent time together for a month before Cyrus Brown married them. Mother had attended their wedding, and she openly admitted to him beforehand that it was still hard for her to accept Ruth into their lives, but she was willing to try. When he'd started his pastorship, Mother and Ruth began to run the bakery together. Ruth started talking to Mother about more improvements in the bakery. She'd suggested having a cookie day, a day when the bakery sold cookies in addition to their breads and pastries.

Their profits had increased even more, and Mother had finally started to respect Ruth. Now, they ran the bakery together, and Mother had finally started coming to their church. She'd even played her flute for the congregation a few times and had received a lot of compliments about her talent. They'd also hired a new assistant for the bakery once he'd become pastor.

He was still active in the abolitionist movement and Ruth continued to assist in the duties. She continued dispensing dried herbs and encouragement to the runaways, and she thrived in her role as a supporter of the Underground Railroad. He scanned the audience before again focusing on Ruth.

"I love you." She silently mouthed the words.

He often daydreamed of what life would be like once their baby was born. He knew Mother would be pleased to have a grandchild on whom to dote.

"I love you too," he mouthed. His beautiful wife then grinned at him, and he returned her smile before he began his sermon.

Cecelia Dowdy is a world traveler who has been an avid reader for as long as she can remember. When she first read Christian fiction, she felt called to write for the genre. She loves to read, write, and bake desserts in her spare time. She also loves spending time with her husband and toddler son. Currently she resides with her family in Maryland.

A Place of Refuge

by Patty Smith Hall

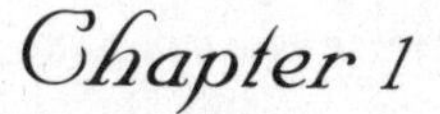

Chapter 1

Abbeville, South Carolina
1857

She was running out of time.

Jorgine Emerson stared out at the lush green fields, the white boles of cotton swaying in time with the horses' hooves. A bumper crop this year for certain. They'd need to harvest their crop and get it to market before the price plummeted. She'd need every spare penny to keep Piney Brooke up and running for another year.

Her home was the only thing she had left on this earth that was hers.

"Really, Jorgine. You're not listening to a word I say."

She took one last look at the ripening field and then turned toward the young woman sitting across from her in the carriage. Millie Shephard had been a friend since the cradle, a fact Mrs. Shephard loved to bring up whenever there was someone close by to impress. The town of Abbeville had been built around the Emerson family, the closest thing to royalty in this part of the state. Thank heavens, Millie was kindness itself without any of her mama's ambitious social climbing.

Jorgine took a deep breath of humid air and sighed. "I'm sorry. So why are we going to the Wallaces' garden party? I didn't think you knew them that well."

"I don't. I mean, we've exchanged pleasantries." Millie's gaze dipped to her clenched hands in her lap. "Mama just says it's a good place to start."

Dear heavens, what was that woman up to now? "A good place to start what?"

Her friend's cheeks turned pink. "Mama feels that it's time I started looking for a husband."

Jorgine shook her head. "We've talked about possible suitors, but you've never mentioned anything about a beau." When Millie didn't answer right way, she leaned forward and grasped her friend's hand.

"Because I don't have one." Millie's green eyes were somber. "Business at the mill hasn't improved since Papa hired freed Negroes and paid them a living wage." She swallowed. "People would rather travel to Spartanburg or Columbia for their lumber rather than buy anything from Papa right now."

"I'm sure folks will get tired of that long trip into town and give their business back to your father. It just takes some time."

"I don't have time, Jorgine." She pulled a white handkerchief from her wrist and sniffed. "Mama fears if I don't make a good marriage now, we might not survive the backlash. I must get married, and to someone with enough money to help my family see this through."

"Oh, Millie. I had no idea things were that bad. Is there anything I can do to help?"

Her friend gave her a watery smile. "Help me find a rich husband? Maybe someone like your Win?"

Your Win. Jorgine's throat tightened at the mention of her fiancé. Winfield Wakefield of the Charleston Wakefields had been handpicked to be her husband by her uncle and guardian, Richard Emerson. Not that Jorgine had been given any choice. Why Papa had asked Uncle Richard to be her guardian when she was perfectly capable of running Piney Brooke on her own was beyond comprehension. Now nearly everything Papa had possessed, including the slaves and the shipping business, belonged to Uncle Richard. Everything but Piney Brooke.

"Your mind is wandering again." Millie gave her a forgiving smile. "Perfectly understandable at the mention of your intended. You must be so excited with the wedding just a few weeks away!"

Jorgine gave her a halfhearted nod. *Terrified* might be a more fitting description. Not for herself. Win had made it perfectly clear that once his senatorial campaign was over, she was free to live at Piney Brooke, which suited her just fine. With the inheritance her father had left her upon her marriage, she might just manage to make their land profitable again.

No, her concern was for her maid, Sally. If the whispers about her future husband's relationships with his female slaves held even a grain of truth, Sally's virtue was in danger.

"You never did tell me how he proposed." Her friend giggled behind her lace glove. "Did he get down on one knee when he asked you to marry him?"

Poor Millie. If she was hanging all her romantic dreams on Jorgine, she'd be so disappointed. The proposal had been more like a business arrangement. "We just agreed that we suited each other. He proposed, and I said yes."

"But he did tell you he loves you?"

She nodded slightly. Not as much as he loved the large campaign contribution her uncle had promised once they said their vows. Jorgine understood her papa's concerns for her future, but why did Uncle Richard have to pick her husband? And why someone as vile as Win Wakefield? Yes, the Wakefields had political clout, but what did her uncle hope to gain from her marriage?

"I've lost you again."

Jorgine caught sight of Millie's hurt expression and sighed. "I'm so sorry. With everything that's going on, I can't keep my thoughts straight."

She relaxed. "It's all right. I can't imagine putting on a wedding of that magnitude. How are you handling it?"

"Fine." If the truth be told, it had been frustrating. All the simple touches she'd wanted for her wedding had been systematically vetoed by Win's mother. "Mother Wakefield has taken over most of the planning."

"What a lovely gesture!" Millie's eyes sparkled. "Your fiancé is a very important gentleman in our state and deserves a wedding befitting his esteemed position."

An esteemed man with a horrible habit, one she couldn't share with anyone. If this news got around town, Jorgine would be more humiliated than she already felt. "Mother Wakefield has more experience arranging such things. As I don't have a mother to advise me, I thought it best to leave it in her capable hands."

"That's so kind of you." Millie studied her for a long moment. "I don't know if I could step aside and let another woman plan every detail of my wedding. Unless it was my mother."

"Of course." Millie's mother chased society's whims like they were the last crust of bread in South Carolina. But Millie had a point. If things had been different, if this union had been blessed with love, Jorgine would have taken great joy in planning all the details of her wedding. As Uncle Richard had told her, this wasn't about silly emotion but the joining together of two great Southern families. "Mother Wakefield enjoys this kind of thing more than I do. Besides, Piney Brooke needs my attention now."

Millie leaned back and snapped open her silk fan. "I can't believe your father left it to you to manage. Mother says it's unseemly for a woman to partake in business."

"It's not as if I'm doing the planting myself, Millie." Jorgine chuckled, tugging at her gloves. "Big Jim tends to all that."

"Don't you ever feel nervous being in that big house all by yourself?"

Jorgine gawked at her. "Since when did having a cook and a lady's maid as well as Big Jim constitute being by myself?"

Millie pressed her lips together. "What I mean is it's nothing like when your father was alive, so why stay when you could live with your uncle Richard?"

"Maybe I want to stay in my own home." Which was the truth. Piney Brooke was the only home she'd ever known. But Millie was right. Piney Brooke was a shell of its former self since her papa's death from a heart seizure five years ago.. It held none of the laughter and joy that had infused the place while Papa was alive, maybe because he always wanted her to know the great love he had for her. Family, though it was just the two of them, meant a great deal to him. "Piney Brooke is where I belong."

"I know. Just be careful." Millie straightened as their carriage turned through the gates of the Wallace Plantation. "I've heard shocking things that no moral, upstanding young lady should hear."

Jorgine's lips twitched. "You were eavesdropping again."

Her cheeks turned pink. "Well, maybe a little. Still, some of those stories about Negro men are terrifying to think of. So please, be careful."

She knew Millie meant well, but she had heard those stories too, tales meant to scare children into behaving. But Papa's slaves had always been so good to her, treating her like she was one of their children, swatting her backside when she misbehaved and kissing her scraped knees when she fell. Big Jim had shared God's saving grace with her when she was still a child. And no one could ask for a better friend than Sally.

She glanced at Millie. Any reassurances she could offer would fall on deaf ears. Best to help her make a profitable match, and the best way to do that was a little confidence. "That green muslin looks lovely on you. It brings out the color of your eyes."

"Why, thank you!" She smoothed the wrinkles from her skirt. "I heard that anyone who is anyone will be here today, so the rumors must be true."

"What rumors?"

Millie snapped her fan together and tapped Jorgine's knee. "Supposedly, Hudson Wallace has returned home."

Dear goodness. The last time she'd seen Hudson, she'd made a cake of herself. She'd been so silly, giving her heart to a man she barely knew. He probably didn't even remember her. "Last thing I heard, he was still in Atlanta charming the ladies."

"His father called him home." Millie opened her fan again. "He wants Hudson to manage the daily running of the plantation while he takes Mrs. Wallace down to Savannah for medical treatment."

"She never has recovered from her bout with pneumonia last winter. Maybe the sea air will help her," Jorgine replied. "Still, Hudson is a poor substitute for his father. His parents may wish they'd left Olivia in charge."

As the carriage pulled up to the brick walkway, Millie let out a tiny squeak. "I wasn't expecting to see Mr. Raley here. He was supposed to be in Charlotte on business."

Jorgine fought to keep from cringing. Why did all her friends act so silly when it came to men? She'd never understood it, maybe because she'd spent her girlhood following her father around the plantation or in Charleston while he worked. She felt at ease with men, enjoyed talking with them—much to her father's chagrin. If love meant acting foolishly, she'd take duty, family, and honor—things that truly mattered—any day of the week.

A servant in red and gold livery waited as the carriage came to a halt. It rocked softly as first Millie then Jorgine was helped down. The other girl didn't waste any time. With a glance toward Mr. Raley, Millie sashayed over to a young man Jorgine didn't recognize and smiled up at him. The gentleman must have realized his good fortune as he offered Millie his arm, and together they walked over to the refreshment table.

Jorgine shook her head. Why couldn't Millie simply be truthful with Mr. Raley and confess her feelings? But she already knew the answer. It wasn't the proper thing to do.

Movement in the far upstairs corner of the house caught Jorgine's attention. She could barely make out Olivia's slender shadow, but the bright colors of the wedding ring quilt she held were unmistakable. Why would her friend be hanging such a blanket from the window of her balcony?

Jorgine sucked in a quick breath. Papa had mentioned a group of people who used quilts and such as a system of welcoming runaway slaves and helped ferry them north to freedom. An underground railroad he'd called it. Was it possible Olivia and her family were involved? But what if she was wrong?

All she could do was ask. Like Papa always said, nothing ventured, nothing gained. If anyone could help her, Olivia would. It was a well-kept secret that she'd taught her father's servants to read. Maybe she could give Jorgine advice on how to help Sally.

Jorgine glanced up at the window once more then hurried toward the front hallway.

Chapter 2

"You have to be more careful, Liv," Hudson Wallace scolded his sister as he folded their mother's treasured quilt. "What if one of the guests saw it hanging off the balcony and knows what it means?"

"When did you turn into a handwringer?" Liv grabbed the blanket out of his hands and refolded it. "And if anyone asks, we'll tell them it had just been washed and was hanging out to dry. As if anyone would dare."

"Still, be careful. You know the penalty for helping runaways escape."

"I know, and I will be more careful, I promise." She laid the quilt on the edge of her bed then turned back to him. "We really need to get downstairs. Pa will be calling up the South Carolina Regulars if we don't put in an appearance soon."

"You go on." Hudson strolled over to the double doors leading to the balcony. "I'll be down in a minute."

Liv gathered her hat and gloves from her dresser and headed for the door. "Don't be too long. Mama's invited most of Abbeville today. I think she's hoping you'll fall in love with one of the local girls and settle down."

"I would've figured every woman of age in Anderson County would be under lock and key given my reputation."

"You and I both know you're using your 'reputation' as a disguise." She leaned against the doorframe. "If any of these women knew what you were doing, they'd fall at your feet and pledge their eternal love."

Hudson scoffed. "I highly doubt that, considering I'd be tarred and feathered if not dead."

Liv pulled the door open then turned back to him. "Dear brother, you simply haven't met the right kind of woman yet." She gave him an affectionate smile as the door closed behind her.

His sister and her romantic tripe. Didn't she realize it was all a lie? Hudson stared out the balcony window at the growing crowd below. Look at them, the pinnacle of Anderson County society trampling through his mother's beloved rose garden, only here to see if the rumors were true that the wayward son had come home.

He took a sip of the warm lemonade Amos had brought him when Father had sent his man to fetch him. Hudson knew his father's reasons for calling him home. Yes, Mother could use a bit of sea air after her brush with pneumonia last winter, but more importantly, they were to organize a sea escape for runaway slaves through the Port of Savannah. A dangerous undertaking to be sure, but his parents were up to the challenge. He and Liv would "conduct" former slaves through their "station" while Father and Mother were gone.

But it couldn't be out of the family home anymore. Running the operation out of Mount

Paran was too dangerous. He would inform the conductors that he would be moving the operations to his property at Thorndike Hall.

A glimpse of honey blond curls below caught his attention, but she was gone before he could discover who it was. He only knew one person with that glorious shade of hair. Jorgine Emerson. His heart sped up at the thought of her. She'd been seventeen last time he'd seen her, tall and slender with an air of girlish innocence about her. The memory of that afternoon seeped through him. She'd come to give him her heart, and he'd ripped it to pieces like a page of thick parchment. Even now, all these years later, he could see he'd had no other choice.

A light knock on the door startled him. Someone looking for his sister? Or maybe a quiet place to escape the crush downstairs? Hudson walked across the room. "If you're looking for the ladies' salon, it's downstairs in the ballroom." He opened the door to find himself staring into a pair of familiar violet-blue eyes. "Jor. . .I mean, Miss Emerson."

She looked as surprised as he felt. Her cheeks were flushed, and her full pink lips parted in a slight O. "Mr. Wallace. I wasn't expecting to find you here." She glanced down the hallway then back at him. "I thought this was Liv's room."

"It is." He hesitated slightly then turned toward the balcony. "I've always liked the view from her room."

When he turned back, he found her staring at the folded quilt on the chair. "I was looking for your sister. I need to speak to her on an urgent matter."

That spiked his interest. "What kind of matter, if you don't mind my asking?"

Her eyes snapped up to meet his. "Nothing for you to worry about."

This wasn't good. Any minute now, someone could discover them, and then what? Jorgine's reputation would be left in tatters. But he had a part to play, a disguise of carefree rogue. Hudson threw open the door and stepped aside, almost daring her. "As you can see, my sister isn't here."

Instead of turning tail and running like he had hoped, Jorgine walked inside.

This isn't the same girl who offered me her heart. Unsure what to do, Hudson closed the door. "Dear heavens, woman, have you gone mad? If someone were to catch you here with me. . ."

"Calm down. No one's going to see me." Her gaze caught on the quilt again, and she walked over to the chair. "Liv and I used to play hide-and-seek in this room when we were children." She picked up the corner of the blanket. "I think I could find a way to conceal myself."

Tarnation! Jorgine was a bright woman. If she put two and two together, his days of helping runaway slaves would be numbered. Best to scare her off. Walking toward her, he gave her a wolfish smile. "A gift from a widowed lady in Atlanta. She thought it might keep me warm at night."

She blushed to the roots of her blond hair yet pushed on. "Why was it hanging from the window?"

A good question, one he had a ready answer for, but Jorgine muddled his thoughts. Turning the questions on her would give him time to think. "Why do you think it was there?"

Jorgine hesitated, almost as if she were weighing her response. Finally, she straightened slightly, her chin tilted in that stubborn little way of hers. "Papa told me of a group of people who use quilts as signals to help slaves travel north. I was hoping Liv might be able to help me with that."

"Why?" The question was out before Hudson could stop himself. Though he knew of

Jorgine through Liv, his sister had never mentioned Jorgine's thoughts on slavery.

"I need to get Sally away from here."

"Sally?"

"My maid," she whispered, then added almost as an afterthought, "My friend."

She spoke with such sincerity, Hudson almost believed her. But a conversation he'd overheard between his father and Elliott Emerson, especially the part where Emerson had refused to free his slaves because "it would hurt Jorgine," still weighed heavy on him. Had she truly had a change of heart concerning slavery? Or was she one of those trying to stop Miss Tubman's work?

Hudson folded his arms over his chest. "Why her?"

"I'm to be married in a month."

There was no hint of excitement in her voice, no longing. Only dull acceptance. Something about it didn't sit right with him. For all her faults, Jorgine deserved to be happy. "Congratulations. Who is the lucky man?"

"Win Wakefield."

No wonder she seemed to dread her wedding. The Wakefields held power in Columbia and were wealthy as Midas, but their riches were built on the backs of slave hunters who trapped runaways like animals for a bit of coin. And Win? There were tales of illegitimate children among his slaves attached to his name. "A state senator, no less. Your father would be proud."

"Papa would be appalled," she bit out then pressed her lips tighter. "He never would have allowed this to happen if he'd lived."

"I see." Though he didn't, not really. "His death freed you to make your own choice of a husband."

"My choice?" Her voice strengthened. "Whenever does a woman have a choice, Hudson? Her entire life is managed by men." She drew in a deep breath. "I just want to make sure Sally is safe."

Dear heavens, had Jorgine heard the rumors about her intended? How could she marry such a man? "Does she have family in the North?"

She shook her head. "I just feel with my impending marriage, Sally might be happier away from here."

"You mean away from Win?"

Color infused her cheeks again, but her gaze never faltered. "Yes."

"You know your fiancé's reputation yet you're going through with the wedding?" Hudson wanted to shake some sense into her. "Are you that desperate for social standing?"

Her head snapped back as if he'd physically slapped her, but there was a fire in her eyes that Hudson found appealing. "You're one to speak on the matter. Look at how your behavior has affected your family's reputation. Why, poor Liv hasn't had a male caller since you left for Atlanta."

Hudson fought to keep from laughing. "Really, Jorgine. I can understand why Win would press for a quick wedding. You look positively magnificent when you're in a snitch. I hope Win realizes what a prize he's won." He gave her a slight bow. "Now, if you'll excuse me, I have guests waiting downstairs."

Jorgine grabbed his arm as he turned to leave. "Please."

There was a vulnerability in her voice that made the muscles around his heart clench.

She'd never been one to ask for help. None of the Emersons did. Too much pride, his father had once said. Yet Jorgine was here, begging not for herself but for her servant girl.

He shouldn't do this, not with so many lives hanging on his every decision, but he couldn't help himself. "I might be able to help you."

Hope lit in her eyes. "You will?"

For some strange reason, he felt a swell of satisfaction that Jorgine Emerson needed him. "You remember the large blueberry bush at Thorndike Hall?"

"Miss Lucille's place?" Confusion wrinkled the smooth skin between her brows. "It's been deserted for years."

A perfect station for Hudson's work with the underground. "You and Sally will go berry-picking tomorrow morning, so bring a bucket."

"I don't know, Hudson. What about Liv?"

He shook his head. No sense landing them both at the end of a rope if this was a trap. "Meet me at nine tomorrow morning in the lane outside the big house."

Jorgine looked ready to stamp her dainty foot. Well, let her pitch a fit if she wanted, but she'd abide by his rules. After all, it wasn't just his freedom at stake. She gave him a terse nod. "Fine, but you're playing games with me."

"I could say the same for you."

Her lush mouth flattened. "I'll be there at nine."

He nodded as he stepped aside for her to pass. She was halfway to the door when he called out, "Jorgine?"

Her skirts rustled softly as she turned around. "Yes?"

Hudson gave her his most wicked smile. "Don't forget the bucket."

Chapter 3

"You've done made a bargain with the devil." Sally jammed another hair pin into Jorgine's thick curls as she sat at her dresser the next morning.

She winced as the sharp metal scraped her scalp. "I know you're angry, but it doesn't give you the right to use my head as a pincushion."

"I'm sorry." Her friend's dark eyes met hers in the mirror. "What were you thinking, asking help from a man like Hudson Wallace? All those rumors about his women in Atlanta. The man is just..." Sally sputtered for the right word.

"A devil. I know, but if he can help us..."

"How do you suppose he can do that?" Sally snapped back.

"I'm not sure." It was a question that had plagued Jorgine all through the night. How could Hudson help her, and more importantly, why? The man had made it clear what he thought of her—another social-climbing, money-grubbing rich girl with no thought to anything except for marrying well. Yet he'd offered to help, and she'd been too desperate to turn him down.

In truth, he was their only hope.

Jorgine brushed Sally's hands away and stood. "I wouldn't have taken the chance if I didn't believe he could help us. I want to know you're settled before the wedding."

"I could stay." She trailed after Jorgine, straightening her sleeve. "Seems you're going to need help more than I will."

"I'm sure everything will be fine after the ceremony," Jorgine said with as much confidence as she could muster. "Win's promised that after the election, I can resign to Piney Brooke while he stays in Columbia. With my inheritance, I intend to set this place to rights, the way Papa always wanted it. The only men working the fields here will be freed men earning a living wage."

Sally went to the small table in the corner, poured a cup from a waiting teapot, and gave it to Jorgine as she sat down. "I wonder what Mr. Win's going to think when he finds out. It won't set well with him or your uncle."

"I don't care." She leaned back in her chair, feeling suddenly defeated. "They planned this marriage without a thought for what I might want. Win wants the Emerson name and my dowry, but I'm not sure what Uncle Richard gets out of the deal. It must be something huge. He wouldn't sell me to the highest bidder unless he gets his pound of flesh."

Sally scrunched up her nose. "Has Mrs. Wakefield set the wedding date yet?"

Jorgine couldn't blame her friend. She didn't much care for her high-handed future mother-in-law either. "No, though she did say she wants it held before the legislature goes home for the summer. That way, the senators and representatives can be in attendance."

"When's that?"

Jorgine sighed. "Two months."

Sally leaned forward and poured herself a cup of tea. "Your uncle Richard will be glad to hear that. He likes hobnobbing with such folks. Nothing like your daddy."

"No one was like Papa," she answered quietly. Even now, five years since his passing, the grief could steal her breath. Papa had been both mother and father to her, teaching her how to run the house as well as letting her come along when he managed the fields. Yet he'd made Uncle Richard her guardian. Why? Had he not trusted her to continue his dream of freeing his slaves and making Piney Brooke a productive farm?

"We're here, Miss Jorgine."

The wagon pulled into the overgrown drive in front of what was left of the Thorndike mansion. What once was described by her father as a magnificent piece of Greek architecture stood in shambles. Broken brick lay in heaps at the bottom of what should have been a lovely stairway up to the porch. The paint left was flaking with large holes of rotted wood. Thorndike Hall held the best soil to grow cotton in all the South, but after Miss Lucille's death and with no heirs to take charge, the place had become a place for vagrants. Even they had abandoned it after the walls started tumbling down.

The perfect place to harbor runaways.

Did it matter? Jorgine hopped down from the wagon then turned and reached inside for the small tin bucket and valise she'd brought. "Are you coming with me?"

"And step on a copperhead?" She shook her head. "My mama raised me with more sense than that."

"But he may want to take you to a safe house right away."

Still, Sally stood her ground. "Then I reckon you can come back for me."

Jorgine rolled her eyes as she gathered her skirts in her free hand. Her friend had never been one to mince words. Still, she'd step into a nest of poisonous snakes to see Sally safely away. "Fine, then stay with the wagon. If you see anyone, head back home. Hudson will help me get home."

"I don't like this." Sally stood, staring down at the weeds. "What if some of your uncle's men come?"

"Then tell them you're out picking berries." High-stepping across the yard, Jorgine headed for the tree line. "Whistle if you see anyone, all right?"

Sally begrudgingly nodded and settled back in the wagon, fanning herself with rapid strokes with her straw hat. With one last glance down the driveway, Jorgine slipped into the woods. It was cool under the lush canopy of newly bloomed trees, refreshing despite the heat and humidity of the late spring morning. It was almost like a day from long ago, when her papa had surprised her with a visit to Miss Lucille's prized blueberry bushes. How safe she'd felt in her father's arms as he lifted her to reach the higher fruit. And the taste! Never had berries tasted so good! If only Papa were here now, he'd know what to do.

Jorgine walked for several minutes, enjoying the coolness, when she came across a freshly worn path. No one had been out here for years. What was Hudson up to?

"Confused?"

She jerked around, her bucket connecting with the man's broad shoulder before she realized who it was. "Hudson, you startled me!"

He rubbed his arm, his mouth curled up into a rakish smile. "At least you know how to protect yourself, though I'd appreciate if you would aim your bucket at someone else."

Was he teasing her? Maybe it would do him good to know just how much she could protect those she loved. "I know how to shoot a pistol too."

His eyes widened as he took her elbow and led her up the path. "I'm shocked that a lady such as yourself would acquire the skill. What does your fiancé have to say about it?"

"I don't know. I haven't asked him."

Hudson threw back his head and laughed. "Any plans to use it on him?"

Jorgine's lips twitched into a smile. Leave it to Hudson to tease her about such a thing. "Only if he gives me reason to."

He leaned his head toward her and her heart skipped a beat. "Good girl."

She stole a glimpse at him. He'd always been a commanding figure even when they were young. Then she'd found a refuge in his company when she and Liv had quarreled, a comforting spirit who treated her with such care and respect, it had been easy to fall in love with him before she was barely out of the schoolroom. And now? She couldn't bear what he'd become—a rake and a scalawag who would break a woman's heart.

Jorgine shifted away from him. "It's not every day I go traipsing through the woods."

"Let's hope not." His voice hummed with humor. "People might get the idea that there's something out here."

"Is there?"

The playful spark in his eyes dulled as he shook his head. "Just an old blueberry bush as far as I know."

She'd known Hudson long enough to know when he was hiding something. "I don't believe you."

If he was insulted, he masked it well. "Are you calling me a liar, Jorgine?"

"I'm sure you've been called much worse."

He chuckled as he pushed a low-lying tree limb out of their way. "Such a sharp tongue for the future wife of a state senator. What will they think of you in Columbia?"

"I don't know and don't care." Jorgine lifted her skirts to step over a fallen tree. "I won't be accompanying my husband to the capital. I'll be here, managing Piney Brooke with Big Jim."

"Not a love match then." His mouth, so relaxed and laughing moments ago, had thinned into a stiff line. "I can see what Win would get out of such a connection. The Emerson name holds a great deal of prestige in the South, which he'll need if the rumors are true that he's considering a run for the presidency. Then you would be first lady of the land." His heated gaze raked over her, making her wish she hadn't left her fan in the wagon. "With your considerable charms, I wouldn't leave you at Piney Brooke if I were your husband."

Jorgine swallowed against the tightness in her throat. He had no right to talk to her in such a way, yet his words gave her a vague sense of pleasure. "My considerable charms?"

His fingers tightened on her elbow. "I know beautiful women. Remember?"

The comment felt like a splash of cold creek water. She must be crazy with worry to consider working with Hudson, but she had no other choice. "How are you going to help Sally escape?"

He must have sensed the change in her because he straightened, then released her elbow and held out his arm to her. "Come with me."

Jorgine glanced back toward the road. "But Sally. . ."

"Is fine," he answered. "Or she was when I checked on her a few minutes ago."

Hudson had looked in on her friend? "That was kind of you."

"I have been known to be that way at times." He held out his arm to her again. "Please, come with me."

Jorgine stepped back, crossing her arms around her waist. "Not until you tell me where we're going and how you plan to help me."

Dark blue eyes glared down into hers, leaving her a little breathless. Why did the man have to be so handsome? "Jorgine, for this to work, you're going to have to trust me as much as I have to trust you. Do you think you can do that?"

Past experience said no, but she knew this man, believed that even after he had broken her heart all those years ago, she could still trust him. Jorgine wouldn't rest until Sally was safe, and Hudson was her only hope.

Jorgine took his arm. "Yes, I can do that."

"Good." Hudson's hand closed over hers. "Then let me show you how it's done."

Chapter 4

Could he truly trust Jorgine?

It was a question that had plagued him throughout the night, really since the moment he'd opened Liv's bedroom door to find her on the other side. She seemed genuine enough in her concern for her maid, but the slave hunters had used those tactics before with great success. They used every means possible to collect their bags of gold. Money that Win Wakefield and his family provided them when they retrieved lost "property."

Yet she'd as much as told him she didn't love Win, didn't plan on sharing a home or a life with him. She must be more innocent than he'd thought if she believed Win would leave her to manage Piney Brooke. No man in his right mind would desert such loveliness, especially his wife. That she had a keen mind and a sharp wit would only endear her to those in Wakefield's circles, an asset that could win him the White House.

"Should we get Sally?" Jorgine asked, interrupting his thoughts. "I assumed you'd be taking her with you today."

He could understand how Jorgine had reached that conclusion, asking her to bring her maid along. But he had to make certain she was being honest with him. "I'm afraid you're going to be disappointed."

"But. . ."

He might be willing to trust her with his life, but he wouldn't endanger his charges, not just yet. "There will be time later."

She breathed out a long sigh. "In other words, not today."

Hudson always knew Jorgine was a smart girl. "Be patient."

Her hand gripped his arm as if to impress on him the urgency of the situation. "I marry Win in two months' time. After that, I can't protect her."

"You could always hit him with a bucket."

"Well, there is that." She bowed her head slightly but not before he caught her mouth curve into a small smile.

Why did her smile make him feel so. . .elated? As if sharing her burden had somehow lightened his own? Strange, he'd never felt that way before, but then, Jorgine always had a way of playing on his emotions. "For now, we need to fill your bucket."

"I thought Miss Lucille's bushes would have died from neglect."

"They've been resurrected."

Her eyes met his, and his breath snagged in his chest. When had her eyes become such a silky shade of blue with threads of silver? Resigned, yet full of hope. Hudson's chest tightened. Wakefield had better understand the treasure he had in Jorgine or. . . What?

"You had them pruned last winter."

Her statement jarred Hudson from his thoughts. He cleared his throat. "Pruned them myself on one of my visits home. I wanted to make certain they produced this year."

"Why?" She glanced up at him. "Mount Paran always has a good crop of berries, and even with the number of people in your household, I can't see how you could use all those preserves."

Jorgine had never seen people starved for food, had never known how much a handful of berries could mean to a person who hadn't eaten in days. But then, how could she possibly know what these people had endured? It was a lesson she'd soon learn firsthand. "The people that I help, some haven't eaten in days when they arrive here. Most arrive at my station with barely the clothes on their back. They don't have time to hunt for food. Some barely have the strength to eat."

"But they're fed at the stations?" She hesitated as if gathering her thoughts. "You can't expect them to keep running without food in their bellies."

The outrage in her voice set his temper to flame. "Most of our departures happen at night, so building a fire, even lighting a lantern, could signal the slave hunters. As for them, they'd rather be hungry than go back to their chains."

Jorgine went still beside him. She could destroy him and his family with the information he'd just given her. He'd be shot, but Liv and his parents, they would suffer the most.

"What can I do to help?"

The question startled him. Surely she was joking. But her somber expression told him otherwise. "You can't be serious."

Her expression tightened. "Why not? I can't bear the thought of anyone going hungry any more than you can. If I can help, I want to."

She wasn't thinking. She wouldn't even consider offering if she'd thought this through. "What about your fiancé? He wouldn't take too kindly to you feeding the very slaves his men are hunting."

Her face paled. "Win owns a slave retrieval business?"

Dear heavens, did Jorgine really have no idea whom she was marrying? "Not just slave hunters. Bounty hunters as well. The largest one of its kind. His family made their fortune from it." He couldn't help but ask. "You didn't know?"

"Why would I? I've only met the man once." Her mouth trembled as her words trailed off. "How could Uncle Richard do this?" She rubbed her fingers against her forehead as if trying to think, then straightened as if she'd made her decision. "You never answered my question. How can I help?"

Bright spots of sunlight dotted the path around them. Just beyond the last row of pine trees sat the clearing, the center of the operation. He was playing with fire, letting Jorgine into this part of his world. Sally could be ferried north, and Jorgine would be none the wiser. It was her simple request to help that had broken his resolve.

He only prayed to God he wouldn't regret it.

The clearing was much like Jorgine remembered. Hundred-year-old oaks circled the field of wheat grass, the flat ground a perfect place for young children to play. Over to her left, a lush bush almost as tall as the crepe myrtle outside the kitchens at home bloomed, the ripe fruit large enough to be seen from this distance.

But there were distinct changes too. Two wooden sheds, large enough to conceal a group of people, hid among the trees on the far side of the meadow. Near the center, a few stumps lay in primitive seating arrangements with a small fire pit in the center for warmth.

Hudson pointed to the larger of the two buildings. "That's where Sally will stay until the conductor comes to take her to the next station."

"How many people does he take at one time?"

"It depends." He led her closer to the first building. "We've had as many as fifteen or twenty at a time, but usually it's more like two or three. A smaller number makes it easier to outrun the hunters."

A cold shiver ran down Jorgine's spine. She was bound to the man who paid the hunters. She pushed the thought away. Sally and these people were what mattered now. "How can I trust the conductor to make sure Sally is safe? Who is this man? Can I meet him?"

Hudson shook his head. "This person puts himself at great danger ferrying these people to the next station. I won't increase their chances of being captured just to calm your fears. All I can say is to have faith, and trust me."

"That's easier said than done." And growing harder by the minute. Why would God allow her to be put in this situation in the first place? Without her papa to guide her? Engaged to a man whose actions rivaled those of the devil himself. Did God even care about her anymore?

Hudson's hand slid over hers. "God has a plan for all of this."

She glanced up at him. "You sound so certain of that."

"It's what I cling to at times."

Hudson had never spoken of his faith, at least not so honestly. But then, she'd never voiced her own, feeling it was a private matter between her and God. "I guess I don't have much of a choice if I want to see Sally away from here."

"You'll feel better once you've seen the process."

Her head snapped around. "You're going to let me help?"

He hesitated. He couldn't change his mind now, not when she found herself so desperate to do what she could for these people. Even if he turned her down, she'd find a way. Maybe Liv knew some way she could get food to these people.

Hudson licked his lips. "The truth is I need all the help I can get, but there are dangers to this. If we're discovered, if anyone finds out that you've been helping the runaways, the life you have won't exist anymore. You'll be a pariah. And if Win finds out. . ."

Jorgine nodded. She didn't doubt the man would probably kill her. Uncle Richard too. Still, her mind was made up. "I understand."

He opened his mouth to speak when the creak of a wooden door turned their attention to the smaller of the two sheds. A few seconds later, a Negro girl, no more than eleven or twelve, peeked around the side of the building.

"Come on out," Hudson said, waving her toward them. "You're safe here."

She took a tentative step and then another as if measuring the promise in his words. As she drew nearer, she straightened her lanky body to her full height. "Are you Mr. Hudson?"

He nodded. "Who might you be?"

The stench of pigs and sweat clung to her like a second skin as she stood in front of them, the fabric of her dress so sheer and torn, it barely hung on her slender shoulders. Her gaze shifted from Hudson to Jorgine. "Mama said I only speak to Mr. Hudson."

Letting go of his arm, Jorgine set the valise down then dragged her lace shawl from her shoulders. She handed it to the girl. "My name is Jorgine, and I'm here to help."

The girl glanced at Hudson. He nodded as if he wasn't quite sure what to make of this. Well, she didn't care what he thought of her. She'd do what she could for these people with or without his help.

Jorgine crouched down and opened her valise. "Are you thirsty?"

The girl's eyes grew wide, and she licked her lips. "Mighty thirsty, ma'am."

"Then I hope you like lemonade." She pulled Papa's whiskey flask from her bag and handed it to her. "My friend Sally says I make the best she's ever tasted. Sweet with just a little bit of tartness."

The girl took the flask with both hands and drew a long swig from the container.

"You carry lemonade in a whiskey flask?" Hudson asked with a note of laughter in his voice.

"It was Papa's." She stole a glance at him and then returned her attention to the girl. "It may seem silly, but carrying it makes me feel like he's close by."

"I'm sorry." His voice lowered to a whisper. "I know you must feel his loss tremendously. I shouldn't have poked fun at you like that."

"Though you do seem to enjoy doing it." Jorgine nodded toward the girl. "Did you know she was here?"

He shook his head. "But they show up like this at times, though usually not this young." Hudson waited until the girl set the flask aside to speak again. "Now, what is your name?"

The girl wiped her arm across her mouth. "Mazie, sir."

"What are you doing out here?"

A defiant light grew in her dark eyes. "I done runned away, sir."

"But you're barely a child." Forgetting herself, Jorgine approached her slowly then draped an arm around her thin shoulders. "What do your parents have to say about this?"

Mazie leaned into her as if searching for comfort. "I don't know where my daddy is, ma'am. Master sold him off when I still slept in my mama's belly. And Mama—" She drew in a shuddering breath. "Mama took sick a while back. Miss Emma—that's the master's great-aunt—she told us there ain't nothing left to be done." Tears glistened in her black lashes. "Both Mama and Miss Emma said I need to run. Said the master's been looking at me in a particular way, funny like." Her face crumpled. "I didn't want to leave Mama, ma'am. Not with her sick like that."

A knot tightened around Jorgine's heart. Poor child. Grieving the loss of everything she'd ever known and sent out into the world alone. She pulled Mazie against her, stroking her back as the girl cried. "Shh. Everything is going to be all right. You're safe now."

"We'll take care of you."

Jorgine lifted her head to find Hudson watching her with an intensity that made her feel vulnerable, as if he could see into every corner of her heart. She shook her head slightly. Why would Hudson care how she felt? And yet she knew without a doubt that he did.

Now was not the time for such thoughts, not with Mazie in such need. Jorgine met Hudson's gaze. "We will help her."

His soft smile made her stomach flutter like butterflies around a honeysuckle bush. "We will."

Chapter 5

"What do you know about Jorgine Emerson's engagement to Win Wakefield?" Hudson buttered a piece of toast and handed it to his sister.

Liv took a bite then lay the rest down on her plate. She lifted the nearby coffeepot and poured herself a cup. "It's turning into the wedding of the season, though I have to say I was surprised by it all. Jorgine usually tells me everything, but she never said a word about Win courting her. I only heard of the engagement when Win announced it at a party last month."

"Jorgine didn't tell you?"

His sister set down her cup and leaned back in her chair. "Why do you want to know?"

Hudson took a bite of his eggs and chewed slowly. Why did he want to know? It had been two weeks since he and Jorgine had come across Mazie at the clearing. Every day since, Jorgine had come as promised, her valise filled with an array of items such as bandages and toweling, hard candy for the children, anything she thought would make the journey easier to bear.

More than anything, she cared for them. It showed in her touch, in the easy way she spoke to each person, always listening and offering encouragement. These men and women had value to her, not as property but as people.

"Are you going to answer my question?"

Hudson pinched the bridge of his nose. "For Pete's sake, Liv. . ."

She laughed as she picked up her coffee cup. "I love when I get the best of you. It happens so rarely. So tell me. Why all the questions about Jorgine this morning? Does it have anything to do with all the time you've been spending together at Thorndike Hall?"

He grimaced. "You're just as nosy as she is with all her questions. Just yesterday, she asked me why the sheds were built the way they were. Said we could have fit a small kitchen with a cookstove in the larger one so we could feed people before we sent them off to the next station."

"She's just concerned about our passengers, that's all."

Hudson knew that. Jorgine lived out her concern every time she came to the sheds. Yet she was engaged to marry a man who made a living from hunting down and brutalizing the defenseless. "She's only helping until we can get her maid to safety."

"Really, Hudson. Do you think so little of Jorgine?" Liv blotted the edge of her mouth with a cloth napkin. "She knows you would have helped Sally escape whether she worked with you or not."

Yes, Hudson conceded. He would never turn his back on someone in need, especially a woman in a helpless situation like Sally. Jorgine would know that. "Then why is she spending her nights out there at the sheds?"

"Maybe because she wants to help."

Yet Jorgine kept her own slaves. How could she give aid to runaways when she refused to free her own? "I guess her father was right."

Liv broke off a piece of bacon and popped it into her mouth. "What are you talking about?"

"Just before he died, Mr. Emerson came to Atlanta to see me. He knew we were part of the underground, supported what we were doing, but he felt using our own home was too much of a risk. He'd bought Thorndike Hall after Miss Lucille passed and offered to sell it to me."

"I didn't know he owned that place."

"I didn't either." Hudson pushed his plate aside then leaned his forearms on the edge of the table. "He sold it to me for less than it was worth. He told me several times during that visit how wrong he'd come to believe slavery to be and how he wanted to help any way he could." He hesitated. "Maybe he sensed he didn't have long and he wanted to make things right with the Lord."

"Maybe, but then why didn't he free his own slaves?" Liv asked.

"I asked him that. He said he couldn't free them because of Jorgine."

"What?" Liv tossed her napkin on the table and sat up. "That's ridiculous."

"I agree." At least, he wanted to believe so. Then why had the man been so unmovable in his decision when Hudson had confronted him? "Jorgine's father thought that freeing his slaves would hurt her."

"I don't know where he got that idea from." Liv took another sip of coffee. "After Mr. Emerson passed, Jorgine gave all of the slaves on Piney Brooke their freedom. It was her uncle Richard who had them rounded up before they got too far away."

Hudson tried to follow what Liv was saying. Jorgine had freed her father's slaves? "What right did Richard Emerson have to retrieve them?"

"He is her guardian."

"And she's a grown woman now," Hudson bit out.

"I do have another theory as to why Jorgine is at the clearing so much." Placing her cup back in its saucer, Liv leaned back again, her eyes dancing with amusement. "I believe she's still in love with you."

His heart did a little flip in his chest, and he scoffed. "She's engaged. The wedding is soon."

"I know. We received our invitation." Liv took a biscuit from the basket in front of her and broke it open. "But everyone knows it's not a love match. Her uncle arranged the marriage with Mrs. Wakefield, at least that's what people are saying. The Wakefields will promote Mr. Emerson's bid for governor next year while Win will have use of the Emerson name and Jorgine's dowry to get elected to the senate."

A marriage of convenience, she'd told him. Still, Richard Emerson in the governor's mansion. "I don't see how Emerson thinks he can win. He doesn't have the political clout or the wealth his brother had."

"Oh my heavens." Liv's eyes were dark with sudden concern. "I thought the rumors seemed odd, but then I overheard that Mr. Emerson had come into money recently." She stared at him. "You don't think he's taken Jorgine's inheritance?"

Hudson shook his head. "Her father probably made provisions for them both."

"Maybe. But it would be easy for Mr. Emerson to steal from her. He is her guardian, after all."

Yes, it would make it easier, but the man couldn't be that foolish. Once she was married, he would relinquish his responsibilities to her as well as her money. Hudson took a sip of coffee before realizing it had grown cold. Was that why Jorgine had agreed to this marriage? To lay claim to her inheritance? It was a common practice. No one would blame her.

Still, it didn't sound like the woman he knew. A woman motivated by money wouldn't put so much of herself into helping others.

"Hudson?"

He glanced over to find Liv watching him, her pale brows gathered in sisterly concern. "Hmm?"

"Are you in love with Jorgine?"

Possibly. Of course, he'd always been a little in love with her for years, but the last two weeks had revealed in her a woman he both admired and respected. But even if he was, and she returned his feelings, she'd made a commitment to marry Win. Breaking her engagement would bring social consequences with it.

"We're friends, Liv." He gave her a halfhearted grin. "Besides, I have my reputation to consider. It's difficult to be a rake with a wife."

"Well then." Her sigh held a note of disappointment as she reached for the small stack of mail she'd brought in with her. "I have some letters I must answer before the dressmaker arrives this afternoon."

Hudson leaned back in his chair. Liv had always harbored the hope he and Jorgine would one day marry and have a family. But it just wasn't possible, not if he wanted to continue his work with the Underground Railroad. Hundreds, thousands of people had escaped because of his ability to collect information on slave hunters, but all that depended on his rakish disguise.

"Hudson."

He glanced across the table to find Liv holding a letter out for him. "It's from Papa. We've been compromised."

Chapter 6

Jorgine leaped out of the seat of the wagon before Big Jim could come around to help her down. "Remember, if Uncle Richard comes by in the morning, have Sally tell him I was up with a headache all night and won't be accepting callers until afternoon, all right?"

"I don't know about this, Miss Jorgine. Don't seem fitting for a young lady such as yourself to be traipsing around alone in the dark." He held up his large, calloused hand when Jorgine opened her mouth to speak. "Mr. Hudson is a fine man doing an honorable thing, helping all those folks like that. But if Mr. Richard finds out you're working with him..." His voice trembled slightly. "Lord save you both."

A cold shiver ran down Jorgine's spine. Big Jim must have overheard the same conversation she had. "I'm sure Uncle Richard was only trying to impress those folks from Charleston."

"He said any man or woman helping a runaway should be shot." Jim lifted her valise out of the undercarriage and set it down beside her. "Said he'd kill his own kin if need be."

Even now, her uncle's words made her go cold, but Jorgine couldn't stop her work now that she had seen the need. She lifted the basket of sandwiches she and Sally had made and settled it into the crook of her arm. "Just because he said that doesn't mean he'll do it."

"Doesn't mean he won't either."

She threw a shawl around her shoulders. "Well, I don't think I'm in any danger from him. I'm not sure what he wants from the Wakefields, but he needs me to get it."

"What about Mr. Hudson?"

That question kept her awake at night. If something happened to Hudson, if her uncle found out what he was doing and went after him, she wasn't sure what she would do. Thank God for small miracles. "Didn't I tell you? Mrs. Wallace is feeling so much better, they decided to cut their trip short and return home. Hudson will return to Atlanta by the end of next week."

Jim studied her for a long moment. "I is sorry, Miss Jorgine."

Not nearly as much as she was. For the first time in her life, she felt a part of something more than herself, something that truly mattered. God had opened this path to her as well as certain truths. *"For God so loved the world."* Not based on the color of their skin, but everyone.

Then there was Hudson. Jorgine drew in a deep breath of cool air. He was nothing like the rogue he pretended to be. In him, she'd found a quiet strength born out of his convictions, someone she could lean on in a world teetering on the brink of war. His faith had helped revive her own after the barren months following her engagement to Win.

A knot formed at the base of her throat. How could she marry one man when her heart belonged to another?

Now was not the time for such thoughts. A large group of runaways was expected this evening, and there was much to prepare. Jorgine untied her bonnet and put it on the wagon seat. "We hope to have everyone moved out before dawn, but that's only if things go smoothly. Hudson will bring me around the back way in case Richard has his men waiting at the front gates."

"I'll be sitting up, waiting."

Jorgine glanced over at him. The dark hair she remembered as a girl had given way to silver, the gentle lines in his face a witness to times gone by. Big Jim was a constant in her life, one of the few people she still trusted. She threw herself against his strong chest. "I wish you were my uncle."

Jim gave her shoulder an awkward pat then folded his arms around her. "It's going to be all right, little girl. God's at work in all of this. You'll see."

"I already do." She gave him a kiss on his whiskered cheek then stepped back, reaching for her supplies. "But you don't have to sit up. Go on to bed."

"I'll be deciding what I need to do." Grabbing the leather strap on the seat, he launched his large frame into the wagon. "You be careful, you hear me. I'll be praying for you both."

Before she could thank him, he slapped the reins against horseflesh and jutted forward. Moments later, the wagon slipped out of sight. She'd tried to convince him and her cook, Jocelyn, to run, offered to help them get settled as she would Sally. But the man had refused. *"Master Emerson told me to watch over you, and I aim to do just that."* Maybe after she married Win, she could convince them to go.

Jorgine gathered her things and glanced around. A large moon overhead cast light over the short meadow on the opposite side of the clearing, away from prying eyes. Hudson always met her near the tree line as soon as Big Jim was gone. So where was he? Her uncle's words exploded through her mind. Had he been discovered? Was Hudson being stood in front of a tree, his hands and feet tied with rifles aimed at his chest, awaiting the fatal bullet? Without thinking, she started toward the woods.

"Jorgine?"

Relief flooded through her at the sight of his tall, lumbering figure hurrying toward her. She wanted to wrap her arms around him then press her head against his chest and listen to his heart beat strong and confident. Instead, she took a calming breath. "You scared the fire out of me."

"Were you worried about me?" There was a hint of amusement in his voice.

"Yes. No." She pressed her lips together. "Uncle Richard said he'd shoot anyone he caught helping the runaways, and when you didn't come right way, I thought. . ." She took another breath. "Forget I ever said anything."

He stepped closer, his hands cupping her face. She breathed again, but this time, her lungs filled of him, of wood smoke and soap. Jorgine leaned into him. "I'm so sorry, sweetheart. It was nothing as dire as all that, but I can understand why you'd be upset. Your uncle should be taken out and horsewhipped for saying such a thing in front of you."

Relieved yet feeling awkward, Jorgine stepped out of his embrace. "He didn't really say it in front of me."

"You were eavesdropping?"

"You don't have to make it sound so vulgar." She shoved her valise at him.

Hudson took the case then offered her his arm. "I just didn't expect a lady like you to lower yourself to that level."

"How do you think women find out half the things they do? Their husbands and fathers certainly don't tell them."

Laughter rumbled in his voice. "Well played."

She dismissed the tiny irritation she felt and pressed on. "You never told me what kept you."

Any note of humor was gone when he spoke. "The passengers arrived early."

"Early?" Her skirts caught on a downed limb as Hudson hurried her into the forest. "But they weren't supposed to be here until after midnight."

Twigs snapped beneath his boots. "The conductor got wind of a raid that was planned for tonight. He thought it best to move them as quickly as possible."

A raid. She'd never considered that possibility. "That was smart thinking on his part to move them like that." Jorgine stopped, Hudson's blistering pace leaving her out of breath. "Could you slow down just a bit?"

"I'm sorry." His words came out a bit breathless. "But we have a situation with one of the runaways, and we need to get back as soon as possible."

Her heart sped up. "What kind of situation?"

Was it her imagination or had Hudson gone a shade paler? "One of the women who arrived this afternoon is laboring with her child."

"Oh dear. That is a problem. Aren't there other ladies to help her?"

Hudson shook his head as he gently pushed her forward. "There's only an older woman who is blind, from what I can gather."

Nerves jangled around in her stomach. "What about her husband?"

His hesitation sent a pang of despair through her chest. "Beaten to death a few days ago. It's why the woman ran. She didn't want her baby born into that."

Jorgine couldn't blame her. The thought of a child being born into forced servitude sickened her. This woman needed her. But should she tell Hudson her only birthing experience had been in the stables? No, he had enough to worry about now. Jorgine picked up the pace. "I'm going to need a small fire and clean water."

"We can't chance building a fire, not with the raiders still out there." Concern crept into his voice. "And the only well on the property is polluted."

"Then we'll have to make do with creek water." She yanked at her snagged skirt, and it ripped. "As long as I have a lantern to clean the scissors, I can manage."

"Are you sure?"

Poor man. She knew how he felt. Right now, she wasn't certain about anything. "Papa always said a baby has a way of making grown-ups feel completely helpless, yet hundreds are safely born every day."

"My papa has said much the same thing." He gave her a slight smile. "Doesn't really matter when it's happening, does it?"

As they broke into the clearing, a loud moan from the larger of the two sheds rent the air. Whether they were ready or not, this child would be born. Turning to Hudson, she gave him what she hoped was her most confident smile as she took her valise. "Would you do something for me?"

Chapter 7

Hudson watched as Jorgine slipped inside the wooden structure, the rustle of her skirts against the floor oddly comforting. She had shown no apprehension at the thought of delivering a child in such primitive conditions. Other women of his acquaintance would've protested at the very idea of delivering a slave's child. Not his Jorgine. She cared too much to leave the woman on her own.

He blinked. *My Jorgine.* He liked the sound of it.

"Sir, was that Miss Jorgine I seen going into that there barn?"

Hudson turned toward the man, one of several who had escaped from the fields outside of Greenwood. The last thing he needed was someone recognizing her. "What's your name, sir?"

"Eli, sir."

Hudson led him to the far side of the clearing, out of hearing distance of the others. When he was certain no one had followed, he turned to the man. "Would you mind telling me why you want to know who the lady is?"

The man slipped off his hat, holding it between clenched fingers. "Iffen that was Miss Jorgine, I'd like to say hello and thank her for all she done."

"Thank her?"

"Yes, sir. You see, Master Emerson was my master up until he passed a few years back." Eli's face grew sober. "That sure was a sorrowful time for all of us, none as much as Miss Jorgine. But the day after she buried her papa, she called us all together and told us we be free." He pushed his hand into his pants pocket and pulled out a coin. "Gave us each a twenty-dollar gold piece. Said it would help us get to where we be going."

Bowing his head slightly, Hudson smiled. The woman would give the last stitch of clothing on her back if she thought it would help. "Why didn't you leave?"

Eli shook his head. "Couldn't just leave Miss Jorgine with a crop in the field and no one to pick it. Truth be told, there weren't no kinder man than Master Emerson, and Miss Jorgine is cut from the same cloth." His eyes narrowed. "Can't say the same about the master's brother."

Hudson's head shot up. "You're not at Piney Brooke?"

"No, sir. Master was barely cold in his grave before Master Richard and his men came to collect us. Told us we be his property now." His voice grew gruff. "Old Silas tried to tell Master Richard we Miss Jorgine's to do with as she sees fit. Master Richard pulled out his pistol and shot old Silas dead right then and there." Eli met his gaze. "I figured it was time to take my leave."

None of this made sense. As her father's heir, Jorgine could do whatever she wished with her property, regardless of Richard's guardianship. Then how could the man legally declare these people were his property?

Unless part of his agreement with the Wakefields was that the courts would make Richard his brother's heir. With his connection in the state house, Win had enough leverage to pull it off.

Fury swamped through him at the thought that someone would take advantage of Jorgine. If Richard and the Wakefields could get away with this, what else would they try? "Jorgine isn't at Piney Brooke alone, is she?"

"No, sir. Big Jim, Miss Jocelyn the cook, and Sally stayed behind."

An old man and two helpless women. No one to keep Jorgine safe. Was that why she'd learned how to shoot? He wouldn't put it past her. She'd see it as her sacred duty to protect her home and those she loved.

Hudson glanced at Eli and nodded. "It was Miss Jorgine. She's helping out until we can arrange for Sally to escape."

"Then she has heard the rumors about Mr. Wakefield?"

"Yes," he conceded. How he wished he could have protected her from hearing the sordid news about her fiancé. But then she never would have come in search of help, and he wouldn't know the woman she'd become. "She's tending to one of the women right now. Once she's finished, I know she'll be happy to see you."

"Thank you." Eli turned toward the clearing then stopped and faced Hudson. "Sir?"

"Yes, Eli?"

"Take care of Miss Jorgine. The good Lord don't make them no better than her."

"Don't worry. I'll take good care of her." Hudson nodded. With his life if need be. "I'd better get that water she wanted or she'll come after me and tan my hide."

Eli chuckled. "Master always said if Miss Jorgine had been born a boy, she would have made a fine general, the way she likes to take over things."

Yes, she was bossy, but always with the best intentions and a kind heart. A woman he could love.

Minutes stretched to hours, punctuated by prolonged moans and the occasional scream. Hudson leaned against the doorframe, strangely comforted by Jorgine's muffled words of instruction and encouragement. The conductor—a Mr. Mims—had arrived almost an hour ago, prepared to ferry their passengers to the next stop. Both had agreed the group should move on with Mims circling back to collect the mother and child once the baby was born. The raiders could be on their trail even now, so the farther the group was away from Anderson County, the safer they would be.

"Breathe, Lizzie. That's it. You're doing good."

Jorgine's voice fell gently against his ears, soothing as a long, cool dip from Sweetwater Creek after a day in the fields. She was more than he'd ever suspected. She loved deeply the person, not their position. Cared about their character, not the color of their skin.

"Hudson?"

"I'm here." He pressed closer to the door. "What is it, sweetheart?"

"I need you." There was a weariness to her voice now. Poor thing, she had to be exhausted. "I wouldn't ask, but..."

"I'll do whatever you want me to." And he meant it, not just for this moment but for the rest of his life.

"Thank you." Her little sigh of relief warmed him. If only he could take all her burdens away so easily. The wooden latch unhinged from its bearings, and Jorgine opened the door. "I know it is unseemly to ask. I should be able to handle this myself, but. . ."

Hudson cupped her cheek, her warmth seeping into his fingertips before lodging in his chest. "This is an unusual circumstance, sweetheart."

His heart soared as she leaned into him as if drawing strength from his nearness. The urge to take her in his arms, to kiss the tiny crease between her brow, grew with each passing moment. Would she spurn his attentions? Or grow soft in his embrace?

A moan toward the back of the room forced him to drop his hand and step back. "What do you need me to do?"

Handing him the lantern, Jorgine wordlessly led him to the farthest corner of the building where a young woman, her rounded stomach bare and glistening with perspiration, lay writhing on the straw-covered floor. With a short breath, she blew out a deep moan, the muscles of her belly tightening with the contraction.

"Lizzie has done a wonderful job, but she's tired and this baby's begging to be born." Jorgine sank down on the floor beside the woman. Taking her handkerchief from her wristband, she mopped her face and neck. "If you could sit behind her and hold her up, that might give her the strength to push the baby out."

Hudson crouched down behind Lizzie, stretching out his legs on either side of hers, then pulled her back against his chest. "Hello, Miss Lizzie. I'm Mr. Hudson. We met earlier tonight."

The woman blew out a puff of air. "I remember."

"If it's all right with you, I'm going to help Miss Jorgine deliver your baby."

Hudson felt her muscles clench. "I's don't care as long as someone gets this stubborn child born!"

He glanced up at Jorgine, who gave him a grateful smile and then turned her attention back to Lizzie. "All right now. This little one is ready to meet his mama, but you have to push, dear."

The woman collapsed against his chest. "I can't, Miss Jorgine. I is too tired." Her head rolled from side to side. "Lord Jesus, help me!"

"Yes, Lord, please help Lizzie," Jorgine began as she pulled what looked to be the remains of a silky petticoat over the lower part of the woman s body. "She's worked hard, Lord, and she's tired and ready to meet her baby. Use this child in a mighty way to bring glory to Your kingdom. In Jesus' name."

Lizzie grabbed his hand, and he held it. "Yes, Lord, use my child for Your glory."

"Amen," Hudson whispered as Lizzie leaned into him and pushed.

For the next few moments, the world faded away and the only sounds he heard were Lizzie's pained cries and Jorgine's gentle words of encouragement. He'd never known the struggle a woman goes through birthing a child into the world, nor the beauty of it. When it was time, his wife would not go through this alone. He would be there, cooing silly words of love and encouragement, holding her hand, being a part of the miracle they'd created together.

Jorgine reached for clean toweling and her scissors. "One more push, Lizzie."

Hudson followed her movement as the woman hunched her body, her groan reverberating through to his chest. He lifted his gaze just in time to see Jorgine's face relax, her eyes aglow with a mixture of awe and profound joy. A tiny mew filled the room as she rubbed the baby vigorously, the smile on her lips almost angelic. "You have a healthy son, Lizzie."

"A boy," the woman whispered as if those were the most beautiful words ever spoken. "My Joe always wanted a son."

Jorgine slid the shawl she'd been wearing from her shoulders and wrapped the child in it before handing him carefully to his mother. "Your Joe would have been proud of you."

Joy so profound she could barely contain it spread across Lizzie's tired face as she drew her son to her chest.

Hudson stood, his throat tightening with emotion. What would it be like to witness the birth of his own son? He glanced at Jorgine. He could almost imagine her with their child, looking at him with so much love it stole his breath just thinking of it. He cleared his throat. "What will you name him?"

Lizzie spread the edges of the shawl to take full measure of her son. When she drew her finger across his tiny palm, he grasped it, making her wide smile grow even more. "Joseph after his papa. And George after Miss Jorgine here."

"Joseph George." Hudson smiled.

Jorgine sniffled beside him, and he turned. Tiny drops of moisture glistened in her lashes. When she caught him looking at her, she blushed. "I've never had a baby named after me."

Hudson wrapped his arm around her and pulled her close to his side. "It's a good, strong name like his namesake."

"Thank you, Miss Jorgine. You too, Mr. Hudson. I'm much obliged," Lizzie said as she ran a finger through the boy's feathery black hair.

"I'm just glad we were here to help." Hudson felt bereaved as Jorgine slipped out of his embrace and walked over to her valise. She pulled out a large cotton sheet, shook it out, and then covered Lizzie and her baby with it. "Once you get him fed, you both need to rest." She turned to Hudson. "When will the conductor be back to collect her and the baby?"

"A couple of hours." Hudson picked up Jorgine's valise while she collected soiled linens. "With the raid last night in Abbeville, you and your son won't be safe until we get you out of Anderson County."

Lizzie nodded, never taking her eyes from her son. "Y'all best be getting some rest too."

When Jorgine returned from disposing the soiled linens in the corner, Hudson took her hand and walked her out. As soon as the door clicked shut behind them, she leaned back against the wooden surface, almost as if it was the only thing keeping her from crumpling to the floor.

Dropping the case, Hudson stood in front her. "You're shaking like a leaf."

Jorgine closed her eyes and sucked in a shallow breath as if it was the first time she'd breathed all day. "I've never been so scared in my entire life."

Jorgine scared? "I don't believe it." Resting his hands on her slender shoulders, he tilted her head back, enjoying the loveliness of her face. "What you did was the bravest thing I've ever seen in my life."

She opened her eyes to search his. "The truth is I've never delivered a baby before. Papa wouldn't allow me in the birthing rooms when my friends began having children. Said it was no place for a lady."

"It seems to me your father underestimated you very badly." Hudson stroked her cheek.

"What would he have said at the strength and resolve you've shown these past few months?"

"I'd hope he would be proud of me." She grimaced. "Still, I shouldn't have kept my inexperience from you, but I didn't see the point in both of us worrying."

He pushed a loosened curl behind her ear, the soft shell a tempting place to leave a kiss. "You couldn't have done a finer job, sweetheart. Do you believe me?"

Jorgine nodded slightly then gave him a tremulous smile. "We delivered a baby!"

Smiling back at her, Hudson cupped her face in his hands. "Yes, we did." Before he could think, he leaned down and kissed her.

Chapter 8

"You've been awful quiet today," Sally commented as she braided a ribbon into Jorgine's hair the next afternoon. "Something troubling you?"

Jorgine glanced at her friend in the mirror. As much as she wished she could tell her friend about the previous night, it would be a mistake. How could she possibly understand the satisfaction she'd felt at delivering Lizzie's baby or the indescribable joy of witnessing his first breath, hearing his first cry? Tears pricked the back of her eyelids even now at the beauty of it.

Yet Hudson had shown her another kind of beauty in his tender kiss.

Jorgine shook her head. "I didn't sleep well, that's all."

"Probably got your nerves all worked up about last night." She knotted her braided hair at the nape of Jorgine's neck then reached for the hair pins. "Big Jim was none too happy with Mr. Hudson bringing you home just before dawn. I overheard Jim tell him it wasn't fitting for a young lady like yourself to be out with a man unless he be her husband."

She could only imagine what Hudson thought. "It couldn't be helped."

"Really." She stuck a pin into one braid then stepped back, her hands on her hips. "You'd best be explaining yourself to me. I'm none too happy with Mr. Hudson either. What if your uncle's men had come by to check on you? What then?" She shook her head. "Mr. Hudson knows better than that."

"I guess that's why he's known as a rake and scalawag." Jorgine sighed. If only Sally knew the real Hudson, the man who had held and encouraged Lizzie during her most painful hour. Her heart melted at the memory. But telling her the truth might put Hudson in danger. Better to let her friend believe the worst.

Sally scoffed. "You mean those rumors about his time in Atlanta?" She began pinning Jorgine's hair again. "Don't believe them."

Jorgine stiffened. "Of course they're true. Why, everyone says so."

"If Mr. Hudson is a rake, then I'm pale as a bowl of sugar." She shook her head again for good measure. "A rogue."

Dear heavens, if Sally suspected Hudson's secret, who else knew? Jorgine met Sally's gaze in the mirror. "Everyone in Anderson County has heard about Hudson's reputation."

Sally glared back at her. "Have you ever actually talked to anyone who's had a flirtation with Mr. Hudson? Can you name one?" Then she added, "I mean, besides you."

"Me?" Jorgine squeaked. "When has Hudson Wallace ever flirted with me?"

"Only every time you see him. It's like he can't help himself with you."

Jorgine shook her head. "You're wrong."

"All right then. Name someone else he's had a flirtation with."

"Well, there's. . ." No, Jorgine had heard that from a friend of a friend. "And there's. . ."

But she'd never actually met the lady in question. Jorgine pressed her lips together. "But the stories from Atlanta. . ."

"Can anyone you know prove they're true?"

Jorgine slumped slightly in her chair. Convincing Sally was harder than she'd anticipated. "Just because we don't have proof doesn't mean Hudson's not a rake." She chuckled. "I mean, who would want a reputation of a never-do-well rake?"

"I've been thinking on that." Sally pulled up a chair and sat down next to her. "I think them stories benefit him."

Sally was too close to the truth. Jorgine huffed. "You think he likes having such a reputation? Do his parents and Liv like it too?"

"Now listen to me," she admonished as she straightened her collar. "Mr. Hudson always acted the gentleman before he went to Atlanta." Sally glanced at her in the mirror. "Even when he broke your heart, he tried to be kind. Then he goes to Atlanta and suddenly he's a rake. It don't make no sense."

Jorgine's heart thudded in her chest. "People change, Sally, sometimes for the worst."

"Maybe. But wouldn't a rogue and a scalawag be the perfect disguise if someone was ferrying people to their freedom?"

It was useless trying to convince Sally of something Jorgine knew to be false. The man she'd worked with these past few weeks was caring, strengthened by the certainty of his convictions and fiercely devoted to the cause with a heart for the downtrodden. Her heart swelled with tenderness at the memory of the genuine joy on Hudson's face when Lizzie's son had been born. She pressed her fingers to her lips.

"Did that man kiss you?"

Heat flooded Jorgine's cheeks. "Why would you think that?"

Sally pointed her finger at her face. "You've got that cow-eyed look Big Jim gets around Miss Jocelyn. Then you touched your hand to your mouth as if you was remembering something sweet." She glanced toward the closed door then whispered, "So? Did he kiss you?"

She'd never been good at keeping secrets from Sally. Jorgine nodded. "It was right after we delivered a baby, and I guess we got caught up in the moment."

"Y'all delivered a baby!"

"Shhhh!" Jorgine pressed a finger to her lips. "Big Jim might have his ear to the door. I don't want to have to explain what happened last night, all right?"

Sally stretched out as if to get comfortable, her slim ankles crossed one over the other. "Maybe you should start from the beginning."

Jorgine told her everything; the hours of intense labor Lizzie had endured and Jorgine's fear of losing them both. Sally went wide-eyed when she heard how Hudson had stepped in to help her and sniffled loudly went Jorgine shared the moment little Joseph had been born. "Hudson only kissed me because I was nervous and he wanted to reassure me."

Sally snorted. "Mr. Hudson don't strike me as the type of man to go around kissing nervous young ladies just to comfort them."

"You thought he was a rogue at first!"

"Like you said, people can change." Sally threw Jorgine's own words back at her. "But that ain't why a man kisses a woman."

"What other reason could it be?" Jorgine traced the lace doily on her dresser. How tender Hudson's fingers had felt against her cheek, warm and reassuring. And when he'd kissed her, it wasn't in the excitement of the moment. It had felt natural, as if they'd both discovered a home in each other's arms. When he had reluctantly broken off the kiss, she'd known she was in serious trouble, and from the look in his dark eyes, she suspected he felt the same way.

"Do you love him?"

She couldn't say the words out loud. Those were meant for Hudson. Jorgine met her gaze and nodded.

"Then you'd best be careful." Sally took her hand and squeezed it. "Your uncle done promised you to Mr. Wakefield. I don't know of any man who would take too kindly to his intended being in love with another man. You know how mean Mr. Win can be. That's why you want me gone."

Jorgine shook her head. "I'd never want you gone. You know that, don't you?"

Her friend continued. "And Lord help us if your uncle finds out. He'll lock you in your room until the wedding and kill Mr. Hudson, that's for sure."

She had no doubt Sally's words were true. "Then we can't let them find out."

But it didn't stop her from worrying. Uncle Richard was desperate for the wedding between her and Win to take place. But murder Hudson? Jorgine had to believe her uncle wouldn't do anything so rash. If he did, he'd have to kill her first.

Chapter 9

Sally, tell Big Jim I'll be right there," Jorgine called out as she hurried up the stairs to her room for the third time. Hudson had sent word this afternoon that he'd booked passage for Sally, but she'd have to leave tonight. Jorgine's valise was bursting at the seams when she'd checked it a few minutes ago, and she realized she'd forgotten the pin money in her nightstand. Sally could use that for food or to establish herself once she was north.

She had barely crossed the threshold to her room when he spoke.

"Niece." Richard Emerson made a dashing figure, leaning against the mantel with the air of an orator ready to deliver a rousing speech to his waiting admirers. Yet she sensed a tension in him, a brooding anger, as if he might attack if provoked. The hairs on the back of her neck stood on end.

Taking a deep breath, Jorgine crossed the room to her dresser. "Uncle Richard, to what do I owe this special surprise?"

"You can cut out the niceties, Jorgine." He stretched his arm across the thick oak mantel. "You and I don't have a great deal of fondness for each other, so why pretend we do?"

"All right then." She glared at him. "Why are you here?"

"Close the door, Jorgine." The menacing tone of his request set her nerves on edge.

"There's no need. No one will hear us."

"Where are your slaves?" He took a few measured steps toward her then sank into a nearby chair. "You didn't free them, did you? There was no one downstairs to answer the door when I arrived."

"And yet you managed all by yourself."

He charged out of the chair after her, lifting his fist as if to strike her. Slamming her eyes shut, Jorgine braced herself for the blow. But it never came. Instead, his hot breath seared the tender skin of her face. "I'll leave it to Win to teach you the proper decorum of a political wife. For now, he doesn't want that face of yours marred by bruises and such." He pinched her chin between his thumb and forefinger. "But you will give me the respect that's due me or you'll pay the price."

Hadn't she already paid enough? Marrying a man she could never love and leaving behind the only man she could. Opening her eyes, she glared at him. "Yes, Uncle."

"Good. Now, take a seat. We have much to talk about."

"What could we have to discuss?" She sat across from him, arranging her skirts as if she were expecting company. "In less than a week, I'm marrying the man you chose for whatever reasons." Jorgine sat straight with her hands folded in her lap. "So please forgive me if I think talking with you is a huge waste of my time."

"You've always had a sharp tongue." Richard reclaimed his seat across from her, his booted foot resting casually on his knee as if this was a cordial chat between relatives. Jorgine wasn't fooled. Her uncle didn't believe in polite conversation; he never had. "I always find it amusing when someone tries to pull the wool over my eyes. It's like they have no idea who they're dealing with."

Nerves caused her stomach to churn. She felt like a mouse being toyed with. "I could see where that would be annoying."

"That's interesting you should say that, my dear niece." His low chuckle held no humor. "Considering you're the one doing it."

Jorgine's mouth went dry. If Richard knew the extent of her involvement with Hudson or her plans for Sally's escape, he would have stopped her before now. Besides, she'd been careful. "I don't know what you mean, Uncle."

"Of course, you'd deny it. What kind of lady would you be if word got around of your involvement in the runaways' escape?" He shook his head. "Underground Railroad. Who do they think they're fooling? Nobody with a brain in their head, that's who."

Jorgine's thoughts scrambled. Richard knew of her work with the slaves, but did he suspect Hudson and his family? It would be best to stay silent rather than incriminate anyone else.

"No witty retorts, Niece? I didn't think so." He shook his head. "Did you really believe you would get away with stealing people's property without anyone finding out?"

"No one can steal a person, Uncle, any more than you can own them," she answered finally.

His harsh chuckle grated on her. "No wonder your father left me in charge of you. I thought it was my penitence after the trouble I gave Elliott in our youth. But now I've determined he must have known you didn't have any sense." He flicked a glance at her. "Your father would have been so disappointed."

"You're wrong. Papa would have believed in what I'm doing. He probably would have joined me if he'd lived." She sat quietly for a moment then added, "It was his desire to free our slaves."

"Then Elliott was as stupid as you are." His face went taut. "Do you realize the scandal you could have caused? Win wouldn't want you. No man would, not even for the precious Emerson name. You'd be a social pariah if the crowd didn't tar and feather you first."

"I doubt they'd go that far."

His nostrils flared as he snorted. "What do you think your 'friends' will say when they find out you, an engaged woman, have been traipsing around at all hours of the night with a rake like Hudson Wallace? They'll not see you as much of a lady then, now will they? You'll be dead to them, and Wallace won't be around to save your scrawny little hide."

Fear shot through her like a bolt of lightning. Dear heavens, he knew all of it, including Hudson's involvement. "What do you mean Hudson won't be around?"

"That boy will be in prison along with the rest of his traitor family, if he is not shot first." Richard turned to her, his eyes hard and menacing. "I'd put a bullet in him myself, but that would ruin my plans."

"Plans?" she whispered.

"A political career, my dear. With the Wakefields in my pocket, I can aspire to any office in the land. Though I'm holding out hope for a Cabinet position in the Southern Confederacy once South Carolina secedes from the Union."

She froze in stark horror. "You're mad."

Richard laughed. "I like to think of myself as more of a visionary, my dear. Much like your fiancé. The Wakefields were barely scrimping by with the monies made in their cotton fields, but Win saw where the true value lay. In the slaves."

Jorgine mashed her lips together in disgust. "Yes. I know all about Win's business, among other things."

"Win is too smart to get his hands dirty, though he has made some wise investments in such companies." His lips turned up at the corners. "Like the one who is going to raid Wallace's operation tonight."

Shock pulled Jorgine to her feet. "No, Uncle! Please! Hudson's done nothing."

But Richard ignored her. "Within a few hours, Hudson Wallace will be in custody." Triumph showed on his face. "Or dead."

Jorgine's heart spluttered. This was all her fault. If she hadn't been so desperate to see Sally safe, then her uncle never would have learned of Hudson's involvement in the underground system. Of course, she wouldn't know what a good man Hudson was either. She'd do anything for him, even die if she must.

"I thought you might say that."

Jorgine blinked in confusion. "What?"

"There is one way to stop the raid on Thorndike Hall." He steepled his fingers over his chest as if to pray. No, men like Richard didn't pray unless it suited him. "But you would have to make it worth my time."

"What would that be?"

Richard glanced around the room, as if taking stock of the furnishings, trinkets, and tapestries for the first time. "I always did envy Elliott this place. With a bit of work and redecorating, this would be a fitting residence for a Cabinet member of the Confederacy."

Bile rose in her throat. Her uncle in the house her father built. "You want Piney Brooke?"

He lazily picked a piece of thread from his wool coat sleeve. "Between your inheritance and the money Win is paying for the Emerson name, I will live very well indeed."

Either Hudson or her home. She knew where her heart lay. "Piney Brooke is yours."

"You've made a wise decision." He stood then walked over to the open door. "For tonight, anyway."

Jorgine whirled around. "What do you mean by that?"

A bulky giant of a man filled the doorway at Richard's nod. "Our arrangement is only for the raid this evening, but there is tomorrow or the next day. But if you agree to my conditions, I can put off the inevitable."

She drew in a shaky breath. What else did she have to give? Her uncle had taken her inheritance, her home. What more could he want? "What conditions?"

"In return for Wallace's safety, you will stay here in your rooms under guard until I fetch you on your wedding day. If you try to escape, I'll kill the man myself."

Chapter 10

Boss, we can't wait much longer. Miss Liv said them raiders are on their way."

Hudson glanced back at the young Negro man his sister had sent to warn him, then turned his attention back to the dirt road. Win Wakefield's men were sighted on the other side of the Miller farm a few miles down the road. A raid on his station was imminent.

But Jorgine was late. "She'll be here. Just a few more minutes."

Shaking his head, the man rejoined the group.

The moments were dwindling down. Where was she? He walked up the road a ways, expecting to hear the sound of a wagon rounding the corner. It wasn't like Jorgine to be late, let alone tonight. Sally was moving north tonight. It was all arranged. She wouldn't miss this opportunity for her friend.

Unless they'd already been captured.

The clatter of wagon wheels approached at such a high rate of speed, Hudson had to jump out of the way or risk being trampled. The wagon barely stopped before Sally jumped down then ran toward him. "Mr. Hudson! Jorgine's uncle! They're on their way!"

Hudson glanced past her to where Big Jim helped an older lady down from the wagon. "Where's Jorgine?"

"Back at the house." Doubling over, Sally sucked in a short breath. "I tried to get to her, but that man put a guard at her door." She glanced up at him. "Jorgine gave up everything to save you, Mr. Hudson. She didn't even think twice when she gave that uncle of hers her inheritance and her home."

Hudson's heart exploded in his chest. "She gave up Piney Brooke?"

"Fool man. She would have given up a lot more." Sally stood, her hands on her hips. "She loves you. She always has."

"I love her too." It felt good to finally say the words. The only thing better would be to tell Jorgine herself. Hudson started toward the wagon. "I'm going to get her."

Sally pulled at his arm. "Mr. Richard aims to kill you."

"I wouldn't mind taking a shot at him either." He reached for the reins then threw himself into the seat. "Jim, you remember the hiding places I showed you up at the house?"

The man nodded. "Yes, sir. I do."

"Get everyone there. No lanterns, no talking. Quiet as a mouse until I give the all-clear." He wrapped the reins around his hand then let go of the brake. "Take whatever food you can find. It could be a long night."

The wagon teetered slightly as Sally joined him on the seat. "I'm going with you."

"Jorgine didn't do all this for you to get yourself caught."

"She's my friend, Mr. Hudson. The only one I've got." She braced herself against the seat. "So you'd best be moving before I get out and find my way back home."

Before he could snap the reins, the beat of a single set of hooves against the clay road jerked Hudson's head up. As the rider came closer, her hair whipping around her like ribbons in the wind, his heart caught in his throat. "Jorgine."

She slid down from her horse and hurried over to the wagon. "We have to hurry. Uncle Richard promised to stop the raid, but I don't trust a word he says."

Hudson jumped down from the wagon, and without thinking, he pulled Jorgine into his arms, his heart full of all the love he felt for this woman. She was everything he didn't know he needed. Even with her hair in knots around her shoulders and her skirts torn, she was the most beautiful sight he'd ever seen. And if she'd let him, he'd spend the rest of their lives telling her so.

"How did you get away?" Sally asked as she clambered out of her seat. "That man was at your door."

Jorgine leaned into him, nestling into his chest. "I shinnied down that dogwood tree outside my bedroom window."

Hudson tightened his hold on her. "You could have broken your neck."

"I know, but this is worth it." She drew in a deep breath. "As much as I like this, we have to go. I don't know if Win's raiders are coming, but we can't take a chance."

The worry in her voice sparked him into action. Holding on to her hand, he slapped her horse's rump then turned to the wagon. Sally was already across the road, heading in the direction of the house. "We have to make a run for it."

Jorgine's fingers tightened around his. "I can barely see."

"Trust me. We don't have far to go." He pulled her into the forest, barely beyond a tall row of massive oaks to a small clump of brush. Letting her hand go, he pulled limbs and twigs away until he uncovered a short rope. He pulled the hinged top open then motioned for her to get in.

"What is this? It looks like a coffin."

A man yelled in the distance. "I'll explain later. Right now, we need to hide."

She nodded then took his offered hand and sat down, fixing her skirts around her before lying down.

Hudson pulled the cover over them then joined her, wrapping his arms around her. "We need to be quiet for now."

Jorgine nodded then burrowed deeper into his arms. He buried his face in her hair and breathed deep, the scent of moss and horseflesh and the clean scent of this woman curling around his heart. The sound of twigs snapping nearby caused Jorgine to lift her head. "They must be. . ."

Hudson bent his head and kissed her. To keep her quiet, he told himself as she wrapped her arms around his neck. When her lips went soft beneath his, he forgot all the reasons he'd kissed her save one. He loved her, more and more with each passing moment. He needed to make Jorgine his wife soon.

"There ain't nobody out here." A rough-hued voice broke them apart. "Iffen they were, they're long gone by now."

"I reckon you're right, Dwight. Don't like being out here in these woods anyway. Folks say Miss Lucille walks these woods at night."

"That's nonsense, Wib. Let's get back. Maybe Mr. Emerson has something else he wants us to do." Twigs snapped as the two men retreated a few seconds later.

Hudson turned over on his back, letting her go. "That was close."

"I didn't mind." There was a hint of a smile in her voice.

"You didn't?" He turned to her, though he could only see the shadow of her face.

"No, you were only trying to keep me safe." She hesitated then continued. "Truthfully, I was too in awe of your abilities."

"Well, I can't take credit. I read that Indians build these kinds of caverns to pull surprise attacks." He caught himself smiling. "I figured they might come in good use as a hiding place as well."

"That was brilliant, Hudson, and I can see where they might come into use." Jorgine found his hand and threaded her fingers through his. "But I was referring to the way you kept me quiet."

Teasing little minx. His hand tightened around hers. "Sally told me what you did. We'll find a way to get Piney Brooke back. It's your home."

"It wasn't a hard choice to make. Not when I realized my heart wasn't there."

Hudson pushed the cover open then sat up, bringing her with him. Night encased them in a veil of moonlight. "Because you love me?"

Her eyes flew open, and he could feel heat flood her cheeks. "Where did you hear that from?"

"Sally says you've always loved me." He touched his forehead to hers. "Is that true?"

Jorgine gave a tiny huff, but his fingers felt the soft smile on her face. "She could have at least let me tell you. And after I made a fool out of myself in front of you all those years ago."

"I don't remember it that way." He kissed the tip of her nose. "You gave me your heart, and I treated you badly. I thought I couldn't work with the runaways and love you at the same time."

"You loved me then?"

"Yes." Hudson kissed her temple. "But nothing like I love you now."

She stilled within his arms. "You do?"

"I always have, Jorgine." Hudson leaned forward and pressed his lips to hers. "I want to marry you if you'll have me."

She wrapped her arms around his neck then leaned back to look at him. "I don't have anything to offer you. Win took my dowry, and my uncle stole everything else. I've only got the clothes on my back."

Hudson gathered her into his arms. "You have always been enough, my love. Just you."

She pressed her cheek to his, her arms tightening around him. "Then yes, Hudson, I'll marry you."

Epilogue

July 1866

"Mama, is this where the blueberry bush is?" Matthew Wallace turned from the window of the family carriage and glanced back at his parents. "You know, the one you and Papa talk about sometimes?"

Jorgine looked over at Hudson before shifting her attention to their seven-year-old son. The spitting image of his father, Matt possessed a thirst for history, particularly his own. She scooted to the edge of the seat to get a better look. "I'm not sure. I'd have to take a closer look."

"Could we stop then?" The boy shifted his focus to his father. "Please, Papa?"

Jorgine glanced back at her husband. Eight years of marriage had only made Hudson handsomer to her. "What do you think, dear? Do we have time for a quick stop before your appointment in Abbeville this afternoon?"

He glanced down at the sleeping child lying next to him. "Ellie is still sleeping."

"Please, Papa," the boy begged. "I want to eat the same blueberries you and Mama ate when you were my age."

Impatient just like his mother. "Darling, as soon as the carriage stops, Ellie will wake up, ready for a romp in the sunshine." Jorgine shifted in her seat. "I would like to stretch my legs too."

He tenderly pressed his hand into her lower spine. "You're not thirsty, are you? I had the hotel pack some cold lemonade for us."

Leave it to Hudson to remember her early pregnancy cravings. She leaned toward him so that only he could hear. "I'm fine; really, I am. I could just use a little fresh air, that's all."

"So you're okay?"

He was always like this early on, so concerned for her and their little one. "Perfectly normal."

"Yes, I know." He pressed his other hand to her flat stomach. "I still like to pamper you a bit, especially now."

"Are we going to stop or not?" Matthew asked insistently.

They exchanged a grin before Hudson rapped on the ceiling. "Seeing as your mother and I could use a walk, why not?"

Matthew did a little jig. "I can't wait to see the blueberries. Do you think we could pick some to take with us?"

"Maybe, but we can't stay long. Papa has a meeting with the mayor this afternoon." Jorgine pushed her son's unruly hair out of his eyes. "Understand?"

He nodded, his blue eyes sparkling with excitement. Jorgine turned to find a similar expression on her husband's face. The carriage had barely come to a stop before Matthew was out the door, closely followed by Hudson. She smiled. Men were just little boys at heart, and she wouldn't have it any other way.

"Mama? Where are we?"

Jorgine knelt down beside her younger child as she rubbed the last of the sleep from her eyes. She kissed Ellie's soft cheek as she pushed her golden curls away from her face. "Papa and Matthew are picking blueberries. Would you like to join them?"

Ellie clasped her hands together. "Booberries? I love booberries!"

"I do too." Retrieving the child's bonnet, she placed it on her head then tied the ribbons. "But there are rules. You must stay close to either me or your papa."

"Yes, Mama."

"Good girl." She helped Ellie to her feet then shuffled to the door. "Wait until I'm down the step; then I'll turn around and help you down. Okay?"

Her golden curls bounced in agreement.

As she turned, she found Hudson waiting for her, his hand outstretched to her. "I'm sorry, my love. Matthew's excitement got the better of me." Once she was safely to the ground, he caught Ellie up into his arms. "I'm very sentimental about blueberries."

Jorgine took his free arm. "And why is that?"

"Well, I once asked a very beautiful lady to meet me here, even though I wasn't certain of her intentions." He glanced down at her, his gaze softened by love. "You see, she was engaged to a very disreputable gentleman."

"I wouldn't call him a gentleman by any means," Jorgine answered, drawing closer to Hudson. "Gentlemen don't turn tail and run in the midst of battle and leave good men to die."

"No." Hudson went quiet for a moment as he often did when talk of the war came up in conversation. As a lieutenant in the Ohio Second Division, he had witnessed the destruction and carnage war inflicts upon its victims. It had been difficult on Jorgine too. Only her work with the runaway slaves and prayer had kept her from constant worry.

Finally, he shook his head. "Anyway, the lovely lady I met."

"Was that Mama?" Ellie asked around the thumb in her mouth.

"Why, yes, it was!" Hudson gave his daughter a kiss on her forehead. "When your mother gave the shawl she was wearing to a young girl in need, I knew she held my heart."

"Just like a princess in one of my books!" Ellie exclaimed.

Hudson smiled down at Jorgine. "Yes, darling girl, just like that."

As they walked across the battle-scarred field, Jorgine mourned the drastic changes. Large craters had been plowed out of the earth by cannon fire and men desperate for cover. The once lush oaks that had provided them shelter in their underground days stood bare and riddled with bullet holes. "I didn't realize the fighting came this close to Abbeville."

"I'd heard rumors," he answered quietly. "But I had hoped it wasn't this bad."

"Do you know anything about Piney Brooke?" Though her home was wherever Hudson was, Jorgine had found herself thinking more of her childhood home since learning they would return to Abbeville. The thought of it being damaged or, worse still, destroyed pained her more than she'd thought it would.

"When the area fell to the Union, the officers used it as a regional headquarters until the end of the war. Your uncle couldn't pay the back taxes from his prison cell, so it was put up for auction last month." Hudson lowered his wiggling daughter to the ground then took Jorgine's hand. "I believe the new owners are repairing it now."

Jorgine's heart sank. With their move to the area while Hudson served as President

Johnson's envoy during Reconstruction, she'd hoped. . . "Do you know who these new owners are?"

Hudson bent down and brushed a kiss against her temple. "We are, my love."

She blinked in surprise. "Truly?"

She felt his smile against her hair. "After we're finished remodeling, I thought you might like to ask Sally and her family down for a visit. I'm sure she'd like to show Robert and the children where she grew up."

Unable to hold back, Jorgine threw her arms around her husband. "Thank you."

A husband who loved her, healthy and happy children, a life of purpose—God had truly blessed her, more than she ever deserved. Hugging Hudson's arm, she smiled up at him. "Let's go pick some berries with our children."

A multipublished author with Love Inspired Historical and Barbour, **Patty Smith Hall** lives in north Georgia with her husband of over thirty years, Danny; two gorgeous daughters; her son-in-love; and a grandboy who has her wrapped around his tiny finger. When she's not writing on her back porch, she's spending time with her family or reading on her front porch swing.

Free to Love

by Terri J. Haynes

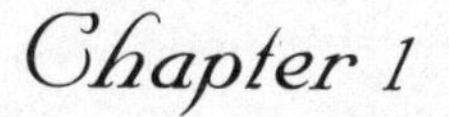

Chapter 1

East Towson, Maryland
1850

Pounding jarred Winifred from the hold of a deep sleep. She bolted upright, sending a quick glance to the still-dark windows. A breeze rustled through the trees surrounding the boardinghouse where she made her home, but other than that, quiet. The fields beyond her window lay shrouded in night. She blinked. Not a hint of warming sun. Her duties at Madison Plantation required that she wake early, but it was still too early to rise for the day. Which meant. . .

The pounding came again, and she rose, quickly putting on a dark gray cotton dress, praying all the while. Once she answered the door, she would not have time to think about anything other than the task before her. She laced her second boot, grabbed a dark scarf to cover her head, and reached for the door. As she opened it, she snatched up the most valuable tool she would need for the moments ahead: a small, worn notebook.

Her mother stood on the threshold, face grim, hand raised to pound on the door again. She lowered her hand and took Winnie's. "Did you hear it?"

Winnie shook her head, needing the movement to clear her head a little more and push away the exhaustion she felt.

"Gunshots." Her mother did not have to say why. They descended the stairs as quickly and as quietly as they could. Another night, another risk. *Lord, let us not be too late.* Winnie's mind imagined birds in flight, soaring above the trees and to their destination. Swift and silent.

Outside, her father, the plantation's overseer, stood with a lantern. "We need to hurry." As they rounded the boardinghouse, he blew out the lantern. They did not need the light. They knew the way even in the darkness, but the moon had shown up to help in their trek, peeking in and out from behind passing clouds.

The night muted their journey through the woods to the Star of Bethlehem Church that sat at the top of a hill on the west side of East Towson. No one spoke but the crickets, frogs, and owls. Winnie often imagined them engaged in lively conversation with their chirps and croaks. Maybe discussing the folks who traveled through the woods' shadows. People looking for freedom that nature already possessed. What would they be saying about Winnie and her parents? Leaving the rest of East Towson's slaves asleep, going to the church to help other souls who risked their lives by running away and entering the wild darkness?

Well done, My good and faithful servants. If her owners knew what she was doing. . . But that was a risk she had to take.

The church, a simple wooden structure with a row of windows, looked out on the East Towson community and the rest of Madison Plantation. It stood guard, speechless but watchful. As Winnie and her parents reached the stairs leading to the front door, a lamp inside gave off the faintest flicker. Winnie frowned. Fugitive slaves were normally immediately moved to a small root cellar beneath the church. When the door opened, Pastor Matthew's drawn face greeted them. "He is in the back."

Winnie removed the wrap from her head. "Not downstairs?"

Pastor Matthew shook his head. "Another group of fugitives arrived earlier today. And he is injured."

Ma sucked in a breath. "Bad?"

Pastor Matthew gave them a sad look as they passed through the door. Winnie inhaled, searching for calm as her mind filled in what Pastor Matthew had not said. Her father remained outside as a lookout. He disappeared into the shadows with swiftness despite his crippled leg.

The faint light gave the church a glow, casting shadows in every corner. Winnie had never gotten used to being in the church after dark. Always so full of life on Sunday mornings. Children laughing, songs sung, praises given, and downcast hearts lifted.

She somehow expected to find the same when she and her parents came for their late-night tasks. But in a way, what they were doing was an act of worship. They would help bear the weighty burden of some broken soul. Someone would know that they were not alone in their struggle for freedom. But in another way, it was an act of disobedience that could cost them dearly.

Pastor Matthew kept his quick pace but spoke over his shoulder as he led them through a back passage. "It looks as though he has been on the run for a while. Up from Virginia. Slave catchers followed him."

Fear seized Winnie, and she almost faltered. Slave catchers were ruthless and determined. They would tear through a town looking for their quarry. Sometimes, when they failed to find the runaway slave, they would instead round up any free blacks they found. Some slave catchers applied to the Madisons if they thought the fugitive they sought was nearby. To be chased by a slave catcher increased the danger, fear, and, in Winnie's heart, compassion. The poor man in Pastor Matthew's office had compounded sorrows upon him.

Pastor Matthew opened the door, and Winnie and her mother entered first. The lamp was a little brighter here. Winnie had to pause and let her eyes adjust. And her heart. She clutched her notebook, bracing herself for the pain. Always the pain. It was the hardest thing to deal with, but it was what she and her parents always found. Physical or spiritual pain, most often both.

In the corner of the room, next to a small table Pastor Matthew used for a desk, was a man lying on the cot Pastor Matthew kept there.

Well, not quite on the cot.

He was so tall that his legs from the calf down hung over the edge of the straw-made bed. He was comely, wide, bright eyes and full mouth, despite the pain contorting his face. Winnie paused before moving to the bedside, trying to reconcile the ugly distortion on such a wonderfully made face.

"Jesus, help," her mother whispered, and moved to the edge of the cot. She knelt, rolled up her sleeves, and began to examine the man. The man flinched like he expected a blow instead of help. It took little time for her mother to finish her examination. From where she stood, Winnie could see the man's injury.

Blood stained the side of his pant leg. There was a small tear in the fabric where the bullet had entered his leg.

Winnie moved to fetch water to clean the wound from a small pail Pastor Matthew filled every night. They never knew when a fugitive might show up. The frequency had increased once Pastor Matthew visited Philadelphia. He never said, but she suspected it had something to do with his meeting with William Still. Not only had fugitive arrivals increased. Winnie had more than once been handed a tightly folded note from slaves accompanying their masters as they visited at the Madison house. The hushed instruction was always, "Pastor Matthew."

At first, she was confused, but she soon learned from Pastor Matthew that those notes brought news from the Southern plantations and that he would deliver the notes to escaped slaves in the North. Now, they had at least one fugitive a month in the cellar, and she expected a note every time the Madisons had company. Tonight was unusual for them to have so many fugitives at once.

"Winnie, I'll be needing bandages and shears too." Concern tightened her mother's voice.

Winnie set the basin of water on a small desk. Beside the desk was a wooden cabinet. She opened and retrieved cut strips of fabric for bandages. Healing supplies often proved more valuable than even safe passage.

Runaway slaves would arrive shot, like this man, sometimes snake-bitten, thirsty, hungry, and sick. It often took all Winnie and her mother's skill to nurse them back to health before they could continue north to freedom. Some of them never made it and died under their care. The quest for freedom ended their lives, and they were buried outside the church under nameless headstones.

Her mother held out her hand for the bandages without looking away from the man. Winnie placed the supplies in her mother's hands and retrieved her notebook.

She took a quick peek out of the window to see if there was any light in the main house. Seeing none, she kneeled at the bedside, the familiar position igniting prayer in her heart. *Lord, give him some comfort.* "Sir," she began quietly. "What is your name?"

The man looked at her, his expression fuzzy with pain. "Hiram." His voice rumbled, but with the slightest hitch, like he fought to get the word out.

She wrote his name, along with a sketch of his physique. Over six feet, probably two hundred pounds, very dark. His hair looked black, but she could get a better look once the sun rose. If he survived. She stole glances at the wound as her mother struggled to stop the bleeding.

"My name is Winnie. This is my mother, Ms. Phoebe. You've met Pastor Matthew. Do you have a last name?"

He shook his head.

"Me either." The man gave her a look of understanding. She was a slave like he was. But judging from the scars on his arms, their experiences were very different. Winnie had never been beaten by her owners. Worked until she nearly collapsed, but never struck. "Were there others with you?"

"Left with three. Don't know where they be. We got separated."

She scooted a little closer and kept her voice steady and low. "Where did you run from?"

At this question, he looked at each person in the room in turn, distrust in his eyes.

She lowered herself closer to the floor and arranged her skirts around her. "'Tis all right, Hiram. You are safe here."

He held his intense gaze on her so long that she started to feel uncomfortable, but she did not look away. He opened his mouth to answer when pounding on the door interrupted them. They all startled.

A loud voice shouted from outside. "Open up!"

Winnie's mother glanced over her shoulder. "Slave catchers."

Pastor Matthew moved to the door. "Probably followed him here. They have a hound."

Winnie's pulse raced as he left the room. She jumped up and blew out the lantern with a quick breath. She crept over to the window that gave her a view of the front of the church, careful to stay completely in the shadows. The slave catcher stood a little shorter than Pastor Matthew, wearing a black hat. The catcher's hand rested on the butt of the pistol at his side.

"I need that light, Winnie," her mother said, hands still working on bandaging Hiram's leg.

"If he sees the light, he might come 'round looking."

Her mother grumbled something but Winnie could not make it out over her thundering heart.

In the darkness, she prayed for Pastor Matthew like she had every other time slave catchers showed up at the church. *Jesus, give him the right words to say.* She also prayed that God would distract the slave catchers and hoped they had not run out of God's favor.

Hiram stayed as still as he could even when Ms. Phoebe pressed a clean rag to his leg. He clenched his teeth to keep from groaning. He could not muffle his heartbeat, which pounded so loud in his ears that he thought everyone in the room and the slave catchers must hear it.

The banging came again, louder, and Hiram's fear rose with it. If he was caught. . . He could not go back. Although these people seemed kind, they could turn on him. He knew it well. He and his three traveling companions had been too trusting with the slaves they had met in Virginia. The three had stumbled across shanties on the edge of a plantation, weary and looking for rest. That was what they thought they had found, but while they slept in the barn the other slaves had alerted the owners of the plantation.

He would have suspected betrayal from these people too, except for the lovely woman kneeling at his bedside. Winnie. He had heard stories of Negroes helping others reach freedom. That horrible night in Virginia made it hard to believe. He couldn't, wouldn't have believed it until now. *What beautiful help.* Winnie's deep, soulful eyes held a sparkle of smarts and the warmth of compassion. And she had not flinched at the sight of his wound. Hiram could not have dreamed after all the pain he had suffered since he left Virginia that he would end up with such an angel at his side.

Pastor Matthew slipped out the door. They all listened in silence as his footsteps sounded through the sanctuary. Hiram measured out the length of the walk, remembering how the pastor had dragged him down the center aisle. When the bullet tore through his leg, Hiram's hope of continuing his journey north died. Certain he could no longer outrun the slave catchers, he had lain down in a soft bed of moss in a copse of trees, panic replacing the frenzy of outrunning the slave catchers.

He had offered one more prayer for help, only to have it answered almost immediately when Pastor Matthew stumbled through the brush, hoisting him up and pulling him into a shallow ditch. They waited in silence for what seemed an eternity before they moved down the hill to a church. Hiram fought to keep from crying out from the pain. Pastor Matthew, in a hushed voice, urged him on with gentle words and firm steps.

The church's front door opening echoed through the empty sanctuary.

"Good evening." He heard Pastor Matthew's polite greeting and marveled at the man. How could he stay so calm when he was harboring fugitives? No matter that he was a pastor, it would not shield him from danger. In the slave catcher's eyes, he was just another Negro.

A louder voice demanded that he be allowed to take a tour of the church to ensure that the escaped slave he was tracking was not hiding there. The slave catcher's voice had a childlike squeak to it that, if he was not a slave catcher, Hiram might have found amusing.

More words were exchanged, but Hiram couldn't hear. A soft whisper caught his attention. He looked at Winnie. The moonlight from outside gave the room enough light to see her in the darkness. She had bowed her head, eyes closed, and her lips moved with the slightest of sound. Hiram's hope rose a little more. As he looked around the room, he realized that both women were deep in prayer. He decided to join them and closed his eyes. *Savior, You carried me this far; keep me and these good people safe.*

After a time longer than was comfortable, the front door closed and Pastor Matthew returned. He motioned for them to remain silent. After a long stretch—Hiram lost track of time with the pain drawing his attention—Pastor Matthew relit the lantern.

"He is gone." Pastor Matthew wiped his brow with his sleeve. "I showed him my papers and that seemed to be good enough for now."

Papers. Pastor Matthew was a free black?

Ms. Phoebe gave him the biggest smile. "Thank God."

"Which brings us to our present situation. We need to find a place for Mr. Hiram to stay." He looked down at Hiram. "I am afraid you are going to have to delay your trip north to heal."

No. He had come too far to stop. "I need to be leaving in the mornin'."

Pastor Matthew shook his head. "You will not make it injured."

"He's right." Ms. Phoebe stood. "You need to heal and rest a while. He can stay in Mr. Samuel's loft."

Pastor Matthew looked at Hiram. "We will wait a few hours before we move Mr. Hiram to his new quarters."

Hiram wanted to argue, but the throb in his leg made it a difficult task. He had been whipped so many times he thought himself immune to pain, but he was not. He would not return to that pain even if he died in the process of escaping. *It would be nice to have a safe place to heal.* But was this place safe? "Thank you."

Ms. Phoebe moved to the door. "We will go and help Paul and Samuel get things ready and come back in an hour."

Pastor Matthew nodded toward Hiram's leg. "This is going to hurt for a few days. I will give you some powder for the pain once we get you over to Mr. Samuel's."

Winnie rose and Hiram almost reached out to keep her from leaving. "I guess we should let Mr. Hiram rest for a while," she said. She smiled at him, but even in the soft light, he could see it was strained. She touched him softly on the arm. A brief touch but it filled him with peace. "Rest well. We will talk later."

Hiram nodded. He was looking forward to seeing Winnie again.

Chapter 2

Hiram's first week at East Towson proved the wisdom in waiting to heal before he continued his journey north. His wound became infected, keeping him confined and, for many days, unconscious. There were times he awakened feverish and unsure of where he was or what had happened. In his twisted nightmares, he awoke believing that he was still in Virginia. But Winnie's face anchored him, confirming that he had indeed escaped.

He wasn't sure how often she was by his side. The haze of pain and fever left his memory full of large gaps. He did, however, figure out some things. Ms. Phoebe and Winnie possessed great care in tending to him. In one of his feverish hazes, he heard Ms. Phoebe and someone else discussing amputation.

But Ms. Phoebe's stern, authoritative voice rang through the cloud of sickness. "By God's help, I will not agree to further suffering for one of His precious creations." Hiram had drifted back to sleep, at peace that he was in the older woman's care. Winnie's voice was the next thing he remembered, encouraging him to drink, something bitter, which he did.

Through God's help, on whom Ms. Phoebe relied, the fever broke one week after he arrived. On the eighth day, he managed to sit up on his own for the first time since they'd laid him on the bed inside the small building. The room swam a bit, and when his vision cleared, he saw Winnie. She sat on a small stool across the room, a bowl of broth in her hands and a big smile on her face.

"Good to see you awake. You've been feverish for several days."

Another man, who stood by the door, grinned too. "Well, praise be to God. I'll go fetch Mr. Paul and Ms. Phoebe."

Winnie brought the broth to Hiram, carefully placing it in his hands. "We were sure we were going to lose you. But we rallied everyone to pray."

Hiram lifted the spoon. His hand trembled with weakness, but he managed to get some of the liquid into his mouth. The faster he healed, the faster he could leave.

Winnie clasped her hands in her lap. She had joy, real joy in her eyes. Something he hadn't seen in anyone's eyes for a long time. "You had us quite alarmed when the infection took a turn."

He looked up from the bowl. Winnie sat, sun to her back, giving her a glow. Behind her, the window framed green fields and trees.

"Where is this place?"

"East Towson, Maryland."

Hiram focused on lifting another spoonful of broth to his mouth to hide his disappointment. He'd hoped he was in Delaware. Traveling only at night confused the distance, making it seem he'd gotten farther than he had. Nevertheless, Maryland was closer to freedom than

Virginia. He'd made it this far. "How far from Pennsylvania?"

"Four days on foot. One by steamer."

He smiled at the thought of steamers. He'd heard much about the big boats. Maybe he would see one as he left Maryland.

Winnie slid to the edge of her seat. "The catchers came around the church a few times. Their dog had your scent, so I took your shirt and hung it in the woods." She giggled. "I moved it every night. Those poor dogs ran the catchers crazy, but they kept coming back every day for a week."

Hiram smiled. She was as smart as he thought. "They won't stop. Got a big bounty on my head."

"You are a—" She glanced at his chest and her words faltered. She swallowed and continued. "You look like you were very valuable to your owners."

He grimaced at the memory. He was very valuable. Young and strong, but that didn't stop his master from mistreating him. Mr. Toley often told Hiram that he got worse punishment because he was so strong. Told him he needed to break his body to break his rebellious spirit. The beatings accomplished neither. The more Hiram suffered, the more he longed to be free. He looked down at the broth in his hands. "Could lift a yoke by myself."

Her gaze stayed fixed on her hands. "The catchers called you Goliath."

Anger flared up in his chest. "My mother named me Hiram after my father." The only thing he had left of the man.

She held his gaze with one filled with compassion. "Good strong name."

He didn't look away. "Thank you." The whole world seemed to quiet as they looked at each other, and it stayed that way until she dipped her head in a soft smile.

Ms. Phoebe and a man Hiram hadn't seen before came into the room, breaking the moment. Ms. Phoebe, with a smile that she had passed on to her daughter, clapped her hands. "Hello, Hiram."

The man moved near the end of the bed. "Hiram, I'm Mr. Paul, Winnie's pa. You sure had us worried and prayin'."

Hiram studied the two, their exuberance odd. No one was ever this happy to see him. "Thank you for caring for me so well."

"Let's see that leg." Ms. Phoebe carefully removed the bandage, and by the look on her face, she was pleased with the process. "A little infection left, but you are well on your way to healing."

Hiram nodded. "And on my way to Philadelphia."

Ms. Phoebe applied fresh bandages. "That will be a while. This has to heal completely. But I think you can go outside for a bit each day so it doesn't get too stiff. But you have to be easy on it."

Hiram heard the truth of her words even though it meant a longer delay. The fever from the infection had sapped his strength, and he could see that he'd lost weight. The first part of the journey had nearly killed him, and he'd been at almost full health.

The idea of going outside filled him with warmth. After years of working in the fields, it felt strange not to have the sun on his back for such a long time. When he worked the fields, he was only inside at night, to be asleep as fast as he could. The out-of-doors called to him. East Towson was a different kind of green than Virginia. There must be different kinds of trees and flowers here. And a different kind of soil. His extended stay would give him a chance to explore the green fields outside the window.

Or I can stay inside if I want. He jolted at that thought. He didn't have to work the fields anymore. Didn't have to rise early and go to bed exhausted. Didn't have to work until he wished for death. Four days away from freedom. That and the time it would take to recover. As soon as he did, he would be on his way.

He let out a deep sigh. "When will I be able to continue north?"

"When you are better," Winnie said.

They sat with him a little longer and then left for Sunday meeting. If East Towson was like Virginia, this would be the only day the slaves had to rest. He gently lifted the bandage on his leg. The gunshot had left a small dent in his leg. Still pink with a little yellow, but it had healed well. There was still a risk of infection. He would have to take the time to heal, as much as he wanted to leave. Because when he stopped again, he would be completely free.

Winnie finished her chores with one final swipe of her rag across the table. She hung the wet cloth over the hearth and was out the back door before Mrs. Madison could find something else that "needed" cleaning. Mrs. Madison filled every moment of the day with work and stood over Winnie's shoulder, inspecting every task. There were times when Winnie longed to protest the unnecessary cleaning she and the other house women did, but she held her tongue. Too much was at stake for her to fight with her mistress.

Since Hiram arrived, Winnie had rushed as much as she could to finish all her work before the night grew too dark. She and Hiram had taken to walking in the growing coolness of the evening to exercise his leg. He had been telling Winnie about his life before he ran so she could record it in her notebook. When Pastor Matthew had asked her to record the stories of fugitives, she'd believed it had one purpose: to be sent to Mr. Still in Philadelphia for his records. Now she saw it performed another purpose: healing.

It was like lancing a festering wound. As fugitives talked, it was as if the poison of their lives flowed out. Most had never had anyone to talk to about the hardships they'd lived through, and Winnie's listening ear and her pen provided them comfort. Their spirits were lifted, but Winnie had cried many tears over those stories. Her heart ached at the pain they'd suffered and, in the same heartbeat, rejoiced at how easy her life was working at Madison House. Her talks with Hiram had been hard to process. His gunshot was another sad chapter in his story.

Her trip from the boardinghouse to where Hiram stayed carried her down a sloping hill, green and soft underfoot. She had traveled this route many days to work in the main house on Madison Plantation. She still remembered the day she and her parents moved to East Towson. They had lived in cramped lodging behind the stables of Madison House, all three of them sharing one room. Her father had asked for permission to move to East Towson, and Mr. Madison had agreed to the arrangement, under a few stipulations.

The move could not impact their work. Also, her family would no longer receive victuals like the rest of the slaves on the plantation. Her father had agreed and stressed every day that Winnie had to do everything exactly right or they would lose their newfound freedom. It wasn't true freedom, but it was the family's first step toward it. It was their road to freedom. A road her parents didn't know they were on.

Winnie looked up at the sky. One day they would walk away free. No ducking in the woods and relying on the help of strangers. *Soon*. For now, she would do her duties with excellence and efficacy. And keep her work at the church a secret. She hid all her journals in her room and helped Pastor Matthew keep all the fugitives hidden from the eyes of the plantation owners. Hiram's extended stay increased the risk of them getting caught, and they would all have to stay alert.

The women of East Towson finished hanging the last of their laundry as children played around them. Nearby, several men were finishing relocating wood. She enjoyed this time, after a day's labor but before the sun had fully set. Life looked normal now. No one under the heat of the sun or the heat of the whip. Now they were just people with children playing underfoot and wives cooking at kettles. Men repairing shoes or windows.

Hiram stood by the boardinghouse door talking with Pastor Matthew. She watched him for a few seconds. He listed to one side, avoiding putting his full weight on his injured leg. Even so, he stood taller than Pastor Matthew. His tattered clothing had been replaced with donated items from some of the larger men on the plantation. The shirts and pants were ill-fitting but better than what he had before.

The clothes did not hide his broad shoulders and thick legs. *What a sight he must have been, lifting and hauling.*

Winnie pushed forward, moving her mind away from her current train of thought. Hiram was handsome, especially when he smiled. But he would be moving north as soon as his leg fully healed. That was clear by his constant questions about how they were going to help him with the rest of his journey. She should care for him as much as she did the other fugitives and no more.

He turned, spotted her, and smiled. "Good evening, Miss Winnie."

"Evening, Hiram. Please call me Winnie."

He looked down at his feet. "Winnie."

At the way he spoke her name, she almost wished she hadn't permitted him to do so. Her knees weakened at the rumbly, wispy way he pronounced it.

They said their good-byes to Pastor Matthew and started walking toward the barn. She steadied herself to fall into step beside him. "How are you feeling today?"

"Stronger."

She craned her head back to look up into his eyes. "You look better."

"That's thanks to the good care I've gotten." He gave her a quick sideways glance. "Very good care."

She felt her face warm at his words. "We want you to be completely healthy for the rest of your journey."

Hiram slowed. "If I could only be so blessed as to find more folks like y'all on my way. Then the trip would be easy."

"You will. We will make sure you do."

A loud cry caught their attention. When she and Hiram turned in the direction of the noise, a pile of logs swayed precariously near three men struggling to keep it steady. One man, a slave named Goldie, had fallen on the ground beside it. If the pile fell, he would be crushed.

Winnie pressed her hand to her mouth and gasped, but Hiram was already in motion toward the group. He arrived as the men lost their battle and placed his large hand at the right points to still the pile. Winnie could see the muscles in his back bulge with the strain.

"Take some of the logs off the top!" he ground out. "Get him out of the way!"

By now, a crowd had grown around the scene. Two other slaves grabbed Goldie and struggled to drag the dazed man out of the path of the logs. Others gathered around, and Mr. Samuel started handing them to anyone nearby. Winnie lifted her skirts and ran to help. She soon had a log in her hands and carried it to the new pile forming a few feet away.

Hiram held the pile steady by himself until it shrank below the danger of falling. Goldie had been moved and now sat on a chopping block. Hiram stepped back and brushed his hands on his pants.

Winnie returned to his side. Hiram stood there, face drawn. "I'm fine. Pretty risky, piling this so high."

"Yes, it was." She eyed the men surrounding the pile. Goldie was on his feet now and stood near the other men who had originally been piling the logs, Thomas and Herbert. They stood with their heads together, whispering. Winnie tensed, straightening her spine. *Not again.*

The three men sauntered over to where she and Hiram stood.

"Thank you, big man." Goldie patted him on the arm.

Hiram looked annoyed. "Someone could have been hurt if I hadn't been here."

Herbert grinned, but there was no mirth in it. "But ya were here."

Winnie moved closer. Now that she thought about it, they'd never had so many logs at one time in East Towson before. The slaves who worked on the plantation would sometimes be able to get a log or two for cooking, but not this much. "Where did that wood come from?"

Goldie drew back a little but kept smiling. "Not to worry yourself, missy."

"Did you steal this from Madison House?"

Goldie's eyes narrowed. "There she goes. Defending her precious Madisons. I guess that comes with working in the house."

Hiram took a step to stand behind Winnie, giving her the impression he was supporting her. "I am not defending them. I am helping us. If you stole that, there will be punishment for us all. We live here at East Towson because the Madisons let us live here instead of in the horrible barns on the plantation."

"They let us." He sneered. "That's right nice of them."

At hearing her words in his mouth, she wilted a bit. *They let us*... "Yes, they do. Haven't you gotten in enough trouble?" How could he forget so soon the pain he'd caused and be willing to inflict more? To bring heartache on more than just his own head?

Goldie leveled a look at Winnie that chilled her through. "You tend to your business and I'll tend to mine." The three men walked past her and Hiram and headed up to their boardinghouse.

Hiram was watching her when she turned back to him. He spoke first. "Is he always like that?"

She opened her mouth to respond, but the words stopped when she saw a thin red line growing in the fabric of his pants.

Winnie pointed to his leg. "Hiram."

Hiram looked down and grimaced.

"You probably put a little more stress on it than you should have." Winnie grasped his arm and led him to the chopping block. More stress because of Goldie, Thomas, and

Herbert. "Let me check it."

"It's all right," Hiram said, moving away from her. "No need for all this worry."

Winnie folded her arms. *Stubborn man.* "But it's bleeding. I need to check it."

He tried to take a step backward and stumbled the minute he put weight on his injured leg.

Winnie mustered all the sternness she could. "Hiram, sit down and let me look at your leg. Now."

At first, it looked like he wasn't going to, but finally he sat on the chopping block and submitted to the examination.

Winnie gently rolled his pant leg above the bandage on his calf. As she undid the bandage, old scars and the new one were revealed. Whip marks crisscrossed his leg. The gunshot wound would blend with his other scars. Only someone who knew it was there would be able to tell it from the others. So much pain.

Her heart ached even more when she finally removed the last bandage. The wound had reopened and was now producing a steady flow of blood.

Hiram's face sank into a deeper frown when he saw it.

Winnie put on as calm a look as she could as she rolled the bandage into a wad. "Put pressure on it and I'll go find my mother." *I'll let Mama tell him his trip will be delayed again.*

Chapter 3

Hiram knew what Ms. Phoebe was going to say to him. That reopening the wound would impact his ability to fly. Knowing that, however, didn't lessen the disappointment when he saw the grim look on her face.

"Well, young man," she said, recovering some of her cheerfulness. "Looks like you'll be staying with us a little longer."

He sighed. He couldn't run. "How long?"

She replaced the bandages. "A few weeks."

His gaze drifted to Winnie. She looked as unhappy as he did, standing there with her arms folded like when she commanded him to sit down. He dared not laugh, but he found humor in the memory. He outweighed her by at least a hundred pounds, but she stood her ground. She had confronted Goldie too. *My little angel has got some toughness in her blood.*

Inside his boardinghouse, Ms. Phoebe gave him some tips to care for the wound while she and Winnie were working during the day. "I know you're disappointed, but you heal fast, so it may not be as long as we think."

"I will take extra care."

Ms. Phoebe patted his shoulder and went back to her work.

Winnie didn't change her stance, a frown on her face. "You need to be careful."

"So you expect me to stand and watch a man get crushed?"

Winnie huffed and began pacing. "Goldie and the others had no business bringing that much timber to East Towson. I'm sure they stole it. If they're caught, we will all be punished on account of it. Maybe a block of wood would have knocked some sense into his head."

Although he'd held his laughter earlier, now he could not. He guffawed.

She turned and looked at him, giving him a stern frown. "Are you laughing at me?"

Hiram tried to stop his laughter but couldn't. "You sure have some fire for being the smallest person on this plantation."

She stood to her full height. "I am not the smallest person. The children are smaller."

"Not much smaller."

Winnie scowled, but footsteps sounded on the stairs. Several pairs. Hiram grumbled at the interruption. So far he'd only seen the sweet, caring Winnie. Her other side fascinated him, mainly because it didn't seem possible that such compassion and fire could live in one person.

Pastor Matthew rushed into the room. "I was hoping you were still here." Mr. Paul and Ms. Phoebe followed him in and closed the door. "I have some news."

Hiram leaned forward on the bed. "You don't look like it is good news."

Pastor Matthew shook his head. "It is not." He pulled a piece of paper from his pocket. "I was down in Baltimore and saw this. There is a new law. The Fugitive Slave Act. It puts into law very harsh penalties for anyone caught helping fugitives. Very harsh."

The room grew still. Hiram felt, like the others, what this law meant. He grappled for words but Winnie spoke up. "Maybe Mama, Papa, and I should stop helping for a while."

Ms. Phoebe put her hands on her hips. "Winnie, how can you say that?"

Winnie looked down at her shoes, and her voice grew soft. "We cannot anger the Madisons."

Pastor Matthew looked at her. "I understand if you want to stop helping for a while, but I would not like to lose you."

"You will not lose us," Mr. Paul said.

Winnie looked at him with horror. "Papa, remember the last time—"

"I won't stop helping fugitives who find their way here," her father replied. "The Madisons have not found out yet, and we will be sure they don't."

Winnie sighed. "Yes, Papa."

Pastor Matthew turned to Hiram. "I suggest you stay inside as much as possible during the day. And stay away from Madison House. I believe the slave catchers went there to ask about you."

Hiram nodded. "Don't have to worry about me, Preacher. I can't go far on this leg." *No matter how much I want to go.* But as he looked at the group of people before him, ones willing to risk their lives for him, his gratitude outweighed his desire to be gone.

The world blurred in front of her. Winnie's back and feet ached, but somehow she kept walking. The sloping hill seemed to carry her toward East Towson more than her steps. Like it was guiding her home. Mrs. Madison's fervor to clean out the attic had earned Winnie a day of pay, a small sum from the coins Mrs. Madison kept in the house. But she had worked Winnie and the other house staff hard. That wasn't all they had to do for the day. Cleaning the attic came in addition to their regular duties.

The day had been hard for another reason in addition to the workload. Halfway through the day she heard Mr. Madison telling his wife that something was missing. She had held her breath. Sometimes slaves would steal coins or food that they thought no one would miss. Mr. Madison's anger, on the other hand, told Winnie that it was more than a few pieces of bread missing. Mr. Madison's raised voice had echoed through the house. "The wood was there last week." Winnie had to cover her mouth to keep from gasping. She knew where the wood was. She had feigned needing something from the kitchen and instead had slipped out the back door to avoid being questioned, too exhausted and angry to trust her mouth to keep Goldie's secret.

She had stood in the sun, hating feeling this tired. Standing there, looking over the green fields, she felt the tug in her stomach. One she felt many times. The tug to start running without care of where she was going. She took one step but stopped. Everything she earned brought her one step closer to walking, not running, away. That thought made her return to her work, weary in body and heart.

It also hadn't helped that another fugitive had arrived at the church last night. He wasn't injured like Hiram and had only run from southern Maryland. Winnie had recorded his story, eyes nearly drifting closed on multiple occasions. The man had family back on his plantation and begged Pastor Matthew to send word to let them know he was okay. They had fed him and given him a small sum of money. He had disappeared into the night despite their admonishment for him to stay.

East Towson had stilled by the time she entered the clearing in front of the boardinghouse. The sun was giving off its last orange light for the day. She spotted Hiram at the side of the house. He sat on the edge of the wooden bench from Mr. Samuel's kitchen. She slowed her approach as she saw what he was doing.

He was leaned over with both hands in a small plot of freshly tilled soil.

He looked up and smiled, and his smile energized her. "What are you doing out here?"

"Planting a garden. I asked your ma about it. She said Mr. Samuel used to grow a garden here, so I figured I'd see what I could grow." He shrugged. "Might as well do something useful."

She took a seat on the bench next to him. She sighed at the relief for her feet. Several plants lay beside him with their roots intact. "What is it you're planting?"

Hiram leaned over and picked up a plant, cradling it in his palm like it was glass. "I don't know. Never seen them before. They are different than what grew on the plantation in Virginia."

She took the plant. "This is thistle. It makes a good tea, and you can eat the leaves."

He nodded, took the plant from her, used his finger to open a hole in the soil, carefully placed the plant in it, and pressed the dirt in around it. He lifted another to her.

She studied it. "This is a weed. Once it starts to grow, you can't kill it." She tossed it over her shoulder.

Hiram laughed, deep and rumbly. "Guess I won't be planting that." He handed her another.

She gasped. "Yarrow. This is a good cure for many ailments. Where did you find it?"

Hiram lifted the plant from her hands with tenderness. "At the edge of the trees behind the church."

"Ma will make sure that grows. She may tend it herself."

Hiram placed the yarrow in the ground and patted the dirt around it. "Tell me about Goldie, Thomas, and Herbert."

Winnie looked at him, her anger from earlier returning. "They have been here all my life. They are. . ." She stopped herself from saying what she wanted, which was *troublemakers*. "They can be difficult. I try to stay away from them."

"I saw them here in East Towson in the middle of the day. Thought that was strange."

Winnie slumped. "Maybe they had a break." She said it knowing Hiram would know better than she did that slaves didn't get long breaks in the middle of the day.

"Maybe." Hiram sounded suspicious and she, stifling a yawn, didn't have the energy to convince him otherwise.

Hiram grew quiet. She knew she needed to get to her boardinghouse and bed, but she couldn't convince her body to move. *A few minutes longer and I'll go.* "Did you find any more interesting plants?"

She didn't hear his answer. The sound of the crickets faded to a whisper. The night warmed, and she felt as if it had cast its cloak over her. So peaceful. . .

She jolted, eyes opening.

The night was dark. She still sat on the bench beside Hiram, but now she sat against him, nuzzled into his side. He had one arm loosely draped around her shoulders. Her eyes widened. She had fallen asleep on him. But now that she was awake, she didn't want to move. His breathing was deep and rhythmic, his body warm compared to the night. That was probably why she'd slept so soundly.

Then he moved. She got ready to speak, but to her surprise, he stood, lifting her off the bench. He picked her up as easily as he would a down-filled pillow, and cradled her. She kept her eyes closed, her neck heating. She should tell him she was awake. She should, but this was a very enjoyable way to get to her boardinghouse. She let her head rest against his chest.

She nearly broke her act when she heard her father's concerned voice. "Is she all right?"

"Yes," Hiram answered. That one word reverberated through his chest and down to her bones. "She fell asleep in the middle of talking to me. I let her sleep for a while. She looked so tired. Then I figured she would be more comfortable at home."

"Put her in her room and her mother will get her ready for bed." Winnie kept her face slack. Her father's footsteps sounded on the stairs up to the loft where she slept. "That girl works too hard. She'll work herself to death."

Oh, Papa. I'm working for a good reason.

Her bedroom door opened, and Hiram carried her to her bed. He laid her down gently.

"Thanks for bringing her home. Don't know what I'd do if anything happened to her."

"Me either."

They left and quietly closed the door. Winnie fell asleep again with a huge smile on her face.

Chapter 4

Months of hard work. Winnie ran her hand over the star-point quilt that would soon join the others for Madison Plantation's annual Quilting Day. A holiday of sorts. The slaves had cooked until the air around the boardinghouses smelled of fried chicken, a rare treat, and cakes. All the work on the plantation had been finished early, and soon the long tables set up in the clearing would be filled to overflowing.

Owners of other plantations came to the celebration too. They would be looking to buy new quilts for their houses, and Winnie and the rest of the Madison quilters would have them in abundance. The profit they made from the scrap fabric quilts would often be the difference in weathering the colder months well or poorly. Winnie's quilts often fetched a good sum of money. She used a little of her money to buy new fabric, but most of her quilts were made from Mrs. Madison's castoffs. She would mend whatever she could use for work dresses, but the rest she used for her quilts.

And she wasn't the only one. The house women of Hampton House did the same, and sometimes they would swap fabric. Even though most of the quilts on display today would share some of the same fabric, Winnie's would stand out. No one else could stitch as neatly as Winnie. She would share fabric, but she kept her sewing technique to herself, never sewing in front of the other women when they had quilting circle. She imagined the other women would laugh if they discovered that her only secret was sewing her quilts much slower than they did, carefully placing every stitch.

She gathered up her quilt and carried it out to the trees on the edge of the gathering. A stretch of twine had been hung between two trees. Other quilts already hung there and she added hers with pride. She ran her hand over it. If she could get twenty dollars for it... She sighed. The quilt represented hours of her free time, her oft-pricked fingers, and many nights' lost sleep. But, like the Bible said, her present affliction could not be compared to what was to come.

She turned to find Hiram standing behind her. She let out a yelp.

He dipped his head. "Sorry. Didn't mean to scare you."

"You are awful quiet for someone so large."

He chuckled. "Not much out here to make noise." He touched the quilt. "This is wonderful."

She felt her face heat to a blush. "Thank you."

They turned and walked back to the clearing. "I hate to miss this." He had helped set up the tables for the celebration, carrying them from each boardinghouse and arranging them. Winnie had tried not to gawk at how strong he was, but it was hard not to notice. Even more fascinating, he would occasionally lift one of East Towson's children into the air for a spin. Her heart soared at the sound of their laughter. How could someone so strong be so gentle-hearted?

She touched his arm. "You won't miss it all. Once the owners buy up all the quilts and the woodwork from the men, they'll be gone."

He grinned. "I will be waiting." He turned in the direction of the church. "Pastor Matthew asked me to help repair some pews in the church."

"I'll come and fetch you when the owners leave."

Hiram nodded but didn't leave right away. He shuffled from one leg to the other, hands in the pockets of his overalls. "I hope your quilt sells well."

"I do too."

"I'm gonna go now."

"Yes." She smiled at him. "The owners will be here soon. I'll come as soon as I can."

Winnie watched him until he reached the base of the hill where the Star of Bethlehem Church sat. His limp was almost gone. She smiled, but it quickly sank into a frown. His healing meant his soon departure.

Winnie searched the crowd for her parents. There was still much to do before tonight. They would eat and dance, laugh and play games. Hints of a life they didn't have, but one they longed for. Pastor Matthew had told them that during their captivity, they would have to be like the children of Israel in Babylon. They would build houses and dig wells, marry and have families. They would continue life even though they were slaves.

Winnie looked forward to the day when her family would be free.

A flurry of activity caught her eyes. The owners were making their way down the hill. Winnie moved closer to get a better look at their dresses. The women were done up finely. Mrs. Madison wore a deep blue cotton dress. Winnie's mind raced with how that color would look paired with the gray dress Mrs. Madison had claimed was too small for her now. Those frocks might come to Winnie for next year's quilts.

Raised voices sounded across the clearing. Winnie turned and spotted Goldie, Thomas, Herbert, and several other men standing between the boardinghouses. Her father stood between them and the clearing.

The men held hoes, rakes, and sticks. They appeared to be arming themselves for something.

Too far away to hear what they were saying, Winnie could tell by their sharp gestures that their words were intense. Her father stood with his hands out in front of him while the others leaned forward, looking like they were ready to push him to the ground. The men pointed in the direction of the owners, but her father held his ground. Their tone grew louder and others turned and took notice.

Papa. If they attacked him, he couldn't withstand them all. She took quick steps toward them. She reached the edge of the clearing as the argument grew. As she passed the corner of the boardinghouse between her and her father, she heard someone call her name. She skidded to a stop when she saw Hiram standing in the shadows.

Her feet stayed glued to the spot. "Papa."

"You need to stay out of it," he said, his voice low.

She took two steps. Before her feet could land for the third, she was lifted off the ground.

She let out a yelp and fought the tight grip around her middle.

"Winnie, stop struggling." Hiram's voice was at her ear. He carried her behind the boardinghouse and set her feet on the ground.

"I have to get to Papa." She tried to sidestep him, but he moved in front of her so she was looking squarely at his chest.

"You can't help your father against those men." He grasped her arms. "Stay here."

She balled her fists. "I can help. Someone needs to talk some sense into them."

"Stay here," he said again, and moved with more speed than she expected. He trotted down to the other end of the building, closer to her father.

She obeyed for one second and then followed. She eased up behind Hiram and peeked around the building.

"I told you to stay back there," Hiram huffed.

The scene in front of them had quieted a little, but not by much. Papa had somehow convinced the men to lower their weapons, but the air between them was still tense.

"I won't let you," her father was saying.

Let them what? "Move out of our way. Our fight isn't with you," Goldie replied.

"You are making a mistake. This ain't gonna go the way you think," Papa said.

Goldie took a step forward. "Move or we'll move you. You are outnumbered."

Horror twisted Winnie's stomach, but before she could act, Hiram did. He stepped out from between the buildings and moved to her father's side. He folded his arms across his chest. Even though there were more men on his side, Goldie and the others shrank back.

"Go away, big man. This doesn't concern you," Herbert said.

"If it concerns Mr. Paul, it concerns me."

The men looked at her father and Hiram, who was standing at his full height, towering over Goldie. "You cannot stop this, Mr. Paul. And you should not try."

A familiar voice laughed, the sound carrying across the clearing. Winnie turned to see Mrs. Madison standing very near the other end of the boardinghouse.

Winnie pivoted and headed directly toward Mrs. Madison. She pasted a smile on her face as she reached the woman. "Ma'am, let me show you which quilt is mine."

Mrs. Madison smiled and took Winnie's arm, turning away from the boardinghouse. "Oh yes. Your work is always so lovely. I don't know when you find the time to create such wonderful quilts. Such detailed work."

Winnie gave a quick look behind her. Her father remained but the men and Hiram were gone. "Thank you, ma'am." As she escorted Mrs. Madison toward the quilts, Goldie's words echoed in her mind. *Cannot stop what?*

Tiny shoots of corn dotted Hiram's little garden. The rest of the seeds he had planted still hadn't sprouted above the surface yet. He bent down with almost no pain in his leg and pulled a few weeds. The day had been the warmest since he'd arrived, but the little garden needed his attention. He wouldn't be here when it was ready to harvest. He would leave it behind.

The thought unsettled him. Moving forward had been his top goal since he'd left Virginia. But two months at East Towson had weakened the urge. He'd never imagined there would be anything he would regret leaving behind other than his mother and brothers. But this little plot of dirt had crept into his heart and had begun to grow there. All of the fields in and around East Towson had grown on him. And the people too.

He spent his evenings talking with Mr. Paul and Mr. Samuel. Despite the fact that they had worked all day in the field, their laughter was easy. The women of East Towson had become quite at ease in asking him to lift a table or repair a window. The children came running to him, begging to be picked up and twirled in the air.

And Winnie. That was going to be the real regret. Celebrating Quilting Day with her, singing, dancing, and playing games, had been one of the best days of his life. She visited him daily after her workday—often exhausted to the point of falling asleep on her feet—but still she came. He felt like he was still in knee shorts when she praised him for how much progress his garden had made. She came to him smelling like sunshine. His heart sank when the day was over and she retired to her boardinghouse.

He went inside and retrieved the bench from Mr. Samuel's kitchen. Could he leave her? Did he want to? Did he have to? Not only that, could he leave with Goldie and the other men acting so strangely as they had on Quilting Day? Thankfully, they had left, skulking off into the woods before the celebration started. Hiram had tried to question Mr. Paul about the reason for the fight. With sadness in his eyes, Mr. Paul had told Hiram not to worry, but his words did little to ease Hiram's concern.

Like clockwork, Winnie arrived as soon as he placed the bench outside the boarding-house.

"Good evening, Hiram." She looked at his garden. "Oh, look. You've got sprouts."

Her excitement made his heart soar. "Yep. There is good soil here. Not like it is in Virginia. We planted only tobacco there, and it was hard on the ground."

She knelt beside the plot and ran her fingers over the rows. "Mr. Samuel tried to get something to grow here for a while, but he couldn't."

Hiram knelt beside her. "Sometimes plants just need a little more care. I hope he can keep them growing after I'm gone." He looked at her to see her reaction and noticed the slightest pucker between her eyebrows.

She stood and dusted her hands. "I wanted to ask you about Quilting Day. What happened with my father and Goldie and the men? What were they planning to do?"

Hiram sobered. "I don't know what they were planning to do." He didn't believe that they had intended to attack Mr. Paul. Their anger had been directed elsewhere.

"I asked my father but he wouldn't tell me what happened. Goldie said my father couldn't stop *it*. Stop what?"

Hiram pressed his lips together. He wouldn't tell her either, but he would talk to Mr. Paul about it again.

Winnie held his gaze for a moment then huffed and took a seat on the bench. "It seems you won't be talking about it either."

Hiram sat next to her. "I thought you said they were always making trouble."

Winnie still didn't look away, but her gaze grew concerned. "Ever since the logs, something has been off with them. Different. Worse than normal."

"I don't think you should worry. The crews in Virginia got restless in the hotter months." That was true. Heat made a man angrier and the weight of his burden heavier.

"I wish I believed you. Goldie is known for his antics."

"How so?"

Winnie turned her face to the fields at Madison House. "He—" She swallowed. "He convinced a bunch of slaves to run, including my father."

Hiram stilled. "Mr. Paul tried to escape?"

Winnie nodded. "This was before Pastor Matthew arrived. They planned for weeks. My father was to run and then send for my mother and me. They didn't get very far. Slave catchers caught them right outside of Baltimore."

"How did they find them so fast?"

Winnie shook her head. "Goldie's mouth can't stay closed. He told several people at Hampton House and in the city about the plan. When those people saw the bounty Mr. Madison put on the runaways' heads, they told the catchers everything."

Hiram squirmed. "What happened to the men?"

"Some of them were sold. Some of them were whipped badly. My father..." She dropped her head. "My father nearly died. I was young, but I still remember Mama telling me to pray every night for Papa. That's why he limps."

"Is that why you haven't run?"

She looked at him with surprise. "Yes. But that's not my only reason."

"What is the other?" Hiram leaned forward. He had wondered why she hadn't run. With the amount of liberty she had, it would be easy for her to walk away and never come back.

"I am working to buy us from Mr. Madison. He promised that after I worked for him for another year, he would set us free. Mr. Madison doesn't want my father around anymore."

"Because he tried to run?"

She nodded. "Mr. Madison believes my father will start another uprising." Hiram could see the tears in her eyes. "Goldie told Mr. Madison that the plan was all my father's idea. Mr. Madison believed him because he doesn't believe that Goldie is very smart. Mr. Madison thinks Papa will cause trouble again and watches everything Papa does."

Hiram resisted putting his arm around her. As the story flowed from her, her slouch deepened. Like the words were sapping her strength despite how strong she was. Working to free three slaves by herself. He knew his little angel was tough, but this was beyond what he'd imagined. "How much longer do you have to go?"

"Another six months, four if I can get extra work after the harvest." She sighed. "Hiram, my parents don't know why I've been working so hard. Please don't tell them, because they would make me stop."

"I won't tell them." Hiram frowned. "But are you sure Mr. Madison will let you go? What if he changes his mind?"

The question seemed to knock the wind out of her. She looked away. "Mr. Madison is a kind master. He lets us work at other plantations to earn extra money. He gave his word."

Hiram grasped her chin and turned her face to him. "But you could be free right now. You could be free in the four days that it takes to get to Pennsylvania."

Winnie shook her head. "And waste all the years I've worked? Besides, if we tried to run and were caught, Mr. Madison would sell my father for sure. When we leave Madison House, we want to leave truly free and without slave catchers chasing us."

Hiram thought over her words. Buying oneself was surely a better way to gain freedom.

If he had his papers, he could travel and work as a free man for hire and not live looking over his shoulder for the slave catchers. But that would have taken years. And his mother and brothers would suffer longer. That he could not bear.

He inched closer to her. "I'm going to miss you when I leave."

She held his gaze, sadness in her eyes. Then she stood. "I have to go." She rushed across the field to her boardinghouse. His heart hoped that her abrupt departure meant she was going to miss him too.

Chapter 5

The day working at the Madisons' house passed in a blur of her unordered thoughts. Winnie fought to focus on her tasks, but Hiram's words haunted her.

What if he changes his mind?

She'd never considered it. Mr. Madison had only ever been a kind master to her. But the truth remained that he was still her master and in control of her life. How much could she truly trust him? Winnie and her parents weren't the only ones Mr. Madison had promised to free. Would he release them all at once and have no one to work the fields?

As she mended shirts, her thoughts tumbled over themselves. Pastor Matthew had told them that some people in the world choose good and some choose evil. Sitting in their well-ordered parlor, she realized that she had always believed that the Madisons had chosen good. She believed they were kind people because they treated their slaves better than other owners. But they had chosen evil. They chose to make their slaves pay for their freedom instead of setting them free.

Wasn't that as evil as those masters who mistreated their slaves?

Mrs. Madison's voice jolted Winnie out of her thoughts. "Almost done there?"

Winnie looked up from her work, and it was as if she were truly seeing Mrs. Madison for the first time. She gritted her teeth and forced herself to smile. "Yes, ma'am."

"I need you to polish some of the silver for my dinner party tonight."

"I'll get to it as soon as I finish here."

Mrs. Madison sighed. "Good. I do not know what I would do without you."

A flame flickered in Winnie's belly. "I guess you'll have to have fewer dinner parties after I'm gone."

Mrs. Madison frowned. "After you're gone? Where are you going?"

Winnie nearly dropped the needle. "When I'm done paying for my freedom. When my family and I leave."

"But that's some time yet." Mrs. Madison waved her hand. "Besides, I treat you well. You're a good, hard worker, and you should be happy here."

Winnie turned her attention back to her work. The Madisons had chosen evil and Winnie's freedom wasn't even in Mrs. Madison's mind. She finished the last stitches with tears in her eyes.

The front door opened and heavy boots sounded in the foyer. "Lillian."

At Mr. Madison's call, Mrs. Madison lifted her skirts and rushed from the room. Winnie placed the folded shirt with the others. She didn't mean to eavesdrop, but Mr. Madison's raised voice made it hard to ignore what he was saying.

"Walters was quite certain. He caught slaves on his plantation meeting in the middle of the day."

"That still does not mean one thing." Mrs. Madison's singsong lilt rang back, softer.

"What else could it mean? The harvest is coming in, and I need all of my workers if I want to get ahead. If any of our slaves are involved, I will not tolerate it."

Winnie eased closer to the door.

"Why not talk to Paul?" Mrs. Madison asked. "If something is amiss, won't he know?"

Mr. Madison laughed, but not with humor. "He's probably the ringleader. I made him foreman so I could watch him."

"I don't believe it. I think Paul learned his lesson from last time."

Papa. Winnie turned around the room, searching for some way to escape unseen. If she exited the parlor's side door, she would end up at the other end of the hallway from where the Madisons stood. Or she could sit and pretend she didn't hear. The Madisons normally talked about all kinds of things around her, as if she wasn't there. But it would be too hard for her to act calm. Slipping through the parlor's second door was the safest choice.

"That's true. He has behaved himself since he moved down to East Towson. But I'm not entirely sure that East Towson clergyman has been completely honest. That slave catcher seemed to suggest that the preacher is hiding runaways in the church." A soft thump sounded, Mr. Madison dropping his hat on the front entry table like he always did.

"My word." Mrs. Madison's skirts rustled, and Winnie could imagine the woman pressing her hand to her heart. "Fugitives? Here?"

"Yes, and now this." Mr. Madison's boots sounded again, heading toward the parlor.

Winnie moved fast, darting to the other door and pressing herself against the doorway. The massive china case sitting against the wall gave her a little cover.

"Do be safe. If what you say is true, this would be a perfect opportunity to do their evil."

Winnie listened as both sets of footsteps headed to the parlor. And as soon as they stepped in the main door, she stepped out into the hallway. They continued talking but Winnie didn't stay to hear. She needed to warn her father.

Hiram sat down in Pastor Matthew's small office, on the very cot he had lain on when he first arrived. First saw Winnie. And now here he was, planning to leave her.

Pastor Matthew smiled at him. "Everything is almost set, Hiram. We believe we can get you out of here in two weeks."

Hiram gaped. He had been here for almost three months, settled into helping with East Towson's chores and tending his little garden. Now, his time to go was close at hand.

"I have arranged with an abolitionist to pretend to buy you."

Hiram drew back.

Pastor Matthew patted Hiram's leg. "No need to worry. The purchase papers will be drawn up with a fake name."

Hiram shifted in his chair. "Okay," was his answer, but he sounded more settled than he felt.

"You can trust this man. He has helped many others get out. Carlton will take you to Philadelphia and direct you to William Still's house. Still is a freed slave who will help you get established, help find you work and someplace to live."

Hiram grinned. A real home. Real freedom. But he would have to leave Winnie. His smile faltered.

"We will go over this again before you go, so you don't have to remember everything now. But do you have any questions?"

"Do you think you could talk Winnie into leaving?"

Pastor Matthew chuckled. "I am a man of God, so I would like to have faith, but that is as far as I can go. Only God could get that girl to leave."

"I talked to her about it the other night." Hiram remembered her words. *"I am working to pay for my family's freedom."* He had never been in love before. But it was love that flooded his heart when she told him her plans. She was already risking her life to help fugitives. And she was giving her life working for her parents' freedom.

"Did she give you a reason?"

"Yes, but she asked me to keep it to myself."

Pastor Matthew gave him a sad smile. "Well, if she changes her mind, I will send her to you in Philadelphia as soon as I can."

Hiram's words faltered. "I did not mean—I wasn't saying. . ."

Pastor Matthew laughed. "I know what you are feeling. I've known since the first day I saw the two of you walking together. You care about her."

"I do." *More than I should, since I am planning to leave.*

"You should tell her," Pastor Matthew said. "Tell her how you feel and that you will wait for her in Philadelphia if she does decide to run."

"But I have nothing to offer her. I can't even offer her the honor of a last name."

Pastor Matthew turned to face him. "You have love to offer her. Freedom to love."

He loved her. Hearing Pastor Matthew say it filled his chest with warmth. But he had not considered it as something to offer. His mother and brothers loved him, he knew, but who else? Love had never been as valuable as strength and freedom. Until now. "What if she doesn't love me in return?"

"Then I would be very surprised." He stood. "Tell her how you feel."

Hiram would have to build his courage first. "I have something else I need to talk to you about. I think Goldie, Herbert, and Thomas are planning trouble."

"Those boys have always been in some sort of mischief."

"I think this is more than that. They were planning to attack someone during the quilting celebration. Mr. Paul had to stop them."

Pastor Matthew gave him a surprised look. "Who were they planning to attack?"

"I don't know, but my guess would be the owners. Goldie and the men showed up at the same time as the owners. They had hoes and rakes."

"Dear Lord." Pastor Matthew bowed his head, his words an honest prayer.

"Winnie told me about the last time and what happened with her father."

"That was before I came, but Paul told me about it when he moved to East Towson." Pastor Matthew stood. "I will be looking for anything unusual with Goldie."

"That may be a good idea for all of us."

Chapter 6

Although Hiram had worried all night about the trip he and Pastor Matthew were to make into Baltimore, it ended up being for nothing. He was sure he would stand out, but the city was a busy place with bustling docks. It was the largest group of both whites and Negroes that he had ever seen in his life. Several times he slowed, gawking at a white man helping a Negro unload crates from a wagon. Or working on securing boxes with rope, like it was the most natural thing in the world. Not in his world, but natural in this world.

He also had the best comfort at his side: Winnie, his little angel. She had shown up at the church minutes before Hiram and Pastor Matthew were set to leave.

"Mrs. Madison needs me to run a few errands in Baltimore." Winnie had been out of breath when she arrived. "I knew you were going into town today, and I thought I would join you."

Hiram had shown his pleasure more than he should have, judging by the way Winnie ducked her head in a blush. The heat, the walk, his worry, none of it bothered him anymore. He allowed himself to be amazed at the city and all its activity. Winnie and Pastor Matthew pointed out churches, businesses owned by free blacks, even schools for black children. But the crowning sight: several steamer ships sitting in the harbor. They crested a hill, and there was the water laid out before them, sparkling in the sun.

"The water," he said.

Winnie giggled. "This is your first time seeing it. I guess Pastor Matthew and I have grown used to it."

The landscape of the city differed in other ways. Modern-looking buildings sat along cobblestone streets. People dressed differently than in the South too. Even the poorest wore nicer clothes and better shoes. Hawkers and newspaper boys called out as they passed, a very different scene from the endless earth and sky on the plantation. The streets were crowded, but they felt freer. Like he could breathe deeper here.

When they reached a street with shops on both sides, Winnie touched his arm, running her finger over one of his scars. *I love when she does that.* "I have to go to the shop over there. I'll meet you two back here in an hour."

Hiram nodded and watched her cross the street to a milliner's shop. She seemed miles away, and he was very aware of her absence.

Smiling, Pastor Matthew nudged him along. "Carlton will be waiting for us at the ironworks."

They approached a large building with tall doors and big puffs of steam billowing from the top. Hiram followed Pastor Matthew inside. The temperature was sweltering, more like the heat of the South that he knew so well.

A man looked up when they entered, flushed with the heat. His sandy-brown hair was plastered to his head. He spotted them and waved them over.

He met them between two long worktables. "Pastor Matthew." The men shook hands. "And you must be Hiram. I am Carlton Gilchrest."

Mr. Gilchrest extended a hand to Hiram. Hiram hesitated. *Will this ever get easier?*

The man grinned and grasped Hiram's hand. "You can shake my hand. I'm only pretending to be your master."

Hiram felt some of the tension leave his shoulders. "Nice to meet you."

Mr. Gilchrest motioned for them to follow. "Let's talk in my office."

As they traversed the tables, Hiram once again saw whites and Negroes working side by side. "What does this place do?"

Mr. Gilchrest looked over his shoulder. "We are a smithy. The best in the city. That is how I met Pastor Matthew." He chuckled. "I admit I was a little angry with our Lord for calling him to sheep and not steel."

The office was small and the desk cluttered with papers. Mr. Gilchrest motioned Pastor Matthew and Hiram to sit in the chairs in front of his desk. The seat was way too small, and Hiram had to wedge himself into it. Mr. Gilchrest sat behind the desk.

Pastor Matthew folded his hands in his lap. "How did Abram and family do?"

"Right fine." Mr. Gilchrest's grin seemed to be something that he wore often. "The little ones were a little afraid, but they did what they were supposed to. William Still set them up in a small house, and Abram is already looking for work."

Hiram swallowed. "I thank you for this."

Carlton waved a hand. "Don't thank me. It is the least I can do."

"You know you don't have to repay anyone," Pastor Matthew said. "You had nothing to do with the slaves your father kept."

"I need to do all I can to undo what he has done." Mr. Gilchrest eyed Hiram. "You didn't happen to come from South Carolina, did you?"

"No, sir."

"One day I am going to help a slave from my father's plantation get free. Then I will have done half enough." Mr. Gilchrest picked up a piece of paper. "I've booked you passage on the *Mary Ellis*. We will sail together as slave and owner next week."

Hiram's eyes widened. "Sail?"

"Yes, right from this port. It is faster and safer once you get on board. Slave catchers normally stay on the dock to look for their quarry. Not always, but most of the time."

"But what if one does follow us?"

"Then I will insist that our dispute of ownership be delayed until we reach land. Once we dock, I will distract the catcher for you to escape." He leaned forward. "All you have to do is set your feet on dry land, and you will be free. No one can take you back then."

Hiram thought of it. Feet touching freedom. He grinned. The grin stayed on his face for the rest of the time they worked through the plans of the escape. They had given him a different name and left his description off the purchase deed, afraid that it would draw attention.

"You need to be at the docks an hour after sunset. I booked passage on the latest ship I could so we could go in the middle of the night," Mr. Gilchrest said.

"I will make sure he is here on time," Pastor Matthew said.

"I know you will." Mr. Gilchrest tipped his head. "In the meantime, I sure could use a man like you here at the ironworks. The pay is fair, and I will pay you daily."

Hiram grinned. He already knew what he would do with his earnings. "I would like that very much."

Winnie arrived at the meeting place before Hiram and Pastor Matthew. She stood near a shop, thinking of Hiram with a heavy heart. She was happy that he would be moving on to freedom. He had suffered more than most who had come through the Star of Bethlehem station. Still, there was gentleness and tenderness in his heart. He would go, and life would be emptier.

As she waited, two young men passed her, deep in conversation, heads almost pressed together. They passed her, then stopped abruptly and came back.

"You from Madison House?"

Winnie shot a glance down the street. She exhaled in relief when she saw Hiram approaching with Pastor Matthew trailing well behind him.

"I am."

The man leaned closer, and she stepped back. Suddenly, Hiram was at her side.

"Winnie?" he asked but did not look at her. Winnie wedged herself between Hiram's shoulder and the building behind her. Safe and secure.

The man held up his hands. "I don't want no trouble. I wanted her to pass a message fer me."

"What message?" Hiram asked.

The man lowered his voice. "Tell Goldie we have thirty armed men. All we need is for him to send the word."

"Thirty men for what?" Winnie asked.

The man smiled, a cold smile that made Winnie hug herself. "To convince our massas to let us go, or die."

The men rushed off before Winnie could ask any other questions. She looked up at Hiram, who watched the men leave with a frown. "I knew those men were up to something."

Pastor Matthew joined them. "Who was that?"

"Men wanting me to tell Goldie that they were willing to join in his uprising against the plantation owners."

"Lord, have mercy." Pastor Matthew grabbed Winnie's hand. "We need to get back and find Goldie."

Hiram carried Winnie's packages, and they covered the distance between Baltimore and East Towson faster than they had come. The sun hung low, bright orange, seeming to urge them on with its setting. Most families had settled for the night by the time they reached the boardinghouses. All three of them searched, but Goldie, Herbert, and Thomas were not in East Towson. Winnie retrieved her packages from Hiram and stowed them in her room. Mrs. Madison would have to wait until the morning for her goods. Unless the riot was to happen tonight. Winnie shuddered at the thought.

Chapter 7

Hiram barely slept the day after their trip to Baltimore. The possibility of a riot overshadowed his excitement over his departure. He had fallen into bed exhausted. The idea that Goldie was somewhere planning something that could possibly harm everyone in East Towson, however, wouldn't leave his mind. More haunting was the fact that he understood Goldie. Many a day he had considered taking the whip from Mr. Toley's hand and reversing the scene. He could have, easily. He was bigger and stronger than his owner.

But he wouldn't have been taking on just his owner. When word got out that Hiram had whipped his master, a posse would hunt him down and have him swinging from a tree. And that was what would happen here at East Towson. The posse would come in, and they would not care who started the riot. All of the slaves would be guilty, and all would share in the punishment. Hiram recognized how dangerous it could be for him. He would be sent back to Virginia and the wrath of Mr. Toley.

Over the next few days, Hiram saw the three men arrive back in East Towson in the evenings after working the fields. They went straight to their quarters. Hiram prayed and prayed that they had lost interest in the uprising.

In that time, his worry decreased. He started helping out at the ironworks in the evening. The darkness provided a good cover for the hour walk from East Towson to Baltimore. The work, hard but not like working a field, distracted him and helped him pass the remaining days.

Tonight, the work had ended early, and he arrived back at East Towson at the same time as Winnie. She was coming into the clearing from the opposite direction, her steps dragging enough to create a cloud of dust around her. But when she saw him, she gave him the broadest smile. His heart hammered, and he smiled back.

I will leave her soon. The thought hit him like a blow to the chest. She would not run, and he could not stay. His stomach twisted. Not only would he have to leave her in slavery, but leave her to suffer whatever consequences came if Goldie did start a revolt.

He closed the distance between them with wide steps and wrapped his arms around her. She stiffened then relaxed into the hug, her head against his chest. If his heart could speak to her, say how it soared at her being this close, she would have heard it clearly.

"Leave with me."

"Hiram," she said, and tried to pull away.

He held on. "Please come with me. I cannot bear to leave you behind. We can have Pastor Matthew marry us before we go. If you got hurt. . ."

He felt her tremble in his arms, and her tears wet his shirt. "I can't, Hiram. I have to buy our freedom. I can't leave my family behind."

"You could get more work in the North than here. You could sell your quilts."

She pulled away from him. "You are asking me to leave my family behind to whatever punishment Mr. Madison gives if those men incite a riot?"

Hiram opened his mouth to contradict her and then realized that was indeed what he was asking her. "I am sorry."

She looked up at him, tears streaming down her checks. "If I could go with you, I would."

"Winnie. . ." The words got stuck in his throat. The words he knew were true. He took a step closer, filled his lungs with air, and said, "Winnie, I love you."

She let out a small gasp, but in the dim lighting, he could see her eyes sparkling. "I love you too."

He pulled her into his arms and she came without resistance. "I don't care how long it takes, I will wait for you. I will send word through whatever way Pastor Matthew has set up."

"Promise me," she said, her voice almost a whisper.

"I promise."

At that, she returned the hug, wrapping her arms around him. When she did, he remembered what was in his pocket.

He stepped back from her and removed an envelope with his pay from Mr. Gilchrest. "I will help you buy your freedom. Here is my pay."

Winnie covered her mouth and shook her head. She was prepared to do it alone.

"Take it, Winnie. The sooner you are free, the sooner we can be together."

She fell into his arms and wept. His little angel.

Winnie started a new notebook. Not of slave stories. This one differed from every other notebook she had, but it was just as precious. She sat in the kitchen chair with the book on her lap. The fire glowing in the hearth gave her enough light. She dated the first page and then entered the sum of money that Hiram had given her.

Hiram, her sweet, gentle man, was helping her get free. She would keep careful records like she had with the fugitives. How different things were now. Before, she was the one arriving to East Towson exhausted from a long workday. Now it was Hiram who staggered to her boardinghouse to give her his pay. Begging him to keep some of his money for himself had proved useless. She had succeeded once, when she all but forced him to buy some better work boots during one of their trips to Baltimore. As she recorded tonight's payment, she smiled at his words to her.

"I am a strong, hard worker. There will always be work for strong people." And every night he seemed to be proving his statement right.

She yawned and finished the entry. She would need to arrange some of her station records. Pastor Matthew had hinted that someone might be visiting to get the records from the last month. That made her smile too. That all the stories she recorded were going to Mr. Still in Philadelphia. The poor souls who had come through the station, whether liberated in this life or the next, would be remembered.

She had just touched her pen to the page when the door opened and her mother rushed in.

Winnie looked up, and seeing her mother's expression, all her fears about Goldie rushed back. "Mama?"

"There is a fugitive at the church. A woman. She came with three small children, and one of the babes is sick."

Winnie sprang to her feet, set the book down on the chair, and followed her mother.

The night's humidity made her feel like she was breathing underwater. Several times she had to swat away mosquitoes. Still, the night smelled of dew and pollen, a soothing smell. She prayed as they walked, for the mother and the little babe. What a great risk this mother took.

They arrived to find the babe not sick, but lethargic with hunger. The mother had not eaten enough food herself to nurse the baby, so they softened some bread in water for the little one. He ate with gusto, and in the darkness of the moment, his hungry sounds and impatient squawks made them laugh. Winnie marveled at how they could find joy even in this situation.

They took the exhausted mother and children downstairs and arranged their bedding. Winnie yawned more than once. She did it so frequently that her mother finally turned to her and said, "Go home and get to bed."

Winnie chuckled. "I guess I am extra tired tonight."

"We are almost done." Mama carried the babe to his mother. "You go."

Winnie started to protest, but another yawn stopped her. "Good night."

The night seemed like a dream as she walked, her tiredness making it hard to focus. All she could think of was sleep. Tomorrow would be another day of hard work at the Madison House. Her mistress wanted to turn all the mattresses. Winnie snorted. She had turned the mattresses last month, but she would be expected to do it again.

Her thoughts drifted and wandered from place to place. Distracted, she almost missed the crunch of footsteps behind her.

She whipped around to find Goldie behind her, grinning. "Miss Winnie. Odd to find you sneaking about this time of night."

"Not sneaking." Her heart rate ticked up. "I—Pastor Matthew needed help."

"Must be real important for you to be out in this dark."

"It was." Winnie struggled for words. But then a question came to her mind. "What are you doing out this late, Goldie?"

He leered at her. "Tending to my business like you are tending to yours."

She held her chin high and put as much confidence as she could into her stance. "Then we should be off to our separate businesses."

As they parted, she walked as fast as she could, resisting the urge to look back. Goldie's business could get them both into trouble, or worse, dead. And so could hers.

Chapter 8

Time to say goodbye.

He had ended his workday at the ironworks early to make the trip down to East Towson for the last time. Mr. Gilchrest had confirmed that everything was in order for tonight. Everything but Hiram's heart. It was time to leave, but his heart wanted to stay a little longer.

The sun had dipped, but not enough to cool the temperatures. He spotted Winnie, her parents, and Mr. Samuel standing in the clearing of East Towson. He picked up his pace. Winnie turned as he reached the outermost house and waved. She wore a big smile. Too big to greet a man who was about to leave. He slowed.

She ran to him. "Come. We have a surprise for you." She dragged him forward.

When they reached the clearing, she led him to Mr. Samuel's boardinghouse and his little garden. It was lined with bright green-leafed plants. She waved her hand. "They grew."

Mr. Samuel stepped up beside him, pride in his eyes. "I did what you told me to."

Hiram chuckled. "Good job. That should get you a little something come harvesttime."

Mr. Samuel clapped him on the back. "Sure gonna miss you."

Hiram nodded, a lump in his throat. "Gonna miss you too."

A few more East Towson residents filed in behind Mr. Samuel, giving their love and prayers for the rest of his journey. Winnie did not move from her place beside him.

Ms. Phoebe hugged him. "I know you stayed longer than you wanted, but I am glad you did. I will be praying that you arrive safely in Philadelphia and that you can get your mother and brothers out."

Hiram swallowed. "Thank you."

Mr. Paul stepped up and gave him a hearty handshake. Sadness colored his features. They left him alone with Winnie. He led her over to the bench next to his garden.

"Are you worried about tonight?" she asked.

"More worried about leaving you here." Once he boarded the ship, he had no way to protect her. He would have to wait months before he saw her again. How was he going to make himself board the boat knowing she was still here?

"Goldie has not been seen for days. Even Pastor Matthew thinks he has abandoned his plans."

Hiram shook his head. He knew the hatred Goldie had for the Madisons. "He will not give up easy. And if it fails, he will try again." Hiram sighed. "I remember the hatred I had for my owner, Mr. Toley. There were times when I could have done what Goldie is planning."

Winnie looked down at her hands. "It is so hard not to hate."

"I could not bring myself to hurt them like they hurt us. I don't think I could have killed another person, but I believe Goldie could."

"I believe he could too."

They sat in silence, the weight of their conversation hanging in the air like the remaining warmth of the day. Hiram took in the scene. This would be the last time he would see these beautiful lush trees and grass. How different it had seemed when he first arrived.

Winnie reached over and laced her fingers between his. He looked down at her and could not miss the tears in her eyes.

He released her hand and put his arm around her. "I know."

He let the remaining time they sat together sink deep into his heart and mind. It would be a long time before he could do this again.

Winnie managed to hold back the tears when Hiram stood from the bench to return to Baltimore. She did not want to make this any harder for him. She watched him until he reached the church and then let the tears flow. She kept reminding herself that he would be waiting for her in Philadelphia. She only had to make it through another six months, and then they would marry. The excitement of being free burned brighter in her mind. She and her parents would be free, and she would be Hiram's wife. She made her way to their boardinghouse, heart heavier with every step.

When they opened the door, her parents met her with sad smiles. Her mother grasped Winnie's hand and studied her face. "I don't understand why you don't go with him."

"I need to tell you both something." Winnie took a breath. "Last year I talked Mr. Madison into allowing me to buy our freedom."

Her parents stared at her, their mouths moving like they wanted to speak, but no words came out.

She continued before they could find their words. "All the extra work I have been doing is to earn money for our freedom."

Papa frowned and folded his arms. "No."

Winnie let out a soft laugh. "This is why I didn't want to tell you."

"The Madisons agreed to let us go?" her mother asked, hope lightening her tone.

"Yes." Winnie exhaled, the weight of that secret off her chest. "They don't trust Papa anymore, and he is not as useful, now that he is lame."

"It is Madison's fault. Believing that fool," her father huffed. "He may have to pay for his mistake."

"I think Mr. Madison realizes he made a mistake with his treatment of you." *I must tell them the rest.* "Mr. Madison suspects there is an attack coming. I overheard him and Mrs. Madison talking about it. Mr. Madison suggested that you were behind the riots. He wants you gone, and once I've worked enough to buy our freedom, we will be."

Her mother shook her head sadly. "That's if Goldie doesn't get us all in trouble again before we can leave."

Winnie moved to the hearth. "If Goldie's plan succeeds, the Madisons won't be around to punish us. But if the riot fails, I fear that the Madisons will change their minds and sell us to separate plantations."

Her father patted her shoulder. "It looks like Goldie's plan is not coming to anything anyway. But if it does, then we will run like Hiram." He let out a huff. "I am not so old I can't run to Pennsylvania."

Her mother moved to Winnie and cupped her face. "I know you wanted to earn our freedom a different way, but any way we get to freedom is good enough for me. You are the best daughter, and I love you."

Winnie was no longer able to hold back her tears. "I love you too."

Her mother wiped her tears. "Your papa and I will start looking for extra work tomorrow. No need for you to carry this burden alone. But tonight, we pray that God protects Hiram."

"Amen," Papa said.

In her room, Winnie undressed and sank into bed. She began to pray, but the weight of the day soon sent her off to sleep.

She had not fallen too deeply into sleep before pounding on her door brought her fully awake. *Another fugitive at the church?* She rose with haste and opened her door. Her mother and father rushed into the room.

"Let me get my notebook."

Her mother grasped her hand, her face grim. "It is not a fugitive."

Her heart thudded in her chest. "What is it?"

Her father grasped her shoulders and turned her toward the window. In the distance, she could see a mob of torch-carrying men making their way down the hill. Night still shrouded them for the most part, but she did not need to be told who they were. She gasped and pressed her hand to her throat.

"We need to leave here now," her mother said, jarring her from her shock.

"Get anything that is important to you and let's go before they get down the hill," Papa added.

Winnie grabbed her notebooks and followed closely behind her parents. She began to pray, but her petitions were unordered. The three of them thundered down the stairs, and Mama opened the front door of the boardinghouse. The view made them all stop short.

Coming down the hill from Madison House was a large posse armed with guns, led by Mr. Madison. The men in it outnumbered the slaves heading down from the opposite direction.

"Go!" her father called from behind them. They rushed out the door and around the side of the building. Winnie's feet moved faster than her mind. She shoved her notebooks in the pockets of her dress.

They turned the corner to find themselves in a crowd of slaves, Goldie in the front.

He reached out and grabbed her. "Where ya going, Miss Winnie? Where is your big man?"

Winnie tried to wrench her arm away from him. "You are all going to die."

"Let my daughter go." Her father grabbed Goldie by the shoulders.

A couple of men took hold of her father and pulled him away. "Where is the big man?"

"Gone," Winnie ground out.

Goldie snorted. "Coulda used him. I guess you will have to do." He began dragging her toward the posse.

"Let me go!" she screamed.

Mr. Madison and the first line of men entered the clearing. They raised their weapons and cocked them with almost a unified timing. "Get yourselves back to your plantations, and we won't kill you for this." Mr. Madison's voice echoed across the clearing. Winnie fought back a whimper. There was no way they could escape now. Even if the owners would not kill them when they returned to their respective plantations, they would be punished. All of them.

Goldie extended his hand. "We are only taking a little walk."

Mr. Madison didn't move. "I know what you are planning to do."

"You don't know nothing. Your sweet little Winnie and her family have been harboring fugitives for years right on your land."

Mr. Madison's eyes widened, but his surprise quickly shifted to a seething anger. He yelled at the crowd of slaves, "Go home!"

"Set us free!" Goldie yelled. The crowd behind him echoed the demand. Winnie looked over her shoulder at her parents. Tears streaked her mother's face, and her father strained against the men holding him.

There was no way out. As careful as they had been, everything was ruined by another slave. Winnie's heart heaved, and she braced herself.

Mr. Madison, seeing that Goldie was not backing down, raised his weapon, aimed, and fired.

The sound of the shot echoed across the field. The bullet hit Goldie, driving him to the ground and taking Winnie with him. She heard her mother scream, and the shots began in earnest. Goldie groaned next to her, and she freed herself from him. Her tears blurred her vision, and in the melee, she could not find her parents. She crawled on her hands and knees through the dropping bodies. *They are no match for guns.*

She reached the back edge of the crowd rushing toward the posse. She crawled past Hiram's garden, sobbing so hard her chest ached. She scrambled to her feet and turned to the crowd. There was a blur of activity.

"Mama! Papa!" she screamed, but if they could hear her, there was no response. She stumbled backward and spotted Mr. Madison. He made eye contact and ran toward her.

She bolted. Shots sounded behind her, but she did not dare look back. She reached the last boardinghouse, and the church loomed in front of her. *Lord, help me.* A yell sounded behind her, and she turned. At the edge of the clearing, her mother stumbled. Mr. Madison was gone.

"Mama!"

"Run, Winnie. Don't stop."

A man from the posse ran from between the buildings, knocking her mother down. Winnie screamed as she watched her mother scooting away from the man.

Suddenly, her father appeared behind the man and clubbed him down. "Winnie, go!"

It broke her heart, but she ran.

Chapter 9

Hiram found it hard to sit still. Mr. Gilchrest's office seemed to get smaller with each minute. Pastor Matthew patted his leg. "Everything will be fine."

Hiram tried to smile, but he was sure he grimaced instead. "Wish we could be off already." He dared not say it, but doubt had begun to creep into his mind. Did he want to be free without Winnie?

"You will be soon enough."

Hiram stood and paced the room. Winnie had not left his thoughts. The way she had looked up into his eyes and told him that she loved him. The warmth of embracing her. The way she touched the scars on his arms, the way she laughed. He sighed, thinking of how long it would be until he saw her again.

"Hiram, you should sit. Rest."

Hiram turned to Pastor Matthew and laughed. "You are right." But he only sat for a second before he stood again. "Is Mr. Gilchrest late?"

Pastor Matthew checked a small clock on Mr. Gilchrest's desk. "He is indeed. That is strange."

Hiram clasped his hands together. "Should we look for him?"

"No. I am sure he has a reason for being late that has nothing to do with your passage tonight."

They waited another half hour in silence. The time seemed to strangle Hiram. He rubbed the back of his neck.

The door burst open, and Mr. Gilchrest rushed in. "Pastor Matthew, our plans may have to change. You need to get back to East Towson."

Hiram and Pastor Matthew jumped to their feet. "What happened?" Pastor Matthew asked.

"An uprising."

Hiram's heart stopped. "At East Towson?"

"I was late because there was a hand from East Towson recruiting men for a posse to put down a riot. I asked as many questions as I could but didn't get many answers. The man was in a hurry to get enough guns to combat the slaves."

Hiram looked at Pastor Matthew and noted the alarm on his usually calm face. "Winnie."

Pastor Matthew rushed to exit, and Hiram followed him.

Mr. Gilchrest grabbed his arm. "No, Hiram. We need to get you on that ship."

He pulled away. "I'm not leaving until I know that Winnie and her family are safe."

Pastor Matthew blocked the door. "Hiram, he is right. I will make sure she is safe and send you word, but having you at East Towson will make everything worse."

"You can't expect me to leave. If there is a posse, they won't care who was or was not a part of the uprising. They will punish everyone."

"I know." Pastor Matthew placed a hand on Hiram's shoulder. "But if they catch you, you will be taken back to Virginia, and then you will be of no help to anyone. Let me go. Winnie and her family may be hiding out in the cellar of the church."

Hiram wanted to argue but could not find the words. Worry for Winnie clouded out every other thought.

Mr. Gilchrest grabbed Hiram's arm. "We need to go now. If all the men from the docks have gone down to East Towson, no one will notice us getting on the boat."

"But—" Hiram's mind desperately worked for the words to convince the men to let him return, but none came.

"Trust God, Hiram. You trusted Him to get you this far. Trust Him to care for His daughter."

Hiram stood for a second and let his heart absorb that truth. "I will pray."

"That is the best thing you can do right now. Godspeed, Hiram." And with that, Pastor Matthew rushed out the door.

"All right, Hiram. Let's get to the docks."

Mr. Gilchrest was right about the docks being empty. They were so barren that it looked as if no one was ever there. They walked at a fast pace, Mr. Gilchrest keeping time with Hiram. The air grew more humid as they got closer to the docks, and a thin fog was forming.

"The boat is there," Mr. Gilchrest said, pointing to a steamer about a thousand yards away. "Walk a little behind me."

Hiram slowed and dropped his head. The stance perfectly fit how he felt. It was going to be hard waiting the remaining time for Winnie to buy her freedom, but even harder waiting for word that she was safe.

"Hiram!" In the stillness of the docks, the voice rang out clear.

"Winnie?"

Hiram stopped short and saw her running up the docks behind them.

"Good Lord," Mr. Gilchrest said from behind him.

They ran to reach her. Before Hiram could even embrace her, Mr. Gilchrest dragged them both into a narrow walkway between the warehouses that lined the opposite side of the docks. Winnie faltered, panting hard, and Hiram held her up.

"Goldie. . . ," was all she managed to get out.

"We know." Hiram tightened his grip. "How bad is it?"

"He told them. . ." She pressed her hand to her throat. "He told Mr. Madison about the station and the fugitives. Told them my family and I were involved."

Mr. Gilchrest shook his head. "Pastor Matthew is on his way to find you."

"My parents." She let out a sob. "My parents told me to run. I went to the ironworks hoping to find you."

Hiram hugged her, knowing in his heart what he needed to do. "You have to run. Mr. Madison knows what you have done. He will sell you for sure. Or worse." He turned to Mr. Gilchrest. "Take Winnie on the boat in my place."

Winnie pulled away from him. "No, Hiram. I can't—"

"Pastor Matthew has helped many others, and now he needs some help."

"I can help them. I can go back," Winnie said.

Hiram knew she was not strong enough for this. "No. I came from Virginia on foot, and Pastor Matthew is no stranger to hard work. We can get your parents and bring them to Philadelphia."

"But the purchase papers are for you."

Mr. Gilchrest shook his head. "The papers do not have a description of the slave."

"Winnie, you have to go. I can fight to get your parents out if I need to, but they will be able to focus on running only if they know you are safe."

Tears flowed down Winnie's cheeks, but the fire was still in her eyes. His sweet, tough angel. "No, Hiram."

A ship horn startled them all. Mr. Gilchrest grabbed Winnie's arm. "Time to go, Miss Winnie."

"No!" She struggled against the man's grasp.

Hiram cupped her face, kissed her, and then let her go. "I will meet you at Mr. Still's house in Philadelphia." He raced down the docks in the direction of East Towson, ignoring her cries.

Leaving her small room in the boardinghouse, Winnie closed the door and hurried down the steps. The house's owner, Mrs. Sarah, a free black, had told Winnie that breakfast was included in her rent, but Winnie had yet to partake of it. Every day for a month, she had dressed and rushed to her job at William Still's office. She even went on Sundays, not to work, but to wait.

Hiram would come. Every day she expected to see him and her parents standing outside the building with smiles on their faces.

She navigated the streets of Philadelphia, which had the same energy and feel of Baltimore, to the Philadelphia Antislavery Society. Mr. Still had invited her to work for him, especially once he heard how she had kept records of the fugitives who came through the Star of Bethlehem station. Although he reassured her that Hiram and her parents were probably well and not harmed by the riot, it was not enough to comfort her. Why hadn't Hiram arrived yet?

She longed to see him and to hear some news of her family. For her first week in Philadelphia, she cried herself to sleep wondering if her parents were dead, maimed, or even worse, sold. She checked the paper that Mr. Still had delivered to the house daily. What of the Madisons? Were they dead? Several times she considered sending a note through the free blacks who visited Mr. Still, but then thought again. If the Madisons had met their demise, there would be no household slaves to receive her message.

Mr. Still had been so kind to search for information, but had gathered none. He was convinced that the riot must not have been bad. There was fear among Maryland owners that a bigger riot was going to happen in Baltimore. Mr. Still told her that if the uprising had succeeded, word would have spread among slaves and whites. She agreed that it was strange that no word had reached him and there was nothing in the newspapers. But what else could delay Hiram?

The city was loud, and the morning air held a thick fog. The mornings were cooler here than in East Towson, and she had to dress warmer and cover her head to keep her ears warm. The society sat only a few blocks from her living quarters, and she covered the distance in five minutes. Maybe today would be the day. She tried to keep her hopes up, but each day that hope waned. If Hiram were going to come, he would have by now. He had been determined enough to make it out of Virginia and determined to save her. She had to believe that he would not stop until he and her parents were free. . .unless he was dead.

She turned the corner of the block, her eyes immediately going to the stairs of the building that housed the society. They were empty. She sucked in a breath, tears ready to fall. Another day of wondering and waiting.

She ducked her head and continued down the way. Birds started their morning song as the sun burned the fog away. Winnie shifted her emotions. Even though Hiram was not there, she could expect other fugitives. They arrived worn but happy that they were finally free. She could understand how they felt. When Mr. Carlton had driven her to the society, the shock of their hasty departure from Baltimore and the heartbreak of leaving her parents behind had left her numb. After a few days, however, her mind began to grasp that she was free. Now her job was to help others realize that freedom was theirs too.

The bell of the church down the block chimed as she climbed the stairs.

"Excuse me, miss." A voice spoke from behind her. A voice she knew.

Her heart stammered as she turned with clumsy steps. At the bottom of the stairs stood Hiram. And not Hiram alone. Her mother, father, Pastor Matthew, and Mr. Samuel stood with him. She let out a yelp and rushed down the stairs to their waiting arms.

Winnie's tears choked her as she embraced her parents. "You are here."

Her mother pressed her tearstained face to Winnie's. "We were so worried about you."

Winnie pulled back to look at her mother. "I was worried about you. I didn't know if you had been harmed during the riot."

Her father patted her arm. "No, we were not. While Pastor Matthew tended to the wounded, Hiram took us to a station house in Baltimore."

"The uprising upset the owners, and we could not go back to East Towson," Pastor Matthew said. "I wanted to try to reason with them, but Hiram's wise advice convinced me that our best option was to run."

Winnie looked over at Hiram. He stood off to the side and wore the biggest smile.

"I am glad I could get them out," he said. "It took a little longer because we had to hide in Delaware for a bit. We came as soon as we could."

"Thank you," Winnie whispered and put her arms around him.

He wrapped his powerful arms around her. "Anything for you, sweet angel."

Terri J. Haynes, a native Baltimorean, is a homeschool mom, writer, prolific knitter, freelance graphic artist, and former Army wife (left the Army, not the husband). She loves to read so much that when she was in elementary school, she masterminded a plan to be locked in a public library armed with only a flashlight to read all the books and a peanut butter and jelly sandwich. As she grew, her love for writing grew as she tried her hand at poetry, articles, speeches, and fiction. She is a storyteller at heart. Her passion is to draw readers into the story world she has created and to bring laughter and joy to their lives.

Terri is a 2010 American Christian Fiction Writers Genesis contest finalist and a 2012 semifinalist. She is also a 2013 Amazon Breakthrough Novel Award Quarterfinalist. Her publishing credits include *Cup of Comfort for Military Families*, Crosswalk.com, *The Secret Place Devotional*, Urbanfaith.com, *Vista Devotional*, and *Publisher's Weekly*.

Terri holds a bachelor's degree in Theology, a master's degree in Theological Studies, and a certificate in creative writing and graphic design, meeting the minimal requirements of being a geek. She and her husband pastor a church where she serves as executive pastor and worship leader. Terri lives in Maryland with her three wonderful children and her husband, who often beg her not to kill off their favorite characters. Visit her website at www.terrijhaynes.com, and check out her blog at www.inotherwords.terrijhaynes.com.

The Winter Quilt

by Debby Lee

Dedication

I would like to thank the wonderful congregation of Crossroads Church for the love, encouragement, support, and prayers over the years. Without you, this book wouldn't have come to fruition. This story is lovingly dedicated to you all.

And immediately there fell from his eyes as it had been scales:
and he received sight forthwith.
—Acts 9:18

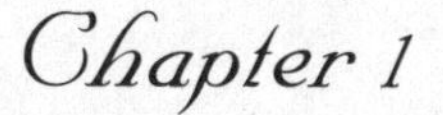

Chapter 1

Newport, Indiana
1840

Coral Martin clutched the handkerchief in her hands and gritted her teeth. She swore she wouldn't look through her hope chest ever again. If she did, the torrent of barely contained tears would burst forth like a breached dam and all composure would be lost.

"Oh, Roland, how am I to survive without you?" The question tugged at her heartstrings until nothing was left but tangled knots and no answers. How could Papa and Mama do this?

Perched on the rough wood bench seat of their covered wagon in the midst of the Indiana wilderness, Coral felt bitterness rise in her throat, filling her mouth with a bad taste. Roland was a good man, a suitable match for her. Yet her parents had dragged her away from all things cultured and refined to this desolate place.

"Coral, I asked you to fetch me another bucket of water, please." Mama's voice contained an uncommon note of impatience.

"Yes, Mama." She tried to keep her words from sounding strained, with little success. She reached for the tin pail then traipsed the soggy banks of the creek. With her head in the clouds, she didn't notice that her shoe stuck fast in the mud until it came off her foot. With her hitched-up skirts in one hand and the bucket in the other, Coral managed to right herself, but not before sticking her bare foot in the cold, gooey mire.

Exasperated, she dropped the bucket to the ground then retrieved her shoe. She placed her rear against a tree to steady herself and put the shoe back on her foot. In the process her skirts were muddied too. Fetching water wasn't this much trouble back home. She tried not to think of the house with the warm brick fireplace, her own bedroom filled with the fragrance of lavender potpourri, and her best friend Ashlynn, who lived just next door. And then there was Roland, of course.

Memories of the man she planned to marry wafted through her thoughts with such clarity she half expected to turn and see him standing beside Papa. Roland was well connected socially in Annapolis and frequented the best parties. His robust laughter at such occasions had always brought a smile to her lips.

Coral blinked back tears while she refilled the water bucket. Not wanting to lose her other shoe along the muddy embankment, she used more cautious steps on the path toward her family's new homestead.

"Here you are." Coral set the pail down by the campfire where her mother set out cups for afternoon tea.

"Thank you," Mama replied. Seven years had passed since they had left London, after the death of William Wilberforce, but Mama still retained her English traditions.

Coral plodded to the back of the wagon to help her father butcher a deer he'd recently shot. Her sore heart ached in her chest, but no matter how hard she tried to be brave, her feelings were evident.

"You miss Roland, don't you?"

Compassion permeated Papa's tone, but Coral found it hard to believe in his sympathy. It had been his idea to leave the security of home and come west, and toss Roland into the wind like yesterday's dishwater.

"He promised he'd write." A tiny flicker of hope burned in Coral's heart, one she stoked as often as her chores permitted. She vowed to see Roland again someday, even if it meant running back to Maryland without her parents' blessing. If fate held any luck for her, she'd be back in his arms by the time the holidays arrived.

Last Christmas they had danced together at Ashlynn's seasonal party. Roland had tried to waltz her under the mistletoe to steal a kiss, but she refused. Warmth flooded her cheeks at the memory.

"We had our reasons for leaving, Daughter." Papa skinned the animal with such ferocity, Coral cringed. She tried to ignore the darkening in her father's eyes and the smoldering expression burning in his features. What reason could he have for leaving that would upset him so?

"My knife is getting dull. I'm going to sharpen it, and then I'll be back to finish up." Papa stepped to the front of the wagon.

Coral heard her father rummage through his tools and decided to help clean up some of the mess. But the slippery container of animal entrails upended in her hands and blood spilled down the front of her muddy work dress.

"Oh!" A disgusted groan escaped Coral's lips. Mama had told her to wear her work apron. Why hadn't she listened? The sticky blood coated her hands and made further cleanup quite impossible. She hoped there was water left in the bucket. Her soggy, mud-coated shoe reminded her of her last venture down to the creek. She didn't wish to revisit the location.

A deep, low voice caught in her ears. Startled, she turned and beheld a tall blond gentleman.

Josiah Williamson stifled a chuckle at the young woman who looked as though she'd rolled in the pool of deer's blood on the ground. Her British accent seemed somehow incongruous with her gory appearance. He'd expect most females to fall into a swoon at being found in such a condition. Not the chestnut-haired beauty before him. Admiration for the lady crept into his surveillance of her.

"The name's Josiah Williamson, ma'am. Would you like some assistance?" Josiah pulled a fresh handkerchief from his pocket and offered it to her. He'd been sent to work with Mr. and Mrs. Martin and didn't want things to go badly before he had a chance to begin. But the young woman shrugged his offer off like a pesky gnat and reached for a pile of rags.

"Thank you for your kind offer, Mr. Williamson, but I don't wish to soil your fine linen. I can manage."

A moment later she added, "Forgive my manners. My name is Miss Coral Martin. If you'll excuse me." She gave a small curtsy. Then she squared her shoulders and hurried toward a bucket by the campfire.

Unable to turn away, he watched as she dunked the soiled rags in the bucket, swished them around, and rubbed them over her hands. Wisps of her hair caught in the breeze and floated about her face.

Josiah gave another stab at being helpful. "Miss Martin, if you'd like, I can escort you to the creek and help you retrieve another bucket of water."

She looked at him with a scowl on her face. Did she have something against being helped, or going to the creek? Or both?

"No, but thank you," she said and then clambered into the back of the wagon.

"I see you've met my daughter," said a burly man who stepped to the back of the wagon.

Josiah nodded and introduced himself. "Afternoon, Mr. Martin. The name's Josiah Williamson. I'm told by mutual acquaintances that you wished to see me."

"Indeed." Mr. Martin set down the knife he was holding. He then offered a firm handshake and stared hard at Josiah. The man's green eyes mirrored those of the young beauty. He seemed protective of his daughter.

Josiah forced himself to focus on the task at hand. "It's good to meet you, Mr. Martin. Mr. Wilbur, the storekeeper, who also works as the postmaster, sent me."

A smile creased the man's face. "Please, call me Sam."

"Very well." The gentleman's distinct English accent gave Josiah a measure of reassurance. A nudging of the Lord prompted him forward.

"I've been sent by Mr. Wilbur to assist you in building your house."

"Pleased to make your acquaintance, Josiah. I could use the help. After all, this isn't like Maryland, where bricks and mortar are readily available. All I have to work with is timber."

Josiah chuckled again. Some folks had difficulty adjusting from life in the city to that on the frontier. He hoped it wouldn't be so with this family. The dwelling he planned to build would provide a very important service.

"I'm more than eager to help you build your house, Sam," Josiah said as he surveyed the surrounding trees for their suitability.

Sam nodded. "I'll finish butchering later. Let's get started on the house."

"That suits me fine." Josiah smiled. He liked the idea of finishing their work as soon as possible.

Together they proceeded toward a stand of trees.

"I have one request." Sam's hard gaze bored into Josiah. "My daughter is to know nothing of the special features built into the house. At least not yet, is that clear?"

"All right." Josiah understood the need for secrecy in this line of work, but Miss Martin didn't seem daft. He was sure she'd find out the truth.

Sam continued. "I'd like to shield my daughter from this ugliness as much as possible. My wife disagrees and thinks we should tell Coral everything about our work."

"Can she be trusted with the knowledge?" Josiah tugged at the collar of his shirt. If their daughter couldn't be trusted, he'd reconsider working with the Martins.

"I trust my daughter explicitly. It's the company she's kept that worries me. Coral is a sweet girl, but she's only twenty, and quite naive. For everyone's safety, I say the less she knows, the better."

Josiah let the matter go and didn't ask any more questions. They had to get to work.

After picking a sizable tree, they sawed it down. Josiah continued to work alongside Sam for a few more hours. Then the lovely Miss Martin approached, and the sweet smile on her face distracted Josiah from his thoughts.

"Papa, dinner is ready."

"Thank you, dear."

"You're welcome to stay and dine with us, Mr. Williamson. We have plenty." Miss Martin cocked her head to the side. An indistinguishable but sweet fragrance hung about her.

Josiah put down his saw. "Thank you for the offer, but I must be getting to town before nightfall."

"Very well, perhaps another time." Miss Martin curtsied and excused herself.

Josiah watched her walk back to the campfire. She seemed polite enough, even after looking the way she did when they'd met. Most ladies would be mortified at such an experience, but this one didn't seem to be.

In spite of the pleasure working near her would bring, Josiah hoped to get the house built quickly. They were already deep into autumn, and winter approached with frightening speed. Winter nights provided extended hours of darkness. Thus, more freedom seekers would be on the desperate pilgrimage north. It also meant frigid temperatures; hence the desperation for safe places to hide them. The freedom seekers needed shelter from the icy winds and falling snow.

A number of oak trees lay on the ground. Josiah admired the work they'd done, but was anxious to come back by sunup the next morning.

He turned to Sam and said, "I'm sorry to miss dinner tonight. Give the ladies my apologies. I have to go now, but I'll come by tomorrow, first light, and help fell more trees." He glanced around to see if he could spot Miss Martin, but she was nowhere in sight.

"See you then." Sam waved a hand at him and strolled toward camp.

Josiah waved back and climbed on his horse. He had important matters to tend to.

When he reached Wilbur's Mercantile in Newport, he glanced around. Would anyone notice this was his second trip into the establishment that day? He hoped he didn't look conspicuous as he hurried into the community's only store.

Bolts of machine-woven fabric lined one wall, and barrels of flour and sugar sat next to the counter in the small building. The smells of leather and spices assailed Josiah's nostrils. His stomach rumbled at the sight of jerked beef hanging up to dry along the back wall.

"Afternoon, Mr. Wilbur. Do you have any packages you need shipped north? I have a friend who is heading that way soon and might be able to deliver them safely."

"Can't say as I do," Mr. Wilbur replied. "But I heard about a package that lost its outer wrapper while passing though Missouri."

Perplexed, Josiah cocked an eyebrow. He watched Mr. Wilbur walk up and down the aisles in his store, inspecting each one. They were the only two people there. The storekeeper then motioned Josiah into the back storage room. Uneasiness churned in Josiah's gut, but he followed the man.

In a hushed tone Wilbur said, "Rumor has it, an escaping slave was caught a few days ago, down in Missouri, and was skinned alive. Might be just gossip, but you never can tell."

Josiah shivered at the cruelty and inhumanity of a heartless society. He prayed to the good Lord above that nothing like that would ever happen to the souls he risked his life and freedom to help save.

Chapter 2

Several nights later, after Papa and Mr. Williamson had gotten a good start on the house, Coral helped her mother prepare dinner over a spider skillet. The aroma of venison lingered in the air. Her flour-coated hands paused over the biscuit dough while she admired the foundation of their new home.

Papa and Mr. Williamson were making great progress. The nights were growing colder, and that morning a light frost coated the wild grasses surrounding the campsite. How nice it would be to live in a real house again. On cold winter evenings Papa would build a fire in the fireplace, and they'd sit around it and read books and newspapers. Mama could unpack all their flatware, the nice dishes, and her favorite English vase.

Coral had her own collection of treasured things in her hope chest. Wrapped in her embroidered linens was her silver brush and comb set and her collection of Jane Austen books she'd brought from England. Lavender-scented potpourri was nestled in her favorite evening dress and kept everything smelling fresh. Then there was her six-sided patchwork quilt. She'd spent hours sewing together the hexagon shapes cut from fine, soft fabric.

Her rebellious heart sailed back to Maryland, and Roland. Had she not prayed and asked God to show her a way to be with him? Much to her chagrin the image of the handsome Mr. Williamson with his blue eyes invaded her thoughts. She shoved the picture from her mind and went back to cutting dough.

A short time later they sat around the makeshift table and bowed their heads. Papa thanked the Lord for the meal, but Coral prayed for something else. Roland had danced with a young Miss Cooper at her summer cotillion last June. She cringed at the memory. Would his head be turned by the money and connections Miss Cooper had? No, not her Roland.

Coral's feelings skittered around in her heart like dry autumn leaves caught in a gust of wind. The Bible said children were to respect and obey their parents. She loved Papa and Mama dearly and knew they would follow wherever God led them, but she believed they were mistaken in coming here. She also knew she should trust God with her circumstances, but why was trusting Him so frightening and painful?

In spite of her hunger, her dinner tasted like sawdust.

"Coral," Mama said, "are you feeling unwell? You're pale and you've hardly touched your dinner."

"I'm fine, Mama." Coral skewered a piece of venison with her fork. Again she thought of Josiah. He hadn't recoiled from her when she'd stood before him coated in blood from butchering the deer. On several occasions he'd helped her fetch water from the creek. Maybe a man from the country could have some manners after all.

"Come, Coral, help me with the dishes," Mama said.

Coral stood, retrieved the bucket, and trudged to the creek.

When she traipsed back into camp, her parents were talking of packages being mailed to Canada. What did they mean by that? They didn't know anyone living in Canada. At least she didn't think they did.

Papa glanced at her. Then he cleared his throat. "I hope we can finish the house before the first snow falls. I don't know these parts well enough to guess when that might be." He sipped from the tin cup Mama handed him.

"Mr. Williamson seems nice enough," Mama replied. "And he's a hard worker. I'm sure it will be done soon."

Coral noticed an odd look exchanged between her parents. Did they have a secret plot to match her up with the rugged woodsman? She hoped not. Manners or not, he wasn't the refined gentleman that Roland was. And how could she trust a man she didn't even know? How could her parents, for that matter?

To change the uncomfortable topic, Coral said, "Papa, when are you going into town again? I need more thread to mend my work dress and apron."

"I hope it can wait until we get the house built. That should be within the month, but I'm running out of nails, and the saw needs to be sharpened. I might ask Josiah to take care of those things for me." Papa studied the sketches he'd drawn of their house.

"Mama, how often do you think a mail rider comes through this wild place?" Coral asked.

"I don't know, dear. Are you thinking of sending Ashlynn a letter?"

"No." Coral shifted her weight. Anxiety washed over her when she replied, "I wrote a letter to Roland."

Papa straightened his stance and said harshly, "I know you miss the lifestyle of Annapolis, but you needn't concern yourself with certain connections there."

Mama shot her a disapproving look and tossed a chunk of wood onto the fire. Sparks spewed. Blue-orange flames hissed and reached upward.

Dismay engulfed Coral. The bucket slipped from her fingers and water sloshed everywhere. She cringed. Not only did she have to make another trip to the creek for more, but she had disappointed her parents.

It wasn't often she saw them so upset. Usually, it had to do with the slave trade. Roland's parents were staunch abolitionists, so he couldn't possibly have anything to do with that. So why, then, would they be so upset when she mentioned her letter to him? The silence filling the atmosphere didn't answer her questions.

"I'm sorry you're heartbroken, my dear," Mama finally said. "Your father has heard of a church social being held at the end of October. Perhaps we could join the festivities."

"A church social," Coral wailed. "What kind of excitement goes on at a church social?"

"The kind that doesn't include the cursing we heard at too many parties in Annapolis. I'd think you'd be grateful to get away from all the arguments over politics."

"Yes, but Mama, what good is it to get away from arguments if I'm also away from the fun?"

"Sacrifices must be made, my dear, and we must trust God to use us where He places us."

Another lapse of quiet ensued, which made Coral angry. Why did her folks talk in such riddles?

Josiah rode his horse into the clearing. The Martins' new home consisted of nothing more than a half-built foundation, but it was coming along. They had been fortunate to find rocks large enough to wedge against the outside corners to give the structure some stability.

That morning he and Sam cut more trees and skinned the bark off them. Then he used a planer to smooth two sides of the logs while Sam cut notches in the ends. That afternoon they stacked them one on top of the other. The resulting walls were only a few logs high, but it was a start. One he was proud of.

While he worked, Josiah tried not to look at the beautiful Miss Martin, but she occupied his thoughts more than he wanted to admit. Both Sam and his wife had told him not to share their secret with her. He understood they wanted to safeguard their daughter, but he worried nonetheless. Did they have other reasons, besides protection, for keeping their work secret? She seemed too sweet to go blabbing secrets of their underground work to others. He didn't want to consider the possibility that she couldn't be trusted.

Wisps of her brown hair came loose from its pins and fell about her face, giving her the look of an angel.

"Ouch," Josiah exclaimed when the planer handle scraped into his palm, causing it to bleed. He reached for his kerchief and wrapped it around the wound.

"Are you all right, Mr. Williamson?" Coral hurried to his side and reached for his hand. "I have some salve I can put on this."

Josiah's pulse quickened at how she held his hand in hers. She cared a great deal about folks. He liked that about her. Perhaps this young beauty could be trusted after all.

Should he speak with Sam about her? Not exactly court her, just spend time with her. It was important that he find out what her father meant when he'd said it was the company she'd kept that worried him. Or so he tried to convince himself. After all, one could never be too careful in this line of work.

"Thank you, Miss Martin, you're too kind," Josiah said after swallowing the lump in his throat.

"You're welcome," she replied. "I'll get that salve right now." She stepped away. A school of fish swam in his stomach as he watched her stride to the back of the wagon and climb inside.

An idea sprang into his mind like an overzealous jackrabbit. He could take her into town to see Mr. Wilbur and see what he thought of her. Josiah chuckled. That's what he would do. He ignored his throbbing hand.

Josiah jogged over to where Coral's father worked. "Sam, may I speak with you a moment?"

"Yes, of course, what's on your mind?" Sam climbed to the top of the ladder with hatchet in hand and chopped at a large knot protruding from the top log.

"Here, I'll hold this for you." Josiah gripped the sides of the ladder and held it steady. He wanted to ask Sam's permission to take Coral to meet Mr. Wilbur. Prudence told him to wait until Sam got down off the ladder before asking, but on this rare occasion he ignored prudence.

"Sam, I wonder if I might—" Josiah wet his lips and swallowed, contemplating his next words. He took a deep breath, ready to forge ahead.

At that moment, the horses, tied to their picket lines near the wagon, whinnied. They pulled at the lines, and one of them bucked and kicked the back of the conveyance. A snake had probably spooked them. He thought of Coral, in the wagon getting his salve. He feared she might be in danger.

"Mind your step up there, Sam. I'm going to calm the horses," he hollered as he went to tend to the animals.

Josiah hurried to the frightened beasts. "There, there, everything is all right now," he soothed. He held his hands up and took a few hesitant steps forward. After a few more gentle words the animals quieted. He stepped alongside them and rubbed their sleek, warm necks.

"Thank you, Mr. Williamson, but I could have handled them." Coral poked her head out from the wagon and smiled at him. Her green eyes twinkled.

A shout echoed.

Josiah turned in time to see Sam tumble from the ladder.

"Papa," Coral screamed. She sprang from the wagon and sprinted to her father. Josiah followed close behind.

They reached Sam at the same moment and knelt beside him. Blood poured from a gash in his lower left leg. Josiah's stomach convulsed at Sam's pale complexion. The poor man grimaced with pain.

"Sam, Coral, what happened?" Mrs. Martin ran from the direction of the creek and knelt beside her husband.

"Papa fell from the ladder. He's badly hurt," Coral wailed.

Josiah stood. "I'll fetch the doctor."

Coral turned to face Josiah. The green irises that sparkled only a moment ago now burned with indignant fire.

"Why weren't you holding the ladder for him?"

Chapter 3

Papa lay on the ground beside the wagon, his ashen face contorted with pain. Coral's heart galloped in her chest as she watched her mother tend the cut on the side of his head.

Mama's hands worked fast and methodically, but the soothing words she expressed to Papa did little to comfort Coral. She tried not to look at the deep blue-purple bruises that colored his swollen knee. He had to be okay. Prayers flew from her lips at regular intervals as she paced from the campfire, around the makeshift table, to her father's side, and back again.

Mr. Williamson had ridden for the doctor in town, but that had been an hour ago. What was taking them so long to get back?

Amidst the concern for her father, Coral also felt a twinge of guilt for snapping at Mr. Williamson. It wasn't his fault Papa fell. She would ask him for forgiveness when he got back with the doctor. Papa would surely be all right after the doctor treated him. *But what if he isn't?*

Her father groaned. A tear slid down Coral's cheek. Another prayer was sent heavenward.

Time seemed to stand still before her ears grasped the sound of horses' hooves in the distance. She rushed to her father and knelt beside him. "It won't be long now, Papa. Mr. Williamson and the doctor are coming."

"Thank you, Lord," Mama said. "Coral, please fetch more water from the creek. The doctor will likely need another kettle heated."

"Yes, Mama." Coral jumped into action. By the time she got back from the creek, the doctor had arrived. He knelt beside Mama, who gave an account of the events.

Coral shifted from foot to foot and chewed on a fingernail while the doctor worked.

Time seemed to crawl again before the doctor spoke. "The leg injury isn't too serious, just a dislocation that I popped back into place. I've stitched his wounds closed. He doesn't appear to have a concussion, but we'll watch him closely for the next two days. He'll need several weeks overall to recuperate, but barring any infection, I anticipate a full recovery."

Coral took deep breaths. Tears of gratitude pooled in her eyes. She rushed to her parents' side and took Papa's hand in hers. Mama kissed Papa on the forehead. Circumstances had righted themselves.

"Thank You, Lord, for Your mercy."

Coral turned to see Mr. Williamson at the table, head bowed in prayer. Touched by the man's compassion, she wished to thank him, but didn't want to disrupt his moments with the Almighty.

"Can you help me wash these bandages, Coral?" Mama asked.

"Of course." Coral was thankful for the distraction from Mr. Williamson. She wiped her eyes before retrieving the tin pail, but hadn't made it three steps toward the creek when Mr. Williamson's deep baritone voice resounded in her ears again.

"Allow me to assist you with that, Miss Martin. And when you're finished perhaps we could go for a walk." Josiah stood, hat in hand, and flashed a smile that could have melted the morning frost.

"Thank you, Mr. Williamson, I'd enjoy that." Coral pushed a wisp of hair from her eyes and tried to fan the heat from her face. Kindness emanated from this man.

"You can call me Josiah." He took the bucket from her. When his hand brushed against hers, a tingly feeling zipped from her fingers straight to her heart.

"And you may call me Coral." She hoped he didn't notice the hitch in her voice as she spoke. Unable to form another sentence, she headed to the creek.

The sound of Josiah's footsteps behind her made her feel safe for some reason. When he placed his hand at the small of her back to maneuver around her, she stifled a gasp.

He dipped the bucket into the flowing water and pulled it up with one hand. Coral noted his strong biceps and expansive chest. Of course he was muscled; he was a carpenter. So why hadn't she noticed it before?

Embarrassed, she turned away. What would Roland, or her parents, say? Thankful no one could read her thoughts, she hurried back along the path toward camp. She didn't dare turn to look at Josiah, afraid her eyes would reveal her growing interest in him.

After returning from the creek, Coral rubbed the bloodstained bandages against the washboard. Every time she rinsed a strip, she snuck a look at the handsome gentleman. He sat on the wagon's bench seat and read the Bible to her father. The rugged carpenter might not be as cultured as Roland, but Roland wasn't nearly as devoted to God as Josiah appeared to be.

"I'll cook dinner tonight so you can go for a walk around the meadow with Mr. Williamson," Mama said. "But don't go so far that I can't see you."

"All right." Now she was sure her parents intended to fix her up with the man. Did they have something against Roland?

Later, after she'd hung the cleaned bandages on a tree limb to dry, Josiah offered his arm to her. She placed her hand in the crook of his elbow.

"Let's walk this way." Josiah pointed down the road that led to town. "There is a lovely meadow a short distance from here. The trees are beautiful this time of year with the leaves changing colors. Perhaps we'll see a doe or a jackrabbit."

"I'd like that." Coral was grateful to get away from camp for a while. "As long as Mama can still see us. I don't want her to worry."

A warm autumn sun cast shadows about them as they strolled past trees. Wild grasses bent and swayed in the breeze as if to wave to the heavens. Coral asked Josiah's forgiveness for being short with him earlier. He readily extended it, which both surprised her and warmed her heart. Roland didn't get over disagreements as easily as this man.

Conversation steered toward Roland for a few minutes. She told Josiah about her friend Ashlynn in Annapolis too. He asked a lot of questions about them. She thought it odd that he seemed so interested in her friends, but assumed he was being polite.

"You seem to know a lot of people." Josiah chuckled. "My closest confidant is the storekeeper, Mr. Wilbur. He's also the town's postmaster."

A spark of excitement ignited in Coral. A postmaster? Perhaps she could get Josiah to take her into town so she could mail her letter to Roland. If she couldn't get away, maybe he'd take her letter to Mr. Wilbur and mail it for her. But how could she convince him to do so and keep the deed a secret?

Supper bubbled in a pot hung over the campfire when Josiah and Coral returned from their walk. He could smell the venison before he spotted Mrs. Martin.

"Your father is sleeping in the wagon, Coral. Mr. Williamson, would you like to stay for dinner?"

"Yes, I'd like that." In spite of the cool temperatures, it warmed him to be around the lovely Miss Martin. He hoped his questions about her friends hadn't raised her suspicions. After what Sam had said about the company she'd kept, he wanted to glean as much information about them as he could.

First thing tomorrow, he'd stop by Wilbur's store and pass their names along. If they were people to be trusted or feared, Wilbur would find out.

He turned his attention to Coral. She placed the plates, cups, and flatware on the table and helped her mother carry the meal from the fire. He couldn't imagine the well-mannered lady before him to be untrustworthy, but she could very well trust the wrong person and thus spill secrets without meaning to. He loathed the deception this line of work required, but until he was sure her circle of friends wouldn't betray them, he would keep quiet.

Josiah's stomach rumbled. In all the hullabaloo that afternoon, they had missed lunch. He inhaled the aroma of the stew and took a big helping. His stomach growled again but proper etiquette told him to wait for the blessing.

Since Sam slept in the wagon, Mrs. Martin did the praying. Afterward, Josiah took a large bite and noticed Coral smiling at him. His middle quivered. This beauty would be the undoing of him. He was taking a shine to her, no doubt, but feelings like that had dangerous ramifications. Bounty hunters were deceptive. They could trap her into divulging information and thus put freedom seekers in danger. How could he court her without her finding out about the work he did?

"The food is delicious." Josiah steered his thoughts elsewhere.

"Thank you," Mrs. Martin replied.

When he finished his meal he tipped his hat, said goodbye, and told the ladies he'd be back the next day to continue working on the house. It didn't matter to him that he'd be working alone. The need to finish the structure pressed at him.

The next morning, before heading to the Martins' homestead, he stopped by Wilbur's Mercantile and gave the man the names of Coral's friends.

"I'll see what I can find out, but it'll take me a few weeks." Mr. Wilbur glanced around the building. Josiah's fingers twitched. Sweat made rivulets down his forehead. Wilbur only checked his store when he had something to tell him.

"What's going on, Wilbur?"

"A package has been lost."

"What do you mean 'lost'?" Josiah leaned forward and placed his palms on the counter.

"I received word that a package was on its way here, but it didn't arrive. I don't know if the package had the incorrect address or if it was intercepted by the wrong party."

Wilbur pushed a poster across the counter as he leaned close to Josiah and whispered,

"Patrollers were in here yesterday and left this. Sheriff Hansen knows about it too."

A wave of nausea slammed into Josiah as he read the wanted poster. His stomach convulsed. This poor soul ran loose in the countryside, lost, frightened, his life hanging by a thread. "Sheriff's good people. He won't stand for any packages being unethically taken, damaged, or destroyed."

"I know, I know." Wilbur nodded. "But the man still has to uphold the law."

"Then we'll have to locate that package and get it back on route before anyone else does." Josiah stomped out of the store. He loaded his wagon with a massive amount of bricks from the supply outside the mercantile, many more than what was needed to build a fireplace.

Anxiety filled him as he drove toward the Martins' homestead. What explanation would he give any patrollers if they stopped him and asked questions about all the bricks in his wagon bed? He couldn't very well tell them they would be used to build a hiding place for freedom seekers.

He called to his horses and the wheels rolled a bit faster. Relief filled him when he arrived at the Martins'. Then Coral stepped from her family's wagon and anxiety set back in. How would he keep her from suspecting anything if she was always underfoot?

"Good morning, Mr. Williamson. Have you had your breakfast yet?" Mrs. Martin stooped by the campfire and stirred a large pot of oatmeal.

"No, ma'am, I haven't."

"Let me dish you up, and then you can start working. Coral agreed to walk with me to the meadow. I'd like to see if there are any dandelions left, and if we're lucky we'll find some wild chickweed."

"That sounds lovely, Mrs. Martin." Josiah exchanged knowing smiles with the lady. How clever of her to divert Coral so he could work on the secret room in the house.

He had hardly scraped the last bite of oatmeal from his bowl before Coral and her mother set out. All morning he worked as fast as he could. Deep satisfaction flowed through him as he slapped a bit of mortar around the last brick that made up the secret wall. If the mortar dried fast, he could build a wooden wall around it and Coral—and any nosy bounty hunters—would be none the wiser.

Exiting the house, he proceeded to the wagon to check on Sam. Before he had the chance, though, Coral rushed into camp and nearly crashed into him.

"Coral!" Josiah exclaimed.

"Josiah." She tugged at his shirtsleeve and pulled him away from the wagon. "I need you to mail this for me," she whispered.

Josiah read the address of the envelope she thrust into his hands.

"I need you to keep it a secret, please." Her beseeching green eyes held him captive, and before common sense had a chance to convince him otherwise, he nodded. She darted toward the meadow. Josiah groaned and turned back to the house.

Brush rustled.

Twigs snapped.

A dark form crouching in the bushes on the creek path caught his attention. His heart paused for a few beats.

Coral paused, pointing to the dark-skinned man emerging from the brush. "Who is that?"

Chapter 4

For two weeks Coral both wondered and worried about the man she'd spotted near the creek. All Josiah had told her was that the man, Amos, was a freedom seeker, recovering from exhaustion, malnutrition, and cut and bruised feet. He had taken Amos away from their homestead, and Coral had not seen Amos since.

"Daughter, will you help me to the table, please?"

Coral hurried to assist her father. He could get around camp now, but his legs were still a bit shaky. Mama added another piece of wood to the fire and stirred a large kettle of venison stew.

Papa combed his fingers through his beard, as if to contemplate his words before he spoke. "We appreciate your keeping quiet about the freedom seeker, but we must have your word that you won't do anything that would put him in danger. Sometimes it can be difficult discerning the intentions of those we call friends."

"Yes, of course." Coral folded her arms across her chest. Granted, she hadn't been involved in her parents' abolitionist groups when they'd lived in Maryland, but she wasn't about to gossip about her knowledge of the runaway, either. Papa and Mama should know that.

"I mean it, Daughter. I don't want you writing to Ashlynn or Roland and telling them about the man you saw. Is that clear?"

"I wouldn't do that, Papa. I won't, I promise." Tears pooled in her eyes. They didn't trust her. Along with a sting of betrayal came a frightening realization. How far did her parents take their abolitionist views? Far enough to work on the Underground Railroad? She suspected as much from Josiah, but from her parents?

A pang of guilt gripped her. They really wouldn't trust her if they knew she'd asked him to secretly mail her letter to Roland. The only thing she'd mentioned in her letter was the weather and how much she missed him. Well, she still thought she missed him, although he occupied her daydreams less and less.

"Samuel." Mama turned to face them. "I have enough beans and flour to make meals for only one more day. A trip into town is necessary. Shall I ask Josiah to escort Coral and me?"

"Why don't we all go tomorrow?" Papa said. "I can get around well enough, and I'd like to speak with Mr. Wilbur, see if he needs any help with his postal business."

"And I still need thread for sewing, especially for my quilt." Excitement stirred within Coral. The notion of shopping in town for a day assuaged any ill feelings she had about her parents not trusting her.

"What about Josiah? Won't he want to come with us?" Coral asked. Heat radiated through her at the thought of spending more time with him. She could get him to introduce her to Mr. Wilbur, and perhaps they could have lunch together. A blush tingled in her cheeks.

Josiah was so kind. With the exception of Sundays, he had worked every day, from first light until dusk, for the past two weeks to finish their house. He even helped with chores.

"We'll ask him when he gets here in the morning," Mama said.

Coral drew so many buckets of water from the creek her arms ached, but at last enough water had been heated to give them all a good scrubbing. She didn't neglect to use her lavender-scented soap. When she laid her head on her pillow that night, she envisioned all the shops in town. One of them had to carry sewing goods.

She had no more than closed her eyes when the zing of an ax hitting wood jolted her awake. She recognized the happy tune Josiah often whistled.

Coral kicked off her blankets, dressed quickly, and applied some of her lavender-scented fragrance to her wrists and neckline. Then she clambered down from the wagon.

The first rays of sunshine peeked over the eastern horizon, coloring the sky with hues of pink and yellow. She paused to admire God's brushstrokes against the vast canvas. In spite of the Creator's handiwork, the morning air still had a bite to it. She shivered and wrapped her shawl around her shoulders.

"Good morning," Mama said. "Josiah has been kind enough to cut firewood for us while your father harnesses the horses for our trip to town."

"Thank you, Josiah." Coral smiled at the man who hadn't even broken a sweat. He flashed a smile at her, nodded, and went back to work. Her heart skipped a few beats. A spot in her middle somersaulted like an acrobat. Roland never made her feel this way—or had he, and she just didn't remember?

Coral pushed the thought from her mind and helped her mother with breakfast. While stirring the last of the oatmeal, she snuck a look at Josiah. He stooped to gather an armload of wood then strode over and piled it near the wagon. Try as she might, she could not picture Roland working as hard as Josiah Williamson. For a brief moment she wondered what good qualities Roland had.

"Coral, stir, before it burns."

"Yes, Mama." She scraped the wooden spoon against the bottom of the pot and tried not to gawk at Josiah.

"I finished hitching the horses," Papa said. "They can eat from their grain sacks while we have breakfast ourselves. Then we can be on our way." He limped across the camp and plopped down on the bench seat. When everyone else came to the table, Coral bowed her head while he said the blessing. She asked God to give her wisdom.

During breakfast Josiah turned to her father. "Sam, why don't you rest in back of the wagon while I drive the team into town? I know the way to Wilbur's Mercantile, and you've asked me to introduce you to him."

"That sounds fine," Papa said.

When breakfast was finished they climbed into the wagon and Josiah took the reins.

Later, when he steered the horses onto Main Street in Newport, Coral squealed with delight. Overjoyed at being around civilization, she squirmed like a child in church. She craned her neck around for a better view of her surroundings. Her mind raced at the different parties she could have at the hotel once they were settled, perhaps. She couldn't wait to write Ashlynn and tell her all about the town. Papa and Mama surely couldn't be upset at that.

Should she write another letter to Roland too?

Josiah pulled the wagon up to Wilbur's Mercantile. Thoughts of Roland sailed out of Coral's head. She wanted to jump from her seat. The establishment wasn't anything as grand as the shops in Annapolis, but she could hardly wait to see the inside. There had to be enough sewing supplies so she could finish her quilt. Josiah alighted from the conveyance and held out his hand to assist her as she climbed down.

They strolled into the building, but not fast enough for Coral.

"Afternoon, Wilbur." Josiah began the introductions. "This is the Martin family I told you about. Sam Martin, his wife, Anna, and their daughter, Coral."

"Pleased to meet you, Mr. Wilbur." Coral dipped a haphazard curtsy to the man then darted to the fabrics and threads stacked against the far wall. She ran her fingers over the smooth cotton plaids and dreamed of the many hexagons she'd cut from all the floral prints and multicolored ginghams. While picking out the right shade of blue to finish the current piece she worked on, the hushed words of the store owner gripped her attention.

"I've been able to repair most of the damage to the package, but someone unfriendly without a claim slip tried to confiscate it. We have to ship it north, and soon, before they come back, or the package will be lost forever."

Something like lightning zipped through Coral.

She knew what they were talking about.

Josiah stepped into the back room of the store. Amos, the lost package that had been found at the Martins' homestead, crouched against the wall. The man clutched a threadbare blanket but was obviously ready to bolt up and fight if danger appeared.

He and Wilbur had worked hard to nurse Amos back to health. The bruises and gashes on his feet had almost healed. The ragged marks crisscrossing his back would be there forever, as would the scars to his mind, but Amos was strong.

Josiah didn't wish to break the fragile trust between them. It had taken Amos three days to regain consciousness after he and Coral spotted him by the creek. Hunger and exhaustion would do that to a man, but Amos hadn't given up. Thanks to some herbal medicine, the fever had broken and he was on his way to recovery.

"I brought you a new pair of shoes." Josiah knelt and held the footwear out to the determined freedom seeker.

"Thank you, sir." Amos's ebony eyes were keenly fixed on Josiah. The man reached for the footwear, held them up, and looked them over. "I'll surely get to freedom with these."

Josiah wondered if Amos had ever owned a pair of shoes. A lump formed in his throat.

"Let me see about getting you something to eat." He stood, strode from the room, and shut the door behind him.

He stormed to where Wilbur stood and said, "That parcel is ready to be shipped. We need to move it today."

"I know that, but Levi has too many packages to process at the moment. Folks showed up at his house looking for this package in particular, so he sent it here," Wilbur said. "He's delivering a wagonload of hay bales to some friends up north sometime soon. He'll take it then and make sure it's safely delivered."

Turning to Sam, Josiah said, "Your house is finished enough. You folks need to move in soon."

He paced the distance along the counter. He noticed Coral standing by the window, a large spool of thread in her hand, eyes as big as two tin plates. Her silence frightened him. Why hadn't he thought to make sure the coast was clear before spouting off? Because it angered him to see freedom seekers stuck in limbo while waiting for logistics to get worked out.

"We'll move in first thing tomorrow," Sam declared. Josiah watched his friend nod at his wife and daughter.

Coral took slow steps as she moved to the counter and placed her spool of thread on it.

He gulped. She could betray them all, but would she?

She nodded at her parents, determination on her face. Elation washed over Josiah. Glory be! This spunky gal was on their side.

Wilbur cleared his throat and said, "Let me get my ledger so I can tally up your order, Mr. Martin."

Josiah and Sam discussed the latest issue of William Lloyd Garrison's *The Liberator* while Coral and Mrs. Martin finished their shopping. For a few wonderful minutes, a semblance of normalcy returned to the store. Josiah felt his muscles relax.

The bell hanging over the door jangled when Sheriff Hansen strolled inside. A man dressed in a fancy suit, with a fancier cravat, followed him.

"I'm terribly sorry to bother you, Wilbur, but this man says he needs to have a word with you." Hansen leaned against the door, not bothering to make introductions.

Uneasiness gripped Josiah as he watched the man look down every aisle of the store. The aroma wafting from his cigar filled the air. Josiah's jaw muscles tensed when the scoundrel smiled, tipped his hat, and bowed at Coral and her mother.

"I'm sorry to bother you folks on this fine afternoon, but I'm looking for this here runaway." He flashed a poster for them all to see.

Nausea churned in Josiah's gut and the fine hairs on the nape of his neck rose.

The sketch on the poster resembled Amos.

Chapter 5

Giddy with excitement at moving into their new home, Coral hefted one end of her trunk while Josiah held the other. Together they carried it into the house and up the stairs. Josiah stopped at the door to her room and set the trunk down. She understood his hesitancy to go further. It wasn't proper for a man to enter the bedchamber of an unmarried lady.

"Thank you," Coral said. Her cheeks warmed. She told herself it was from the exertion of carrying things into the house, but she knew better. She had to fan the heat from her face nearly every time she conversed with the strong carpenter. Was that a blush she noted on his cheeks as well?

"You're more than welcome, and thank you kindly for distracting that bounty hunter so Wilbur and I could hide Amos."

"It was the only humane thing to do. Besides, what Papa said at the store is true; he heard it straight from Levi Coffin. Bounty hunters can't search your property without first obtaining a search warrant."

"You don't know how much it pleases me to see you advocating for the freedom seekers." Josiah swiped at a lock of blond hair that fell in front of his eyes and flashed a smile as bright as the morning sun.

A drop of sweat rolled down Coral's temple. Half mortified, she cleared her throat and opened the trunk in search of a fresh handkerchief. The scent of lavender wafted up to tickle her nostrils. She paused before digging into her things. What was she thinking? She couldn't unpack her unmentionables in the presence of a man, and it would be rude to tell him to leave.

Josiah coughed and tipped his head toward the ceiling and then to the floor. "If you'll excuse me, Coral, I need to help your father plan the next leg of Amos's journey." He stepped away. His footsteps echoed in her ears as he clomped down the stairs. Then she heard him speak to Amos.

"We'll be moving you soon. Until then, eat heartily and get some rest."

"Thank you, Mr. Williamson."

Respect for the weary freedom seeker flooded through Coral. How brave these people must be. They risked their lives for a chance at a better life. In that moment she knew she'd do anything to ensure the safety of those who knocked on her door for help.

At one point she had doubted her father's decision to move to Indiana, but perhaps the Lord had brought her family here after all.

Days in Annapolis had been filled with parties, fancy dresses, and carriage rides through the city. She hadn't realized how empty those days had been. But this place, this place, held something different. Something she hadn't sought before. Something that stirred her spirit.

Purpose.

A chance to fuel hope in the oppressed, a chance to serve those in desperate need.

"What an honor, Lord," she whispered. "Thank You for the opportunity."

A flush crept into her cheeks again, and this time it had nothing to do with the kind-hearted carpenter. Her heart beat a tad faster. She let out a giggle. Life in Indiana was going to be all right. She hummed her favorite hymn while unpacking.

Delighted with her new bedroom, she hung up her dresses and spread a heavy coverlet over her bed. Tomorrow she would sew the last few hexagons into her quilt and begin working on the trim. Soon it would be finished, although she didn't know what purpose it would serve. She doubted she and Roland would ever be together. That wasn't what she wanted anyway, not anymore.

"Please, God," she prayed, "let this quilt be used to bring glory to Your name."

Mama's voice drifted up the stairs as she offered Amos a bowl of hot stew. A prayer for the man's safety flew from Coral's lips.

The tiny crawl space nestled behind a bookcase next to the fireplace wasn't very big, but it provided a good place to hide if bounty hunters came looking for him.

Coral's thoughts once again turned to Josiah. He had compassion and a willingness to serve that Roland didn't. She harrumphed, her mind made up. "First chance I get, I'll write him another letter and tell him I'm staying put."

From the depths of her trunk, she pulled another bottle of lavender fragrance and a doily she had tatted. She placed the doily on her dresser and set the glass bottle on top.

Before she could admire the effect, the sound of hoofbeats thundered from the front yard below. A commotion resounded from the kitchen. Her heart jerked.

Hiking up her skirts, she rushed down the stairs. She rushed into the living quarters in time to see Papa and Josiah scoot the bookcase back into place. Amos was hidden. Good! She exhaled with relief, but who had arrived?

"Papa, who is it?" she cried. Fear skittered across her skin. She heard the rider dismount. Mama reached out and grasped her hands.

Bang, bang, bang.

"Martin, open up!"

"It's Wilbur," Josiah exclaimed.

Papa flung the door open.

"I just heard from a stationmaster up the road," Wilbur said. "That bounty hunter has obtained a search warrant and is on his way back into town."

"How much time do we have?" Papa asked.

"A quarter of an hour, maybe, and this time he has bloodhounds with him. We have to get Amos out of here, now!"

Josiah let out a low whistle then smacked his fist into his palm. "God have mercy. Those bloodhounds will smell him a mile away. They'll catch him for sure."

"Well, we can't sit here and do nothing," Papa said. "I'll hitch the horses and get the wagon ready." He grabbed his hat and a lantern and hurried from the room.

"I'll help you." Wilbur followed Papa.

"I'll pack some food." Mama turned toward the kitchen.

Coral stood still, seemingly rooted to the floor. She watched Josiah pace the room. He stopped in front of the fireplace.

"Jesus, please spare Amos. Show me what to do, Lord," he prayed.

"Oh, I have an idea." Coral ran up the stairs, grabbed her lavender bar of soap and bottle of fragrance, and ran back downstairs.

"We can use these." She held the items up for Josiah to see.

A perplexed expression covered his face.

She grinned at him and then explained. "Help me get him out of the hiding spot. We can wash him real quick with my lavender soap and then spray him with my lavender perfume. That should throw off the bloodhounds, shouldn't it?" She hoped, prayed.

A smile creased Josiah's face. He laughed aloud. "Coral, you're a smart young lady."

Together she and Josiah moved the bookcase. Amos stepped from the tiny space. A wildness flashed in his eyes. This man looked ready to fight for his freedom. Something flashed in Coral as well. If need be, she too would battle the principalities of darkness for the sake of this man.

"Don't worry, Amos," she said. "We're going to take care of you. That is, if you don't mind smelling like lavender."

"Smelling like a lady beats a lashing from the whip." Amos tugged off his shirt.

Coral splashed water from the kettle onto a few rags. She and Josiah scrubbed Amos. Agony throbbed in her chest as she wiped the cloth over the ragged scars on his back. A lump formed in her throat so thick it hurt to breathe. She had to look away.

The cruelty that blinded some folks both saddened her and made her angry. Coral gritted her teeth and continued to wash Amos's back.

Papa and Wilbur burst through the back door.

"The wagon's hitched. Is he ready?"

"Just a moment, Papa," Coral said.

Josiah helped Coral rinse the soap off Amos and dry him with towels.

Mama appeared and handed a garment to him. "Here's a clean shirt." Amos wiggled into it with amazing speed.

"One last thing." Coral yanked the stopper off her perfume bottle. She doused Amos with the fragrance. "Lord Jesus," she prayed, "let it be enough."

"If anyone asks you about the scent of lavender, tell them it's from this." Coral held up a lace-trimmed handkerchief to Josiah.

Their fingers touched when he took it. Warmth swept over him. Did she feel it too? The fire flashing in her emerald-green eyes told him it was possible.

"Now go, go!" She gave him a shove. He ran from the house and out into the backyard, by the barn.

"Hurry, man, hurry," Wilbur implored. "I can hear the hounds."

Josiah stuffed the handkerchief into his pocket. He helped Sam and Wilbur move hay bales over the secret compartment in the back of the wagon. Fear chomped at his heart, but he managed to wrestle it into submission. Never had he been this close to getting caught with a freedom seeker. He shuddered to think what would happen if someone wanted to search the wagon.

It wasn't time in jail that frightened him the most. He was sturdy and could afford to pay any fines. It was the thought of the freedom seekers being dragged back to cruel masters that sent waves of terror coursing through him.

Josiah leapt onto the wagon seat. "I know where the next station is. You two hold off the bounty hunters."

"I'll keep them searching the house as long as I can. Godspeed to you, man," Sam called over his shoulder as he limped toward the house.

"With God's mercy, we'll make it to the next station without getting caught." Josiah prayed Coral and her mother had the sense to burn anything Amos left behind, anything that might point to his having been in the house.

Josiah snapped up the reins and called to the horses.

The animals took off at a gallop.

Chapter 6

Mama tossed pieces of dry wood onto the fire. The flames sizzled and popped as they burned all the evidence of Amos's stay with them. Coral rushed upstairs to hide her now empty lavender perfume bottle and the remnants of her soap.

Her lacy nightgown lay across her pillow. She seized it, along with a spare petticoat she'd mended earlier, and stuffed them into her trunk. The thought of those rough men searching her bedroom made her nauseous. Then she thought of Amos and shook her head. It was selfish to think only of one's self at a time like this.

Coral steeled herself and hurried back down the stairs. She'd delay those brutes for as long as possible, and if that meant allowing them to search her room, then so be it. When she reached the foot of the stairs, she smiled and nodded at Mama.

The racket of baying hounds echoed in the night.

Fear punched her in the stomach. She pursed her lips. What little faith she had. She shook her head and turned to the Lord. "Mercy, Jesus, be with us." The words rolled off her lips and fear dissipated.

The back door was flung open. Papa burst inside and slammed it shut. He rushed into the living room. Bounty hunters pounded on the front door.

"Open up, Martin," said the brusque voice outside.

Hastening to Coral's side, Mama clutched her so hard the breath went out of her.

"Lord Almighty, keep us in Your hands," Papa prayed. She watched her father square his shoulders. In response, she straightened her spine and stood taller.

Time seemed momentarily suspended, like a small silver spoon dropped into a jar of thick honey.

With slow, methodical ease, Papa undid the latch and opened the door.

Three men stood in the entryway. The tall one, the lead bounty hunter from Wilbur's store, shoved a piece of paper at Papa. Two hounds barreled under Papa's legs. They approached Coral and sniffed at her skirts, then the floor, and barked.

"The dogs are on to something," the shorter man said. A wicked grin spread across his stubble-covered face.

"You and your men are welcome to search our house," Papa interjected. "There's an opening in the kitchen floor that leads down to the cellar. You're free to look there."

"And don't forget my room upstairs." Coral wanted them to look anywhere besides the living quarters where Amos had been. The tall one eyed her, smiled, and then clomped up the stairs. She squeezed her eyes shut. *Time, Lord, give Josiah and Amos time.*

She averted her gaze to the kitchen. The cellar door lay open. For a moment she wondered what might happen if she shut and locked it. Too bad all three men weren't down there, or she'd do just that. It took some strength to stifle her chuckle.

The cellar door banged shut, jerking her back to the present. The men finished searching the kitchen and the tall man came back down the stairs. The three men gathered in the living room, and she cringed at the way they looked at Papa.

Mama piped up. "It's bitter cold out there tonight. Shall I make you all a cup of hot English tea?"

Coral gulped at the lump in her throat. Mama treated these men as she would any guest in her home.

Her mother continued. "Perhaps some biscuits and cheese to take with you. You're bound to get hungry later on."

Coral gulped harder the second time, but the lump in her throat stayed put.

She watched the taller man stride over to Mama and stare at her. His muttonchops twitched as he worked his jaw muscles. Then he looked to Papa, to Coral, and back to Mama.

After a slow minute passed he said, "He ain't here, men; let's go."

Before she could blink twice, the men were gone.

A quiet hung about the house well into the evening. Coral hardly spoke a word, and neither did her parents. The close call rattled her more than she cared to admit. Still, her resolve was not weakened.

Four nerve-wracking days after that wild night, Josiah still had not returned. Every evening, and countless times while slogging through her chores, Coral prayed for his safety, and Amos's. She wished Josiah would come home and inform them that Amos had made it to the next station. Many times she feared something awful had happened, even now as she donned her shawl and then stepped outside.

Moments later she carried an armload of firewood inside and deposited it in the wood box next to the hearth. The shawl did little to combat the chilly winds that blew across the homestead. When she went out for another load, she wrapped her shawl tighter around her. Her teeth chattered in the cold and she could see her breath.

She hurried back inside and dropped the wood where it belonged.

"Thank you, dear," Mama said. She placed a log onto the flames and turned the spit. The roasting meat smelled heavenly. Coral's mouth watered. Doing extra chores while Papa recuperated had increased her appetite. The physical exertion felt good but left her little time to work on her quilt. Her thread supply had dwindled again anyway.

Maybe Papa would allow her to take the wagon into town for more. Thankfully, the wagon had been returned the day after Josiah took it. While shopping for thread she could ask Mr. Wilbur if he'd heard anything.

"Mama," Coral began, "I'd like to be more involved in aiding the freedom seekers. I have a passion to help them, and I'm sure it's from God."

Mama wiped her hands on her apron and smiled big. Her cheeks turned pink. "I'm sure the calling came from God. Your Papa will be pleased to hear of your devotion, but he'll be afraid for your well-being too."

"I really want to help."

Mama said, "Are you sure your desire to help isn't rooted in the idea of being around Josiah more?"

Warmth flooded through Coral. Thoughts of Josiah had certainly filled her mind the past few weeks, but could what she felt be called love? With minimal discomfort she'd recovered from the loss of Roland, but she still wasn't sure if she wanted to venture that direction again. "I—I don't know."

Noises outside snagged her attention. At first she thought the bounty hunters had returned, but she didn't hear the hounds baying. The sound of hoofbeats grew louder, and the voice didn't sound familiar. Papa opened the door and there stood a man dressed as a Quaker.

Darkness covered the land by the time Josiah rode back into Newport. He jumped down from his horse and tied the reins to the hitching post. He took a quick walk around the outside of Wilbur's store, but there was no sign of him. No light shone from inside the building either. The man had probably gone to bed. No sense in waking him.

Josiah unsaddled his horse and led it to the stable in back. Four days and nights of smuggling Amos north had plum worn him out. After brushing down the exhausted animal, he bedded down in the tack room. Tomorrow he'd tell Wilbur about the adventures with the hopeful freedom seeker.

His head hit the pillow, but before he could even stretch, he heard a voice.

"That you, Josiah? I thought I heard you ride in," Sheriff Hansen said.

"Yep, what can I do for you?" Josiah yawned so big he thought his jawbones would come unhinged.

"I know what you're doing, helping slaves escape. And although I can't abide slavery, the law's the law, twisted as it is."

Josiah gave his friend a long look. "I know man's law, but I follow the higher law of God."

Hansen nodded. "I agree on all accounts. Why do you think I've looked the other way so many times? I just wanted to warn you to be careful. I pray God soon ends the scourge of slavery in this country, but the way folks get into such a state about the issue, I don't think that'll happen in our lifetime. Maybe never."

Although it was dark, Josiah could easily see the moral quandary his friend was mired in, and he ached for him. "I'll do my best to keep you out of it. Now, it's late—why don't you head back home and get some sleep."

Hansen sighed. " 'Night Josiah."

The stable door creaked open, then closed. Josiah sank into a deep slumber.

The sun peeked through the knotholes in the walls and the room warmed considerably by the time Josiah awoke, but the rest had done him good. He stuffed a cold biscuit in his mouth and strolled over to the mercantile.

Not more than two steps into the building, he ran into the Martin family. His eyes lingered on Coral for a long moment until he heard Sam clear his throat. Josiah swallowed and stepped over to him. He'd tell him about Amos—not all the details, but enough to alleviate any worries.

"Sam, just the man I wanted to see," Josiah said. "I was going to ride out to your place later today to speak with you. Mr. George DeBaptiste, the barber up in Madison, wanted me to thank you for the package you sent him."

"Thank you kindly. I hope it arrived without incident." Sam cocked an eyebrow.

Josiah nodded. "I delivered it myself, safe and sound."

Sam smiled, turned to Wilbur, and said, "A Quaker named Strauss showed up at my place late last night. He just moved into town and wants to know how he can mail packages."

Before much more could be said, Wilbur glanced around the store.

"Josiah, you mind tending things for a minute? I need to show Sam something in the storeroom."

"Sure."

The two men headed to the back. Josiah turned to watch Coral and her mother shopping for thread near the bolts of fabric. When Coral glanced up and locked eyes with him, he winked at her. He laughed aloud when her cheeks took on a pink hue and she dropped a spool of thread.

"Mr. Williamson." Her admonishment didn't match the smile playing on her lips. She bent to pick up the thread.

He pulled her handkerchief from his pocket and admired the lingering scent of lavender before he sauntered closer to her. "Here, I thought you'd like this back."

"Thank you." Coral took it and placed it in her reticule. "Perhaps you could dine with us some evening."

"I'd like that." He leaned against a barrel of dried beans.

Before she could set a date for her invitation, her father and Wilbur emerged from the back.

"Let's tally up our wares and get back to the house. I need some rest." Sam wiped beads of sweat from his forehead and leaned against the counter. Mrs. Martin and Coral fussed over him like a pair of mother hens. Not more than a few minutes passed, and they were gone. The dinner invitation would have to wait.

Josiah purchased a bag of dried beans and some coffee, but cut short his conversation with Wilbur. All he wanted was to get home and begin the next building project. He wasn't a pauper, but he couldn't neglect his customers either, or he'd starve through the winter.

The bell above the door jangled. The dandy who burst inside had wealth enough, judging by his fancy attire. Something about the man made Josiah uneasy. He locked eyes with Wilbur. "I'll stay a bit longer, in case you need me."

"Much obliged." Wilbur nodded and cast a warning look at two freed women in the fabric section. The wide-eyed women clutched a bolt of calico and appeared frightened at the newcomer's presence.

Josiah wandered to the hardware section and estimated the price of a pound of nails. He tried to be inconspicuous, but paid enough attention to assist Wilbur if necessary.

The dandy strutted over to the women and yanked the material from their hands. When he growled threats to them, Josiah took two steps toward him.

Wilbur's boots pounded on the wooden floorboards as he stormed to the scene. "See here now, I run a respectable establishment. I don't take kindly to the use of coarse language, nor do I tolerate folks who threaten our free citizens. You'll have to leave."

The man jutted his chin in the air and voiced a string of profane words that weren't fit for decent folks' ears. Wilbur stood his ground and threw the dandy out of the store. No more than what the scoundrel deserved. Josiah laughed, tipped his hat to the ladies, and left.

Late that night, after darkness had fully fallen, Josiah met Wilbur at the farm of Mr. Strauss, the new Quaker in town. They rode their horses into the barn and dismounted. A man who couldn't have been a day over twenty came forward and shook their hands.

"Welcome."

No twitching, no stammering, no averting his gaze when he spoke. What the man did have was a firm handshake, a look in his eyes. A good sign he could be trusted.

"Sam couldn't make it, but he sends his regards," Josiah told him.

Josiah and the two men talked about their faith, slavery, the community, and safe places for runaways. They even drew maps in the dirt.

During a lull in the conversation, Josiah heard the chickens in the nearby henhouse squawking and clucking. He cocked an ear in their direction. The chickens continued. Dogs barked. His horse added a whinny to the cacophony.

Josiah rose and placed a hand on the pistol in his holster. Wilbur ran his foot over the drawings in the dirt and ducked behind a stack of hay bales. Mr. Strauss grabbed a pitchfork and began pitching hay into the horses' stalls.

Josiah reached for the lantern hanging on a nail by the door. He stepped outside and held it high. "Who's out there?" he hollered.

No one replied.

Three steps into the barnyard, he called again. "Is anyone out there?"

A large haystack rustled. Several pieces of hay blew off of it and into the wind. Two dogs sniffed around the base of it. Were they bounty hunters' bloodhounds, or did they belong to the Quaker? Upon closer inspection Josiah spotted a scrap of cloth protruding from the yellow-gold stalks. Someone had been spying on them!

That spy could be a slave patroller, an informant, a malicious Southern sympathizer, someone who could have them all arrested.

A flash of anger shot through Josiah like a bolt of lightning. Nobody would put the freedom seekers in harm's way if he could help it.

With his free hand he pulled the pistol from his holster. Tramping over to the haystack, he realized his dilemma. He didn't want to kill anyone, and prayed he wouldn't have to, but the spy could be somebody intent on taking them all down.

When he reached the haystack he cocked his pistol with as much noise as possible.

Twice he cleared his throat and then said, "Come out, or I'll shoot."

He watched in growing amazement as a young woman made her way out of the haystack.

Chapter 7

In Mr. Strauss's barn Coral sat on a hay bale receiving some harsh words from Josiah. At least he'd holstered his pistol, small comfort that it was. Tears brimmed in her eyes. Determined not to let him see her cry, she gulped and bit them back.

She had only wanted to find out more about smuggling freedom seekers. She thought maybe she could attend the meeting and learn some useful information. Then those barking dogs had given her a fright. She was sure bounty hunters lurked in the shadows. She had climbed into the haystack to hide from them. How was she supposed to know they belonged to Mr. Strauss?

"I appreciate your sympathy to the cause, Coral, but you have to understand how dangerous this is."

Warmth spread through her in spite of the chilly atmosphere. She knew Josiah wanted her to be safe. She couldn't fault him for that. If Papa and Mama found out what she'd done, they would be angry with her too.

"How did you get here?"

"I told Papa and Mama I didn't feel well and retired early. Then I snuck out and rode Papa's horse here. Brownie is as gentle as a kitten. I've never had a bit of trouble with him."

Josiah turned and addressed Wilbur and Mr. Strauss. "I think we're finished here. I'm escorting the lady home."

Once outside, Coral located Papa's horse. He stood on the other side of the haystack, eating his fill. That's probably what kept him from running off. Josiah helped her into the saddle; then he climbed on his own horse. Together they left the Quaker's farm.

Silence hung between them, and Coral preferred it that way. It was better than any hurtful comments Josiah might say. Lost in her thoughts, she feared what her parents might do if they found out what she'd done. Josiah had mailed her letter to Roland and kept that a secret. Could he be trusted to keep this a secret as well?

The moon hung full and bright in the sky along with a spattering of gleaming stars when they reached home. As quietly as possible, Coral urged the horse across the familiar backyard. She dismounted, opened the barn door, and led the animal inside. She walked the faithful creature into a nearby stall and filled his manger and water trough.

A noise startled her. She turned to see Josiah standing in the entrance.

"You know. . ." Josiah's words were calmer now. "It's not just bounty hunters and ruffians that put you in danger. It's also the wild animals that lurk in the night that could do you harm."

She nodded. He was right.

He grasped her by the shoulders. "Promise me, Coral, you won't do this again. It would break my heart to see you hurt."

She gazed at him. How safe this strong man made her feel. Her breath hitched in her throat when he pulled her into his arms and held her close. The feelings that swam through her made her dizzy. She pulled away.

"Josiah, I. . ." Heaven help her, she wanted him to kiss her. He ran a finger along her cheek. He wiped a stray hair from her eyes. His husky breathing gave her goose bumps. For a second she thought he would kiss her.

Shouts and hoofbeats echoed from the front of the house.

Bounty hunters?

"Get inside, now!" Josiah wrapped his horse's reins around a post. Coral sprinted into the house through the back door. She raced into the living quarters to see Papa thundering down the stairs. He grabbed his shotgun from its perch above the door.

Josiah rushed into the room.

Papa stared at him with wide eyes. Then his eyebrows crunched together. He looked ready to aim his shotgun at Josiah. "What are you doing outside at night with my daughter?"

"It's not what you think, Sam."

Mama dashed down the stairs. "Samuel, what is it?"

Someone pounded on the front door and hollered, "Coral, open up."

Coral rushed to throw open the door, and gasped. "Roland!"

Josiah noticed Sam's grim expression. Mrs. Martin wrung her hands. They didn't look pleased to see this Roland character. And yet Coral led him inside, gentle as you please. His body tensed. Much as he wanted to, he refused to say something unkind.

"Roland," she began. "I'd like you to meet Josiah Williamson. Josiah, this is Roland, a, um, friend from Annapolis."

Josiah recognized this man. He was the one who'd made rude comments to the two free women in Wilbur's Mercantile.

The man wore a fine-tailored waistcoat and matching tan trousers. The money from his beaver-skin top hat and silk cravat could clothe a dozen runaways.

Even though his insides wove themselves into a knot, Josiah thought it best to be polite.

"Pleased to meet you." Josiah extended his hand and prayed God would forgive him for the half-truth. He wasn't at all pleased to meet him. In fact, he thought Roland was a mangy weasel, but something told him he shouldn't go out of his way to get on the man's bad side just yet.

Roland extended his hand. Josiah shook it, noting how soft and smooth it felt. The gaudy rings on Roland's fingers flashed in the dim candlelight. Before he could stop himself, Josiah calculated how many runaways could buy their freedom with those rings.

Josiah looked long at wide-eyed Coral. She matched his gaze. Her expression was unreadable, but the way she fussed about the man twisted something in his stomach. He tried to convince himself she was merely being polite, but he sensed there was more between them than he wanted to know. He wondered what was in the letter Coral had penned to him.

"Let's make sure we have enough bread rising for breakfast," Mrs. Martin said. She grabbed hold of Coral's sleeve and tugged her into the kitchen area.

Sam hung his weapon back on its pegs above the fireplace. He looked at Roland and scratched his head. "How did you find us?"

"Well, I—" Roland maneuvered around. His gaze lingered on Coral.

Sam faced Josiah and said, "If you'll excuse us, please." The deep tone of his voice made Josiah worry about Coral.

"No, really, perhaps I could stay."

Sam's eyes seemed to plead with Josiah. "Please, Mr. Williamson, I need a moment with my daughter and Roland."

Josiah nodded, gulped, and exited through the back door with slow, uneasy steps. Roland was sure to tell the Martins about the letter from Coral, the letter Josiah had mailed for her. What would they think of him now? More frightening still, how would it affect their work with the freedom seekers? He pleaded his case before the Lord as he rode home in the moonlight.

Chapter 8

Coral poured Roland's tea with hands that shook. She couldn't bear to look at Papa, who spoke with Mama in the kitchen a few steps away. How disappointed in her they must be. She now understood the consequences of her actions. If only she'd realized earlier, she'd have never sent Roland the letter telling him of their whereabouts.

"Coral, dear," Roland said. "If your parents give their blessing for us to get married, you can come back to Annapolis with me."

He smiled at her, but his display of affection made her cringe. From the kitchen she heard both her parents gasp. She didn't want to go back to Annapolis. She wanted to stay here and help runaways with Papa and Mama, and with Josiah.

Roland guided her to a chair and she sat. To her horror, he got down on one knee and pulled a ring from his pocket. The dim light in the room glinted off the large blue sapphire. She clenched fistfuls of her skirts, her breath suspended. Months ago she'd have given anything for a moment like this. But things had changed. She had changed.

Roland cleared his throat and straightened his shoulders. Ever so formally he said, "Miss Coral Martin, will you do me the honor of becoming my wife?"

She turned her eyes to her mother and father. Deep frowns creased their faces. Mama hung her head and sighed. Coral had gotten herself into this; it was up to her to set things right. She breathed deep, intending to say something, but Roland interrupted.

"If you say yes," he said, "we'll have the finest house in Annapolis. You'll have the grandest dresses and wear the fanciest jewelry. After all, I have a very lucrative income derived from the slave-catching business."

Coral felt as if she'd tumbled down the stairs. Her torso ached, her lungs screamed for air, but she couldn't suck in a breath. Papa and Mama rushed into the room.

"Now see here, Roland," Papa growled, "Mrs. Martin and I will not be giving our blessing for you to marry our daughter."

Roland stood and faced her father. "This is between Coral and me."

Air finally found its way into Coral's lungs. Now she knew why her parents disliked Roland so much. He was a slave catcher!

Why hadn't they told her the truth about him? She'd ask first chance she had. For now, she'd deal with the skunk before her.

"I'm not marrying you, Roland. I don't love you, and I despise what you stand for." Coral stood, hands clenched at her sides. Her heart pounded with fury. He knew her parents' views on slavery. They'd discussed it many times. Yet he came here and proposed, and gloated about money he made in capturing runaways. If she married Roland, he'd likely blackmail her and her parents for information about their contacts. She wasn't going to let that happen.

"You need to leave." She placed a hand on her hip and pointed at the door. He took two steps to stand right in front of her. Fire burned in his eyes. His jaw muscles twitched. His face turned a deep shade of red she'd never seen on him before. Refusing to back down, she squared her shoulders and stood firm.

"Fine," he snarled. Three long strides took him to the door. Before leaving, he turned. "I know what you folks are doing here. Mark my words, I'm going to make you pay for this."

The door shut with a loud bang.

Coral burst into tears. "I'm sorry, Mama, Papa. I didn't know." She held her hands over her face. She had placed them all in danger, but how could she have known? Her parents hadn't told her about him. Anger simmered and reached a boil.

"Why did you let me go riding with him? And you allowed him to escort me to so many parties. If you knew he was mixed up in slave catching, why did you let me spend so much time with him?"

"We didn't know," Mama soothed. "We found out when he turned in some of our friends in Annapolis. We left then and thought the danger to you was past."

"We should have told you earlier." Papa sighed.

"We're sorry, dear." Mama wiped the moisture from her cheeks. "Please forgive us."

Coral dabbed her tears with her shirtsleeve. She'd forgive her parents. They had done what they thought was best. For now, they had to deal with Roland's threats. Oh, what a mess.

Mama poured them all a cup of hot tea.

Papa reached for the Bible. He and Mama bowed their heads in prayer. They were a family rooted in faith, and they would get through this.

The next afternoon Josiah hammered away on a bookcase for Sheriff Hansen's office. Twice he cut boards too short. Then he dropped the auger on his foot. Next, his hammer missed the nail and smashed down on his finger.

Josiah yelped. It was time to take a break. Walking to the water bucket, he filled the dipper and drank. He wrapped a bandanna around his aching finger, but he realized no matter how hard he worked, he couldn't forget the sight of Coral and Roland together.

He chastised himself for mailing her letter to Roland. Whatever had gone on between them, Josiah didn't want to know about it. His mission was to help the freedom seekers. He wouldn't allow himself to be distracted by the shenanigans of those two. If Coral wanted to set her cap for that fancy-feathered peacock, she was free to do so. Sheriff Hansen needed his bookcase.

Hours later, the sun said good night as it dipped below the horizon. A sliver of moon climbed into the inky-black sky but did little to illuminate his way. He carried the furniture into Hansen's office. The sheriff wasn't there. The deputy said he was out on some urgent business.

Josiah shrugged and placed the bookcase against the far wall. "Tell Hansen I'll collect my pay later." Then he headed for home.

About a mile outside Newport, a band of men stopped him in the road.

Bounty hunters.

The tall one he recognized from Wilbur's store. The one who'd chased after Amos. Who were these men chasing now? He said a silent prayer, asking God for mercy for these men's prey.

A county lawman rode to the front of the pack. "Easy does it now, boys. I have jurisdiction over Sheriff Hansen, and I have the papers to prove it." He waved them high.

Holding his hands in the air, Josiah said, "I'm not looking for any trouble."

"No," the tall hunter said. "You just look for runaway slaves, don't you, Mr. Williamson? Least, that's what Amos says."

Josiah sucked in a breath. His heart raced like a bloodhound hot on the trail of a runaway.

"Lord, have mercy."

He was caught.

Chapter 9

The cold, hard bench beneath Josiah did little to soothe his aching body. He adjusted his weight and tried to get comfortable, but one didn't live in luxury within the confines of a jail cell.

The bruises on his ribs and the cuts marring his face would heal. It would be painful for a while, but it was worth it. No matter how many times he'd been questioned, threatened, and punched, he'd not divulged the names of his contacts. Especially not the Martin family.

His assailants questioned him about Amos with relentless intensity, but he'd managed to keep the information secret. The men didn't seem to know much about his involvement with the runaway. The comments on the road had probably been just to trap him. He hung his head. How could he have fallen for such a ploy?

His pride had taken a beating along with his body, but he had to stay strong to keep the freedom seekers safe. Worry gnawed at his sanity. Could he take another beating and still keep quiet about his contacts? What if he was sent to jail for a very long time? He wouldn't be much help to the runaways in that situation.

An agony-filled groan escaped his mouth as he rolled off the bench onto his knees. He bowed his head and prayed.

Hansen would be back tomorrow. Josiah hoped the sheriff's presence would mandate his release, but if his friend's hands were tied, he was in trouble. They all were. His thoughts honed in on Roland. If he had to guess the identity of who turned him in, it would be him.

Josiah suspected the man was in cahoots with the bounty hunters, but the question was, could he prove it? Wilbur had asked around about him a few weeks ago, but the investigation turned up nothing.

The air in the cell cooled and made him shiver. Climbing back onto the bench, he wrapped the threadbare blanket around him. It didn't do much good, but like it or not, he was stuck there for the night.

Once again he shifted his weight in search of a less painful position. A high-pitched squeak told him a rat was near. Morning couldn't come soon enough.

Josiah tried to sleep. What seemed like seconds later, his eyes popped open. Hounds barked in the street just outside. Fear snaked its arms around him and tightened its grip. In his mind, there was only one reason the bounty hunters would come back. To string him up.

"Oh please, Lord, I don't want to die, not here, not now." He was willing to give his life for the cause, but that didn't make dying any easier. Besides, there were so many more runaways he could save, if given the chance.

He could hear them now. Their loud laughter and slurred obscenities were exacerbated by their inebriated state.

Keys jangled. The jailhouse door was flung open.

"Lord, be with me," he prayed. If this was his time, he needed to be right with his Maker.

The tall lawman motioned to someone outside. "Get in here."

Sam, clothing torn, face bleeding, shackles rattling, stepped into the jailhouse.

When the shock dissipated, anger inundated Josiah. "Sam, are you all right? What have you done to him? He's an old man, for pity's sake."

The captors paid him no mind. They opened the cell door, shoved the ailing Sam inside, and clanged the door shut.

"You monsters should be ashamed of yourselves," Josiah hollered as they departed, laughing. His attention turned to Sam. A gash on Sam's forehead bled, and his limp was prominent. Guiding him to the bench, Josiah helped him sit.

"Water," Sam croaked.

Josiah hurried to the bucket and drew a dipperful of warm, dirty liquid. The man drank three dippersful before he could say more.

Sam grasped Josiah's shirtsleeve. "Promise me, if I don't make it, you'll find a way out of here and take care of my wife and daughter."

Another tentacle of fear gripped Josiah. "Don't talk like that. Hansen will be back at sunup, and he'll get us out of here."

"Listen," Sam pleaded. "Wilbur and Hansen are working to expose Roland, but in the meantime, don't let him near my daughter. If necessary, take Anna and Coral back to England; there's money hidden away—"

The jailhouse keys rattled again.

Did evil *ever* sleep?

The door swung open.

Roland strolled inside, twirling the keys to the jail cell around his finger. "Which one of you will be the first to answer my questions?"

For three days Coral visited Papa and Josiah while they were in jail. Every night she prayed for a Christmas miracle of their release. As her prayers floated toward heaven, a light snow fluttered to the earth. A white blanket of pristine snowflakes coated the ground, and still, the ones she loved faced the confines of federal prison.

Congestion had settled in her father's chest. His hacking cough echoed off the walls at the last visit. She didn't know how much longer he would last. If anything happened to him, Mama would take it hard.

On the fourth day of their imprisonment, she rode into town. She climbed down from the wagon and traipsed to the jailhouse. She had brought a basket of warm bread and jam Mama had made. Slices of fresh cheese and boiled eggs accompanied the meal. Papa and Josiah needed to keep their strength up.

Coral also brought a blanket and some warmer clothes from home. She hung the basket of food over her wrist and carried the rest of the items inside.

Sheriff Hansen stood to greet her as she entered the building. Lord bless the sheriff, he allowed her to have lunch with Papa and Josiah.

Pale and weak, Papa was unable to do more than lie down. Coral felt sick to her stomach to see him that way. Lunch was a bittersweet affair. She was elated to see the men she cared about, but heartbroken to see them in jail.

Papa nibbled a piece of cheese and refused the bread and jam. He coughed hard and curled up on a narrow pallet someone had placed in the corner. She bit her lip until she tasted blood to stifle the cry rising in her throat. The threadbare blanket she stretched over him would have to suffice until she could bring something heavier.

"Josiah," she said, as she stood and prepared to leave, "I'm working hard on a quilt for Papa. I'll bring it in as soon as it's finished, but until then here's some heavy clothes for him. Please help him stay warm."

The tall, blond carpenter looked down at her. "You know I will."

Adoration, respect, and perhaps love swelled to a crescendo within her. Love, yes, she loved Josiah. She loved his strength and compassion, his willingness to suffer for the sake of freedom seekers, and his dedication to God above all else.

What all she had gone through to learn what it meant to love someone. How precious a treasure love was, one not to be squandered. She remembered the scripture where Paul walked on the road to Damascus and God had struck him blind. Later, something like scales fell from his eyes and God enabled him to see again and to focus on things that really mattered. Coral thought she now knew what that felt like.

Mr. Wilbur and Levi Coffin entered the building.

"Good news, folks." Mr. Wilbur placed a pile of paperwork on Sheriff Hansen's desk. "We found a loophole in the bounty hunters' arrest warrants."

"But the circuit judge doesn't come to town until after Christmas. That's a week away. What are we supposed to do in the meantime?" The sheriff shook his head. Coral surmised he'd rather be home with his family on Christmas as opposed to keeping watch over the prisoners.

"I'll go home now so you men can work out the particulars, but I'll be back first thing in the morning." She wished she could bring her father home with her, but that wasn't possible. The air had an icy bite to it. Her gloved hands ached with cold, so she wrapped her shawl tighter around herself and reached for the reins. She feared the cold would sink its teeth into Papa and never let go. Another prayer passed from her lips, that Mr. Wilbur and Mr. Coffin could do something for her father and Josiah before it was too late.

A week went by and Christmas Eve came, with no change. Upon arriving home from the jail, weary and heartsick, Coral unhitched the wagon, put the horses in their stalls, and gave them plenty of grain. In this weather they ate more. Famished herself, she finished in the barn and strode into the house.

After the supper dishes were washed and put away, Coral sat down with her mother by the fireplace. The nearly finished quilt beckoned her from its basket, and Coral busied herself putting the final stitches in place. An hour later it was done. Self-satisfaction surged through her. The making of this quilt was no small feat, especially in such a remote town where supplies were not readily available.

She held it up for Mama to admire. Tomorrow she'd take it to the jailhouse and give it to her father. With the major project completed, she relaxed a bit with her favorite book, *Sense and Sensibility*.

Later that evening someone knocked on their door. Coral's heart jerked. She prayed it wasn't a message from the jail bearing bad news about Papa, or worse yet, someone coming for Mama. A shudder went through her, imagining what she'd do without her folks near.

Mama must have sensed her tension as she answered the door. "Don't fret, Coral. We're in God's hands."

"I know, but I'm praying anyway," Coral said.

"Come in, Mr. Wilbur," Mama said. A dark-skinned man and woman followed Mr. Wilbur inside. Coral knew next to nothing about midwifery, but the woman looked to be about nine months pregnant.

"My name's Gideon; this is my wife, Tella Sue. We been runnin' for two days straight, but them pattyrollers is still on our trail. Our massa said he'd take the hide off any slave he catches escapin'."

Mama stepped forward. "You are safe here, at least for the time being. Have a seat by the fire. Coral, add some wood, please. I'll set the teakettle on."

Mr. Wilbur tipped his hat and stepped to the door. "I need to get back to town. I'll do what I can to throw off any patrols headed this direction."

"Come stand by the fire; you must be freezing," Coral said.

The couple moved to the fireplace. The woman appeared as frightened as a rabbit caught in a snare. Gideon soothed his wife and pulled her close to his chest.

Coral placed two logs on the embers and poked at the coals until flames rose and crackled. Her throat tightened as she imagined what these two people had gone through to get this far. She tried to reassure them, but her voice wavered. "Try not to worry; you're safe here. I do hope Mama brings some biscuits with the tea. You must be half starved."

"Thank you, ma'am," Gideon said. "Massa threaten to sell our chile, but as long as I got breath I ain't gonna let that happen."

"I'm so sorry," Coral muttered. Pitiful words for such a dire situation. She moved to help her mother in the kitchen, but Gideon's request made her pause.

"Ma'am, you mind if Tella Sue have a seat? We don't have no shoes, and her feet been hurtin' her something powerful."

"Of course, where are my manners?" Coral guided Tella Sue to a chair then bent to unwrap the rags from the woman's feet.

Coral's entire being tightened. A gash on one heel, scrapes and bruises on both ankles, a missing toenail. *Lord Jesus, have mercy.* Anguish gripped her, but respect and admiration gripped her tighter. What this woman had sacrificed to get her child free.

"Here, let me help you." Coral nearly choked on the words. Steam rose from the hot water she poured from the tea kettle into a bowl. She dipped several rags into the water. Carefully, so as not to cause the woman any unnecessary pain, she wiped and cleansed her injured feet. Next she smeared salve into the wounds. Lastly, she wrapped them with fresh cloths.

Humility stirred within Coral. A holy love for this family took root in her being and grew tall and unwavering.

"There you are, Tella Sue." Coral stood just as Mama entered the room with a tray. Gideon whispered something in his wife's ear.

Curiosity piqued in Coral as she watched the woman unwrap three layers of tattered cloth from her middle. A tiny baby yawned and stared at Coral with big, dark eyes. Tella Sue wasn't pregnant after all.

Christmas Eve. Church bells pealed, and Josiah's throat constricted. Who wanted to be in jail on Christmas? His situation paled in comparison to those enslaved in the South, but he had a small taste of how the men, women, and children in bondage must feel.

He was stuck, not in chains, but under the control of those with selfish intentions who were driven by greed and a lust for power. This didn't make him want to give up, however. It drove him to fight harder against the tyranny of slavery.

Coral possessed that same determination. In spite of the cold and hunger, he smiled. The thought of her face warmed his heart. What a team they would make, if he could stay out of prison. But he did face prison, and as much as he cared about her, he wouldn't want her there as well.

Thoughts of Paul and Silas, when they were in chains, seeped into his consciousness. They too had been beaten and thrown in jail. Yet those brave men sang praises even from the depths of darkness. Should he ask God for an earthquake?

Sam coughed again and turned on his side. Josiah rose and went to him.

"Its Christmas Eve; let's at least pray." Using what little strength he had, Josiah dropped to his knees on the cold, hard floor. He wouldn't ask for an earthquake, but getting out of jail tomorrow would be nice. Prayers tumbled from his heart as he lay down and slipped into a fretful sleep.

The next morning Josiah awoke and looked out the tiny window. A light snow had fallen during the night. Hope for a Christmas miracle filled his whole being. At least he would see Coral and Mrs. Martin, providing nothing deterred them.

Hours later, Sheriff Hansen escorted the ladies into the building. Overjoyed as he was at their presence, it tore at Josiah's heart for Coral to see him locked up. She beamed as bright as the afternoon sun, however, and didn't seem to be bothered.

"I finished the quilt. Josiah, please take it to keep you and Papa warm at night." Coral held up the quilt, and he admired her handiwork. The bright colors were striking, and the pattern was intricate and beautiful.

The sheriff carried the baskets of food into the cell. Then he held the door open and allowed the ladies to walk in. He closed the door with a bang and relocked it.

"I'll leave you folks for an hour, but don't get any funny ideas." The sheriff tipped his hat and was out the door.

Coral spread a red-checked tablecloth on the floor while Mrs. Martin unpacked the food. The roast turkey, potatoes, and cooked squash looked and smelled better than anything he'd ever expected to experience in a jailhouse. He'd have to thank Sheriff Hansen and pray blessings on him for the kindness he showed.

There was no tree to decorate, and no presents either, but Josiah considered it a delight to be with such fine folks on Christmas. Too soon their time together ended. Hansen strolled back into the building. The man seemed fidgety, causing Josiah to suspect something was amiss.

"Time's up, folks; I'm sorry." Hansen unlocked the cell door.

Mrs. Martin looked on the verge of tears but didn't lose her graceful composure. "We know visits like this are unusual, so we thank you, Sheriff," she said. She pulled her husband into an embrace, one Josiah hoped wouldn't be the last.

Before Coral could step away, he wrapped his arms around her. "Pray, Coral, and trust God."

"I have been praying, and will continue to do so."

Hansen interrupted the moment. "Let's go, ladies."

He guided the women from the premises. When the ladies left, he let someone else in and then shut the door. Josiah recognized Mr. Strauss, who was still new in town. Something was up; he could sense it. The two men walked to the cell.

In a hushed voice Hansen said, "Those bounty hunters are out of town for a few days to be with their families. They don't know it yet, but word has it that court didn't go well for them. All charges against you two have been dropped."

"Praise God," Josiah said. He glanced at Sam shaking with fever on the pallet, covered by the quilt. If they weren't out of there soon, the man might die. "How long before we're out of here?"

"Since it's Christmas, I'm letting you and Sam go now."

Josiah raised his hands in the air. "The miracle I've prayed for, thank the Lord." He lowered his arms, sobering. "Hansen, you won't have any kind of trouble for doing this, will you?" he asked.

Hansen locked eyes with Josiah. "I have the paperwork signed by the judge right here. Levi just delivered it, but he said if you're released, those men vowed to trap you again, maybe shoot you on sight."

Josiah growled and clenched the bars so hard pain surged through his fingers.

So much for his Christmas miracle.

Chapter 10

December 31
New Year's Eve

If God was merciful, 1841 would be a year of new beginnings.

Coral walked into Sheriff Hansen's office. In her arms was the quilt she had labored on for so many months. Papa brought it home when he was released from jail, and Mama had enough blankets to keep him warm, so he'd given it back to her.

"Afternoon, Miss Martin." The man stood and tipped his hat to her in greeting.

Overcome with gratitude, Coral cleared her throat, swallowed, and pushed forward before she lost her nerve. "I want to say thank you for freeing my father and Josiah."

"You don't have to thank me." Sheriff Hansen's face turned pink, and he waved a hand at her. "I was just doing what was right for two decent men. Mr. Coffin and I sent Roland on his way. I can't make any promises, but he shouldn't be bothering you anymore."

"Well, I want to give this to you as my way of saying thank you." Coral handed him her token of gratitude.

The sheriff ran his hand over it. He smiled, but shook his head and handed it back. "That's very kind of you, Miss Martin, but I have plenty already. Give this to somebody who needs it more than me."

Coral sighed. How many times had she prayed over this quilt? She trusted God to lead her to the right recipient, but who would that be? It wouldn't be for her wedding to Roland, that much was certain. Papa didn't need it to keep him warm at night now that he was out of jail and recovered from his ordeal. Sheriff Hansen didn't seem to want it either.

She left the jailhouse and climbed into the back of the wagon. She felt dejected and hung her head. *All that work on the quilt, Lord. Does anyone want it?*

Papa emerged from Wilbur's Mercantile and climbed onto the wagon seat. "Don't look so sad, Daughter. Your mother is planning a nice dinner this evening." He chirruped to the horses. It was a quiet ride back to the homestead.

Coral walked into the house and placed a log on the fire. Poor Mama scurried about the kitchen in a near frenzy and needed help. She basted the roast goose on the spit above the fire while Coral stirred up a chocolate cake.

Tella Sue and Gideon had spent the week resting and regaining their strength. The wounds on Tella Sue's feet had healed, and she and Gideon were itching to go north to Canada where they could raise their daughter without the fear of her being sold off.

"I do hope you can stay just one more night." Coral bounced the baby on her knee. She wanted a life, a love, like Gideon and Tella Sue. Like Papa and Mama. Her thoughts turned to Josiah. She wondered if he felt the same way she did. He said he'd come for dinner that night. A blush crept into her cheeks.

"Tella Sue, can you take the baby? I need to go up and dress for the party."

The doting mother took her infant, and a smile lit up her face as if she knew why Coral wanted to look her best that night.

In the confines of her room, Coral donned her best dress. There was no lavender soap to wash with or perfume to wear, but Amos's freedom was worth that small luxury. All the freedom seekers were.

Later that evening Josiah and Sheriff Hansen arrived.

"Sir." Josiah addressed Papa. "Do you mind if I have a moment alone with your daughter? We won't be but a few steps out the back door."

Coral glanced from Papa to Mama, and back to Papa. They both smiled at her. She tried in vain to fan the heat from her face.

"Go ahead, dear," Mama said. "I'll set the table."

Josiah led her into the backyard. The moon carved a small crescent of light in the coal-black sky. In the distance the creek bubbled. The tune accompanied the crickets chirping in the woods nearby.

Josiah interrupted nature's melody. "I didn't have the chance to shop for you since I was in jail on Christmas. I hope this makes up for it." He pulled a box from his coat pocket.

"For me? Thank you." Coral untied the ribbon and unwrapped a bottle of lavender perfume and a cake of lavender soap. Her heart swelled.

Josiah coughed, cleared his throat, and said in a croaky voice, "There's more."

More? What more could she possibly want? A kiss, perhaps. She shook her head. She shouldn't be thinking such things.

Josiah knelt down on one knee. He pulled another box from his pocket, this one much smaller than the first. "Coral Martin, I've come to care very deeply for you over these past few weeks. And I would love nothing more than to spend the rest of my life with you. Will you do me the honor of becoming my wife?"

A host of butterflies swarmed in her middle. Tears flooded her eyes and spilled down her cheeks. She giggled like a child but managed to give him an answer. "Yes!"

Josiah sprang to his full height and encircled her in his arms. "I love you, Coral. I'll make you proud. I'm going to build you the coziest house. It won't be a mansion but—"

He paused midsentence and then touched his lips to hers. The music of the chirping crickets, the gurgling creek, and the whinnying horses built to a crescendo in her ears. Her knees went weak. She leaned into his embrace and tasted the sweetness of his kiss.

Placing her head on his chest, she listened to the sound of his heart beating and looked to the sky. The stars glistened like diamond dust flung from one corner of the heavens to the other. She breathed a prayer of thanks to God.

Hand in hand, they walked into the house. Coral's mind was awhirl with thoughts of a new beginning. Perhaps her quilt would be of use to her after all.

The kitchen was frighteningly quiet when they stepped back inside. Her mouth went dry. Wilbur had arrived while Josiah had proposed to her, and he bore some distressing news. Bounty hunters were back. They were angrier than ever at Josiah for getting out of jail.

"Sorry to disrupt the festivities, ma'am." Wilbur tipped his hat to Mama. "But we need to move some packages tonight."

Coral's heart stumbled and then fluttered in her chest like hummingbird wings. Much as she would miss the family of freedom seekers, she wanted them safe. Wilbur was right. They needed to go.

Gideon entered the kitchen. Tella Sue followed, snuggling the baby in the same three threadbare cloths she had arrived with. Those thin pieces of material to keep a baby warm, outside, on a winter's night?

Not if Coral could help it.

Coral bounded up the stairs and burst into her room. She flung open the lid to her hope chest and stared at the colored hexagons that made up the quilt. Slowly, she ran her fingers over the soft, smooth fabric. She closed her eyes as memories of stitching the pieces together danced in her mind. For the second time that night, tears streamed down her cheeks.

Wiping them away, she stood and pulled the heavy quilt from her hope chest. There was no time to waste. She rushed from her room and descended the stairs two at a time.

"Here, Tella Sue." Coral held out the quilt. "Use this to keep the baby warm."

"Oh, Miss Martin, surely you don't mean for our child to have such a fine gift?" Tella Sue and Gideon stood wide-eyed.

"Trust me, God *wants* you to have this. *I* want you to have this."

Tella Sue's jaw dropped, and then her mouth snapped shut. She lifted her chin and nodded her head. "We thank you, Miss Martin. You can rest assured our baby will know the story behind this quilt and where it came from."

Papa cleared his throat. "Finish saying your goodbyes; it's time to go."

When had he entered the room? Coral hadn't noticed. Tella Sue reached out and grasped her in a hug so tight the baby yelped.

Papa and Wilbur led the family out into the night and, with God's grace, into a promised land where fear had no place and the hounds of the enemy couldn't touch them.

Sheriff Hansen plopped his hat on his head and said, "I'll keep watch out front." He crossed the room and stepped outside.

"Coral, help me finish dinner. Your father, Josiah, and Mr. Hansen will be hungry when they're done, and it's mighty cold out there. I'm sure they'll want something warm to eat."

For three-quarters of an hour Coral helped her mother. The clock was about to chime seven when she heard voices in the front yard. Feeling bolder than ever, she stepped to the front door, opened it a crack, and peeked outside.

Bounty hunters.

Sheriff Hansen stood tall and said, "There are no slaves in this house. Do you think I'd be here if any illegal activity was taking place? Now get out of my county."

Respect for the sheriff rose in her. The man could face jail if caught aiding the runaways. While it was true, the family wasn't there, he still took the risk when he wasn't obligated to. After some tense minutes she watched the bounty hunters ebb into the darkness, in the opposite direction of Gideon's family. She closed the door and dropped into a chair. What dangerous times they lived in.

A moment later, the sheriff came back inside and rubbed his hands together. He strode to the fireplace and held his fingers over the warm flames.

"That was a kind thing you did, Sheriff," Coral said.

Sheriff Hansen cast a sideways glance at her. A shy smile spread across his face. "It was nothing." Humility laced his gentle, quiet tone.

"I mean it," Coral continued. "It may not seem like much to you, but it is to that family. I know that those of us here appreciate the godly man you are, your unselfishness, and all you do to stand up for what's right."

The back door banged open. Papa and Josiah entered.

"Are the bounty hunters gone?" Josiah asked.

Sheriff Hansen nodded.

"Thank the Lord," Mama said. "Let's eat."

Coral's family, along with Josiah, Mr. Wilbur, and Sheriff Hansen, took their places at the table. A hush fell over the room as everyone bowed their heads. She slipped her hand into Josiah's and then closed her eyes.

Papa said the blessing. "Thank You, Lord, for all Your bounty. Please, protect Gideon and his wife and child. We ask for mercy and pray for healing upon this country that seems so bent on tearing itself apart. We pray that eyes would be opened to see nothing but Jesus in all His glory."

Josiah squeezed her hand. She believed healing was possible for America, with large measures of God's grace, with His compassion, with a heaping of forgiveness, and, most of all, with His love.

Debby Lee was raised in the cozy little town of Toledo, Washington. She has been writing since she was a small child and has written several novels, but never forgets home. The Northwest Christian Writers Association and Romance Writers of America are two organizations that Debby enjoys being a part of. As a self-professed nature lover and an avid listener of 1960s folk music, Debby can't help but feel like a hippie child who wasn't born soon enough to attend Woodstock. She wishes she could run barefoot all year long, but often does anyway in the grass and on the beaches in her hamlet that is the cold and rainy southwest Washington. During football season, Debby cheers on the Seattle Seahawks along with legions of other devoted fans. She's also filled with wanderlust and dreams of visiting Denmark, Italy, and Morocco someday. Debby loves connecting with her readers through her website at www.booksbydebbylee.com.

The Song of Hearts Set Free

by Darlene Panzera

Therefore all things whatsoever ye would that men should do to you, do ye even so to them: for this is the law and the prophets.

—Matthew 7:12

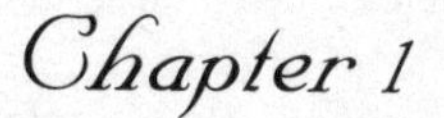

Chapter 1

Jersey City, New Jersey
November 1851

Annie Morrison and her dearest friend had not taken more than five steps past Morrison's cabinet shop when Louisa clutched her arm and let out a startled gasp.

"Perhaps we should cross the street," Louisa suggested, her voice tight. "Quick."

Annie followed Louisa Strong's cautious gaze toward the dashing young man with brown hair who stood on the wide, bluestone sidewalk a half block ahead. He appeared innocent enough, wearing a large fold-down collar over a loosely tied cravat; a fancy shawl-collared vest; a black, loose-fitting frock coat; and fashionable plaid trousers.

"Why?" she asked, dropping her voice to a whisper. "Whatever is wrong?"

"He's *staring* at me."

Louisa made a sharp turn to cross the cobblestone street, but Annie drew her back with a swift tug. Just in time, too, for Louisa narrowly missed being run over by a team of horses pulling a heavily laden delivery cart.

As the clattering of hooves subsided, Annie released her breath and reprimanded her friend with a sharp look. "You must be more careful."

Louisa nodded. "Yes, everyone these days seems to be taking sides, either for or against the abolitionists."

"I *meant*," Annie clarified, "you should be more careful of the roadway. Although I do fear your nightly activities are going to get you into trouble."

Louisa's brows shot upward. "Do you think the young gentleman might know my secret?"

"I doubt this man suspects anything. I'd say he's staring because he is *smitten*," Annie teased.

Louisa cast another glance up the sidewalk; then her shoulders relaxed and a devilish smile played upon her lips. "I daresay you're right."

"You can hardly blame him, when you are so beautiful," Annie said, eyeing the blond curls tucked into her friend's bonnet.

"Except he's not staring at me, like I first supposed," Louisa said, her smile broadening. "He's staring at *you*!"

Annie shot a second glance toward the handsome young man, and their gazes met for the briefest second before she let out a startled gasp of her own.

Louisa was right.

Morrison's Cabinetry relied upon its delivery wagon to transport the custom cabinets built by Annie's father and her brother, William. However, one of the wooden wheel axles had broken that very morning, leaving them in an unexpected bind. Thankfully, Louisa's family had offered the use of their wagon for the day.

Annie was glad, too, for Louisa's company. It wasn't proper for a young lady to traverse the town alone. But together, they were free to explore the shops while Will off-loaded the cabinets they'd brought in from their countryside home to their father's shop in the heart of Jersey City.

Her thoughts were still on the young man who had been staring at her when Will called over to her that it was time to go. She hated to leave the bustle of the vibrant city behind; its luscious smell of fresh-baked breads from the bakery, the mouthwatering taste of sweet treats from the confectioners, the soft feathers adorning the assorted hats for sale at the milliners, the ringing cadence of the blacksmith's hammer, the *clip-clop* of horses' feet, the shrill whistles of the approaching trains, and the deep, bellowing toots of the steam-powered ferries out on the river.

Her mother said each sound blended together to form a cacophony of music only a city lover could appreciate. But Annie didn't believe that was true. She adored both the country and the city, welcoming the variety each had to offer.

Except she wasn't sure she liked catching the attention of the bold young man on the sidewalk. She'd much prefer an honest country boy over a pompous, well-to-do city dweller's attention. Especially after her time spent in the company of Henry Pennington, a banker who proved he was no gentleman after pledging his undying love to both her *and another* on the very same day.

"Annie!"

Snapping out of her reverie, she took her brother's hand and stepped up to sit in the middle of the wagon's bench seat beside Louisa. A moment later Will joined them, and taking the reins, he turned their team of horses toward the stream of other horse-drawn buggies and wagons heading north past the train terminal.

"Why are we going this way?" Annie asked, her shoulder bouncing against her brother's as they drove over the bumpy roadway.

Will shrugged. "Daniel Walker says the sheriff and his posse are searching for a group of runaway slaves over on Paulus Point. I figure it's best if we don't get in their way."

Louisa leaned forward to look over at him. "You spoke with Daniel? When?"

Will smirked. "While you two were off trying on hats."

"Oh! I would have liked to have seen him," Louisa said, her tone wistful. Then, breaking into a huge smile, she looked at Annie and confided, "Yesterday, he proposed."

"He did?" Annie grabbed hold of her friend's hand and exclaimed, "Why didn't you tell me earlier?"

"I thought to wait until we could both surprise you with the news, but I simply cannot wait any longer," Louisa gushed, her face aglow. "He asked permission from Father first, of course. I suspected as much when I saw Daniel approach him after the morning sermon. Poor Daniel held his hat crushed in his hands, and his face was as red as my mama's raspberry jam."

Annie laughed. "I suppose it would take nerve for anyone to ask Reverend Thomas Alexander Strong permission to marry his daughter. He said yes, of course?"

Louisa's green eyes danced with excitement. "He did. And so did I. We're to be married on the twenty-fourth of April."

Annie caught her breath. "Why, that only gives you six and a half months to plan."

"It only gives *us* six and a half months to plan. You will help Mother and I make the arrangements, won't you? And stand up with me as my maid of honor?"

"Whoa! Hold tight!" Will interrupted, his voice tense. "Runaway wagon!"

Annie turned her head just in time to see a frenzied pair of horses pulling a careening cart, and indeed—there was no driver. William jerked the reins of their own team to the left, then to the right, in what Annie supposed was an attempt to avoid a direct collision.

Too late. Another passing wagon forced the spooked runaways to weave once more into the path before them. One of their horses reared, and the wagon carrying Annie, Louisa, and Will turned over on its side.

Louisa screamed as Annie fell over on top of her. Their skirts were tangled and likely soiled, but as they scrambled onto their hands and knees along the steep embankment, it was the ominous whistle of the oncoming train that curdled the blood in Annie's veins.

For there, on the tracks below, lay her brother. And it didn't look like he was getting up.

"William!" The shout that left her lips sounded far away, almost as if it had come from another person. And yet he lifted his head.

Twisting out of Louisa's grasp, Annie lunged forward, but this time it was her friend who pulled *her* back.

"Annie, no! There's no time!"

Glancing at the inbound train, Annie's heart screeched to a dead stop.

Was there no hope?

Then from out of the trench on the opposite side of the tracks, a black man, covered in filth, reached out a hand and pulled her brother toward him. Annie sucked in her breath and craned her neck, straining to see if her brother was all right, but couldn't, for the massive steam engine blocked her view as it sped between them.

Annie glanced back at Louisa, who sat with her hands clasped together and her head bent over in prayer. Annie hadn't thought to pray. It had all happened so fast, there hadn't been time. But in the next few seconds, during which she waited for the train to pass, she decided she should pray also. She only hoped God remembered her name. For she hadn't prayed as she ought for a while now. Not since He allowed Henry Pennington to break her heart.

Scrambling down the embankment, Annie and Louisa crossed the tracks in search of Will. They found him in the trench from which the black man had come.

"Will, thank God," Annie exclaimed, peering down at him. "Are you hurt?"

"No," her brother replied, shaking his mussed, sandy-haired head, then nodded to the bleeding wound on the foot of the man in filthy overalls beside him. "But he is."

The man Will referred to looked up and held her gaze, the whites of his eyes emphasizing his dark pupils and even darker hair and skin.

"Are you one of the fugitives the sheriff's men are after?" Louisa asked, keeping her voice low.

The black man didn't answer, but Will stood up and said, "We have to help him."

"Will, we—we can't," Annie whispered. "You know what the townspeople think of the abolitionists." Shooting Louisa an apologetic look, she said, "Papa doesn't want us to get involved."

"Louisa's family can hide him with the others in the church basement," Will insisted.

"We haven't any more room," Louisa exclaimed, giving them each a desperate look. "You'll have to hide him at your place."

"Take him home with *us*?" Annie's stomach tightened. "It's illegal to lend aid to a slave's escape. Papa would never approve."

"Annie," her brother implored. "He saved my life."

"Well, then let's just thank him and be on our way," she suggested.

Will's eyes widened as he glanced at the man beside him, who tried to stand. "He hurt his ankle saving me and is unable to walk. I can't just leave him."

"If the sheriff's men find him, they could shoot on sight," Louisa agreed.

"Misses, I ratha' die than let them ship me back," the man vowed.

Annie opened her mouth to protest, but Will gave her a look that brooked no further argument.

"He saved *my life*," William repeated, his voice firm. "Papa will understand."

Maybe he would. But that didn't ease the tension flowing through every one of her nerves.

What if they were caught?

Isaiah Hawkins made sure to keep his profile hidden within the shadows of the darkened threshold of the livery stable as he watched Louisa Strong unlatch the hidden compartment beneath the bench seat of her family's wagon. He'd long suspected the Strongs were active in the Underground Railroad, the secret network of people who helped Southern fugitives escape north, but he hadn't believed—until now—that William and Annie Morrison were abolitionists as well. The Morrisons had always so unerringly presented a neutral standing on the topic of slavery whenever publicly questioned.

Yet there they were, glancing about as if to make sure no one was watching and then helping the man climb into the wagon's secret hiding place.

Except that "cargo" wasn't meant for them.

Isaiah had planned to be at the train station early, but got waylaid by the clothier in the men's shop who, suspecting he held opposing views, refused to sell him the garments he wished to purchase. Isaiah had hoped the elegant threads might help the man transition more believably into Northern society. But only by donning the attire himself, and forking over an exorbitant amount of coin, was he finally allowed to walk out the door.

Except the victory was short lived. For although the state of New Jersey had outlawed slavery, slave catchers, motivated by huge rewards, were often afoot trying to retrieve what Southern plantation owners claimed as their property. And today they'd enticed the sheriff to help them hunt down the group arriving on the morning train.

Which had made retrieving his intended cargo quite difficult. Isaiah had taken a quick scan of the tracks and seen the sheriff and his posse chase down three of the black men. But the fourth still had not been found. The one with the dark imprint of a horseshoe branded into his side. The one *he'd* been meant to transport. Not Louisa Strong or the Morrisons.

Now—he had to devise a way to get him back.

Chapter 2

Isaiah retreated further inside the livery stable and found his brother arguing with a short, red-faced man, who claimed the team of horses he'd hired took off without him.

"Lucky for you, Mr. Felding," Tom grumbled, "my men were able to catch Mitsi and Pike before they reached the end of the street." He jerked his head toward the two chestnut geldings who now stood in their stalls, bathed in sweat. "What did you do to spook them?"

"It wasn't me," the indignant man replied. "It was those dark-skinned varmints running about the place."

Taking a step closer, Isaiah narrowed his gaze. "Varmints?"

"Those pesky Southern slaves who think they can hitch a ride north. I saw three of them jump from the train and scurry across the road. I wouldn't have worried so much about hitting them, but the sheriff's deputies were in pursuit and would have been run over if I hadn't—"

"Jerked back on the reins?" Tom demanded. "Mr. Felding, you said you had experience driving a team of horses, but apparently you do *not* know what it's like to have your mouth tugged back far enough to swallow your tailbone, do you?"

Mr. Felding scowled. "You weren't there."

"I was," Isaiah said, his distaste for the man souring each passing second. He looked his brother in the eye and added, "This fellow yanked so hard that Mitsi and Pike had no choice but to rear. And when he fell out of the wagon and the team realized they were free, they ran as fast as they could to get away from him. Several other wagons had to swerve out of the way. One turned over."

Tom sucked in his breath. "Anyone hurt?"

"No," Isaiah said, and clenched his jaw. "But the diversion did cause me to lose my cargo."

Tom shot him a look of alarm then glanced back at the short, huffy man and pointed toward the door. "Our business here is done."

Mr. Felding's eyes widened. "No refund?"

"You will owe *me* if I find out you've damaged the horses or my wagon in any way," Tom warned.

"Owe *you*?" Mr. Felding glanced around the building and stomped his foot. "Be careful you don't keep any of those *varmints* around here," he retorted, "or I'll shut you down."

Isaiah reached behind a wooden bin, pulled out two rats, and held them up by their tails. "You mean these guys? They won't hurt anyone."

Mr. Felding shot him a condescending look, letting him know that wasn't what he'd meant, then turned and walked away without another word.

"Good riddance," Tom growled.

Isaiah set the wriggling upside-down critters back on their feet and watched them run through an opening in the side wall. "Looks like we've made ourselves an enemy."

"I'm afraid we have bigger concerns than Mr. Felding," Tom whispered. "You lost your cargo?"

"Couldn't get to him in time." Suppressing a pang of guilt, Isaiah quickly explained what had happened with the Morrisons and asked, "Do you think they'll hand Kitch over to the sheriff?"

"Not if Louisa Strong was with them. Only problem is, they don't know that Kitch is supposed to be on the eight o'clock ferry."

"And if we don't get him across the river in time," Isaiah muttered, "the crew will change and we might not have another opportunity to ship him to New York for another week."

Tom shook his head. "It's too dangerous for Kitch to hang around Jersey City for that long. I'll go over to the church and see if Louisa's family is hiding him there."

"And then what? Tell them you're an abolitionist? What if we're wrong about the Strongs and they're more sympathetic toward the South than we thought? I thought we decided to trust no one, to work only with those we already know have our backs."

"What other choice is there?"

Isaiah met his gaze, and for a moment he could hear the gunshot that took out their father echo through his head all over again. What if a similar gunshot took out one of them? Despite his misgivings, he knew one thing for certain. Their father wouldn't have wanted either of them to live a life of fear. He'd say, *"Stand up for what you believe in and help your fellow man, no matter the cost."*

Straightening his shoulders, Isaiah nodded. "I'll ride out to the Morrisons'."

After Annie and Will drove Louisa back to her house, around the block from the First Presbyterian Church where her father pastored, she climbed down from the wagon and told them to go straight home without stopping to speak to anyone.

"I'll bring you instructions in the morning," Louisa promised.

Annie nodded toward the secret compartment beneath the front seat where they'd hidden the man. "What should we do with him overnight?"

"Hide him in your root cellar."

"But our cellar is not very large. . .and certainly not as dry as it should be this time of year."

"I don't think he cares about the conditions," Louisa assured her. "A little discomfort is nothing when running toward freedom."

Annie didn't believe she'd ever want to spend a cold November night inside the bottom of their root cellar. The one on her family's small homestead was nothing but a hand-dug hole in the ground with a wooden hatch her father had built to lay over the opening. Most of the fresh vegetables from summer that they had stored inside had already been eaten, except for some of the hardier root vegetables, like the potatoes, carrots, and turnips. And with the excessive moisture from recent rain, even some of them had begun to rot, giving the cellar a pungent stench that was most unpleasant.

However, before they could hide the runaway anywhere, Annie and Will's parents came outside, and they had no choice but to show them who they'd brought home.

"We couldn't just leave him," Will explained, taking the injured slave's arm and helping him hobble to his feet. "Not after he risked his life to save mine."

For a moment both of their parents stared at the black man before them, not uttering a word. Then after a quick glance at one another, their father finally broke the silence and said, "No, of course not."

From the wary expression on her mother's face, Annie wasn't sure if her mother agreed, but there was no taking back what had already been done.

"I'll get some bandages to wrap that ankle." Her mother gave their guest a slight nod before picking up her skirts and heading into the house.

"Don' mean to cause you's any trouble," the man said, his voice low. "I's be on my way soon as I's can."

"What's your name?" Will asked.

"They's call me Kitch."

"That's an unusual name," Annie commented.

The man glanced at her and shrugged. "They's had me work in the kitchens, so's I guess that's why they's call me Kitch."

Annie smiled. "My mother and I cook."

Kitch shook his head. "I's chop and bring in wood for the stoves."

"Oh." Annie frowned, not knowing what else to say. She'd been named after her grandmother on her father's side. She'd never heard of someone being named after the location where they worked. Somehow it didn't seem very respectful. Didn't he have a real name given to him at birth?

"What made you run, Kitch?" Annie's father asked, leaning on the cane that helped support his own injured leg as he and Will helped the man sit down.

"I's runs so I's can be free."

Annie stared at the newcomer, waiting for him to elaborate, and when he didn't, her curiosity got the better of her, and she asked, "Why do you want to be free?"

His dark brown eyes flickered with an intensity she had never seen. "I's runs," Kitch told her, "so I's free to decide what *I's* wants to do, 'stead of doin' what my massa says I's *has* to do. I's runs so I's free to help others run. I's runs so I's not whipped for singin' praises to my Lord."

Annie gasped. "You were *whipped*?"

"An' branded." Kitch lifted the hem of his shirt to reveal a dark scar in the shape of a horseshoe on the lower left side of his abdomen, just above his hip. Then in his broken Southern accent, he went on to explain how his master marked everyone he considered his property, slaves and animals alike.

Was that why this man had said he'd rather die than return to his master in the South? If someone had dared to whip her. . .and brand her with a horseshoe. . .she'd be tempted to run away too. She loved to sing. She couldn't imagine being whipped for singing, especially for singing songs of praise. Surely God could not condone such harsh treatment either.

Annie tore her gaze off the man's scar to glance at Will, then her father, who both looked just as bothered by the imprint as she was.

Louisa had whispered about some of the horrors that supposedly happened in the

South, but Annie had thought some of the stories may have been exaggerated. And she'd never really thought about the freedoms she and her family enjoyed, such as the freedom to make their own decisions, the freedom to help their fellow man, and the freedom to sing and worship God. How could she blame Kitch for also wanting such basic rights?

When her mother returned with several strips of clean cloth, Annie helped her remove the man's tattered shoe and wrap his ankle to give it better support.

"You should stay off your feet until your injury heals," Annie's mother told him.

Kitch shook his head. "I's gotta keep movin'."

"Where are you headed?" Will asked, handing the man his water canteen.

The man lifted the canteen to his lips and took several greedy gulps before replying. "Moses says I's suppos' to take a boat across the river."

"The ferry to New York?" Will exclaimed, raising his brows.

Kitch nodded, and Annie couldn't help but continue to stare at the black man, as if he were a puzzle she couldn't quite put together.

"Who's Moses?" she asked.

For the first time since they'd met, Annie caught a glimpse of a smile. "She's the one who sings the song that tells us to follow the North Star an' helps us find the way to the tracks."

Will frowned. "Us?"

"Four from my massa's cotton fields. Two more from up the road."

"And this woman who helps you," Annie's mother said, "is she a slave?"

Kitch shook his head. "No, ma'am. Not no more. Moses is as free as a bird, flutterin' among the trees, singin' 'Sweet Chariot,' and lettin' us know when it's safe to run. I's thinks she's an angel."

The faint *clip-clop* of several horses sounded in the distance, and when Annie turned her head toward the road, she stiffened. "The sheriff! And four of his deputies! Kitch, you've got to hide."

Will and her father each took Kitch under the arm and, lifting the slave to his feet, helped him hobble toward the root cellar behind the house. Annie flung open the wooden door, and they slid Kitch down the sloped entrance of the enclosure. Then they resealed the opening and spread a pile of dead leaves overtop to hide its location.

"Hello, Sheriff Davis," Annie heard her mother say, as she rounded the corner of the house with her father and Will. "What brings you out this way?"

"We had six runaways jump the train this afternoon," the sheriff told them as he reined his horse to a stop. "There's a hefty reward being offered for their return. Dead or alive."

Annie held her breath, and for a moment she thought her heart stopped beating. Kitch was in real danger. And so was she. . .and her family. The stronger laws, enforcing the Fugitive Slave Act the previous year in 1850, gave the sheriff and his deputies the authority to punish those caught assisting Southern runaways. Her family could be heavily fined. . .or even jailed, if they were caught.

"You haven't seen any of those black folks running around your place, have you?" Sheriff Davis continued.

"No," her father said, shaking his head. "I can't say I have."

"What about you, Will?" the sheriff asked, stepping closer.

"No, sir," her brother answered, lifting his chin. "I haven't seen any *runners* over here."

From the unchanging expression on the sheriff's face, Annie didn't think he caught on, but Will's slight emphasis had her attention. As did the almost imperceptible nod she received from her father.

"Annie?" Sheriff Davis gave her a direct look.

Reverend Strong preached that one should never lie. But what about a half-truth, or a misdirection of the truth, to protect those she cared about?

"N–no," she said, trying to quell the guilt playing havoc with the insides of her stomach. "I haven't seen anyone. . .*run*."

Actually, she hadn't. With his hurt ankle, Kitch could barely walk.

"Mind if we search the inside of your house and have a look about your barns?" the sheriff asked.

"No, sir," Annie's father answered, swinging his cane. "Go right ahead."

But as soon as the uniformed officers were out of earshot, her father huddled both her and Will and their mother together and said, "Kitch can't stay here. I'll take him to the ferry as soon as it's dark."

"You can't," Annie's mother exclaimed, wiping his sweaty brow with her handkerchief. "You've been sick all afternoon and need to go back to bed."

"That's right, Papa." Annie studied her father's face and realized he did look pale. That was why he didn't come with them to the cabinet shop. And no one dared mention the fact he wouldn't get far on his lame leg. "Will and I can take him."

Her father thumped his cane. "No. I won't let you two place yourselves in more danger. It's best I—"

Her father swayed, and Will reached an arm out to steady him.

"We'll be careful," Annie promised.

Will nodded. "She can keep watch while I take Kitch down to the ferry and help him sneak aboard."

Their father hesitated, gave them a beseeching look, then squeezed their hands in his and whispered, "Please. . .don't get caught."

Isaiah had never been to the Morrisons' house but knew they lived on the outskirts of the city, near the woods. Not wanting to draw attention with a wagon, or even a steed, he'd decided to travel on foot. And when he got closer, a neighboring farmer had pointed him in the right direction. For a price. The information had cost him a quarter-day's wages. But finding Kitch and getting him onto the eight o'clock ferry was of utmost importance.

First, Isaiah checked to see if Annie and Will had hidden Kitch in the barn. He called out softly. No answer. Only a few snorts from the horses and a couple of startled squawks from the chickens. Next, he looked inside the toolshed. No sign of him.

Moving toward the dark, two-story house, he wondered who would answer the door if he knocked. He didn't see any lamplight. Had the family already turned in for the night? He didn't relish the idea of waking them, especially if Annie and Will had not told their parents about Kitch.

Deciding to take a different approach, Isaiah went around the side of the house and studied the upstairs windows. Two had beige curtains and an empty sill. The accompanying rooms could belong to either Will Morrison or his parents, but he couldn't be sure which was which. Pink, frilly, tied-back curtains framed the next rectangle pane, and a small stuffed animal in the shape of a cat sat on the bottom ledge. No doubt, this had to be Annie Morrison's bedroom window.

He'd talk to her first. If only he could get her attention. Picking a few pebbles off the ground, he pulled back his arm and then gently launched the first one toward the glass, hoping it wouldn't break. The slight *ping* as the pebble glanced off its target should have been enough to draw Annie to the window. Except the sweet face of the brunette beauty he'd glimpsed in town earlier that day never appeared.

Isaiah tossed two more pebbles against the window. He drew his arm back to toss up a third when he caught sight of a lantern swaying in the darkness beside him.

"What do you think you're doing?" a hushed voice hissed.

Startled, Isaiah dropped his arm. He recognized the deep, scratchy voice. It belonged to Sheriff Davis.

"I was. . ." Isaiah swallowed hard, his mind racing for a plausible excuse.

"Trying to court Miss Morrison without her father's permission?" the sheriff demanded, raising his lantern.

Isaiah flinched, nearly blinded. "I. . . Yes, sir."

"I wouldn't recommend it." The sheriff smirked. "Mr. Morrison has a mean shot with a rifle, and I'd pity any fella who got on his bad side, if you know what I mean."

"Yes, sir. I do."

"You'd do best to move along now, young man," the sheriff instructed. "You never know who you might find hiding out here in the dark these days, or if they might be friend or foe."

Nodding, Isaiah stepped away from him and took one last glance up at Annie's window. Lucky for him, it didn't appear she was home.

Or he'd have a whole lot more explaining to do.

Annie hid behind a tree and peered across the open stretch of land before the waterfront docks. The moon had not yet risen, but a series of lanterns illuminated the boats and alerted her to the whereabouts of other people patrolling the vicinity.

"I see three. . .maybe four men loading boxes onto some of the other boats," she reported in a terse whisper. "But the path to the ferry is clear."

"We've got to be sure," Will warned, shuffling closer with the injured man under his arm.

Annie glanced over at them, and a faint glimmer of light, reflected from the distant lanterns, fell on the pale, horsetail wig they'd stuck into a bonnet and placed on Kitch's head. They'd also powdered his face and wrapped him in their mother's dark blue, hooded mantle, hoping that if they were spotted, he might look like a woman. . .from a distance.

"I'll go first," Annie instructed. "And when you see me wave, *run*."

She pulled her own mantle tighter about her to ward off the bitter evening chill, and when she reached the docks, something cold touched her nose. Snow! More flakes fell, dimming the visibility. But the unexpected change in weather also presented them with the perfect camouflage to sneak Kitch aboard the ferry to New York without being seen.

Encouraged that God must surely be on their side, Annie waited until two ferry workers disappeared belowdecks, and a third went through a door into the top deck cabin, then raised her arm and waved. But her confidence froze when a strong hand shot out from behind her, wrapped around her wrist, and brought her arm back down.

"You must learn to be more discreet," someone murmured in her ear.

Annie jumped, her heart pounding, and spun around to see who had caught her. Her boot slipped on the dock's slushy surface, and she pitched sideways toward the icy waters of the Hudson. She would have fallen in, too, if the young man had let go of her.

But he didn't.

With a sharp intake of breath, she glanced up from her precarious position and realized he was the same young man who had been staring at her earlier that day. However, this time he wore a simple, plain pea coat with matching trousers, instead of fancy attire.

A second later, Will arrived with Kitch.

"Annie, we've got to hurry if—" Will broke off when he saw she was with someone and stopped up short, his eyes wide.

"I'm Isaiah Hawkins," the young man said as he pulled Annie up straight. "And I'm here to relieve you of your 'cargo.'"

"Our *what*?" Annie demanded.

Isaiah pointed to Kitch. "I'm the one who was supposed to meet him at the train station."

Several loud voices broke out farther up along the waterfront, and Annie's pulse quickened as she spotted the approaching lanterns. Then the unmistakable, scratchy, deep voice of the sheriff met her ears, and her stomach wrenched tight. Had he followed them?

Worse, a couple of barks let her know they were accompanied by dogs. Annie hadn't particularly cared for dogs since her neighbor's German shepherd chased her up a tree like a squirrel when she was six. From the fearful expression on Kitch's face, it appeared he didn't like the creatures much either.

With wide eyes, he wrenched free of Will's grasp, but his injured ankle couldn't support him. Thankfully, Will was able to re-catch him before he went down.

"Quick!" Isaiah whispered. "Give him to me. I'm here to help."

Will gave him a quick nod, but Annie hesitated, still unsure.

"You can trust me, Annie," Isaiah insisted.

Could she? How was she to know Isaiah wouldn't turn them all in to the sheriff the moment he arrived? *And how does he know my name?*

Isaiah held her gaze a moment longer, and when she gave him a nod as well, he took Kitch from Will, opened a hatch on the back of the ferry, and stashed the runaway slave inside. A few sailors emerged from the front cabin and Annie feared Isaiah would be hollered at for trespassing, but as he worked with the other men to untie the ropes from the pier and pull up the anchor, she realized Isaiah was part of the crew.

Had he hidden slaves on the ferry before? Did the rest of the crew know about it?

She wished she could stay to watch the vessel cross the river. . .and make sure

Kitch was safe. But the approaching lanterns, which bounced along the waterfront, grew brighter. And before Sherriff Davis and his men could reach them, Will took Annie's hand in his.

And they ran.

Chapter 3

Sunday morning, Annie sat rigidly upon the wooden church pew beside her parents and prayed for forgiveness for wearing her brother's trousers beneath her skirts the night they'd taken Kitch to the ferry. She wished she had the courage to wear the scandalous new Bloomer dress, which flaunted a fashionable skirt over trousers, in public. The looser style would allow her greater freedom and not suppress her internal organs with the whalebone-fitted corset she loathed.

However, most clergy, including Reverend Strong, denounced the wearing of pants by women, saying it usurped male authority. She wasn't sure where God stood on the matter, but despite her discomfort, she was grateful that her life was finally getting back to normal.

The first few nights after she and Will had helped Kitch board the ferry to freedom, she'd had nightmares of dogs, large ones with sharp, deadly teeth, chasing her, pouncing on her, and ripping the flesh from her bones.

The last two nights had been different. Her dreams had become blissfully muddled, bouncing back and forth between her friend Louisa's reassuring smile, Will and her parents' expressions of concern, and a pair of grayish-blue eyes that always seemed to be watching her, waiting to see what she would do next.

"Tell me more about the handsome young man who helped you get your cargo aboard the ferry," Louisa said, sitting down beside her.

Annie shifted in her seat. "I never said he was *handsome.*"

"You didn't have to," Louisa said with a smile. "I could tell by the expression on your face when you explained to me why my instructions were no longer necessary."

That conversation had been five days ago, the morning after she and Will had helped Kitch escape. Apparently, Louisa had not forgotten.

"When you slipped and the ferry worker helped you regain your balance, did he smile at you?" Louisa pressed.

No, but his eyes did. At least she thought they did. Annie frowned. Everything had happened so fast. Could it have only been her overactive imagination? After all, she'd also mistakenly believed Henry Pennington was in love with her.

"I'm. . .not sure if he smiled or not," Annie confessed. "What do you know of Isaiah Hawkins?"

"He and his brother arrived six months ago from somewhere in Pennsylvania," Louisa whispered. "I overheard someone say their father passed away, leaving them a substantial inheritance, which they used to buy the livery near the train station."

"They must go to another church, because I've never seen them here," Annie mused.

Louisa agreed and leaned her head closer. "There are also rumors that a notorious slave catcher is headed our way. A man by the name of Simon Augustus Cole. It's said he treats abolitionists the same way he treats slaves—with coldhearted contempt."

Annie shuddered. "Then it's a good thing we aren't hiding any more slaves. I mean *cargo*."

Louisa bit her lip. "Actually," she confided, "three shipments arrived late last night. The sheriff and his deputies have been watching our house around the block, so we hid them in the church basement."

Annie's gaze dropped to the floor, and she imagined that if she could see through the wood, she'd be able to see the slaves huddled beneath them at that very moment.

Fearful of being caught. Whipped. Being chased by dogs.

"Who else knows?" Annie asked, glancing about to make sure no one was listening in. "Have you told Daniel?"

"Not yet," Louisa said, her brows pulling tight. "He doesn't know what we do, and I'm afraid to tell him."

"If he's to be your husband, you owe him the truth," Annie warned. "What if Daniel finds out from someone else?"

"You're right," Louisa admitted. "But what if he doesn't like the fact I'm involved? What if he decides he no longer wants to marry me?"

"Then he isn't the right man for you."

"But I *love* him," Louisa said, a catch in her voice.

"You can rethink your involvement," Annie offered. "And stop before you get caught."

Louisa looked heavenward. "But what would God have me do?"

"Stay safe?" Annie suggested. "Can't you let *God* help the people from the South?"

"God *is* helping them, Annie, by using people like you and me."

Annie shook her head. Maybe God had used her to help one slave, but surely she and her family were now done and could go back to minding their own business. Why couldn't Louisa do the same?

"Mama is organizing a special women's group," Louisa said excitedly, her green eyes lighting up. "Perhaps you and your mother would like to join? We're putting together care packets for the poor."

"You mean the poor runaways that the church harbors?" Annie clarified.

"Whatsoever ye would that men should do to you, do ye even so to them," Louisa said, quoting from Matthew 7:12.

The scripture had been the first Bible verse they had both memorized as children, and had tried to live by as they grew into adults.

To compound Annie's guilt over wanting to stay neutral on the topic of slavery, Louisa's father, Reverend Strong, delivered a sermon on the good Samaritan, a biblical story of a foreigner who showed compassion on a wounded man when others would not. The one who had helped was said to have been a neighbor to he who had been in need.

Reverend Strong finished by asking the congregation, "Are *you* a good neighbor? Who have you been compelled to help? Is it the friend you greeted in church this morning? Those who look like you and talk like you? The people who agree with you on political issues? Or is it possible God would have you be a 'neighbor' to those even of a different color or background, maybe even from a different region or race?"

The congregation looked around at each other, and one man stood up and walked out. After a few seconds' pause, another family followed, their scowls displaying their disagreement over the issue at hand.

Unperturbed, Reverend Strong moved in front of the pulpit and continued to look each person in the eye. "Who was a neighbor to the wounded man in today's teaching? Was it someone who was prejudiced or indifferent or afraid of the inconvenience or cost? I ask you again, who was a *neighbor*?"

"The one who had pity on him," a clear voice rose from the back.

Annie's heart lurched, and with a gasp, she spun around in her seat. *Isaiah?*

Beneath his top coat, he was dressed in a dark brown waistcoat and trousers and wore his hair slicked over to the side, sharpening his features and giving him yet a different look than the other two times she'd seen him. A freshly scrubbed, *gentlemanly* look that somehow made him appear even handsomer than Henry Pennington.

Her cheeks grew warm as Isaiah met her gaze. Then he sat down in the last pew and bowed his head. Perplexed as to what prompted his sudden arrival, Annie glanced over at her parents, but they had no idea who the young man was. And Will wasn't there to guide her. He'd caught their father's sickness and remained at home in bed with a low-grade fever.

Turning back toward Louisa, she said in an urgent whisper, "It's *him*."

"The same young man who was staring at you in town is. . .Isaiah Hawkins, the handsome ferry dock worker?" Louisa murmured, lifting a brow.

Annie's heart fluttered inside her chest like a caged bird. "What do you suppose he is doing here?"

Louisa's mouth curved into a smile. "After the service, be sure to go over and ask him."

"Me?" Annie could barely breathe as she fought a surge of panic. She wasn't usually the one who took the initiative. Not like Louisa or Will, who were both a year older than her. She peeked at Isaiah over her shoulder then turned toward Louisa and asked, "What shall I say?"

After the service, Isaiah stood outside the double doors of the church waiting for the rest of the congregation to emerge. After twisting the wide brim of his brown bowler hat around in his hands, he spotted the Morrisons. Squeezing the edges of his hat tight, he walked toward them, his attention on Annie, who looked off in another direction, as if searching for someone. Then he put his hat back on his head and approached her father.

Shaking his hand, he introduced himself, then asked, "Mr. Morrison, may I speak to your daughter?"

Annie's gaze snapped toward him, and her mouth popped open to form a small O.

Her father gave her a questioning look, and at her nod, Mr. Morrison said, "Yes, Mr. Hawkins, you may."

Mr. Morrison and his wife then promptly stepped aside to give them a few paces of privacy, as if such a thing were possible while standing in the middle of the milling crowd of people who were all eagerly bent on conversing with one another.

Annie pulled her white silk gloves from the pocket of her wool mantle and slid them on before looking at him. But when she did, she smiled.

His pulse kicked up a notch and he swallowed hard, suddenly unsure of what he had wanted to say. Or how to say it.

Finally, he drew in a deep breath and grinned back at her. "I wanted to let you know that the cargo was delivered safely and is now headed up through New York to Canada."

Annie nodded. "Thank you. I *was* concerned."

"Do your parents know?"

"Of course. My father would have put him on the ferry himself, if he hadn't been sick. And my mother is the one who thought up the disguise."

Isaiah glanced around to make sure no one was eavesdropping. "How long has your family been a station?"

"We're *not*," Annie said, glancing around as well. "Our involvement was. . .one time only."

"That's too bad," he said when she met his gaze. "I had hoped we could work together."

Annie shook her head, and fear entered her eyes. "It's too dangerous. If we were caught. . . the fine would devastate our family. We could lose everything."

"I know the risks."

"How long have you been a ferry worker?" she asked in a hushed whisper.

"I'm not," Isaiah informed her. "I'm a 'watcher.'"

Annie frowned. "What's that?"

"The captain pays a few of us to ride the ferry and keep watch over the docks on either shore. I'm supposed to be on the lookout for thieves who might want to steal the ship's *real* cargo."

"Does he know what you are really doing?"

Isaiah shook his head. "Only some of the crew."

"Aren't you afraid of being caught?"

"I am," Isaiah admitted.

"And yet, still you put your life on the line. . .for people you don't even know." Annie pursed her lips. "Why?"

Isaiah chuckled. "Because I am their 'neighbor,' Miss Morrison. And because. . .it's the right thing to do."

Chapter 4

Whoa! Easy, Blue." Isaiah drew back on the reins and brought the fidgety blue roan to a stop beside the grassy embankment west of the tracks, several hundred feet from the Jersey City train terminal. The young horse didn't care much for the noise of the incoming trains, but Isaiah's brother, Tom, hoped that with time and training, they'd be able to use Blue to pull a carriage for paying customers. For now, they took turns driving him past the tracks each day to show him there wasn't anything to be afraid of and used him to pull the carts and wagons carrying their incoming supplies. Earlier that morning, Isaiah had picked up a full load of hay from one of the outlying farms, at a better price than the feed store in the heart of the city, a perfect cover to hide his *other* intended cargo.

If it arrived.

He'd come to this section of the tracks the last three days in a row, waiting. But each day the train passed right on by, with no drop-offs for him to collect. That's the way it was with the Underground Railroad. Sometimes you were told someone was coming, but you didn't know when. And sometimes you didn't know they were coming at all...until they showed up.

Of course, there were also the ones who took a different route than originally planned. Which is what he was beginning to suspect had happened with the pair headed his way. While he waited at the train tracks, his expected cargo could be headed toward the city on foot or by boat from the east.

All he knew was that a woman, dressed in a fine green cloak and bonnet, had come into the livery on Saturday and told him to expect a double delivery this week, most likely aboard the New Jersey Railroad.

The distant chugging of the steam-powered engine drew closer, and Isaiah climbed down from the wagon seat to stand by Blue's side, not only to keep a firm hold on the horse to keep him from rearing, but also to whisper words of encouragement.

The train slowed as it passed, hissing and chugging, but although Isaiah kept a sharp lookout, he didn't see anyone jump. Not even his horse jumped. He gave the roan a gentle pat. "You did good today, Blue. Much better than yesterday. Wait until I tell Tom. Maybe he'll mix an extra treat with your grain tonight."

Blue's ears pricked forward as if he liked that idea. No doubt the horse understood the word *treat*. Horses were much smarter than some people gave them credit for.

So was he. Most people in Jersey City thought he was only a ferry-dock laborer when he wasn't helping his brother with the livery. What they didn't know was that he'd graduated from the Dickinson School of Law. And once he had enough money saved, he planned to open his own law firm. One that sought justice for *all* people, not only the rich and the free.

Blue's eyes widened, and the roan let out an aggravated snort.

Isaiah followed the horse's gaze and scanned the embankment near the tracks. "Hey, boy. Did you see something?"

Releasing his hold on Blue's reins, Isaiah took a few steps forward, and a small dark face with bright eyes peered over the edge of the embankment. *A child?*

Whistling the tune of "Wade in the Water" to put her at ease, Isaiah extended his hand to help her up and found that a dark-skinned woman, whom he assumed was the mother, followed behind.

The woman eyed him with caution. "You know the true name of Moses?"

"Harriet Tubman," Isaiah whispered.

"Praise God in heaven above. I'm Emmeline, and this here is my Lucy." Smiling, some of the tension left the woman's face, although the wariness in her eyes remained. "That your wagon?"

Isaiah nodded. "Quick. Let's get you aboard."

The livery had been the intended destination, but when Isaiah spied the crowd gathered on the street outside, he decided to leave the wagon beside the blacksmith's shop and paid the owner's son to keep watch.

"I'll be right back," he murmured to his two passengers hidden beneath the hay then hurried up the street to find the cause of all the commotion.

As he edged closer, Isaiah spotted the sheriff. Tom and his wife, Henrietta, stood off to the side, their expressions grim. And the fugitive they'd sheltered the previous night stood between two of the sheriff's deputies, enslaved in handcuffs.

"Hawkins and his wife should be handcuffed too," a man from the crowd shouted. "Send them south with the slave, if they are so fond of them!"

A few people threw up cheers to support the scoffer. Others from the crowd, not so much.

Louisa Strong was one of those who opposed them. "Mr. and Mrs. Hawkins are prominent members of our community and do not deserve your judgment."

"Be that as it may, Thomas Hawkins will be fined a sum of six hundred dollars," Sheriff Davis announced.

"No!" Isaiah exclaimed, breaking through the crowd.

The sheriff raised his brows. "Do you wish to be fined also?"

Isaiah clenched his jaw and stared the sheriff straight in the eye. "Not unless you have proof of my involvement."

"This runaway," the sheriff said, pointing toward the slave, "was hiding inside Hawkins Livery."

"So?" Isaiah challenged.

"The closet he hid in was *locked.* From the outside. Who do you suppose put the lock on that closet door, son? Was it you?"

"Isaiah, stand down!"

The order came from his brother, and a swift glance in his direction showed Tom's anger. . .and fear.

Again, Isaiah heard the gunshot that had placed a bullet straight into his father's forehead. Heard Tom scream. Then himself. Heard the Pennsylvania sheriff his father had been arguing with say anyone who dared question his authority would be fired upon next.

"No repeats," Tom warned.

Isaiah held his gaze and nodded. "No repeats."

Taking a step back, Isaiah disappeared into the crowd and made his way back to the wagon.

Late in the afternoon, on Thursday, Annie put on her warmest work coat, gloves, and fur-lined boots and followed her mother out to the barn to help distribute the animals' second feeding before it got dark. The chickens often escaped their coop and ran to and fro, but at feeding time, most of the hens came running.

Annie dipped the metal scoop into the bucket of dried corn, barley, and oats and dumped the mix into the wooden box tray feeder, while her mother refilled their water. The dairy cow, which not only gave them milk, but produced the cream they needed to make their own butter and cheese, stood in a stall beside their two horses and let out a loud *moo.*

"Don't worry, Polly, you're next," Annie promised.

She gathered the grain buckets for the larger animals and turned to walk toward them, when Isaiah Hawkins stepped out from the tack room.

"Gracious!" Annie exclaimed, jumping with a start and spilling some of the feed. She glanced over at her mother, beside her, who took a pitchfork off the wall and pointed the sharp prongs at their surprise guest.

Isaiah put out a hand. "I mean you no harm, ma'am."

Her mother frowned. "You're the young man who came to church on Sunday?"

Isaiah nodded, and Annie hid a smile as her mother put the pitchfork down. Anyone who stepped through the doors of their church was someone they could trust, as far as her mother was concerned. Annie wasn't sure she agreed with her, but in this case, she was glad her mother had relented.

"He's the one who helped Will and I sneak Kitch on the ferry," Annie told her. "Isaiah and his brother own Hawkins Livery."

This information seemed to make her mother relax even more, and she stepped forward to shake Isaiah's hand. "What can we do for you, Mr. Hawkins?"

Isaiah sent Annie an apprehensive look and nodded toward the hayloft above. "I picked up two shipments from the South this afternoon, but I can't hide them at the livery because the sheriff and his deputies found the cargo we'd been hiding and shut down the place. I tried to drop them off at the church, but the Strong family is also being watched."

Annie followed his gaze toward the hayloft above their heads, and her mouth fell open. "You brought them here?"

Isaiah nodded. "There was no one else I could trust."

"You shouldn't have come," Annie warned, shaking her head. "The sheriff searched our place a week ago. We can't—"

"Let me see them," her mother said, cutting her off.

Annie glanced at Isaiah, wondering if she could trust him or if he'd end up getting them all in trouble. Didn't he say his own family had been caught? And the sheriff was watching Louisa's family as well? Her stomach twisted in knots, but she leaned forward, as curious as her mother to see who Isaiah had hid in their hayloft.

He went up the ladder, and when he came down, he carried a small black girl, no older than four years, in his arms. A thin woman, dressed inappropriately for the winter weather in a thin black dress, descended the rungs behind him.

Annie glanced at the woman then back to the child, her black, wiry hair sticking out at odd angles, tangled with hay and small sticks. The young girl's eyes widened when she saw them, and she buried her face into Isaiah's shoulder.

"She's so young," Annie exclaimed. "I had no idea children came up the Underground Railroad."

"What's happened to you?" her mother asked the woman. "Why are you here?"

"My massa put my Lucy up for sale," the woman told her. "If we didn't leave, I was never goin' to see her again."

Annie glanced at her own mother and tried to fathom how she would feel if put in their situation. From her mother's haunted expression, it appeared she shared her thoughts.

"They separate families?" Annie asked, her voice soft as she drew closer.

The child's mother snickered. "They sell us off to the highest bidder at the auction."

Annie knew the slaves on the Southern plantations were not given certain rights. Women of all color, even white, were not given certain rights either, such as the right to speak out in public or cast their vote in elections. But she'd had no idea that some of the plantation owners in the South did not treat their slaves with the respect she'd come to believe they received. She'd had no idea that slaves were whipped, separated from family, and sold like cattle.

Unbidden, tears sprang to her eyes, and her heart swelled in her chest with sympathy toward these two slaves who had traveled hundreds of miles just to make it this far.

"We have to help them, Annie," her mother said softly, her voice choked.

She nodded and glanced at Isaiah. "What do we do?"

Chapter 5

Annie brought clean towels into the washroom, where her mother helped Emmeline bathe little Lucy and pick the small twigs from her hair.

"We're going to need to use butter to smooth out the matted tangles," Annie's mother instructed, "and fresh water for Emmeline's bath."

Annie nodded. The caked mud they had scrubbed off the young girl's body had turned the tub almost as brown as the child's skin.

So different from her own.

And yet the tender look Emmeline gave Lucy was just as strong and full of love as the look Annie's mother gave her. A fact she pondered while retrieving the needed items to clean up their guests.

"We ran, the two of us, on foot, and hid along the clay riverbanks till we could run for the trees," Emmeline told them as she washed herself with a sudsy cloth.

"How did you know which way to go?" Annie asked, working the clean butter into Lucy's hair with her hands. She'd never touched a black person's hair before. The texture was course and wiry, but the tight spirals did soften with the butter, enabling them to drop down and touch her shoulders.

"Moses sang us a song leadin' the way," Emmeline said, her face relaxing for the first time since she arrived.

"Moses?" Annie asked, remembering Kitch had spoken of a woman by the same name. A former slave. A woman who helped slaves escape by singing encoded songs to signal when it was safe to run. "Did she come with you?"

"Moses took us as far as Pennsylvania then put us on the train tha' came here," Emmeline explained.

Lucy smiled and sang in a soft, high-pitched voice, "Wade in the water, wade in the water, children, wade in the water, God's a-going to trouble the water."

Annie frowned. "What does it mean?"

"The song is 'bout the Israelites' escape from Egypt in the book of Exodus," Emmeline explained. "Moses led them through to the Promised Land just like our Moses leads us to *ours*, the land of the free."

The woman they described sounded like a brave soul, who risked her own life, again and again, to help others. Someone not afraid to do what she believed was right.

"I'd like to meet this Moses," Annie declared, then gasped when she realized what that would mean. *More danger.* "What are the words to the rest of the song?"

"There are many verses," Emmeline said, and smiled. "One told us to hide in the riverbanks to escape the dogs chasing our trail."

Annie's stomach clenched. "Did you say. . .dogs?"

After both Emmeline and Lucy were given a clean change of clothes and fed a generous helping of bread, cheese, and dried beef, Annie led them up the stairs to the secret room behind the hall bookcase, where her grandfather, who had built the house, would retreat to hide his cigar smoke from Grandma.

The small "parlor" had remained a family joke for anyone who needed time alone, and the *perfect* place to house their new guests, even though Emmeline had insisted that she and Lucy would be fine in the barn. But Annie's mother wouldn't hear of it and insisted they'd be much warmer and more comfortable upstairs.

Until they could make it to the ferry. Isaiah wasn't scheduled to work for another two nights. Emmeline and Lucy would need to stay with Annie's family until then.

Her mother introduced the newcomers to her father and Will as soon as they arrived home from the cabinet shop. Then Annie's family gathered around the dinner table, and her father said grace.

"Lord, give us the wisdom to discern Your will for our lives and for the lives of those we harbor under our roof. We humbly ask for Your protection and guidance. Thank You for this food before us, and as Thanksgiving approaches, help us to remember to be thankful for *all* our blessings and give to others as You have so generously given to us."

"Amen," Annie chorused along with them at the end, and shifted in her seat.

Could God truly be counted on to protect them? What was *His* position on slavery? Surely a loving God couldn't fault them for taking in Emmeline and little Lucy, even if it *was* against the law. Not if He was a God of compassion.

"I know we said we wouldn't take in any more runaways," Annie's mother said as she passed a plate of roasted potatoes and herbed carrots. "But they truly had nowhere else to go."

"We can't let Emmeline and Lucy be separated," Annie agreed. "They need each other. Families ought to be allowed to stay together."

Will nodded. "I thought the slaves in the South were shown basic human decency."

"Some are," her father said. "Your grandfather owned a couple of slaves before moving up here, but he always treated them fairly. He didn't break up families."

"What happened to Grandpa's slaves?" Annie asked, intrigued. She'd never had slaves or servants.

"Your grandfather sold them when he needed money to move my mother, my two sisters, and myself north, to New Jersey. He'd inherited the land we live on from a great-uncle. After buying the supplies to build the house and barn, there wasn't money left over to repurchase slaves or hire help. We learned to do for ourselves."

"As should the South," Will said vehemently.

"Will!" Annie's mother scolded. "It's not for us to judge how others should do things."

Annie frowned. "Would you have us stay neutral?"

Her father finished chewing a bite of stewed chicken and set down his fork. "Your *great*-grandfather fought in the Revolutionary War, which founded this country. I had thought it our patriotic and Christian duty to obey our government, as long as it remained true to God's Word. But when I increasingly see the two divided into opposite sides, one has to question which he ought to follow."

"Dad, do you mean—?" Will asked, his face expectant as he awaited an answer.

"Of course, there *are* dangers," her father continued. "If caught, we must be prepared to pay the consequences."

Annie looked around the table at each of their faces, trying to make sense out of what was being said. "Does this mean we're going to become a station on the Underground Railroad?"

Her parents exchanged a glance, and then her father's eyes twinkled. "What do you think, Annie? Should we?"

Her father had never asked her opinion before. He sought out Will's opinion on social issues, but never hers. After all, women usually had no say on such matters. She sat up straight in her chair, honored, and with a surge of confidence ricocheting through her entire being, she thought of Kitch, Emmeline, and little Lucy, and met her father's gaze head-on.

"Yes, Father, I—I believe we should."

Isaiah stood on the wharf, waiting for both the ferry and the Morrisons to arrive. Squinting, he gazed toward the First Presbyterian Church. Reverend Strong kept watch over the area from the bell tower, the tallest point in Jersey City. He had sent word through Louisa that he would light a lantern and place it in the top window when it was safe for Annie and Will to bring Emmeline and Lucy down to the docks. By this time of night, Annie and her brother should all be hiding in the woods, waiting for the signal. As was he.

There!

The lantern had been lit, giving off a bright, golden glow that could be seen for miles. Turning his gaze toward the tree line, he searched for Annie's cloaked party of travelers.

"Did you hear the news?" a fellow crewman asked, coming to stand beside him.

"What news?" Isaiah asked hesitantly.

"We have a new captain," the crewman said ominously and gave him a pointed look. "I thought you ought to know."

A new captain? What happened to the other one? And how will that affect tonight's mission?

"Thanks," Isaiah said appreciatively. But he couldn't suppress the sudden prickling sensation running down his arms, warning him to be careful.

The lanterns lighting the approaching ferry drifted closer across the river, and Isaiah's pulse kicked up a notch. Would the new captain be sympathetic to the cause? And if not, how was he to sneak Emmeline and Lucy on board without being seen?

Once the ferry dropped anchor and the ropes had been tied around the pier posts, the crewmen off-loaded and reloaded several wooden crates, carrying various shipments of supplies. The captain must have remained inside the front steering cabin.

Keeping watch, Isaiah spotted the silhouettes of several figures emerge from the edge of the trees, then stop.

Glancing about in all directions, Isaiah made sure the coast was clear, then whistled the tune "Wade in the Water," the signal he and Annie had agreed on to let them know they should come out of hiding and run toward the dock.

Except there were three figures instead of the four he'd expected.

"Where's Will?" he asked as Annie ran toward him, carrying Lucy, whom she transferred into his arms.

"He and my father never came home from the cabinet shop. Mother has poor eyesight in the dark, and so that only left me to show Emmeline and Lucy the way."

"That was a brave thing to do," Isaiah said, his tone filled with admiration.

"Me? Brave?" Annie shook her head and with a smile said, "Lucy is the brave one. She took my hand and ran so fast, I couldn't turn back even if I wanted to."

"Is that so, Lucy?" Isaiah asked the child in his arms.

Lucy nodded, and with wide eyes that spoke of uncertain danger, she sang softly,

"Oh, go down, Moses, go down,
Way down into Egypt's land,
Tell old Pharaoh,
Let my people go!"

"Emmeline, watch your step," Isaiah said hurriedly as he lifted the lid to the trapdoor leading to the secret cargo hold in the back of the boat. "Once you climb down, I'll hand Lucy to you."

However, before he could do anything, Annie whispered, "Behind you!"

Isaiah spun around with the child in his arms, and tightened his hold as he locked gazes with a man with white hair and a beard whom he had never seen before. But the stranger's unmistakable hat and uniform gave away his identity. Isaiah froze and judged the distance between them to be about ten feet. Lucy's soft but passionate song had most likely drawn the man's attention. Or Isaiah's own whistling.

For a moment, they all just stared at each other, and Isaiah swallowed hard, adrenaline surging through every limb. The captain's testimony against them would be enough to send both his and Annie's families to jail. But the older man's gaze shifted from Isaiah toward the girl in his arms, then over to the open hatch in front of them, where Emmeline's head poked through.

Isaiah tensed, ready to spring off the boat and lead the child to safety, but the captain turned his back on them and said in a low voice over his shoulder, "I saw nothing."

A wave of relief washed over him as Isaiah met Annie's gaze.

"He's letting us go?" she asked, her eyes incredulous as the captain walked away.

Isaiah nodded. "Quick! Let's get Lucy below."

Annie gave the child a quick hug; then Isaiah handed her down the hatch to her mother and closed the lid.

"Will they be safe?" Annie asked.

"I won't let anything happen to them," Isaiah promised, and extended his hand to help her step back off the boat and onto the dock. "Do you trust me, Annie?"

She glanced down at her gloved hand in his, and in the soft glow of the lantern light, he saw her expression soften. "Yes, I suppose I must, if we are to continue working together."

"Does that mean. . . ?" he asked, searching her face for an answer.

Annie nodded. "Our family has decided to become a permanent station on the Underground Railroad."

"Great news," Isaiah assured her. He knew he should let go of her hand, but found he couldn't. Instead, he bent his head and kissed it. Then she pulled away, a smile on her lips, and he added, "I look forward to seeing you often."

"I look forward to seeing you too," Annie said, and gazed up at him shyly. "But what shall we say if other people take notice?"

Isaiah grinned. "The sheriff already thinks I'm courting you. I say we stick to that excuse."

Annie's smile broadened. "If you say so, Mr. Hawkins."

He would have said more, continued their little banter, but the ferry whistle blew, signaling their departure, and the crew came out to untie the lines.

His last glimpse of Annie showed her running across the field toward the safety of the dark tree line, her long cloak billowing out behind her. But halfway across the field, she stopped and reached out her hand to give him a small wave.

And even though she couldn't see, he smiled in return.

Annie's heart raced as she ran up the hill and through the trees toward home. She tried to convince herself it *was* from the exertion, but by the time she arrived at her own house and into the waiting arms of her anxious family, she knew the cause was due to something else.

Someone else.

None other than the intriguing Isaiah Hawkins.

Chapter 6

Annie arrived back home, exhausted, and planned to go straight to bed, thankful the ordeal of getting Emmeline and Lucy to the ferry was over. But when she saw the solemn looks on both her parents' faces, she knew something was terribly wrong. Her gaze flew toward her brother, Will, who sat hunched over in a chair beside the fireplace, and when he lifted his haunted gaze to meet hers, she grew even more alarmed.

"What happened?" she asked, going to his side.

"I've been pressed into the service of Simon Augustus Cole," Will spat, his tone bitter.

"He came into the cabinet shop with the sheriff and his men," her father explained. "They searched every nook and cranny of the building."

Will nodded. "He even wanted a look inside the sailing skiff I've been building in the back. But they didn't find the fugitives they were looking for."

Annie gasped. "Emmeline and Lucy?"

"Yes," her mother whispered, her eyes wide. "Are they safe?"

"They're on their way across the river," Annie assured her.

"The sheriff says Cole has the right to demand help from any man he chooses," her father said, his voice low. "And he chose *me*, but when I told him I couldn't mount a horse with my gimpy leg. . ."

Annie glanced back at her brother. "He took Will."

"I have to help him round up runaway slaves until he and his men take them back to Georgia at the end of the month," Will informed her.

"That's not fair," Annie protested. "You should be given a choice."

"I was," Will sneered. "Help Cole or go to jail."

"That's blackmail," Annie exclaimed.

Her father scowled. "Unfortunately, it's the law."

"Rumors have spread that Mr. Cole isn't just after slaves," her mother added. "He's determined to catch all those who help them."

Without assistance from the abolitionists, what would happen to the Southern fugitives who needed them, like Kitch, Emmeline, and Lucy? How would they make the journey north on their own?

While Annie was happy to see their short-term guests escape, she was also sorry that they had to travel so far to reach freedom. Would she ever see them again? Would there ever be a time when they could stay in Jersey City and not fear getting sent back south?

Annie looked at her father. "What shall we do? Stop helping the people who come to our door?"

"No," her mother said determinedly. "We just won't tell Will. It will be safer for him—and *us*—if he can honestly say in good conscience that he doesn't know where any fugitives are hiding."

"I won't come into the house without calling out and giving you fair notice," Will told her. "And if, perchance, you have someone with you, whom you don't want me to see, you must do the same, so there is no interaction between us."

A wave of sorrow flooded over her, bringing tears to her eyes. She and Will had never been on opposite sides before. They'd always been a team, working together. Now this horrid slave catcher, with his dominating authority, had managed to drive a wedge between them.

While she, Louisa, and Isaiah worked to help the slaves escape north, Will would be working with Simon Cole to return them to the South.

After Isaiah finished his evening shift aboard the ferry, he trudged slowly back to the livery. Surprised to find half the wagons and carriages missing from the interior of the building, he went in search of his brother and asked optimistically, "Did we have a good day of business?"

"Not in the way you'd hope," Tom answered. "No leases, but about a half dozen sales. The good news is that I got a good price for them. Although still not enough to pay the entire fine."

The fine for harboring the runaway slaves.

"This is my fault," Isaiah said, leaning against one of the remaining wagons. "If I hadn't antagonized that red-faced little man—"

"We don't know for sure if Mr. Felding is the one who squealed," Tom said, taking a harness off a nearby bench and hanging it up on a hook along the wall.

"He said if we were hiding any slaves, he'd shut us down." Isaiah clenched his fist. "I think he must have been spying on us. If I hadn't been working on the ferries, I could have kept better watch."

"Your work on the ferry brings in extra money," Tom reminded him. "And helps those who need a free passage to the promised land."

"Not anymore," Isaiah said, and cringed. "I got fired."

"*What?*" Tom exclaimed, his eyes widening.

"The ferry had a new captain tonight," Isaiah said, and blew out a frustrated breath. "He caught me hiding Annie Morrison's cargo in the back hatch. He feigned indifference, but when we returned to the wharf at Jersey City, the new slave catcher, Simon Augustus Cole, and the sheriff were waiting for us. They insisted on searching the boat."

Tom frowned. "But your cargo had been dropped off on the opposite shore."

"Yes, but they rattled the captain pretty hard. And after they left, the captain said he feared he wouldn't be needing me anymore."

"No doubt with less income, we'll have to tighten our belts," Tom said, rubbing a hand over his jaw. "But we'll manage. I'll tell Henrietta to add more broth to her chicken-noodle soup to make it stretch further."

"I'll get another job," Isaiah promised.

"We'll also need another way to transport the runaways across the water," Tom said, furrowing his brows. "Another boat."

Isaiah nodded. "I've already spoken to a fisherman who has agreed to help. Not *everyone* is on Cole's side."

Tom gave him a good-natured slap on the shoulder and grinned. "Praise God for that, eh?"

Chapter 7

Over the next several weeks, Annie's admiration for her adventurous, kindhearted pretend beau grew every time they met, every time they shared a look or smile, every time they helped a new fugitive escape across the river toward the "promised land."

During one escapade, when they'd had to wait for the fisherman's boat to arrive, they'd hidden in a small shack along the shore, the back half embedded in the hillside and the front obscured by tall clumps of dried reeds. It was there that Isaiah had told her about his father, who had been shot by a sheriff two years before.

"Dad stood on our back porch, proud and defiant, and stood up for a free man, a friend of ours, whom the slave catcher insisted was a runaway," Isaiah said, his expression pained as he choked out the words. "The echo of that pistol. . .is something I'll never forget. Then the gun turned toward me and I—I couldn't move. I couldn't say a word. I just stood there, my father's body not five feet away."

Annie shuddered to think how she would have responded in his situation. She'd probably scream and crumble to pieces. But later, after she got over the shock of what had happened, she'd be *angry*.

"What happened to. . .your friend?" Annie asked.

"The slave catcher took him south and sold him back into slavery. We never saw him again. Tom and I are still trying to find him. We'd been hoping Kitch would have some information for us when he arrived, but he said there was no news."

"That's why you became abolitionists?" Annie asked, rapt with attention.

Isaiah nodded. "Tom and I vowed that day to help as many of the fugitives escape as we can. That way, our father's life was not taken in vain."

Annie could see the tenderness on Isaiah's face when he spoke of his father, a man he clearly loved and admired. And when she and her mother joined the other women from church to assemble care packages for the needy, Annie couldn't help but wish Isaiah's affection for her was real.

Sometimes, when he held her gaze, it seemed as if the sparkle in his eyes was genuine. But she knew he was only *pretending* to court her, so as not to raise suspicion from the sheriff and his deputies; a ruse to keep the lawmen from discovering their true mission.

Helping the Southern fugitives.

During the second week of December, Annie sat at the round wooden table in the church basement with Louisa, their mothers, and the other women caught up in the abolitionist movement. Each of them had been supplied with a needle and thread, which they pulled through squares of folded muslin material. They'd decided that pillowcases would be easiest for them to sew and their recipients to carry. The soft sack "care packages" could hold an assortment of small, lightweight clothes, toiletries, and food supplies.

Annie had also been shown how to sew a small pocket into the inside to hold hand-drawn maps detailing how to get to the ferry, through New York, and across the border to Canada, should the travelers get separated from their agent or guide.

Two of the fugitives would be leaving the hidden room opposite them this very night, as soon as they were married. Annie finished her work, and as she held it up for the others' inspection, she wondered if *she* would ever get married.

"I've invited Daniel to the wedding," Louisa confided.

Annie raised her brows. "You told him. . .what you do?"

Louisa nodded. "Daniel met Jourdon and Rhina when he came over last night. He learned how they'd met when the slaves from their two neighboring plantations came together for a prayer meeting."

"And then they fell in love," Annie said dreamily.

Louisa nodded. "Jourdon went on to explain how he was freed as a thank-you for his years of service, when the widowed mistress of his plantation sold everything and went to live with her sister. But I'm. . .not sure Daniel believed him until Jourdon showed his signed papers of release. Then Daniel got real quiet when he heard how Jourdon had worked for seven years to buy Rhina's freedom, but her master just took his money. . .and refused to let her go."

"Until Harriet Tubman helped her escape," Annie said, again wondering what it would be like to meet this modern-day Moses.

Louisa smiled. "I'm hoping that once Daniel sees the wedding, he'll understand why we need to help them. If Jourdon and Rhina didn't run, they'd never be together. They'd never have a chance to have the happiness we share."

"What if he doesn't understand?" Annie asked worriedly. "What if he turns them in?"

"To do that, he'd also have to turn *me* in, and he'd never bring harm to me or my family," Louisa assured her.

However, later that night, Daniel was as fidgety as a cat with its tail on fire as he stood beside Louisa and watched the fugitive slave couple she'd been hiding exchange vows.

Annie had gathered a few pine branches and green holly sprigs with bright red berries into a bouquet for the bride to carry down the aisle. And Louisa let Rhina wear one of her own dresses, a simple, pale pink gown trimmed with rosebud ribbon. Mrs. Strong provided the lace veil.

But what made Rhina the most beautiful bride Annie had ever seen was not her attire. It was the way she looked into Jourdon's face as she professed her undying love and promised to remain faithful and true. . .till death parted them one from the other.

Jourdon repeated the same words back to her. . .with tears streaming down his face, and Annie wept along with him, her heart so full of joy for these two who had overcome such odds to be together.

Glancing at Isaiah, Annie could see by the smile on his face that the ceremony had touched him too, and when he shifted his gaze to look at her, she saw that tender expression enter his eyes again, as if Isaiah truly cared for her.

Smiling, her heart beat a little faster. Perhaps if there was hope for Jourdon and Rhina, there was hope for her too.

Isaiah had agreed to help the bridal couple escape down to the waterfront. But it seemed to Annie that Daniel couldn't wait for the ceremony to end, so he could make his own escape.

Poor Louisa! She'd so hoped Daniel would support her views.

Reverend Strong pronounced Jourdon and Rhina husband and wife, but instead of celebrating their union with a kiss, a rapid pounding on the basement door had the bridal couple staring at each other in alarm.

"Who is it?" Louisa's father called out.

"Will Morrison," replied a muffled voice.

Annie's heart leapt in her chest as she drew closer to the heavy wooden entrance that had been bolted with two strong iron pegs. "Will? What do you want?"

"The sheriff, Cole, and their men have the church surrounded. They'll be closing in within the next ten minutes."

Oh no! They were trapped? How would Jourdon and Rhina get to the docks? And how did Will know they were there? Annie had been careful not to tell him where she was going that night. Had he followed her?

Turning, Annie glanced around at their small entourage. "We can provide a decoy. Louisa, if you pull up the hood of your mantle and run out the door with Daniel, the sheriff might think you are Jourdon and Rhina. Meanwhile we can help them escape out a window on the opposite side of the building."

"Yes!" Louisa cried then turned toward Daniel, whose face had turned almost as pale as his blond hair.

Shaking his head, he backed away. "No. Louisa, I'm sorry, but I can't be a part of this."

"Annie and I can be the decoys," Isaiah volunteered.

"But then who will take them to the boat?" Annie whispered.

"It's too dangerous for them to run to the boat tonight," Isaiah whispered back. "They'll have to hide somewhere else until it's safe."

"Where?" she asked, taking the white veil off Rhina's head and placing it on her own.

"There's the driftwood shack, near Paulus Point," Isaiah told her. "Louisa can lead the way."

Louisa nodded. "I've hidden people there before."

"I'll go with them," Reverend Strong said, pulling on his coat. "Godspeed to you both, Isaiah and Annie."

"And to you," Annie answered in return.

She only had enough time to blow Jourdon and Rhina a kiss; then Isaiah grabbed her hand, and they hurried up the basement steps and ran out the front door, with the shrill barking of dogs closing in on their heels.

Isaiah had been afraid Annie might trip and fall, but she held on to him with one hand, picked up her skirts with her other, and kept up at a brisk pace as they ran down the hillside into the woods—exactly where the sheriff and the slave catchers would expect them to go.

"Didn't know a woman could run so fast," Isaiah muttered when they stopped behind a tree to catch their breath.

"A woman can do *extraordinary* things when pressed to do so," Annie said, her chest heaving as she drew in another gulp of air. "Especially when being pursued by a pack of sharp-toothed, ferocious beasts!"

Isaiah grinned. "Don't worry, I will protect you."

"One bit me when I was a child," Annie said with a scowl. "I still have the scar on my hand."

The high-pitched yappy barks from the dogs on their trail grew louder, and Annie squeezed his hand and took off again, this time leading *him*.

His own adrenaline kicked up a notch, but he attributed it more to the fact he was running away with *her*, than being chased by the authorities and their hounds.

He admired her quick thinking and calm presence of mind back at the church when she'd suggested using a decoy. And her deep compassion for the fugitives she helped escape was unmistakable. No doubt someone with that much heart. . .also needed love in return. The soft longing on her face at the wedding had him wondering what it would be like to share his life with someone. But not just anyone.

Someone like. . .her.

"They're gaining on us," Annie said, her voice shrill.

"Turn left," Isaiah instructed, guiding her through the trees. "Now right. . . Left again . . . Over that big log."

Annie shook her head. "I can't."

"Why not?"

"It's too big."

Isaiah stopped up short, wrapped his arm around her, and lifted her up and over. Then he joined her on the other side and pulled her behind another big tree.

"Wait!" Annie cried. "I lost the veil. The dogs—they'll find it and—"

"Too late."

The leaves rustled and the barks were so loud, Isaiah judged them to be less than fifty feet behind. "Annie, run!"

She ran but, after a few feet, turned and bumped into him, knocking him down.

"We're surrounded on three sides," she cried. "Sullivan's Gully. There's nowhere to go but back."

However, that, too, was not an option.

Isaiah jumped to his feet as the dogs charged, but before he could step in front of her, Annie clenched her fist and shouted, "Stand down, you big bullies!"

Her stern voice rang with such authority, the dogs stopped up short and nudged one another uncertainly as if not sure what to do.

"We've got them cornered!" a voice shouted.

A rush of footsteps followed, and several lanterns lit up the clearing, one held by Simon Augustus Cole, the others by some of his men.

The sheriff entered the clearing behind them and did a double take. "What are you two doing out here?"

"I—I was out taking a walk. . .when your dogs decided to *chase* me," Annie accused.

"It's not decent for a young lady such as yourself to be out in the woods at this time of night, Miss Morrison," the sheriff said, narrowing his gaze. "Especially when in the presence of a strapping young man and unaccompanied by a *chaperone*."

Annie folded her hands together and bowed her head as if properly ashamed.

Next the sheriff turned to Isaiah. "Mr. Hawkins, do you remember what I told you about

Mr. Morrison's aim with a rifle?"

Isaiah nodded. "Yes, sir."

The sheriff let out a loud *harrumph*. "Do the right thing, lad, and ask to *court* the girl."

"Yes, sir," Isaiah replied.

"The darkies must have slipped off in another direction," Cole said, clearly annoyed. "Leave these two be and let's get a move on."

"I'm thinking I should see to it that Miss Morrison here finds her way safely back to her house," the sheriff countered.

"I *said* get a move on," Cole drawled in his thick Southern accent. "Unless you want me contacting someone higher up about your reluctance to help."

Sheriff Davis glanced over at the slave catcher, his face rigid, then bowed his head, much like Annie had. "No need to be saying stuff like that, Cole."

"Then give me the proper respect I deserve," the slave catcher taunted.

"Yes, sir," the sheriff muttered.

"What was that, Sheriff?" Cole said with a smirk.

"I said. . .yes, sir!" the sheriff repeated with more spunk.

"That's what I like to hear." Cole chuckled then looked at Annie with a glint in his eyes that had Isaiah bristling. "I trust you can escort Miss Morrison home, Mr. Hawkins, with her reputation intact?"

"Yes, sir!" Isaiah said, copying the same tone as the sheriff, so as not to rile the slave catcher's temper.

"Good man, Mr. Hawkins," Cole said with an approving nod. Then he turned around and, with a wave of his hand, motioned his men onward.

Isaiah released his breath, unaware he'd been holding it.

Beside him, Annie did the same then met his gaze in the moonlight and smiled. "We did it."

"We did," Isaiah said with a grin. "And you faced down a dog."

"A whole pack of dogs," Annie agreed, smiling broader. "And they cowered before me."

"Like the sheriff cowered before Cole," Isaiah said, recalling the lawman's expression. "He's afraid of him. We might be able to use that to our advantage."

"How?"

"I don't know."

Annie tilted her chin up, and Isaiah glanced at her lips and had trouble concentrating on anything other than the fact he was so proud of her and how she'd held up under such extreme pressure this night.

"Annie," he said, lowering his voice, even though they were now utterly alone. "I have something I need to ask you."

"Yes?"

He cleared his throat, drew in a deep breath, then looked straight at her. "I was wondering if I have your permission to properly court you?"

Annie laughed. "My, you took the sheriff's instructions seriously, didn't you? Please, don't tease."

Isaiah shook his head. "I'm not teasing."

"You're. . .not?"

"I've never known anyone like you," he coaxed. "You're beautiful, smart, compassionate, fast on your feet. . .and very brave."

"Now that I've faced my fear of dogs?"

"I thought you were brave even before that," Isaiah assured her. "Who else would volunteer to run headlong into the dark woods as a decoy to help others escape?"

Annie continued to hold his gaze; then her lips slowly curved into a smile, and she placed her hand in his. "You'll have to first ask permission from my father."

"I'll speak to him first thing in the morning," Isaiah promised.

Chapter 8

Isaiah arrived at Morrison's Cabinetry bright and early. He'd been unable to sleep a wink as he thought of the bridal couple hidden in the shack along the northern banks of the Hudson.

Unfortunately, the fisherman's boat Isaiah had planned to put them on had been mysteriously sunk the night before. The broken wooden mast, laden with bullet holes, swung cockeyed—the only thing still sticking above water. And Isaiah hadn't been able to find safe passage aboard any of the other sailing vessels in port to take his newly wedded "cargo" across the river. His mission this morning was to ask Mr. Morrison if he could build him a boat.

Isaiah also planned to ask about Annie.

Quick to shut the door behind him on his way into her father's shop, he rubbed his hands together to ward off the chill from the gusty wind he'd encountered on his short walk over from the livery, two blocks away.

"Can I help you?" Mr. Morrison greeted, setting down the handsaw he was using on his worktable.

Relaxing as he drew near the heat of the woodstove, Isaiah drew comfort from the cedar-scented air, produced by the fresh wood shavings scattered across the floor. The shop reminded him of his own father and how he'd whittled wooden whistles for both him and Tom one Christmas. A holiday that was fast approaching.

I'll need a gift for Annie. If she'll have me.

With the image of her smiling face vivid in his mind, Isaiah gained courage and continued forward. "Good morning, Mr. Morrison. I was wondering if I could—"

Behind the elder, gray-haired man stood Annie's brother, Will, who glanced up from the elongated cabinet frame he was hammering and gave Isaiah a friendly nod. And behind *him*. . .was a small wooden vessel with a twelve-foot mast and a strong rudder. The white sails had been tucked and tied, but they were all there, just waiting to be unfurled. His pulse leaping, Isaiah eyed the sleek design and judged it would hold about five people.

Mr. Morrison followed his gaze then asked, "Is all. . .well?"

"As well as it can be, except. . .I was wondering if I might trouble you to lend me the use of your boat?"

Mr. Morrison cast a hesitant glance toward his son then looked Isaiah in the eye. "The boat in the back belongs to Will—who has recently been recruited to help Simon Cole and the sheriff round up Southern fugitives."

Isaiah caught the warning in his tone, glanced between the two of them, and said, "I. . .see."

"What do you need the boat for?" Will asked, his eyes widening.

Mr. Morrison shook his head. "William, it might be best if you don't ask. You don't want to have any reason for Simon Cole to look at you funny, if you know what I mean."

Will scowled. "I'm tired of being left out. You know I'd never reveal any information that could put anyone in harm's way."

Isaiah walked over to stand before him. "Will, I need the boat so I can go. . .fishing. Do you think your skiff could handle a trip across the Hudson and back?"

"Yes, I believe it could," Will said, breaking into a grin. "The rigging is sturdy enough. . .and the interior can hold a lot of *fish.* I started building it several weeks ago, thinking I might have to do some fishing myself. No chance of that now."

Isaiah glanced at the boat again. "Think you can help me cart it down to the docks?"

"That might be too dangerous," Mr. Morrison protested. "I can go with you."

Will frowned. "Dad, with your leg?"

"I've got a limp, Will, but I'm not feeble," Mr. Morrison said, tapping his cane. "I may not be able to run like you and Annie, but I can help this young man take the boat off the wagon and set her in the water."

"Sir, there's something else I would like to speak to you about," Isaiah said, and his stomach broke into a fit of excited but nervous jitters. "I'd like to speak to you about. . .Annie."

Mr. Morrison smiled. "My daughter speaks very highly of you."

"I was hoping you might allow me the privilege of—"

Before Isaiah could finish, the front door to the shop opened, and a gust of cold air swirled inside, along with Simon Cole and three of his men.

"Ah, Mr. Hawkins," Cole drawled. "Just the man I wanted to see."

"Oh?" Isaiah hesitated, exchanging a look of alarm with Annie's father. Then, giving Cole his full attention, he said, "I can't imagine why."

Cole took a few steps closer. He reeked of alcohol and stale cigars. "I want to offer you a job, that's why. I heard you are no longer working on the ferry, and I decided you might make a grand addition to my team."

"Sorry," Isaiah said, noticing Cole's men blocked the door. "I need to help my brother at the livery."

"We heard about that hefty fine the sheriff handed your brother, Tom," Cole said, and grinned. "Didn't we, boys?"

Cole's men nodded and grinned along with him.

"Must be tough, trying to come up with that much cash without going out of business," Cole pressed.

Isaiah lifted his chin. "We'll manage."

"And then, of course, there's that baby his missus has on the way."

"Baby?" Isaiah did a double take, and before he could recover his composure, Cole caught on.

"You didn't know?" Cole asked. "Well, I did just find out myself this morning. Seems Doc Riley is worried poor Mrs. Hawkins won't have enough to eat to keep both her and the baby strong. Of course, if you joined up with me, I might be able to persuade the sheriff, since we're *such* good friends, to reduce that hefty fine so's it's not such a burden on you all."

Join up with Cole?

Heat rushed up Isaiah's neck and spilled over his tongue. "I'd rather go to jai—"

The door opened behind Cole, and Isaiah's attention shot to the scantily dressed, shivering man one of the sheriff's deputies had handcuffed and brought in.

Oh no. Isaiah swallowed hard, and his gut wrenched. *Not him.*

"What have we here?" Cole asked, his brows lifted in surprise. He glanced at the shiny silver ring on the black man's left hand, let out a hearty chuckle, then slapped his thigh and announced, "Looks to me like we caught ourselves a groom! What do you think he'd fetch down south? Twenty dollars?"

"I'm a free man," Jourdon retorted.

"No," Cole said, as if the man had the intelligence of a small child. "You are a *slave*."

Isaiah bristled. He knew it didn't matter whether Jourdon was free or not. Cole would take him anyway and sell him to some wealthy Southern plantation owner. Because all Cole cared about was the money. And because the black people up north had no rights. Just like his black friend Nathaniel, whom his father had died trying to defend.

With an amused smirk, Cole turned back around, and with his eyes gleaming, he gave Isaiah another devilish grin. "What's it going to be, boy? Are you going to help me round up these darkies and reduce your brother's fine, or not?"

"Oh, Annie, it's just terrible!" Louisa exclaimed, opening the side door of the church and letting her in. "Cole's men broke into the shack in the middle of the night. Jourdon and Rhina climbed out a window and ran along the water's edge, but had to cut inland because they were being chased by the men on horseback. They just barely made it through the woods and back to town. Rhina said she pounded on the church door, but when no one answered, she remembered I'd told them about my family's house around the block."

"Where are they now? In the church basement?" Annie asked, following her down the stairs.

"Only Rhina."

"Where's Jourdon?"

Louisa's expression grew solemn. "They got him."

"Cole's men? But he's a free man!"

"They don't care, Annie. That's why all the black people need to leave Jersey City and head to Canada. Even though this is a free state, no one with black skin is safe here. Cole will take him south and sell him to the highest bidder."

Annie shuddered. "Where do you suppose Cole is keeping the fugitives?"

"There are rumors that his men guard them out in the woods somewhere. But now that they have Jourdon, I'm worried they might come back here looking for Rhina. She's not safe here, Annie."

"We can hide her in the secret compartment of your wagon and drive her down to the waterfront this afternoon. Isaiah spoke to my father and said he'd bring Will's boat around Paulus Point at three thirty. He can at least still get Rhina safely across the Hudson."

Louisa took a white envelope from the pocket of her top skirt. "In the meantime, why don't we take the old cedar path to the post office? I'm sending word to William Still, a prominent abolitionist in Philadelphia, with hope that he might be able to contact Harriet Tubman. If anyone can help free Jourdon from Simon Cole's clutches, it's her."

Annie agreed, and as they set off arm in arm, she told Louisa about how she and Isaiah had led the sheriff, Cole, and his men astray the night before.

"You should have seen him, Louisa," Annie gushed. "Isaiah held my hand the entire time, making sure I never tripped, like a true gentleman."

"Gentlemen do not run with their ladies through the woods," Louisa teased. "They take them to lavish balls and twirl them around on the dance floor."

Annie ignored her and smiled. "Then he complimented me by calling me 'brave' when I stood up to the pack of dogs chasing us."

"He did well to compliment your bravery," Louisa assured her. "I myself am so proud of you! Although I daresay Mr. Hawkins would have done better to compliment the effect you have on his *heart*."

"He may not have used words," Annie confided, her face warming by the mere thought of him. "But when Isaiah looked at me with those sparkling, gray-blue eyes. . ."

"How could you see what color his eyes are in the dark?" Louisa demanded.

Annie laughed. "I've seen them in the daylight. But the color is beside the point. The point is. . .he asked if he could court me."

"I've seen the way you two have been gazing at each other," Louisa said, smiling. "You and Isaiah will make a great couple."

"I do hope so," Annie admitted, and sighed. "Even though I know what we do is dangerous, I love how Isaiah risks his own life to help others and how he stands up to the sheriff and Cole and his men."

"Sounds like you're in love."

Noting the sudden lack of enthusiasm in Louisa's tone and in the expression on her face, Annie stopped in the middle of the path. How careless she'd been when pouring out her feelings for Isaiah to not remember that her dear friend's own relationship was in question.

"I'm so sorry, Louisa," Annie apologized. "I shouldn't have been so insensitive."

"You weren't," Louisa said earnestly. "I'm happy for you, I truly am. I've wanted you to meet someone else. . .and be happy again, for so long."

With a start, Annie realized Louisa was right—she hadn't been happy since Henry Pennington left town with that other girl. Even though two years had passed, she had not forgiven him. Until she met Isaiah.

"Any word from Daniel?" Annie asked softly.

"None." Brushing away a tear, Louisa shot a glance heavenward then gave her a forlorn look. "I'm so afraid, Annie. I'm so afraid our engagement is off."

"I'm sure it's too early to jump to conclusions," Annie soothed.

"Our views are so different," Louisa said, and shook her head. "If he can't abide my involvement in the Underground Railroad—"

Annie tensed as a boisterous laugh, undoubtedly male, carried through the trees to their right, followed by the snap of a whip.

Louisa raised a finger to her lips, warning her to keep quiet; then in silent agreement, they moved closer, edging forward from bush to bush to keep themselves out of sight. Then as they peered between the branches of a large, green-leafed rhododendron, Annie caught a glimpse of a group of men standing in a semicircle.

Amongst them was Cole, who held the whip, a few of his men whom Annie recognized from the night before, and. . .

Isaiah—

With a leather horse harness in his hands, which he put around a dark man's neck.

Was that. . . ? Annie gasped. No! It couldn't be! But the edge of the black man's ragged shirt lifted as he stumbled forward to reveal the curve of a familiar dark scar. *Kitch?*

What was he doing here? Didn't Isaiah help him escape?

Confused, Annie continued to stare at the scene unfolding before her, with dread pitting the bottom of her stomach. Surely Isaiah couldn't be one of them. Not willingly. Not after telling her about how the slave catcher had shot his father.

Unless. . .it had all been a lie.

"Hold tight to the reins and drive that darkie back to our cabin," Cole instructed. "In the mornin' we'll chain him to the others and make ready to head south."

Annie held her breath, waiting for the man she loved to stand up to the wretched Southern slave catcher, to flash him a belligerent look or show the least bit of defiance. But to her deepening sorrow, she heard Isaiah respond with an enthusiastic, "Yes, sir!"

And then. . .she saw him *smile.*

Isaiah sailed around Paulus Point and waited in the skiff, pretending to fish for over an hour. There were many other boats sailing back and forth from the Jersey City docks to the tall buildings of New York, looming above the opposite shore. It would have been a perfect day to blend in and transport his intended cargo. . .if they had showed. After glancing at his pocket watch for what seemed the hundredth time, he finally brought the boat ashore.

Where is Annie?

Fearing something had gone dreadfully wrong, he ran the distance to her house, hoping she'd just miscalculated the time.

He knew that wasn't like her, but hated the other alternatives running through his head. She was smart. Fast. But perhaps she'd had to take a detour. In which case, she wouldn't be home. . . . But when he arrived, with his heart racing and his lungs out of breath—she opened the door.

"Where were you?" he whispered. "Is the cargo safe?"

"What cargo?" she asked, feigning innocence. "We don't have any cargo here. It's best you leave, Mr. Hawkins."

Annie attempted to shut the door, but Isaiah stopped her by wedging his boot into the narrow opening.

He glanced past her into the house. Perhaps the sheriff had paid a visit and was listening in the background. "Are you. . .alone?"

"Quite."

Isaiah frowned, confused by her obstinate expression. "What's. . .wrong?"

"I won't be played a fool a second time," Annie said with a lift of her chin. "I made that mistake two years ago, and I *won't* be making it again."

"What are you talking about?" Isaiah demanded. Was she talking in code?

"I saw you today," she accused, her tone bitter. "With Cole. And *Kitch.*"

Isaiah thought back to the loathsome incident in the clearing of the woods, and he sucked in his breath. "Annie, I had no choice."

"You seemed to be enjoying yourself well enough, Mr. Hawkins. I'd thought you and I shared the same views, but it seems you were only using me as a pawn to get my family in trouble. When were you planning to turn us in?"

"I'm not," Isaiah insisted, opening the door wider. "You must believe me."

"Rumor has it Simon Augustus Cole wants to abolish those who want to abolish slavery and ruin his good business. I *trusted* you. But it appears you have done well to set me up. Worse, you did it by toying with my affection and pretending interest in a possible courtship."

"I was never pretending, Annie," Isaiah said, his throat hoarse. "And I would never do anything to place your family in trouble. Cole came into your father's shop this morning and enlisted my help, the same as he enlisted Will."

"You had a *harness* around Kitch's neck, like a *horse*!" Annie cried, her disgust in him undeniable. "If Cole enlisted you against your will, then why were you *smiling*?"

"I assure you, it was nothing but an act."

"Of course that's what you would have me believe." Annie scowled, her expression growing as fierce as the night she shook her fist at the dogs. "What is Kitch doing here? I saw you put all those fugitives on the ferry to New York, but how do I know they ever got off *safe*? How do I know you haven't been working with Cole and his accomplices this whole time?"

"I would rather go to jail than work for Cole," he said vehemently, "but I wouldn't be doing anyone any good while sitting in a cell. Cole says if I cooperate, he'll get the sheriff to lessen my brother's fine, which we need or the livery will close. And I figure if I play along and make Cole think he can rely on me, then the first chance I get, I can find a way to slip up and let Kitch and the others go free."

For a moment, a flash of doubt crossed her face. As if she almost believed him. Then she shook her head. "I'd like to trust you, Isaiah. . .but if I'm wrong about you—and my judgment in character *has* been wrong in the past—"

"You know me, Annie," he pleaded, the ache in the back of his throat nearly unbearable. "You're *not* wrong about me. I won't let you down."

Her lower lip wavered, and in her sad, red-rimmed eyes, he saw longing. And regret. "I'm sorry, Mr. Hawkins," she whispered. "But if you're working for Cole. . .then we're on opposite sides. And I can't endanger my family."

Chapter 9

Annie curled up into a ball on her bed and squeezed her eyes shut. The insides of her stomach twisted and turned, leaving her feeling hollow and empty, and incredibly sick.

What if Isaiah had been telling her the truth? What if he did have a plan to let the slaves escape? Or had she misjudged him as much as she'd misjudged Henry? Perhaps she just wasn't a good judge of character to have allowed both men to fool her so easily.

Well, she wouldn't dwell upon either one of them again. Crying over what couldn't be changed was never anything but a waste of time.

If only she could tell that to her heart.

Why, God? Why can't I find someone who loves me? Am I not smart enough? Pretty enough? Do You even care?

She'd heard some people say they heard God's voice speak to them all the time, encouraging them to do the right thing, to take the right path. Except she'd never heard God speak to her, and she didn't even know what path she was on.

Perhaps she could ask Reverend Strong to speak to God for her. Surely as a minister of the church, God would listen to *him.* Drying her eyes, she vowed to ask him right after the morning service. First, she'd sneak down to the basement and bring Rhina a jug of fresh milk and a few dried apples.

Luckily, she and Louisa had found out that Isaiah couldn't be trusted *before* taking Rhina to his boat. Staying in the church basement might be dangerous, but they'd decided Rhina would be safer there than walking straight into the hands of a suspected slave catcher.

Ignoring her parents' concerned glances, Annie sat in the back of the wagon, cuddled under a lap blanket, as they drove into town. They'd been aware of her foul, "unladylike" mood after Isaiah had left the evening before, but hadn't made comment. Since Simon Cole had arrived to terrorize the neighborhood, foul moods had seemed to run amuck. Her brother, Will, had been in a foul mood just this morning, and left, taking the horse, saying he needed to take care of something important before church.

From what she'd heard Cole say in the woods, Annie suspected he was needed to help prepare the slaves for the move south.

Indeed, the entire town seemed astir as Annie's father drove their wagon past the courthouse. A small crowd was gathered on the stone steps, between two of the four majestic structural pillars, unusual for a Sunday, when most people were focused on visiting the various places of worship. More folks hurried along the streets. And when Annie's father hitched their horse and wagon with the others in the back field, the sheriff and his deputies rode past at a furious pace, kicking dust up over everyone's Sunday best.

Shaking off her mantle, dress skirts, and bonnet, Annie slipped through the First Presbyterian Church's double doors and down the stairs to the basement. Unlatching a second door to her right, she knocked five times then entered the room where Rhina was hiding.

"I brought you milk and apples," Annie said, removing the items from the inside folds of her hooded mantle.

"Thank you, miss," a deep voice replied.

Annie jumped back. "Rhina?"

"I'm here, miss. Jourdon too. And Kitch."

Annie rolled back the rug and lifted the grate off the trapdoor beneath. Then she peered into the hole and gazed down at Rhina and the two men beside her. "Jourdon. Kitch. How. . .did you get here?"

"Mr. Hawkins made it look like one of the other men lost the keys to the handcuffs; then when Mr. Cole went to search for them, Mr. Hawkins and young Mr. Morrison helped us escape."

"When?"

"Early this mornin'."

Was *that* where Will had gone? To help Isaiah?

"You're not wrong about me," Isaiah had told her. *"I won't let you down."*

His words from the day before filled her with guilt. *Oh, why didn't I believe him?* And joy. Now that she knew Isaiah was a man of his word, she also realized he must have been telling the truth about how he felt about *her*. He'd said, *"I was never pretending, Annie."*

"What about the other fugitives Cole captured?" she asked, her spirit lifting as she handed down the food.

"They were freed as well," Louisa said, rushing into the room. "Simon Cole is storming mad and searching the entire town. It's best everyone stays hidden."

Rhina, Jourdon, and Kitch nodded, and Louisa replaced the grate and straightened the braided rug overtop.

"I—I need to find Isaiah," Annie said, heading for the door.

"Come with me," Louisa said, grabbing her hand. "I think I saw him sit in one of the pews toward the back."

Isaiah searched the congregation seated inside the church and spotted Annie's mother pulling both her and Louisa into the space beside her in the front row. He'd have to wait until the sermon was over to speak with the woman he'd come to adore.

And tell her he'd willingly go to jail rather than help Cole, if it meant she'd forgive him and believe his feelings for her were true.

Ironically enough, Reverend Strong had picked this Sunday to preach about the enslaved Israelites and how Moses, being led by God, had asked the Egyptian pharaoh to "let his people go."

Would the story inspire the abolitionists in the congregation to take action against Cole and demand he let the Southern fugitives go?

From the scared, nervous looks flitting around the room, Isaiah didn't think so. Especially when Cole burst through the front doors, disrupting the service, and ordered his men to search the entire building.

"This is a disgrace!" Reverend Strong thundered from the pulpit. Turning toward the sheriff, who also entered the church, he demanded, "Are you going to let him get away with this?"

The sheriff grimaced. "I'm bound by the law to help him."

"Then *break* the law," Reverend Strong said, shaking his fist in the air. "And do what you know by God is right."

Tensions in the room escalated when someone called out, "Found them!" and Rhina, Jourdon, and Kitch were hauled into the middle of the assembly.

"This church is the real disgrace," Cole taunted. "Led by a preacher who'd rather break laws than abide by them. Instead of a fine, I think this man needs some time behind bars to contemplate the seriousness of his actions."

Sheriff Davis hesitated, and despite the chill in the room, a bead of sweat ran down the side of his face as he took out a pair of handcuffs. "Reverend Strong, I'm placing you under arrest."

"Chances are, he didn't act alone," Cole drawled, releasing a grin. "Lock up the missus, and their daughter too."

The congregation let out a collective gasp, and all who were sitting jumped to their feet. Including Annie.

"No!" she cried, as the deputies tried to pry her hands away from her friend.

Isaiah worked to make his way toward her. If she spoke out too loudly, the sheriff and his men might decide to lock Annie away too. But from the roaring chant of hostile voices, it appeared a mob had formed outside the church, and when someone threw in a flaming torch. . .

The mass exodus of people turned everything into utter chaos.

Annie found herself swept out the door with the rest of the crowd, like a small piece of kelp caught in the current of an angry sea.

The mob who had incited the incident threatened to burn down the church! *God's church.* For providing a safe haven for fugitives! And instead of standing up to them, the congregation had run away in fear. Annie was scared too. Afraid for herself; for her best friend, Louisa; for their families; and for her community.

Dear God, what has this world come to?

Annie frowned, her wits shaken. Indeed, where *was* God in all of this? Didn't He see what was going on? Wasn't He going to send someone to stop the madness?

"I'm sending you."

The words popped into her head like a soft whisper. At first, she didn't know if she'd imagined it or if someone beside her had actually spoken the words aloud. Surely it couldn't have come from. . .

God?

She glanced upward, still not sure she'd heard His voice, but with firm resolve, she knew in her heart and with every fiber of her being that if no one else would speak out against the injustice surrounding them, then by golly, she *would.*

Despite the risk it might pose to her family.

"Stop!" she cried, spinning around. If only she could get at least one person to listen to her. "Can't you see what Simon Cole is doing to us?"

But she was too short to be either seen or heard. An insignificant voice from an insignificant person. Or was she? Squeezing through the crowd, she climbed atop the back of a wagon someone had parked along the street and surveyed the scene on either side of her.

To the south stood the courthouse, where the laws that were enacted were supposed to protect the rights of the people. To the north stood her beloved church, with its tall, illuminated bell tower pointing toward the heavens. And in the middle, standing on the street before her, stood Simon Augustus Cole, crowing like a celebrity as he tore off Kitch's coat and threw him down in the dirt by her brother's feet.

"This is the second time this here darkie has slipped away from me," Cole said, tossing Will the whip. "Why don't you teach him a lesson?"

Annie glanced at the whip and at poor Kitch, anticipating the worst. But in a surprise move that brought joy to her heart, her brother tossed the whip back toward the slave catcher, and in a clear voice that turned many heads, he said, "I will *not.*"

"Are you defying my order, son?" Cole asked, narrowing his gaze. Turning toward the crowd, he said, "Anyone who protects one of these slaves is no better than a slave himself. And disobedient slaves deserve to be *whipped*!"

Annie's heart nearly stopped when Cole drew back the tail end of the long, brown leather whip, preparing to strike, his eyes targeting her brother. But before the slave catcher could lash out, another man stepped forward and took Will's place.

Isaiah! Oh no, not my Isaiah!

Annie winced. The same moment, a shot rang out. Opening her eyes, her gaze flew first to Isaiah, who remained unharmed—*thank the Lord*—then toward the shattered remains of Cole's whip, strewn on the ground. Noticing everyone else had turned toward the direction from which the shot had been fired, she followed their lead and spied her father, leaning against the side of his cabinet shop, a long-barreled rifle in his hands.

"Simon Cole would make slaves of us all," her father said, addressing the crowd. "But there won't be any whippings on *my* watch."

"Nor mine," Annie said, and spun around to face the slave catcher straight on. "Simon Cole, how *dare* you treat people that way! It's inhumane!"

"You—a mere woman—dare to judge me?" Cole growled, spotting her atop the wagon. "You have no more right to speak to me than one of these slaves! Women are to remain silent."

"I will not!" Annie protested. "The people in our town have remained silent too long already, while you've searched our homes, fined and jailed our loved ones, and enslaved us in *fear* with your cruel bullying."

"That's right!" someone shouted supportively from the edge of the crowd. Daniel. With an outraged scowl, he was weaving through the crowd, his gaze steadfast on Louisa, who stood handcuffed with her parents in the sheriff's company.

Encouraged, Annie pointed toward Jourdon. "That man, whom Cole has bound, is *not* a slave. He is a free man."

Cole rolled his eyes and let out a derisive laugh. "You have no proof."

"Neither do you have proof that he *is* a slave," Annie argued.

"I do not need proof," Cole countered. "The law says my word is good enough."

"I'll give you proof," Isaiah said, walking toward the three fugitives. First, he asked Jourdon for his papers and held them up in the air. Then he walked toward Kitch and pulled a square, folded paper from *his* front shirt pocket. "This letter was sent by courier just seven days ago." Addressing the crowd, he read, "*I, Benjamin DeWitt, heir of DeWitt Manor in South Carolina as of December 1st 1851, upon the death of my father hereby declare, that the former slave by the name of Kitch, a tall, robust black man identified by a horseshoe-shaped scar on the lower right side of his abdomen, is released from his service to this plantation to go henceforth into the world. . .a free man.*"

Kitch was free? Annie could hardly believe it!

Neither could Cole. "Rubbish!" the slave catcher sneered. "The letter is a phony. Probably given to him by one of the abolitionists."

"No!" Annie protested. "The letter is real. Kitch, lift up your shirt."

Heads strained to lean over each other as the crowd watched Kitch lift the hem of his shirt to reveal the large horseshoe scar that had been branded into his side. Several people turned their faces away in horror; others couldn't help but stare. But the murmur that erupted among them clearly showed they were dismayed.

So was the sheriff. "Let me see that letter, Mr. Hawkins."

When Isaiah handed it to him, Annie saw the sheriff wince.

"Benjamin DeWitt and I studied at The Citadel in Charleston together," Sheriff Davis announced. "This *is* his signature."

Knowing the lawman was afraid of Cole, she prompted, "Are we going to continue to let Mr. Cole intimidate us?"

"No, we are *not*," the sheriff replied.

Taking a key ring from his pocket, he took the handcuffs off the wrists of Louisa and her parents. "Reverend Strong, my apologies. I cannot arrest you for housing free men."

"What about the woman with them?" Cole protested. "They haven't proved *she's* free."

"Simon Cole," the sheriff announced, "as a disturber of the peace, you are no longer welcome in this town. I suggest you leave or I'll have my men put you on the next train south. And. . .if you *ever* show your face in Jersey City again, I'll arrange to have some false charges trumped up against *you*."

The entire crowd buzzed with excitement as they murmured back and forth to one another, followed by clapping and several cheers.

"What about *this* man?" Isaiah asked, grabbing hold of a red-faced little fellow, who looked like he'd wanted to slink away unseen. "He's the one who incited the mob to burn down the church."

"Arrest him," the sheriff ordered, motioning toward his deputy.

"And these three?" Annie asked, pointing toward Rhina, Jourdon, and Kitch.

The sheriff looked at the three fugitives and said, "May God go with you. . .as you head *north*."

"Yes, sir," Kitch said with a big, toothy smile. "Thank you, sir."

As the sheriff walked over and released them from their bonds, Annie's heart soared, making her feel floaty, exuberant, almost giddy with both relief and joy.

This was who she was meant to be—someone who helped others and gave a voice to those who had none. . .slaves. . .women. Perhaps others would like to join her, and together they could make a difference for future generations.

Isaiah broke through the crowd, and although she knew it would be most unladylike, she picked up the hem of her petticoats, climbed over the side of the wagon, and ran to him like a wayward tramp. Her bonnet flew off her head backward, but she didn't even care! Her heart beat fast, leaving her breathless and excited all at the same time, as if by confronting Cole she'd just faced a *hundred* dogs!

"Annie, you were amazing," Isaiah said, his gray-blue eyes gleaming as he swept her up in his arms and twirled her around. "I'm so proud of you!"

"So am I," Will said, coming up from behind and looping an arm around their shoulders.

"I was so worried for you both when Cole raised that whip!" Annie exclaimed.

"Lucky for us, your father is a mean shot with his rifle," Isaiah said with a grin.

Annie glanced over at her father and mother, their faces overwhelmed with emotion as they crossed the street to make their way toward them, past the sheriff, past Louisa and Daniel, Reverend and Mrs. Strong, and around Rhina, Jourdon, and Kitch.

"It wasn't luck," she said, her heart swelling with gratitude for all the wonderful family and friends who populated her life. "I'm convinced it was God's plan all along."

Chapter 10

The day after their release, Jourdon and Rhina waited along the banks of the Hudson River, in the late afternoon, for their journey across the water to their "promised land." Kitch had come down with Isaiah and the Morrisons to say goodbye but had informed them he wasn't ready to cross over into Canada quite yet.

"What will you do?" Isaiah asked.

Kitch gave him a toothy smile. "Tell your brother I's found out where your friend is bein' held down south, and I's gonna go fetch him."

"I'll be sure to tell Tom," Isaiah promised, his throat tight. "We can't thank you enough."

"Goin' to get my own brother too," Kitch confided. "Seein' 'em go free will be all the thanks I's need."

Isaiah glanced at Annie as Jourdon took Rhina's hand. The boat should have been here by now. Had something happened to waylay Will?

Unperturbed, Jourdon suddenly broke into song.

"Swing low, sweet chariot,
Coming for to carry me home.
Swing low, sweet chariot,
Coming for to carry me home."

From the north, a deep woman's voice joined in like a faint echo upon the water, and a moment later, William Morrison's small skiff sailed toward them through an opening in the fog.

Isaiah frowned. "Who is that with him? The woman singing?"

"An angel," Kitch said reverently.

Annie smiled. "Harriet Tubman, the Moses of her people, come to take Jourdon and Rhina home."

Isaiah didn't think the legendary lady was much bigger than Annie. Her left eyelid drooped a bit more than her right, but her face glowed with an internal light as she stepped out of the boat to make their acquaintance.

"Heard about what you two did," Ms. Tubman said, looking at both him and Annie as if sizing them up. "Makes me look forward to coming through your station."

"You mean. . .we might be working together?" Annie asked, surprised.

Ms. Tubman nodded. "When I need to pass this way."

"It was Annie who helped rally the town to finally take a stand," Isaiah said proudly.

A faint rose color blushed Annie's cheeks as she said, "We might not be able to end slavery, but we can help fight the evil in our little part of the world."

"Indeed, we can, Miss Morrison," Harriet Tubman agreed.

Isaiah glanced again at Annie, as he'd done at least a hundred times already this day, and knew it was time to make his own stand.

Just as soon as his nerves calmed down long enough to allow him to speak.

Annie sighed as the bridal couple climbed into her brother's boat with Ms. Tubman, who would be accompanying them north. She wondered what kind of life they would have in Canada. Which led her to think of her dear friend Louisa, who had made up with her fiancé, Daniel, and was due to wed the following spring.

"If there's hope for us, there's hope for you too," Louisa had told her.

Except, Isaiah kept glancing away every time she looked at him. They hadn't made eye contact once. He hadn't smiled at her either.

"Annie," he said, taking her elbow and drawing her aside. "Can I have a word?"

Oh no. His face was too serious, and she feared he might say something awful, like he might be leaving with Kitch to go find his Southern friend and bring him home. Or that the livery hadn't been able to pay the fine, and he and his brother would be relocating elsewhere. Or. . .maybe he just didn't like her anymore. . .the way she hoped.

Her knees wobbled as she waited for him to say something. It wasn't like him to dawdle. "Isaiah, say what's on your mind and get on with it," she said, searching his face for a telltale sign that he still cared.

Smiling, he turned his head and gave her a direct look that shot straight into her soul and lifted her spirit so high, she thought she'd lift right out of her boots.

"I'm sorry I didn't stand up to Cole sooner," Isaiah said, taking both her hands in his.

Annie held his gaze. "I'm sorry I didn't trust you."

"If I'd been in your shoes, I wouldn't have trusted me either," he assured her. "But I hope you trust me now, when I tell you—I love you, Annie Morrison."

Warmed by the words she'd wanted to hear, she smiled with relief. He wasn't going to leave her behind, she was sure of it now.

"I'm quite fond of you too, Mr. Hawkins," she said, bursting into a smile.

Isaiah quirked his brow. *"Fond?"*

"Did you express to my father your wish to court me?" Annie teased.

"No, I did not," Isaiah said, shaking his head.

She hesitated. "You didn't?"

"I asked his permission to ask for your hand in marriage," Isaiah said, the confidence in his voice returning.

"Marriage?" Annie gasped. "What did my father say?"

Isaiah chuckled. "He said I have his blessing, if I can convince you to accept my proposal."

"He did, did he?" Glancing behind her, she caught her father's eye and laughed when he gave her an encouraging wink.

"Annie," Isaiah said, dropping to one knee before her. "Will you do me the honor of becoming my wife?"

He looked so handsome, with his dark hair flopping over his forehead and waving in the cool, gentle breeze. "Isaiah," she said softly, her voice choked with the amount of happiness bubbling up from within. "I love you too."

"My dear lady," he admonished, "you *still* have not answered my question."

"Yes, I will marry you," Annie said, then frowned. "As long as we are agreed that I can continue to speak my mind."

Isaiah grinned then stood and held her gaze. "I wouldn't have it any other way."

Drawing closer, he pressed a light kiss upon her lips that sent Annie's hopes soaring and her heart silently singing the song of the slaves she'd helped escape, a song of joy and promise for those who believed in a better life, a better future.

The song of hearts set free.

Darlene Panzera is a multipublished author, speaker, and writing coach of both sweet contemporary and Christian inspirational romance. Her career launched with *The Bet*, a novella included in bestselling author Debbie Macomber's *Family Affair*, which led her to publish nine more titles with Avon Impulse, a division of HarperCollins. The final installment of her newest three-book series, Montana Hearts, debuted May 2016. Darlene is also a member of RWA and serves on the board of the Northwest Christian Writers Association. When not writing, she loves spending time with her husband and three kids, serving her church, teaching at conferences, and feeding her horse carrots. Learn more about Darlene at www.darlenepanzera.com.

Freedom's Flight

by Penny Zeller

Cast thy burden upon the LORD, and he shall sustain thee:
he shall never suffer the righteous to be moved.
—PSALM 55:22

Chapter 1

Ridge Gap, Tennessee
1856

Annalise Van Houten followed her aunt and uncle toward the First Church of Ridge Gap, Tennessee. The stately brick building loomed over an otherwise modest town square.

Yet for all of the church's opulent outer appearance, inside its doors, hypocrisy reigned. Hypocrisy that Annalise wanted no part of.

She cast a glance across the street and up the road. A steeple rose above a humble white church. It reminded her of the church she attended with her parents in Virginia before their deaths.

A place of true worship.

"Come along, Annalise, or we shall be late," Aunt Lavinia rebuked.

At twenty years of age, shouldn't Annalise have a right to choose where she wished to worship?

Not if I am constantly under the control of Aunt Lavinia and Uncle Phineas.

"Aunt Lavinia, might I attend the church just up the road for this time only?"

And all the other times until I'm at least ninety-five...

Aunt Lavinia stopped and turned abruptly to face Annalise. Thankfully, Uncle Phineas was discussing with one of the elders the rewards for runaway slaves.

"Surely you jest, Annalise. First Church has always been our church. Why would you desire to go elsewhere?"

Retorts came to Annalise, most of them unacceptable to Aunt Lavinia. Half-truths filled her mind. But she couldn't, wouldn't lie. "I—"

"Are you doing your best to shame our good name by attending a paltry church with no parishioners of high social standing?"

"No, I just... It reminds me of the church I attended with my parents."

"Feeling nostalgic, are you?" Aunt Lavinia narrowed her eyes, but they seemed to soften for one brief moment.

"I promise, Aunt Lavinia, that no one in our social circle will be the wiser as to my choice in where to worship. Nehemiah can deliver me to the front door and retrieve me when it's over."

"What if the church you wish to attend has a longer service? We won't be waiting around for you."

"I would not expect you to, Aunt Lavinia."

"Won't you miss being able to discuss individuals' fashion, or lack thereof, with the other women in the congregation, as we do at our church?"

Not in the least. Besides, they are your friends, not mine. Annalise hadn't been able to make any friends in her new home. She pushed aside the disheartening thought. "I promise to sit in the back of the church and watch the door for Nehemiah. Have him retrieve me when the services at First Church have concluded, and I will leave posthaste."

"I really should ask your uncle." Aunt Lavinia turned her perfectly coiffed head toward her husband. "On second thought, he is in a deep discussion with Percy Hiram." She lowered her voice and rolled her eyes. "You know how they get when they discuss runaway slaves that have made it all the way to Canada. Phineas becomes a sourpuss for the remainder of the day. Best not to ask him anything if you desire a favorable response."

"I agree. Perhaps this is a situation better handled without him."

Did I really just say that? Annalise rebuked herself for allowing the words to tumble from her mouth.

"I suppose you are right. Run along then."

Ten minutes later, she found herself in the back pew of the Ridge Gap Bible Church. Due to her tardiness, parishioners were already singing hymns when she arrived. The sound of their voices lifted to the Lord filled Annalise's heart, and she merged her voice, singing with devotion to her Savior.

The church was full, almost to capacity. Annalise noted immediately that she stood out among the rest of the women with her elaborate dress. A few glances her way made her feel self-conscious, but she quickly dismissed the thought. Finally, she was in a place where she could fully worship the Lord.

A handsome young man approached the weathered podium and introduced himself as the Reverend Matthias Sorenson. His love for the Lord was evident as he began to preach. What a contrast between the sermons of Ridge Gap Bible Church and First Church!

All was quiet at supper. That is, until Aunt Lavinia decided to speak. Annalise watched her aunt dab at the corners of her mouth with exaggerated fanfare. "Annalise, your uncle and I would like to announce a guest who is coming for a visit tomorrow evening."

Annalise inwardly groaned. Aunt Lavinia's "guests" were never a good thing.

"His name is Dale Hiram, and he's the son of an esteemed acquaintance, Percy Hiram." Aunt Lavinia tapped her long nails on the table. "You would do well to make it a point to be gracious and congenial."

Uncle Phineas glowered from across the table. "Not like the immature actions you indulged in with the last fine young gentleman your aunt attempted to introduce to you."

Annalise shivered, even though the house was stifling from the high humidity. Beulah, one of the slaves, did her best to fan the family, but the constant flow did little to reduce the summer heat. The man Aunt Lavinia had attempted to introduce to Annalise last time was far from a young man. At least forty in Annalise's estimation, his eyes had traveled up and down her body, and his leering expression had caused vomit to rise in her throat.

"Don't be too harsh with her, Phineas. She is young and naive as to the importance of finding a suitable husband."

"She's twenty years old. Hardly a child," growled Uncle Phineas.

"True, and I was embarrassed for days by her actions. The women in our social circle fussed unmercifully." Aunt Lavinia's wide forehead puckered. "It took some time to rectify the situation." She paused and let out an exaggerated sigh. "Annalise, please do attempt to appreciate that we only want what is best for you. Or do you intend to be a spinster and reside here in our home upon our merciful act of charity for the remainder of your days?"

Never would I desire such a fate! But Annalise didn't allow the thought to escape her mouth. While she never would have chosen to reside with her aunt and uncle, it was the only home she had, and Annalise didn't wish to suddenly become homeless.

"Move the fan faster, Beulah," snapped Aunt Lavinia. "I declare. If you do not do better than the ghastly job you are doing, we will have no choice but to sell you."

Annalise tossed Beulah a sympathetic glance. The poor woman was doing her best. How her hand could not fall off from the constant motion was beyond Annalise.

Uncle Phineas scowled. "I never wanted her in the first place. We inherited several slaves from your parents when they died, Annalise. We have six of them left in this household. Many were sold because of their refusal to do an adequate job."

"And many of them," quipped Aunt Lavinia, pointing a long, crooked finger at her niece, "had to leave because you became friends with them."

The accusation made Annalise's stomach hurt. She had always thought of the slaves they owned as friends. Yes, her parents had kept slaves, but they were treated well. Of course, Annalise's parents were godly Christian folks. Her aunt and uncle were the opposite. They called themselves Christians, but none of their behavior exhibited such beliefs. Wealth and power were their only concerns.

"Did you hear what I just said, Annalise?"

"Yes, ma'am."

"Good. Then you'll do well to treat the slaves as they deserve to be treated."

As animals? As less than human? Never.

"You should be grateful we allow you to live here at all. Your father was not on the best of terms with his sister. And I, quite frankly, never cared for the man," sneered Uncle Phineas.

Nor did he care for you, Uncle Phineas.

"True, indeed." Aunt Lavinia tapped her nails on the table. "Your father and I were never close, and he made his feelings known about his disapproval of my marriage to Phineas. It's only out of the goodness of our hearts that we allow you to live here with all the freedoms most people wish for."

Freedoms? What freedoms? You allow me to live here only to manage the funds left behind by my parents.

Annalise bit her lip. To retort would do no good. She'd tried it once.

That was the day she had realized just how evil her aunt and uncle could be.

That night was the same as many nights at the Thorn household. Annalise's only reprieve from her aunt and uncle's watchful eyes was when she turned in for the night. Her small room on the second floor was her sanctuary.

Her lady's maid, Jinny, helped Annalise into her nightdress. The tears began to fall.

Tears over the loss of Annalise's beloved parents. She missed them so! Why had the cholera taken them so soon?

Why hadn't God taken Annalise too?

Such a fate would be far better than what she now had to endure.

Tears over leaving her life in Virginia, only to be brought here to reside with Aunt Lavinia and her horrid husband, Phineas.

Grief over the way the slaves at the Thorn household were treated. Abuse of the slaves was rampant. Beatings, a daily occurrence. Whenever Uncle Phineas tired of any of the slaves, he merely sold them to the highest bidder.

If they survived his wrath.

Annalise's parents had never once sold a slave. They had never once allowed one to be beaten.

Only six of the Van Houten slaves remained—Beulah, Jinny, Tandey, Nehemiah, and two other male slaves in the fields.

Annalise had never condoned slavery. But what could she do?

How could one person make a difference?

And with Aunt Lavinia and Uncle Phineas watching her every move, she had no freedom.

Lord, I beseech Your help, for right now, I feel helpless.

Chapter 2

Annalise walked down the boardwalk and past the shops. The freedom of having five minutes without the presence of Aunt Lavinia's oppressive personality refreshed her. She would certainly take advantage of the few minutes while her aunt chatted with one of her high society friends.

"Hello, Miss Van Houten." Sheriff Bleyer interrupted Annalise's thoughts.

"Sheriff."

The sheriff swaggered toward Annalise and cornered her. Something about his stance and unrelenting stare left goose pimples on Annalise's arms. He was a man of the law, so surely she was overreacting. "Tell me, Miss Van Houten, how are you takin' to attendin' Ridge Gap Bible Church?"

Was it Annalise's imagination, or was there a note of sarcasm in the sheriff's voice? "It is a Christ-loving church."

"So you enjoy attendin'?"

"I do."

How did the sheriff even know she attended the humble church? As soon as the question popped into her head, Annalise pushed it aside. Of course he knew. Nothing was a secret in Ridge Gap, least of all when Phineas and Lavinia Thorn's niece decided to attend another church.

How scandalous!

"From what I understand, you've been attendin' for the past two weeks now." His never-blinking, gimlet-eyed stare unnerved her.

"Sheriff Bleyer, I have every mind to believe you are interrogating me."

The sheriff appeared shocked. "Not at all, ma'am, not at all." He turned and gestured toward the Ridge Gap Bible Church. "Just wonderin' how you like the place is all."

"I like it fine, Sheriff. Perhaps you should attend sometime."

"No thank you, ma'am. I prefer First Church," he said, a self-righteous gleam in his hardened hazel eyes. "Have a good day."

Annalise watched Sheriff Bleyer strut down the boardwalk. Why had he chosen to intimidate her?

Matthias saw her from his position near the mercantile.

The lovely woman who had attended church services twice now.

But she didn't take any notice of him. Instead, she chatted with Sheriff Bleyer.

The enemy.

Matthias watched the woman point in the direction of the church. Was she discussing something she'd discovered about the church with the sheriff?

Something akin to three members of the church assisting slaves in escaping to freedom?

Worry niggled at him.

The last thing they needed was to have their plans exposed. Too many lives were at stake. Matthias thought he had paid close enough attention to the newcomer. Now, he wasn't so sure. Traitors, as he knew full well, didn't look the same. Cloaked in dishonesty and selfishness, betrayal was second nature to them.

Which was why Matthias couldn't afford to be gullible.

He should have made time to ask her about herself last week. But the parishioners had been overly eager to discuss the sermon afterward, depriving him of the chance.

"Reverend, so nice to see you." Portly Mrs. Robinson bustled her way out of the mercantile and nearly collided with Matthias.

Matthias reluctantly drew his eyes from the scene of the woman and Sheriff Bleyer. "Hello, Mrs. Robinson. Nice to see you as well." Matthias grunted inwardly at how unconvincing his voice sounded. Not at all fitting for one leading the flock.

"Why, Reverend, if my eyes don't deceive me, I would say you might be captivated by that young lady."

Could Mrs. Robinson speak any more loudly or be any more obvious? Matthias knew red crept up his freshly shaven face.

Lovely woman? Yes. Captivated by her? Perhaps. A possible threat? Yes.

Mrs. Robinson glanced from him to the woman, then back to him. While Mrs. Robinson was a dear woman, she quite often partook in gossip. Should she truly believe Matthias was "captivated," as she said, word would spread throughout the church—and the town—within minutes.

"Now, Reverend, there is no shame in being mesmerized by a lovely young lady's beauty. Why, when I was a few years younger, my husband—you do know that Harold and I have been married for forty years, don't you?"

"Yes, ma'am." Matthias kept his gaze on the woman, but his attention on Mrs. Robinson.

"Anyhow, when I was a few years younger, long before Harold and I married, Harold was enchanted by my loveliness. I was quite comely, and he could scarcely take his eyes from me when we were introduced that fateful day. Now, forty years and four months later, we are still happily joined in matrimony. That could happen to you too, Reverend. Even if that lovely young woman is far above your station."

Far above his station or not, Matthias had no interest in a woman who might endanger those seeking freedom and those who helped them attain it.

That evening, Matthias pushed the food around on his plate. Betsy had done a fine job making the meal, but he just wasn't hungry.

"You're in deep thought," observed Betsy.

"Haven't spoken a word all evening," added her husband, Adam.

"What's on your mind, Matthias?"

Matthias eyed his younger sister. So often, he had given thought to what would happen to her if the opposition knew.

He must never allow her to be implicated. He would take complete and utter responsibility before he allowed her to even be accused.

"Did either of you see the woman who has been attending church these past two Sundays and sits in the back pew?"

"The one in the fancy gown?"

"Yes."

"I noticed her too," added Adam. "Never seen her at our church before. What do you reckon she wanted?"

"Perhaps to worship?" teased Betsy.

"Funny, Bets. I'm concerned about why she was there," said Matthias.

"It's a peculiar day when we become concerned why folks attend church." Betsy let out a soft laugh then continued, her overly large eyes appearing even larger. "I admit I wondered who she was as well. Folks of high society don't usually attend our church. Maybe she meant to attend First Church and became lost."

Matthias didn't think that was likely, but he didn't mention it. Always the optimist, his sister likely would think him absurd for even considering the woman's affiliation with the enemy. "Did she appear to be listening to the sermon?"

"Devoutly," answered Betsy. "Matthias, what is this all about?"

"I saw her speaking with Sheriff Bleyer today."

Adam stopped chewing his roast chicken and narrowed his eyes. "She was speaking with Sheriff Bleyer? Did you happen to hear the conversation?"

"No. But I did notice her pointing to the church."

"Oh, Matthias, you are always such a distrustful sort," declared Betsy. "She probably needed directions."

"My concern is that she may have been sent by Sheriff Bleyer, Phineas Thorn, or one of the others to find out if we are involved in assisting the slaves to freedom."

Betsy tilted her head to one side. "Because she was merely speaking to Sheriff Bleyer?"

"Bets, I know you try to see the best in others, and I commend you for that. But sometimes we have to be realistic."

Adam nodded. "Especially after nearly losing our lives with Gene's deception."

The three were the only ones who knew the details of their former friend's treachery. Had the Lord not been watching over them, Matthias and Adam would have already been hanged or, at the very least, been doing time in the county jail in their former town.

"I watched her for a while, well, as best as I could with Mrs. Robinson doing her best to distract me."

Betsy began to laugh. "That Mrs. Robinson is quite ornery."

"That she is. Of more serious concern, we can't have anything or anyone thwart our plans, and with Sheriff Bleyer nosing around..."

"Oh, Matthias. You're so leery. The woman may have heard that you have wonderful sermons and how you encourage folks to live for our Savior. You do have a reputation here in Ridge Gap."

Matthias knew Betsy was only good-naturedly chiding him. Still, he couldn't let go of his worry.

"Trust, Matthias, just trust."

"I'm trying, Bets, but it doesn't come easy."

"Cast thy burden upon the Lord, and he shall sustain thee: he shall never suffer the righteous to be moved." The words from Psalm 55:22 burrowed into his heart.

Now if only his mind could believe it.

Chapter 3

The following Sunday, Annalise again attended Ridge Gap Bible Church. After a month of listening to Pastor Sorenson's sermons, she found herself digging deeper into God's Word and full of gratitude that Uncle Phineas and Aunt Lavinia allowed her to continue attending the church.

She had also exchanged pleasantries with some of the other folks at the church. Perhaps they would accept her, even if she was not at all like them. For they had the most important thing in common—Jesus.

Without hesitation, Annalise had become friends with Betsy Woods, Reverend Sorenson's sister.

One afternoon after church services, Annalise wandered outside, waiting for Nehemiah to retrieve her. She scanned the road. Where was Nehemiah? Of course, with her aunt and uncle deciding not to attend church today, Annalise could have been forgotten.

She returned inside and heard soft voices.

"The Faith Train will be leaving again in two days." Reverend Sorenson's voice.

The Faith Train?

"We still need more clothes for the runaways. Betsy, do you have enough fabric to sew three pairs of trousers and three shirts?"

Runaways? As in runaway slaves?

"I do. That's a lot to sew in such little time."

"Perhaps one of the ladies from church could join you in sewing. You could mention that the clothes are for the less fortunate in our community," suggested Reverend Sorenson. "That is the truth," he added.

"Indeed," answered Betsy, "I have just the person in mind. Annalise Van Houten has considerable experience in sewing from her boarding school days. I can tell her it's for the less fortunate, and I am sure she would be willing to assist."

Me?

Annalise sucked in her breath and willed her heart not to pound loudly enough for the others to hear. *Why would they be speaking of such delicate matters as runaway slaves? Could they not get caught and hanged if someone other than me had crept back into the church?*

"You must be sure not to tell her who will be the true recipients of the clothes," said Reverend Sorenson. "We don't know if we can trust her. She is Phineas Thorn's niece after all."

Why could you not trust me? Annalise shoved the pang of disappointment aside. *I certainly did not ask to be Uncle Phineas's niece.*

"I'll not let on," answered Betsy.

Lord, please don't let them hear me. . . .

Annalise tiptoed her way to the door and pushed it open. She stepped into the sunlight once more. Had she really just heard a conversation about runaway slaves?

Nehemiah arrived then and escorted Annalise into the carriage. Two things were for certain: More than anything, Annalise wanted to be part of the Faith Train and aid the slaves. And for some reason, she desired Reverend Sorenson to know he could trust her. Even with such a sensitive matter.

"I never imagined I would use the skills I acquired at the boarding school to sew clothing items for the less fortunate," said Annalise. She and Betsy had spent the morning stitching trousers and shirts.

Would her new friend someday tell Annalise the truth of who would wear these clothes? That they were likely so the slaves had a change of clothes for their first days of freedom?

Betsy giggled, interrupting Annalise's ponderings. "Nor had I imagined that I would be sewing at all, given that I abhorred such a task until I was married and had no other choice."

The sewing circle was the one place that Aunt Lavinia allowed Annalise to frequent besides church. In Aunt Lavinia's mind, the sewing circle furthered Annalise's chances of marriage in the near future by advancing her sewing skills. Annalise would take any opportunity that presented itself to be free of the strict confinement of the Thorn Plantation.

And help the "less fortunate" at the same time.

She hadn't admitted that the sewing circle contained only her and Betsy.

"I am thrilled you accepted my invitation," said Betsy. "It has been delightful getting to know you through church."

"And you as well." *Not to mention finding out tidbits about your older brother.*

But although Reverend Sorenson was a handsome man who obviously loved the Lord, one thing was clear. He did not trust Annalise or her intentions.

Never had she been more thrilled to be a part of a plan to free those so wrongly held in captivity. Mother and Father would be proud. Although they owned slaves, they never treated them the way Uncle Phineas, Aunt Lavinia, and their friends did. Annalise had prayed long and hard that the Lord Almighty would show her a way to make a difference.

And show her, He had.

A noise interrupted the women's comfortable camaraderie and conversation. Annalise peered out the window at the wagon that had just arrived.

"It appears Matthias and Adam are here for the midday meal." Betsy placed her stitching on the table.

"May I help you prepare the meal?"

"Certainly."

Grateful that Betsy never judged her because of her privileged circumstances and the fact that Annalise had never prepared a meal in her life, Annalise rose to assist her friend.

Reverend Sorenson entered the room while Mr. Woods remained in the wagon. "Betsy, Miss Van Houten."

Was it Annalise's imagination, or did his startling warm gray eyes hold her gaze for a tenth of a second?

"Reverend."

Reverend Sorenson turned his attention to Betsy. "Reckon we are behind on the delivery, so Adam and I will have to take the food and eat it on the road."

"Give me just a moment, Matthias, and I will have it ready."

Annalise stared out the window. Why had Mr. Woods not entered the house with Reverend Sorenson? Why had he remained in the wagon, swiveling his head about as if on the lookout for something or someone?

A slight movement in the back of the wagon caught Annalise's eye. She fixated upon the canvas tarp covering the goods to be hauled to the next town. Annalise moved closer to the window and leaned her head toward the glass. Was an animal in the back of the wagon? Something moved again, an ever so slight ripple under the tarp.

"Miss Van Houten?"

Reverend Sorenson's voice interrupted her investigation. Without taking her eyes from the tarp, she answered a simple, "Yes, Reverend?"

"What is it you are staring at?"

"I seem to detect some movement in the back of your wagon." She returned her focus to him.

His brows knit together in concern. "A movement, you say?"

"Yes. There it is again."

Just then, a dark head came from under the tarp. Annalise saw the full features of a man. Mr. Woods abruptly turned and said something to the man, and the man again hid beneath the tarp.

"Reverend, did you know there's a man in the back of your wagon?"

Reverend Sorenson squinted out the window.

"And Mr. Woods just spoke with him."

Betsy and Reverend Sorenson shared a knowing glance and the reverend shook his head, as if answering an unspoken question.

"Here's the meal, Matthias. Have a safe trip." Betsy excused herself and rushed to the side of the wagon. Mr. Woods planted a hurried kiss on his wife's waiting lips.

"Miss Van Houten, I reckon you won't repeat anything about possibly seeing something in the back of the wagon. Do I have your word?"

Possibly seeing? My eyes certainly did not deceive me.

Was it more of a request or a demand? Annalise had never heard Reverend Sorenson take on such a somber tone. Even when he spoke of serious matters in his sermons.

"I won't say a word to anyone."

"You will put countless lives at risk if you mention anything you have seen or imagined that you saw."

"I certainly didn't imagine seeing anything. I did, however, see a man poking his head up from under the tarp. A slave to be exact."

Reverend Sorenson appeared to be pondering his next words. He took a deep breath. "I pray you say nothing of what you saw here today, Miss Van Houten."

Who would she tell? It wasn't as though she had many friends in Ridge Gap, and she rarely spoke of anything of real importance to Uncle Phineas or Aunt Lavinia. "Why are you transporting a slave?"

"Sometimes the Lord calls us to save a life. It is my prayer that you don't jeopardize that."

"Reverend Sorenson, I know about the Faith Train. I overheard you, Betsy, and Mr. Woods speaking of it. But believe me, I won't breathe a word to anyone. I've also figured out that the clothes I am sewing are for the runaways. Am I correct?"

Reverend Sorenson's concern was apparent in his troubled features. "How do I know I can trust you?"

"Rest assured, Reverend, you can trust me. I like slavery no more than you do."

"How can that be when your uncle owns more slaves than anyone in the area?"

The insinuation caused Annalise distress, and her face reddened. "I am aware of my uncle Phineas and his wicked ways, and I assure you that I am nothing like him."

"Bets never should have allowed you to sew clothes with her today."

Annalise prayed she could tamp down the anger that rose within her. "Why ever not?"

"Because if she hadn't, you would not have seen the cargo. We should never have been so careless."

"Reverend Sorenson, please believe that I will not tell a soul about the cargo."

His voice was soft, barely above a whisper. He leaned closer and looked Annalise directly in the eye. "I must be able to trust you."

Annalise wasted not a moment in her response. "You can."

Reverend Sorenson eyed her with apparent mistrust before hurrying to the wagon. Within minutes, he and Mr. Woods traveled out of sight.

Leaving Annalise to wonder if the reverend believed a word she had promised.

Less than an hour later, barking dogs interrupted Annalise's focused attention on her sewing. She and Betsy were nearly finished for the day, and Nehemiah would be arriving any moment to retrieve her. Betsy hadn't spoken a word about the slave or about the "delivery."

And Annalise hadn't asked.

Her mind still pondered Reverend Sorenson's words. He didn't trust Annalise, and oh how she wanted to earn his trust.

"Oh dear!" exclaimed Betsy. "Try not to speak much. These men are rather abrupt and awful in their accusations."

"What men?"

Before Betsy could answer, two men on horseback with dogs yapping at their heels stopped at the house and pounded on the door.

Betsy's nervous demeanor from just seconds before switched into a relaxed and calm disposition. Holding herself with considerable poise, she stood and opened the front door. "May I help you?"

"Yah," scowled the first man. "We're bounty hunters lookin' for a runaway slave."

The other man nodded but said nothing. Instead, he perused the room.

"The slave is about yay high," the first man said, holding his hand in the air above his own head to indicate the height of the slave. "Large nose, missing a front tooth. Have you seen him?"

"I have not. My friend here and I have been sewing all morning, and it's been rather quiet."

"How 'bout we come in?" Without awaiting Betsy's answer, the two men forced their way into the house, nearly toppling Betsy off her feet.

"My husband and brother will be returning soon." Betsy fetched the rifle from its place.

"No need for weapons, ma'am. We're just lookin' for a fugitive slave is all."

"I've told you I haven't seen him." Betsy kept the rifle trained on the men, and Annalise had no doubt her friend would use it.

Annalise's heart raced. The men could mean them harm, and no one would hear their cries for help.

"Have you seen any slaves?" the man asked, coming a little too close to Annalise. The foul odor on his breath combined with dank body odor nearly made her vomit.

Lord, please make my voice calm. "I have not. But I will keep my eyes open for such a person."

"You sure neither of you ain't seen him? A farmer down the road told us he saw the slave come this way. There's a hefty reward for him."

"We have not seen him," said Annalise, grateful that her voice did not quiver.

"If you do see him, be sure to let us know. We'll be stoppin' back by this evenin' or tomorra mornin'."

"We will do that," answered Betsy.

The men and their dogs retreated, leaving Annalise quite sure her legs might topple right out from underneath her. "What a frightening experience."

"Yes, it was."

"I take it those men have come here before?"

"Never when Adam and Matthias weren't here, until today."

"Betsy, please answer me honestly: Are you, your husband, and Reverend Sorenson a part of the Faith Train?"

Betsy offered a stoic expression.

"Reverend Sorenson doesn't trust me not to tell anyone. I would never do that, Betsy. Never would I put lives at stake."

Betsy sighed. "I know you wouldn't, Annalise. You proved that today."

Now if only Annalise could persuade Reverend Sorenson to believe her.

Chapter 4

Annalise heard him before she saw him. His abrasive voice echoed through the front parlor.

She cringed.

Dale Hiram, the son of the wealthy Percy Hiram and one of the most callous men Annalise had ever had the misfortune to meet, was a guest at the Thorn Plantation.

Annalise attempted to scuttle past the front parlor and up the stairs to her room.

She didn't succeed.

"Annalise, is that you?"

She stopped, one foot on the bottom stair, and held her breath. If she failed to answer, would Aunt Lavinia forgo the question?

"Annalise, come into the front parlor," demanded Uncle Phineas, his obnoxious voice booming throughout the house.

Annalise squared her shoulders and gathered her courage.

And prayed.

Dale Hiram sat at the far edge of the parlor, his cognac-colored eyes seeming to stare right through her as she entered the room.

"Aunt Lavinia, Uncle Phineas, Mr. Hiram," she greeted.

Aunt Lavinia nodded her head toward Annalise. "Do come in and sit a spell. Mr. Hiram is here as our honored guest."

Honored guest, indeed. Annalise did her best not to show her true opinion of the man she had met thrice before. She sat on the sofa and placed her hands in her lap.

"Mr. Hiram has been discussing his interest in both the Thorn and Hiram futures. As you know, he is quite wealthy in his own right. Furthering that wealth would be of substantial benefit to both the Thorns and the Hirams."

Of course. Uncle Phineas can think only of monetary topics and the furtherance of his massive wealth.

"I've been successful in obtaining more acreage and slaves. Soon I will be the wealthiest man in the entire state." Mr. Hiram steepled his fingers and leaned back against the sofa.

If you think you are being impressive, Mr. Hiram, you are sorely mistaken.

Mr. Hiram leered at Annalise, his eyes traveling from her head to her toes and stopping somewhere in the middle. An eerie grin formed on his overly thin lips.

Annalise shivered, although the temperature in the mansion was far from frigid.

One look at Uncle Phineas, Aunt Lavinia, and Mr. Hiram brought Annalise a frightening revelation. They intended for her to be courted by the very man she despised.

Chapter 5

"Miss Van Houten?" Annalise was nearly out the church door to wait for Nehemiah when she heard Reverend Sorenson's voice.

"Hello, Reverend." Warmth crept up her face. Why did he seem to have some odd effect on her? It wasn't as though he liked her. He certainly didn't trust her.

"Tell me, what brings you to Ridge Gap Bible Church?"

Annalise shifted and peered out the front door. Was Nehemiah here to retrieve her? Best not delay if he was. Aunt Lavinia and Uncle Phineas having to wait even for a minute could cause them to decide she couldn't attend the church of her choice. "I appreciate your profound sermons, Reverend."

Reverend Sorenson eyed her with suspicion. Did he wonder why she continued to gaze about, searching for the Thorn carriage? "Thank you. It's important to me to preach directly from the Bible."

"And you do a fine job of it, to be sure." Annalise took another glimpse out the church door. No sign of Nehemiah yet. Perhaps Aunt Lavinia had been delayed while speaking with one of her friends.

"So how is it that you came to live with Mr. and Mrs. Thorn?" His voice wasn't accusatory, but there was a slight edge to his words.

"Aunt Lavinia is my father's sister. When my parents died, I came to live with them. I unfortunately had no other choice."

His handsome face still held suspicion. But should it be a shock? Many in Ridge Gap weren't fond of Uncle Phineas and his pompous and vile personality.

"I'm sorry about your parents." His expression softened with compassion.

"I am nothing like the Thorns." Had those words just passed from her lips?

"I would reckon not."

Had his opinion of her changed since that day at Betsy's house? That would relieve Annalise. His opinion mattered to her. She again gazed out the door.

"Are you looking for someone?"

"Yes. Unfortunately, if I am not ready to leave right when Nehemiah arrives at the door, I may not be able to attend this church in the future."

"We wouldn't want that. I wouldn't want that."

Reverend Sorenson's gaze held hers.

And Annalise's heart beat faster, if that were possible.

People waved their goodbyes as they passed, but Reverend Sorenson remained standing directly in front of Annalise.

Peculiar that she found herself rather enjoying their camaraderie. "This church reminds me a lot of the church I attended with my parents when I lived in Virginia."

Reverend Sorenson's mouth turned upward. "Might I take that as a compliment?"

She returned his smile. "Absolutely, Reverend, for it is a compliment, to be sure."

At that moment two things happened: One, Nehemiah arrived with the carriage. And two, the conversation marked a turning point in Annalise and Reverend Sorenson's association.

Over the next three weeks, Matthias found himself looking forward to seeing Annalise Van Houten at church. They had decided to call each other by their given names and had spoken about a variety of topics during their few precious moments while Annalise waited to be retrieved by the Thorns.

The Thorns.

While Matthias had grown fond of Annalise, the realization of her relationship with Phineas Thorn concerned him. Surely someone as likable, smart, and lovely as Annalise wouldn't betray him and the Faith Train. Would she?

And beautiful she was. There was no doubt that Matthias was drawn to her. If only he could trust her.

Chapter 6

Over the next few weeks, Annalise and Betsy grew closer, and Annalise began to see more of Matthias. At times he would assist Adam on the small farm where the house was located. At other times, Matthias mentioned taking deliveries or visiting those who needed his assistance. Annalise knew what that meant because of her accidental eavesdropping. If only the reverend would trust her to help with the runaways.

Then maybe she could make a difference in the lives of others.

And be part of the Faith Train.

What would he say if she asked him?

Annalise wandered out to the porch when she heard Matthias's wagon approach. Perhaps if she caught the reverend after one of his "deliveries," he might be amenable to granting her request.

"Good afternoon, Annalise." Matthias flashed her a handsome smile, and she did her best to maintain her composure. Goodness if the man wasn't dapper! There was something about him that caused a pleasant jittery sensation deep within her stomach.

With a struggle, Annalise reminded herself of the task she wished to undertake. "Good afternoon, Matthias."

"Reckon I've been on my feet most of the day. Care to sit a spell?" Matthias pointed to the two chairs on the porch. He gazed about the property from left to right.

Annalise nodded. "Thank you."

"I want to thank you for not telling the bounty hunters about the cargo in the wagon." He paused. "Betsy told me."

The admiration in his voice touched her. "You are welcome. Was the man a runaway?"

"Annalise, your parents owned slaves, correct?"

Matthias must have discussed this with Betsy, for other than Annalise's aunt and uncle, only Betsy knew. "Yes, but—"

"Then it's possible that you might have the same opinion about owning slaves."

"My parents were quite different than Uncle Phineas." Annalise struggled to keep her voice low. How dare Matthias insinuate that her parents were evil like her uncle!

"Truth is truth, Annalise. You live at the plantation and see the treatment that the slaves receive. Phineas Thorn is known for being one of the most brutal slave masters in the state, and you are his niece."

Annalise felt the color rising in her cheeks. "I do not know how to convince you that I am nothing like Uncle Phineas. My parents owned slaves, yes. But they treated them kindly and with dignity. I grew up with the friendship of two of them—Jinny and Tandey. Who, by the way, I would love to see escape. To suggest that I am like my uncle is the worst misrepresentation of the truth I have ever known—a complete falsehood!" She stood. "I'd best be gathering my sewing items. Nehemiah will be here soon."

Matthias stood and reached for her arm. "Annalise, please understand. I must be cautious. So many lives are at stake."

"If only you knew how I detest the prospect of slavery. While I am not a slave, I do know a thing or two about lack of freedom, for I experience it every day. Mind you, it is nothing like the slavery you seek to eradicate, but it is a form of bondage I shall endeavor to escape from. They even intend to tell me whom I shall marry." The thought of Dale Hiram disturbed her.

Her pulse raced and her mouth grew dry. Matthias's insinuation brought about a range of emotions from anger and sadness to frustration and anguish.

"Annalise." He fixed his gaze on hers. "I'm sorry if I offended you. You must understand."

"While I am not usually prone to temper, I'll not understand your position in accusing me of being someone I am not."

Matthias took a deep breath. "All right then. Yes. The man you saw was a runaway."

His remark caught her unawares. Did he finally believe her? Feeling guilty that it took nothing short of a tirade to convince him, Annalise offered a prayer seeking forgiveness—combined with a prayer of gratitude. "And is the runaway—the cargo—is he safe now?"

"That I don't know. My role is only to transport them to the next place and pray. God takes care of it from there."

"So you do not know the other people aiding the runaways?"

"No. It's safer that way."

"Might you have a position for me within the organization?"

A flicker of something crossed his face. Uncertainty perhaps? Lingering fragments of mistrust and doubt? "Annalise, you need to understand that the Underground Railroad can be dangerous. If someone is caught aiding a slave's escape, they can be jailed, flogged, hanged, or worse."

"I'm willing to take that chance. I desire to serve the Lord in this way and make a difference."

"There aren't any open positions."

"Surely, Matthias, there must be something I can do."

Matthias rubbed his chin. "You can assist by continuing to sew clothes for the runaways. But you cannot tell anyone, Annalise. I'm taking a risk just by telling—and involving—you."

"I won't tell a soul." She paused, grateful for the change in his opinion of her. It mattered for more than fulfilling her desire to make a difference. It was important because she truly wanted him to think well of her.

"But are you sure there isn't something more I can do? It seems so insignificant."

His kind eyes searched hers. "It is far from insignificant. Each part done to aid this cause is important. Each person on the Underground Railroad has a different role to perform. If one role remained unfilled, the entire plan would fail." He paused. "Are you familiar with 1 Corinthians 12:12–27? It discusses how each part of the body is important and no less critical than any other part—just as each person in the body of Christ. So it is with the Faith Train. Sewing clothes for the runaways is as important as transporting them. It's just a different role."

"I only want to make a difference in the lives of others."

"And you are, Annalise. You are."

Matthias's words meant more to her than she could ever explain.

Chapter 7

Over the following weeks, Annalise spent more time at Betsy's house sewing clothes for the runaways. Aunt Lavinia continued to believe it was a sewing circle, and Annalise prayed the Lord would forgive her for omitting the complete truth.

And lying about the man in the wagon.

Matthias had given a sermon last Sunday about how, while God does not excuse lying, it can be necessary to save a life as did Miriam and Rahab in the Old Testament.

Not only was Annalise aiding the Faith Train, but she was also coming to know a great deal more about the man who was winning her heart.

A man of the cloth named Matthias Sorenson.

"Care for a walk?" Matthias asked one afternoon.

Annalise set down her sewing needle and fabric. Today had been productive. "I would love a walk."

Together they strolled through the privacy of Betsy and Adam's property. The birds chirped, and the air smelled of pine. "Thank you for your hard work on the clothing."

"I'm thrilled to be putting my skills to good use. My mother would be proud."

"You miss your parents."

"I do. They were dear people who loved the Lord and were taken home far too soon. What about you? Where are your parents?"

"They are in Ohio."

"And do they work for the Faith Train as well?"

Matthias shot her one of his grins. "Yes, they do. But again—"

"It's a secret. I know. Have I ever in the two months I've been assisting shared any information with anyone?"

"Reckon you haven't." He offered his elbow, and she placed her hand through it. It felt natural to be walking through the forest with him. She had grown to appreciate his wisdom, his sense of humor, and his passion for assisting the downtrodden.

They stopped a short distance in front of the river. "They say that when the runaways cross the Ohio River, they are crossing the Jordan River," he said, watching the clear water trickle over the rocks.

"I can see the parallel."

"As can I." He turned toward her and took both of her hands in his.

Annalise figured her heart stopped right then and there.

"Annalise, I know we come from different stations in life, but I reckon I enjoy spending time with you."

"I do too, Matthias."

"If we are ever caught in what we do..."

"God will protect us."

"Annalise, if we are ever caught in what we do. . .if it's God's will that we are caught, promise me something." He rubbed his thumb on her hand.

Her knees felt weak from his touch. How could she even speak at a moment like this? "All right," she whispered.

"Promise me you will not come forward and state your role on the Faith Train. Act as though you know nothing. Promise me."

"But what if you go to jail. . .or worse?"

"Promise me you won't tell of your involvement. I need your word, Annalise."

"I—"

"Promise me."

"All right, Matthias, I promise you, but. . ." *I've grown quite fond of you and wouldn't want to see anything happen to you.*

"Thank you."

They stood facing each other. Annalise wished he would kiss her. Wished they could court each other and plan a future.

For he was the man she was quickly growing to love.

Matthias wished he could kiss her. Not a tiny peck, but a true kiss telling of his affection for her. During the many hours spent with her at Betsy and Adam's house and those times spent after church services while she awaited her ride home, Matthias had grown fond of her company. She amused him with her sense of humor. Tugged at his heart with her tenderness toward the slaves. And her beauty was an added benefit.

If only they could court. But it wasn't possible. He was a poor preacher who didn't even own a home. And she was a wealthy Southern belle whose aunt and uncle expected her to marry well.

Still, he would dream. . .and pray about such an opportunity with the woman of his affection.

Without a second thought, Matthias reached over and stroked her cheek. Her blue eyes gazing back at him were almost his undoing. What would it be like to spend every moment with her? To love her and care for her? To have her as his mate, not only in marriage, but also in his work on the Faith Train?

Don't be a cad, Matthias. Such thoughts are too unlikely for you to even consider. "Matthias, what will I do if they make me marry Dale Hiram?"

"Dale Hiram?" Matthias shook from his daydream of loving Annalise forever to the unpleasant thought of one of his biggest nemeses.

"I fear Aunt Lavinia is pushing for us to court. I cannot court him, Matthias. I cannot."

"Surely they would not force you to marry someone you do not love."

"You don't know them." A tear glistened in her blue eyes, making them twinkle even more than usual.

That couldn't happen. Not when he wanted to court her and someday make her his wife.

Whoa. Marriage? Matthias shook his head. Too soon for such thoughts. But didn't a man sometimes know—truly know—that God had picked someone just for him, even after a short while?

Annalise shifted, and without another thought, he took her into his arms. He knew not what to say to alleviate her fears of having to marry Dale Hiram. He knew not how to solve what could become a horrible life sentence for Annalise.

So instead, he held her close, never wanting to let her go.

Chapter 8

Annalise heard voices downstairs and cringed. She always detested it when Percy Hiram, Dale Hiram, Edgar Oret, and her uncle had their "secret" meetings. Coarse words and copious imbibing always took place. Slaves, especially the women, were even more mistreated by Uncle Phineas and his cronies during these "secret" meetings. Annalise dared not be in their presence during these times. Even Aunt Lavinia found somewhere else to be. Annalise cocked her ear toward the conversations and thought she heard an additional voice.

She tried to identify the voice. She hadn't heard it often, but it seemed familiar.

Then it came to her.

Sheriff Bleyer.

The thought of the lawman participating in the evil Uncle Phineas and his friends concocted made Annalise's heart race. She had always suspected there was something not quite right about Sheriff Bleyer, even more so after his interrogation about her church attendance.

Annalise crept down the staircase as quietly as she could manage. Her stockinged feet padded on the wood steps as she gripped the handrail.

As if it could protect her.

She remained on the alert, glancing frequently to and fro as she proceeded toward the library, where the men were.

"I know there's somethin' goin' on with that Reverend Matthias," said Sheriff Bleyer. Then a pause. "Pour me another drink, Phineas."

"Good thing your deputy is handling matters tonight, Bleyer. Wouldn't do you any good to get caught drunk," chortled Percy Hiram.

Annalise heard the chink of a bottle hitting a glass. She kept her head pressed back against the wall, even though the temptation to jut her neck forward a bit and see what was going on was almost impossible to resist.

"I agree with you on the good reverend," snarled Uncle Phineas. "He's too friendly toward slaves. Even saw him helping one who had dropped her load of parcels from the mercantile once. I say we do something about it."

Sheriff Bleyer's voice seemed too eager when he answered, "Like what?"

"You're the corrupt sheriff, you think of something," snapped Percy Hiram. "If we get him out of the way, the church will no longer be a problem. I reckon others in that *place of worship* should be hung for assisting slaves."

"Don't your niece go there?" Edgar Oret asked.

"Yah, I seen her there 'afore," said Sheriff Bleyer. "Asked her about it once. She didn't give no indication she thought somethin' was amiss. But then, she don't seem like the most intelligent woman."

Annalise narrowed her eyes. She was indeed an intelligent woman! For just that comment, she ought to let Sheriff Bleyer know her opinion. But she stuffed down the pride that reared within her and continued to listen to the conversation.

Dale Hiram slurred his words. Too much whiskey perhaps? From the odor floating up the stairs, it would appear the men had overindulged in cigars as well. "Why don't y'all do something about that niece of yours, Phineas? Make her stop going to church or something?"

Annalise bristled. No one, not even the tyrannical and dictatorial Uncle Phineas, would stop her from attending church and worshipping God.

"Don't you see, Dale? Having her there can help us."

"How so?"

"She can be a spy of sorts."

Never.

Sheriff Bleyer let loose a mean laugh. "No way is she gonna agree to that. She ain't like you, Phineas."

"True. She is too much like Lavinia's brother." Uncle Phineas's voice rang harsh in Annalise's ears. "A pathetic coward if there ever was one."

How dare you!

In preparation of spitting, Percy Hiram hawked, a gross sound that made Annalise cringe. Pity the slave who would have to spend an inordinate amount of time scrubbing the hardened sputum from the wood floor. "Can't believe you don't make that girl mind you better. If you'd force her to marry Dale, all this would be solved. She would finally be controlled the way she ought to be."

The thought of marrying Dale Hiram sent shivers of nausea from Annalise's head to her toes.

A sound made Annalise jump, causing her to smack her head against the wall.

"What was that noise?" Percy Hiram asked.

"I'll go take a look-see," offered Sheriff Bleyer.

Annalise sucked in her breath. If she thought marrying Dale Hiram a nightmare, she could only imagine what Uncle Phineas and his cronies would do to her if they discovered her eavesdropping on the stairs.

With the swiftness of a doe, Annalise retreated upstairs to her room. She was certain everyone on the plantation heard her pounding heart, especially Uncle Phineas.

Loud footsteps barged up the stairs. Would they find her? Realize she was the one they heard? Punish her?

Lord, please, I beg of You to protect me.

"Don't see no one," announced Sheriff Bleyer.

Annalise let out the breath she had been holding and prayed for calmness.

Moments later, she opened the door and poked her head into the hallway. No sign of Aunt Lavinia. Good. The woman was still reclining in her room.

The sounds of the men had grown louder. Annalise took a step into the hallway, keeping her hand on the doorknob of her room. For what? Security perhaps?

"Since we believe the good reverend is to blame for these most recent escapes, there is only one solution." Annalise shuddered at the cruelty in Uncle Phineas's voice.

Percy Hiram cleared his throat. "What's that?"

"We hang him for his crimes."

The men joined in a chorus of vile laughter.

"Let's enjoy the rest of our evening, shall we? Tomorrow night, we'll discuss plans to rid ourselves of that gutless namby-pamby once and for all."

"Hear, hear!"

Annalise froze. She must, no matter what the cost, listen to the men's conversation tomorrow. Then she would tell Matthias what she had learned.

Lord, grant me courage.

Not to intervene would surely put Matthias's life at risk.

Annalise tiptoed to her door and cracked it open. She had wanted a somewhat peaceful evening reading a book in the library or knitting in the parlor. She missed those quiet times of togetherness with her parents.

They would never again be possible.

And there would be no peace while she resided at the Thorn residence.

The knocker on the front door had sounded at half past seven. Sheriff Bleyer, followed by the Hirams and Edgar Oret, entered the mansion.

Annalise had spent much time praying in preparation for this very moment. The moment when she uncovered her uncle's plan to have Matthias put to death because of his work with the Underground Railroad.

Surely, Lord, that is not Your will. Matthias has been such an instrument in assisting the slaves to freedom. Lord, I beseech You to preserve his life.

The men gathered in the library, and Annalise envisioned Uncle Phineas taking the most comfortable spot in the room, the leather chair adjacent to his cherrywood desk. Rather than use the desk for writing, as most folks did, Uncle Phineas would prop his large feet on top of it, scuffing the fine wood.

It wouldn't have mattered so much if the desk hadn't been Father's cherished writing desk. The desk where he so eloquently penned poems for Mother.

Uncle Phineas's feet clomped on top of the desk, and she imagined him settling his rotund self into the leather chair and tipping the whiskey flask toward his mouth.

"Gentlemen, thank you for joining me on this fine evening."

Uncle Phineas's voice made Annalise's blood curdle. *This fine evening? The evening when you unveil your vile plans to take someone's life?*

"I've been doin' some followin' of our good reverend," said Sheriff Bleyer. "Seems he does have a way with the colored folk. Like they trust him or somethin'."

"What do you mean?"

"Yesterday, he walked by a slave and tugged on his right ear. Had to be some sorta code or somethin'. Reckon the slave seemed to understand what the good reverend was doing, for he nodded and went on his way."

"Doesn't surprise me none," interjected Percy Hiram. "Whenever folks engage in illegal activities, a shroud of deceit under the cloak of a code seems reasonable."

Uncle Phineas interrupted Percy Hiram with a curse toward one of the slaves, demanding she retrieve something to eat for him.

Likely Jinny. Poor, poor dear.

That wasn't the worst the young slave woman had experienced at the hands of Uncle Phineas.

"Where were we? Oh yes, discussing a secret code between the good reverend and a slave. That's good investigative work, Sheriff. Didn't think you had it in you."

Rather than take offense, Sheriff Bleyer chuckled. "Even a man with no law trainin' can do some investigatin' when the moment calls for it."

"Our goal is to prove that Reverend Sorenson is guilty. He has some friends that might look unkindly upon us apprehending the man and tossing him into jail for a hanging the following day," said Dale Hiram.

Annalise strained to hear the voices. Dale Hiram's, especially, was a lower, more foreboding voice. Schooled at the best of universities, and now a rich plantation owner, according to Aunt Lavinia, he would be the perfect match for Annalise.

Especially to secure the family fortune.

Annalise cringed. For one, there was likely nothing left of her family's fortune. Secondly, the only man worse than Dale Hiram was Uncle Phineas. Even Percy Hiram wasn't as bad as his evil son.

And Percy Hiram was a reprobate if there ever was one.

Sneaking forward as quietly as she could, Annalise was taken aback by the new portrait of her uncle that hung in the hallway.

Startling at the glooming glare of Phineas Thorn, Annalise jumped back. The floor creaked.

"Miss, are you all right?"

Annalise jumped again at Jinny's voice as she rushed down the hallway with a stack of clean linens. Annalise held a finger to her mouth and shook her head.

The slave woman appeared to understand. She nodded and went on her way.

But not before Annalise saw the bruise darkening beneath Jinny's left eye.

Jinny had to be next to know the taste of freedom.

Annalise slid against the wall again and did her best to listen to the conversation on the floor beneath her. The men had, unfortunately, lowered their voices.

Or perhaps Uncle Phineas had closed the door to the library.

Whatever the reason, Annalise struggled to make out any of the words being exchanged between the men.

Chapter 9

Annalise took another step down the banister. Then another.

Lord, please keep me safe.

She held her breath all the while her heart raced. Where was Aunt Lavinia? Would she emerge at any moment and catch Annalise attempting to eavesdrop?

"Now that's an idea and a half," Uncle Phineas thundered.

What idea?

She must move closer.

"Annalise!"

Annalise straightened her posture and scurried up the stairs to her room.

"Annalise!"

"Yes, Aunt Lavinia?"

"Oh, there you are." Aunt Lavinia patted her curly gray hair.

Annalise willed her heart to be still. What if Aunt Lavinia had found her on the stairs? What if...

"You look bedraggled, Annalise."

The statement was more of a chastisement than a concern. Just like most of Aunt Lavinia's comments.

"I was just preparing to retire for the night."

Lord, forgive me for that bold untruth.

"I see. Well, I thought I heard some clamor. Is everything quite all right?"

"Quite all right, Aunt Lavinia."

"Very well. It must have been your uncle and his unruly cronies."

"Indeed."

Aunt Lavinia eyed Annalise with suspicion. "Good night, then."

"Good night, Aunt Lavinia."

Please hurry and retire to your room so I can return to hear the men's plans.

Taking one more glance back at Annalise, Aunt Lavinia proceeded to her bedroom. A few moments later, Annalise heard the door close and lock.

Perhaps, Annalise hoped, the men would be drunk and would repeat their plans. She waited a few more minutes, anxiety permeating every ounce of her being. *Lord, grant me the wisdom to know when it is safe to eavesdrop again.*

With the utmost prudence, Annalise skulked down the long hall and to the top of the stairs, all the while keeping a close watch on Aunt Lavinia's door. The men's rowdy voices carried up the stairs, although Annalise was unable to discern their words. For the third time in as many days, she continued carefully down the stairs and toward the library until she could distinguish their words.

"It's a task that must be undertaken."

How much had she missed due to Aunt Lavinia's "concern"?

"I agree. Who we gonna use as the bait?"

Bait?

"How about my slave Horace? The reverend doesn't know him, from what I recollect."

"This might just work. Yes, Dale, let's use Horace. Give him the details tomorrow. Tell him if he errs, he'll be hung immediately with no questions asked. After a good beating," Uncle Phineas added.

"I'll tell Horace to act as if he wants his freedom. He'll seek the good reverend out and ask how he can be assisted in his escape endeavor. Horace will do his best to convince Reverend Sorenson that he needs his freedom. Isn't that how it all works?" Dale Hiram snarled. "Horace is a good-for-nothing slave as it is, so if he gets himself hung, he'll rightly deserve it."

"And," added Percy Hiram, "Reverend Sorenson is a good-for-nothing preacher, so it's the perfect match for a perfect plan."

Annalise gasped, covering her mouth with her hand. *This plan mustn't succeed.*

"Good. Then he's perfect for the job. Sheriff Bleyer, be at the ready to bring Reverend Sorenson to the Ridge Gap town square after he decides to help our decoy. Percy and Edgar, you start the crowds rioting about the injustice of one of our own—a reverend of all things—breaking the law. It won't take much to bring the reverend to justice. Folks won't stand for a criminal on the streets of Ridge Gap, preacher or not. As Lavinia would say, 'It's absolutely scandalous.'"

The men chuckled at Uncle Phineas's comment.

Anger rose within Annalise. How dare they make unkind comments about Matthias. And how dare they plot the murder of an innocent man.

She had every mind to barge into the library and rebuke them in the harshest way possible.

Much as the idea held appeal, it would do no good. They would likely throw her in jail for being a sympathizer. Then where would Matthias be? How could she assist the man she was growing to love?

And how could she aid in the escape of more slaves?

Instead of giving in to the temptation, Annalise retreated to her room.

She had a big day tomorrow.

Chapter 10

Never had Annalise willfully disobeyed.

God's mercy was upon her with Uncle Phineas and Aunt Lavinia in town for the day.

Lord, please alleviate the case of nerves permeating me.

For if she failed at her attempt to warn Matthias, his life—and the lives of others, including her own—would be at stake.

Annalise swung open the barn door. Tandey, the stable slave, was grooming Annalise's black horse, Eclipse. "Good afternoon, Tandey," Annalise greeted him with a low voice. "I would take Eclipse on a ride."

"Will it be the sidesaddle for you, miss?" A glimmer shone in the young slave's eye as he reached for the saddle and placed it on Eclipse's back.

"Yes, Tandey," Annalise answered with her own smirk. Besides Annalise and her father, Tandey was the only other person who knew that Annalise had, on more than one occasion, ridden bareback. The memory of Father allowing Annalise to ride bareback with him through the vast fields of the Van Houten property while Mother attended a tea party warmed Annalise's heart. He had allowed it thrice more, on the condition that no one must know that he, Hayes Van Houten III, had allowed his well-bred, high-society daughter and only child to partake in such an unladylike activity.

Annalise, of course, had agreed. Tandey, barely four years older than her and a slave who had been born on the Van Houten plantation, had taken particular delight in Father's demand for secrecy. He had laughed for minutes as he watched Annalise clutching the thoroughbred she rode.

Mother would have suffered from the vapors had she known the truth about Annalise and the bareback rides on those hot summer days so long ago. It was the only secret Annalise held from her beloved mother. A secret necessary as Mother, bless her heart, wasn't nearly as forward in her thinking as Annalise was.

Four times riding bareback for several hours each time without the irritation of that bothersome sidesaddle had made Annalise practically an expert. Under Father's patient guidance, Annalise had been convinced she could win a riding contest with the best of the best.

Although Father hadn't been *that* permissive.

Annalise smiled at the memory, thankful for the reprieve from the burdens that overwhelmed her.

Moments later, she rode slowly through the barn door and out into the open. Glancing down to ensure that her riding habit was draped carefully over her ankles, Annalise continued past slaves picking cotton in the fields, past the creek, and past the pecan grove. Riding sidesaddle was a torturously slow process.

Annalise did her best to act as though nothing was amiss on this hot and rather humid day. She held her head high, as she'd been taught in those riding classes Mother enrolled her in from a young age.

The sun was high in the sky, indicating that Annalise didn't have much time before her aunt and uncle returned home. She must hurry if she desired to be effective in her discreet warning to Matthias.

How can one hurry with this most ridiculous excuse for a saddle?

Eclipse neighed, as if he heard her question and agreed.

Some miles later, Annalise spied the cluster of trees she sought. Pulling gently on the reins, she brought Eclipse to a stop and dismounted. Then, methodically, albeit swiftly, Annalise removed the saddle and hid it safely in the center of the trees, covering it with grasses and branches to disguise its presence.

She again mounted Eclipse, thankful for the pair of tan trousers beneath her riding habit. With a light tap of her heel to his flank, Eclipse took off at a gallop. Annalise clutched the horse's mane and tightened her legs around his flank, welcoming the warm breeze.

Lord, please don't allow anyone to see me.

Rarely had anyone taken the shortcut through the forest, a path Annalise was thankful to have stumbled on while out for a walk one day.

She ducked her head, as low tree branches hovered. Birds chirped, and the smell of wildflowers filled the air.

If only she could be free like this all the time, without the constraints of Aunt Lavinia and Uncle Phineas and their desire to marry her off to someone like the abhorrent Dale Hiram.

Think not of Mr. Hiram right now. There are more demanding tasks at hand.

So Annalise thought of Matthias as she rode briskly through the trees. She thought of his warm gray eyes and his handsome smile. Of his servant's heart and his desire for justice. Of his strong arms and dapper appearance.

Of how he had almost kissed her.

Or so she had thought. Maybe she had imagined it.

Either way, no matter who her aunt and uncle desired to court and marry her, Annalise's heart would forever belong to Matthias Sorenson.

Which was why she must reach him and warn him of the slave bait plan her uncle and his comrades had concocted.

It wouldn't be much farther to Betsy and Adam's house. Annalise urged Eclipse to gallop faster, and Annalise leaned low, pretending that she was one of the contestants in the bareback races Father had taken her to during the town's Founder's Day.

Only this race was for a life.

Chapter 11

Matthias heard her before he saw her. A vision of beauty astride a black horse tearing through the pasture toward his sister's house. He rubbed his eyes and did a double take.

"Annalise?"

A mixture of elation and concern filled Matthias. Why was the woman he had recently grown so fond of riding toward Betsy's home? And bareback?

"There's something wrong," he muttered.

Betsy joined him on the porch. "Now, now, Matthias. Don't always think the worst."

"No, Bets, there is something wrong." Matthias felt it in his entire being. He marched down the two steps of the porch and hurried to meet Annalise. From the look on her face as she drew nearer, Matthias knew his assumption was correct.

Something threatened the Underground Railroad and his role in it.

"Matthias!" Her voice alone caused him concern.

"Annalise? Is everything all right?"

"May we step inside?"

Even though she had apparently ridden a great distance from her home to his, her beauty had not been compromised. A strand of blond hair cascaded near her right cheek, and Matthias resisted the urge to reach for it.

Her uneven breath that came in almost gasps caught his attention. "Are you all right?"

"Please sit and have some tea," offered Betsy.

"I regret that I don't have the time for formalities, but thank you just the same, Betsy."

Her face showed grave concern, and he longed to embrace her and tell her all would be well—to hold her in his arms and shield her from whatever burdened her.

But he couldn't very well embrace a woman he wasn't courting; nor could he reassure her that all would be fine.

For what if it wasn't?

Her blue eyes lit with fear. "Matthias, you must be careful."

"Whatever do you mean, Annalise?" Betsy moved toward Annalise.

"Matthias's life is in danger."

"Danger?" Had he heard her correctly?

Annalise's words tumbled out in rapid succession, one word overlapping the other as she laid out the trap her uncle and his cohorts were setting to catch Matthias. She told of the slave bait plan and the planned riots. Annalise leaned toward him and whispered, "They know you are part of the Underground Railroad."

"How can they know?"

"I'm not sure." She looked at him with a troubled expression. "Surely you don't think I'm the one who revealed your role in freeing the slaves?"

Matthias shook his head. "No, Annalise, I do not think you would ever share such information intentionally. However, you may have—"

The hurt in her eyes was almost more than he could bear, and he regretted his insinuation. "Annalise, it's just that you may have unknowingly—"

"Never, Matthias, never!" Her voice went up an octave, and tears streamed down her face. "You must understand that I would never lead them to you. Why would I?"

"Annalise, I'm sorry, I just. . . If they're watching you, as I believe Sheriff Bleyer to be doing, he may have ascertained my involvement—and yours."

"With so much at stake, I would be an utter fool as to allow that."

Matthias again longed to draw her into his arms to comfort her. Only this time the comfort was for the hurt he had just caused her. "I only meant that such a mishap is possible given your uncle's suspicions of you and Sheriff Bleyer's observations of your comings and goings."

"I believe this conversation is over. Matthias, I rode out here risking my life to tell you that yours is in grave danger. Don't think for a second that they will not draw you into this trap if you are not wise and disregard the slave's request. Do not give in when a slave asks for help. No matter what. Do not offer to assist him. For if you do, Uncle Phineas plans to have you hanged."

"Thank you, Annalise. Thank you for telling me. But it will be difficult for me to turn away a slave in need."

"You must. There is no other choice. It could be the very slave Uncle Phineas uses to trap you. I must go." Her voice took on a sarcastic tone Matthias had never heard from her, and her eyes narrowed. "I'm sorry if you believe I am to blame for their knowledge of your role in the Faith Train."

Before he or Betsy could respond, Annalise marched toward the door. "Goodbye, Matthias. Betsy."

Matthias wanted to go after her. He wanted to explain his error and seek her forgiveness. But she rode through the woods away from the house before he could convince his own two lethargic feet to move from where he stood.

What have I done? Lord, please forgive me.

Chapter 12

Tears flowed, spilling over her cheeks and down her neck. How could Matthias believe she had led Uncle Phineas and the others to him? Hadn't she proven herself? What more must she do to convince him?

And to think she had entertained the fanciful thought of courtship with Matthias. What a fool she had been.

Annalise continued through the woods toward home. She swiveled her head to and fro to be sure no one had seen her. That no one had followed her. Thankfully, she saw no one, save the creatures that made the woods their home. And Annalise heard no one except the birds chirping on the humid July day.

When she reached the place where she had hidden the saddle, Annalise stopped Eclipse and dismounted. Digging through the brush to uncover the sidesaddle, she placed it on her horse then started toward home. Glancing at the sun's position, Annalise knew she had little time before Uncle Phineas or Aunt Lavinia began to wonder where she had ventured.

Freedom did not exist in the Thorn household. Not for the slaves and certainly not for Annalise.

Annalise forced herself to now ride at a much slower pace sidesaddle than she had astride. To not do so would surely end in disaster when she was inadvertently bucked from the horse. As she rode at a sluggish speed, Annalise's mind reverted to Matthias and his accusation. Would her dried tears be evident to Aunt Lavinia? All the more reason to hurry home and into her room to wash her face before being called to the noonday meal.

Her heart broke into a thousand pieces. How could Matthias think she would ever lead Uncle Phineas or any of his cohorts to him? How could Matthias believe that Annalise would be so daft as to not ensure that no one knew of the covert operation of which she was now a part?

"Annalise, it's just that you may have unknowingly. . ." His words kept ringing in her ears.

"I only meant that such a mishap is possible given your uncle's suspicions of you and Sheriff Bleyer's constant observations of your comings and goings." Annalise's heart beat even faster at the thought. Had she done something to make the sheriff suspicious? She recounted her actions from the past days and weeks.

No. She could not think of a thing that would have made Sheriff Bleyer wary of her actions.

And then the audacity. . . Annalise almost said those words aloud as she recounted Matthias's other words during their conversation: *"Thank you for telling me. But it will be difficult for me to turn away a slave in need."* So Annalise had risked her life in eavesdropping, further risked her life in riding a great distance—scandalously astride, no less—and risked her life going to tell Matthias what she had overheard.

All for naught.

Annalise gritted her teeth. Had it all been in vain? It would be if Matthias decided to help the slave posing as a potential runaway in need. Why could Matthias not heed her advice? Why was the man so obstinate?

Because he has a compassionate heart.

The words impressed on her heart, but Annalise chose to ignore them. Compassionate heart or not, Matthias was downright foolish to not take seriously her words of warning.

And then to suspect her of leading Uncle Phineas and Sheriff Bleyer to the organization.

A combination of anger, irritation, and self-pity rose within Annalise. She never should have become involved in the Faith Train.

Had she even been of help?

Annalise added self-doubt to her list of emotions.

She never should have allowed her heart to be stolen by the handsome man with broad shoulders who preached the Word of God Sunday after Sunday.

Chapter 13

The stable came into view after what seemed like a lengthy trip. Annalise allowed a sigh to escape her lips. At least she was no longer crying, for the moment anyhow.

The acres and acres of plantation worked by dozens of slaves reminded her of how important her job was—even if Matthias's comment had diminished that importance in her mind.

"Annalise!"

At the sharp mention of her name, Annalise nearly fell back off Eclipse. She turned her head to see Uncle Phineas on horseback. Had he followed her? Did he know where she had gone?

Fear rippled through her.

Uncle Phineas would not show mercy, even to a relative, if she were caught helping runaways.

Annalise willed her voice not to tremble. "Hello, Uncle Phineas."

"Where have you been?" His harsh voice stirred panic in every part of Annalise's being.

So much for pleasantries.

"I said, 'Where have you been?'"

Think quickly, Annalise.

"I have been out for a ride. Such a lovely day."

Uncle Phineas stopped his horse in front of Eclipse. "Out riding where?" His evil dark eyes bored through her.

"Out yonder."

"Yonder?"

"Yes, Uncle Phineas. Is everything quite all right?"

"That depends on you, Annalise." He practically spat her name.

No surprise there. Annalise knew Uncle Phineas's feelings for her. She pondered his response. Should she feign innocence? Reply with a syrupy retort? However Annalise responded, she feared she would stir up more wrath in her volatile uncle. *Lord, please give me the words to speak.*

"It appears there is something going on that you're not telling me."

"Uncle Phineas, I merely went for a ride through your lovely property."

"Be assured, Annalise, that I will discover whatever it is that you are scheming. You are not beyond the law, no matter who you are. If you are, as Sheriff Bleyer suspects, doing something to assist slaves, not only will you be punished to the fullest extent possible, but I will see to it that every slave on the plantation takes a beating for your poor choices."

Annalise bit back her trepidation. Uncle Phineas had already punished Jinny, Tandey, and the others for her wrongdoings.

"Speaking of which, I gave Tandey a good beating today for allowing you to ride by your lonesome."

"No—"

"What is it about the slaves that concerns you so, Annalise? If you think for a moment they deserve freedom, you are sorely mistaken." He waved his hand at her. A hand that Annalise feared was about to connect with her cheek. A hand that had waved many a whip toward the backs of slaves.

She jolted back, nearly falling out of the saddle.

"Get to the house, Annalise. And no more riding without a chaperone."

Panic infused her at Uncle Phineas's condemnation. "Yes, sir."

Uncle Phineas had certainly whipped Tandey. The young man groaned as he mucked the stables. Annalise's heart broke at the sight of the lacerations and dried blood that crusted on his arms. She could only imagine what his back must look like.

Annalise breathed in with relief to see that Uncle Phineas had not followed her. She must be careful. Speaking to Tandey would only cause another whipping.

"Oh, Tandey," she whispered. "I'm so sorry."

Tandey smiled at her, his eyes kind, and nodded. "Don't worry about me none, Miss Annalise." His voice was low as well. For he knew—knew all too well—what would happen if Uncle Phineas heard him speak to Annalise.

"Someday, Tandey, I promise, I will see to it that you are freed."

Tandey assisted Annalise from the horse. "Don't speak of that, Annalise. It could put you in danger."

"I know that, Tandey, but I promise. Both you and Jinny. Then you'll be free to marry and start your own family in freedom."

A smile lit Tandey's ebony face. "If only it could be so."

"It will be, one day."

A sudden flicker in Tandey's eyes told Annalise that he dared to believe her words. Honestly, she shouldn't be making such promises. But she meant what she said. Someday her dear friends would be free.

And hopefully so would she.

Chapter 14

If Annalise had hoped to slip unnoticed into her room, she was mistaken. Aunt Lavinia lurked just inside the parlor. "Is that you, Annalise?"

"Yes, ma'am."

"Goodness, but your face looks atrocious. All red and burned from the sun. Do you not know you will cause freckling from being so irresponsible?"

Annalise reached a hand up to her face. Could Aunt Lavinia see the dried tears that scarred her cheeks? "Yes, ma'am."

"Where were you anyhow? Your uncle Phineas has the mind to punish you for taking off like that without telling a soul."

"I went on a ride about the plantation." *Sorry, Lord. I know I went beyond the plantation. Please forgive me for that minor falsehood.*

"A ride about the plantation, indeed. Does it take so long for you to do so? You do realize that your insensitive actions caused a slave to be beaten. Was it worth it, Annalise?"

Aunt Lavinia knew full well Annalise's compassion for all people, slave or free, and she chose often to use it against her niece. "It was a mere ride about the plantation. It reminded me of the times I did so with my father. *Your brother*, who was a kind and godly man."

The words came out harsher than Annalise intended, and Aunt Lavinia recoiled ever so slightly before regaining her composure.

Blame it on the dreadful day. What with the urgency of meeting with Matthias without being caught, his suspicions of her, Tandey's beating and knowing it was all her fault, and the entire ordeal of assisting runaway slaves, it was enough to thrust Annalise into a deep melancholy.

"You will not speak to me in that manner, Annalise. Remember that your uncle and I gave you a home when you were orphaned. Who else would be so patient and gracious? Your antics deserve nothing less than vagrancy. Where would you be then? Your words and your actions are drawing you ever closer to being ousted from this home. And if you are indeed contemplating assisting runaway slaves, as Phineas believes you are, you will be punished for your shenanigans. Believe you me, neither your uncle nor I will be there to rescue you from the clutches of Sheriff Bleyer."

Annalise knew that even her sun-reddened face blanched at Aunt Lavinia's words. It was one thing to be punished for her disrespect of her aunt, but quite another to be accused of assisting runaway slaves. At least Aunt Lavinia had said the word *contemplating*. Perhaps that meant that Uncle Phineas was not sure of Annalise's role in the Faith Train, but only assumed it.

Aunt Lavinia looked Annalise square in the eye. If she was awaiting an apology, it would not be forthcoming. For it wouldn't be honest, nor made with a pure heart. She bit her lip.

Lord, help me control my anger.

"Yes, ma'am," she finally said, proud of herself that she had avoided gritting her teeth while doing so. "May I go to my room to freshen up?"

Aunt Lavinia narrowed her eyes. "Yes, you may."

Annalise plodded up the stairs, careful not to make any additional noise. Not only were her steps heavy, but her heart also. When she entered her room, she collapsed on the bed.

She grasped her feather pillow and mourned. Mourned the loss of her beloved parents. Grieved that she must reside with her aunt and uncle. Lamented over Matthias's suspicions and lack of trust. Sorrowed over the punishment Tandey had received because of her choice to go for a ride. Bemoaned her own lack of freedom.

Pushing her face into the pillow, Annalise willed the tears to stop. But they wouldn't. Sobs choked her body, and her shoulders shook.

"Miss Annalise?"

Annalise hadn't heard a knock at the door. When she turned her face, she saw Jinny standing in the doorway. "Do you want that I should bring supper to your room?"

Supper sounded about as appetizing as eating a dirt clod, even if it was one of Henrietta's delicious meals. "Yes. Thank you, Jinny."

Jinny softly closed the door behind her. Taking a risk that could get her beaten or worse, Jinny sat on the edge of the bed and patted Annalise's arm. "I'm sorry, Miss Annalise."

Annalise leaned her head on Jinny's shoulder, and Jinny wrapped a thin arm around her. "Now, now. Let those tears fall."

"I'm so sorry, Jinny."

"For what?"

"Tandey was beaten because of me. Because of my choice to go for a ride. I'm so sorry."

"Now, now. Don't fret. You've been a good mistress. Always caring for us and looking out for us from the time your parents done owned us. It wasn't your fault none, but the master's."

"Thank you, Jinny, but I am sorry, and I will make it up to both of you someday."

Annalise made sure her voice was lowered. If Aunt Lavinia heard her speaking to Jinny, there was no telling what Uncle Phineas would do to Jinny. "Matthias doesn't trust me," she croaked in a hoarse whisper, forgetting for a moment that Jinny had no idea who Matthias was. "Maybe I should just marry that hideous Dale Hiram."

"Don't you dare do such a thing," Jinny gasped, her big brown eyes growing even larger with concern. "That man is horrid, and you and I both done know it."

"But if Matthias doesn't trust me—"

"Your sorrow is speaking for you now. You and I both know you have feelings for Matthias, just the same as I have feelings for Tandey. Everyone makes mistakes, and maybe his words just didn't come out right is all. I don't know about the situation none, but I'm sure this Matthias fellow cares for you."

"You're right, Jinny. I need to show him grace. He's carrying a large burden right now. It's just hard not to be doleful after all that's happened today."

"I done saw your aunt's wrath poured out on you." Jinny patted Annalise's shoulder. "Now you just cry some good tears because then you'll have to put on a happy face so as your aunt doesn't suspect you all the more."

Annalise sighed. "You're right, Jinny. Whatever would I do without you? Remember those days back at our other home? We would play with our dolls and have such jubilant times."

"Oh, I remember them days." A smile lit Jinny's sweet face.

"It was the most wonderful thing having a friend the same age."

"Yes, it was."

"Did you ever feel scared for your life at our old home, Jinny?"

"Never, not once. I did miss my mama and papa like you do now, but your folks, they took good care of me and treated me well. Almost like I wasn't owned at all."

"Thank you for being a good friend, Jinny."

"I'm always here for you, Miss Annalise. You know that. Times is tough, but the Lord, He watches over us and He has a plan. A mighty good plan for His children."

Guilt overwhelmed Annalise. Jinny's life had taken a turn for the worse after Mother and Father passed. She'd been beaten and worse at the hands of Uncle Phineas and his slave masters. "I have no right to complain after all you've been through."

"Pain is pain. We both suffered enough of it for sure. Don't you apologize none for being sad. Didn't your mama say that tears are God's way of washing all that sadness away and making way for a smile?"

"She did indeed. Jinny, do you know what we are?"

"In a whole heap of trouble if your aunt hears us talking."

"That too. But we are good friends in the Lord."

"Yes, we are, and we be praying for each other."

"Yes, and someday, somehow, I'm going to see to it that you and Tandey are freed."

Chapter 15

Matthias stood behind the pulpit, ready to preach the sermon. His eyes scanned the crowd. Would Annalise be there after his accusatory words?

Matthias swallowed hard. He never should have expressed that concern. Since he had come to know her, Matthias had realized how different she was from his first assumptions about her. He *knew* Annalise would do nothing to compromise the Faith Train, whether intentional or accidental. He knew that with every fiber of his being. Just like he knew that he was falling in love with the beautiful Southern belle with a heart for others.

Lord, please give me the opportunity to apologize.

Matthias again scanned the rows of pews. No sign of Annalise. Had she been apprehended by her uncle? Worry wormed its way into Matthias's heart.

"Cast your cares upon Me."

The prompting in Matthias's heart propelled his mind to remember the sin of worry and how it had grasped so fiercely onto him throughout his life. Wasn't that the topic he was preaching on this very day? Not to worry. Not to fret. Not to fear. But to cast all of his cares on the Lord. That the Lord would sustain him.

The last thing Matthias desired was to be a hypocrite. He had prayed time and time again that the Lord would free him from the bondage of worry and fear. For how could a man of the cloth doubt that his precious Savior would protect him? And a man of the cloth couldn't preach about it when he himself didn't live it.

Matthias shoved the thoughts of guilt aside. He hadn't slept much as of late, between his concern for Annalise, his regret over the insinuations he had made to her, and the prospect of preaching on a sermon that would likely help him more than it would help his congregation.

One of the elders cleared his throat, catching Matthias off guard, and he brought his mind to the present. His congregation stared at him expectantly, awaiting his wisdom from the Word. Matthias wouldn't fail them.

Lord, please give me the words You wish for me to speak. Help me to digest and apply each word of truth from Your Bible that I am about to quote. Free me from the fears and worries that overtake my mind. And Father, please give me the opportunity to apologize and reconcile with Annalise.

"Good morning. Let's open with a word of prayer."

After the opening prayer, the singing of several hymns, and the announcements, Matthias again took his place behind the pulpit. That's when he saw Annalise walking down the aisle toward her newfound place beside Betsy and Adam.

Thank You, Lord.

His eyes connected with hers, and she looked away. *Lord, another chance with her. Please?*

Matthias set aside the turmoil roiling inside him and addressed the congregation with a renewed sense of peace.

Annalise had been drawn in by Matthias's sermon. Oh, she was always captivated by the words of the gifted young man she had grown so fond of in recent months, but this time something about him was different. Almost as if the words Matthias spoke were directed toward something more personal.

She hadn't slept well over the past two nights, going over and over the words Matthias had said and what he really must think of her. Annalise wished she could request that he do a sermon on dwelling on a topic repeatedly. She needed advice when it came to that trap she found herself in whenever something upsetting, frightening, or irritating happened.

Their eyes had connected several times throughout the church service. Those gray eyes that carried within them a tenderness toward others that Annalise had never before seen. Those eyes that she longed to gaze into without interruption.

Annalise pulled her mind back to the service. She ought not think about such things of a man who wasn't courting her, and especially in church. Annalise offered a prayer seeking the Lord's forgiveness.

And Lord, would You please allow Matthias and I to reconcile?

When the service concluded, Matthias walked toward her. "Annalise?"

"Hello, Matthias."

"Could we speak after the other parishioners have left?"

Annalise nodded. She wanted nothing more.

It took some time for Matthias to offer goodbyes to the faithful members of his church. In the meantime, Annalise spoke to the people who had embraced her when she first arrived, even though she was different from them. Some congregants still eyed her with suspicion, but for the most part, she had been accepted because each person in the church had one important thing in common: their love for Christ.

"Thank you for waiting, Annalise."

Her heart leapt at his voice. Feelings of elation filled her when in his presence. Were she to someday marry him. . .

I can no more marry Matthias than turn Uncle Phineas into a decent man. Besides, how can I even begin to think of marriage when we are not courting? And wasn't I irritated and saddened about Matthias's words just this morning? The word *capricious* came to mind, and she almost giggled at the description of herself.

"Annalise. . ." Matthias reached to place a hand on her arm.

A swarm of butterflies zipped up her arm. "Yes?"

"I am so sorry. Please forgive me for my accusations. I sometimes become so consumed in worry about the Faith Train failing that I forget God is in control. I know I upset you with my words, and I pray you will give me a chance to make amends."

"I forgive you, Matthias. You must understand that I would never, ever do anything intentional, accidental, or otherwise to compromise the Faith Train. I have too much vested in it myself, and I care deeply for those we assist. I have been extra cautious at all times of Uncle Phineas's watchful eye."

His hand slipped from her arm to brush her fingertips before returning to his side. "I know that, Annalise. I do. I can't tell you what a huge benefit you have been to the organization. We would not have been able to accomplish as much without your help. And with your sacrifice--and I'm certain it was a sacrifice—to come and warn me about the slave bait your uncle is planning, there is no way I can thank you adequately. You may have saved my life and the lives of countless others with that act of bravery."

Matthias's eyes almost seemed misty—something one wouldn't expect from a man so masculine and seemingly tough when moving slaves through the network.

But Matthias had a tender side. A side that Annalise was quickly growing to love.

They spoke in hushed tones, for even the church could have someone listening who was set to thwart their plans. "Please promise me, Matthias, that you won't give in to the slave that Uncle Phineas sends."

"But how will I know who he is? Slaves approach me weekly with the code, expecting my assistance—our assistance—in securing their freedom. How will I know which one is false?"

"They have a slave chosen just for this purpose." Annalise wished she could recall the name of the slave. "But you are right, it will be difficult to know. Sheriff Bleyer and the others know of your code with the tugging at your right ear."

"They do?"

"Yes."

Matthias shook his head. "Then we must develop a new code."

"Yes. But until then, potential runaways will be using that code. You mustn't assist any slaves for the next few weeks until I can glean further information from Uncle Phineas and his cronies."

"A few weeks is a long time to refuse help to someone. Especially those who are innocent."

"I agree, Matthias, but it must be done. You know that."

Matthias appeared reluctant.

Lord, please help him to see.

"You are correct, Annalise. This one error could stop our entire mission. As it is, we are sending a telegram tomorrow to others in the network that we are delaying sending more slaves for the next few weeks. I don't like it, but it's something we must do. Betsy, Adam, and I spoke of it last night."

"We can again offer our assistance once Uncle Phineas has given up on his plan."

"But will he ever abandon his plan?"

Annalise doubted it. "Likely not. But in the meantime, as you say, we can develop other methods of spreading the word about how help can be accessed for those in slavery."

"Yes."

"Because, Matthias, I couldn't endure it if something happened to you. Uncle Phineas is bent on hanging you, whether a judge finds you guilty or not. And a judge would, given Uncle Phineas's influence."

"Annalise, I'm not about to allow myself to be hanged. I have too much to live for."

They stood for a moment, their eyes and hearts connected in this moment of time. Would they ever have the freedom to express their feelings toward each other? Two people from different social classes. Annalise with such strong restrictions placed upon her life by her nefarious uncle. How could they ever hope to court, let alone marry?

And did Matthias feel as she did? Annalise pushed the thought aside. There was another pressing matter.

"Matthias, when Uncle Phineas relents somewhat, promise me one thing?"

"Anything."

"Promise me we will do all we can to help Jinny and Tandey escape."

"I promise I will do everything in my power."

If the two were allowed to escape, perhaps they could marry, as they had dreamed of for some time. Something most folks took for granted.

Matthias couldn't take his eyes from her. Not only was the woman before him lovely, kind, spirited, and brave, but she was also a woman of forgiveness.

And the one who had captured his heart long before even he knew it.

"If only you didn't have an uncle Phineas, I would ask to take you on a Sunday drive."

The corners of Annalise's mouth turned up in the pleasing smile Matthias had grown to admire. "It just so happens that Uncle Phineas and Aunt Lavinia are in Knoxville until tomorrow. A Sunday drive would be most delightful."

Chapter 16

Spending time with Matthias was nothing short of a dream come true. Aunt Lavinia and Uncle Phineas so rarely left town that when they had announced their trip to Knoxville, Annalise feared she hadn't heard correctly.

Yet here she was in a buggy that Matthias had rented from the livery, traveling down the road toward a lovely picnic spot he had picked out just for them. While Annalise knew the time with Matthias would be short since there was no telling when her aunt and uncle would really return and no telling who might see them, Annalise planned to make the most of every moment.

"This is a lovely spot, Matthias."

The location for the picnic was a plush spot near a river. "I had to have somewhere special to take someone special."

Had it been only two days ago that Annalise had doubted her feelings for Matthias? Only two days ago that she had given thought to marrying Dale Hiram? *Thank You, Lord, for reconciliation.*

Matthias lifted her from the buggy. Setting her down, he held her at the waist, his eyes looking into hers. "Annalise. . ."

Would he kiss her? She hoped so! Was it scandalous that she hoped for that? They stood for what seemed like a lengthy time gazing into each other's eyes. Matthias reached up with one hand and touched her cheek. "You're beautiful."

Annalise attempted to find words to respond, but couldn't. Any response remained stuck in her throat. He leaned toward her, his lips pressing against her forehead and his arms finding their way around her waist once again. Annalise closed her eyes and relished the moment, feeling safe enfolded in the strong arms of the man she had come to care for. He smelled like a combination of pine trees and soap. Her pulse quickened, and she wondered if Matthias could hear her heartbeat.

Annalise could remain here forever.

Matthias whispered in her ear. "Shall we have our picnic?"

She leaned back and gazed up at him. "We shall."

He smiled the crooked smile that showed all the more the dimple in his chin. "I'll retrieve the basket."

With the basket of food that Betsy had prepared in one hand, Matthias reached for Annalise's hand with the other and led her to a spot by the river. "What a blessing to have your aunt and uncle out of town."

"Indeed. Although who knows how long they will be gone."

"We will make the most, then, of the time we are given." They said grace before eating the fried chicken Betsy had prepared.

"It's a frightening time with all that's going on."

"Yes, but let's not speak of that right now. Instead, let's speak of another pressing matter."

"Another one?" Wasn't all they had experienced enough?

"Yes, the pressing matter of falling in love with a beautiful woman named Annalise Van Houten."

Of all the things Annalise thought Matthias would say, she hadn't figured he would say that. Had she heard him correctly? "I beg your pardon?"

"I know you are accustomed to finery. I can't offer you that. I've been a reverend and before that a farmer. I don't have much to offer you. I don't even own a home. I do, however, own a fine horse." His mouth quirked to one side.

"I don't care if you don't own a fine home, Matthias."

"Someday—and it's looking like it might be sooner than I had expected—I will be leaving Ridge Gap. I will continue to do the work that the Lord has called me to—that of preaching and helping the runaways. Neither calling will amass a small fortune with which to support a wife and family."

"The Lord's work offers rewards much more important than money and possessions. A wise reverend once preached on that very topic."

Matthias grinned. "So you were listening."

"You didn't think I'd dare sleep through your sermons?"

"There was that one time when it appeared your head was bobbing, and I figured you to be nearly asleep."

"Well, if I remember correctly, that was a sermon on the book of Numbers."

Matthias chuckled, a deep, throaty laugh that Annalise realized she didn't want to go without hearing for even one day.

He stopped, and his face took on a serious demeanor. He reached for her hands and held them in his. "Annalise, life with me won't be easy. It will be full of worry at times and the type of adventure that can cause stomach upsets."

"Stomach upsets? Matthias, you are a romantic at heart. I know life with you won't be easy. You are making a difference in the lives of countless people. Every day, you undertake assignments, most of which I am unaware of."

"It's for your safety and for the safety of the Faith Train that we don't know the exact details, nor the others involved in the undertakings of freeing the slaves."

Such secrecy was necessary should one of them be caught and questioned. What one didn't know, one couldn't share.

"Anyhow, I guess what I'm failing miserably at trying to say is that I wish to court you and, Lord willing, marry you someday." He paused. "May I court you?"

"Yes, Matthias, yes, you may."

"I can't exactly ask your uncle for his blessing or permission, and I know he intends you to marry Dale Hiram."

"I'll not marry Dale Hiram. Ever." *Yet two days ago, you believed that to be your only option.* Annalise pushed the rebuke aside.

"I've spent time with the Lord seeking His guidance as to whether courting in secret is acceptable. If you'll have me, I'd like to make you my wife. Although, as I said, I can't offer you anything."

"You can offer me the most important things, Matthias. Your love and devotion."

"You will have both of those. You'll also have my orneriness at times."

"And you shall have mine. Along with a bit of stubbornness thrown in for good measure."

They laughed again, causing Annalise to forget that she must return to her life in short order.

"So it doesn't bother you that I don't have much? That we may have to live in a meager log cabin?"

"Will I be with you?"

"Yes."

"Then a meager log cabin will do just fine. You see, Matthias, right now I am a prisoner in the home of Aunt Lavinia and Uncle Phineas. I would prefer living in a shack in freedom than living in a mansion in bondage. Unfortunately, I suspect my aunt and uncle have squandered my inheritance, so I may have nothing to offer either. We could have used that money for so much good."

"I never loved you for your inheritance, Annalise. I fell in love with you for your benevolent heart and your willingness to sacrifice yourself for another. And, of course, your beauty." He grinned.

"I am content just to have the honor of being your wife."

"You've made me a happy man." Matthias leaned forward. "May I kiss you?"

Before Annalise could answer, Matthias had leaned forward. Their newfound love was sealed when his lips found hers in a combination of gentleness and passion.

Chapter 17

If only all of her life could be as peaceful as the Sunday and Monday that Aunt Lavinia and Uncle Phineas were in Knoxville. But it was not to remain so. On Tuesday, not only did they return, but Aunt Lavinia presented Annalise with some disturbing news.

"Dale Hiram is to be our guest tonight. You will do your utmost to be pleasant and worthy of his affections."

If only Annalise could escape the clutches of her aunt and uncle. Her mind continued to retreat to the delightful time she had spent with Matthias during their picnic. What would it be like to spend every waking moment with the man of her affections? What would it be like to make a life with him, rather than the life she was living against her will?

She might never know.

Dale Hiram arrived at the Thorn household promptly at 7:00 p.m. Annalise sat in the front parlor, awkwardly facing him as he attempted idle chitchat with her. His leering gaze and arrogant attitude induced nausea. His harsh, darkened eyes pierced through her without blinking, and his jaw was set firm in his motionless face. Mr. Hiram locked onto Annalise's shifting gaze, seemingly willing her to accede to his overt domination. Barely taller than Annalise, he exuded an air of superiority.

"Mr. Hiram, as you know, has one of the largest plantations in the area. You would do well to appreciate that he has chosen you as the future Mrs. Hiram," gloated Aunt Lavinia.

The future Mrs. Hiram? The thought caused Annalise's chest to constrict and her breathing to become labored. *Never!*

Mr. Hiram puffed out his chest. "I intend to expand my plantation to the border of Father's land. I recently purchased the acreage on the north side."

And I should find this impressive? I'm being married off to the first bidder since I no longer have an inheritance and nothing left to offer a greedy aunt and uncle.

"We feel that based on current circumstances, it would be in the best interests of everyone involved for you to begin courtship with Mr. Hiram posthaste. As Mr. Hiram and I have discussed, your wedding shall commence as soon as we are able to arrange it."

As soon as they are able to arrange it? "This is highly unconventional." Annalise's voice shook.

"While it is short notice and much needs to be done before the wedding, I am confident that between Mr. Hiram's mother, myself, and the ladies in our society, such a feat can be achieved without much fanfare."

"With all due respect, shouldn't there be a longer courtship period? After all, Mr. Hiram and I barely know each other."

A slight flicker in Mr. Hiram's sinister glare told Annalise that he was not happy with her suggestion. His words confirmed it. "Now, now, Miss Van Houten. Is a long engagement necessary? Your family and my family are of equal social standing. Would this not make for a match that would combine affluence in the most beneficial manner?"

But I am betrothed to another, a man I love. Annalise, however, couldn't mention this. Neither her aunt nor her uncle would find Matthias of suitable social standing to court, much less marry, her. *Lord, please, I beseech Thee to assist me in this most horrific matter. Show me a way to escape.*

"Have you nothing to say in response to Mr. Hiram's statement?" Uncle Phineas asked, daring her to respond.

"I simply feel that we should have a longer courtship." *Thereby giving me ample time to escape the clutches of this bondage.*

Uncle Phineas pounded his fist on the table beside the overstuffed chair on which he sat. "Nonsense! I'll not hear of it. The joining of the Thorn and Hiram families will suit us all quite well."

"But I am a Van Houten." The words escaped Annalise's lips before she could restrain them.

Uncle Phineas gritted his teeth, his red face rivaling Aunt Lavinia's rosebushes. "You will do as we say, and you will be grateful for the opportunity, Annalise."

"But—"

"Perhaps for her squabbling, we should hasten the wedding all the more," suggested Aunt Lavinia, a malevolent smirk lining her hateful face.

"Aunt Lavinia, please."

"Not to worry, *my dear*. Any objections, Mr. Hiram?"

"No objections at all, Mrs. Thorn. The sooner I make Annalise my wife, the better for everyone."

The tears fell, and she could not stop them. She wished she could retreat to her room, but knew better than to leave the presence of her menacing relatives. Instead, she prayed fervently, and when she finished, she tuned out the remainder of the conversation between her uncle and Mr. Hiram.

But when she excused herself to her room after supper, she heard the words of her future husband loud and clear: "Now that we have that matter settled, Phineas, let's rid ourselves of Reverend Sorenson."

Chapter 18

Matthias walked up the boardwalk after his visit to the livery. He had accomplished much on this Tuesday, despite his mind being elsewhere.

On a lovely Southern belle with sparkling eyes, for instance.

He couldn't stop thinking about Annalise and how they had spoken of courtship and someday marriage. He couldn't stop thanking the Lord that Annalise had given him a second chance after his careless words. If only he had more to offer the woman who had stolen a place in his heart.

"Love and devotion are the most important things you can give someone," Bets had declared when he'd told her Annalise had accepted his courtship. "The two of you will be able to serve the Lord even more so than individually. You have found your true helpmate, Matthias."

Whistling, Matthias thought of how he had successfully sent the telegram to his parents in Ohio that the "parcel" he was sending would be the last for some time. He hadn't mentioned his plans to leave and move to Ohio in the coming month. That was not something he could send in a telegram. Not with the nosy Mr. Burns honing in on every word.

Besides, Matthias needed to address his congregation and tell them he had been called to another congregation. Most importantly, he had to discuss his plans with Annalise and reassure her that he would return for her next spring.

Matthias had secured a wagon for today's load of "potatoes." He had managed to get Tandey and Jinny off the plantation, but the delivery was risky, especially given Mr. Thorn's preoccupation with Matthias's supposed role in the Faith Train. He had worried most of the night, but the Lord continued to help Matthias overcome his fears daily.

The Lord Almighty would deliver both Tandey and Jinny to their freedom.

Matthias had to believe that. Just as he had to believe that the Lord would protect him, Annalise, Betsy, and Adam.

A slave ambled behind his owners, carrying a large sack of flour. Masters Matthias did not recognize. The slave tugged on his ear, and Matthias did a double take.

Another person seeking freedom whom Matthias was called to assist.

He lingered by the mercantile, eyeing the slave and awaiting a moment of time to confront him.

Within moments, the slave had turned and headed back toward the mercantile, presumably for a second load. Matthias purposely ran into him. "Watch where you are going," he said.

"Sir, can you help me escape?" the slave asked, his voice more of a hiss.

Something indiscernible in the slave's eyes caught Matthias off guard. A jolt sent warnings through him.

But why? Never before had warning signals presented themselves in such an odd manner. Or at all, for that matter.

"Sir, can you?" The slave took a rapid glance back toward his master, then at Matthias, then back at his master once again. A shifty demeanor radiated from him, as the slave transferred his weight from one foot to the other.

Was he concerned his master would inquire why the slave had so brazenly confronted Matthias in public?

Matthias stared at the man. He should say yes and give the man hope of freedom. While Matthias didn't know any of the conductors on the railroad between here and the "promised land," he did know that once the man reached Ohio, Matthias's parents would be eager to help him continue his journey to Canada.

"Uh. . ." Matthias had never been speechless before when asked this question. Why was this time different? How many slaves had he assisted? At least twenty-five, counting Tandey, and that was just in the past year. Matthias took in his surroundings and noticed that the master had not been waiting for the slave, nor insistent upon his quick return.

Something wasn't right.

"Please promise me, Matthias, that you won't give in to the slave that Uncle Phineas sends."

Annalise's words pierced Matthias's mind, almost as if they were spoken aloud.

Was this the slave Phineas Thorn had sent? How would Matthias know for sure?

"Reverend Sorenson!" Mrs. Robinson's voice sounded from across the street. Her hand waved frantically in Matthias's direction. "Oh, Reverend Sorenson! May I have a moment of your time?"

Lord, are You trying to tell me something?

"The Lord your God which goeth before you, he shall fight for you." The Lord's impression on Matthias's heart was not audible, but it left no questions.

Matthias cleared his throat. "I'm sorry, but I don't assist slaves in running away. You'd best get back to work, or I will tell your master." Matthias held the man's gaze.

The man quirked an eyebrow, as if pondering whether to believe Matthias's words. "Yes, sir," he finally said, and shuffled dejectedly away with his head held low.

"Reverend Sorenson, I'm so glad I caught up with you." Mrs. Robinson's round face loomed as she bustled near him. "Did you not hear me calling?" She knit her thick eyebrows together in concern.

Oh, Matthias had heard her all right. For Mrs. Robinson might easily have been the tool the Lord used in saving many lives that day.

Before the recent turn of events, Annalise never would have imagined herself to be a busybody who eavesdropped on the conversations of others. But it had become necessary.

She rounded the corner of the parlor where Aunt Lavinia and Uncle Phineas sat on overstuffed chairs. The pungent odor of Uncle Phineas's cigar swirled toward her. Add that to the list of things she wouldn't miss when she left.

"Reverend Sorenson didn't fall for our plan with the slave, so the men and I are talking about taking further steps. That man needs to be stopped." Uncle Phineas paused. "While I cannot prove it, I have every reason to believe that he is why two more of our slaves have gone missing."

"I am sure you are right about him, Phineas. If you and the menfolk decided to take extreme measures, it wouldn't be the first time blood has been shed upon your direct order."

Annalise sucked in a deep breath. Were Uncle Phineas and his cronies planning to take Matthias's life? *No, Father, please don't allow that to happen!*

Uncle Phineas chuckled, a low, rolling, thunderous laugh that caused chills to ripple up Annalise's spine. "I am quite cunning, if I do say so myself."

"Indeed."

"On a more serious note, if we continue to lose slaves, we will no longer have a plantation. I cannot afford to keep purchasing new ones to replace those the good reverend has helped to escape. We have already used all of the money Annalise's parents left when they died."

Aunt Lavinia laughed, a high-pitched cackle. Annalise squeezed her eyes shut. Her aunt and uncle had wasted all of her family's fortune? That quickly? Without her knowledge? While Annalise had suspected the loss of her inheritance, this confirmed the greed of her aunt and uncle.

"When do you plan to execute your scheme against the reverend?"

"Next week. Sheriff Bleyer, Percy, and I discussed some of the details at Percy's home last night."

Annalise heard Aunt Lavinia clap her hands. "Splendid! After that, we will plan the wedding for Annalise. The sooner we are rid of her, the better. Dale Hiram will put that impertinent young woman in her place."

She had to leave the life she knew. Her aunt and uncle's plan to fatally harm Matthias, their plot of forcing Annalise to marry Dale Hiram, and the loss of Annalise's entire inheritance confirmed her decision. There was only one thing to do.

Beg Matthias to take her with him when he left Ridge Gap.

The second Nehemiah stopped the carriage, Annalise leapt from it, not waiting for the slave's assistance. She had to catch Matthias before services started.

He sat in the front pew, likely praying, as he always did before delivering the sermon. "Matthias!" Her voice sounded breathless. Only a matter of minutes remained before members of the congregation arrived.

"Annalise, so nice to see you." Matthias unfolded his hands and stood. He took a step toward her. "What's wrong?"

"Matthias, you have to take me with you when you and the others leave. Please."

"What happened?"

She took a deep breath then began to speak, her words sounding jumbled, even to her own ears.

"Annalise, please slow down." He gently reached for her upper arms as a look of concern spread across his handsome face.

Where should she start? And with so few moments of privacy? "Matthias." She lowered her voice. "I am so thankful my uncle's first plan did not work. But Uncle Phineas, Sheriff Bleyer, and the others are not going to stop. They want to destroy the Faith Train and everyone involved, especially you."

"Annalise—"

She shook her head and put a soft finger to his lips. "Please hear me out, Matthias. They are planning to take your life."

A look of alarm crossed over Matthias's face, and Annalise fought the bile that rose in her throat. "This will happen next week."

"We plan to leave in two days."

"Good." She closed her eyes and offered another quick prayer heavenward. "Matthias, take me with you," she begged. "Please. By the time you return for me, my marriage to Dale Hiram will have already occurred."

Matthias shook his head and a look of determination lined his face. "Annalise, I will never allow them to marry you off to Dale Hiram. I don't want to lose you."

"Then please take me with you."

Matthias removed his hands from her arms. "It will be dangerous taking you from Thorn Plantation."

"You recently assisted Jinny and Tandey from that very place." She jutted her chin out. She must get away from her aunt and uncle at any cost.

A sparkle lit his eyes, and he smiled. "Why do I think I can ever win a battle with you?" He placed a kiss on her forehead. "Annalise, we will take you with us, but I must make one request: that you will find me fitting to be your husband."

"Are you proposing?"

"What better place than in the Lord's house?"

Annalise giggled, a laugh that felt good after all the trepidation she had experienced. "My answer is yes."

"That's the answer I was hoping for." Matthias paused, looking at the door as if expecting a parishioner to walk through it at any moment. "I love you, Annalise."

"I love you too." And she did, with every part of her being.

"After church, we will discuss the plans for your escape." His words settled her fear for the time being.

Matthias hadn't been looking forward to bidding his congregation farewell. He would miss the fine folks of Ridge Gap and this little church that had been his place to serve the Lord for such a short time.

"It is with mixed feelings that I must say good-bye to this congregation. Some of you have known of my plans before now, while this is the first time others of you have heard this news." He paused and gazed out at the faces of the people of whom he had grown so fond.

"The Lord has called me to another place to serve Him. The life of a reverend is never dull when we have absolutely surrendered to His will. However, I would not have it any other way."

Sniffles erupted, and Matthias found he was having a difficult time containing his own feelings. "Until a permanent replacement is found, Mr. Lawton will lead the church."

His eyes met Annalise's gaze.

He loved her.

And soon, Lord willing, they would begin their new lives together in Ohio.

"Annalise, are you coming in for the evening?" Aunt Lavinia poked her head out the door where Annalise sat on the veranda in a rocking chair.

"Soon, Aunt Lavinia, soon. For now, I am taking a moment to escape the heat of the house."

Aunt Lavinia narrowed her eyes. Would she accept Annalise's weak excuse? "Very well, Annalise. But neither your uncle Phineas nor I will wait up to accommodate your ridiculous antics of sitting outside until the wee hours of the night."

Wee hours was right. If that's what it took to proceed with her plan, then that was what Annalise would do. "Do not worry. I will be in soon."

Without so much as a kindly farewell, Aunt Lavinia stepped back into the house, leaving Annalise to her thoughts.

And to the three very long hours that awaited her.

In the distance, she could hear singing, likely from some slaves, as they finished their nighttime chores. A whiff of something cooking reached her, and Annalise's stomach growled. Good thing she had packed a sandwich in her carpetbag.

She glanced to where she had hidden the only items she would be taking with her to her new life. From an exhaustive supply of fancy dresses to three meager ones. Annalise's life was about to change.

For the better.

She begged the night to come faster as she slowly rocked in the chair. Every few minutes, Annalise checked the pocket watch she held in her lap. She mustn't be late to meet Matthias and the others.

Sometime later, all of the lanterns in the house and elsewhere grew dim. The only sound was the snoring of Mr. Talon.

Mr. Talon.

The hideous man Uncle Phineas had hired three days ago to provide surveillance over the plantation at nightfall.

That man unsettled her. From his leering at her when Uncle Phineas first introduced them to his spiteful words toward the slaves, Annalise knew Mr. Talon was not a man she wanted to cross paths with. His name fit him well, as his face had the appearance of a pinched bird beak. He reminded Annalise of a bird of prey settling his eerie gaze on his victim.

He was somewhere near the barn. The man would take no mercy on her if he found her sneaking off into the night during his watch.

Lord, please, please be with me as I go forward with this plan. Let it be successful.

At the proper time, Annalise stood, reached for her carpetbag, then slowly meandered down the steps of the veranda. Constantly looking to and fro, she tiptoed past the barn, where she eyed Mr. Talon lying on the ground. Obnoxious wheezing sounds came from his open mouth and a bottle of whiskey sat beside his right hand. A rifle lay across his chest.

She almost turned back to the house.

No, I must keep going. I must. For if she didn't, Annalise would be married to Dale Hiram and forever be his prisoner.

And a life without Matthias was a life she didn't want to live.

Out of the eyesight of Mr. Talon, Annalise took to a run. She must only make it to the gate at the edge of the plantation where Matthias and the others would meet her. It wasn't that far. Not really.

Why, then, did it feel as though it was an eternity from the house to the gate? She willed her breath to quiet. Her heart rumbled in her chest, and her carpetbag slid off her elbow and clunked against her wrist. Clasping it in her hand, Annalise increased her speed.

A noise startled her. Mr. Talon? Could he have discovered her presence?

She glanced behind her and thought she saw something. Or someone. Had Aunt Lavinia or Uncle Phineas realized she hadn't returned to the house?

A thought rammed through her mind. Was this how the slaves felt as they escaped?

For she didn't doubt for a moment that her life would be at risk if she were caught.

Ahead was the gate. Just a few more steps. . . Once she was in the wagon, a friend of Matthias's would take them to the next town where they would stay the night before embarking on their journey to Ohio.

Would they make it there safely?

As Annalise crossed over from one side of the gate to the other, she nearly collapsed from exhaustion and gratitude.

Strong arms lifted her and carried her to the waiting wagon.

Epilogue

Things had been a flurry of excitement over the past two months. After Annalise and Matthias had traveled safely to their new home in Ohio, Matthias, with the assistance of so many others in the Underground Railroad network, had helped Tandey and Jinny complete their journey to freedom. And Annalise could finally put her heart at rest knowing that her dear friends were safe.

Matthias squeezed her hand, and Annalise gazed up at the man she had married just one short week ago.

How I love him!

For now, Annalise and Matthias would reside in a humble cabin about a mile from Matthias's parents, who also had a position in the Faith Train. Betsy and Adam resided not far from them.

Annalise and Matthias had joined not only in matrimony, but also in a role the Lord had placed them in, aiding slaves in reaching freedom.

Only He knew what was planned for them at the next juncture.

When Matthias leaned in to plant a passionate kiss on Annalise's waiting lips, she knew one thing to be true.

She had found freedom.

While **Penny Zeller** has had a love for writing since childhood, she began her adult writing career penning articles for national and regional publications. Today, Penny is a multipublished, award-winning author of inspirational books. She is a homeschool mom of two and actively devotes her time to coaching homeschool PE and teaching at her local homeschool co-op. Her passion is to assist and nurture women and children into a closer relationship with Christ. When Penny is not writing, she enjoys spending time with her husband and children while camping, hiking, canoeing, reading, running, gardening, and playing volleyball.